Saurgan

Saudamos

A Tromek
Portal

Shadamehr's Keep

mpire

Dwarven Mountain

Dwarven Territories

Karkara

New
Vinnengael

ak 'Vir
Karnuan Portal

Forden

Saumel (The City of the Unhorsed)

Enesh 'Sar

SEA OF STIAGA

Gatu 'Sar

Rehu

SEA OF

Goresh 'Sar

SEA OF SAGQUANNO

f the Orks

ORKAS

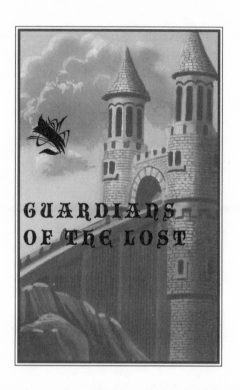

GUARDIANS
OF THE LOST

The Sovereign Stone Trilogy by
Margaret Weis and Tracy Hickman

WELL OF DARKNESS
GUARDIANS OF THE LOST
JOURNEYING INTO THE VOID*

*Forthcoming from Eos

An Imprint of HarperCollins*Publishers*

GUARDIANS OF THE LOST

Volume Two of the Sovereign Stone Trilogy

MARGARET WEIS

and

TRACY HICKMAN

A. DuKianney

Thanks to Joy Marie Ledet for the artwork on the part and chapter openers, Alan Gutierrez for the artwork on the title and half title pages, and Stephen Daniele for the endpaper and interior maps.

EOS
An Imprint of HarperCollins*Publishers*
10 East 53rd Street
New York, New York 10022-5299

ISBN: 0-06-105179-9

Library of Congress Cataloging-in-Publication Data

Weis, Margaret.
Guardians of the lost / Margaret Weis and Tracy Hickman—1st ed.
p. cm.—(The sovereign stone trilogy ; v. 2)
ISBN 0-06-105179-9
I. Hickman, Tracy. II. Title.

PS3573.E3978 G83 2001
813'.54—dc21   2001040770

First Eos hardcover printing: November 2001

Eos Trademark Reg. U.S. Pat. Off. and in Other Countries,
Marca Registrada, Hecho en U.S.A.
HarperCollins ® is a registered trademark of HarperCollins Publishers Inc.

Printed in the U.S.A.

FIRST EDITION

10 9 8 7 6 5 4 3 2 1

www.eosbooks.com

ACKNOWLEDGMENTS

The world of Sovereign Stone came from the mind and heart of renowned fantasy artist, Larry Elmore. We want to gratefully acknowledge his creation and his continued help and support as we bring his vision to life with our words, as he brings it to life with his art.

We would also like to thank the people of Sovereign Press, producers of the Sovereign Stone role-playing game, who have worked with Larry and with us to share this world with those intrepid adventurers who want to explore it and have adventures of their own. In this, we gratefully acknowledge the contributions of Don Perrin, Tim Kidwell, and Jamie Chambers. We want to acknowledge Jean Rabe and Janet Pack for their work on the taan and artists Stephen Daniele, Alan Gutierrez, and Joy Marie Ledet for the interior art in this book.

Finally, we would like to thank our editors, Caitlin Blasdell and Jennifer Brehl, for their wisdom, their patience, and their own adventuring spirit!
—Margaret Weis and Tracy Hickman

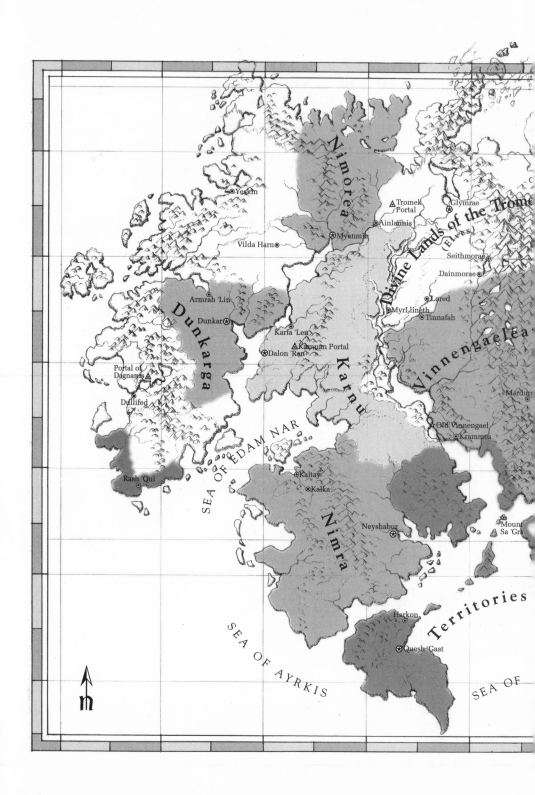

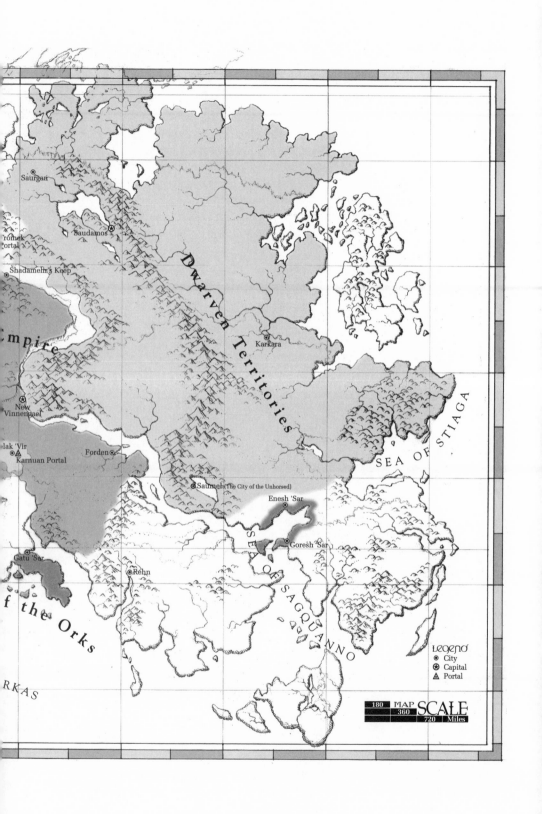

Saurgan

Saudamos

romek
ortal

Shadamehr's Keep

Dwarven Territories

Empire

Karkara

New
Vinnengael

lak 'Vir
Karnuan Portal

Forden

SEA OF STIAGA

Saumel (The City of the Unhorsed)

Enesh 'Sar

SEA OF SAGQUANNO

Goresh 'Sar

Gatu 'Sar

Rehn

f the Orks

RKAS

Legend
⊙ City
✪ Capital
△ Portal

180	MAP	SCALE
	360	
		720 Miles

BOOK

I

GUSTAV KNEW HE WAS BEING WATCHED.

He had no proof, nothing more solid than a feeling, an instinct.

Instinct had kept Gustav the Whoreson Knight alive for seventy years. He knew better than to ignore it.

He had first experienced the sensation of being watched three days ago, on his arrival in this godforsaken part of the wilderness. He had been following an old trail that ran along the Deverel river. The trail was probably made by animals, although the humans who had once lived in this area might have borrowed it. If they had, they had long since returned the trail to the deer and the wolves, for theirs were the only tracks Gustav saw.

Knowing it likely that he was the only person to have set foot in this region for the past hundred years, Gustav was understandably disquieted to awaken his first morning in camp to the distinct impression that he wasn't alone.

He had no proof that someone was watching him. His nights, spent in a tent in the wilderness, were quiet, peaceful. He sometimes woke, thinking he heard stealthy footfalls outside, but he found he was mistaken. His well-trained war horse, who would have alerted him had there been anyone lurking nearby, remained placid and calm, undisturbed, except by flies.

During the day, while he proceeded with his investigation, Gustav tried every trick in the book—a book he could have written—to catch sight of the person who was dogging his steps. He watched for the glint that might have been sunlight reflecting off metal, but saw nothing. He made abrupt stops, trying to hear footfalls that continued on after his ceased. He searched for signs that someone else was in the vicinity—foot-prints on the muddy river bank where he performed his daily ablutions, fish heads from the stalker's supper, broken sticks or bent branches.

Nothing. Gustav heard nothing. He saw nothing. Instinctively, he felt everything, felt the stalker's eyes watching him, felt those eyes to be hostile.

Gustav was not one to be deterred from his quest by an unsettling feeling, however. He had come here on a search he had begun forty years ago and he had no intention of departing until he had concluded that search. He had been exploring for three days and had found nothing yet.

He was not even certain he was searching in the right location. His only guide was a brief description taken from the mummified body of one of the monks of Dragon Mountain. Having quested for years, only to come to one dead end after another, Sir Gustav had returned to the Temple one final time.

The monks of Dragon Mountain were the repository of history in Loerem. The monks and their agents traveled the continent, seeing history as it was made and recording it on their own bodies. Preserved after death by the sacred tea the monks drank while they were alive, their bodies and all the knowledge that was recorded thereon were housed in the vaults of Dragon Mountain. Anyone on Loerem could travel to the mountain in search of knowledge of the past and find it among the slumbering dead.

Gustav had studied the historical records dealing with every race on Loerem specific to the time period in which he was interested. He had found innumerable possible sites where the object of his quest might be located. He had visited all those sites and a hundred more and had come up empty-handed. Was there a fragment of information he might have missed? Anything at all which might provide him with a clue? Had the monks truly studied all the records?

An acolyte listened to the elderly knight with intense interest and, by permission of the monks, took Gustav to the sacred vault. The two of them examined the mummified remains of the historians who lay there, each with their tattooed histories entwined around the composed limbs. Gustav recognized every corpse. After long years of association, he and these corpses had become friends.

"You say you have read them all," the acolyte stated. "But did you think to include this one?"

The monk paused beside a body of a human female who lay at the very end of the long row. Gustav looked at the body and could not recall that he had ever seen her before.

"Ah, likely not." The acolyte nodded. "Her area of expertise was the study of the pecwae race. Your earlier guides probably felt that the pecwae could have no possible connection to the Sovereign Stone."

Gustav considered this. "I cannot think that they would, but I have exhausted all other possibilities."

"Have you?" the acolyte questioned gently. "Have you considered the possibility that the portion of the Sovereign Stone for which you seek was destroyed in the blast that leveled the city two hundred years ago?"

"I have considered that, but I refuse to believe it," Gustav replied calmly. "The gods gave us our portion of the Stone, as they gave a portion to the other races. Ours is mislaid, that is all. Let us see what this chronicler of pecwae has to tell us."

The acolyte perused the tattoos on the body, murmuring to himself and shaking his head. The tattoos were magical. The historian transfered his or her thoughts onto the flesh by means of tattoos that would later transfer those thoughts to the monks trained in the magic. By placing his hand on the tattoo and activating the spell (the magic is a carefully guarded secret among the monks), the acolyte received into his mind all the images and words and thoughts of the monk detailing this portion of history.

Gustav watched the acolyte's face, watched the information pass over it like wind over a still lake. The ripples of thought cleared. The acolyte's eyes brightened.

"I have something," he said cautiously. "Do not build up your hopes too much. It is nothing more than an oddity, but it falls into the correct time frame."

"I'll take anything," Gustav said, hoping he did not sound as desperate as he was beginning to feel.

At age seventy, the knight was nearing his own eternal slumber. A valiant warrior, he had looked Death in the face, had even shaken hands with the gentleman on more than one battlefield. Gustav did not fear the unending silence. He could look forward to his final rest, if only he could be assured that his rest would be peaceful. If he was forced to leave the world before his quest was complete, he imagined himself as one of those pathetic ghosts who are doomed to wander in torment, searching and never finding.

"The clue has to do with the tomb of a bahk," the acolyte explained. "A bahk known as 'Guardian.' "

Gustav listened as the acolyte told the story of a starving bahk, his pecwae saviors, and the unusual circumstance of the bahk's burial. When he came to the part stating that the bahk had been buried with a magical treasure, Gustav's interest was piqued. He asked the acolyte to repeat that part again. Was it possible that the sacred and powerful Sovereign Stone had been resting all these years on the moldering body of a monster? Gustav could hardly believe it, but this was the last and only clue he had to follow.

The description that the monk provided of the location of the tomb was general in nature. The history-recording monks use landmarks as markers, for they are well-aware (none better) that artificial boundaries established by man have a way of shifting with the political tides. As it was, the land would have been called Dunkarga two hundred years ago but was now known as Karnu, after a civil war had ripped the nation apart.

The monk described a mountain that was shaped like the beak of an eagle west of an immense river that ran north and south and was west of Dragon Mountain. The burial site of the bahk was somewhere betwixt and between river and mountain. Gustav had determined that the river must be the Deverel. Going by the historian's guidelines, which included such directions as: "within the shadow of the mountain peak at midday" and "seventeen days' journey from the mountain's base," he arrived at what he considered to be the likeliest location.

Gustav deduced that the old camp site must be somewhere close to a source of water, for to dig a well or build an aqueduct would simply never occur to the pecwae, who are generally regarded to be the laziest people on Loerem.

The Deverel river formed the border between the Empire of Vinnengael and the kingdom of Karnu. Had Gustav been traveling through any town along the border, he would have found armed guards from both sides glowering at each other across narrow points in the waterway, maybe chancing a lucky shot with an arrow, for the two human kingdoms were currently, if unofficially, at war. As it was, Gustav explored a wilderness area that had probably not been occupied by any civilized race since the pecwae left it a hundred years before.

A Vinnengaelean by birth, Gustav would have faced open hostility or perhaps even worse if he was discovered in Karnu land and his true identity revealed. He had no fear of being discovered. The Whoreson Knight had a talent, gleaned from his years living in the streets and the alleyways of New Vinnengael, that allowed him to pass unremarked through enemy towns and cities. Gustav was, when he wanted to be, just another solitary old man wandering the back roads, trying to outrun death. No one looking at him would have taken him for a Dominion Lord.

Setting up his base camp about a mile west of the riverbank, Gustav began his search for the tomb of the bahk. He went about his daunting task methodically, first dividing up the area into grids, afterward spending his days walking the grids in a set pattern. One hundred steps north. Turn east one hundred steps. One hundred steps south. Turn west. One hundred steps back to the starting point. When he had completed one square, he began another.

Three days. He had found nothing yet, but he was not discouraged. He had four more squares in the grid marked out, four more left to explore. If he was not successful here he intended to move ten miles south along the river and start the process over again.

All this time, someone was watching.

The morning of the fourth day, Gustav woke from a light sleep that had not been particularly restful. He had wakened in the night no less than three times imagining he'd heard something outside his tent. Every time he woke up, he'd been forced to go relieve himself. A weak bladder, just one of the disadvantages of growing old. The knight emerged groggily from his small tent to find that the day promised to be a fine one, clear and sunny. The season was early summer, the time when the leaves are still shiny green, before the dust of dry weather coats them and the heat wilts them and the worms gnaw them. Gustav looked carefully at the ground around the tent, saw no footprints other than his own.

Gustav walked to the river, performed his ablutions and took a refreshing swim to clear sleep's cobwebs from his head. He saw no tracks along the river. He carried water for his horse, made certain that the animal was tethered in an area where there was sweet grass and clover, and then set off to the starting point for today's search.

Walking through the brush, the sun warm on the back of his neck, Gustav halted abruptly. He took off his boot, peered into it irritably, upended it and shook it, as if he suspected that it had acquired some unwelcome company during the night. As he did so, he listened with all his ears and darted glances left and right.

The birds sang blithely, bees hummed among the bee balm, flies buzzed past him.

Gustav replaced his boot and continued on his way. He wore his sword while he was exploring, something he rarely did, and as his eyes scanned the ground for some trace of an old pecwae camp, he also looked for trampled grass or perhaps a bit of cloth caught in a bramble. His ears were pricked and alert so that if a squirrel a hundred yards distant chittered in anger at being disturbed, he heard it.

"The gods be thanked that at age seventy I have my hearing and most of my eyesight and my teeth," Gustav said to himself, grinning, as he walked.

With the exception of his enforced nightly sojourns into the shrubbery, the advancing years had used him kindly. His eyesight had diminished somewhat, not long range, but short. After about age forty, he had been forced to hold a book to his nose to read it. An ork sailor had sold him a remarkable invention—two pieces of magnifying glass contained in a wire frame that he placed upon his nose and, with their aid, he could read once more. This weakening of the eyes had been the only harsh symptom of advancing years, that and a certain stiffness in the joints when he woke in the morning, a stiffness that a brisk walk usually corrected.

He was thinking that he'd been especially lucky in keeping his teeth— he'd seen too many old men slurping their supper from a soup bowl— when he came upon the clue for which he had been searching.

Even in his excitement and gratification, the knight continued to listen to the forest sounds, trying to pick out the one sound that had no place there. Hearing nothing except what he was supposed to hear, he bent down to examine his find—a ring of stones, charred black with fire.

Located in the center of a stand of fir trees, the ring had been here a long, long time, so long that weeds and plants had grown up all around the stones. He might have thought them a natural formation, but that no act of nature had formed the stones in that circular pattern. Hands had placed the stones here. Hands had built the fires that had blackened them. Pecwae hands? Gustav needed more clues.

He expanded his search beyond the ring of stones. Pecwae have few personal possessions and what they do have they carry with them when they leave. He was elated, therefore, when he came across the shards of a broken clay pot not many yards from the fire ring. Fitting the pieces together, he found it to be a small pot such as might have been used by small hands.

Gustav continued his search, patiently going over every bit of ground and was rewarded at last. A flash of metal caught his attention. Kneeling down, using his dagger, he carefully pried the shiny object from the ground in which it had been partially buried. He unearthed a small silver ring that might have fit a human child. He had no doubt that it was a pecwae ring, however, for in it was set one of the turquoise stones which the pecwae value beyond gold, considering them to be magical.

How did such a valuable ring come to be lost? Gustav wondered, turning it in his fingers. Was it tossed away in a lover's quarrel? Dropped while fleeing in panic from some enemy? Or had the gods set it here as a sign for him? Gustav closed his hand over the treasure and continued his search.

Although he found nothing else, the ring convinced him that this was a pecwae camp. But was it the camp the monk had visited? There remained only to look for the burial mound. Gustav walked a circle round the campsite, expanding the circle outward with every rotation. The trees grew sparsely here, a possible indication that long ago the ground had been cleared for farming. The pecwae were not farmers, but the Trevenici humans who were their protectors would have tilled the soil and left their mark. On the edge of a brush-covered rectangle of land that might have once been a field of grain or corn, Gustav came upon a mound, a large mound, covered over with grass.

He glanced at the sun. Still several more hours of daylight left. He walked around the mound, examining it minutely, bringing to mind the monk's description.

After they had placed the body of the bahk inside, the pecwae sealed up the tomb's entrance with stones piled on top of one another, then covered these over with a layer of mud.

And there it was. The crude stone wall. Gustav halted, not so much in elation at his find, but in alarm.

According to the historian, the pecwae had covered the stones with mud. Over the intervening years, grass and weeds would have taken root in the mud, partially hiding the stone wall. Gustav should have found the wall only with great difficulty, but it stood out quite plainly.

The grass and weeds had been torn off and tossed aside. Finding small clods of dirt with the grass still clinging to them, he picked up one of the clumps, examined it. The grass was still green, just starting to wilt. Someone else had been here.

Gustav examined the stones in the wall. He could see signs that they had been removed and then replaced, to make it look as if they had not been touched. The knight knew better. The pecwae are not builders. They would have done little more than pile one rock on top of another, never giving any thought to fitting them or to putting mortar between them. The dirt of the ages would have crept in among the stones. There should have been spiders, worms, ants crawling among them.

These stones were free of dirt. The insects had been displaced.

Gustav cursed. He cursed himself mostly, cursed his own methodical, plodding nature. While he had been marching off squares in his fool grids, someone else had found the tomb. While he was counting footsteps, someone else had opened the tomb.

Gustav sat down in the grass to rest and drink from his waterskin and to consider this unlooked-for development. Someone had found the bahk's tomb only days before he had done so.

Coincidence? The tomb had remained untouched, unnoticed for a hundred years. Of course, it might be possible that someone else could have taken it into his head to search this remote locale for the tomb at the same time that Gustav did, but he considered that highly unlikely.

Someone knew he was coming.

Gustav thought back over all he had done and said the past few months. He had never made any secret of his quest for the Sovereign Stone. But Gustav tended to be a private man, keeping his own counsel. He was not the sort to tell every stranger he met in an alehouse his business. The monks of Dragon Mountain knew he intended to try to locate the tomb. History gatherers, the monks are not history makers. If one of the monks had wanted to come on this journey, he would have come, bringing with him his full retinue of hulking, devoted bodyguards. Gustav had not enjoined the monks to keep his destination secret. He had seen no need to do so and they might have revealed it to anyone asking.

Someone had opened the tomb and presumably someone had entered it. Grave robbers? Gustav doubted it. Your ordinary run-of-the-mill grave robber would have dashed off with the loot, leaving the tomb unsealed. Someone had gone to a good deal of trouble, expended a lot of time and effort to replace those stones.

"Someone doesn't want to discourage my exploration," Gustav murmured. "Whoever it is wants me to think that the tomb is unviolated. He fears that if I come to the tomb and discover it open, unsealed, I will go away without entering. Which just proves that this person doesn't know me very well." Gustav smiled, though his smile was grim. "He has been waiting all this time for me to find the tomb. He's taken care to keep himself concealed. He wants me to go inside. Why? That is the question. Why?"

He had no answer, at least none that made sense. One fact was certain. Whoever this someone was or whatever it was this someone wanted, Gustav did not intend to disappoint him. He began to dismantle the stone wall.

The task did not take him long. The stones had been stashed back in a hurry and were all higgelty-piggelty. He soon cleared the opening.

Cool, moist air scented with the musky odor of freshly turned earth flowed out of the mound. The sunlight permitted him to see a short distance inside and he was agreeably surprised to find that the tunnel was still intact after all these years. He had figured that a dirt tunnel dug by pecwae, who would not have bothered to shore it up with timber, would have inevitably collapsed shortly after it was built. Smooth-sided, the tunnel was about five feet in height and about four feet wide and it disappeared into darkness.

Had the watcher entered the tunnel? If so, there should be some sign. Crouching down outside the entrance, Gustav examined the floor and the walls, searching for footprints.

He found prints—small, naked pecwae feet. A great many, passing back and forth, so that only a few tracks close to the tunnel wall were clearly visible. The dirt on the tunnel floor was dry, hard-packed, the images of the feet preserved. These were the marks of those who had built the tunnel, not the marks of a trespasser.

Gustav could envision the pecwae chattering excitedly in their high-pitched voices. He felt a connection to them extend back through the years and he was glad to think that they had loyally honored one who had served them faithfully to the very end.

Gustav rose, walked back out into the sunshine. He looked around, listened carefully, but heard nothing, saw no one. He felt the eyes watching him, as usual. Placing his knapsack on the ground, he opened it and removed items he would not need inside the burial mound—food, his map. These he left outside. He retained a small oil-burning lantern, flint and tinder to light it, lockpicking tools and water.

Certain he had everything he would require, he slid his arms through the straps of the knapsack, settled it on his back, and prepared to enter the mound. On the threshold, the knight paused. Turning, he placed his hand deliberately on the hilt of his sword and cast one long, significant look behind him.

"I know you are here," he said to the unseen watcher. "I am ready for you. Do you not imagine you can take me unaware."

He did not bother to wait for an answer.

Turning, stooping, he entered the burial mound.

GUSTAV HAD TAKEN ONLY A SINGLE STEP INSIDE THE BURIAL MOUND WHEN he sensed the magic.

Gustav had no skills in the arcane art himself, a fact he had bitterly regretted as a child, having mistakenly imagined that magic could solve all his problems, ease all his griefs, make everything right. Years brought wisdom and a better knowledge of magic and the sacrifices required of those who practice it. The years also brought magic to him in the form of the enchanted armor that is a gift of the gods to the Dominion Lords, those holy knights chosen of the gods who undergo the Transfiguration.

When a Dominion Lord undergoes this miracle, he gives himself wholly to the gods. His flesh is transformed into the element that is associated with his race. Human Dominion Lords are changed to stone. Elves give themselves to air, orken to water and dwarves to fire. When the miracle is complete, the Dominion Lord emerges alive and well and exalted from touching the minds of the gods. As a reward for his faithfulness and to assist him in his pledge of defending the defenseless, the Dominion Lord is granted wonderful, magical armor.

This armor bestows many gifts upon the Dominion Lord—gifts of magic, gifts of strength, gifts of wisdom and insight. All gifts are dependent upon and designed to suit the personality of the Dominion Lord and take into consideration his or her own skills and the life they choose to lead thereafter. The gods know more of a man than he does, they see into the heart, and the gifts that are given may not at first be understood. The gods saw Gustav's long quest before him. They gave him the ability to sense the presence of magic, a skill possessed by only those who have undergone magical training. The armor did not give him the power to use magic, however, knowing that his skills did not lie in this area.

But though Gustav could not use magic other than the magic of his armor, he could sense magic, as an orken sailor can sense an approaching storm or a dog the coming of an earthquake. Gustav halted to light the wick inside his oil lantern. Known as a "dark lantern," popular with thieves, the lantern had a sliding panel that could be raised to emit light or lowered to shut the light off. He flashed the light around, but could see nothing.

He tasted the magic, rolled it on his tongue, the only way he could describe the sensation he experienced whenever he was around magic. The taste was not foul. It did not flood his senses with bitter bile, as happened to him when he was in close proximity to the accursed magic of the Void. Yet, there was an implied threat. He was being warned to leave, warned against trespass.

Lifting the lantern, Gustav advanced a few more cautious steps, flashed the light off the walls of the tunnel, shifted the beam from ceiling to floor. The pecwae are skilled in the use of Earth magic, particularly the magic of stones, and will often guard their tents by surrounding them with stones of warding and protection. They might have inlaid such stones into the walls of the tunnel or embedded them in the floor.

Search revealed nothing, however. The walls were made of dirt and were unadorned. Not so much as a pebble. Not pecwae magic, then.

As Gustav entered deeper into the tunnel, the sense of danger and foreboding increased and he drew his sword. Perhaps the spirit of the dead bahk lingered here, unable to leave the mysterious object the creature had so long treasured. Perhaps it was not the spirit of the bahk at all, but something more sinister. Old burial sites drew other beings—some with flesh and blood and some without.

The knight had now left the sunlight behind. He relied solely on his lantern for light. The tunnel extended farther than he had imagined it would, farther than was realistic, given the size of the hill. Either the tunnel had opened up into a chamber or the magic was affecting his senses. Fortunately for his aching back, he was no longer forced to stoop. He could stand upright.

Darkness dropped on him, thick and soft and heavy as some large, lumbering animal. Gustav could see nothing for the darkness. He was completely, utterly blind. He felt with his hand to determine if he had accidentally allowed the panel to drop down, shut off the light, although he knew perfectly well he had not committed such a careless act. A child of the streets, forced to earn his living by nefarious means, he had been skilled in the use of dark-lanterns since the age of ten.

Intending to relight the lantern, Gustav turned to go back to gain some sunlight for his task.

He found his way blocked by a solid wall of earth.

Gustav was uneasy, but also intrigued, more intrigued than fearful. He was blessed with an excellent sense of direction. He had walked in a straight line. He had not turned off the path or taken a misstep. The tunnel should be open behind him. Yet it was not.

Fumbling in the thick darkness, he managed to relight the lantern, held it up to examine the wall.

It was made of earth.

He set the lantern on the floor beside him to mark his place. Laying his knapsack beside the lantern, he walked along the wall that had suddenly sprung into being, feeling it with his hands, counting his steps. After twenty paces, he still could not find a break. He tried to dig into the wall with his fingers. The earthen wall was solid as if it had been built of bricks.

The tunnel had sealed shut behind him. He was the one entombed.

Gustav had faced death many times in his seventy years. He had fought men, monsters, dragons and spirits and he had overcome them all. He had survived several accidents, one near drowning and attempted murder. He had known despair and terror. He had known fear. Most important, he knew how to use fear to his advantage. Fear is the spur that pricks one to life.

Gustav had known fear, but never panic. He knew panic now, as he pictured the death he would die—slow and tortured, starving, dehydrated, alone in the thick and smothering darkness.

His mouth went dry. His palms sweat. His bowels spasmed, his stomach constricted. A nerve in his jaw began to twitch uncontrollably. He was about to summon the magical armor of the Dominion Lord and it was at that point that he regained control of himself, even to the point of seeing the ludicrousness of the situation. Summoning the magical armor would be akin to a child diving beneath a blanket to protect himself from a lightning bolt. The armor didn't bolster his thought processes. He had to think through this danger.

"There has to be a way out," he muttered to himself, angry at his loss of self-control. "You just haven't found it yet and you won't find it if you lose what wits the gods gave you."

Then the darkness lifted and he saw the eyes. Small eyes, burning bright red, close to the ground and coming nearer with shrill squeals and chatterings and the scrabbling sound of innumerable clawed feet. As the first of the creatures swarmed into the lantern light, he saw they were rats—hundreds of rats, thousands of rats. The floor of the tomb heaved and rippled in a black-furred wave, rolling toward him. Half-starved and wild with hunger, the rats would strip the flesh from his bones in moments.

Gustav ran back to where he had placed the lantern, grabbed it up and swung it at the vermin to drive them away. Fearful of the bright light, the rats hung back, red eyes gleaming, like an army awaiting the order to attack.

Whirring noises buzzed in his ears. An insect landed on his cheek and almost immediately, he felt a small, stinging pain. He put his hand to his face, crushed a mosquito between his fingers. At the same instant, ten other mosquitoes stung any part of his flesh that was exposed—his face, his neck. More mosquitoes flew down his back, stinging and nipping. He could feel them crawling underneath his leather cap, biting painfully at his scalp. Hastily sheathing his sword, he put the lantern at his feet to ward off the rats and began to slap the mosquitoes. He jumped around and shook his arms and legs in an effort to try to dislodge them. Anyone who saw him performing this macabre dance would think he had gone mad.

In the midst of his torment, something grabbed his sword arm. Gustav turned swiftly. No hand had hold of him. His arm was in the grasp of an enormous tree root that was winding itself around his elbow. Another root snaked out and caught hold of his ankle. A third clutched at his left arm.

A veritable cloud of mosquitoes surrounded Gustav, stinging every part of him. He was forced to close his eyelids to keep them out of his eyes. The army of rats moved in to attack. Heedless of the lantern's flame, they swarmed over his feet, screeching and scratching and clawing. The tree roots began cutting off the circulation in his arms. With a desperate heave, Gustav broke free of the roots. Flailing his arms, he stumbled backward.

The wall was gone.

Gustav retreated down the tunnel. The mosquito infestation diminished. He could still hear the buzzing sound of their wings, but the cloud did not follow him. The rats, too, ceased their assault. He looked back over his shoulder. He had left his lantern on the floor behind him and by its light he could now see what he had not been able to see when he had been inside the tomb.

The lantern light illuminated a large chamber, undoubtedly the burial chamber. His tormentors were lined up before it, watching him depart. The rats did not come after him. The tree roots hung limply from the ceiling. The mosquitoes whirred but did not pursue him.

Gustav understood.

He had been warned. He would not be permitted to enter the burial chamber.

"It is as if the very Earth itself is guarding the tomb," he muttered, scratching at the mosquito bites and slapping at the few still infesting his clothes.

He halted his scratching, no longer feeling the stings.

"The very Earth is the guardian," he repeated. "Of course! Earth magic! Nothing else could have called out Earth's legions. The rats and insects and trees threatened me, but they did not kill me. Not this time. This time was the warning. Next time, they will kill. What are they protecting?"

He guessed the answer.

"Is that possible?" he asked himself, awed.

His heart swelled with elation so that its beat grew erratic. Suddenly weak, he leaned back against the wall, trying to calm himself.

"After searching all these years, have I truly found what I seek?"

He could think of nothing else that the Earth would strive so valiantly to protect.

The Sovereign Stone. Each portion of the sacred stone had been empowered by different magicks: the elven portion was powered by Air magic, the dwarven portion by Fire magic, the orken portion by Water magic. The human portion of that sacred artifact was empowered by Earth magic. Earth magic that would protect the blessed Stone from those who had no claim to it.

Such as the person who had been watching him.

That person must have entered the tomb, only to meet with the same deadly threat as Gustav. Forced to retreat, the person was now waiting and watching to see if Gustav fared better.

Gustav straightened. His heartbeat returned to normal. He walked back down the tunnel, walked toward the lantern light—his beacon in the darkness. The rats screeched at him in fury and began to grow in size until they were as big as hounds. The mosquitoes changed to monstrous creatures. He could see his image reflected a hundred times in a single bulbous eyeball. The tree roots looped into nooses, prepared to seize him by the neck and strangle him. Behind him, he heard clods of earth come crashing down. The tunnel had been closed off. He was sealed inside.

The first had been a warning. Now Earth meant his death.

Gustav smoothed the fine, hand-tooled gauntlets he wore and, lifting his hands, he clapped them together. A thunderclap reverberated throughout the chamber, the sound so loud that it stunned some of the rats, who flopped over on their sides, and caused some of the mosquitoes to drop from the air. The tree roots shivered and wavered.

The magical power of a Dominion Lord flowed from the gauntlets, slid over Gustav's body like quicksilver. In less time than it took him to draw two deep breaths, he was accoutered, head to toe, in helm and armor that shone silver in the lantern's light.

Gustav lifted his visor and raised his voice.

"I am Gustav, known as the Whoreson Knight," he announced. "I was made a Dominion Lord by the grace of the King of Vinnengael, Giowin the Second. I underwent the Transfiguration in the year after the Fall one hundred and forty-nine. At that time, I was granted the blessed armor and my calling, Lord of Seeking. True to my calling, I have studied long and quested far to find what was lost two hundred years ago. I seek that portion of the Sovereign Stone that was given to King Tamaros by the gods and then given into the keeping of his eldest son, Prince Helmos, Lord of Sorrows."

Gustav ceased speaking, waited to see what reaction, if any, had been caused by his words and, more important, to see the reaction of the Earth magic to the blessed armor of a Dominion Lord.

The red eyes of the rats blinked and flickered as if in doubt. Their furious chattering died away. The tree roots again hung limp, though the ends twitched. The mosquitoes buzzed near him, but did not attack. His audience remained hostile, but they were at least listening to him.

Gustav took another step forward, to show that he was not afraid, to show that he believed with all his heart he had the right to be here. He took another step and another and now he was among the rats. He had no need of the lantern light. His armor gave off its own light, pure and argent. The vermin parted at his coming, allowed him to proceed forward, but they flowed in behind him, surrounding him. The mosquitoes buzzed near him. Tree roots swayed ominously, brushing against him as he passed, just to let him know that the mysterious power which guarded this place was not yet fully convinced.

"Why have I come? I seek the blessed Sovereign Stone," he told the power. "Not for my own use. I am an old man. My days are numbered. My death is imminent. I come in the name of humanity.

"The elves, the dwarves, the orks—each race has its portion of the Sovereign Stone to bless the people and grant power to their Dominion Lords. Bereft of ours, we humans have been forced to make do with what little blessed magic remained in the housing of the stone discovered on the body of King Helmos. We have Dominion Lords, but their numbers diminish. Few of the young pass the Transfiguration now. The wise fear that if the Sovereign Stone is not soon recovered, we human Dominion Lords that now exist will be the last."

Gustav fell silent again, waiting, listening.

Nothing moved, but everything watched him.

He drew his sword, named *Bittersweet Memory*, from its sheath. The rats gibbered angrily, the tree roots coiled, ready to lash out. The darkness deepened, so that even the light cast by his magical armor was dimmed.

Gustav made no threatening move. Kneeling on the ground, he placed his hands on the sword's blade beneath the hilt and held it up, an offering.

"Guardians of the Sovereign Stone, look into my heart and see the truth. I have searched for the stone the greater part of my life. Grant it to me. I vow that I will guard it with my life. I will bring it safely to my people, whose need for its blessed power has never been more urgent."

An unseen hand drew back the dark curtain. In front of Gustav was the well-preserved body of a bahk, lying on a brightly colored blanket, looking very much as it might have looked had it been buried only a day before, not a hundred years ago. The bahk was enormous, one of the largest Gustav had ever seen. The bahk must have measured twenty-five feet from his two huge feet to his horned head. The pecwae had taken good care of their protector, evidently; seen to it that he was well-fed. The bahk's protruding snout and gaping mouth of razor-sharp teeth were frozen in an expression that made the hulking creature appear inoffensive, far different from others of its kind. Most bahk have faces seamed with cruelty and hatred. This bahk smiled, as if he had died with the knowledge of a job well done.

Hulking, shambling, huge beasts, bahk were newcomers to Loerem, having arrived—most scholars believed—when the magical Portals shattered, opening into other lands, maybe even into other worlds. Fearsome looking beasts with hunched shoulders, their spines protected by a bony carapace, bahks are fierce predators and, so most people believed, cruel and vicious with no love for anything except magic and slaughter.

Yet here was one named Guardian, who had lived for years among the gentle pecwae and died honored and loved.

Gustav felt a momentary sense of shame for all of the bahk's brethren he had killed without remorse. Like most of the other races of the world, he had assumed that the bahk were monsters without a soul. Here was proof to the contrary.

Stones of all kinds had been piled around the body. Turquoise glinted blue in the silver light, amber shone with a golden hue, mica sparkled, quartz gleamed. None of these stones was the Sovereign Stone, the sacred treasure Gustav sought, nor did he expect to find it among them. He rested his sword on the floor of the tomb and rose to his feet. Moving slowly, hands folded in respect, he approached the body. The rats crept after him. He could hear their clawed feet scrape on the floor. The mosquitoes whirred near. The tree roots quivered.

A box made of silver lay on the breast of the bahk. The box was of pecwae work, measured the length of his hand, and was as wide as his hand with all the fingers fully spread. The box was covered with the images of birds and animals, flowers and vines, all etched into the silver. Each animal had turquoise stones for the eyes. Inlaid stones made up the petals of the flowers: red jasper, purple fluorite, lapis lazuli, while the lid of the box was adorned with the largest turquoise Gustav had ever seen. Veins of silver wove through it like cobweb. The box itself was a creation of beauty and wonder. The lid was hinged, held in place by a silver latch that could be opened with the flick of a finger. The latch was well-worn. Apparently the bahk had opened his treasure box many times to admire his possession.

Gustav started to reach out his hand to touch the box. Of a sudden, he hesitated.

"This box is the final guardian," he realized.

The magic of the box was powerful. He could feel it vibrate. The box would kill any common thief who might have escaped the tomb's other guardians.

A thief such as himself. A thief such as he had been.

Gustav had renounced that life years ago. He had lived every day since in remorse for his past sins. He had done what he could to atone for them. But what if none of that counted?

The magic of the box was deadly. The magic would not hesitate to kill anyone it considered to be unworthy of claiming the blessed artifact.

His hand trembled above the silver box and, suddenly, he smiled.

"So, Gustav," he said, having from long years of traveling alone come into the habit of talking to himself, "you have spent forty years of your life searching for this and now you fear to touch it. How Adela would laugh, if she were here to see this. I must remember to tell her. If I survive . . ."

His hand closed over the silver box.

A tingle like chill water coursed through his body. That was all. Nothing more.

Slowly, respectfully, he lifted the bahk's huge head and carefully removed the ornate silver chain to which the box was attached from around the bahk's enormous neck. Holding the box, he studied the latch, taking care not to break it. His fingers shook so that he was forced to make several tries, then at last the latch gave way. He opened the box and looked inside, stared in awe and in rapture, deep and profound.

The Sovereign Stone was a triangular jewel with four sides, forming a wedge. Smooth, hard, cold as ice to the touch, without flaw, the crystal caught the light and fractured it, split it into a rainbow of color that dazzled the eye. According to the records left behind by King Tamaros of blessed memory, each piece of the stone looked exactly like the others and when all four pieces came together, they formed a pyramid.

Falling to his knees, Gustav prayed fervently to the gods.

"Thank you for granting me this. I will be faithful to my vow. My life, my soul be forfeit if I fail." His voice was choked with emotion. Tears stood in his eyes.

He spent long moments savoring the euphoria of his triumph, enraptured by the fulfillment of his life's quest. He could not take his eyes from the Sovereign Stone. Never had he seen anything so remarkable, so radiant, so wondrous. Truly, he could believe that it was a gift of the gods. He imagined the face of King Tamaros smiling down on him, granting him his blessing.

At length, Gustav sighed deeply and, with a final prayer, he replaced the Sovereign Stone back inside its silver box and closed the lid. He thrust the box inside the breastplate of his armor. He found he could not leave, however. He was drawn once more to look upon the bahk, the strange and unlikely guardian of the Sovereign Stone.

How had the bahk come by the stone? That was a mystery of the gods, a mystery never likely to be solved. The Sovereign Stone had been kept secret and safe all these years. Perhaps it was Gustav's imagination, but he thought the corpse of the bahk looked bereft, forlorn without its box. The spirit of the bahk lingered here still, and although he did not begrudge Gustav's claim to the Sovereign Stone, the bahk missed its treasure, as a child misses a loved toy.

Gustav reached his hand to his breast, clasped there a jewel he wore on a chain of gold. The jewel was a sapphire, the color of his wife's eyes. The jewel was a love-token, the first she had ever given him. Thinking to wear it always, he had left instructions in his will that he was to be buried with it. Gustav gave the chain a swift, sharp tug.

The chain broke, came off in his hand. Gustav brought the jewel to his lips, kissed it, then slowly and reverently, he laid it to rest upon the breast of the bahk.

"Forgive me for taking what you most valued, Guardian. In return, I leave behind that which I most value. I wish for your sake it was magic," he added softly. "But the only magic this jewel contains is her love for me and mine for her. Farewell, Guardian. May your spirit find rest after your long and faithful watch."

The jewel sparkled in the light of his armor. Perhaps, again, it was his imagination, but Gustav fancied that the bahk smiled.

3

RETURNING TO THE PLACE IN THE TUNNEL WHERE HE HAD LEFT THE DARK-
lantern and his knapsack, Gustav took time to rest. He was well aware of
the limitations age had placed upon his body and he knew better than to
try to pretend he was thirty again.

Seating himself comfortably on the floor, he opened the knapsack and
began to remove the contents. When the knapsack was empty, he placed
the silver box with its precious treasure—a treasure that was the heart and
soul of a race—inside.

Gustav had specially commissioned the knapsack long years ago precisely for this occasion. The magus at the Temple in New Vinnengael had
done her work well. She had listened with polite gravity while Gustav explained why he needed such a special carry-all. He had paid for such politeness, he reckoned. The magical knapsack had cost him his life savings,
as well as his modest town house in the city. He'd even been forced to sell
his horse to raise the money. All for a dream.

No wonder people thought him mad.

What they could not know, of course, was that the house meant nothing to him without her in it. Or rather, she was too much in it. She was
everywhere in the house. He could not sit in his chair of an evening but
what he would raise his eyes and see her spirit sitting opposite him. She
poured his wine. She laughed at his small witticisms. She pricked the bubble of his pomposity. She sang to him and played the harp. When he
asked the servants if they enjoyed her music, they stared at him in alarm
and fled the premises.

Gustav spoke the single word that was required to activate the magic.
The magus had told him to select a word he would be certain never to forget.

"Adela," he said softly.

The silver box containing the Sovereign Stone vanished. The knapsack appeared to be empty. Gustav felt a momentary qualm of fear. The magus had warned him—or so he vaguely remembered—that the magic was so effective at concealing the object placed inside the knapsack that even though he knew how the magic worked, he would be tempted to doubt.

"Adela," he said again and found himself looking down at the silver box with its marvelous jeweled-eyed animals.

Gustav opened the box, looked inside, just to reassure himself. The Sovereign Stone lay within, its sharp edges glinting in the lantern light. Gustav recalled the tale that when the Sovereign Stone had been handed to Prince Helmos by his younger brother, Prince Dagnarus, one of the edges had cut Helmos, drawn blood. The story had it that when the blood of the martyred prince fell on the stone floor, the stones cried out a warning against Dagnarus, a warning that had gone unheeded.

Gustav shut the box. He spoke his wife's name again and the silver box disappeared. Hefting the knapsack experimentally, he was interested to note that it even felt empty. He tried to recall the magus's explanation about "layering folds in the earth's aura" and "pockets in time," but, truth to tell, he had found her rather boring and pedantic. He didn't understand magic, didn't want to understand it. That's why he was paying her for it. He wanted to know only that it worked. And so it did.

He wondered where the magus was now. Probably dead. Most everyone he had known from those days was dead.

The important task accomplished, Gustav considered whether or not he should divest himself of the blessed armor of a Dominion Lord. The tree roots were now ordinary, dirt-sucking tree roots. The rat army had departed, leaving behind only a few stragglers, who were in mortal terror of the lantern light. Outside the tomb waited the person who had been watching him so patiently and secretly, the person who had wanted him to enter the tomb. Gustav decided to remove his armor. His plan was to lure out the watcher, to talk to him, understand his game. A single clap of his gauntlets and the magical armor vanished.

Gustav repacked the knapsack, so that it looked the same as any other traveler's knapsack, adding to it a few bits of pecwae jewelry that had been placed with the corpse. He regretted having to take them, but he needed something to show the unseen watcher. Resting, Gustav drank water and began to consider what he would do next. The first part of his quest was accomplished. Now he must embark upon the second part—the safe delivery of the Sovereign Stone to the Council of Dominion Lords in New Vinnengael, a city that was over two thousand miles from his current location. For the first time in two hundred years, the four parts of the Sovereign Stone would be joined together again and, or so it was believed and fervently hoped, this joining would bring peace to warring nations.

"At that point, my life's work will be over," Gustav said to himself. "And I can join you, Adela."

He had meant to join her earlier. Driven mad by grief for her loss, he had lifted the cup of poison to his lips and was about to drink when her hand had dashed it to the floor. The cup had been knocked from him with such force that he had later found it some ten feet away from where he had been sitting. It was then he had known that he had yet to fulfill his purpose in life. It was then that he had resolved to start his quest in search of the Sovereign Stone.

Adela's faith in her knight had been fulfilled.

He hoped and trusted that the second part of his quest would be much easier than the first. His journey would take months, but he should arrive before the start of winter. He foresaw no delays, no obstacles, except the one that was waiting for him outside the tomb. He did not anticipate trouble. No one knew he was carrying the Sovereign Stone, not even the watcher out there waiting for him.

Gustav emptied the waterskin and rose, wearily, to his feet. The tension, the battle with the forces of Earth magic, and his own pent-up excitement had taken their toll. He was tired past reckoning and he had yet to deal with the unseen someone. Fortunately, he could always summon the magical armor, or, if he were ambushed, the armor would act of its own accord to defend him.

Emerging from the tunnel, Gustav blinked in the bright sunlight. He halted at the entryway, astonished to realize that it was still daylight. He would have been less surprised to step outside into the middle of a snow bank, for it seemed to him he had spent months, not hours, inside that tomb.

He kept his hand on the hilt of his sword and listened, using his ears while his eyes were growing accustomed to the bright light. He thought he heard a rustling sound, as if someone hiding in tall grass had made a movement, but, if so, all movement ceased, for he did not hear the sound again. When he could see, he looked closely at the tall grass and peered into the shadows of the trees. Nothing was out there, yet he felt the eyes on him, more intensely than ever.

Gustav was starting to become annoyed.

"Stop skulking about and show yourself!" he shouted irritably. "I know you are out there! Tell me why it is you have been watching me thus long and patiently. Tell me why it is you hoped that I would enter that tomb."

No takers.

Gustav held up the knapsack. "If you are curious, I will show you what I found in there. Nothing of immense value, if that's what you're expecting. Pecwae baubles. Nothing more. Your time and mine have been wasted seemingly. Come, join me, and we will share a skin of wine together and laugh over what fools we were to think we might find treasure in a pecwae burial mound."

The grass whispered, but that was the wind. Tree branches creaked, but that, too, was the wind. There came no other sound.

"The Void take you, then," Gustav yelled and, hoisting his knapsack on his shoulder, he set off for his campsite.

Gustav faced a dilemma. He could either ride off with his treasure now, tired as he was, and risk being attacked on the road by the unseen watcher, or he could have a meal, rest and maybe even get some sleep. If he had brought along a companion, they could have split the watch, but he had not, and he did not regret it. His motto had long been: "He travels fastest who travels alone." Gustav liked few people well enough to endure their company for months on the road and those he did like were too busy with their own pursuits to set off on an old man's quest.

He concluded he had better be fed and rested, rather than try to run away from danger when he was so tired he could barely put one foot in front of the other. Always fight on ground of your own choosing, if that is possible—an axiom of his former commander and mentor. If the unseen watcher was planning an attack by night, hoping to catch Gustav witless and befuddled, he would be in for a surprise.

Trudging back to camp, Gustav kept close watch, but he saw nothing, nor did he really expect to. By now, he knew the watcher well enough to have a healthy respect for his woodcraft skills. Just as well he had no companion. Anyone with him would have decided by this point that the old man was barmy. No sign or sound or sniff of anyone out there and here was Gustav preparing to be attacked during the night.

By the time he arrived back in camp, darkness had fallen. Gustav tossed the knapsack carelessly into his tent. Having checked his snares on the way back, he cut up and roasted a fine, plump rabbit over his campfire. He made much of his horse, to appease the animal for having been without company all day, made certain the horse was fed and had plenty of water. This done, he doused the fire. Leaving his horse flicking at flies with its tail, Gustav entered his tent.

Once inside, Gustav removed two small silver bells from his bed roll. Keeping the clappers muffled, Gustav hung the bells on the tent supports, near the top.

"An old thieves' trick, appropriate for an old thief," Gustav said to himself with a smile. A touch, no matter how gentle, on the fabric of the tent would set the bells to ringing. He had carelessly left his cooking pots in front of the tent flap for the same purpose, hoped that he himself didn't forget they were there and tumble over them when he had to make one of his trips to the bushes.

Figuring that he had done all he could to make certain the watcher didn't catch him unaware, Gustav wrapped himself in his blanket and, using the knapsack as a pillow, lay down on the ground. He kept his sword and a pile of dwarven sulfur sticks close to his hand.

Gustav was not one to fret and worry or to lie awake, staring into the darkness, listening for the snap of a twig. Sleep was as essential to the warrior as sword or shield or armor. Gustav had trained himself to sleep and sleep well at will. He had gained fame by once sleeping through an ork siege. His comrades later told tales of catapult-flung boulders smashing into the walls and flaming jelly turning men into living torches. Gustav, who had been awake three nights running battling orks, had finally had a chance to sleep and he meant to use it. His comrades had been considerably startled when Gustav rose up the next morning and walked out among them. He had slept so soundly they had assumed he was dead and had been—so they claimed—on the verge of tossing his body onto the funeral pyre.

Worn out from the day's exertions, he slept soundly, counting on his horse and the traps he'd laid to warn him in time to confront any intruder.

It was not the clanging of pots that woke him, or the ringing of the small silver bells. It was a dream.

Gustav could not catch his breath. He fought to draw air into his lungs and he was losing the battle. He was dying, suffocating. It was the knowledge that he was dying that jolted him out of sleep. He woke with a gasp, his heart racing. The dream was very real, left him half-convinced that someone was inside his tent, trying to smother him. He looked around, but concentrated more on listening.

The night was dark. Clouds covered the moon and stars. He could see very little inside his tent. The bells had not rung. The pots had not been disturbed. Yet something was there.

His horse sensed it. The animal snorted uneasily, hooves raked the ground. Gustav lay back on his bedroll. The feeling of being smothered had not left him. He found it difficult to breathe, as if he had a weight on his chest.

The air was tainted, smelled foul. Gustav recognized the stench immediately. He'd once happened on a battlefield three days after a battle. The corpses of the unburied dead lay bloated and rotting in the hot sun. The most hardened veterans in the Vinnengaelean army heaved up their guts at the horrible smell.

The silver bells shivered. Their chiming was flat, discordant. He heard the sounds of stealthy footfalls drawing near. His horse shrieked suddenly, a scream of terror such as he'd never heard from the well-trained beast, and there came a crashing sound, the thudding of hooves. His horse, trained for battle, who had not flinched when facing the points of a hundred spears, had broken free of its tether and fled through the brush.

Gustav could empathize with his horse. He himself had faced a hundred spears and he had not experienced the fear he felt come over him now. He was in the presence of evil. Diabolical evil. Ancient evil, from beyond the creation of the world. Attuned to magic of all kinds, he recognized the foul magic of the Void.

The magus out there was no cantrip parsing hedge-wizard. He was a sorcerer wielding a power such as Gustav had never before encountered. A power he was not certain he could contend.

The footsteps came nearer. The stench of Void grew worse, turning Gustav's stomach. Breathing the foul air was like trying to breathe oil-covered water.

A hand touched his tent. The bells chimed again, but Gustav could not hear them for the pounding of blood in his ears. Sweat beaded on his forehead. His mouth dried, his palms were wet. He had two choices. He could rise up, clad in his magical armor, and accost the sorcerer outside his tent or he could lie here and wait for the sorcerer to come to him.

Gustav grimly decided to play possum. He wanted to see this Void magus who had spent so much time and patience following him. He wanted to know the reason why. Closing his eyes and keeping them closed required an extraordinary effort of will. He tried, as best he could, to calm his jagged breathing.

He heard a ripping sound—the intruder slashing open the back of the tent. The silver bells jangled wildly. Gustav thought that it would be only logical for him to wake now and he snorted and grunted and half-sat up, rubbing his eyes with one hand, his left hand.

The intruder entered the tent, moving on hands and knees. Gustav could not see clearly, for the thick darkness.

"Who's there?" he called out in a sleep-fuddled voice while, at the same time, the thumbnail of his right hand scraped against the tip of the sulfur stick.

Flame flared. Gustav thrust the fire into the face of the intruder: a woman's face, a face of astonishing, breathtaking beauty. Blue eyes, large and lustrous, full red lips, hair the color of maple leaves in autumn. She wore a dress of rich green velvet, the bodice cut low. She was on her hands and knees. Her white breasts fell forward, heavy, ripe and tempting.

"I am lonely," she said softly. "I need somewhere to spend the night."

The smothering feeling, the stench of rotting flesh.

Gustav stared fixedly at the woman and the illusion shattered, burst apart, as if it had been made of ice and he'd struck it with a hammer.

Beauty disappeared to be replaced by horror.

The beautiful face deteriorated into the face of a long-dead corpse, a skull with a few clumps of decayed flesh still clinging to it. There were no eyeballs in the bony sockets, but there was malevolent and cunning intelligence. No pity, no mercy. No compassion. No hatred, no greed, no lust. He saw, in the eyes, the Void.

The Void. As it had been before the gods came and the world was created. As it would be when the gods departed and the world came to an end. He saw, in the eyes, the emptiness in his own heart when Adela died.

Gustav saw his own death in the empty eyes. He could not fight this thing. He could not move to defend himself. The power of the Void emptied him, drained him, drained his will to live.

The sulfur match went out, burning Gustav's thumb. The pain reminded him that he lived and that, while he lived, he could fight. Before the flame vanished, he had seen a small knife made of bone in the corpse's skeletal hand.

The corpse lunged at Gustav, stabbing at him with the knife. So swift and skilled was the attack—aiming straight for the heart—that Gustav had barely time to grab his sword. He would have died, but for the magical armor of the Dominion Lord that flowed over his body.

The knife in the corpse's skeletal hand struck steel. The armor turned the blade from the heart, but did not stop its entry. Few weapons can penetrate the blessed armor and this was one—a weapon of Void magic. The blade missed the heart, stabbed Gustav in his left shoulder.

The pain was terrible, a stinging, burning pain that slanted through his flesh and struck to his very soul. The pain shriveled his stomach, caused him to gag.

The corpse made an unearthly sound, muffled scream, as if it were crying out in fury from the grave. Fighting against the debilitating pain that was making him sick and dizzy, Gustav raised his sword. The corpse was close to him. He could feel the rasping of its nails against his armor. He plunged his blade into the corpse's chest.

He had expected bone, but the blade struck steel armor. The blow jarred his sword arm so that he very nearly dropped the weapon. Yet, he could tell by a grunt of pain that he'd managed to inflict damage on his murderous assailant.

Gustav took advantage of the corpse's momentary distraction to escape the confines of the tent. Kicking aside the pots he had placed in front of the tent opening, he staggered out into the night and turned immediately to face his opponent, who would not be far behind him. His armor glowed silver in the darkness.

His attacker emerged from the tent and rose to her full height. By the silver light of his own blessed armor, Gustav looked upon his antithesis.

The figure wore armor that was blacker than the darkness. The design of the armor was hideous, like the carapace of some monstrous insect, with razor-sharp spikes at the elbows and the shoulders, and a helm that was formed in the shape of the head of a mantis with bulbous eyes of empty nothingness. The creature had abandoned the small knife and held in her gloved hands an enormous black sword with wicked, serrated edges. Now Gustav knew what it was he fought.

"A Vrykyl," he breathed.

Creatures of myth and legend. A nightmare come to life. There had been rumors, reports that these ancient demons once more walked Lo-erem. It was said that they had been responsible for the destruction of Old Vinnengael.

The Vrykyl swung her blade, a stroke intended to test the skill and strength of her opponent.

Gustav parried the stroke with his own blade, but the Vrykyl's power-ful blow nearly knocked the weapon from Gustav's hand. Forced to spend a moment recovering, he could not follow up his advantage and he felt the first twinges of despair. He was far more skillful with a sword than this Vrykyl, but the Vrykyl had the strength of Void magic, the strength of one who has no muscles that will start to ache or heart that will begin to fal-ter. He was wounded and he was old. He could feel himself already start-ing to weaken.

Gustav had one chance and that was to end this fight quickly. His mag-ical weapon, blessed by the gods, had the ability to penetrate the accursed armor. He had only to find a vulnerable spot and strike a killing blow.

He waited and watched, grim and patient. The Vrykyl saw his weak-ness. She rushed at him, sword raised, thinking to cleave him in two with a death-dealing stroke. The Vrykyl was darker than dark, a hole cut in the night. Gustav balanced, thrust, used all his strength to drive his sword into the Vrykyl's midriff, beneath the breastplate.

The sword penetrated the armor. The shock was paralyzing, sent jolts of teeth-jarring pain throughout Gustav's arm. His hand went numb, he could no longer hold onto the sword.

But he had hurt the Vrykyl. Her shriek split the night. The horrifying sound sent shudders through Gustav. He stood clutching his arm, trying to rub some feeling into it, trying to halt the jangling of his nerves.

The Vrykyl fell to the ground, screaming and writhing. The magic of Gustav's blessed sword entering the Void brought substance to the Void, filled it with light, bringing an end to the darkness that sustained her.

His right hand was useless. Gustav wondered if he would ever regain the feeling. The wound in his shoulder burned and throbbed and he started to feel a numbing chill spread from his shoulder throughout his body. Using his left hand, gritting his teeth against the pain, Gustav leaned over the wounded Vrykyl and yanked his sword free. The blade was clean, bore no trace of blood.

The Vrykyl's screams ceased. She lay on the ground, her body twisted in its death throes.

Gustav collapsed near his enemy. He spiraled down into darkness, fell into the emptiness of the Vrykyl's eyes.

Gustav felt something tickling his cheek. He woke with a wrenching gasp, the horrid memory of the bone knife of the Vrykyl fresh in his mind. His eyes flared open. He stared up in terror, to find that the tickling sensation on his face came from the muzzle of his horse.

Gustav gave a shuddering sigh. He lay back on the grass, looked up to find the sun was shining high in the sky. The warmth was wonderful to feel, eased the pain in his shoulder. The horse, remorseful that he had failed in his duty, nuzzled his master in what was first an apology and second a demand to be fed.

Gustav lay a moment longer, basking in the sunshine, and then he lifted his right hand, wiggled the fingers. The feeling had returned. He gave another sigh of relief and sat up, carefully, so that the blood didn't rush from his head.

He was no longer wearing his armor, which would have acted to protect him while he was unconscious, had there been any threat. Shoving aside his shirt, he examined the wound. It was not serious, at least to look at, being nothing more than a small puncture, such as might have been made by an ice pick. The wound had not bled much, but the flesh around the wound had turned a strange whitish blue and, when he touched it, he could not feel his touch, as if the skin were frozen.

He tried lifting his arm and gasped in pain. Moving gingerly, he looked over to where the Vrykyl had fallen, feeling a grudging curiosity to see what the loathsome thing looked like in the light of day.

The Vrykyl was gone.

Alarmed, Gustav jumped to his feet. He searched around the area hurriedly, thinking that perhaps he had mistaken the location of the corpse.

He found nothing. It was as if the Vrykyl had never been. He might have thought he had dreamed the entire nightmare encounter, but for the wound in his arm. And there were other signs that a fight had occurred.

Now that he examined the area closely, he could see where the grass had been torn and trampled. He could also see signs where something heavy had been dragged through the brush.

He had not killed the Vrykyl. He had only wounded it.

In his mind's eye, he saw the injured Vrykyl hauling her body along the ground. Gustav touched his numb shoulder, recalled the deadly little knife the creature had wielded. No ordinary knife could penetrate the armor of a Dominion Lord. Her knife had been enchanted with Void magic—powerful Void magic. Gustav wondered why the Vrykyl hadn't tried to slay him while he lay unconscious.

Perhaps she lacked the strength. Perhaps she had counted him dead, as he had assumed she was dead. Perhaps . . .

Perhaps she had not found what she sought.

Gustav followed the trail of broken grass stalks and gouges in the earth. The trail led directly to his tent. Gustav opened the tent flap and caught his breath. The air was tainted with the foul and oily taste of Void magic.

He looked inside for the knapsack, found what was left of it. The Vrykyl had torn it to shreds. The objects that had been in the knapsack were strewn about. The dark lantern had been smashed, its glass shattered, its case bashed and dented. The tinderbox had received the same treatment. His spare clothes were cut to ribbons as was his blanket.

At least he had the answer to his question. The Vrykyl had been searching for the Sovereign Stone.

The more he thought about this, the more sense it made. The Vrykyl had learned of his quest—he had made no secret of it. She had been following him. She had discovered the tomb and had attempted to enter, planning on seizing the Sovereign Stone herself. The Earth magic that had acted to thwart Gustav would have risen up in fury against a Vrykyl. She could not take the Stone. And so she had retreated and waited for Gustav to bring it out to her.

She had attacked him in the night, hoping to kill him and recover the Stone. She had not counted on meeting a Dominion Lord and thus she had failed. After the fight, wounded though she was—and she had been terribly wounded, of that Gustav was certain—she had dragged herself to the tent and torn apart everything in search of the Stone. Frustrated, not finding it, she had been forced to depart to nurse her wounds.

Gustav was under no illusion. She had permitted him to live only because she was certain he would lead her to the Sovereign Stone.

Gustav picked up a small strip of leather, a remnant of the knapsack. Undoing his thick braid, he twisted the leather in among the locks and rebraided the gray hair tightly around it. Then, unable to breathe the fetid air, he left the tent. Back in the sunshine, he gratefully drew in a deep breath.

Further search revealed the Vrykyl's trail. It led away from the tent. He had removed his saddlebags and his saddle from the horse and she had searched those, too. The saddlebags were in tatters. The saddle bore marks of her long nails. She had then limped on, heading northward.

About a hundred paces away, Gustav discovered signs of a horse that had been tethered to a tree. His own horse had fled the Vrykyl in terror. Gustav wondered what sort of Void magic spell the Vrykyl had cast on the poor animal to induce it to serve the hideous creature.

The horse's hooves left gouges in the earth, heading northward. The Vrykyl was gone for the time being. She had been forced to leave because she was wounded and needed whatever succor the dreadful creatures used to heal themselves.

Gustav sighed deeply and stood long moments, searching the land in all directions. He saw nothing. He heard nothing. Yet he still had the feeling he was being watched.

Returning to camp, Gustav went about his normal routine. He fed and watered his horse. He ate something himself, though he could not have said what, for he could not taste it. All he could taste was the foul smell of the Void magic, that was all-pervasive. His meal finished, he dragged his saddle and bridle and the maltreated saddlebags into the tent with the rest of his possessions. He soaked his bedding and the saddle with lantern oil. Using what was left of the tinderbox, he created a spark, dropped it onto the oil-soaked rag that had once been his blanket.

The fabric caught fire instantly. Gustav watched for a moment, making certain it spread. When the flames began to lick the sides of the tent and the heat became intense, he left. He stood outside the tent, watched the conflagration build, watched to see that everything was consumed. Thick, black smoke roiled into the air. Satisfied that very little would be left, he mounted his horse. He had only the clothes on his back, his sword and scabbard, his saddle blanket his magical gauntlets and a piece of the magical knapsack.

He must ride long and hard this day. Not accustomed to riding bareback, he knew that his body would be stiff and sore at his journey's end. Gustav was under no illusion. The Vrykyl would attack him again. He had to find some way to send a message to the Council of Dominion Lords. He had to find some way to tell them of his great success and to warn them of their dire peril.

Gustav was relatively certain he would not live to tell them himself.

4

THERE WAS IN THE PART OF LOEREM NEAR WHERE LORD GUSTAV TRAVELED, a place called Wild Town. The day Lord Gustav set fire to all his possessions that had been touched by the Vrykyl, two people walked into Wild Town. It does not seem possible that these two disparate incidents should be related, yet, in the near future, they would be.

Wild Town was something of a misnomer. The place was neither very wild—though it liked to think it was—nor could it be classified as a town. Wild Town might be considered more nearly a member of the fungus family, for it had grown up overnight at a crossing of two roads, one road leading south to a town that was a town—the settlement of Vilda Harn— and the other road leading to a ford on the Little Blue river.

Wild Town consisted of seven ramshackle shacks. Four of these shacks were, in order of importance: a tavern, a brothel, a blacksmith shop, and a Temple of Healing that came complete with a somewhat faded, but still impressive looking gilt sign. The other three shacks were currently occupied by vermin, both two-legged and four-legged.

Wild Town boasted a market, if one calls four stalls a market, and a well of remarkably clear, cold water. A ragged child sat by the well all day, collecting coppers and providing the community mug, which—for an extra copper—he would clean with the tail of his tattered and filthy shirt.

A seasoned traveler, passing through Wild Town, would have given the place either a look of disgust or a look of pity, depending on his nature, and ridden on. The two young men entering Wild Town were far from seasoned and they gazed on its tumble-down buildings and faded, wrinkled whores with awe and wonder. In their eyes, the whores were the most beautiful women they had ever seen, the shacks were the most magnificent structures conceived of by man, the market was the financial center of the universe and the tavern a place of danger, a rite of passage into manhood.

"Look, Jessan," said his friend, reaching up a small, slender and long-fingered hand to tug on the taller youth's arm, "that woman with the yellow hair is waving at you."

"Of course, she is, Bashae," Jessan replied, shrugging. "Likely she has never seen a Trevenici warrior before. Nothing but soft city men, such as that one over there."

His disparaging glance fell on a scrawny fellow in baggy, patched robes squatting on a large brick that formed the doorstoop of the Temple of Healing, fanning himself with a leaf from an elephant-ear plant.

"What does that sign above him say?" Bashae asked.

Jessan had been hoping his friend would ask him that very question. Jessan's uncle Ravenstrike, a mercenary warrior in the Dunkargan army, had taught his nephew to speak a smattering of Elderspeak, the common language of all races on Loerem. Raven had taught his nephew to read some, too, teaching what he considered to be the most important words for a warrior to learn to recognize, "temple" and "healing" being chief among them.

"Truly!" Bashae was awed. He could speak Elderspeak, but he could not read any language, even his own. "A Temple of Healing. That is where we must go. At once."

"Wait." Jessan caught hold of his friend's thin arm, dragged him back. "Not yet."

"But this is what I came for," Bashae argued. "I came to trade the jewelry for healing salves and potions."

"Yes," said the more worldly-wise Jessan, "but you never sell your wares to the very first buyer. You must show them around, create interest and excitement." He himself was carrying a load of fine fur pelts.

"We must first go to the market," he announced, although he eyed the blacksmith's longingly. He had come to barter for steel arrowheads, to replace the crude stone arrowheads he made himself.

The young men walked on. The whores called after them—or rather they called after Jessan. The women mistook Bashae for a child, although the pecwae was, in fact, eighteen—the same age as his friend. Jessan heard their shouts, but he could not understand what they were saying and thus had no idea that they were yelling at him.

Two people of different races watched Bashae and Jessan walk the one street of Wild Town, watched them with an interest born of intense boredom. One was a merchant, a member of the elven race, who had only recently come to Wild Town to set up his stall in the marketplace. He was bitterly disappointed with the place, that he had been led to believe was a prosperous, thriving community. He planned on packing up and leaving any day now. The other was a dwarf, whose name was Wolfram.

His name meant Wolf's Son, a common name among dwarven males, who believe that they are descended from wolves. Wolfram was vague as to why he himself was in Wild Town—not that the elf had asked. Once, during the glory days of Old Vinnengael some two hundred years before, the elves had been persuaded that they should take an interest in the other races of the world. This interest had proven disastrous for them. The fall of Old Vinnengael had resulted in a rupture between the elven ruler, the Divine, and the elven warlord, the Shield of the Divine. Every House of the Tromek nation had been involved in the devastating struggle for power that followed. Though peace had finally been declared, there was still much bitterness and bad blood between the Houses.

Thus Wolfram had been extremely surprised that the elf had deigned to speak to him at all, much less be so friendly and chatty. Wolfram figured the elf was on some sort of secret assignment. The elf liked nothing better than to talk about the politics of Dunkarga, particularly of rumors of war in the northwest part of that nation.

Wolfram saw the elf's pointed ears twitch like a dog's when he noted the arrival of a Trevenici youth. If anyone in Dunkarga would know about wars and battles, it would be a Trevenici, who fought as mercenaries in the Dunkargan army. The elf and the dwarf watched with interest as the young men came closer, both inwardly chuckling at the gaping wonder with which the two young men viewed the grubby buildings.

Wolfram had a belly laugh at the discomfiture of the whores, who could not persuade the handsome Trevenici, with his half-naked, oiled, and strongly muscled youthful body and his valuable fur pelts, to look at them twice.

The elf immediately rearranged his wares to their best advantage.

"You're wasting your time, friend," said Wolfram. "Neither of those young men will be interested in your lacquer boxes and silk scarves."

"Indeed?" the elf asked politely. "And why is that?"

"Both the pecwae and the Trevenici live simply. They never know when they may have to pick up and move and so they do not load themselves down with useless possessions."

"A pecwae," the elf repeated. "Do you make sport of me, sir?"

The elf's hand went to the curved-bladed sword he wore on his hip.

"No, I do not," said Wolfram. "That is a pecwae. You've never seen one before, I take it."

"The little people? The ones who speak with animals and can disappear in a twinkle of the eye? Bah! They are the stuff of legend. You are trying to trick me, and that is an insult which my honor will not permit me to abide. That is a human child."

"Look closely, friend," Wolfram advised. "You will see that although he is the height of a human child of eight, he has the features of an adult. That one is probably about twenty, or so I should guess."

The pecwae and the Trevenici passed close by the elf's stall, heading for the booth of a fur-peddler that was two down. The elf stared hard at the pecwae and lifted an eyebrow. In his turn, the pecwae stared, gaping, at the elf. He attempted to draw the attention of his friend, but the Trevenici was intent upon his business and did not look around.

"I see that you are right. That is not a human child," said the elf. "I am not prepared to say what it is, however."

"It's a pecwae," said Wolfram irritably. "You'll find several colonies of them in these parts. Where there are Trevenici, there you'll find pecwae."

The elf was not easily convinced, but since it would be insulting to the dwarf to continue to express doubts, the elf politely changed the subject.

"But what of the young warrior? He will be interested in my wares. Undoubtedly he has a woman waiting for his return, a woman whose beauty will be enhanced by one of my silk scarves."

Wolfram grunted and shook his head.

"No, he has no woman. Among the Trevenici, only a blooded warrior is allowed to take a mate. That young man has yet to fight his first battle. He probably still has his birth name."

"Not a warrior?" The elf looked doubtful. "He is young, certainly, but he is of fighting age. How can you tell he is not already a seasoned veteran?"

"Because he wears no trophies," Wolfram returned. "A Trevenici veteran would be decked out head to toe with shrunken heads and fingers and toes or any other body parts cut from his dead enemies."

"You jest, surely!" the elf exclaimed, shocked. "They mutilate the dead? I have heard that these Trevenici were barbarians, but I never imagined that . . . that . . ."

"They could be this barbarous?" Wolfram concluded dryly. "They don't consider it mutilation. They consider it a compliment to the dead, in fact. The Trevenici cut off body parts from an enemy who has particularly impressed them in battle. They believe that this not only displays their own valor and will therefore strike terror into the hearts of any who oppose them, but they also honor the fallen. If you travel to Dunkar, you will likely see more of them, for the Dunkargans hire Trevenici mercenaries to fight in their army. But perhaps you already knew that?" Wolfram added casually.

"Me? I know nothing of such barbarians. And if I had any plans of traveling south to Dunkar, you have just dissuaded me," the elf said lightly. "I shall most certainly be heading in the opposite direction."

"And if you are walking north tomorrow, I will fly up in the air like one of your damn kites," Wolfram said to himself, grinning into his beard.

He lingered near the elf's booth, watching the young men approach the fur peddler's stall. The Trevenici spoke a word of greeting in Elderspeak, then indicated his pelts. The fur peddler appeared guardedly interested. The Trevenici slung the pelts off his shoulder, spread them out on the counter. He exhibited the fine quality of the fur, running his hand through it and lifting the pelts to show the skin.

The fur peddler shook his head, but Wolfram could tell the man was impressed. The Trevenici could tell, as well. This young man was no yokel with hay-seed in his hair. He knew what he was doing and although his Elderspeak was crude, he knew enough of the language to make his points. Someone had taught him well.

The pecwae had no interest in the furs. He could not take his eyes off either the elf or the dwarf, but stared at them with all his might. The dwarf found it amusing. The elf was offended.

"They are taught no manners, whatever they are," the elf stated, a faint flush staining his pale cheek.

"We stare at him. He stares at us," said Wolfram.

The pecwae fidgeted, digging his bare toes in the dirt and looking around. Eventually, finding that this bargaining was likely to take up a considerable portion of the afternoon, the pecwae said something to his friend and wandered off.

He came straight to the booth. He was only about four feet in height, not as tall as the dwarf. His hair was brownish blond and very curly. He wore his hair cut short, revealing his long and pointed ears. His eyes were an intense blue color, round and large. He had a small, sharp chin and a full-lipped mouth. His teeth were blunt, like the teeth of a cow or a horse, for they had no need to tear meat. The intense blue eyes went from the elf to the dwarf and from the dwarf to the elf. The pecwae was awed, enchanted, but not in the least daunted or disconcerted.

"Jessan"—the pecwae jerked a thumb in the direction of his companion—"say that you are an elf and you"—the pecwae turned a pair of astonishingly bright eyes on Wolfram—"a dwarf. Is true?"

The pecwae's voice was shrill, high-pitched and piping. His Elderspeak was halting and barely understandable. The Trevenici are the only other race on Loerem who can speak the pecwae language, known as Twithil, and even they can only speak and understand a portion of what is said, for many of its sounds soar far above the human range of both speech and hearing.

"I am of the Tromek," said the elf, with a chill bow.

"I'm a dwarf," said Wolfram bluntly.

"I'm a pecwae. I make this," said the pecwae proudly and, reaching into a pouch attached to a leather thong that he wore draped over one shoulder, he pulled out a handful of jewelry that flashed in the sunlight and deposited the jewelry on the counter.

The elf had never seen anything so lovely. Sighing with pleasure, he reached out his hand to touch the beautiful pieces.

"Skystone," said the pecwae, watching with pride as the elf lifted the necklace to the light.

"Stunning!" the elf breathed.

Even the dwarf, who had no interest in jewelry, was taken with the work. Wolfram might have no love for jewelry, but he knew gemstones and that turquoise was the finest he had ever seen. Veins of silver streaked each nugget. The blue was the color of the summer sky reflected in a smooth lake. His fingers itched to touch it and he had to restrain himself from snatching it from the elf's hands.

"I will trade you one of my boxes for this," said the elf. "Whichever you want. Take your pick."

Wolfram had to bite his tongue to keep silent. Elves believe that turquoise is magical, has the power to protect the wearer from harm. A necklace like this, made up of at least thirty turquoise nuggets—the largest the size of the dwarf's large thumb—would be worth the price of a small house in any Tromek city. Wolfram cursed the luck that left him dirt poor when such a wonderful opportunity had come his way.

The pecwae cast a polite glance over the boxes. "Nice," he said and reached out his hand to gather up the jewelry. "Not for me." He looked at the Temple of Healing. "Potions."

"Ah, I understand." The elf was effusive. "You want healing potions. I have money. I will pay you money for the necklace and you can buy your potions at the Temple."

The pecwae looked blank.

"He doesn't understand the concept of money," Wolfram told the elf.

"What? Doesn't understand money?"

"Show him," suggested Wolfram. "I'll explain."

The elf was dubious, but a glance at the turquoise necklace that was disappearing back into the pecwae's pouch made up his mind. The elf left the booth, entered the covered wagon in which he lived, and returned a moment later with a small bag of coins. He took out several very large, shiny phennigs.

The pecwae found the coins, decorated with the head of a former Emperor of New Vinnengael, interesting. He admired the engraving, but, beyond that, had no idea what to make of them.

"This is money. You take that for the necklace," Wolfram said. "If you take these coins to the Temple, the man there will give you potions in return."

The pecwae looked at him in astonishment. "Why? Worth nothing. Copper."

Wolfram grinned and jerked his thumb at the elf. "He has other coins that are worth more in his pouch. Coins made of silver."

The pecwae nodded, his blue eyes glittered. He was bright, this one, quick to catch on. He shoved the coppers back to the elf. "Skystone worth more."

The elf cast Wolfram an angry glance.

"He's not a child," Wolfram said. "Nor is he a sheep to be sheared. He made that silver jewelry. He knows the quality and value of metal. You won't fool him with such tricks."

The elf reached into his bag and drew out two argents and laid these on the counter. The pecwae studied them and was more interested, obviously recognizing their worth. While his head was bent, he cast a sidelong glance at the dwarf. Wolfram made a very small movement with his head.

The pecwae held up ten fingers.

The elf held up five fingers.

The pecwae, now on firm ground, shook his head.

Finally, sighing deeply and looking as though he'd been forced to sell his grandmother, the elf rooted through the coin bag and dug out ten argents. The pecwae took these, examined each one, and placed them carefully in his pouch. He handed over the turquoise. The elf disappeared into his wagon with it. He was a long while inside, probably finding the best place to hide it. After all, even for ten argents, he'd made an excellent bargain.

By his standards, so had the pecwae. Wolfram knew the Temple priest. The man had probably not seen ten silver argents in a year. The pecwae would leave loaded down with all the potions and salves he could carry.

"That is beautiful skystone," said Wolfram. "Where do you find it?"

"Near camp," the pecwae answered.

His gaze shifted momentarily to his Trevenici friend. Jessan, he'd called him. Wolfram had been right. Jessan was a birth name, meaning Lasting Gift, a common name for children among Trevenici. The young man had yet to achieve his adult name. That would happen only after he completed the ceremony of becoming an adult, when he would take the name the gods would give him in a vision. This name would be revealed only to those close to him. To all others, the young man would select a name in Elderspeak, a name of his own choosing.

The pelt bargaining was nearly complete. The peddler had spread a great many steel arrowheads on the counter. The Trevenici was studying them with a practiced eye.

"We find silver near camp, too," the pecwae added, as an afterthought.

"Do you mine it?" Wolfram asked.

"Mine?" The pecwae didn't understand.

Wolfram made a chopping motion, as if wielding a hammer.

The pecwae shook his head. "The Earth would be angry and that would ruin the magic."

"Then how do you obtain it?" Wolfram asked.

"My grandmother sings it out," said the pecwae.

"Eh?" The dwarf thought that perhaps he'd translated the word incorrectly. "Sing? As in yo-yo-yo-heh-heh?"

"You call that singing?" The pecwae grinned. "It sounds more like the cawing of a crow. My grandmother's voice is the most beautiful voice in the world. She can imitate the calls of every bird so well that they mistake her for one of their own. She can sing up a wind or sing away rain. She sings to the Earth and the skystone tumbles out into her hand."

Wolfram raised an eyebrow. "Just as the words suddenly tumble out of your mouth."

A slight flush overspread the pecwae's cheeks. He grinned, shame-faced.

"Raven—that's his uncle"—he jerked a thumb at his friend—"told us not to let on that we understood what people were saying. That way, we'd find out if they were trying to cheat us."

Wolfram grunted. "Uncle Raven is wise."

Of course, Wolfram didn't believe a word about the grandmother singing the gemstone out of the earth. Still, he knew that pecwae were extremely lazy and would do anything to avoid working at a task. He wondered idly how Grandma really managed to obtain the skystone.

"This my friend, Jessan," said the pecwae in introduction, shifting back to the crude Elderspeak, though his eyes sparkled with fun when they met the gaze of the dwarf. "My name Bashae."

"Wolfram," said the dwarf in Elderspeak. He could have communicated with the two in Tirniv, for he spoke the language of the Trevenici, probably one of the few outsiders on Loerem to do so, almost certainly the only dwarf. Wolfram knew better than to let on that he understood, however. The Trevenici do not like to hear outsiders speak their language, which they consider sacred. Though they make exception for the pecwae, Trevenici will become hostile if they hear an outsider speak the holy words.

Jessan regarded Wolfram with cool appraisal. He was not friendly, but he was not mean nor distrustful, either. Guarded would be a good word to describe this young man, Wolfram thought. Self-possessed, for one so young. Confident, sure of himself, even in what must be a strange and unfamiliar situation. His face was well-molded, with a strong nose and jawline. His hair was dark red, thick and lank. He wore it twisted into a tail that hung down past the middle of his back. His skin was bronze from having lived most of his life outdoors.

Though not a warrior, he would be trained for warfare. All Trevenici youth, male and female, are trained warriors. He wore leather breeches. His chest and arms were bare, save for an exquisite necklace of turquoise and silver and a large silver bracelet. His pelts were gone. Tucked into his breeches was a fur bundle, undoubtedly containing the arrowheads his bargaining had won him.

"We go to Temple now," Jessan said in pidgin Elderspeak.

"I know the man at the Temple," Wolfram offered. "If you like, I could go with you and help you explain what you need."

"We do fine," said Jessan and, with another curt nod, he put a hand that was both protective and commanding on the shoulder of his friend and turned away.

The pecwae made no demur, but docilely accompanied his friend, obviously accustomed to following where the Trevenici led. Before he left, however, Bashae flashed Wolfram a smile of thanks and waved his hand.

Wolfram scratched his chin. All in all, a pleasant morning's diversion. He was about to turn away, planning to go spend his last copper on a mug of tepid ale, when he felt the burning sensation on his arm. He had not felt this sensation in so long that, at first, he mistook it for a bug bite and absent-mindedly scratched it. He was under no illusions the next moment, for the burning sensation grew stronger, as if he brushed his hand through the flame of a candle.

Wolfram glanced swiftly around. No one was paying him any attention. Reflecting on the fact that no one would have paid him any attention if he'd dropped down dead in the street, Wolfram walked over to stand in the shadow cast by the elf's wagon. The dwarf rolled up the long sleeve of his homespun shirt and peered down at a bracelet on his wrist.

The bracelet was made of silver set with five gems: ruby, jade, sapphire, pearl and onyx. Each of the gemstones had started to glow, heating the silver metal that was now starting to grow extremely warm. Wolfram stared at the bracelet in astonishment. This had not happened to him in a long time. Years, in fact. So long that he had begun to think that perhaps he had lost favor with the monks. He was immensely pleased, glad to think he still had the opportunity to turn a nice profit. He touched the stones, one by one, in a certain order and the burning ceased immediately.

Wolfram looked expectantly at the elf's wagon, but received no response from the bracelet. Pondering, the dwarf glanced around. As his gaze flicked over the two young men, the bracelet's warmth increased markedly.

"Well, well," said the dwarf and, rolling down his sleeve to cover the bracelet, he started off after them.

The gaudy gilt painted sign board nailed to the outside of the Temple of Healing was adorned with the symbols marking true Temples of Healing, those run by members of the Church who had received their training in the Temple of the Magi in New Vinnengael. Wolfram guessed that the supposed "Revered Magus," who was sitting fanning himself on the doorstoop, might have actually been to New Vinnengael and that he might very well have seen the grand Temple of the Magi, but that was as close as he came to being aligned with the Church. The man was a hedge-wizard if ever Wolfram had seen one.

Thin and unremarkable in appearance, the erstwhile magus watched the two approach with a pathetic interest. Once he determined they were heading his direction, he scrambled to his feet and pounced on them the moment they opened their mouths.

"My name is Brother Elias and I am a healer of extraordinary skill." He looked eagerly from one to the other. "Are you feverish? Coughing? Heart palpitations? Vomiting? I have cures for each of those complaints. Let me take your pulse."

He reached out his hand to Jessan, who favored the man with a cold stare.

"Not sick," he said. Indicating Bashae with a wave, Jessan added, "He buy potions."

Bashae produced two of the silver argents he'd received from the elf.

Although extremely disappointed to find out that they weren't suffering from some disease that would take lots of time and money to cure, Brother Elias perked up immensely when he saw silver flash in the pecwae's hand.

"I recognize a colleague," he said, his eyes on the coins. With grave dignity, he led his charges inside the tumble-down "temple."

Brother Elias gave out that he was a healer, but local opinion held him to be a potion peddler. About the best that could be said for Brother Elias was that he'd not poisoned anyone. Yet.

Wolfram wandered that direction. Moving around to the side of the Temple, he squatted in the building's shadow—almost more substantial than the building itself—and settled down comfortably below a hole in the wall that passed for a window.

Wolfram was now able to hear everything said inside the building. He hoped that the pecwae knew as much about potions as he knew about gemstones, otherwise he was liable to be plucked clean as a cooked goose.

Brother Elias started off with his best merchandise, offering a love potion guaranteed to make the object of your affection fall swooning into your bed. At this, the pecwae chuckled and the Trevenici took offense. Seeing the way the wind blew, Brother Elias cleverly switched horses in midstream and offered up a salve that was certain to heal any wound received in battle, from an arrow through the throat to a spear taken in the belly, without leaving so much as a scar. This was more kindly received. The Trevenici was interested. At this juncture, the pecwae took charge.

"Let me smell it," said Bashae.

A loud snuffling sound, then Bashae said to Jessan in Tirniv, "It's nothing but bear grease."

There came the sound of shuffling feet, a scrape of metal, and Jessan's voice, cold with anger, "You are no better than a thief. I should cut off your ears."

Brother Elias gave a whimper and, by the sounds of it, fell back against the wall that shook most alarmingly.

"No, don't do that, Jessan," Bashae told his friend. "He does have some potions I want and he'll need his ears to hear what I say to him." He then added, sternly, "I think you should wait outside."

At the sound of footfalls, Wolfram regained his feet and hastily left the Temple. A glance over his shoulder showed the Trevenici youth, grim and glowering, taking up a stance outside the Temple with as much earnest purpose as if he had been assigned to mount guard on the king's treasury.

Wolfram sauntered past, head down, apparently deeply absorbed in his own business. Coming to the crossroads, Wolfram glanced back, saw the Trevenici still standing in front of the Temple. Wolfram, moving fast, dove into the cover of a patch of weeds. Ducking down among long, tasseled grasses and sweet-smelling sage, he settled himself to wait for the two to pass by him on their way out of town.

5

About an hour later, the two young men approached the dwarf's resting place; the pecwae chattering excitedly to his friend, describing the various items he'd purchased from the priest.

"You acted sensibly, Bashae," Wolfram said. Rising up out of the grass, the dwarf brushed dust and seeds off his breeches. "Buying the raw ingredients, not the finished product. That man was no true healer."

The Trevenici youth glared darkly at the intrusive dwarf.

"Keep walking, Bashae," Jessan said to his friend.

"He wasn't a healer?" Bashae asked, walking backward in order to speak to Wolfram. "Why would he lie about something like that?"

"Because people pay good money for healing," Wolfram said, following along. "He mixes up a few potions, then spends his day squatting on that doorstoop underneath that lying sign. People come up and tell him what ails them. He hands over the potion, takes their argents and goes back to sitting on the doorstoop."

"But what happens when they're not healed?" Bashae questioned sensibly.

"Oh, sometimes they are, you know," Wolfram replied. He had caught up to the two by now. "Sometimes they manage to get better on their own. Sometimes, by accident, one of his potions works. And, sometimes, his patients die. But then they can't very well come back to place blame."

"Neither my grandmother nor I would ever ask for anything to heal a person," Bashae said, thoughtfully scuffing dirt with his bare feet. "She says that healing is in our bones just like magic is in the Earth's bones and that the Earth gives of her bounty and so we give of ours."

"An estimable woman," Wolfram stated. "I would like very much to meet her." The dwarf fell into step with the pecwae and the Trevenici. "I'm going your way. Mind if I tag along?"

"How do you know which way we are going, Dwarf?" Jessan returned shortly.

"Your way is my way," Wolfram returned. "My way is any way. All ways are the same way—in the end," he added reflectively.

Jessan maintained a dignified silence. The Trevenici do not discuss the afterlife with outsiders, considering that topic too sacred to be bandied about during casual conversation.

They continued on down the trail that was nothing more than two wagon ruts worn across the prairie. The land in these parts was flat and barren, covered with tall, rustling grass that had dried up and turned brown in the sun's heat. The trail ran straight and true with never a turn until it reached the Little Blue river. A stand of cottonwood trees, some ways distant, marked a creek or a pond. The Crackerneck Mountains could be seen to the northeast, but they were far away, a smudge on the horizon. The sun was edging its way into the west. This was summer and there were still several more hours of daylight left for travel.

Bashae showed Wolfram his purchases: apple bark from the north lands for female troubles, feather foil from the south to treat the swelling joints of the elderly, green tea from the elven lands. Wolfram described some herbal treatments used by the dwarves. Bashae listened with interest, making special note of the ingredients. This topic exhausted, Wolfram went on to tell about his people, the pony riders, who live their lives on the backs of their shaggy beasts, roaming the hills far to the east.

Wolfram knew a great many stories. He knew how to be entertaining. He knew how to win over a sulky audience. His livelihood depended on his charm, something for which dwarves are not particularly noted, but which Wolfram had cultivated over the years. Jessan never said a word, but he listened attentively and, occasionally, during some especially exciting encounter with elven warriors or orken raiders, the Trevenici would either nod his approval or glower his disapproval, depending on circumstance.

They halted toward nightfall. Jessan produced a packet of venison strips and actually shared them with Wolfram, a mark of favor. Bashae ate dried berries and chewed on the root of some plant, which he also offered to the dwarf. Wolfram politely declined. Dwarves are meat-eaters.

The night air cooled rapidly in early summer. Following the meal, the two young men lay down on the still-warm ground and both were immediately asleep—the sweet and uncomplicated slumber of youth. Wolfram could not remember a time when he'd slept like that. He lay down, but he remained awake, listening to Jessan's deep breathing, watching Bashae's hands and feet twitch in his sleep like a dog on a dream-hunt. Sighing, Wolfram sat up. He peered again at the bracelet on his arm. The burning had ceased. The gems glowed faintly in the darkness. A sign that he was obeying instructions.

Wolfram had no idea why these two youths were of such importance. He looked forward eagerly to finding out. Rubbing the bracelet, thinking fond thoughts of the silver argents his mission would bring him, Wolfram lay back down. He was on the verge of drifting off when Jessan awoke and announced that it was time they were moving on.

Wolfram had forgotten this custom of the Trevenici warrior—to sleep only a few hours and then, if possible, continue the journey during the night.

The dawn was still many hours away, but one could see fairly well by the lambent light of moon and stars, for there were no trees to cast shadows. The three trudged down the trail. Wolfram had more stories, but was not in the mood to tell them. Perversely, he was sleepy now and that made him grumpy, right when he needed to continue to exude charm. He had noted that Jessan was starting to keep closer watch on landmarks, guessed that soon they were going to leave the trail, strike out across the open prairie.

About an hour into the march, Jessan came to a halt beside a group of stones that had been sorted into a pile alongside of the trail. The trail ran east and west. Jessan looked to the north. He left it to the pecwae to speak.

"We turn off here," Bashae announced. "Thank you for the stories and thank you for helping me with the elf."

Jessan muttered something that Wolfram couldn't catch.

"A good journey to you, sir," Bashae added politely.

Wolfram felt a small twinge of warmth from the bracelet, but he didn't need the prompting. He knew well enough that he was supposed to stick with these two, though for what earthly reason, he couldn't tell.

"Thank you," he said, equally polite. "I would like very much to continue to travel with you. I hope to consult with your grandmother," he added, speaking to the pecwae. "A woman of vast wisdom."

Bashae looked to Jessan, who shook his head. He did not so much as glance at the dwarf, but continued to gaze to the north. "No," he said.

Wolfram could always trail them the next day, but he would need to be accepted by the Trevenici people and he didn't want to start off by seeming to have sneaked up on their dwelling places like a thief. He was thinking over what arguments he might use when, unexpectedly, the pecwae came to the dwarf's rescue.

"Let's take him with us," said Bashae, speaking in Tirniv.

Jessan shook his head.

"No one in our village has ever seen a dwarf," Bashae argued. "Not even your uncle Ravenstrike. Think what a sensation it will cause when we bring Wolfram into our village. And he will be our dwarf. No one else can claim him. Bear Paw will be sick with envy, for all his trophies. What's a puny, shriveled up old head compared to a real, live dwarf!"

Jessan appeared to consider this.

"Especially to Bright Dawn," Bashae insinuated cleverly. "She's never seen a dwarf and she's seen lots of shriveled up old heads."

Wolfram stood looking ignorant, not supposed to be understanding any of this. He supposed he should feel insulted, being valued like a freak at the fair, but if this insured his continuing with the two young men, then he would willingly put on a good show.

"You're not afraid of him, are you?" Bashae asked with every appearance of innocence.

"Of course not," Jessan returned, with a disparaging glance at the dwarf.

"Then let's take him," Bashae urged.

The pecwae had handled this very cleverly. If Jessan refused now, he would later and for all time be accused of being afraid of dwarves. Jessan seemed to realize he was being maneuvered into a corner, but didn't know how to escape. Wolfram obtained a much clearer idea of the relationship between the pecwae and Trevenici. One accustomed to living life by walking always a straight path was bound to trip over one who darted around him in circles.

"The dwarf can come," Jessan said in no very gracious tone.

"You can come with us," Bashae stated excitedly, turning to Wolfram. "We talked it over, my friend and I. I told him that my grandmother would be very interested in speaking with you and he agrees with me."

Wolfram said what was polite, thanking both young men for allowing him the pleasure of their companionship and the very great honor of bringing him into their village. Jessan kicked over the pile of stones, scattering them, and the three resumed their travels. Wolfram wondered how far they had to go, but didn't like to ask, fearing that he might appear to be angling for information for some sinister purpose.

They did not travel a straight route, and the dwarf guessed that the Trevenici was deliberately taking a circuitous route in order that the dwarf would not be able to find his way back to the village. Wolfram, who was starting to grow very weary, could have assured Jessan that he had no such intentions, but that would have made it seem like he did have such intentions. Wolfram kept his mouth shut, therefore, and concentrated on staying awake.

The night deepened. A large patch of darkness rose up on their right, blotting out the stars. Wolfram sniffed, smelled water, identified the patch as a stand of trees surrounding a lake. Bashae said something about his waterskin being empty and the two young men bent their steps in this direction. Wolfram was pleased at the idea of a halt, if only for a short time. By laving his neck and face with cold water, he hoped to wake himself up.

They entered the grove of trees. Leaf-laden branches cast heavy shadows. Their way slowed. They heard the sounds of nocturnal animals out hunting. An owl hooted overhead, proclaiming this his territory. Another owl called out in the distance, maybe in dispute. A rustle in the brush was a fox having a look at them, according to Bashae. Wolfram almost stepped on a stoat, who snarled in irritation and slithered out from beneath his foot.

Leaving the trees behind, they emerged from the shadows and came to the banks of a still, placid lake. A herd of deer was drinking from the water. Startled, they flipped their white tails and dashed off, although Bashae called out after them, telling them not to be afraid. Wolfram watched this with interest. He had always heard pecwae could communicate with animals, but he'd never seen one do so until now.

The deer were not impressed, however. Wolfram heard them crashing through the trees.

Bashae smiled, shrugged. "They didn't believe me. You two are wearing deer hides. I can't really blame them."

Wolfram could not blame them either. Walking to the water's edge, he cupped his hands and drank. The water was cool and tasted of the earth. He splashed some on his face.

"What is that strange light out there?" Jessan said in a sharp tone.

Wolfram wiped his eyes free of water, peered out to see a patch of shining silver glimmering on the surface of the inky black and star-studded water. He had noticed the light earlier, but had given it little thought.

"The moon," he said, yawning. "A moon glade."

"The moon set an hour ago," Jessan said.

Wolfram woke up. Scrambling to his feet, he glanced involuntarily at the sky. "You're right."

He stared back at the shimmering surface. The silver patch was about twelve feet from the shoreline, and, now that he studied it more closely, he could see that the light was not a reflection of moonlight shining down from above. The silver light floated on the surface of the lake like an oil slick, rising and falling with the movement of the water.

The ripples created by the startled deer did not disperse the patch of silver, did not break it up into tiny waves of silver and of black. The shining light remained intact, slid right over the ripples, as might a silk scarf, dropped upon the water. Wolfram's hand closed over the bracelet on his arm.

"I'll be . . ." he said, awed.

"Let's go see what it is," Bashae cried, excited. Flinging down the water skin, he was three steps into the lake and Jessan was splashing in after him before the dwarf realized what the young men were doing.

Wolfram plunged into the water. Grabbing hold of the pecwae's thin arm in one hand, he caught hold of Jessan's wrist with the other.

Angrily, Jessan jerked his wrist from the dwarf's hold, glowered at Wolfram. Trevenici don't like to be touched by outsiders, but this was not the time to indulge in formalities. The young man had halted and that was all Wolfram wanted.

"Don't go near it," the dwarf warned. "I know what it is. Keep away from it."

"What is it?" Bashae asked, staring at the light.

Jessan continued to glower at the dwarf, but he stayed where he was, about shin-deep in the water. Instinctively cautious and wary, he would at least wait to hear what Wolfram had to say.

"That is a Portal," Wolfram explained. "One of the magic Portals." He jerked his thumb at it. "You walk into it and there's no telling where you might come out. Maybe some place nice and maybe in the middle of an elf war encampment, where they'd spit you before you could say 'boo,' or maybe in the middle of a pool of boiling hot mud. You do know what a Portal is, don't you?" Wolfram added.

"My uncle speaks of them," Jessan replied coolly. "He says that there are none in this part of the world. The nearest Portal is in Karnu."

In his mind, that settled the issue. Uncle Ravensbeak or whatever his name was had said there were no Portals here and so, of course, there could be no Portals.

"The nearest *known* Portal," Wolfram emphasized. "There are a great many unknown Portals—rogue Portals that were created when the four Great Portals in Old Vinnengael were torn asunder by the blast that leveled that city. This is likely one of those." He backed up out of the lake, drawing Bashae with him.

Jessan frowned, his dark brows lowering. He continued to stand in the water. "If what you say is true and this is one of the magical Portals, then why has no one discovered it before now?"

"I know!" Bashae cried. Reaching land, he shook himself like a dog. "Because no one ever comes to this lake at night. You wouldn't be able to see the light in the daytime."

That's true, Wolfram realized. The lake is far from the trail. Travelers would not know of its existence. And, even if someone did stumble across it, the Portal's eerie glowing light would not be noticeable for the sun's beams dancing across the water. Even in the night, a casual observer would mistake it for moonlight, as had Wolfram himself.

"Come away, lad," he said.

Jessan remained in the water, staring at the pale, glistening light. "Where do you suppose it would take me?" he asked.

"Who knows? Perhaps not even the gods," Wolfram said, wondering what in the name of the gods he would do if the young man decided to see for himself.

The two were not his charge, not his responsibility. He was not answerable for them. If they disappeared into a Portal, then that was their concern. He knew the way back to the main trail. He'd obviously found what it was the monks had sent him to find. He had only to note the location and report back. Yet, he kept a tight grip on the pecwae.

"Perhaps it goes to the bottom of the lake," he said. "Perhaps it goes to the other side of the world. Or to the gods themselves. If you've never been in a Portal before, it can be very disorienting. Like a cavern. You have no sense of what is up and down, which way is north or south. You can become easily confused."

He was suddenly inspired. "Take word back to your people. Send a party of warriors to trace its route—"

The Portal flashed, its light suddenly shining stronger and brighter. Faint sounds could be heard emanating from the Portal, the thudding sounds of pounding hooves, or perhaps a beating heart.

Wolfram sucked in a breath and scrambled backward away from the water, dragging Bashae, who was quick to follow him. Thankfully, the diminutive pecwae are blessed with a strong sense of self-preservation.

"Jessan, come away!" Bashae urged.

The sounds of hoofbeats grew louder. Jessan, startled and uneasy, edged his way back onto the bank, though he kept his rapt gaze riveted on the glowing light.

Horse and rider leapt out of the Portal, white foam water cascading around them. The horse's nostrils flared. The beast was galloping at full speed. Shaking water from its mane and head, the horse scrabbled desperately with its front hooves to find purchase on the lake bottom. The rider was a knight whose silver armor shone brilliantly in the Portal's light. Obviously a skilled rider, he bent low over the horse's neck, urging the animal on.

The horse made landfall and splashed through the lake, sending up fountains of water that shone white against the lake's black surface. Amazed at the astonishing sight of man and horse leaping out of the lake, Jessan stumbled backward and nearly fell. He came close to being ridden down by the maddened steed, but the well-trained horse sensed the human in his path and jumped over him.

"A god!" Bashae breathed, awed. His hand clung so tightly to Wolfram's that the dwarf winced.

At first, the astounded Wolfram thought the pecwae might be right, but something about the knight's armor was familiar to the dwarf. Recovering from his shock, he stared more closely at the rider as the horse clamored up onto dry land.

"No," said Wolfram softly. "But close. He is a Dominion Lord."

The knight halted his steed. Twisting, he turned to look back at the

Portal. Jessan stared with all his might at the knight, whose wet armor glistened like fish scales in the starlight.

The knight raised his visor. "Where am I?" he called, a note of urgency in his voice.

He looked around him, taking in trees and lake and vast sky and empty prairie and turned to Jessan. "Where am I?" he asked more urgently still.

Jessan could not reply. He could do nothing but stare.

"Damn it—" the knight began.

"I'll tell you where you are, Sir Knight," said Wolfram, stepping out of the shadows of the trees. "You stand on Trevenici lands, north of Dunkarga.

"Dunkarga," the knight repeated.

Wolfram could not see the knight's face very well in the half-light of stars and Portal, but he could tell by the slump of the armored shoulders that this was not the answer the knight had hoped to hear.

Wolfram pointed. "The capital Dunkar is some seven hundred miles to the south."

"Dunkarga," the knight said again. He sounded weary to the point of falling. "*Not* Vinnengael, as I had hoped and prayed." He shook his head, then looked back at the Portal. They could all hear the faint sound of hoofbeats, coming nearer. "Very well. My brave Fotheral is foundering. He can go no farther. And neither can I. I must make my stand here."

Sliding off his horse, the knight drew his sword, then, with a word of command, he sent the horse galloping into the trees. Glancing behind him, he said sternly, "Take these young ones and flee, Dwarf. That which is coming through the Portal in pursuit of me will mean your death."

"What . . . what is it?" asked Wolfram, who had the disorienting sense that he was in a strange dream.

"A Vrykyl, a creature of the Void," the knight answered. "Fell and powerful." He looked back grimly at the Portal. "I fought it a fortnight ago. I thought I had inflicted a death wound, but the thing managed to heal itself. It has pursued me since. When I found the rogue Portal, I hoped . . . I prayed it would lead me to New Vinnengael."

He smiled slightly, shrugged. "The gods have answered so many of my prayers, I have no right to complain that they did not heed this one."

Wolfram was no longer paying attention. He was already heading for the trees. A creature of the Void so powerful that not only had it dared to fight a Dominion Lord, but had managed to send this knight fleeing before it must be powerful indeed. Wolfram sensed danger, like the coming of thunder on a sweltering summer's day, and he wanted nothing to do with it. Bashae ran alongside him.

"Make haste, lad!" Wolfram called over his shoulder to Jessan. "The knight is right. We must get out of here!"

Jessan lifted his head proudly and the dwarf knew what the young man was going to say before he said it.

"You mistake me if you think I would flee in the face of danger. No one of my people has ever run away from an enemy," Jessan stated. Drawing his knife—the only weapon he carried—he took up his stance beside the knight.

The knight did not smile, nor did he berate the young man or scold him for a fool, as Wolfram might have done. The hoofbeats drew nearer still, the Portal's silver light began to dim, as though it were a moonglade and a cloud had moved to swallow it up.

"I thank you, sir, for your offer," said the knight. "My name is Gustav. I am a lord of Vinnengael. I have no squire, as you can see. You could serve me in that office, if you will." He gestured with his sword and now Wolfram noted that the knight held his left arm stiffly, did not make use of it. "Go stand with my horse. Keep him from bolting. And make ready to bring me another weapon if I am disarmed."

Jessan gripped his knife tightly and for a moment Wolfram feared that the young man would defy the knight and stand his ground. Jessan knew his limitations, however, as he would have known them on the field of battle. Nephew to a Trevenici warrior, Jessan was accustomed to obedience, accustomed to taking orders. The knight was the elder and he was in command. He had treated Jessan with respect and given him a task he could perform with honor.

"My name is Jessan, son of Clawing Bear. I will not fail you, sir," Jessan replied.

He had spoken in Tirniv, a rare honor for the knight, though he was too preoccupied to notice. He simply nodded and turned back to face his foe.

Jessan ran to the horse that stood in the trees. The beast had not shown the least inclination to bolt. Wolfram, who knew horses, as all dwarves know horses, recognized it to be a highly trained destrier, one that would remain where its master told it to remain though the sky fell down. Quick-thinking, this knight, and even in his dire predicament, understanding of proud young men.

Bashae wrenched his hand loose of the dwarf's hold and went to the horse. Stroking its neck admiringly, he spoke to it softly. He used Elder-speak, the language the horse was most accustomed to hearing, and asked the beast if it needed water. The horse heard and understood, seemingly, for its mane twitched. It did not take its attention from its master, but stood tense and alert, waiting to be summoned. Jessan removed a battle-ax from the saddle and stood holding it tightly, white-knuckled, waiting, like the horse.

The darkening, murky water started to churn and roil. The feeling of evil was palpable, absorbed all sound, so that Wolfram heard nothing except the beating of his heart and that seemed to be the echo of nothing.

"A Vrykyl, he says. I should clear out of here," Wolfram told himself. Sweating and panting, he tore his gaze from the turgid water. "This is not my fight." He backed up a step. "These young ones are not my concern. Nor is the knight, the gods bless him." He backed up another step. "I've done what I came to do, found what I was sent to find. My next task is to stay alive long enough to report it. The knight himself told me to flee and I find myself in complete agreement."

Perhaps it was fate, perhaps the gods. Perhaps it was the dwarf's own irresolution, or maybe the bracelet on his arm. Perhaps it was nothing more than the work of an industrious gopher. Taking a third step backward, his intent to turn and run for his life, he felt his boot heel sink into a hole in the soft ground. He gave a startled yell and toppled over, wrenching his ankle.

The dark water frothed and bubbled. A black horse bearing a black-armored rider burst out of the Portal. The Portal's eerie light did not touch either of them, did not shine on the horse's wet fur, did not glisten on the black armor. The evil absorbed all light, so that the stars vanished and the dark became absolute, stilled the wind, drew the air from the lungs. The darkness of the horse and rider absorbed the light and the Portal's glow faded, became pale and wavering.

The Vrykyl wore armor of her own, armor that was black as the Void that forged it. Adorned with wicked-looking spikes on the shoulders and elbows, the armor would turn blade or bludgeon.

The dwarf had heard legends of Vrykyl—the undead knights of the Void—but he'd never believed in them. He wasn't certain he believed in them now. He much preferred to think that he was dreaming and that shortly he would wake to laugh at his fear.

The black horse thrashed through the water, thundering straight for the knight in silver. Lord Gustav lowered his visor and waited on the shore to meet his foe. Void magic spread out in waves from the rider. The very trees seemed to flatten before it, like stalks of grain in a violent windstorm.

Half-blinded, wholly terrified, Wolfram huddled close to the ground, praying only that the Vrykyl would not see him. The knight's horse whinnied, its feet thrashed the ground. Bashae whimpered and Jessan gasped in horror. Hearing the ring of steel against steel, the dwarf dared lift his eyes.

The Vrykyl saw her opponent dismounted and bereft of a shield, which the knight's useless left arm could not hold. She had him now, she thought, and sheathed her sword to take hold of a gigantic mace. She began to swing the mace with an unnaturally powerful stroke.

The mace made a hideous whirring sound, as of hundreds of devouring locusts, as it sliced the air. The Vrykyl intended to strike a blow that would crack open the knight's armor. If the blow and the magic did not kill the Dominion Lord, the attack would leave him dazed, wounded, and vulnerable to a second strike.

Gustav stood poised and calm, his sword raised. The Vrykyl charged straight for the knight, her mace swinging a vicious, cutting stroke. Gustav didn't move.

Wolfram wondered if the knight was just going to stand there and die, wondered where that would leave the rest of them.

Gustav shouted words in Vinnengaelean. "Bittersweet memories," he called out.

Silver blue light gleamed from armor and sword. As he swung the blade to defend himself against the mace, the magic of the blessed weapon encountered the cursed magic of the Void. Sparks flared. The air vibrated with the shock. Gustav's blade sliced through the Vrykyl's wrist, severing her hand from her arm. The Vrykyl's weapon and the mailed glove that held it dropped to the ground.

Gustav staggered backward, stunned. The sword weighed heavily in his grasp, almost too heavy to hold. He raised his head, looked at his opponent, hoping to see the Vrykyl fall.

The terrible blow would have stopped any mortal. The Vrykyl was briefly amazed by the loss of her weapon, but that did not halt her attack. Reining in her horse, the Vrykyl wheeled, and spurred the beast straight at the knight.

We're all dead, thought Wolfram. The Vrykyl will slay him and then kill the rest of us. The dwarf glanced at the young ones. Jessan stood holding the horse's reins without knowing that he held them. He watched the battle with eyes that were wide and luminous with excitement. Bashae, shivering in terror, peered out from under the horse's belly.

Wolfram set his tongue against the back of his teeth and made a sound—a buzzing, clicking sound. Placing his hand to his mouth, he amplified the sound—the buzz of a swarm of insects the dwarves call the horsebane fly.

The buzzing sound mimicked the strange clicking noise made by the hordes of the tormenting flies right before they strike. The knight's horse, well-trained though it was, whinnied in alarm, jerked its head, and rolled its eyes wildly, trying to locate the stinging, biting insects that could drive horses mad with pain, send them plunging over cliffs to escape. Jessan and Bashae suddenly had their hands full, both trying to keep control of the panicked steed.

Wolfram prayed to the Wolf that the Vrykyl's horse was flesh and blood, mortal, not some nightmare creature of the Void.

His prayer was answered. The ears of the Vrykyl's horse pricked. Its eyes swiveled in its head. The horse reared straight up, hooves lashing out in panic. The Vrykyl fought to calm the creature, but could not. The horse reared and bucked. She fell from the saddle, landed on her back on the ground.

Knowing her danger, the Vrykyl sought immediately to regain her feet. Encased in her armor and missing a hand, she could not move easily or swiftly and floundered on the ground like an overturned turtle.

Gustav seized his advantage. Grasping his sword, he ran to stand over the Vrykyl. She made a last, desperate attempt to save herself, flailing about with her good hand to try to seize the knight's leg.

Gustav shouted out again in Vinnengaelean.

"Love of Adela," he cried and drove the point of his blue-flaring sword straight into the Vrykyl's breast.

The sword splintered with a shattering crack, its blue light flashed and then went dark. The Vrykyl screamed, a terrible sound that was more fury than pain. Blessed light filled her empty darkness, ending the power of Void magic to sustain her existence. The scream sounded long, a keening wail of rage and rending magic.

Wolfram gritted his teeth and clasped his hands over his ears. The last sight he saw before he squinched his eyes tight shut in terror was the knight, armor shimmering with fading blue light, slumping to the ground beside his fallen foe.

6

CAUTIOUSLY, AMAZED THAT HE WAS STILL ALIVE, WOLFRAM OPENED HIS eyes. The Portal's light gleamed bright on the surface of the rippling water. Bashae calmed the knight's horse, stroking the animal on the neck and speaking soothing words. Jessan, mindful of his duty, ran to the aid of his fallen knight.

Wolfram regained his feet, grunting and grimacing in pain. His ankle was not broken—he could not hear anything crunch—but he'd sprained it badly. So much for running away. Like it or not, his lot was cast with the young ones for awhile, at least until his ankle healed. Or, if the Vrykyl's horse were still around, he would take it and return to impart his news and claim his reward.

He searched for the horse, heard its hooves beating on the ground some distance away. So much for that idea. Wolfram limped over to where Jessan stood beside the fallen knight and his dead foe.

The hilt of the knight's sword—all that remained—lay on top of the black breastplate. The Vrykyl's armor had cracked in two, but there was no sign of blood.

"The knight will want a trophy," Jessan said. "If he dies, we will place it in his grave with him."

Jessan still held the knight's battle-ax. Before the horrified Wolfram could stop him, Jessan wielded the ax and with one swift stroke, severed the Vrykyl's helmeted head from the armor-covered body.

Wolfram froze, panic-stricken, waiting for the Vrykyl to rise and seize Jessan by the throat, for Void magic to swirl out of the black armor and steal their souls.

The helmet rolled off through the grass. And then Wolfram saw why there was no blood.

There was no body.

Jessan squatted down to take a closer look. "*Garlnik!*" he swore in Tirniv. "Where . . . where is it?"

Well might he ask. Nothing remained of the Vrykyl but a pile of greasy, gray dust.

The sight frightened Wolfram more than the most hideously mutilated corpse, raised the hair on the dwarf's arms and neck and prickled the hairs of his mustache on his lip. The taint of Void magic was so thick it made him queasy.

Jessan was not bothered by it. Trevenici are very literal minded. They believe in what they can see, what they can feel, what they can touch. They know that there are certain things in nature that cannot be explained. What keeps the bird in the air and the man on the ground? No one knows. Does this matter to the bird? Not in the least. Nor does it concern the Trevenici. Thus they view magic—without awe, without even much interest, so long as it has nothing to do with them.

Down on all fours, Jessan peered into the empty black armor in search of the body. "Where did it go?" His voice echoed hollowly. His breath displaced the greasy dust, sending it into the air in little puffs.

Wolfram felt a fear-laugh bubbling up in his throat. He choked it back, knowing that once he started, he would not be able to stop.

His tongue was thick, his mouth dry. "Leave it be, son."

He put his hand on the young man's arm.

Jessan cast the dwarf a fierce, proud look and Wolfram swiftly withdrew his hand, noted that it trembled visibly.

"It's a creature of the Void," Wolfram tried desperately to explain. "A thing of evil. Best not to come too close or look too hard or ask too many questions."

Jessan glowered, eyes dark and accusing. "Pah! You are a coward. You tried to run away. I saw you."

"So should you, if you had any sense," Wolfram returned. "And because of me, you're still alive, young warrior. But don't thank me on that account!"

Favoring his hurt ankle, he limped as far from the black armor as he could manage. "You should tend to the knight now," he said over his shoulder. "He made you his squire."

"That is true." Jessan left off poking and prodding the black armor—much to Wolfram's relief.

Jessan knelt down, searched for some means to remove the man's helm. His hands fumbled at the visor, hoping to lift it, but it seemed to be welded shut. There were no visible fastenings, buckles or leather straps.

"How does this come off?" Jessan asked helplessly.

Staring in awe-struck confusion at the knight's intricate armor, he reverently touched the gleaming helm, that was fashioned in the image of a fox's head. Jessan was not the least impressed by a vanishing corpse, but the beautiful armor of the Dominion Lord brought the young warrior near to tears.

"I have never seen the like," he added, awed. "Not even Uncle Raven's armor is as wonderful as this."

Wolfram could well imagine that. Uncle Raven's helm probably doubled as his stew pot.

"You won't find the secret to that armor," Wolfram advised the young man. "He's a Dominion Lord. Their armor is magic, given to them by the gods."

"Then why does he lie injured?" Jessan demanded, personally affronted. "Surely the gods would protect him."

"Not from that evil," said Wolfram, glancing askance at the empty black armor. "That was a Vrykyl, a creature of the Void, as I keep trying to tell you. Still, you have a point. I did not see the thing hit him. Perhaps the knight has only fainted."

"Bashae!" Jessan summoned his companion peremptorily. "Leave the horse. He can look after himself. Come here and see if you can figure out what is wrong with the knight."

"The horse grieves for his master," Bashae reported, approaching their group with wary awe. "The horse spoke to me of their journey. He says that their foe attacked his master almost a fortnight ago. The master battled it and thought he had killed it. But the thing did not die. It has pursued them since. Though they could not see it, both horse and master felt its evil presence trailing them. His master was wounded by the thing the first time it attacked. He has grown weaker since and these last few days he could not eat."

"Strange," said Wolfram, frowning and scratching his chin. "Why would the thing pursue the knight? Usually creatures of the Void kill and have done with it. Odd this is. Very odd." He rubbed his arm. The bracelet on his arm was warm to the touch.

Bashae knelt beside the knight. Reaching out, he rested his small hand on the knight's breastplate. At his touch, the breastplate changed to liquid silver. Bashae squealed in dismay and scrambled backward, took refuge behind the horse. Jessan sucked in a hissing breath. Something had at last impressed the unimpressionable Trevenici.

The armor flowed over the knight's body and disappeared, leaving him clad in plainly made, trail-stained breeches and a leather jerkin, such as any traveler might wear.

"I told you the armor was magic," Wolfram said irritably. He examined the knight's face, moved closer. "I'll be swiggered. Lord Gustav, he said his name was. And I never recognized it. The Whoreson Knight being chased by a thing of the Void. Now I just wonder . . ." He stared down at the knight, musing, his thoughts a tangle of new and possibly profitable possibilities.

"What made it do that?" Jessan asked, eyeing the knight warily.

Looking around, Wolfram located the pecwae, who was crouching behind the horse.

"Come back, Bashae," the dwarf called, waving his hand. "It was your gentle touch that lifted the enchantment. See if you can determine what is wrong with him. Come along." He motioned again. "Nothing will hurt you."

But even as he spoke, he looked again at the black-armored figure. He did not like hearing that Gustav had thought he'd killed it, only to have it rise again and pursue him. Albeit, Wolfram reminded himself, that was the horse's version. Wolfram loved horses as all dwarves love horses, but he had no great faith in the beast's perspicacity.

"He's an old man," Jessan exclaimed, examining the knight's lined face, his gray hair and beard. "Old as Grandmother Pecwae. And yet he is a warrior."

Small wonder he was astonished. Few Trevenici males or females live to a peaceful old age.

"Yes, he is old," said Wolfram. "He is the eldest of the human Dominion Lords and the *most honored*." He added that, in case the knight could perhaps hear him. What was truly said was that this knight was the most addled.

Bashae squatted near Gustav. The pecwae laid his ear on Gustav's chest, listening for the heartbeat. He opened an eyelid, peered into it. He opened the mouth, examined the tongue. Shaking his head, he looked over at the black armor.

"You say that thing was evil?" Bashae asked.

"Most assuredly." Wolfram was fervent.

Bashae nodded. He raised up, sniffed the air, very much like a hound on a scent, and then left them, darting into the darkness. He returned after a few moments, bearing a sprig of fragrant smelling leaves in his hand.

"Sage," he said, waving it in the air. "Strike a light," he ordered.

Jessan brought out tinder and flint, struck off several small sparks. Bashae held the sprig to the flame. The dry leaves soon caught fire. Bashae let the sage burn a moment, then blew out the flame. Murmuring words in his own language, he waved the smoking sprig over Gustav, beginning with his head and working his way down to the feet.

"This will drive away the evil," Bashae explained.

Last, he held the sage to Gustav's nose, letting the knight inhale the smoke. This had the desired effect of rousing Gustav, whether because the evil had been driven away or because the knight thought he was about to be asphyxiated is open to question.

Gustav came to his senses, coughing and choking. He stared at them a moment without recognition, then the memory of the battle returned full force. Waving smoke out of his face, he struggled to sit up.

"Ease yourself, Lord Gustav," Wolfram said, laying a restraining hand on the knight's chest. "Your foe is dead."

Gustav looked around. His gaze rested on the black armor.

"Truly? Did I slay it?" He shook his head, frowned. "You must not trust it. I thought I killed it once before."

"Unless a pile of dust can reassemble itself, the thing is dead, my lord."

"I would not put it past the Vrykyl," said Gustav quietly. "Destroy the armor. Bury it. Sink it in the river." He paused, his eyes focused on the dwarf. "I know you . . ."

"Wolfram, my lord," he said with a clumsy nod of the head. "You've seen me before, perhaps you'll recall where." Jerking his thumb at Jessan and Bashae, Wolfram leaned closer to whisper. "I try to keep myself to myself, if you take my meaning, my lord. I don't like to brag of my connections."

"Yes, I understand." Gustav smiled slightly, then caught his breath with a sudden gasp as a spasm of pain shuddered through his body.

Bashae put his thin arm around the knight's shoulders. "You should lie down, my lord," he said, taking his cue from Wolfram, probably not at all certain what a lord was. Bashae helped ease the knight to the ground. "Where are you hurt? Can you tell me? I am a healer," he claimed proudly.

"I know you are," Gustav said, drawing in a shivering breath. "Your touch is most gentle." He lay still a moment, eyes closed, resting. Then he moved his hand to his breast. "I am wounded here." He opened his eyes, looked full at Bashae. "But there is nothing you can do for me, gentle friend. My wound is mortal. I die by inches every day. Still, I am a tall man." He smiled again. "The gods will carry me a little farther. Let me rest and then help me to mount my horse—"

"You cannot ride, my lord," Bashae protested. "You can barely sit up. We will take you back to our village. My grandmother is the best healer in the world. She will find a way to help you."

"I thank you, gentle friend," Gustav said. "But my time is not my own. I am on urgent business. I cannot rest. The gods . . ."

But even as he spoke, the gods took the matter out of his hands. Pain sharper than a sword lanced through him. Clutching his breast, he lost consciousness.

Quickly, Bashae felt for the heartbeat.

"He's alive," he reported. "But we must take him back to our village with all possible speed. Jessan, you lift him onto his horse. I'll explain to the animal what I want it to do." He looked at Wolfram. "Can you ride?"

Could he ride! Wolfram's thoughts went to the days when he had ridden like the wind across the rolling tundra of his homeland. To the days when he and his horse had been one being, flowing into each other, hearts and minds joined. The image was so vivid and painful that it brought stinging tears to his eyes. Yes, he could ride. But riding was forbidden to him now. It was on the tip of his tongue to say so, when it occurred to him that if he did not ride, they would leave him behind. Leave him behind with the accursed black armor.

He stumped swiftly over to the horse. The animal was admittedly taller than the short, stocky beasts he was accustomed to riding, but he could manage.

Wolfram vaulted onto the horse's back. The animal was restive, but the dwarf took the reins with a strong hand, patted the neck and clucked reassuring words. The horse relaxed, comforted by both the dwarf's touch and the pecwae's voice. Jessan lifted Gustav into place onto the horse's back. The elderly man was not heavy. The flesh had melted from his bones these last few days. Wolfram helped them position the wounded knight in front of him, wrapped his strong arms around him, steadying him on the horse's back.

"Go along," Jessan told Bashae. "I'll catch up with you."

The saddle blanket in his hand, he headed for the dark armor.

"Ah, good lad!" Wolfram called out. Sink the armor in the lake, Jessan, as the knight said. Hurl it as far as you can into the deepest part."

"What?" Jessan stared at him. "Drown good armor? Are you mad?"

He spread the blanket on the ground. Lifting a piece of the armor, he tossed it onto the blanket and Wolfram realized that the young man meant to carry the armor back to camp. If the dwarf could have climbed down off the horse, he would have raced over there, injured ankle or no, and dumped the accursed armor in the lake himself. As it was, he was so overcome with shock he could only choke and sputter.

"No! Don't! It's cursed. The knight himself said we should destroy it. Bashae!" He appealed to the pecwae, who had taken the reins in his hand and was leading the horse out of the woods. "Bashae. Tell him. Warn him. He mustn't—"

"Oh, he wouldn't listen to me," Bashae said. "Now that you mention it, that armor did make me feel sort of unhappy and frightened. But don't worry. My grandmother will know how to remove the curse." He tugged on the horse's reins and the beast picked up speed.

Wolfram wished desperately that Gustav would regain consciousness. The knight would surely insist that the armor should be destroyed and perhaps with his authority he could convince Jessan to leave it behind. But Gustav had sunk into a deep sleep and nothing the dwarf did or said could waken him.

Wolfram looked back over his shoulder to Jessan tying the corners of the saddle blanket over the armor, making a bundle of it. He slung the bundle over his shoulder and started out after them.

Wolfram shuddered so that the tremor went through his body and into the horse, who shied nervously, causing Bashae to issue a sound scolding.

DAY WAS DAWNING. ROSE-RED STREAKS VIED WITH PURPLE AND SAFFRON to light the sky. A beautiful sunrise, presaging a fine day. Jessan watched the colors deepen and glow, felt a corresponding glow within. He had long dreamed of this—his return from his first journey away from his village. For once in his life, his dreams had fallen far short of reality. He made certain to give proper thanks to the gods, as he gave them his morning greeting.

When he judged that they were about a mile from their village, he took over the leading of the knight's horse, sent Bashae on ahead to make the Grandmother aware that her services would be needed, give her time to prepare a fitting place to house the wounded knight. Bashae readily agreed to the undertaking, not sorry to have the chance to be the first to astonish his people with his remarkable tale.

Although Jessan would relinquish to his friend the glory of imparting astounding news, he himself would enter the village in triumph, bringing with him his very own knight with amazing powers, his very own dwarf, and armor of a quality that he trusted confidently not even Uncle Raven had seen before now. The village would be talking of him for years on end. His was a tale that would be handed down to his children's children.

Bashae sped off, his feet kicking up small puffs of dust as he ran along the narrow dirt trail which led from the Trevenici encampment to a nearby, meandering river. Pecwae can run extremely fast and maintain their speed for long distances—a trait that had undoubtedly contributed to their survival in a hostile world. He would reach the village long before the plodding horse. He would tell his tale and they would all come running from their farming and other occupations to hear the news. He could hardly wait and he went over and over in his head what he was going to tell them.

Arriving in the village, Bashae grabbed hold of the first elder he could find and blurted out his story, his words coming so fast that they clogged up his tongue. The elder Trevenici understood very little of what the pecwae was jabbering about, but he gathered that it must be important. Grabbing a ram's horn, he blared out the warning that would bring his people from their labors. This time of year, the field workers would be tending the newly planted potatoes and onions. Hearing the horn call, the Trevenici threw down their spades and ran back to the village in excitement. They were not alarmed. The horn's call meant interesting news. Drumbeats sounded when the village was under attack or when someone died.

"What is that racket?" the dwarf demanded peevishly. He had been dozing and now he blinked his eyes, looked around. "Where's Bashae?"

"I sent him on ahead to prepare the Grandmother for our coming," Jessan replied. "She will have all ready for the knight when we arrive."

"That's good," Wolfram said, grunting. "Though I doubt there's much can be done for him."

"The Grandmother has performed many wonders of healing," Jessan said. "She is much honored among our people. I would advise you to say nothing against her."

He cast a stern glance at the dwarf, hoping that would settle him, but the glance lost much of its effect because Wolfram wasn't looking at the young man. The dwarf's gaze was fixed on the bundle Jessan carried slung over his shoulder.

"What are you going to do with that armor, young man?" Wolfram asked, his tone tense, urgent. "Here would be a good place to bury it. Bury it deep. Deeper than you bury the dead. If as you say we're close to the village, I'll take the knight on in. You can stay to deal with the armor."

"So you can return and dig it back up and sell it," Jessan said coolly.

Wolfram sighed deeply, looked away.

Jessan smiled, pleased to think he had guessed and thwarted the dwarf's nefarious scheme.

His entry into the village was a triumph.

A Trevenici village consists of a collection of dwellings made of hard-baked clay and logs with thatch roofs built in a circle around a central point—a ring of stones, the Sacred Circle, placed there in solemn ceremony by the first people to establish the village.

Dedicated to the gods, each stone has a special significance. The circle grows as members add to the stones' numbers, placing stones to mark special occasions such as marriages, deaths and births. Once the circle is established, no one is permitted to step inside, for it is believed that the gods frequent this sacred area and that they would be offended if mortals trespassed. So holy is this site that not even the village dogs will enter it. They go out of their way to avoid it.

In the old days, it was said that any animal or person who violated the sanctity of the Sacred Circle was put to death. The one time the violation of the Circle had occurred among Jessan's people, the harsh sentence was not carried out, though there were many who argued in favor of corporal punishment. Eventually the elders decided against it, in view of the fact that, judging by the answers the person gave in her defense, she was incapable of understanding the severity of her crime.

The homes built near the circle house the elders, the founding members of the village. When children grow up, they build their own dwellings behind those of their parents. Thus the village expands outward generationally. Trevenici homes are snug and well-built, a contrast to the ramshackle dwellings of the pecwae, located a short distance from the Trevenici. Pecwae structures are made of anything that comes to hand when a pecwae takes a notion to build a dwelling place—skins, branches, rocks, mud or a happy combination of all of these. Fond of living out-of-doors, friendly to all sorts of weather, even the most inclement, the pecwae are generally content to live and love in the open, seeking refuge in caves during the coldest months or when danger threatens. This settlement of pecwae probably would not have built dwelling places at all, but they were strongly encouraged to do so by their Trevenici neighbors.

The village of Trevenici and pecwae had been on this site for almost fifty years. All of those who had first settled here were now dead. Their dwellings, occupying the first circle around the Sacred Circle, were now used as granaries, meeting places, or houses for the sick and infirm. Four irregular rings of houses expanded outward from that inner circle. This was a thriving village, located in a propitious area, for Dunkarga was always at war with someone and relied heavily on Trevenici mercenaries to swell their ranks. And if Dunkarga was ever accidentally at peace, their kinsmen and fierce enemies, the Karnuans, could be counted on to hire any mercenaries currently unemployed.

The people of the village gathered around the outside of the Sacred Circle, their traditional meeting place. The elders stood at the north end of the circle, where the first stone was always laid. The Trevenici people spread out behind them, holding children on their shoulders in order to see. Blooded warriors stood in their own group. There was a full contingent of these, for Jessan's arrival was the second important event to happen that day. The first was the return of the warrior Ravenstrike from the capital of Dunkarga. At the sight of his uncle standing among his friends, his dark eyes warm with approbation, Jessan felt his heart swell with pride.

Bashae stood there, as well, in a place of honor before the elders, pointing and explaining and telling his tale. Near him stood the Grandmother. Her position alongside the Trevenici elders was unusual, for it is rare that pecwae are so honored by being permitted to join the elders of the Trevenici. But the Grandmother was an unusual pecwae.

She was taller than average. In her youth, she had stood almost five feet in height. Age had shrunk her, but even now she was still among the tallest of her people. Her face was wrinkled and wizened so that it resembled a walnut and it was difficult to find her mouth amidst all the other lines. Her bright, clear eyes and thick white hair were her distinguishing features. Her name had been long forgotten, even by herself. She had been known for years as Grandmother Pecwae. She did not know how old she was, except that she was older than anyone in the village. She remembered when the first sacred stone was laid. And she had been a grandmother even then.

She had buried all twelve of her children. She had buried twenty of her grandchildren and two of her great-grandchildren. Bashae was a great-great-grandchild and her favorite of them all, for he was the only one to have a serious turn of mind, like her own, and who took an interest in healing.

Most pecwae wore little in the way of clothing, just enough to keep from shocking the sensibilities of the Trevenici. Grandmother Pecwae was different in this regard as well. She wore a chemise made of fine-spun wool and, over that, a long, full wool skirt that tied around her waist. Both skirt and chemise were decorated with thousands upon thousands of colorful beads, made of all kinds of substances—tiny vertebrae from fish, bone, shell, stones, wood and precious metals. Long strands of beads adorned her skirt, each strand ending with a stone set in silver. Turquoise were the most numerous, but other stones included rose quartz, red jasper, leopard jasper, amethyst, lapis lazuli, opal, bloodstone, tiger-eye, azurite, malachite, and more beyond reckoning. Her skirt was so heavy with the stones and beads that it was widely believed she relied on the magic of the stones to help her bear its weight. The beads flashed in the sunlight, the stones swung and clicked together rhythmically when she walked.

Jessan entered the village in triumph, the reins of the horse in his hand, the heavy bundle of armor on his back. He gave the elders a nod in place of a salute. He bowed to Grandmother Pecwae and grinned at Bashae, who came to take his place beside Jessan, as was the pecwae's right, for he had also shared in this enterprise. Jessan slung the bundle onto the ground. The armor rattled and made a metallic clunking sound that drew curious looks from the warriors. Jessan then made a proper salute to the elders and to his uncle, who nodded and raised his hand in return.

Raven shifted his gaze to the wounded man in the saddle and slightly frowned. Jessan thought he knew what his uncle was thinking.

"The man doesn't look like much now," Jessan admitted, wishing that the knight was still wearing the wonderful, magical armor. "He is hurt and he is very old. But he fought with courage and skill. He fought on foot, against an opponent who was mounted and better-armed. His name is Gustav and he comes from Vinnengael. The dwarf says that he is a . . . a—" Jessan paused, trying to think how to translate it into Tirniv. "A lord of a dominion."

Jessan kept a close eye on his uncle, hoping Raven would be impressed.

"A Dominion Lord?" Raven asked the dwarf in Elderspeak.

"A Dominion Lord," said the dwarf. "From Vinnengael."

"One of their most honored," Jessan added, thinking this reflected well on him.

"What's a Dominion Lord doing here in our lands?" Raven wondered, incredulous.

Jessan took in a deep breath, about to further amaze them with his tale of the shimmering light in the lake through which the two knights had most unexpectedly appeared, but he was interrupted.

"Enough talk! You men, take him down off the saddle before he falls off." Grandmother Pecwae issued orders. "Carry him to the healing house. He doesn't look good," she added in an aside to Bashae in Twithil, "but we'll see what we can do."

Several warriors hastened to do the Grandmother's bidding. Bashae stood near, worried and anxious and proprietary. Accustomed to dealing with the wounded, the men slid Gustav from his horse and, holding him gently in their arms, six of them bore him slowly and solemnly to the healing house that stood near the Sacred Circle. Bashae walked at the knight's side. Grandmother Pecwae walked with stately mien behind, her skirt swinging, beads flashing, stones clicking.

Jessan was eager to show his uncle the gift he had brought him, but he had to find some way of ridding himself of the dwarf, being still convinced that Wolfram wanted the armor.

"This is my dwarf," Jessan said, exhibiting Wolfram.

Raven and many of the warriors nodded wisely; well-traveled, they had encountered dwarves before. But most of the land-tillers and all of the young unwed females stared at the dwarf in surprise and wonder that was highly gratifying to Jessan.

Raven came forward to put his arm around his nephew, showing all the village his pride in his kin.

"The name is Wolfram," said Wolfram, sliding nimbly down off the back of the horse. "I'm a friend of the knight."

"Then you will want to go with him to the healing house," said Jessan. "The Grandmother may have questions only you can answer."

"I might be in the way," said Wolfram, his gaze flicking to the bundle Jessan carried.

"You will not be in the way, Wolfram," Raven added. "Your prayers may be of value to intercede with the gods on his behalf." Raven gestured to a friend. "Escort Wolfram to the healing house."

The dwarf had no choice now but to do as he was told. He cast another lingering glance at the bundle of armor, then trudged reluctantly after the warrior toward the lodge where they had carried Gustav.

The elders gathered around Jessan, along with the warriors and other members of the tribe. Bashae had told his version of events. Now was time for Jessan to tell his.

He launched into his tale, repeating much of what Bashae had said. He confirmed the appearance of the strange shimmering light in the lake, the light that had opened to disgorge two men on horseback.

"The dwarf said it was a Portal," Jessan explained.

"I have heard that rogue Portals exist," one of the elders said. "If this is one, we should explore it, find out where it leads."

"The knight can tell us," said another. "We should lay claim to this Portal for our village. I have heard that the Karnuans have grown very wealthy from the fees they charge to travelers entering their Portal."

"That is because their Portal leads to the great empire of New Vinnengael," a woman's voice said. Her voice was low and rough and came upon them unexpectedly. Absorbed in Jessan's story, no one had seen or heard her approach. "Your Portal probably leads to some cow pasture. Besides," she continued, her tone mocking, "what good is a door in the middle of a lake? You will drown half your travelers before they enter."

The woman stepped into the circle of listeners. Her name was Ranessa, a birth name, though she was in her mid-twenties. She was the sister of Ravenstrike, Jessan's aunt. Those near her eyed her askance and moved away from her, so that they would not come in contact with her. She was not ill-looking, or rather would not have been if she had taken some care about her appearance. Her long, thick black hair was uncombed, flew wildly about her head, straggled down into her face. Her brows were black and heavy and formed a straight line across her forehead, giving her a severe and stern expression. Her eyes were a peculiar shade of brown with a red cast to them. Her skin was alabaster white—a stark contrast to the sun-bronzed Trevenici.

Ranessa bore no resemblance at all to her elder brother and in civilized places there would have been whispers about her fathering. Such doubts would never occur to the Trevenici, for that would have been to impugn the honor of the family. Sometimes such oddities occurred, such as those born with marks on the skin or shrunken limbs. The gods had their reasons for these happenings, reasons that they did not see fit to make known to men. Ranessa was not shunned for the fact that she looked different or that she was sharp-tongued and ill-tempered. She was shunned for the fact that one morning the village had awakened to find the nine-year-old girl asleep in the very center of the Sacred Circle.

According to Ranessa's story, she had wakened from a dream in which she was flying through the sky like a bird. The dream had been very real and very wonderful and when she woke from it, she had cried because it had not been real. Thinking that she might truly be able to fly, she had left her parents' dwelling place and gone to the house of healing that stood near the Sacred Circle. She had climbed up onto the roof, spread her arms, and launched herself into the air. She had landed flat on her belly inside the circle of stones. The fall had been painful, knocking the breath from her body. But the worse pain was the knowledge that her dream had been a lie. She had wept bitterly, never thinking about where she was, and had cried herself to sleep.

Some in the village had wanted her put to death, but the elders, after listening to her tale, had judged her to be crazy. No one in the village was allowed to harm her, but from that day to this, they all avoided her.

The elders looked exasperated and uncomfortable. Jessan and his uncle exchanged glances. Ranessa was their responsibility.

"You should not be out in the hot sun, Ranessa," Raven said kindly, taking her by the hand. "Let me walk you back to your dwelling."

Ranessa lived on her own. She had moved out of her parents' house after her father's death. Her brother had offered her a place in his dwelling, but she had scornfully refused and he had built a house for her. She lived there alone, leaving it only to go on long, rambling and seemingly aimless walks that would sometimes last for days. She would always return from these half-starved and irritable, with a sneer on her lips as though she knew quite well that many had hoped that this time she would leave them for good and that her return was a cause for disappointment.

"I go where I choose, Raven," she said, snatching her hand from out of his grasp. "I want to hear my nephew's story." Her lip curled. "If for no other reason that it makes a welcome change from the dreary monotony of this place."

Jessan continued with his tale, trying his best to look anywhere but at his mad aunt. Beneath the gaze of her strange eyes, he was self-conscious and his story of his first meeting with Gustav was somewhat jumbled. But when he came to the battle, he forgot Ranessa, forgot his uncle, forgot the elders. He once again relived the glorious fight and he described the scene with a warrior's attention to detail, not forgetting to give the dwarf due credit for his mimicry of the horsebane fly.

The villagers rewarded Jessan with their nods, and their liking for the dwarf markedly increased. When Jessan described how the knight had plunged his sword clean through the chest of his enemy—armor and all— several of the warriors lifted their voices in shouts of triumph, while others spoke prayers for his recovery from his wounds.

"He will not recover," Ranessa stated in ringing tones, her voice cold and harsh. "His death is on him. As for the thing he killed, it was dead when he killed it. And it is not dead now."

Turning, her black hair whipping like a flail, she cast them a look filled with enmity and scorn and stalked off. At her departure, everyone let out a collective sigh. Her presence was like a dark cloud over them and the sun seemed to shine more brightly when she was gone. Jessan cast a wry glance at his uncle, who merely shrugged and shook his head.

"What is that you have wrapped in the blanket?" his uncle asked, to take his mind off their crazy relation.

Jessan had been prepared to proudly reveal his treasure, but Ranessa's strange pronouncement put him in mind of the knight's warnings. The young man was forced to admit to himself that the lack of a body inside the armor—while convenient—had been a bit unnerving.

"It is a gift," Jessan replied. "For my uncle."

No more was said. Gifts are private and personal matters. One does not flaunt one's good fortune before others, good fortune that might foment jealousy and discord in the village.

The elders stated their pleasure in Jessan's and Bashae's safe return, commended their courage and then departed, heading for the house of healing to inquire after the wounded knight. The rest of the villagers added their good wishes, then went back to their work.

"Come to my dwelling place, Jessan," his uncle said. "Bring your bundle. That is a gift for me?"

"Yes, Uncle," Jessan said, as they walked through the village together.

"From Wild Town." Raven frowned. "You have not squandered what you earned, Nephew?"

"No, Uncle. I traded the pelts for steel arrowheads. They are good quality. I inspected them, as you taught me. I have them here." Jessan patted the pouch that hung from his belt. "The gift that I brought you is from the field of battle. The spoils of war. Armor from the knight's foe."

"Such armor rightly belongs to the knight," Raven said.

"He does not want it," Jessan replied, shrugging. "He said we were to bury it or sink it in the water. But you will see, Uncle. This armor is very valuable and not to be wasted. I think the poor man was raving," he added confidentially.

"It is possible," Raven conceded. "I am curious to see this wonderful armor. Did you bring your aunt a gift?"

Jessan hesitated. The only other object he had on him that he could give her was the knife he had taken from the body of the black-armored knight. The knife was a curiosity, for it was made of polished bone, not metal. The bone blade was sharp, but so thin and fragile-looking that Jessan wondered what possible use the dead knight could have made of it.

Hilt and blade were one, fashioned from the bone of some animal. The knife was obviously old, for the bone was yellowed and worn smooth. Jessan wanted to keep this unusual knife, considering it a battle-trophy. He would cherish the knife and do it honor. His aunt would probably use it to gut fish.

"No, I didn't bring her a gift. Why should I, Uncle?" Jessan asked. "She hates me. She hates everyone. If Bashae and I had died out there, it would have been all the same to her. She shames our family, Uncle. You don't know what happens when you're gone. She says hurtful things to everyone. She laughed when she heard that Briarthorn's baby was stillborn. She said that we should rejoice, not grieve for a child that had been spared a world of suffering and torment. I thought Elkhorn was going to kill her when he heard about it. I had to make them a gift of meat to ease the insult. And when I tried to talk to Ranessa about it, she called me a foolish little boy and said that it was well my mother was dead, so that she would not see what a fool she had brought into the world."

Jessan's voice trembled with anger. His memories of his mother were few and they were sacred to him.

"Ranessa has a talent for hurting people. Do not take what she says to heart, Jessan," Raven said. "I don't believe she means it."

"I do," Jessan muttered.

"As for Elkhorn, he confronted me with the tale the moment I set foot in the village. I will add a gift of a weapon as an apology. He did say that you had handled the situation as an adult."

Raven eyed his nephew, saw the young man unhappy and downcast on what was a special day. "Never mind. We will say nothing. Now come show me this wonderful armor."

He put his arm around his nephew's shoulder. They walked companionably to the dwelling they had shared since Jessan's parents had died and left him orphaned. Jessan thought of telling his uncle about the knife, of showing it to him. He was reluctant to do so, however. He knew what his uncle would say. The knife had belonged to the dead knight, therefore it now belonged to the knight who had bested him. But the knight was dying, he had no use for the knife, anymore than did the corpse from which it had been taken. The dying knight had not wanted the armor. He wouldn't want the knife.

I helped the knight in battle, Jessan reflected. I earned the right to this knife. I earned the right to carry it. I'll show it to my uncle, but not just yet. We would only argue about it and I don't want anything to spoil this day.

Jessan touched the bone knife at his belt. The bone had a warm feel to it, as though it shared his pleasure at their secret.

8

Gustav looked upon the hideous face of a mummified cadaver. The skin was withered and brown as old parchment, pulled taut against the bones of the skull, the lips were stretched in a rictus grin. The eyes of the corpse were the eyes of the living with a frightening intelligence in their cold and empty depths. Those eyes searched for Gustav.

Or rather, they searched for what he bore.

The eyes scanned the horizon, starting with the edge of the world. The eyes moved by increments, studying every person they encountered, questing, seeking, probing. They had not found him yet, but they were drawing nearer and nearer and when they touched him, the eyes would devour him, drown him in the fathomless darkness.

Hide! He must hide! They were almost upon him . . .

He woke with a gasp and a shudder to find eyes staring down at him. These eyes were black, but not empty. These eyes were bright and soft and quick as a bird's, set in a face that was nut-brown, nut-shell wrinkled.

"Easy, lie easy," said the old woman, speaking through a mouth that had no lips. Gustav was reminded of a nut-cracker he'd once seen in the Vinnengaelean court. "Dreams may touch you but they cannot seize you."

Gustav gazed up at the face in baffled confusion, then looked at his surroundings. He was naked, his body covered above and beneath with several layers of wool blankets. Hot rocks, wrapped in blankets, had been placed around him. He had the feeling he was inside a permanent structure, though he could see little of walls or ceiling through the fragrant smoke rising from a bowl near him. Occasionally the person with the nut-cracker smile would use a red feather of the cardinal to waft the smoke over him.

The bone-numbing cold that had been creeping steadily over his body ever since he'd been attacked by the Vrykyl receded. He had the sense of being pleasantly warm, of being safe, of being able to rest without fear of hearing footsteps outside his tent or the galloping hooves of his pursuer. He would have liked to have rested here for a long while, but he dared not linger. The eyes had not found him but that was only temporary. They were still searching for him and, even here, they must soon catch him.

"Thank you . . ." he said and was astonished and irritated to hear how weak his voice sounded. "Thank you, goodwife," he said again, more strongly. "I must go now. If you could . . . hand me my clothes . . ."

With great effort and true regret, he struggled to rise from his warm bed.

He was barely able to lift his shoulders.

He exerted his will, he fought to sit up, but, in the end, he was too weak. He sank back down. Sweat beaded his forehead and lip. His muscles trembled as if he had tried to lift a heavy load, when he had tried only to lift his wasted body. He thrust aside the thought of failure, held it at arm's length.

"I have not eaten," Gustav said. "I will feel better with some food in my belly. I need only food and a few hours rest. Then I will be able to continue my journey."

He told himself this as he held failure, held death, away with a hand that was so weak he could not even lift it from the blanket.

He closed his eyes against the knowledge with bitter despair, felt two hot tears seep beneath the eyelids and roll down his cheeks. He lacked the strength to wipe them away.

A small nut-brown hand did that service for him.

"You have taken grievous hurt, Sir Knight," said Bashae softly. "You must lie still. The Grandmother says so."

The pecwae shifted his gaze to the old woman who squatted comfortably beside Gustav. "He tried to ride away even after the fight, Grandmother. He said he was on urgent business, something about the gods. He said he was dying, but I knew you could heal him, Grandmother."

The old woman's hand hovered over Gustav. He felt something cold and hard being placed on his forehead. The hand went to his bare chest and again there was a sensation of cold. He saw, to his astonishment, that the Grandmother was adorning his body with rocks.

"What—" he asked, frowning.

"Bloodstones," she said. "To draw out the impurities. Now is not the time to make decisions. That time will come soon, but you must be stronger. You will sleep now."

Gustav felt sleep steal over him. He was about to give in to it, when he noticed the dwarf, who had been crouched in a corner, out of the way. Gustav's eyes opened wider. Wolfram dipped his head in awkward acknowledgment.

The sight of the dwarf started a new chain of thought in the knight's mind. He wanted to continue stringing together the links of the chain, but he was too weary. First one link fell from his mental grasp, then another. But they would join together for him. He had only to be patient. Sleep, sweet sleep, dreamless sleep, flowed over him.

He felt the hand of the old lady place one more stone upon him, this one on his breast.

The stone was a turquoise.

He did not dream of the eyes again.

Raven's dwelling place that he shared with Jessan was large, the dwelling of a married man. The dwelling was a single room with a hole cut in the roof to allow smoke to escape when the home fires were kindled in the winter. Sunlight poured in holes cut in the walls, holes that allowed the air to circulate. The holes had no coverings now during the summer months. Only when winter's winds blew cold would his uncle hang blankets over them to keep out the chill and the snow. The fire pit was cold and swept clean. The dwelling's floor, hard-baked dirt, was covered with deer skins.

If a woman had inhabited the dwelling, there would have been baskets and pots containing dried beans, berries and corn meal. Hand-woven blankets, with her own special pattern, would have covered the floors and hung on the bare walls. If she was a warrior, her shield would stand next to that of her husband's. As it was, Raven's shield stood alone. There was no food in the house. Jessan ate his meals with Bashae, bringing gifts of fish and deer skins in payment. (While the pecwae will not eat the flesh of any mammal, they will eat fish, creatures the pecwae find to be stupid and uncommunicative.)

Raven had once had a wife, but she had died in childbirth. Their tiny son had not long survived her. Shortly after, he had traveled south with a contingent of warriors to sell his services to the army of Dunkarga.

Thirty-two years old, Raven was tall and well-built. His hair had once been as red as Jessan's, but was now a dark auburn. He had his share of battle scars and wore them proudly, along with an assortment of trophies, including his favorite, a necklace of finger bones strung around his neck. His eyes were gray and narrow beneath heavy brows—in these heavy brows he resembled his sister but that was the only feature the two shared in common. An enemy that sought to tell by Raven's eyes what he was going to do invariably failed.

Ravenstrike had adopted Jessan when the young man's warrior parents had both died fighting in Karnu. The young man, then age sixteen, had moved into the dwelling place, living there by himself when Raven was gone. Jessan was old enough that he would soon be ready to take up the warrior life. One of the reasons Raven had left Dunkar to return to his village was to take Jessan back to the city with him. It was time the young man found his warrior's name.

Jessan deposited the bundle on the floor. His face flushed with the excitement and pleasure of the gift-giver, he opened the bundle.

The ends of the horse blanket fell back. The black armor shone sullenly in the sunlight that formed a bright pattern on the floor.

Jessan was not watching his uncle. He was looking at the armor with the pride of acquisition and so, thankfully, he missed his uncle's initial expression of alarm and disgust. The black armor, lying on the floor, looked like the desiccated carapace of some enormous insect, whose head had been torn off and whose shell had been hacked to pieces.

Jessan expected his uncle to express his pleasure. Hearing nothing but an indrawn breath, Jessan looked up quickly, worriedly, to see what was wrong.

"Don't you like it, Uncle?"

By that time, Raven had managed to work his face into some semblance of a smile.

"It is fine armor," he said. "The finest I have ever seen."

That was the truth. It was fine armor. It was also the most awful, hideous looking armor Ravenstrike had ever seen. His admiration for the knight who had battled this apparition increased four-fold. Raven was not sure but that he would have fled the field had that monstrosity ridden at him. And he was a man who could not wear all the trophies he had taken in battle or else they would have weighted him down so he would have been unable to move.

Jessan's face relaxed in a smile. "I thought you would like it, Uncle. The knight wanted to throw it in the lake. Can you imagine? Waste good armor like this?"

Raven discovered that he'd involuntarily taken a step back from it. He couldn't understand his reaction, was half-angry at himself. It wasn't that the armor came from a dead man. Raven had hacked off fingers from every one of his victims and taken valuables from the bodies. What need have the dead of swords or breastplate? This was fine armor. His friend, the army's blacksmith, could repair the hole made by the knight's sword. The strange-looking spikes that jutted out from the shoulders and elbows would turn any blade or even a spear.

"Would you like to try it on? I will help you with it," Jessan offered eagerly.

"Uh, no," Raven said. Seeing Jessan's smile start to fade, the older man added quickly, "It is bad luck to put on armor when there is no battle in the—" He paused, looked toward one of the windows.

"What?" Jessan followed his gaze.

"I thought I heard something," he said. Walking over, he peered out the window, but if someone had been listening, the person was gone now. "That's odd. Why would someone be spying on us?"

"The dwarf," Jessan guessed. "He wants the armor for himself. He tried to trick me into leaving it back on the trail so that he could return and claim it."

It was on the tip of Raven's tongue to tell the lad to give the armor to the dwarf and be rid of it, but he swallowed the words before they had a chance to inflict pain.

Jessan crouched down to begin examining the armor more closely, proudly exhibiting its finer points.

Raven forced himself to overcome his squeamish reluctance and squatted down on his haunches beside his nephew. "I see no blood," he said. "And yet the knight's blow must have struck to the heart."

"There was no blood," Jessan said. "There was not even a body. Just piles of dust." He grinned at his uncle's astonishment. "I know! Strange, isn't it?"

Raven felt the hair rise up on the back of his neck. The sight of his nephew touching the armor made his stomach shrivel. This armor was about death and suffering. Yet, he had seen death before—battlefields littered with the bodies of the dead, the carrion birds pecking out eyeballs, the pi dogs fighting over chunks of flesh, and he had never blenched.

"Wrap it up, Jessan," he said harshly. "You should not keep it in plain view."

"You are right, Uncle." Jessan busily tied the ends of the bundle back over the armor and stowed it in a corner.

"Perhaps we should not even leave it in the house," Raven suggested, knowing he would never sleep at night if the armor was around. "If the dwarf is intent upon stealing it, this is the first place he would look."

"Right again." Jessan pondered. "But what should we do with it?"

"You could take it to the storage cave," Raven suggested. "When we are ready to leave for Dunkar, we will stop and pick it up."

He had spoken of leaving casually, so casually that, at first, Jessan did not catch the implication. He replied with a dutiful, "Yes, Uncle," and started to head out the door with the bundle on his back.

Raven watched, grinning to himself. Jessan came to a sudden halt. His head jerked around. Seeing his uncle's grin, Jessan dashed back into the dwelling.

"You said 'we'!" He was panting with excitement. "You said 'we' travel to Dunkar! Do you mean it, Uncle? Am I to go with you this time?"

"It was the reason I returned," Raven said. "I have spoken to my com-

manding officer. He says that another one of our family will be most welcome. Worth three of any other."

"Thank you, Uncle," Jessan said huskily. "I will not let you down. I—"

He could not speak further. Shaking his head, he turned and bolted out
the door, the armor clunking and rattling as he ran. Raven was not offended at this sudden departure. He had seen the tears of pleasure glimmering in the young man's eyes. Jessan would need time to compose
himself alone and in private, another reason Raven had sent him with the
armor to the cave.

As to the armor, Raven would have to find some means to dispose of it
before they left on their journey. The Little Blue river ran deep and fast
and it was not far from camp. He could toss it in the river and be quit of
it. He could always tell Jessan that it had disappeared of its own accord.
Not unbelievable. After all, the body the armor held had disappeared. Jessan would be disappointed, but in the excitement of traveling to Dunkar,
he would soon forget all about it.

His mind still on the armor, Raven went to the house of healing, hoping to question the knight about both the armor and the dread foe who
had worn it. When he arrived, the Grandmother told him that the
knight was asleep and must not be disturbed. Raven looked in the door,
saw the man, saw the gray tone of the flesh, heard the shallow, rapid
breathing and thought that, for once, Ranessa's dark pronouncement was
accurate.

The knight had his death on him.

The village held a feast in honor of Jessan and Bashae and their guests
that night. Bashae brought Wolfram along with him—the two having
been dismissed from the knight's side by the Grandmother. Now that the
armor was safely hidden away, Jessan could take pleasure in the dwarf's
company. An artful story-teller, Wolfram held the Trevenici and pecwae
enthralled with his tales of the far-distant lands he had traveled and the
people who inhabited them.

The acquisition of the dwarf added to the regard in which the Trevenici
held Jessan. Bashae willingly gave his friend the credit, though bringing
the dwarf along had really been the pecwae's idea.

Jessan told Bashae of his good fortune. Bashae was disappointed to lose
his friend, but he knew that this was the dream of Jessan's heart and so he
congratulated him and spoke of how Jessan would return with so many
trophies that he'd have to hire a wagon to transport them all.

The feast wound down. No one could eat another bite of roast venison
or swallow another morsel of roasted corn. Before the feast had started,

the villagers had gathered the choicest morsels and placed them in a basket to be given to the Grandmother, who had refused to leave the dying knight. Bashae offered to take her the basket. Jessan offered to accompany his friend.

The night was warm, the air soft and throbbed with the croaking of tree frogs.

"Grandmother!" Bashae called softly, parting the blanket that hung in the doorway. "We have brought food."

The Grandmother came out to meet them, the stones and beads clicking and ringing. Accepting the basket without a word, she turned to go back inside.

"There's a jar of broth for Lord Gustav," said Bashae. "I thought he might be able to drink it."

The Grandmother halted, her hand on the blanket. She shook her head. "His body would not accept it. Do not worry," she added, seeing the cast-down expression on Bashae's face. "He has no need of the food of this world anymore. He prepares to feast with the gods."

She disappeared inside the healing house, letting the blanket fall behind her.

Bashae sighed deeply and brushed his hand across his eyes. "I do not want the knight to die."

"He is an old man," said Jessan. "And a warrior. He dies an honorable death having vanquished his foe. Your sniveling dishonors both him and you."

"I know," Bashae said. "I don't know why I feel this way. I guess because he's not ready to die. He has something that he has to do—urgent business, he said—and I am afraid he won't live to do it."

"That's true of everyone," Jessan said practically. "We all leave something unfinished behind."

"I know," Bashae said again.

The two started walking toward the pecwae camp. Bashae kicked the dust of the road, stared bleakly into the night. The moonlight touching the stones of the Sacred Circle caused the white rocks to gleam white, making the darkness around them seem darker by contrast.

"Would you ask your Uncle Raven to come talk to the knight, Jessan? Perhaps there is something your uncle could do to help him."

"I'll ask him," said Jessan. "But we don't have much time. *We're* leaving for Dunkar in two days," he added, with proud emphasis on the plural.

"I remember. Still, I wish Raven would just talk to him."

The two parted, yawning their goodnights. Jessan returned to his uncle's dwelling, where he found Ravenstrike already asleep. Jessan lay down on his blanket. He had a strange dream that night that two eyes were searching for him, scanning the horizon, hoping to see him silhouetted against it. He woke during the night, troubled, but he could not tell by what.

By next morning, he did not remember the dream. Nor did he remember that he was going to tell his uncle about the knife.

It was as if he had owned the knife all his life.

9

GUSTAV WOKE TO PAIN THAT TORE AT HIS VITALS LIKE THE CLAWS OF A black vulture. He stifled a groan, but the old woman was quick to hear even that small sound. She no longer fussed over him with her rocks and her feather-wafted smoke. She sat cross-legged on the ground at his side, her wizened hands folded in the bead-adorned lap of her skirt and gazed down at him sternly.

"It hurts you, does it," she said, more a statement than a question.

He could not lie to her. He nodded sparingly. Any movement seemed to increase the pain done by the claws. He could almost fancy he felt the hot air of the black wings beating at him.

"I can do nothing for you," she said flatly. "The pain is caused by the evil magic that festers inside your body." She leaned forward, pierced him with her bright, bird-like eye. "Let go your hold on life. Your soul has escaped the evil that sought to claim it. When you abandon this body, your soul will soar free."

She moistened his lips with water. Gustav could no longer swallow. He was ready to die. Adela waited for him and he longed to join her. Yet he could not, he must not leave this world. Not yet. He shook his head feverishly.

"You carry a great burden," said the Grandmother. "You do not want to leave this body because you think that once you lay down the burden, no one will pick it up. You think that if you die your hope will die. That is not so. You have done your part. The burden is meant to pass on. Others will take up where you leave off. So the gods have intended."

Gustav stared at her in wonder and concern. Had he been babbling of his quest in his pain-filled wanderings?

The Grandmother chuckled—a throaty, hearty chuckle, not the cackle he might have expected.

"Don't worry. Your discipline is strong. You have kept your lips sealed. But it was not difficult for me to see. And the dwarf has told me much."

Wolfram. Yes, he would know of the Whoreson Knight's life-long quest. Gustav recalled that yesterday he had considered entrusting the Sovereign Stone to the dwarf. Not a perfect choice, by any means. Gustav knew little of Wolfram, other than he worked for the monks of Dragon Mountain. One of the Unhorsed, Wolfram had been banished from his tribe, almost certainly for some criminal act. Now he earned his living as an information gatherer and peddler. Wolfram could be counted on to take the Stone to the monks, especially if Gustav made it worth the dwarf's while. Yet Gustav felt a reluctance to hand over the sacred Sovereign Stone to the dwarf. The decision did not feel right to him.

The Grandmother eyed him. "You refuse to die until you know who will take this burden. If you are satisfied, then you will depart?"

"Are you in such a hurry to get rid of me, Grandmother?" Gustav asked weakly with a faint smile, using the name he had heard everyone use in her presence.

"Yes," she said bluntly. "I am a healer. Your pain is my pain. You are trying to decide who will take up the burden. You should not be the one to make such an important decision. Your judgment is clouded. You are half in this world, half in a realm of darkness."

Gustav sighed. He knew very well she was right. "Yet, the burden was laid on me by the gods. If I do not make the choice, who will, Grandmother?"

"You have provided the answer," she responded, laying a cool cloth on his burning forehead. "The gods gave you the burden. They will choose the one who will take it up when you lay it down."

"And how will they do that, Grandmother?"

She glanced toward the blanket that covered the door. "The next person who walks through that door will be the chosen of the gods."

Gustav turned the notion over in his mind. It felt right to him. The gods had entrusted the Sovereign Stone to him. The gods had given him the strength to defeat the Vrykyl, though it had cost him his life. He had done his part. The gods would do theirs.

Gustav drew in a deep breath and nodded his head. His gaze fixed on the blanket covering the door. The Grandmother sat back and watched with him.

"Uncle," Jessan said that morning, "Bashae is worried about the dying knight. He thinks the man is troubled by this unfinished business of which he spoke when we first found him. Bashae asked if you would visit him, see if there was anything you could do to help ease him."

Ravenstrike shook his head. "The man is a Vinnengaelean and a Dominion Lord. They are supposed to be magical, although I don't know how much of that is true. I have no idea what I could do to aid him. And my leave time is almost up. We must be on the road day after tomorrow."

"I know." Jessan grinned with excitement at the thought. "I told Bashae that. But perhaps just speaking to the knight will help. It would mean a lot to Bashae."

Raven shrugged. "Very well. I will speak with the knight this day without fail and if it is in my power to assist him, I will. You have much to do if you are to be ready to ride with me in two days time. You have the arrowheads, now you must make the arrows. You will need an eating knife, a hunting knife and a fighting knife. Hammerblow will make them for you, but you need to assist him and to keep an eye on him. He is lazy and will take short cuts if you allow him. You must have a leather shirt and breeches for the journey—"

"All right, all right, Uncle," Jessan said, raising his hand to defend himself against the barrage.

"And those are today's orders. There will be more tomorrow," Raven called after the young man, as he departed for the blacksmith's, whistling a marching tune.

Ravenstrike left his dwelling, intending to go visit the knight and offer his services to the dying man. The dying have a claim upon the living and, although pressed for time, Raven would do what he could to bring ease to the man's last remaining hours. If that meant finding a young warrior and dispatching him to Vinnengael to deliver a message or deliver the body or whatever else the knight requested, Raven would see to it that the man's wishes were carried out. His steps and his thoughts had turned to the house of healing, when he heard a hissing noise behind him.

Raven continued walking, did not turn around. He knew very well who was making the hissing sound, knew it was directed at him. He decided not to respond. His sister could speak to him in a normal voice. He would not answer a snake's tongue.

"Raven!" Ranessa called sharply. She raised her voice with its shrill edge. "Raven!"

Sighing, Raven halted, turned around. Ranessa stood in the shadow of her dwelling, beckoning to him imperatively with a hand curled like a bird's claw. She was wrapped in an old blanket cast over the loose-fitting leather dress she wore slung over her body. She was filthy, had no care what she looked like.

Yet, why should she care? Raven thought, his steps slowing in reluctance as he approached her. She will never marry. No man will have her.

The morning air was cool, but pleasant. Ranessa shivered beneath her blanket, while Raven went bare-armed and bare-chested. She had built a fire inside her dwelling to warm her.

"Yes, Sister, what is it?" he asked, striving for patience.

Ranessa scowled at him, her large brown eyes narrowed against the bright sunshine. "The evil that Jessan brought with him. What has he done with it?"

"It is armor, Ranessa," Raven said. "Nothing more—"

She drew close to him. Her hand pressed against his chest.

"Jessan brought the evil to us," she said, her voice low, hollow. "He gave it to you. You are responsible. The two of you. The evil poisons every-thing around it. Death will come to the people if it is not removed."

She drew closer, her eyes open wide, so wide that he could see himself reflected in their strange brown-red depths. And as he saw himself in her eyes, he saw his own thoughts in her mind. He feared the same about the armor, but he had not been able to express it. That troubled him. He didn't like sharing thoughts with a mad woman. He tried to step back, but he had allowed himself to be cornered by her against the side of her dwelling. There was no place for him to go, not without shoving her out of the way, and he was loath to touch her.

"Where did you put the armor?" she demanded in soft, sibilant tones.

"The armor is stowed someplace safe," he said thickly.

"Poison," she said, staring at him through a tangle of thick black hair. "The poison will bring death and misfortune to the people. And the fault will be yours. Yours and Jessan's unless you end it."

Shivering, though the morning was warming fast, she turned abruptly and vanished inside the smoky darkness of her dwelling.

Raven remained standing outside her dwelling a moment, waiting for his heartbeat and his breathing to return to normal. He pondered uneasily what he should do. He tried to convince himself that it had been the mad-ness speaking. But, if so, then the madness was growing on him, as well, for he felt the truth of her words in his heart.

He was particularly bothered by her use of the word, "poison." The armor was stashed in the cave with the food that was meant to feed the vil-lage should there be a drought or the crops were flooded out or the rains didn't come.

Still thinking of Ranessa's warning, Raven once more headed for the house of healing, to visit the knight. But as he came to the point where two roads converged—one road leading to the healing house and the other leading to the cave, Raven saw movement out of the corner of his eye. Looking back he was disconcerted to see the dwarf, Wolfram, strolling out from behind Ranessa's dwelling.

The dwarf had his hands thrust into his pockets. He walked with a limp and nodded his head in friendly fashion to Raven as he passed him by. Raven gave Wolfram a sharp glance, wondering if the dwarf had over-heard Ranessa's words. Then Raven recalled that if the dwarf had heard anything, it wouldn't matter. No dwarf could speak Tirniv.

"Ranessa is right about one thing," Raven admitted to himself, wiping sweat from his forehead. "The armor is causing me nothing but trouble. The sooner I rid myself of it, the better. Jessan will be so caught up in the excitement of leaving that he will forget about it."

Raven altered direction, took the road that led to the cave. Caught up in his troubles, he did not see Wolfram change his direction. Had Raven looked back, he would have seen that he now had two shadows—his own long, tall shadow and another shadow that was short and squat and moved nearly as quietly as the first.

Bashae slept late that morning, worn out from the adventurous journey. The sun had climbed far into the sky before Bashae rolled out from under the blanket in the Grandmother's dwelling. He stretched pleasantly, dozed a few more moments, listening drowsily to the scoldings and fret-tings of the birds, preoccupied with nest-building.

He came out of his tent to find only about half the pecwae up and stir-ring. The rest were asleep, some in their crude lean-to style shelters, oth-ers lying on the ground, covered over with blankets of leaves, visible only when inadvertently stepped on. The only excuse a Trevenici had for not rising with the dawn was that he had died during the night. By contrast, few pecwae ever saw a sunrise.

The pecwae consider sleep a time when they visit another world, a world in which they are able to perform the most wondrous feats, a world that is frightening and beautiful, a world in which they are immortal, for though terrible things might happen in the sleep world, the pecwae who visit it gen-erally return to this one. Seeing no need to forcibly leave one world just to come to another—especially if they are doing something important or pleasant in the sleep-world—few pecwae see any need to rise early.

Bashae ate berries and bread left over from last night's feast and then de-cided he would take some food to the Grandmother and see how the poor knight was faring this morning.

Bashae was on his way to gather fresh berries when he came upon Palea, returning from the direction of the Trevenici village. Palea was a year or two older than Bashae and his intended mate, whenever they each got around to it. They were already casual lovers and had been since the age of fourteen. Palea had borne a child, but whether Bashae was the fa-ther or not was uncertain. Children were raised by the pecwae community at large and the mother in particular.

"Have you been to the Village?" Bashae asked. "Did you see the Grand-mother?"

Palea shook her head. "I took her some food, but the basket you gave her from last night was sitting outside the dwelling and it was still full, so I just added mine to it and left. I thought perhaps she might be visiting the sleep-world and I did not want to disturb her."

Bashae nodded in understanding. No one ever woke anyone unless it was a most dire emergency, for fear that the person wrenched unexpectedly from the sleep-world might not be able to find his way back to this world. Such a person, caught half in the sleep-world and half in this world, would be most confused. This was what had happened to Jessan's aunt Ranessa, so the Grandmother said.

Worried about the knight, Bashae set out for the house of healing.

Wolfram had an easy job, trailing Ravenstrike. The suspicion that he might be surreptitiously followed would never occur to the honest and un-complicated mind of the Trevenici warrior. He never once glanced back. Wolfram kept to the shadows of shrubs and bush more out of force of habit than necessity.

The dwarf had, of course, understood every word that had passed be-tween Ravenstrike and his sister, just as he had understood much of the conversation he overheard between Raven and Jessan.

Wolfram had taken an early dislike to the sister, a dislike tempered by a certain grim amusement. He found it ironic that the girl, who was clearly as mad as a marmot, was the only one who could see the evil currently at work in the village. His amusement was replaced by alarm, however, when he noted that the silver bracelet grew warm whenever he was in the mad woman's presence. He couldn't imagine what interest the monks could have in a crazy person. He had none, certainly, and he planned to keep his distance.

He trailed along after Ravenstrike, planning to see what he'd done with the armor. The bracelet on his arm tingled pleasantly, so that Wolfram fig-ured that he was doing something right.

The storage cave was located about a mile from the village, far enough so that it would not be discovered by raiders and close enough to access at need. The cave was well-hidden. Wolfram would have never found it on his own. Even when Ravenstrike was standing right in front of it, the dwarf still couldn't spot it and was concerned to find that he'd lost sight of the Trevenici, who appeared to have vanished into thin air.

Poking around the rocks, searching for tracks and traces, Wolfram dis-covered the entrance quite by accident. His weak ankle gave way and his boot slipped. He sat down heavily, slid on his backside along a smooth rock face and crashed through a screen of tree limbs cleverly woven to conceal a large hole in the ground.

Amidst splintered branches and dried leaves, Wolfram fell about four feet through darkness, landed on a hard-packed surface with a startled yelp and a thud.

So much for stealth. Wondering just how many bones he'd broken, Wolfram looked up into the grim face of the angry Ravenstrike.

"Oaaah!" the dwarf moaned. His eyes rolled up. His head fell back with a thunk. He lay very still.

He heard the Trevenici squat down beside him. He felt the man's hand on his arm. Fingers kneaded his skin and suddenly pinched him, hard. The pain was intense and the supposedly unconscious dwarf let out a howl. Wolfram sat up, glaring.

"I am accustomed to dealing with malingerers in the army," said Raven. "What do you mean by following me?"

He was speaking Tirniv. Wolfram blustered. "I don't know what you're saying. Speak a civilized tongue, can't you?"

"I think you know," Raven said, still in Tirniv. He was a persistent bastard. "Why would you follow me if you didn't know where I was going?"

"I was lost," Wolfram said, sulkily, still in Elderspeak. He patted his hands over his body, decided that he hadn't broken anything. "My foot slipped and I fell into this blasted hole. I'm not spying on you, if that's what you think."

He glanced around nervously, hoping to find the exit. The Trevenici would be extremely protective of their valuables. Most likely the penalty for a stranger stumbling upon this cache was death.

"I'm hurt," he added in a pitiful whine. "I think I broke something."

Raven's large hands clasped hold of each armbone and legbone in turn. Wolfram gasped and groaned at every touch. The Trevenici was not gentle and if no bones were broken now, Raven might remedy that. No bones were broken, however. The Trevenici brushed off his hands and rose to his feet. He looked down grimly at the dwarf.

"I'm thinking you chose a very convenient place in which to get lost," Raven said, continuing to speak Tirniv. "You are not hurt. Get up."

"I guess nothing's broken, after all," Wolfram said and stood up. He backed away as far from Raven as he could, all the while searching for a way out. "Well, I'll leave you to whatever it is you're doing in this hole . . ."

"You can't escape this way," said Raven. "The exit is behind me."

Wolfram's eyes involuntarily shifted to a place behind Ravenstrike. Too late, he realized his mistake. He tried to cover it.

"Is that the way out?" He pointed.

Raven was tight-lipped. "Where did you learn our language?"

Wolfram gave up. He'd already sentenced himself to death. They couldn't very well kill him twice.

"I get around," he muttered in Tirniv. "I didn't want to let on that I knew how to speak your language. I know it's sacred to you. I respect that."

"I can't imagine that there is anything you respect, Dwarf," Raven returned. "I believe that you came among us deliberately to spy on us. Jessan said that you were the one who proposed accompanying him and Bashae to the camp. What I can't figure out," he added dryly, "is why. What did you think you could find in our village? Gold? Silver? A cache of precious gems? Or valuable armor, perhaps?"

Wolfram breathed a bit easier. He wasn't out of this hole yet, so to speak. But at least Raven hadn't killed him outright. So long as Wolfram had use of his tongue, he trusted he could fend off disaster.

"Turquoise," growled the dwarf. "I came in search of turquoise. The pecwae told me his grandmother could sing it out of the rocks."

"Turquoise?" Raven was astonished. "Why, it's not worth anything."

"Not here, maybe," Wolfram stated, "but in Tromek lands, the elves will pay dearly for it. As for the armor"—he shuddered and the shudder was not faked—"batter it and burn it and bury it and then pray you've done enough to rid yourself of it."

"Or perhaps give it to you," Raven suggested slyly. "Let you deal with it for us . . ."

"Not to me!" Wolfram reared back, hands raised in warding. "Not to me!" He shook his head. "I won't have anything to do with it. I don't care what you do to me."

This response was obviously not the one the Trevenici had expected. Raven rubbed his chin. He was clean-shaven, like all Trevenici men. He eyed the dwarf in perplexity.

"The armor is magic, then?" he asked.

"The worst kind of magic," Wolfram answered fervently. "Void magic. You've heard of that, haven't you?"

Raven's face darkened. "I know it is the magic of death."

"Death, pain, suffering." Wolfram shook his head. "Your sister is right. It will bring evil upon your people. You have to get rid of it." He looked at the warrior intently, took a step forward to see his face better. "But then, you already know that, don't you? You knew it was evil the first time you laid eyes on it."

"I . . . felt there was something wrong with it," Raven admitted. "But what could I do? My nephew gave it me as a gift. To refuse it would have hurt him."

"Better that sort of hurt than the kind the armor could bring down on you," Wolfram said.

"Why? Tell me what sort of creature wore it? What must I fear from it? It's nothing more than metal . . ."

"Metal that is not made of the iron of the earth," Wolfram said. "Metal that was not fashioned in any forge in this world. The metal of that cursed armor came from Death's forge and Death himself wielded the hammer. Ask the knight. Ask Lord Gustav, if you don't believe me."

"I believe you," said Raven slowly. "Or rather, I believe what I feel in my heart. In truth, I came here to destroy the armor . . ." He glanced at the dwarf with lowered brows. "But what do I do with you?"

"Don't let me stop you. I'll find my own way back to the village. Just show me the way out—"

"After you know the way in? I don't think so. I don't want you paying a return visit. Nor do you need to know what all we have stored in here."

Reaching out his hand, Raven seized hold of the dwarf's slouch hat and pulled it down over his eyes.

"Hey! What the—!" Wolfram roared.

Raven grabbed hold of the dwarf's groping hands, trussed them securely behind his back, using the dwarf's own belt to hold them.

"My breeches'll fall down!" Wolfram protested.

"I'll hold them up," Raven replied.

There came the sound of striking flint, the smell of pinetar and the whoosh of flame. The dwarf could see the glimmer of orange light through a hole in the felt hat. Raven took a good grip on a handful of material at the back of the dwarf's pants and gave Wolfram a gentle shove forward.

"I can't see!" Wolfram moaned, stumbling. "You're going to drop me in a pit!"

"It would serve you right if I did. But I won't. Here, now! None of that. Stand up and walk or I'll drag you like a sack of potatoes."

Wolfram walked, guided by Raven's prodding and pushing from behind. He knew when they'd reached the larder, for he could smell lavender, basil and other herbs, the musky smell of potatoes, a strong odor of apples, and blood from freshly killed meat hung to age. Raven shoved him to the left. They walked at a slant, downhill, for a short distance and then Raven came to a halt so suddenly that he jerked Wolfram off his feet.

"Ho!" Wolfram yelled. "Watch it—"

"Shut up!" Raven's voice was tense, taut.

"What?" Wolfram demanded in alarm. A Trevenici warrior was not easily daunted. The dwarf squirmed to free his hands and tried, simultaneously, to shake the hat from his head. "Cut me loose, damn you! Cut me loose!"

Raven's hand plucked the hat from his head, his hand gripped the dwarf hard by the shoulder.

Torchlight flared. Disoriented and blinded by the sudden light, Wolfram blinked his eyes and looked all directions at once, fearing every sort of monster known to inhabit caves from klobbers to bone crushers. Raven held him fast and finally the dwarf was able to see well enough to distinguish a large bundle on the cave floor. Recognizing the saddle blanket Jessan had used to wrap up the armor, Wolfram stared, blinked again, and took a step backward, only to bump into Raven.

The blanket was covered with splotches of some dark substance.

"What is that?" Ravenstrike demanded, holding the torch so that the light played on the splotches.

"How should I know?" Wolfram said and tried vainly to fall back another few steps. The warrior's rock-solid body blocked the way. "What are you doing?" He gasped in horror. "Don't touch it!"

Raven had drawn near to the blanket, hand outstretched. At Wolfram's warning, the Trevenici hesitated. Curiosity was too strong. Gingerly, he took hold of a dry corner of the blanket and pulled it back. The fabric clung to the splotches, like a bandage being removed from an oozing sore.

"It looks as though . . ." Raven hesitated, repulsed. "As though it is bleeding!" He bent nearer. "And look at this."

He pointed to the bodies of several small rodents lying stiff and rigid near the bundle of sacking.

Wolfram coughed, choking. The armor gave off a peculiar stench, acrid and bitter and oily. He found it difficult to breathe. The dwarf muttered every charm against evil known to his people and he threw in a couple he'd learned from the orks for good measure.

"Leave it alone. Don't touch it. The mice touched it and look what happened to them! Come on!" Wolfram gestured. "Let's get out of here. Quickly!"

"I can't leave it," Raven said, turning a dark glance on the dwarf.

"And what will you do with it?" Wolfram countered. The blotches were spreading, even as he watched. Some of the oily substance had leeched through the cloth, stained the rock.

"Tie it to a rock and sink it in the river," Raven said grimly.

"And who swims in the water of the river?" Wolfram demanded, his voice rising. "Who eats fish from the river? Who hauls river water to the crops?"

"You are right," Raven said, thinking this over. He looked helpless, baffled. "I have fought in countless battles. I have faced death in many terrible forms and never blenched, but this . . . This clenches my gut and twists inside me like a meal of tainted fish. I cannot leave the armor where it is. Perhaps if I burned it—"

"The smoke," said Wolfram. "Poisoning the air."

"I will bury it."

"And poison the ground."

Raven clenched his fists. "Is my sister right? Is this poison? Will this evil bring death to my people?" He glared at Wolfram. "You know something about this Void magic! Answer me!"

The dwarf stared in revulsion at the bundle. He shook his head. "I know only what I have told you. But there is another who can advise you. The knight. He fought the Vrykyl. He warned that the armor should be destroyed. We'll ask him."

"If he yet lives," Raven added.

He cast one last, grim glance at the bundle, then turned swiftly to leave. Wolfram had to scramble to keep up.

"You're not going to blindfold me?"

"There is no longer need," Raven replied shortly.

Wolfram understood. It wasn't that Raven trusted him now. The Trevenici people would move all their goods from this accursed cavern and never come near it again.

"Hey, Jessan!" Bashae yelled out. He was near the house of healing, just about to enter, when he saw his friend walking on the other side of the Sacred Circle.

Jessan carried several pieces of leather in his hands. Bashae ran around the Circle to join him.

"Where are you going?"

"To find you," Jessan said, halting. He looked ruefully at the swatches of leather. "I am making breeches to wear to Dunkar but I am all thumbs. I have broken two needles and I was coming to see if you had any I could use."

"You were coming to see if I'd ask Palea to sew them up for you," Bashae said, grinning. "Otherwise why bring them along? Don't worry. She'll do it. I'll take you to her. But first, I must visit our knight. You should pay your respects to him. Or say good-bye," he added in softer tones.

"I don't have much time," said Jessan, glancing in the direction of the house. His face grew solemn. He thought of the brave man who lay inside. Compared to him, Jessan had all the time in the world. "I can spare a few moments. I will come."

They walked around the Sacred Circle and came to the house of healing. They paused at the front, uneasy in the presence of death.

"Should we call out?" Jessan asked in a low voice.

"Better not, in case he's sleeping," Bashae returned. "We'll just slip inside quietly and see how he's doing."

Bashae put his hand on the blanket that hung over the door. He pushed it aside. Moving softly, silently, he entered the dwelling first. Jessan came immediately behind.

"Ah," said the Grandmother. "The chosen."

A DEVOUT AND FAITHFUL MAN, GUSTAV DID NOT QUESTION THE GODS' choice, but he did feel that perhaps the gods could have used better sense. Why had the gods chosen to send two youths on a mission of such importance, especially when any number of older, trained and experienced warriors were at hand?

"Chosen? Chosen for what, Grandmother?" Bashae asked, understandably confused.

The Grandmother cast a glinting glance from beneath red-rimmed puckered eyelids at Gustav. The knight gazed long at the two young men who stood respectfully, silently before him and it was then that he began to understand the wisdom of the gods.

Whoever was searching for the Sovereign Stone, whatever intelligence belonged to those eyes that plagued his dreams, would be looking for those older, trained and experienced warriors and might never notice callow youths.

There were other reasons, too. When he had been the age of these two youngsters, Gustav had been an adept thief on the streets of New Vinnengael. He had used his youth to his advantage, pleading an innocence which in reality he had lost around the age of six.

Bringing the Sovereign Stone to the Council would be a mission fraught with danger for Gustav, but that same mission might not be difficult at all for these young men, who would certainly never be suspected of being in possession of a lost artifact of such immense value. He would not need to tell them the true nature of what they carried. All they would be required to do was to take a nondescript looking knapsack to the elven realms and deliver it to a certain person.

Gustav had proof of their courage. Both young men had acquitted themselves well in the battle with the Vrykyl. They had acted with quickness, dispatch and common sense by bringing him to their village, or so the Grandmother had told him, and he had no reason to doubt her. Still, the young lack experience and the wisdom of years. They are wont to act in haste, learn bitter lessons later.

"Chosen for what, Grandmother?" Bashae repeated, his brow furrowing. "I don't understand—"

"Hush!" she said peremptorily.

The Grandmother turned to Gustav. "Is it to be, Sir Knight?"

Gustav looked at each young man intently, delving to the heart. He had come to be a good judge of character during his seventy years and he was satisfied with what he saw. Here was courage and loyalty, no question about that. As to the rest, he either had faith in the gods or all he had said and done these last years of his life was hypocrisy.

"The gods have chosen well," he said quietly.

"I think they have," said the Grandmother, though her eyes narrowed as she looked back on the young men. She had heard the knight's sigh and guessed what he was thinking. Slapping her knees, she motioned the two to step forward. Bracelets clicked and jangled on her thin arms.

"Come here, both of you. Sit down." She gestured to a place in front of her. "Listen to my words."

Bashae did as he was told, moving with alacrity. Jessan hung back. "I would like to, Grandmother," he said, "but I am leaving tomorrow with Uncle Raven to travel to Dunkar and I have much to do. I came only—"

"You have more time than some of us," the Grandmother said snappishly. "Time enough to listen to an old woman. Sit down, Jessan."

The young man had been raised to respect his elders and he had no choice but to obey. He did not sit, however, but squatted on his haunches, ready to jump up and leave the moment he was dismissed.

"Lord Gustav has a request to make," the Grandmother said. "This will likely be his dying request," she added sternly in Twithil, the language of the pecwae. "He will not live to see another sunrise."

Jessan's attitude became more respectful. Bashae edged closer to the dying knight. Solemn and wide-eyed, he put his strong, sun-browned hand over Gustav's pale and wasted hand.

"We are ready to carry out your request, Lord Gustav," said Bashae gently. "What is it you want us to do for you?"

Jessan sat silent, but he indicated with a brief nod that he was attentive.

Gustav smiled. "I thank you both. I know that I am dying. Do not grieve for me. I have lived a good, long life. I achieved all I wanted to achieve. The gods have blessed me and now, even at my end, I am further blessed."

He drew in a shivering breath, clamped his lips over a gasp of pain. The Grandmother wiped the chill sweat from his forehead. When the agony had passed, he continued speaking.

"I do not grieve for myself, but there is one person who will grieve for me."

"Your lady wife?" asked Bashae softly.

Gustav smiled again as the image of Adela came to his mind. Her face eased his pain. She waited for him beyond the pale, growing more real to him the nearer he drew to her. He would be very glad to go to her, to give up this burden, to be free of the agony. But not yet . . . Not yet . . . And these young ones would not understand.

How could he describe his relationship with Damra? A Dominion Lord like himself, she had been his friend for a long time, despite the disparity in their ages. She was the elder in years, but still young by elven standards. He was the elder in wisdom and experience. They had met in New Vinnengael, during a meeting of the Council. She had been interested in his quest, interested in the Sovereign Stone. She had invited him to visit her in the elven realm.

An image of Damra's simple house—beautiful in its simplicity, like all elven manors—built into the side of a mountain peak, came to his mind. It was in her house he had sought refuge in those terrible days after Adela's death. There, with Damra's help, Gustav had found the will to go on with his own life.

"Yes," Gustav said, trusting that both Damra and the gods would forgive him for his misrepresentation, "she is my lady love."

"She must be very old," said Bashae.

"Yes, she is old. Older than I am. But strong and beautiful, still."

Bashae was polite and nodded. Jessan obviously thought the old man was babbling. The Trevenici shifted restlessly, eager to race off on his own errands.

"She is an elf, you see," Gustav added and that brought raised eyebrows and looks of astonishment, even from Jessan. "Elves live longer than we do and the infirmities of age come to them far more slowly than to us. I have a token that I want to give her in remembrance of me. A love token. I need trusted messengers to carry it to her in my name."

He glanced at the Grandmother, who nodded firmly. Gustav shifted his gaze to the two young men. "I prayed to the gods to send me a messenger. You two are the ones the gods have chosen."

Unprepared for this startling development, the two young men stared at him, neither of them fully grasping nor comprehending the import of his words. Then the meaning hit Bashae like a blow on the head. He gaped and pointed his finger at his own small chest.

"Me?" he said.

"And Jessan," said the Grandmother.

"What?" Jessan leapt to his feet. He looked from the knight to the Grandmother and back. "But I can't. I must go to Dunkar with my uncle to become a soldier."

"His is a request made by the dying," the Grandmother said sternly in Twithil.

"I am sorry," Jessan said, uncomfortable but steadfast. He took a step backward, edged toward the door. "I would like to help, but I must go with my uncle." He made a vague gesture with his hand. "There are many trained warriors, older warriors, who would be honored to do the knight's bidding."

"But, Jessan!" Bashae cried, bounding up to face his friend all in the same excited move. "He wants us to go to the elven realms! The elves, Jessan! Us! You and me! All by ourselves!" He paused, turned back to the Grandmother. "And you sanction this, Grandmother? You think it is all right if we go?"

"The gods have chosen," said the Grandmother. "What we mortals think does not matter."

"There, you see, Jessan? What an adventure! You must come! You must!"

"You don't understand, Bashae," Jessan said in a stern voice; his dark brows furrowed. "All my life, my uncle has promised me that he and I would be warriors together. I have wanted nothing else since I was old enough to remember." He shifted his frown to the Grandmother. "The gods chose Bashae, perhaps. They did not choose me."

Turning on his heel, he walked swiftly from the house of healing.

"Be easy," said the Grandmother to Gustav and to Bashae. "The gods have mixed the dough. The yeast has yet to work."

Gustav drew in a ragged, pain-filled breath. "But my time dwindles."

"Easy," the Grandmother repeated gently and bathed his forehead. "The hands of the gods are kneading the bread, even as we speak. Bashae, go make ready for the journey. You will require food, water, warm clothes, and a blanket. Make haste. Return here at sunset."

"Am I to go alone, Grandmother?" Bashae asked, somewhat daunted by the task.

"Have you no faith in the gods?" the Grandmother returned sharply.

"I guess so," Bashae said slowly. "But Jessan's awfully stubborn."

The Grandmother scowled so fiercely at this that Bashae deemed it was time to depart.

Gustav rested his hand on his knapsack, a knapsack identical to the one the Vrykyl had thought she'd shredded. He had used the magic of the knapsack to recreate it from the bit of leather he'd salvaged. The Sovereign Stone remained hidden inside, undetected by the Vrykyl. By Gustav's own command, the knapsack had been placed near him when he was first brought to the house of healing. He had never let the knapsack from his sight. If he slept, the knapsack was the first object he sought when his eyes opened.

He looked at the Grandmother. He needed privacy, but he could not in honor ask her to leave him when she had devoted so much time and care to him.

Rising to her feet, her beaded skirt swirling and clicking around her bony ankles, the Grandmother said, "The stiffness of old age. I must walk it off or it will set in for good and they will have to carry me around like a child. I have set water close by here, if you thirst."

"Thank you, Grandmother," Gustav said. "You are a wise lady. A very wise and noble lady."

"Me! A noble lady! Ha! That's a good one!" The Grandmother gave her deep chuckle. Pausing at the entryway, she turned her head. "I will tell the dwarf you want to speak to him." She gave a bobbing curtsey that seemed very spry and departed.

Gustav no longer questioned her ability to know his thoughts almost better than he did. He was leaving the realm of the physical, drawing nearer every moment to the realm of the spirit. What he would have laughingly questioned a month ago seemed perfectly plausible now.

Gritting his teeth against the pain that brought tears to his eyes, Gustav said softly the word, "Adela!" and, fumbling only slightly at the buckles, he opened the knapsack.

Gustav woke from a troubled dream of seeking eyes to find two pairs of real eyes regarding him intently. The dwarf was here, as was a Trevenici warrior. Gustav slid his hand beneath the blanket that covered him, reassured himself that the Sovereign Stone was safe and well-hidden.

"Water, please," he gasped, coughing.

Wolfram quickly moved to lift the water basin to the knight's lips. Gustav could not drink it, however. He shook his head. The dwarf, with a look of concern, let a trickle run down the knight's throat, daubed water on the knight's parched lips.

"Thank you," Gustav said, breathing easier. He turned his gaze upon the warrior who stood near the entrance, not wanting to put himself forward until recognized. "You are Jessan's uncle?"

Raven gave a respectful nod and drew nearer deferentially.

"You know what I have asked of Jessan?" Gustav said.

"Yes, the Grandmother told me," Raven replied. He squatted down beside the knight. "She also told me what Jessan said. He did not mean to be disrespectful. I apologize for him."

Raven paused, obviously trying to think through his words. "At any other time, I would not have understood the gods' choice to make this journey. I would have said they were mistaken. I worry about Jessan's youth and inexperience, not in regard to his courage or his honesty. But"—Raven was clearly uneasy, kept glancing at Wolfram—"something unexpected has occurred. Something beyond all my knowledge and understanding. I begin to think that perhaps the gods know what they are about, after all."

"What has happened?" Gustav looked from the dour face of the dwarf to the dark-avised face of the warrior.

"You tell him," said Raven, drawing back into the shadows, but keeping his eyes fixed on Gustav, watching every change and nuance of expression.

"It's this way, my lord," said Wolfram, hunching nearer. "You recall the accursed armor that fiend from the Void was wearing?"

"Yes, why, what of it? It was destroyed, wasn't it?"

Wolfram shook his head dolefully. "Not for lack of trying, my lord. But the young man was set on keeping it. Brought it back to the village, a present for his uncle." He jerked his thumb at Raven.

"Gods' sanctity!" Gustav tried to sit up, but he was too weak. "A terrible mistake. The armor must be destroyed. It must!"

"Yes, my lord," said Wolfram dryly. "We're all agreed on that point. But, the question, is—how?" Lowering his voice, he bent low over the knight to whisper. "The armor's started to bleed, my lord. Bleed or leak or something. Liquid black as pitch and greasy, like lamp oil. And deadly, too."

"We found the corpses of two rodents who'd ventured near it," Raven said, his tone heavy. "Perhaps they drank it. Perhaps they simply stepped in it. Whatever they did, they were dead."

"Which means, lord," Wolfram continued, "that we can neither burn the armor nor drown it nor bury it. Not without the likelihood of deadly poison contaminating everything around it. So what is to be done?"

"You must take it away from this village," said Gustav. His voice was strong and firm. The danger had kindled a last spark in his fading eyes. "Far away."

"Aye, that much is clear. But then what, my lord? Wherever it goes, it carries this curse with it!"

Gustav thought a moment, then gestured for Ravenstrike to come closer. "Jessan said that you were intending to travel to Dunkar. Is that true?"

"Yes, my lord. I am a soldier in the army of King Moross. I travel back to Dunkar tomorrow to return to my duties. My leave is almost over. If I do not return, they will count me a deserter."

"Return, by all means," said Gustav. "There is a Temple of the Magi in Dunkar, I think."

"Yes, my lord."

"Take the armor to the High Magus. He will know what to do with it. Take it in secret. Show it to no one. Discuss it with no one."

"The High Magus!" Raven breathed deeply in relief at the thought of handing this deadly problem over to someone else. "Of course! He is very powerful in magic, so my commander says. I will take it to him and ask him how to remove the curse from our people. As for Jessan, he will go on this mission for you, a mission that takes him north in the opposite direction, far from the armor. Who knows but that the curse has some sort of fatal hold on him? This mission will allow me to withdraw my promise to him with honor and will allow him to leave the village in honor. Truly," Raven said reverently, "the gods are wise."

"If they were so blamed wise, why did they allow the boy to cart off the armor in the first place?" Wolfram muttered, but he made certain that neither of the other two heard him.

Gustav shuddered. His strength was giving out. His eyes closed in exhaustion. Yet, he had energy enough to reach out a wasted hand, catch hold of Wolfram as he was about to leave.

"I must . . . speak with you," Gustav said so weakly that the dwarf understood the words only by reading the man's lips. "Alone."

Raven departed. Wolfram remained behind, though reluctantly, it seemed.

"Yes, my lord?"

"You are in the employ of the monks of Dragon Mountain—" Gustav began.

"Not actually in their employment, my lord," Wolfram quibbled. "Seeing as how I travel a good deal, I bring them little tidbits of news now and again."

"Yet I have seen you there on more than one occasion," Gustav said.

"They make it worth my while, my lord," Wolfram said slyly.

"Indeed." The knight smiled. "I have need of a messenger to the monks, Wolfram. You are the obvious choice—"

"My lord, I would do anything for you, indeed I would," Wolfram said solemnly, scratching at the bracelet on his arm, "but I have already been given an errand and I—" He paused. "What's that?"

With much effort and at the cost of some pain, Gustav reached beneath his blankets and drew out a silver box, decorated with gemstones. Wolfram eyed the box suspiciously, not offering to take it.

"I need someone to carry this box to the monks," said Gustav.

"Ah, now!" Wolfram rubbed the side of his nose with a finger. He still made no move to touch the box. "And what might be inside this box?"

"The contents are secret," said Gustav, "and may be revealed only to the monks."

"The journey to Dragon Mountain is long and travel is dangerous these days, my lord," Wolfram observed. He frowned. "Particularly for those who have ought to do with those who have run afoul of the Void."

"I understand," Gustav said gravely. "And I will see to it you are well compensated. I have left instructions inside the box for the monks to distribute all my worldly wealth to the bearer of this box."

"And all your worldly wealth would be—"

"Land in New Vinnengael, all my chattels and houses on said land. And the contents of a strongbox hidden in the castle. My seneschal knows the location and he has the key. Also inside this box is my signet ring. Thus the seneschal will know that whoever comes bearing that ring comes from me."

Wolfram looked at the box and his eyes glittered, but he still made no move to take it. "Answer me this, my lord. Was the foul creature that attacked you seeking you or was it seeking that box? I'm thinking," he added, stroking his mustaches, his gaze narrowing, "judging by the magnanimity of your offer, that it was the box first and you as bearer of the box second. And that whoever bears the box runs a great risk. Am I near the mark?"

"In a manner of speaking," Gustav replied. "You will be in danger if you accept this charge. I don't deny it."

"From those creatures the Vrykyl?"

"I cannot say. I do not know if more of them exist. If they do, I trust and hope we have thrown them off the trail."

"And these two young ones," said Wolfram craftily. "You're sending them off on another mission. Does their journey have ought to do with this box?"

The dwarf's shaft had lodged squarely in the black. So near the center that Gustav knew a lie would not be believed.

"You are the killdeer with the broken wing," he said at last.

"Meaning danger follows me and leaves the young alone."

"You are being paid well to run the risks," Gustav observed.

Wolfram turned the matter over again in his mind, as he turned the bracelet on his arm. "Your estate? It's a large one?"

Gustav's lips quivered. If he'd had strength enough, he would have laughed. As it was, he said, "Yes, it is a large one, Wolfram the Unhorsed."

The dwarf did not take kindly to this title. He eyed the knight, then leaned forward to whisper hoarsely, "Has this ought to do with your mad . . ." He coughed, embarrassed. "Your quest, my lord?" he amended.

"The reward is very rich," said Gustav.

Wolfram spent another moment in thought, then reached for the box. "My lord, I am yours to command."

"As you see, the box is sealed," Gustav said, handing it over to the dwarf. "The seal must not be broken. That is a prerequisite. The note inside says that if the seal is broken, the deal is off."

"I understand, my lord," said Wolfram. He studied the box, turning it this way and that. "Pecwae work, if I'm not mistaken." Holding the box to his ear, he shook it. "Sounds empty." He shrugged. "You can trust me, my lord. I'll see to it that it reaches its destination safely."

Wolfram thrust the box into his shirt front. He was about to ask a few more questions, poke and pry and try to trick the knight into revealing something more about the box and its mysterious contents. But Gustav's eyes closed. His breathing was shallow and labored. His strength was spent and his life nearly so.

Wolfram's face grew solemn. Every man who looks upon the deathbed of another sees his own, so the elves say. Dwarves believe that in death, the spirit enters the body of a wolf and so continues on.

"May the Wolf receive you," the dwarf said softly, resting his rough and callused hand briefly on the hand of the knight. Clutching the box to his breast, Wolfram left the house of healing. He very nearly bumped heads with the Grandmother at the entrance.

"He's asleep!" Wolfram said in a loud whisper.

"Humpf!" the Grandmother snorted.

Entering the house, she was not particularly surprised to find her patient's eyes wide open.

"Don't worry," she said to him. She daubed his lips with water, replaced the cloth that had fallen from his forehead. "They will come. They will *both* come. The gods have chosen."

"Let them come soon," Gustav said, sighing. "For I am very tired."

"But, Uncle, you promised!" Jessan said.

Even as he spoke the words, he knew he sounded like a whining child denied a plum and he was not surprised to see his uncle's face darken with displeasure. He could not very well withdraw the words he had spoken. He could only try to explain himself.

"Uncle, I am the only person of my age in the village who has not taken a warrior's name." Jessan did not count Ranessa. No one counted Ranessa. "I had a chance to go south to Karnu with the others, but I waited for you. Family should be together, you always say, and I agree with you. Family *should* be together, Uncle. Take me with you to Dunkar!"

"I cannot, Jessan," said Raven. "The gods have made their choice."

Jessan lost his temper. "The gods! Hah! Yes, if the gods have taken the form of a dried-up old pecwae woman. A woman who has gone addled, for all we know! Uncle, I—"

Raven's backhand caught Jessan across the mouth, knocked him to the floor. Raven had not pulled his punch. He meant the blow and the lesson it carried with it to sink in.

Jessan sat up, shaking his hurting head. He spit out a tooth, wiped blood from the corner of his split lip. He cast a brief glance at his uncle, looked quickly away. He had never seen Raven so angry.

"A warrior does not speak of the gods with disrespect," Raven said, his fury shaking his voice. "The gods hold a warrior's life in their hands. I am surprised that they have not closed those hands into a fist, instead of opening them to grant you a great honor. Furthermore, a warrior does not speak of his elders with disrespect. To do so is the mark of a mean and sniveling coward."

Slowly, Jessan rose to his feet. He faced his uncle squarely, stolidly, knowing that he had done wrong and accepting of his punishment. "I am sorry, Uncle," he said. "I spoke the words thoughtlessly." He wiped away more blood with the back of his hand. "Please forgive me."

"I am not the one you insulted," Raven said grimly. "Ask the gods for forgiveness."

"I will, Uncle," said Jessan.

"You cannot ask the Grandmother for forgiveness for that would mean you would have to repeat what you said of her and I trust words like that will never again fall from your lips. But henceforth the least little thing she requires of you, you will do for her without fail and without protest. Thus you will make reparation."

"Yes, Uncle," Jessan replied, subdued and saddened.

He knew then that, for some reason, his uncle did not want to take him to Dunkar. There could be no other explanation. Although a devout man, Ravenstrike could have argued his way around the gods if he had wanted to, of that, Jessan was certain. He could not imagine what he had done to offend his uncle.

Raven stood glaring at his nephew a moment more, then, relenting, he flung his arms around the young man and held him close.

"You will be venturing into strange lands, Jessan," Raven said, pulling back to hold the young man at arm's length. "Lands where I have never gone. Lands where none of our tribe have ever traveled. You will meet strange people, see strange customs, hear strange languages. Treat all with respect. Remember that to them, you are the stranger."

Jessan nodded. He could not trust his voice to speak.

"I will take my leave of you now, Jessan," said Raven. "When you return from this journey, travel on to Dunkar. I will be waiting for you."

"Thank you, Uncle," Jessan said, his voice cracking.

The moment was awkward. Both men felt it to be so.

"I didn't think you were leaving until tomorrow, Uncle," Jessan said, at last.

"Something has come up," Raven replied evasively. "I've had news. I must return to my post."

"Don't forget the armor," Jessan said.

"I won't," Raven replied dryly. "Trust me."

"I don't know what's come over him," Jessan told Bashae. "Raven's been acting oddly ever since I gave him the armor. Oh, he says that he's pleased with it, but I don't think he means it. You know, I wish I'd done what the dwarf said and chucked that armor in the ravine. Raven says I'm not to go to Dunkar, after all. I am to go with you."

Bashae gave a whoop of delight. Seeing his friend's downcast face, he said contritely, "I'm sorry, Jessan. I know you really wanted to go with your uncle. What reason did he give?"

"My uncle says that this mission the gods themselves have chosen is far more important than joining the army of Dunkarga. I can always do that when I come back. I've been thinking it over. Maybe he is right. It will be an adventure, as you say. Traveling to the elven lands. No one from our village has ever gone that far."

Bashae did a little dance, clapping his hands. "And I will be the first pecwae to travel so far. I'm glad you're coming. I should have been terrified to go by myself, but if you're along, I'm not afraid."

Jessan sighed and shook his head. He wished he could feel the same enthusiasm, but he was too bitterly disappointed. He glanced up at the sun, which had passed noon's zenith some time ago and was sinking toward the west. "I have to go. My uncle wants to leave soon. You go on to the knight. I'll meet you there."

Turning, Jessan stalked off.

"This has been without doubt the worst day of my life," he muttered to himself. "I'll be glad when it's over."

At least, he thought, feeling a shred of cold comfort, everything that could go wrong this day had gone wrong. He couldn't imagine anything worse that could befall him.

He had gone only a short distance when he heard feet pattering after him and a breathless voice shouting his name. He turned to find Bashae dashing up to him.

"Oh, Jessan! I'm glad I caught you. I forgot to give you the good news," Bashae said, panting in happy excitement. "The Grandmother has decided to come with us."

11

RAVENSTRIKE WAS READY TO DEPART. THE VILLAGE HAD TURNED OUT TO wish him well, along with the dwarf. Wolfram stood holding the horse's bridle, stroking the animal's nose and speaking softly to the beast. Raven was going to ride the knight's horse. The warrior had at first refused to accept such a princely gift, but Gustav had said, quite rightly, that he would never ride again. Gustav knew very well that if the horse was left behind in the village, the practical Trevenici would hitch the animal to the plow. Better the proud war horse should end his days on the battle-field.

Raven stood chatting with the village elders, who had all gathered around to admire the horse. The neatly rolled tarp was attached to the back of Raven's saddle. Saddle bags held Raven's clothes and a supply of food. He was dressed in long, fringed leather breeches and a leather shirt. He wore all his trophies.

At the sight of Jessan's approach, the circle of people who gathered around Raven parted to allow the young man inside.

"Well, Nephew, I am ready to go," Raven said, turning to Jessan with a smile. He clapped a hand on Jessan's shoulder. "May the gods walk at your side on your journey, Jessan."

"I'm going to need them," Jessan said glumly. "The Grandmother has decided to go with us."

The image of two proud young men going off on the adventure of their lives accompanied by their grandmother came vividly to Raven's mind. A corner of his mouth twitched. Seeing his nephew's unhappy face and cast-down spirits, Raven hastily swallowed his laughter.

"Then truly you have a great responsibility, Jessan," he said gravely. "This is a solemn trust we give into your hands."

The village elders murmured and nodded.

"I hope you will be worthy of it," Raven added, "and make me proud."

Jessan raised his head. His face cleared. Raven had given him back his honor. "I will, Uncle."

Raven embraced and kissed his nephew. He embraced the elders, exchanged the ritual kiss, then mounted his horse. Wolfram stepped back and Raven was ready to ride when Ranessa suddenly thrust her way through the crowd.

"What is this, Raven?" she demanded in her harsh voice. "No farewell kiss for your sister?"

Raven gazed down on her, his expression dark. He had spoken with the elders about her care. He had hoped to leave before she was aware of his departure.

She looked up at him through her black, disheveled hair. Slowly Raven dismounted and walked over to his sister. He came only as close as was necessary to give the dirty cheek a brushing kiss, but Ranessa seized his sleeves, digging her nails into the leather, and dragged him near.

"You take the curse from the village," she said to him, her voice harsh and urgent. "That is good, Brother. Do not worry. You will save the people, though you yourself will be lost. Lost," she repeated.

Raven knew Ranessa was mad, growing madder every day it seemed. Yet, at her ominous words, he felt a chill. He tried to pull away from her, but she sagged into him, rested her forehead on his broad chest. He was amazed to see the tracks of tears down the dirt-streaked face.

"You have been good to me," she mumbled into his chest. "Better than I have deserved. I am a torment to you." She raised her tear-stained face, her eyes were dark and shining and wild. "If it brings comfort, know that I am a greater torment to myself than to any other."

She gave him a kiss, a kiss that was nearer a blow, for it was swift and hard, left his jaw aching. Then, turning on her heel, she walked out of the circle. Those in her path had to move swiftly aside, or she would have trampled them beneath her bare feet.

Raven stood staring after her, bemused and uneasy, rubbing his sore jaw. The next day, he would find that her kiss had actually left a bruise mark.

Everyone looked uncomfortable. All felt she had ruined an otherwise triumphant departure. Raven determined that the best he could do was leave immediately, before she took it into her head to come back. He mounted his horse, waved his hand and headed south, the direction that led to Dunkar. The people in the village shouted good wishes after him until he was out of sight. Then they left to begin the arduous task of searching for another cave in which to store the foodstuffs, as well as the village's wealth.

The elders departed to the house of healing, to help speed another man on another journey, far longer and entering realms unknown. Different from Raven's journey, or so they thought.

In the house of healing, Gustav grew weaker by the moment. Each breath was a hard-fought battle against a foe he had faced many times before. He had no regrets. Death was an enemy to whom he could lose with honor. Gustav longed to break his sword, sink down on one knee and proclaim himself beaten, though not defeated. He had yet to finish his business in this world. He had yet to pass on the prize for which he had spent his life searching, given his life to defend. He would give that prize to two young men. And the Grandmother.

"I'm near the end of my life and I've never been farther away from my tent than the river," she said to him, after telling him her astounding decision. "I've never seen an elf. I would have never seen a dwarf, but that my nephew caught one. An elf would be harder to catch, so I imagine."

"But your comforts," Gustav argued, mildly protesting. He could not very well speak out against elderly adventurers. "The journey will be long and hard."

"What comforts?" The Grandmother snorted. "I can't sleep at night for the aching in my bones. I might as well not sleep on the road as not sleep in my stuffy tent. I can't taste my food anymore so it doesn't matter what I eat."

"I will lie in a strange land after my death," Gustav said. "I do not mind. I have no children to tend my grave in my homeland. But you have borne many children and grandchildren, so Bashae tells me. They all lie buried here. Do you not want to be buried with them?"

"Not particularly," the Grandmother said, grunting. "They were a disappointment to me, all of them. Always expecting me to take care of them in this world and I've no doubt they expect the same in the sleep-world. All lined up with their empty food plates, waiting to be filled. Well, they're going to go hungry. Let them look for me. Do them good."

Gustav smiled. "Send for your nephew," he said.

Bashae had been waiting outside the tent. He came in, moving softly and quietly, and knelt down beside the dying man.

"In this knapsack," Gustav told Bashae, "is the token to be given into the hands of Lady Damra. You must give it to her and to no one else."

He struggled to lift the knapsack. To his wasted arm muscles, it felt as if it were made of solid iron.

Bashae took it from him gently.

"Yes, lord," said Bashae.

"You may open it," said Gustav.

Bashae peered inside. "This ring?" he said, drawing out a ring made of silver, adorned with a purple stone.

"Yes, the ring," said Gustav. "Give it to Lady Damra. Tell her that inside the knapsack is the most valuable jewel in the world and that it comes from me, who searched for such a jewel a lifetime. I give it to her, to carry to its final destination."

Bashae cast a doubtful glance at the Grandmother. "The jewel is only an amethyst!" he said in a loud whisper.

"Perhaps they are worth more to the elves," the Grandmother told him. "Like turquoise."

"Of course," said Bashae, recalling the greed in the eyes of the elf in Wild Town. "That must be the reason."

"It is important that she receive the knapsack, as well," Gustav said earnestly. "The Lady Damra gave me that knapsack. It is magical and it is also very valuable."

"Magical!" exclaimed Bashae, awed and excited. "What does it do?"

"The Lady Damra will show you," said Gustav. "I no longer have the strength. Do not tell anyone of its magic. Promise me that. If you do, they might try to take it from you and that must not happen."

"Yes, my lord," Bashae said solemnly, and he looked a little uneasy.

That was well, Gustav thought. He didn't want to frighten the young man, but he hoped to impress upon him the seriousness of the mission. He trusted that the two who were taking up his quest would have a safe and uneventful journey. It was for that reason he'd given Wolfram the box which had held the Sovereign Stone. If the eyes he saw in his dreams were truly searching for the stone, perhaps they would be drawn by the residual magic left in the box. The Stone itself, hidden away in its magical pocket of time, would be very difficult to detect. With the cursed armor of the Vrykyl traveling in one direction and the box with its aura of blessed magic traveling in another, pursuit should be drawn away from the two young men. And the Grandmother.

At his bidding, the young warrior, Jessan, entered the healing house. Bashae showed him the knapsack, went over their instructions, keeping one eye on Gustav the entire time to make certain he had it right.

Gustav beckoned the young warrior near.

His expression solemn in the presence of death, Jessan knelt at the knight's side.

"Take the Big Blue river to the Sea of Redesh," Gustav said, his voice now nothing more than a whisper. He had to pause many times to draw breath. The simple movement was no longer reflexive, but had to be performed deliberately and with painful effort. "Travel the sea north to the city of Myanmin in the southern part of the land of Nimorea. In the city of Myanmin, go to the Street of the Kite Makers. Ask for a man named

Arim. Tell him that you come in my name and that I beg, for the sake of our long friendship, that he will guide you to the house of Lady Damra."

"Yes, my lord," said Jessan. "The landlocked Sea of Redesh, the city of Myanmin, the Street of the Kite Makers, a man named Arim. And if I cannot find him, we will find your lady ourselves if we have to turn the elf nation upside-down."

Gustav swallowed, closed his eyes. He no longer had the strength to move his head. When he spoke, Jessan had to bend over him to hear the words.

"You are . . . human. The Tromek will not allow you into their lands . . . without a go-between. The Nimoreans . . . are accepted . . ."

His voice died away. His eyes gazed intently at Jessan, who appeared to ponder this a moment, then gave an abrupt nod. "I understand, my lord. We would be prohibited from entering elven lands, but this Nimorean, Arim, can both vouch for us and guide us."

Gustav was pleased with the answer, still more with the thought behind it. He had completed his task. The burden was his no longer. He had handed it on. He had done all he could to make certain that the Sovereign Stone arrived at its destination safely. Now he could release his grip on life and hold out his hands to Adela.

He closed his eyes. He stood on a strip of sand, shining silver in the bright sun. The wide, living, moving, breathing sea spread out before him. The sun gilded each wave with gold. The waves lapped at his feet, each one drawing closer. The gulls wheeled in the air overhead, wing-beats strong against the wind. Small brown birds hopped over the sand, wings tucked in close, skittering away from the waves each time one came too near.

A wave flooded over Gustav's feet. When the water retreated, the wave sucked the sand out from under him. Each wave took a little more from him, a little more.

He waited there on the beach, waited for Adela to come to him and lead him out beyond the waves to calm water.

The elders of the village entered the house of healing and ranged themselves around the bed of the dying knight. They wore their finest clothes, decked themselves with all their trophies. They spoke in turn, beginning with the eldest, each telling the tale of some valiant warrior, now dead, evoking his or her spirit to come to the house of healing. They told the tale of Lone Wolf, who had remained on the battlefield with a wounded comrade, fighting and finally succumbing to overwhelming numbers rather than leave his fellow soldier to die alone. They told the tale of Silver Bow, who fired arrow after arrow at the eyes of a marauding giant, standing courageously in his path when all others had fled. These and more tales they told until soon the house of healing was crowded with dead heroes.

The elders were in the midst of the tale of Ale Guzzler, when the blanket over the doorway was thrown aside. Ranessa entered the house of healing.

She was wrapped in her blanket, that she held close around her body. Her legs were bare. For all anyone knew, she might have nothing on beneath it.

The elder who was speaking fell silent. He glared at this intrusion in outrage. Ranessa had no right to be here. She had no reason to be here. She was an insult to them and to the dying knight. One of the elders rose to his feet, placed his hand on her arm.

She jerked away from him. "Leave me be, Graybeard," she said coldly. "I will not stay. I came to see. That is all."

"Let her remain," said the Grandmother suddenly and unexpectedly.

Ranessa stepped forward until she stood over the dying knight. She stared down intently at Gustav for the space of ten heartbeats. She turned on her heel and, just as abruptly as she had come, she departed.

The elders glanced at one another, shook their heads, raised their eyebrows, and picked up the tale of Ale Guzzler where it had been left off.

The knight did not seem to notice the untoward interruption. He did not give any indication that he heard the tales. He was, to all appearances, slipping peacefully away into death, when suddenly his eyes flared open. He gave a hoarse shout of anguish. Spasms twisted his body.

"The evil seeks to take him to the Void," the Grandmother pronounced.

The elders watched complacently. The Grandmother had warned them to prepare for the battle. It was for this very reason they had summoned the spirits. Legions of dead Trevenici heroes were now surrounding the knight, fighting the Void for his soul.

The battle was swift and hard, but soon over. The knight gave a great, shuddering gasp. His body relaxed. The lines of pain and anguish smoothed from his face. He opened his eyes. He lifted his hands.

"Adela," he said and the breath that pronounced the word was his last.

The Grandmother closed the eyes that no longer held life's gleam.

"It is finished," she said, adding with satisfaction, "We won."

That night, by the light of the stars, six strong warriors carried Gustav's body to the site where the Trevenici gave the dead back to the earth. He was laid to rest in the burial mound with other Trevenici, a great honor for the knight.

The entire village turned out next day to bid farewell to the departing travelers. It is not in the nature of the Trevenici to mope or sulk or wail for what cannot be. When Jessan rose early that morning and made ready to leave, he was in a good humor, looking forward to lands unvisited, sights unseen. He traveled lightly, carrying only his bow, that he had made himself, under Raven's tutelage, the arrows with their new steel tips, some food, a waterskin and the bone knife.

He swept his uncle's dwelling clean, rolled the blankets neatly and stacked them against the wall. This done, he had one more task to perform before he could join his traveling companions. Gritting his teeth, he went to bid good-bye to his aunt. He had no doubt that she would say something terrible to him, just as she had said to his uncle, and that he would start his journey with the bad taste of her ill-omened words in his mouth. By going to see her in her dwelling, he hoped to spare himself the public humiliation Ravenstrike had suffered at her hands.

"Aunt Ranessa," Jessan called, standing outside her dwelling.

No answer came from within.

Jessan waited a moment, hope rising in his heart. He called again and still there was only silence. Thrusting aside the blanket, hoping fervently he would see nothing untoward, he poked his head inside the dwelling. The smell of rot and decay nearly made him gag. He glanced swiftly about. Ranessa was not there. He had no idea where she had gone. Probably on one of her rambles. He left hurriedly. He had done his duty. No man could say otherwise.

He was to meet Bashae and the Grandmother near the Sacred Circle. As he drew closer to his destination, he heard such wailing and weeping that he wondered who else had died besides the knight. Quickening his steps, he arrived at the Circle at a run, only to discover that the wailing was from the pecwae, deploring the Grandmother's departure, begging her to stay.

Only the white crown of the Grandmother's head could be seen, rising above a puddle of sobbing pecwae, who seemed likely to drown her in grief. The Trevenici elders were there, exchanging amused glances. Bashae was there, too. He stood apart from the crowd, looking embarrassed. His embarrassment deepened at the sight of Jessan, who noted that the dwarf, Wolfram, was also present, watching and grinning.

"What is going on?" Jessan demanded, feeling a warm and unpleasant flush start at the back of his neck and consume his face. "Everyone's laughing at us."

"I'm sorry, Jessan," Bashae said, his face red. "It's not my fault. The Grandmother said this might happen and we tried to slip away before anyone was awake, except that the Grandmother doesn't move very quietly. She sewed some little silver bells to her skirt—"

Jessan muttered a curse beneath his breath. "Haul her out of there!" he ordered Bashae in a low tone, with a sidelong glance at the elders. "And let's get started!"

Bashae waded into the pecwae. He was completely submerged at one point, only to resurface when he reached the Grandmother.

"Jessan's here, Grandmother," he said. "We have to go—"

The word brought a wail that raised the hair on Jessan's head.

"Silence!" shouted the Grandmother, and the wail subsided to a whimper. "I'm not dead. Though I wish I was. Then I'd be spared this caterwauling. Palea, I leave this silly lot in your hands."

The Grandmother looked very fierce, but she patiently allowed all the pecwae to kiss her cheek or her hand or the hem of her rattling, jingling skirt. When at last she managed to extricate herself, she was red-cheeked and her usually neat hair, which she wore pulled back in a severe bun, straggled about her face.

"Go home," she told the pecwae and flapped her skirts at them as if they were so many chickens.

Palea kissed Bashae a casual farewell. She held a small child in her arms, who kissed Bashae and addressed him by the name of father. There was nothing in this, however, for every young pecwae addresses all his elders in the same manner. The pecwae departed, with many lamentations, and dignity was restored.

After that scene, the Trevenici kept their farewells short, to Jessan's relief. They said they expected to see him return with many trophies and his adult name chosen. Never mind that this meant they expected Jessan to go forth to battle and carnage. Other people might wish travelers a peaceful journey. Not the Trevenici.

Jessan accepted their wishes with thanks and made a formal request for one of the tribe's boats. The request was granted and that was that. The elders turned next to the dwarf, who would be accompanying them as far as Big Blue river.

"No trophies for me," said Wolfram. "I leave that to the young. A safe journey and a fast one is what I want, for riches galore await me at journey's end."

The elders did not quite know how to respond to this. The dwarf's statement was certainly unlucky, for to count upon blessings not yet received was the surest way to anger the gods and cause those blessings to be withdrawn. Looking pitying, the elders bid Wolfram farewell.

Wolfram shouldered his pack, waved good-bye, and set off walking. Jessan led the way out of the village. Bashae walked behind, carrying food and a rolled blanket for the Grandmother. She brought an iron stew pot that hung by its handle in the fork of a stout walking stick, carved out of an oak branch in which the knot holes had been inlaid with agates to resemble eyes. The agate eyes stared about in all directions, keeping watch. Several pouches also hung from the end of this stick and swung back and forth as she walked. Wolfram brought up the rear, waving and grinning.

The villagers were starting to disperse, to go to the fields or to their other tasks, when the sound of horses' hooves brought them up short. Jessan turned eagerly. It was in his mind that his uncle might have had second thoughts and come back for him. Instead, he saw his Aunt Ranessa.

Mounted on his uncle's horse, she wore leather breeches and a fringed leather shirt, which Jessan recognized as having once belonged to himself, but which he had outgrown.

She rode the horse bareback, and it was clear that neither she nor the horse cared for the situation.

Ranessa passed the villagers without a glance. She rode straight to Jessan's group and there reined in the horse, pulling too hard on the reins and causing the animal to whinny in protest. Wolfram winced in sympathy.

"I have had a dream," she said. "I have been told to go with you."

Jessan decided that he would tie her to a tree before he permitted her to come, when he noticed that her gaze was fixed not on him. She looked at the dwarf.

"Come, Dwarf," Ranessa said to the astonished Wolfram. "Mount up behind me. Walking is too slow. We must make haste."

"But . . . but . . . I, I, I . . ." Coughing, Wolfram cleared his throat and finally found words that made sense. "Out of the question," he began to say tersely, then he suddenly put his hand over his wrist. "What?" he demanded in astonishment. "No." He groaned. "Don't ask this of me."

For long minutes he stood with his head bowed, deep in thought.

"What's wrong with you?" Ranessa asked, frowning. "Are you mad?"

"Me mad!" Wolfram repeated, his jaw sagging. "Me!" He glowered at her, rubbing his arm and shaking his head. "I must be, to have agreed to this."

One of the elders seized hold of the horse's bridle. "We cannot allow this, Ranessa. Your brother left you in our care at his departure. We would be remiss in our duty to Ravenstrike to let you leave—"

"Oh, shut up, you blithering old man," Ranessa said angrily. There was the flash of steel. "Take your hand off the bridle or leave it there permanently when I sever it from your wrist."

She held a sword as awkwardly as she rode the horse, but there was no doubt that she intended to use it. At a glance from the elder, the rest of the Trevenici villagers moved to surround the horse.

"Stand clear! I warn you!" Ranessa shouted, panicked as a hare trying to escape the hounds. Her fear translated to the horse. Not liking his rider, not liking the people closing in on him, he rolled his eyes and bared his teeth, appeared ready to bolt.

"Leave her be!" said a voice.

The Grandmother thrust her way forward. She glared around at the Trevenici. "Why should her dreams be honored less than the dreams of another? If it was any of the rest of you"—the Grandmother pinned them all with her sharp eyes—"you would act as the gods commanded. True?"

That was true. The adult name often comes to a warrior in a dream.

"The dream bids her go," the Grandmother said. "If you prevent her, you will be thwarting the will of the gods."

"She may go, then," said the elder, stepping back. "But the dwarf is free to go with her or not as he decides."

"That's what you think," Wolfram muttered. "She can come with me," he said aloud. He eyed Ranessa grimly. "But I won't ride behind you like a mewling babe. And put that sword away before you cut your tits off!"

Walking over to the horse, Wolfram rested his head against its head. The horse nuzzled Wolfram gratefully. The dwarf glowered up at Ranessa, who glowered back. The war of wills continued for a moment, then Ranessa lowered her eyes before his. She managed, after several futile tries, to return the sword to its leather sheath. Sullenly, she shifted her position to sit farther back, leaving room for the dwarf in front.

Wolfram removed the bit from the horse's mouth and tossed away the bridle and reins. Dwarves have the ability to become one with their mount, the two acting in concert out of mutual affection and respect. Wolfram swung himself up onto the horse's back.

"Dig in with your knees like this, girl," he instructed her. "Hold onto my vest if you must. If you fall off, I'm not stopping for you."

He pressed his heels lightly into the horse's flanks, clucked a certain way with his tongue and the beast cantered off, making for the river. Wolfram sat the horse with ease. Ranessa jounced up and down, doing her best to follow his instructions, holding onto him for dear life.

Jessan heard a collective sigh of relief sweep through the village like a refreshing breeze.

"I wonder what your uncle will say," Bashae said.

"Not much he can say," Jessan replied with a shrug. And that was true enough. The gods had spoken.

He noted that a group of pecwae were heading this direction, one shouting that someone in the camp had cut his finger and that the Grandmother must come to tend to it. Fortunately the Grandmother had gone conveniently deaf. Clutching her walking stick, she stared grimly northward.

"Let's go," Jessan said and, with that, they left the village.

When they passed by the burial mound, Jessan called a halt.

"Show him," he ordered.

Bashae wore the knapsack slung over one shoulder. It was so large and he was so small that the knapsack bumped against his knees when he walked. Jessan had offered to carry it, but Bashae had refused, saying that the knight had given it to him and told him to keep it safely in his possession until he placed it into the hands of the Lady Damra.

Bashae lifted the knapsack. "I'm doing as you asked," he called.

A ripple passed through the long grass that covered the mound and the leaves of the walnut trees that shaded the mound rustled and stirred. But that was the wind.

For good or for ill, they were on their own.

12

CARRY THE ACCURSED ARMOR TO THE TEMPLE OF THE MAGI IN DUNKARGA.
Such was the counsel of Lord Gustav to Ravenstrike and the counsel was
wise and good. Yet the Void intervened.

The High Magus of the Temple of Magi in the city of Dunkar was considered to be the most powerful person in the realm, more powerful than
the King of Dunkarga. The current king, one Moross, was a deeply reli-
gious man. His detractors whispered this was so because he was glad to
place the blame for all his woes on the shoulders of the gods. "It is in the
lap of the gods," was his favorite doleful pronouncement, thus freeing
himself from any responsibility.

Fortunately for Moross—or unfortunately, as it turned out—the High
Magus of the Temple of the Magi in the city of Dunkar was a strong man,
wise and intelligent, who was glad to guide his king in all important matters. The High Magus of Dunkar was held in awe by all who knew him.
Strict and stern and joyless, he had gained his exalted position through
hard work and sacrifice and he saw no reason why others should not do
the same. He demanded complete loyalty and total obedience. The novi-
tiates went in healthy fear of him, his people revered him, his magi respected him.

These qualities, as well as his exalted position and the influence he
wielded over the weak-willed and weak-minded King Moross of
Dunkarga, made the High Magus of the Temple of Magic of Dunkarga an
ideal target for the Vrykyl.

And thus, the High Magus had died a year previous at the hands of a
Vrykyl named Shakur.

The eldest and most powerful of all the Vrykyl ever brought into
hideous being, Shakur had used the blood knife—a knife made of his own
bone—to steal the soul of the High Magus. Shakur replaced the image of

his real body—that of a rotting, loathsome corpse—with the image of the High Magus. Shakur was now able to use this subterfuge to encompass Dunkarga's fall.

The battle between Shakur and the High Magus had been hard-fought. To avoid having to fight powerful magicks, Shakur had stabbed the High Magus while he slept. The High Magus had died without a cry, but the man's soul, standing on the edge of the Void, fought to avoid being drawn into that chasm of eternal darkness. The soul of the High Magus had attempted to cast Shakur into the oblivion that both tempted Shakur and horrified him. Having fought such battles for over two hundred years, Shakur had emerged victorious.

Shakur had considered murdering the king himself. But Moross was known to be a man who fluttered with every wind that blew, while the High Magus was held to be the true power behind the throne. Thus Shakur chose the High Magus. His choice had been a good one. Shakur's poisoned words had so filled the poor king with terror that the man jumped at the sight of his own shadow.

On this night, the night Gustav lay dying, the High Magus walked the halls of the silent Temple. The inmates slumbered peacefully, unaware of the proximity of that which would turn blissful dreams into nightmares.

Shakur entered his own quarters, passed through his private library, his sitting room and solarium, shutting and locking doors as he went. Arriving in his sleeping room, he shut and locked that door. He had little fear of being disturbed. Few liked him, and no one would ever think of dropping by his room for a cozy midnight chat. Shakur did not believe in taking chances, however. Either in life or in death.

Having insured his privacy, Shakur was startled to hear a voice speak to him from out of the darkness.

"It is about time," the voice said coldly. "I have been waiting these past three hours and you know that I am not a patient man."

Shakur knew the voice, knew it as well as another knows the sound of the beating of his own heart. Shakur had no heart to beat, but he had the voice.

Shakur turned slowly, taking care to hurriedly order his thoughts, before he confronted the speaker.

"My lord," he said humbly. "Forgive me, but I did not know of your arrival. Had you informed me—"

"—'you would have sped to my side on the wings of love,'" said Dagnarus. "Isn't that what the poet says? Except in your case it would be on the wings of hatred, wouldn't it, my dear old friend?"

Shakur was silent and he kept his thoughts silent as well. Dagnarus, Lord of the Void, was master and creator of the Vrykyl. He carried upon his person the Dagger of the Vrykyl, a powerful artifact of Void magic.

Two hundred years ago, Dagnarus had used that dagger to end Shakur's life, change him into the dreadful being he was this day. True, Shakur's life had been a miserable one. There was not a law on the books of any civilized nation that he had not broken, starting with matricide. He had given himself freely to the Void and thus it was that Dagnarus ensnared him.

Dagnarus rose to his feet. He wore the black armor of the Lord of the Void, armor that is the direct opposite of the blessed armor of a Dominion Lord. Dagnarus's armor had been blessed, but not by the gods. His armor was of the Void. The black metal was malleable, flowed over Dagnarus's flesh like a coating of viscous oil.

He did not wear the helm, that was bestial and terrible to look upon. He had no need to hide his face. Unlike the Vrykyl, who were ambulating dead, Dagnarus was a living man. He had been a comely young man when he gave himself to the Void. He retained that form through the power of the Void. His hair was thick and auburn. He wore it long, drawn back in a club at the nape of the neck in the fashion of elven warriors. He was handsome with a rakish air. He could be charming, when he chose.

Two hundred years ago, Dagnarus had been a royal prince of Vinnengael. His brother, Helmos, was king. The Sovereign Stone had been a gift of the gods to their father, King Tamaros. Although the gods warned Tamaros that his understanding of the Stone was yet imperfect, he chose to use it to try to establish peace between the races. He split the Stone into four parts with disastrous consequences. His young son, Dagnarus, looked into the center of the Stone and saw there the Void and within the Void, the opportunity to gain the power for which he had always lusted.

Each race had been granted a portion of the Stone, to use to create the powerful, magical paladins known as Dominion Lords. Longing to attain such power for himself, Dagnarus tried to become a Dominion Lord. In so doing, he gave himself to the Void and was made Lord of the Void. He obtained great power, but at a terrible cost. He also obtained the Dagger of the Vrykyl and was thus able to bring into existence those dread beings.

Dagnarus declared war upon his brother the king. Their two armies met and fought in the capital city of Vinnengael. At the height of the battle, Dagnarus sought his brother in the Temple of the Gods and demanded that Helmos give up the Sovereign Stone. Helmos refused. Dagnarus murdered him and claimed the Stone. In that moment, the powerful magicks that were swirling about the vortex of the Void created by Dagnarus could no longer be controlled. The magic exploded, shattering the Portals and destroying much of the once proud city of Vinnengael.

The Void carried Dagnarus to safety, preserving his life by means of all the lives he had acquired through the Dagger of the Vrykyl. Dagnarus was horribly injured, but he lived and he had his prize, the Sovereign Stone. Either by happenstance or by the wish of the gods, a new Portal—a remnant of those shattered in the magical blast—had opened near where Dagnarus lay injured. Although no one knew it at the time and few know it still, the Portal opened into a new part of the world not previously known to those living on Loerem.

Through this Portal wandered a creature known as a bahk. The bahk was young and the young of this species are not noted for their intelligence. Lost and hungry, the bahk wandered into this new world in search of food. The bahk are drawn to magic as bees to honey and this young bahk was drawn to the Sovereign Stone. The bahk was huge and strong; Dagnarus weak and injured. Dagnarus did his best to fight to retain his prize, but he was no match for the bahk. The creature seized the Stone and departed. Dagnarus despaired. In that moment, he came as close to death as he ever had or likely ever would.

He did not die, however. The Void would not let him. Drawing on the lives he had stolen through the Dagger, Dagnarus managed at last to drag his maimed and wounded body into the very Portal through which the bahk had entered. Here Valura, his former lover and now a Vrykyl herself, came in response to his call. Here Shakur and the rest of the Vrykyl came. He sent them back out into the world with one order—find the Sovereign Stone.

As they searched, Dagnarus remained safely hidden within the Portal until he had fully healed and recovered his strength. Then it was that Dagnarus began to plan the campaign that would at last restore him to power. But he never lost sight of his main goal, his true objective.

For two hundred years, he had sought the Sovereign Stone and now, on the eve of his great war to conquer Loerem, the Sovereign Stone had reappeared. Dagnarus's joy was complete.

"The gods themselves are vanquished," he had said on hearing of the Stone's discovery. "Mortals do not stand a chance against me."

But the gods, it seemed, still had a fight or two left in them and as for mortals, if they went down, they would go down swinging.

"You take a great risk coming here, my lord—" began Shakur.

"Nonsense," said Dagnarus impatiently, prowling about the chamber. "The armor cloaks me in shadow. I am the darkness, I move with the darkness. If someone should walk through that door right now, he would not see me unless I choose otherwise."

"I mean, my lord," said Shakur, "the risk of leaving your army at this critical juncture. You have before expressed doubts about the bestial taan warriors and their unpredictability. Who knows what they might do in your absence?"

"I am their god, Shakur. The taan fear me as their god. They would all fling themselves off the top of Mt. Sa'Gra if I commanded it. Besides, I am not going to be away from them for long. I had to find out. Have you heard from Svetlana?"

"No, my lord," Shakur replied. "I have not. You know well that I have not. For how could I hear if you have not heard?"

Created by Dagnarus, Lord of the Void, the Vrykyl are bound to serve Dagnarus. They have no will of their own, other than that which their lord permits them to have, and their thoughts are always linked to the thoughts of their dread liege lord. The Vrykyl maintain contact with each other through the blood knife and thus Shakur in Dunkar heard through the whispers of the blood knife the same words that his lord Dagnarus heard in the emptiness of his soul.

Dagnarus clenched his fist. "Tell me what you know," he said tersely.

"My lord, you know all I know—"

"Tell me!"

Shakur knew better than to argue.

"Svetlana told me that the Sovereign Stone was in the possession of a Dominion Lord, one of the blessed of the gods. This news worried me, my lord, as you are aware, for I told you of my fears regarding the power of these knights."

"Yes, yes," Dagnarus said, trying to brush this aside.

Shakur would not let it be brushed aside, however. He was not going to be blamed.

"If you recall, my lord, I suggested that I go to Svetlana to aid in the retrieval of the Stone. You said no, that I was needed here."

"And so you were, Shakur," Dagnarus said. "In these critical times, when rumors are spreading about war in the west, the absence of the High Magus would have looked most peculiar, started people wondering. You had to be here to calm Moross, to allay his fears."

Shakur bowed in acknowledgment. "I suggested other Vrykyl—"

"They are spread across the continent," Dagnarus interrupted tersely. "Some busy subverting the orks, others working with the dwarves. The Lady Valura is in elven lands. They all seek the other portions of the Stone. As for this Dominion Lord who discovered the human portion, he was old and decrepit and half-mad. A stranger in a strange land, he should have fallen easy victim to Svetlana."

"Svetlana wounded the Dominion Lord with the blood knife, but he wounded her grievously during the battle and he managed to escape." Shakur shook his head. "Svetlana's thoughts turned to hatred and revenge. She went berserk. She lost sight of the true objective. Her only thought was to pursue the knight who had so humiliated her."

"At that point you should have gone after her," Dagnarus stated. "My armies are close now. You can be spared."

"How could I, my lord?" Shakur demanded. He had known all along he would be blamed. "I had no way to find her! She was silent. I could do nothing but wait to feel her blood knife kill again. I calculated that she would need a soul to replenish her power and then I could reestablish contact with her. Days passed and I felt nothing."

"I, too, have lost all contact," said Dagnarus. "What has happened to her? What has happened to the Stone? I must know, Shakur!

The human portion of the Stone has been found and, not only that, it has been found on the eve of battle. Why else would this happen if the Stone were not meant to come to me? I want you to go in search of her, Shakur. I want you to find her and the Stone."

"You know very well that such a search would be a waste of time, my lord," said Shakur. "You know very well what has happened to her. The Dominion Lord destroyed her. The Stone has once more eluded you."

"No!"

Shakur felt the word lance through him. He felt the very earth quiver with the conviction of the Lord of the Void. Those who slumbered within the walls of the Temple felt it as well, tossed restlessly and uneasily in their sleep.

"My lord," said Shakur, speaking hesitantly, "would it not be better to concentrate your efforts on pursuing the war, rather than squander our efforts and resources in this pursuit of the Sovereign Stone? We have lost one Vrykyl already and what have we gained? What do you hope to gain? You don't need the Stone to be the most powerful force in Loerem. You don't need the ability to create Dominion Lords when you have the Dagger of the Vrykyl. This pursuit has brought trouble upon us already. I think you should abandon it, my lord. Your armies will win the world for you. You don't need the Stone."

"Yes, I do, Shakur," said Dagnarus. He fell silent and was silent for so long that Shakur thought his lord had departed and was startled when he once more spoke. "I am about to tell you something that I never told you before, Shakur. I have never told anyone."

Shakur knew Dagnarus lied. He had told Valura. He told Valura everything. But Shakur said nothing, made no comment.

"I tell you this now, Shakur," Dagnarus was continuing, "because you are my lieutenant and it is time that you know of my true plans, my ultimate goal.

"When we returned from the land of the taan and I emerged for the first time from the Portal, walked again on the soil of my own homeland, I made a journey, a solitary journey. Do you recall, Shakur?"

"I do, my lord. I was opposed to your going by yourself. I considered it too dangerous."

"Yet, what could harm me?" Dagnarus said dryly. "No, this was a journey I needed to make on my own. Where do you suppose I went?"

"I have no idea, my lord."

"I went to the heap of ruins they are now calling Old Vinnengael."

Shakur could think of nothing to say. He was astonished and yet he was not. He had often been told that the criminal is ever drawn back to the scene of the crime.

"I went to that place in search of the Sovereign Stone. Not such a foolish quest as you might suppose. A bahk had taken the Stone from me. I had received reports that numerous bahk were to be found in the area of Old Vinnengael, drawn there by the wayward magicks that yet pervade that accursed place. And it is accursed, Shakur. I am not a coward. I have proven my courage in battle countless times. I wore the armor of the Void and carried the magic of the Void as my weapon. Yet, I tell you, there were times during my journey when I knew fear, when I thought that perhaps I had overreached myself.

"This is not the time to recount my adventures, however. I could not find any trace of the Sovereign Stone. I knew then that it was not there. I could have departed, but I hoped to find some clue as to the Stone's whereabouts. I fought my way through the ruins and the magic to the very center of what is now left of the Temple of the Magi.

"No other had been there before me. I know that, because no other could have survived the going. I stood amidst the rubble and wondered why I had come. There was nothing here for me. I was about to leave, when my foot struck against something. I looked down to see a skull. The flesh was gone from the body, yet I knew him by the robes he wore. It was my whipping boy. Gareth.

"As I stood staring at the body, the events of that terrible night came back to me with such force that it seemed to me I lived them all over again. And then, as the memories began to fade, a voice spoke to me. 'My prince,' said the voice, and I recognized it. It was Gareth who spoke."

"A waking dream, my lord," said Shakur, who didn't like where this tale was heading. "He was in your mind. You imagined you heard him."

"So I thought myself," said Dagnarus. "So I hoped—with all my heart. I do not mind admitting to you, Shakur, that when I heard his voice speaking to me from the grave, my blood ran chill. I have never been one to look behind me. What's done is done. The strong man faces forward, never looks back. Yet, sometimes, unbidden, I do look back and when I do, I see the reproach in Gareth's eyes. I see his blood upon the wall and the light of life fading. Of all I knew, he alone was true to me and faithful. He deserved better of me."

"He was a traitor, my lord, a coward and a weasel," said Shakur bluntly. "Whatever punishment you meted out, he richly deserved."

"Did he? Well, perhaps you are right." Dagnarus's introspective mood had ended. "However that may be, the voice was not my imagination,

Shakur. Gareth's spirit appeared to me there in the ruins of the Temple of the Magi."

"And what did his spirit have to say to you, my lord?"

"Some very interesting things, Shakur, so you may dispense with the sarcasm. I asked why he continued to remain in the world, why he had not gone off to some well-deserved rest.

"'My spirit is so bound up with yours, my prince, that it is not free to depart until either your spirit is free of the Void or utterly consumed by it.'

"'You know what has happened in the world since?' I asked him.

"'I do, my prince.'

"'Do you know where I may find the human portion of the Sovereign Stone?'

"'I do not, my prince. The Stone has passed beyond my ability to see. In truth, I believe that the gods hide it from me. I have, however, discovered something else that might be of use to you.'

"'You were a loyal friend, Gareth, and you continue to be. What is it you have discovered?'

"'All believe that the Portal to the Gods was shattered, as were the other Portals. They are wrong. The Portal to the Gods remains intact.'

"His spirit gestured, Shakur, to where the Portal had once stood. The doorway had collapsed. I could see nothing but ruin. Seeking to test his words, I walked in that direction. I had taken only a few steps, when I felt the wrath of the gods like a hot wind from a raging fire.

"'What is that to me?' I asked. 'I care not what the gods do or think.'

"'It might be everything to you,' Gareth replied. 'I have learned that if someone enters that Portal bearing in his hand all four portions of the Sovereign Stone, the Stone will come together again. Four will be one.'

"'And one will rule four!' I said.

"'I know nothing of that,' Gareth said and his voice was bitter. 'The gods speak to me no more. I am not permitted into their blessed presence, so heinous were my crimes. Yet, this I do know. You are the only person now in Loerem who has the power to bring all four pieces of the Stone together.'

"'Well, then,' I said, 'what else could this mean but that I am meant to rule over all of the others?'"

Shakur said nothing, but Dagnarus could hear even his silences.

"I am not a fool, Shakur. I was skeptical myself. 'Tell me this, Master Whipping Boy,' I said, 'if the gods speak to you no more, how did you discover all this?'

"He did not want to answer me. He sought to evade my question. Using the power of the Void, I pressed him hard and at last his spirit, under constraint of the Void, had no choice but to respond.

"'Your brother told me,' he said at last. 'Helmos. He told me this as he lay dying.'

"'You lie,' I returned in anger. 'Helmos was dead when I left him. You were dead. And if you were not then, you would have been after the blast.'

"'Not so,' Gareth replied. 'The blast expanded outward from the Portal. The Portal itself was unharmed. Over time, the unstable structures have disintegrated and collapsed. Then, it stood in peace and serenity. I felt my death upon me, yet I could not depart without begging forgiveness of your brother—'"

"The traitor," Shakur intoned. "It is as I have always said, my lord. I wonder that you still trust him."

"I never trust anyone, Shakur, as you should know by now. To my mind, this proves the veracity of his tale. Gareth dragged himself over to the dying Helmos. Helmos forgave him and then whispered these words. 'The Sovereign Stone must be made whole again. The four pieces must be brought here to the Portal. Whoever does so will gain the gods' greatest blessing.'"

"Do you *want* the gods' blessing, my lord?" Shakur asked.

"If it means ruling over all of Loerem, I think I could stomach it," said Dagnarus. "Thus you see, Shakur, why the discovery of the human portion of the Stone is so significant, coming at this time. I have now only to lay my hands on it and the other three and there will be no one who can stop me."

"Indeed, so it would seem, my lord," Shakur replied. "Still, you put a lot of trust in one whose last act was to betray you . . ."

"Gareth?" Dagnarus gave a shrug. "He was always weak. As it turns out, Helmos's forgiveness availed the whipping boy nothing, for his spirit is doomed to remain imprisoned in the Temple where lies his body. He serves me still. He has no choice. The Void constrains him. If I need him, he is bound to come do my bidding. So long as he returns to his body at night, his spirit is free to roam the world at my command."

"Then why do you not send him in search of the Sovereign Stone, my lord?" Shakur asked, nettled.

"Because his last act was to betray me," Dagnarus replied.

"I understand, my lord."

"I thought you might. Now you know my reasons for what I do and why the recovery of the Stone is so important. I will send the Vrykyl Jedash to assist you. He is the closest within call."

He paused a moment, then he spoke again, "Shakur, you will find the Sovereign Stone. You will."

No threat was issued, but it was there. Dagnarus could not only inflict pain on his Vrykyl, he could, with a single word, drain the magical power that kept Shakur's corpse shambling through this life. Much as Shakur loathed this existence in which he walked as a shadow in the land of the living, with no rest, no pleasure, no joy, he feared the Void more. Its empty darkness gaped always at his feet, eager for the single misstep that would cause him to fall into that eternal abyss.

"I will find the Sovereign Stone, my lord," promised Shakur.

RAVEN BEGAN HIS JOURNEY BY RETRIEVING THE ARMOR FROM THE CAVERN, wrapping it in the tarp he'd brought for the purpose. He was forced to touch the various pieces to place them on the tarp. The feel of the metal was slimy, oily, and although he wrapped his hands with cloth, like bandages, the foul ooze from the armor penetrated the cotton, leaving patches of oily residue on his skin.

Once the armor was safely packed, he washed his hands, washed them several times over, but, although the residue came off, he could still smell the horrid odor or imagined that he could.

He was unable to convince the knight's horse to carry it. Every time he then strapped the armor on the horse's back, the beast bucked and plunged as if the armor were a load of stinging nettles. Finally, Raven was forced to make a litter out of tree branches and strap the litter to the horse. Placing the armor on the litter, he dragged it behind him and he was able to set out on his journey. Every time he passed a stream or an oasis or well, he halted to scrub his hands again.

Dunkar, the capital city of Dunkarga, was over seven hundred miles away. The journey normally took him a few weeks of leisurely riding and it was a trip he always enjoyed.

He did not enjoy this one.

First came the dreams. Night after night, the moment Raven fell asleep, he dreamed of the eyes searching for him. He didn't know why, but he was terrified lest the eyes should find him. He spent all his sleep-time looking for places to hide from the eyes. Just when it seemed they must see him, he would wake, drenched in sweat and shaking. They had not found him yet, but every night, they came closer.

His sister's words haunted him. *You will save the people, though you yourself will be lost.* He had the dreadful feeling that if the eyes ever once looked into his, they would draw him inexorably into their emptiness and his sister's prophecy would prove correct. His one consolation was that Jessan and the others were far away, safe from this curse.

After a week of these terrible dreams, Raven eventually gave up trying to sleep. He wanted nothing more now than to reach Dunkar and the Temple of the Magi. He would have ridden day and night but he was forced to halt to rest the horse. When such stops were necessary, he built immense bonfires to keep away the eyes. After three days of this, his body took over and imposed sleep upon him. An old campaigner, he'd often dozed in the saddle and he found he could do so again. Once he left the wilderness of Trevenici lands and reached Dunkarga, the road to Dunkar was a King's Road, well-traveled and broad. Near the capital city, the road was actually paved. The horse knew its business and followed the route with only minimal guidance. Raven had the feeling the horse would be as relieved as he would be to rid itself of the Void-tainted burden.

The lack of sleep took its toll on Raven's mind as well as his body. He spent most of one afternoon in violent argument with a dwarf, who was riding on the back of the horse with him. Their combined weight—his and the dwarf's—were too much for the horse to bear. Raven told the fellow repeatedly to jump off, but the dwarf ignored him. The dwarf continued to sit behind him, gloating over the wealth he was going to win when he came to some mountain or other. At length, Raven jumped down off the horse. Drawing his sword, he threatened to cut off the dwarf's ears if he didn't dismount. By now, Raven had reached a well-traveled section of road and it was only when he saw the stares and heard the laughter of his fellow travelers that Raven realized he was threatening nothing but air. He was hallucinating.

He had no idea how long he was on this nightmare journey. Half-stupefied, weary beyond caring anymore what happened to him, Raven rode day after day and wondered if he would be forced to ride forever. Then came the day he lifted his head and saw Dunkar on the horizon. Tears came to his eyes.

Graceful minarets and twisting spires alternated with squat bulbous-shaped domes to form a border of black lace on the hem of sunset's splendid red-golden robes. The capital city of Dunkar was far distant yet, but at least it was in sight, for which blessing Raven thanked the gods. He would reach Dunkar long after nightfall, but he would reach it.

He stopped at a roadside well only long enough to water his horse and splash the cold well-water on his face and wash his hands. He was weary to the point of collapse, but he was not going to spend another night on the road in the company of the accursed armor. He pushed himself, pushed the horse and when the beast came to a halt and stood with its head down, shivering, too exhausted to go farther, Raven slid off its back and, leading the horse by the reins, walked the remainder of the way to his destination.

Dunkar was a walled city. The gate on this, the main road, was well-guarded. Approaching the guard house, Raven called out loudly to announce his arrival. Few ordinary travelers journeyed so far into the night. The guards would be suspicious. As it was, the sound of Raven's own voice startled him. He didn't recognize it and his fuddled mind wondered for a moment who it was who had shouted.

Guards came out bearing torches that flared painfully in Raven's bleary eyes. He blinked gummed eyelids, held up a shielding hand. Fortunately, he was well-known among the soldiers. Dark looks changed to welcoming grins.

"Captain!" said one, "we weren't expecting to see you back so soon."

"Get out of here, Captain," said another, laughing. "No soldier in his right mind returns from leave early. They'll come to expect that of all of us!"

"What'd you bring us, sir?" asked a third, holding the torch over the bundle. "Spirits? A haunch of venison?"

"Keep your hands off that!" Raven snarled.

The soldier stepped back, a startled expression on his face. "Yes, sir!" he said, making a mock of his obedience. He exchanged wondering looks with his comrades.

Raven couldn't explain. He was too tired.

"Just let me through," he ordered.

The soldiers did as they were told, but sullenly and with an ill will. Raven knew he had fallen in their estimation and the knowledge bothered him, although it shouldn't. He was not in this business to be liked. The next block, he was practically weeping at the thought that they all hated him.

"Gods!" he said to himself, wiping the sweat from his face. "I'm going crazy. Crazy as my sister." The thought terrified him and fear jolted him back to reality. "Just a little longer. A little longer and we'll be rid of it."

Guiding the stumbling horse, he wended his way through the empty, narrow streets, heading for the Temple of Magic.

"But, Captain," the porter said, peeping at Raven through the grate, "what you ask is impossible. I cannot permit you entry at this hour of the night!"

"Then I will dump this in the street," Raven said savagely and raised clenched fists. He kept tight hold of his sanity in those balled fists. "And you must suffer the consequences. I haven't slept in days!" Someone was shouting now, making a hell of a racket. He had the dim realization that maybe it was he himself. "You'll let me in or by the gods I'll—"

"What is the matter, Porter?" came another voice. One of the magi of the Temple had been crossing the courtyard. Hearing Raven's shout, he came to investigate. "What is all the commotion? Some of us are trying to sleep."

"This officer"—the porter pointed through the closed gate at Raven—"insists that he must come inside. I told him to return in the morning, Brother Ulaf, but he refuses. He says his business is urgent and will not wait."

"Perhaps I can help him," said the magus. "Open the gate and let him enter."

"But the rules—"

"I will be responsible, Porter."

The porter, muttering, opened the gate. Raven led his horse with the litter bearing its strange and terrible burden into the Temple's courtyard. The porter locked the gate behind. Brother Ulaf turned to Raven with a pleasant smile that faded when he studied the man closer. "Captain, you don't look well. What is wrong?"

"This is wrong!" said Raven in a hollow voice. Taking out his knife, he cut the straps that bound the litter to the horse. The wooden poles fell to the cobblestones with a clatter. "Come closer. You'll see what I mean."

Brother Ulaf, mystified, drew nearer. Bending over the bundle, he reached out a hand to touch it. Raven had no need to warn the magus. Brother Ulaf gasped and snatched his hand back. Appalled, he looked at Raven.

"It reeks of Void magic," he said sternly. "What is it?"

"Your problem," Raven said. "Not mine." Taking hold of the reins of his horse, he turned to leave.

"Wait!" Brother Ulaf's voice snapped.

He was young, perhaps in his late twenties, but he had an air of authority that Raven recognized and to which he instinctively reacted. He remained standing, his head bowed with fatigue and thankfulness that he had handed over his burden.

"Joseph," said Brother Ulaf, "bring a lantern."

The porter, shaking his head, headed for the stairs that lead to the Temple proper.

Brother Ulaf tucked his hands in the sleeves of his robes and remained with Raven in the darkness. No lights shone from the Temple windows. Even those who stayed up late studying would have gone to bed by now. Neither man spoke. The young magus stared in horrible fascination at the bundle. Raven stood straight and rigid, as if on parade, looked straight ahead.

The Temple of the Magi was an imposing structure, the second largest in the city, next to the king's palace. Its gleaming white dome and four spiraling minarets could be seen for miles. Its gardens were legendary. Only the Temple of the Magi in New Vinnengael was larger—a sore point to the Dunkargans, whose Temple had been the largest in the years after the fall of Old Vinnengael, until the Vinnengaeleans had built their Temple in its new location.

Dunkarga was an impoverished country, following the ruinous civil war with its brothers, the Karnuans. The Dunkargans could only watch with seething jealousy as the wealthy Vinnengael empire poured immense amounts of money into building a new temple, mainly—so the Dunkargans felt—to spite them. Now all the Dunkargans could do was sneer at the new Temple, proclaim it ostentatious and boorish and take comfort in the fact that their Temple was far older, dating back at least three centuries. The great king Tamaros had once visited their temple, something which the people of New Vinnengael could not say.

A light flared in the windows of the entry chamber, streamed out onto the white marble stairs. Joseph was returning with a lantern.

"Bring it to me," Brother Ulaf said to the porter. "Go back to your duties."

The porter handed over the lantern and retreated to the gatehouse. Lifting the lantern, Brother Ulaf looked Raven full in the face.

"What is your name, Captain?"

"Raven, Revered Magus."

"You are Trevenici?"

"I am."

"Where is your village located?"

"It is only a small village, Magus," Raven replied. "Of no importance."

Brother Ulaf raised an eyebrow, but said nothing more on that score. He glanced back at the bundle. "I ask again, Captain, what is it?"

"It is . . . or was, knightly armor, Revered Magus," said Raven. He raised a hand to shield his burning eyes from the light. "Evil armor. I am not a magus, but I think this armor has been cursed by the Void."

Brother Ulaf shifted the lantern, held it over the bundle.

"Would you unwrap it, Captain?" he said, straightening.

A strong shudder went through Raven. He shook his head and took a step backward. "No," he said, unable to even phrase the refusal politely. "No," he repeated doggedly.

Brother Ulaf eyed the warrior doubtfully and then he reached down himself. With a swift and sure movement, he grasped hold of a corner of the bundle and tugged it open. The lantern light gleamed on a portion of the armor, glittered on the black spikes. Raven's disturbed fancy pictured an insect's black jointed legs.

Brother Ulaf gazed at the armor in silence for a long time, so long that Raven's burning eyelids closed.

"How did you come by this?" Brother Ulaf asked.

Raven woke with a start. Fortunately, he had his answer prepared or he would have never been able to articulate it. He looked back at the armor, saw that the magus had covered it up with the blanket again.

"I found it, Revered Magus," he said. "On the banks of the Sea of Redesh. I was out hunting . . . came across it. There were signs of a . . . fight." He rubbed his eyes. "The knight who wore this was dead. I didn't see anyone else."

The Magus peered at Raven intently. "What did you do with the body?"

"I buried it," Raven said.

"Why take the armor?"

Raven shrugged. "I am a warrior. The armor looked to be well-made, valuable. A shame to let it go to waste. Only later, I found out . . ." He swallowed. "I found out it was . . . like that. Horrible. I knew I had done wrong and I brought it here to turn over to the Church."

"You buried the body, you say. How did this so-called knight die?"

"A sword thrust, through the chest. You can see it went through the armor."

"Strange," murmured Brother Ulaf, "for such well-made armor. You did not see the battle? You heard nothing? You saw no one else around?"

"No, Magus," said Raven. "I did not." He was growing impatient. "I have told you all I know. I have brought you this armor. Do with it what you will, just so long as I never have to look at it again. I bid you good-night."

Turning, he stumbled in his exhaustion and almost fell. He caught himself on his horse's flank, pressed his head into the warm flesh and stood there waiting for the mists that shrouded his eyes to pass. He was aware of the magus's voice, continuing to ask questions, but Raven had provided all the answers he was going to. He ignored the voice and, when the man dared lay a hand on his shoulder, responded with a low snarl that was so fierce and feral that the hand was immediately removed.

When at last Raven felt he had the strength to pull himself up, he crawled into the saddle and, with a mumbled command and a knee in the flanks, urged the horse forward. The beast was glad to comply and bolted from the courtyard with the wild, rolling-eyed stare of a horse that has been about to step on a coiled snake.

Raven let the horse have his head, not particularly caring where they were going, so long as it was away from the Temple and the horrid bundle. He slumped over the horse's neck, with only dim awareness of where they were. He guided the horse by instinct and knew that the animal stopped only when he became aware of cessation of movement. He recognized the barracks, but he did not have the energy to dismount and so he remained on the horse, head lowered, slumped in the saddle. He might have stayed that way until morning had not two of his fellow Trevenici walked by, having just come off watch on the city walls.

"Captain," said one, resting his hand on Raven's arm.

"Eh?" Raven grunted, raised bleary eyes.

"Captain, you are back early—"

Raven felt himself slipping from the saddle, but he made no effort to halt his fall. He was home, in the Trevenici camp, among friends, comrades. He was safe. The burden was gone. He was rid of it.

Strong hands caught him, strong arms cradled him, strong voices shouted for assistance.

Raven paid no attention to any of it. At last, he could sleep in peace.

Brother Ulaf stood in the courtyard, staring intently at the bundle that reeked of Void magic. Confronted with this unexpected situation, he had to decide what to do and he didn't have much time to make up his mind. The porter Joseph was a notorious gossip, harmless, but loving to talk and this would be all over the Temple by morning. Ulaf had no doubt that the gods had guided his steps so that he happened to be the one passing by the gate at this particular time. It was his responsibility to figure out what the gods wanted him to do, how best to act. Having made up his mind at last, Ulaf acted with his customary decision.

He peered inside the gate house. Joseph sat on his stool with his head bowed, as though dozing. Ulaf smiled slightly, not fooled.

"Joseph," said Ulaf peremptorily, "I want you to go wake the High Magus."

Joseph jerked his head up, stared open-mouthed at Ulaf.

"Go on," said Ulaf. "I will take responsibility."

Joseph hesitated, hoping that Ulaf would think better of it. Ulaf frowned at the delay and eventually, with much reluctant scraping of feet and fumbling for the lantern, Joseph departed, heading back into the Temple.

Ulaf watched until the porter had entered the Temple and shut the door, then he hastened back to the bundle. Joseph would be in no hurry. He would undoubtedly try to find someone to complain to or at the very least attempt to foist this onerous duty off on someone else.

Ulaf had considered asking for Joseph to leave the lantern, but changed his mind almost immediately. As a newly made Revered Magus, Ulaf was supposed to have only the most cursory knowledge of Void magic— enough to know to keep away from it. He should not be down on all fours pawing through this strange bundle. The night was dark, clouds covered the stars, and the Trevenici had happened to drop the bundle in the shadow of the gate.

Ulaf glanced around to make certain no one else was out taking a late night stroll. Seeing the courtyard empty, as was only reasonable at this hour, Ulaf bent over the bundle, twitched off the blanket and studied it, smelled it, poked it and prodded.

When Joseph, looking aggrieved, returned to say that the High Magus was coming and that he was not at all happy about having been wakened at this ungodly hour, he found Brother Ulaf where the porter had left him, his arms folded in the sleeves of his robes, standing a seemly distance from the bundle, regarding it with wary uneasiness. Ulaf had made one change, that he trusted the porter would not notice. Ulaf had not replaced the blanket over the armor, but had left the armor uncovered.

Lamps were lit. A man appeared at the top of the stairs, a dark, robed figure against the bright light. The High Magus was a man of stately mien, perhaps in his sixtieth year, with white hair and a white-streaked black beard. The man's face was patrician, with fine-honed features and deep lines that indicated a strong will and an iron disposition. The High Magus frowned slightly at the sight of Ulaf, who pretended not to notice. Ulaf knew very well that he wasn't liked, wasn't trusted. The fact that Ulaf was a Vinnengaelean among Dunkargans was enough to account for the distrust, but Ulaf was aware that the ill feelings of the High Magus ran deeper than that.

"Brother Ulaf," said the High Magus, his voice crisp and alert. If he had been sleeping, he was quick to wake. "I am told that you need to see me on a matter of urgency that could not wait until morning."

He laid an irritable emphasis on the latter words.

Ulaf bowed, as was proper. Approaching the High Magus, he spoke in a hushed voice properly tinged with horror.

"I did not know what to do, High Magus. I thought that you should be informed." Ulaf made his eyes round in the lantern light. "I've never seen anything like it."

"Like what, Brother Ulaf?" the High Magus snapped. He had no use for what he considered the histrionics of a Vinnengaelean.

Ulaf gestured respectfully. The High Magus turned to look at the bundle on the litter.

"Joseph, bring the lantern."

Joseph hastened to comply, held the lantern light directly over the dark armor that did not shine in the light, but seemed to suck it up, diminish it. The High Magus took a step toward it, then he stiffened. He was expert at controlling his facial expressions, but Ulaf—who was watching closely out of the corner of his eye—saw the swift contortion that passed over his features.

"Void magic, High Magus," Ulaf felt called upon to point out.

"I am aware of that," the High Magus snapped. "Give Brother Ulaf that lantern before you drop it, Joseph, and return to your post."

Ulaf took the lantern from the shaking hand of the porter, who was staring at the dark armor with wide-eyed terror. The porter started to leave, but he couldn't take his eyes from the horrid bundle, and nearly tripped himself.

"Wait, Joseph!" said the High Magus. "Where did this come from? How did it get here?"

"A-An officer brought it, High Magus," Joseph stammered.

"What officer?" the High Magus demanded. "What was his name?"

"I-I don't know, High Magus. He wanted to come inside and I-I said he couldn't. And then the brother here—" Joseph looked helplessly at Ulaf.

"I happened to be passing by, High Magus," said Ulaf deferentially. "I heard the soldier at the gate. He was most distraught. He threatened to dump this in the street. I thought—"

"Yes, yes," said the High Magus. He cast a frowning glance at the armor. "He came inside and left it." He shifted the frown to Ulaf, who bore it meekly. "I assume you questioned him. Asked him his name, how he came by this . . . this . . ."

"I did, High Magus," said Ulaf, "but he was not very cooperative. He was a Trevenici," he added, as if that explained everything.

"His name?" the High Magus persisted. "There are a thousand Trevenici soldiers in the Dunkargan army."

"I regret, High Magus . . ." Ulaf lowered his eyes. "It didn't occur to me . . . The armor was so frightful . . ."

The High Magus snorted. "You, Joseph?" he demanded of the porter. "Did you get his name?"

"I-I-I . . ." Joseph stuttered.

"What rank was he then?" The High Magus looked extremely put out.

Ulaf was chagrined. "I am sorry, High Magus, but I know so little of the ways of the Dunkargan military . . ."

Joseph could only shake his head.

"Go!" the High Magus ordered and Joseph fled thankfully back to his gatehouse.

The High Magus turned his gaze to Ulaf. "Did you even bother to question this Trevenici about how he came by this accursed armor, Brother Ulaf?"

"Indeed, I did, High Magus," Ulaf stated.

In his enthusiasm, he was waving the lantern about and accidentally shot a beam of light directly into the eyes of the High Magus, who flung his arm over his face and backed away precipitously.

"I beg your pardon, Your Grace!" Ulaf gasped and hastily lowered the lantern. "I did not mean to blind you—"

"Continue," the High Magus muttered.

"According to the Trevenici, he came across the armor while he was out hunting. The armor being quite . . . er . . . well made and no one being about to claim it, he thought he would appropriate it for his own use. He quickly discovered that the armor was cursed and decided to bring it to the Temple, in order to be rid of it."

"And what happened to the knight who wore this armor?" the High Magus asked. Glancing down at it, he pointed to the hole in the breast-plate. "Such a wound would be mortal."

Ulaf felt that he was under intense scrutiny, though he could not see the High Magus, who remained standing in the dark, careful now to keep his face out of the light.

"The Trevenici had no idea, Your Grace," said Ulaf. "He could find no sign of a body. Of course, the man was lying," he added disdainfully. "He did not want to admit that he had stripped the dead. We all know and de-plore the barbaric ways of the Trevenici."

The High Magus made no comment, neither agreeing nor disagreeing. He remained silent, staring down at the armor. Ulaf was respectful of his superior's musings for a moment, then he said, tentatively, "I find it ap-palling to think that there may be knights—paladins, if you will—dedi-cated to the evil practice of Void magic, Your Grace. Where do you suppose such a knight might have hailed from? What was his objective? What killed him? For certainly he must have been very powerful."

Again, Ulaf was aware that he was being scrutinized.

"I, too, would be interested in answers to these questions," said the High Magus. "One reason I deem it imperative to speak to that Trevenici. Could you recognize him again, if we find him, Brother Ulaf?"

"Oh, yes, I am certain of it, Your Grace," said Ulaf without hesitation. "I can even give you a description of him."

He proceeded to do just that. The High Magus listened with interest at first, then shook his head.

"You have described a Trevenici male, Brother Ulaf. Did you notice nothing more specific about this man? Scars? Body paint? Adornments?"

Ulaf lowered his eyes. "The night was dark . . . I was excited . . . One of these barbarians looks the same as another to me . . . Perhaps Joseph . . ."

The High Magus grunted and made a dismissive gesture, well aware of the limited scope of Joseph's power of observation. "If you can tell me nothing more of importance, Brother Ulaf—"

"I am sorry, High Magus—"

"Then you should go to your bed. Please say nothing of this matter to your fellow brethren. I would not want to start a panic. The armor is an-tiquated and archaic and *Vinnengaelean in design.*" He emphasized the latter. "Nothing like this has ever been seen in Dunkarga. I think therefore that this is a Vinnengaelean problem."

Ulaf bowed, but said nothing.

"Since the armor is Vinnengaelean, a report of this matter should be immediately carried to the Temple in New Vinnengael. You had not intended to leave us quite this soon, Brother Ulaf, but you are the logical choice as messenger—"

"I would be only too happy to carry news of this to the Temple, Your Grace. I can be ready to depart in the morning or at Your Grace's pleasure."

"Excellent. I will write the report this night. I know this means that you will have only a few hours sleep, but you should be ready to ride at first light."

Ulaf bowed again.

The High Magus bent down and began to wrap up the armor in the folds of the blanket.

Ulaf knelt to help, but the High Magus waved him away. "The fewer who have contact with this, the better. I will deal with it. Go to your bed, Brother Ulaf. You will need your rest."

Ulaf returned dutifully to the Temple. He walked the narrow corridors to his own cell, but only to fetch and light a dark lantern. Making sparing use of the light, Ulaf hastened through the main living quarters of the Temple until he came to the kitchen. He exited through the kitchen door that led outside to the cook's herb garden.

Once outdoors, Ulaf dared make no more use of the dark lantern, for fear even a quick glimmer of light would be noticed. His eyes soon grew accustomed to the darkness. Treading softly, he took his place behind a trellis supporting bean vines and waited.

Within a few moments, he saw a bulky figure in the darkness—the High Magus, carrying the armor wrapped in its blanket, walking around to the back of the Temple.

"I was right," said Ulaf softly to himself. "He's going to hide it in the wine cellar."

Ulaf had considered where the High Magus might hide the cursed armor on the Temple environs. Ulaf had no idea if such armor could be immediately destroyed, but he doubted it. Yet it had to be placed where it would not be discovered and where it could do no harm. Ulaf had been forced to touch the armor during his investigation and although he had wiped his hands numerous times on his robes, he still had the sensation that the terrible ooze was on his fingers.

The wine cellar contained bottles of wines served only at the table of the High Magus and thus it was always kept locked. The High Magus was the only person who had keys. The wine cellar was located below ground, to keep the wines at a constant temperature all year round, and was accessible only by a door located in the back of the kitchen gardens. The wine cellar was the logical place.

Ulaf watched the High Magus squat down to unlock the cellar door. Suddenly, the High Magus lifted his head, stood up straight.

"Is that you?" the High Magus said quietly.

Something approached through the garden. Ulaf stared.

"A Vrykyl," he breathed.

It was as if night had taken on the form and shape of a man, could walk like a man and use arms and hands like a man. Night wore armor as a man wore armor. Armor of darkness. Armor that was darker than the dark. Armor that was hideous in aspect, with spikes of darkness that stuck out of it like the pincers of a poisonous insect. The armor was very like the armor wrapped in the blanket held by the High Magus.

The Vrykyl walked up to the High Magus. The two conferred in low voices; Ulaf could not understand them. But it seemed to him by the tone and the fact that the Vrykyl occasionally bowed that the High Magus was issuing instructions.

The Vrykyl appeared about to depart, then it stopped. It turned its insectoid helmed head this way and that, as if searching for something. Ulaf held his breath and froze as still as the rabbit when the hounds are near.

"What the devil are you waiting for, Jedash?" the High Magus demanded. "I told you to leave. We have no time to waste. You must intercept and destroy this wretched spy."

"I thought I heard something." The voice from the helm was horrible, cold, hollow.

"Owls. Wolves. Rats." The High Magus waved his hand. "Go find someone to deal with the Trevenici. Have him search their barracks, search everywhere. It is probable that he will be tainted with Void. Let that guide the person you send."

"I was thinking of letting Commander Drossel deal with this, Shakur."

"Drossel." The High Magus frowned. "There was some question, once, as to his loyalty."

"Only to Dunkarga, Shakur. His loyalty to us is assured. He will, however, expect a reward."

"He has the favor of Dagnarus, Lord of the Void. That should be reward enough." The High Magus sounded irritated. "What more does he want?"

"Elevation in rank. A private meeting with Lord Dagnarus."

"The fool!" the High Magus muttered. "He doesn't know when he is well off. Promise Drossel that, then, Jedash, if nothing else will satisfy him. Report back to me when it is done. I will have further instructions for you."

"Yes, Shakur."

The darkness bowed and departed. The High Magus, lugging his bundle, descended into the wine cellar. He pulled the door in place after him and Ulaf heard the key grate in the lock.

Ulaf breathed again. He had seen many strange and terrible things in his life and he had imagined himself inured to anything. He had never before seen a Vrykyl in its true form, however. His hands trembled, cold sweat trickled down the back of his neck, and he had to wait a moment to calm the wild gyrations of his heart. Moving silently and stealthily, he made his way back to the kitchen, where he crouched in the dark shadows of the pantry and held consultation with himself and the lord he served, a lord who was far away in location but always close in thought.

"You were right, Shadamehr," he murmured to his unseen liege. "The High Magus is a Vrykyl and he has Vrykyl serving him. I knew the moment I flashed the light into those dead eyes and now this more than confirms your suspicions. He speaks of Lord Dagnarus, Lord of the Void." Ulaf sighed deeply and shook his head and added softly, "The gods help us, my lord, you were right.

"My life is not worth tuppence. I know too much. This false High Magus rids himself of me by sending me to New Vinnengael in the morning. I'll wager that the instructions he has given that creature of his have to do with me, for the Vrykyl must make certain I never reach New Vinnengael to tell what I have seen. I am 'the wretched spy.' I am to be waylaid on the road, my body shoved into a ditch. Or worse."

Ulaf considered a moment more, weighing his options. "It is time for Brother Ulaf to disappear. He will vanish in the night and no one the wiser. The High Magus will know or guess that I have discovered his secret, but that cannot be helped. My work here is done. I have confirmed my lord's worst fears. It is my duty to return to report to Shadamehr as fast as possible. Already, we may be too late . . ."

Ulaf had long had his escape planned—his first objective whenever he began any assignment. Within thirty minutes time, Brother Ulaf would be gone from the Temple and Ulaf the mendicant or Ulaf the mercenary or Ulaf the itinerant merchant would be traveling the roads that led from Dunkarga back to New Vinnengael and from thence to the lands of his liege lord and master, Baron Shadamehr.

"He said the name Shakur. Shakur," Ulaf muttered to himself, leaving his robes neatly folded in the pantry, for the cook's helper to discover and exclaim over in amazement the next morning. "Where have I heard that name before? Some old legend, I fancy. Never mind. My lord will know."

He remained in hiding until he saw the High Magus returning from the wine cellar. When his steps faded away, Ulaf made ready to depart, taking only the dark lantern and his new identity with him. Yet, as he was about to leave the Temple of Dunkarga forever, he paused and looked into the night.

"The gods go with you, Captain Raven. I wish you had told me the truth. It is possible I could have helped you. As it was, I did what I could to shield you, but I fear that will not avail you much. What evil fate brought this upon you and why, I cannot explain. The ways of the gods are a mystery to mortals and that is as it should be or else we would go mad. I pray for your sake some good comes of it."

With this prayer, Brother Ulaf departed and was seen no more in this world.

14

RAVEN'S SLEEP WAS NOT RESTFUL SLUMBER. IT WAS A STAGGERING RUN through a hellish landscape of endless burning sands. He was chased, hunted, and there was no tree to hide behind, no water to slack his torturing thirst. The eyes searched for him and if he stopped, even for a moment, they would find him . . .

He could not wake from this nightmare. His body was too tired, he was sunk too deep in sleep to be able to drag himself out of it. When, after almost twelve hours, he did manage to rouse himself, he felt worse than when he'd collapsed on his blankets. He woke with a shudder to find that his blankets were soaked with sweat. Shivering, he roused himself and went to the privies, where he was sick as a poisoned pup.

He felt better afterward, for it is always good to purge the body of ill humors. Going to the well that was in the barracks, he drank almost an entire bucketful of water. This water was the first Raven had drunk in many days that did not have the oily taste of that accursed armor and it was sweet as sun-ripened pears to him.

He was still groggy and fuddle-headed, but he thought he could eat something now and keep it down. The smell of garlic pervaded the barracks and made Raven's stomach rumble. The Dunkargans are passionately fond of garlic, use it in almost all their cooking. He had never eaten garlic before coming to Dunkarga, but he had quickly developed a taste for the pungent bulb. The Dunkargans not only enjoyed the taste, but maintained that it warded off illness. Certainly, the Dunkargans appeared to be unusually healthy, rarely succumbing to the more virulent diseases that often struck those living in cities. His mouth watering, Raven headed for the Trevenici cook fire. He was intercepted by one of his comrades.

"Commander wants to see you right away," said Scalplock, thus called because of his impressive array of enemy scalps that hung from his belt.

He jerked a thumb in the direction of the Dunkargan barracks, near where the Trevenici mercenaries made their camp. "Drossel."

"Which one is he?" Raven growled. There were so many Dunkargan commanders in this army, he could never keep them straight.

"Short, dark-skinned, bandy-legged, squints," said Scalplock succinctly.

Raven nodded. He knew the man now. Raven continued on to the cook fire. He would see the officer in his own good time, which might mean after supper or next week.

Raven was just finishing his meal and thinking he would go back to sleep again, when he became aware of a pair of black boots with the flowing white trousers worn by the Dunkargan military tucked into the tops standing in front of him. Squatting cross-legged on the ground, Raven looked up to see Commander Drossel looking down.

"I have an important matter to discuss with you, Captain Ravenstrike."

Raven shrugged. He had finished eating, but he didn't feel all that good. Still, he knew Dunkargans. Once they got an idea in their heads, they would never rest until they had acted on it. If Raven didn't talk with the Dunkargan now, this commander would hound him and he would have no peace at all. Best to get it over with. Raven eased himself to his feet and accompanied the Dunkargan officer to the barracks.

Finding a quiet room in the large blockhouse, Drossel took Raven inside. The room was empty except for a table and a couple of chairs. There were no windows, only openings in the top portion of the walls where blocks had been left out to provide for air circulation. Raven felt stifled the moment he entered, ill-at-ease.

Commander Drossel pointed to a chair. Raven remained on his feet, knowing that to sit down was to prolong the stay. Drossel smiled and pointed to the chair again. To make his offer more palatable, the Dunkargan indicated a crockery pot and a couple of small crockery mugs on the table. Steam rose from the pot. An enticing aroma filled the room. Raven sniffed appreciatively.

"We have a lot to discuss, Captain," Drossel said, apologetically, as if he knew how Raven felt about being cooped up in this small room. "Coffee?"

Not all the Trevenici liked the Dunkargan hot drink known as coffee, claiming that it smelled better than it tasted, but Raven happened to be one who did. He sat down in the chair and watched in approval as the commander poured the thick, syrupy black liquid into the small mug. The coffee was laced with honey, but it was still bitter to the taste. Raven took a very small sip, his eyes puckering at the bitterness. Once past that, he could enjoy the rich flavor of the roasted beans and the honey.

"You are back from leave early," Drossel commented, sipping at his own coffee.

Raven shrugged, made no comment. That was his business, none of this officer's.

Drossel went on to remark, laughingly, that most soldiers had to be dragged back kicking and screaming from leave. Raven didn't pay much attention. Dunkargans were known to waste breath on talk that said nothing. He sipped at his coffee. He had not drunk coffee for a long time. The beans were expensive and he had never learned the art of making the brew. Raven did not remember that coffee had this relaxing effect. The last time he had drunk some, he had felt jumpy and twitchy. This time, all his muscles seemed to go limp. His eyelids drooped. He had to concentrate to hear what the Dunkargan was saying.

Drossel watched Raven intently, then came around to sit on the table, quite close to him.

"You paid a visit to the Temple of the Magi last night, didn't you, Captain?"

Raven blinked at the man. Raven had no intention of answering and was astonished to hear his own voice doing just that. "I was there, yes. What of it?"

"You handed over some armor you had found, I believe," Drossel continued pleasantly. "Black armor. Very strange armor."

"Cursed," Raven said. He didn't want to talk about this. Talking about this armor was dangerous, but he couldn't seem to help himself.

"Where did the armor come from, Captain?" Drossel asked, his voice losing the pleasant quality, sharpening. "You said you found it. Where did you find it?"

Raven tried to get up to go, but he couldn't walk properly, stumbled like a drunken man. Drossel steered Raven back to the chair and the questions started again. The same questions, over and over and over.

Raven saw the armor, black and oily; he saw Jessan unwrapping the blanket, giving him the armor; he saw Ranessa lunging at him with her sharp nails like talons; he saw the dying knight Gustav; he saw Bashae running into camp, telling his story; he saw the dwarf, Wolfram, panting and frightened. Raven didn't like the dwarf. He remembered that quite clearly. He saw all this at once and he knew he didn't want to be talking about any of it, but his mouth plucked images from his brain and spewed them forth.

Only sometimes, when the danger was so bad that he could barely stand it, was he able to stop the words, but that took an immense amount of effort on his part, effort that was painful and left him sweating and shivering.

The next thing Raven knew, he was being carried from the room by two soldiers, who grunted under his dead weight. They dumped him in his tent, muttering about drunken barbarians who couldn't hold their liquor. He lay on ground that seemed to be constantly falling out from underneath him, stared up at the tent poles that writhed and twined in his blurred vision, and he did not sleep so much as pass out.

Drossel went to the Temple of the Magi to report his findings.

Shakur knew the moment he looked at the black armor brought in by the Trevenici that the armor was Svetlana's. But how had her armor come to be in the possession of a Trevenici? What had happened to the Dominion Lord and, most important, what had become of the Sovereign Stone?

Now, after speaking to Drossel, Shakur had answers. He did not have all the answers—curse the stubbornness of the Trevenici—but he had enough.

Taking out the blood knife, Shakur placed his hand upon it and sent his thoughts to his master. The link was quickly connected. Dagnarus had been waiting eagerly to hear from Shakur.

Having positioned his forces to attack Dunkar, the Lord of the Void had departed, traveling northward. He was currently in the mountains of Nimorea, not far from Tromek, the elven nation. Neither the Nimoreans nor the elves were aware that an immense force of fierce warriors from another part of the world threatened their lands. Dagnarus held his taan on a tight leash. They marched at night, keeping under cover, using the magic of the Void to conceal their movements. Another taan army lurked outside the capital city of Dunkar and still a third was hidden in the wilderness of Karnu. Dagnarus was now poised to begin the conquest of Loerem.

"What news?" Daganarus's thoughts thrummed through Shakur's veins like the warm blood that no longer circulated in his decayed body. "Where is Svetlana? Have you recovered the Stone?"

"Svetlana is dead, my lord," Shakur said bluntly.

"Dead?" Dagnarus repeated, his anger burning. He had never reacted well to bad news. "What do you mean, dead? She is a Vrykyl. She is already dead!"

"Then she is deader," Shakur returned wryly. "She died by the hand of the cursed Dominion Lord. I have seen what was left of her, my lord. I know. Her armor was brought in by a Trevenici warrior."

"And where is the Stone?"

"I do not know for certain, my lord. It wasn't with her. But I have made inquiries and I have some ideas. One of our agents has questioned the Trevenici."

"What did he say?"

"The man was reluctant to speak, my lord. He resisted the truth potion, but we managed to learn a great deal. The Dominion Lord killed Svetlana, but not before she managed to fatally wound him. The Trevenici found the knight. He was dying. He had with him the Sovereign Stone—"

"Did the Trevenici tell you that? Did he see the Stone?"

"No, my lord. The Dominion Lord would never reveal such a treasure to a pack of barbarians. We know from Svetlana that the Dominion Lord was in possession of the Stone. According to the Trevenici, the man was desperate to complete some quest before he died. What else could that quest be but to take the Stone to New Vinnengael?"

"That makes sense," Dagnarus conceded. "What else did you find out?"

"The knight died. He was buried with great honor in the village. Now here is the interesting part, my lord. After his death, a dwarf, who was with the knight and may have even been a traveling companion, departed the village. At the same time, another group also left the village. We do not know much about this second group, for every time our agent pressed the Trevenici, he grew agitated and resisted the agent's probings. Our agent assumes that someone in this group is close to the Trevenici and that he is protecting them."

"The agent found out nothing more from this Trevenici?" Dagnarus demanded angrily. "Question him again. Don't use some fool potion. He has the information I need. Tear him into little pieces until you find it!"

"He is Trevenici, my lord. He would reveal nothing under torture," said Shakur with finality. "His disappearance would start the other Trevenici asking questions. They would search for him, perhaps alert those in his village . . . If I might suggest a different course of action, my lord?"

"Very well, Shakur. You are a cunning bastard. What do you propose?"

"We know the location of his village. I will send my mercenaries in company with a bahk to the village with orders to obtain what information they can from the villagers. With its uncanny ability to sniff out magic, the bahk will be useful in discovering the Stone if it remains in the village—"

"You will not find it in the village," Dagnarus returned with finality. "The Stone has been sent on. It moves in the world. I sense it, feel it, taste it . . . How could I not, Shakur? For two hundred years, this shard of rock, this bauble, this jewel has been the object of my dearest desire. I paid for it with my blood. The Stone is stained with my blood. In my dreams, I see it. I reach out to seize it . . . and it slips away. The Stone travels north, Shakur. The Stone travels north . . . and it travels south."

Shakur had to work very hard to keep his thoughts in check, but apparently he failed, for Dagnarus came back to say, "You think me mad . . ."

"Not so, my lord," Shakur thought hastily, scrambling, "Suppose this knight found a way to split the Stone? Two hundred years ago, it was split into four separate parts. Could it not be further divided?"

"No! Impossible!" Dagnarus was firm. "I saw the Stone. I handled it. The

Stone was meant to be split into four separate sections. Five, if you count the Void. But no more. Not the sharpest sword blessed with the strongest magic could cut it."

"And yet, it appears that the impossible has happened, my lord," Shakur observed.

"Has it? I wonder. Consider this: The Dominion Lord is sick, dying, desperate. But he is also smart and clever. Clever enough to find the Sovereign Stone, clever enough to defeat and kill one of my Vrykyl. In order to send on the Stone, he cannot count on finding people who are as clever or wise or smart as himself. Svetlana accomplished that much at least. She brought about the death of the one man who might have bested us. She forced the Dominion Lord to pass the Stone to those weaker and more vulnerable. The Dominion Lord would do his best to ensure the Stone's safety. But he can no longer watch over it, guard it.

"What would he do? He would do what I would do myself. When I send a messenger to the general of my armies, I do not tell the messenger the nature of the message he carries. Thus if he is captured, he cannot reveal what he does not know. If I were sending the Sovereign Stone to the Council of Dominion Lords in New Vinnengael, I would not tell the one carrying the Stone the nature of what he has in his possession. I would tell him he carries something of value, but no mention of *how* valuable. And do you know what else I would do, Shakur?"

"You would send out a decoy, my lord."

"Exactly. I know that Vrykyl are searching for the Stone. I fear that they may have the ability to sense its powerful magic. I send out a decoy . . ."

"But the Stone cannot be split or duplicated—"

"That is true. We know, however, that the Vinnengaeleans continue to create Dominion Lords from the residual magical power left behind in the setting that they found on Helmos's body. Let us assume that the Stone was housed in some case or had been hung on a chain—"

"Of course, my lord! That is the answer. The knight sent out two parties. One with the Stone and the other carrying something that is meant to draw off pursuit. One messenger is the dwarf. The other, the group the Trevenici was so loath to talk about."

"I like your idea, Shakur. Find that Trevenici village. See to the matter personally, don't leave it to mercenaries. Question the inhabitants and if they have the least knowledge about the Sovereign Stone, drag it from them. That done, kill all of them. Destroy any man, woman or child who ever saw the Dominion Lord or who knows anything at all about the Sovereign Stone. I do not want other Dominion Lords hearing of its recovery and setting off in search of it."

"Yes, my lord." Shakur was uneasy and his uneasiness was impossible to hide.

Dagnarus was quick to take note. "What is it, Shakur?"

"I regret to report that the brother who interviewed the Trevenici when he arrived here with the armor has disappeared. As I told you, I had taken steps to insure that the meddlesome Brother Ulaf did not return alive to New Vinnengael with word of Void-cursed armor. Jedash hid in ambush along the road, but Brother Ulaf did not appear. Sometime later, the cook discovered a cast-off robe that was identified as belonging to Brother Ulaf. No one saw him after the encounter with the Trevenici at the gate. His bed was not slept in. He apparently fled during the night."

Dagnarus's anger could be painful if he chose, for he held absolute control over the Vrykyl through the Dagger of the Vrykyl. It seemed to Shakur that he was never free of the Dagger, that he still felt the blade in his back, the burning pain that stole his life and gave this horrid nonexistence in return. When Dagnarus was angry, the Dagger twisted and the pain was excruciating.

Shakur waited, but the pain did not come.

"As to this missing brother"—Dagnarus gave a mental shrug—"he saw the Vrykyl armor. Perhaps he even touched it. He was terrified and so he fled."

"It is a possibility," said Shakur, not convinced and unable to suppress his doubts, no matter how much it might cost him. "But I do not think so, my lord. He claimed to be a Vinnengaelean and so I thought nothing of the fact that he was unusually stupid and thick-headed. But now I wonder if that was just an act."

"Bah! Even if he was not what he appeared, what did he find out? He saw some Void-tainted armor. Nothing more. He may tell all the world, if he likes, but the information will do them little good."

"Still, my lord—"

"Do not argue with me, Shakur," Dagnarus warned. "My dearest wish has been granted. I am in a good mood and therefore willing to overlook this lapse on your part."

Shakur bowed. "What are your plans now, my lord?"

"Taking the Stone's discovery as a sign, I wait no longer. This night, I will send orders to proceed with two of the three planned assaults. Tomorrow, my troops will launch attacks against Dunkar and the Karnuan Portal."

Shakur was astonished. "Is all prepared? Are your armies in place?"

"As to Karnu, I will attack with the troops I have there now. The Karnuans have sent most of their army through the Portal to the opposite end at Delek 'Vir to protect against a Vinnengaelean attack. Once I hold the western end of their Portal, they will not be able to send these troops back. When Dunkar falls, the troops in that city will sail across the Edam Nar and attack Karnu's capital Dalon 'Ren from the sea, while another army attacks overland. Not my original plan, but one that will work, since the downfall of Dunkarga is assured."

Dagnarus sensed his vassal's disapproval. "It is assured, isn't it, Shakur?"

"All is in place, my lord. You have only to say the word. But how does starting the war of conquest now help with the recovery of the Sovereign Stone?"

"The Stone must reach the Council of Dominion Lords in New Vinnengael. Its bearers could travel overland, but the way is fraught with danger and it would take them six months of hard journeying at least, perhaps longer. The Dominion Lord would have impressed on his bearers the need for speed. He would have told them to take one of the magical Portals that leads to New Vinnengael, thus cutting the journey's time from six months to a few weeks. The closest Portals are the Karnuan Portal and the elven Portal. I will capture the one at Karnu. If the bearers try to enter there, we will take them."

"And what of the elven Portal, my lord?"

"I am not ready to attack Tromek yet. The situation here is too delicate. The Lady Valura works at acquiring the elven portion of the Stone, and I dare not do anything to upset her plans. I am here, however, and if the Stone goes to elven lands, I will know it. Whichever way the Stone travels, the bearers will find their way blocked. I suppose you can leave your post at the Temple without occasioning too much comment?"

"The start of the war will give me an excuse to absence myself, my lord. In the guise of the High Magus, I will tell the king that I am leaving Dunkar, traveling to the Temple of the Magi in New Vinnengael, where I hope to put a stop to this great evil. No one will question my departure, nor will they question the fact that the High Magus never returns."

"There will probably be few left alive to question," Dagnarus said, with another shrug.

RAVENSTRIKE WOKE FROM HIS DRUGGED SLEEP WITH THE NAGGING, UN-
easy feeling that something had gone horribly wrong for him in the night.
He remembered an officer talking to him and asking him questions, questions that Raven had not wanted to answer, but which he had ended up
answering. Sitting up on his mat, he clutched his aching head and tried to
recall the events of the previous night. The memories slid out of his grasp
as if they were coated with the oily ooze of the black armor. He had been
poisoned. The poison had made him say what he did not want to say.

He was able to remember disjointed words and sometimes the fragment
of a sentence and these were enough to disturb him deeply. Because of the
poison, he had placed the tribe in danger. He had to return to the tribe
immediately to warn his people of their peril.

What that peril might be, he did not know and could not say, but that
did not matter. Unlike city humans, the Trevenici are accustomed to relying on their instincts and to acting immediately on those instincts without
stopping to try to rationalize or define them. Thus city humans marvel to
see a Trevenici duck in time to save himself from the thrown spear, although he could not possibly have seen the spear coming. If asked to explain this, the Trevenici will have no answer, except to say that if city
people would leave their walls they might smell something besides their
own stench.

Raven was under no illusions. The accursed black armor was the cause.
He had tried to do the right thing by bringing the armor to Dunkar, by
"taking the curse from the people," but now it appeared that he had done
everything wrong.

Raven stumbled out of the Trevenici camp, ignoring the calls of his
fellows who were roasting meat for their breakfast. He headed for the barracks, determined to find the officer who had poisoned him. Unfortu-

nately this proved difficult because Raven could give no coherent account of the meeting. He could not remember the captain's name. He could not recall what the man looked like, beyond the fact that he was short, swarthy and had a black beard. That description might fit any male in Dunkar. Those he questioned only laughed at him and told him that he should never try to drink a Dunkargan under the table.

The sun rose and burned off the morning fog that lay both on the lowlands and in Raven's head. He was never going to find the man who had done this to him and he was wasting precious time. Returning to his campsite, he rolled up his sleeping mat. He snagged a waterskin and some dried meat, enough to last for many days on the trail, for he would not have time to stop to hunt for food. His fellows were curious, for they knew he had just come back from a visit to his people. He told them only that he had heard that the tribe might be in danger and, after that, no one asked any more questions. Every Trevenici's first duty is to the tribe. His fellows wished him well and said they would see him in the northlands.

Raven saddled his horse. He was leading the beast from the stables when horns sounded the alarm. The city was under attack.

Rumors of war had swirled around Dunkar for months. Reports came in from outposts on the western borders that they had been attacked by savage creatures. Then stories came to Dunkar of caravans looted and burned, entire villages wiped out. Since the reports emanated from the sparsely populated western territories, hundreds of miles away, and brought with them only a whiff of the smoke of war, the people of Dunkar sniffed, but did not pay much attention. They were far more concerned with their bitter enemy, the Karnuans, to their east.

The reports continued to come in, the whiff of smoke on the air was now a thin curl of smoke that could be seen rising on the horizon, for villages that were within a month's ride of the capital were now under attack. The flow of travelers into the city reduced to a trickle and those people who did come had strange and terrible tales to tell of people vanished or found murdered in the most cruel, savage ways. Word went around the streets of Dunkar that a patrol sent out had not returned and was long overdue.

Anxious women hung about the guardhouses, asking after missing husbands and brothers. The officers answered them brusquely or not at all. Soldiers who went drinking in the ale houses no longer shouted and laughed good-naturedly over dice games, but sat hunched over their ale, looking grim and talking in low voices.

King Moross, whose hatred of the Karnuans ran deep, was determined to blame this on the Karnuans, as well. The High Magus was loud in denunciation of the Karnuans. The high ranking nobles agreed with His Majesty and those who did not held their tongue, for the king's pleasure, once lost, was not easy to regain.

The Seraskier, the current head of the Dunkargan army, did not hold his tongue. He told His Majesty bluntly that this strange army came from the west and that it had nothing to do with Karnu. He gave it as his opinion that the Karnuans might well be facing the very same threat as the Dunkargans. The city of Dunkar was in danger. His reports indicated a massive force headed this direction, and he wanted to press into service all able-bodied civilians, double the guard on the wall and send for reinforcements from their sister city, Amrah 'Lin, to the north.

The High Magus was there to whisper in the king's ear, refuting the Seraskier's advice.

King Moross valued the opinion of the High Magus, but he also valued his Seraskier, Onaset, the first high ranking officer the king had ever found who had not been corrupted by Karnuan gold. King Moross went so far as to approve the doubling of the guard on the city wall, but he would not press civilians into the military, fearing that such dire measures would send the city of Dunkar into a panic.

King Moross might as well have issued the order, for panic set in the very next day, when the Dunkargans looked out to see the morning sun illuminate an immense army marching over the grasslands to the southwest. The people of Dunkar stared in shocked disbelief. Never had they seen an army this big. If this was an attack by Karnu, then they must have emptied their land of soldiers.

"Karnuans, do you think, sir?" asked one of his officers, as Seraskier Onaset hastened to the wall to have a look for himself.

After studying the enemy until his eyes ached and burned, Onaset shook his head.

"They're not Karnuan. Karnuan soldiers march in disciplined ranks. These appear to have no order at all," he said.

He called for his aide to bring him his spy glass, an orken invention he had seized from a captured pirate vessel, and trained it to the west.

With the glass he saw that what had appeared at first to be ragged patches of armed soldiers flowing across the plains at random were actually battle groups who were maintaining some sort of order. The ragged patches shifted formation, flowing into circles with their standards in the center. He could see tents going up.

Onaset looked closely into one of these camps. He had received reports from scouts describing their attackers as being creatures more like beasts than men, although they walked upright as did men and had hands and arms like men. They could wield weapons with as much skill as men, or perhaps more. Still, Onaset was not prepared for the sight of these creatures, like no creatures ever seen before on Loerem, with their long snouts filled with razor-sharp teeth, and their green and brown mottled hide that was reputed to be so tough they had no need to wear armor.

He watched the creatures until his eyes began to water so that he could no longer see. He handed the glass to his trusted officers with the curt order that no matter what they saw, they keep their comments to themselves. His next order was to immediately close the two main gates and the smaller wickets. No one was to enter the city, unless he had damn good cause. No one was to leave it. Aides departed to carry out his commands. Onaset returned to staring out over the battlements.

One of his officers gave a low whistle. "Gods help us," he muttered, "there are humans down there!"

"What is that you say?" came a sharp voice.

Onaset turned to find King Moross climbing the stairs that led to the battlements. Moross was in his late forties, a saturnine man, good-looking with black hair and beard streaked with white, making him look older and lending him dignity. His robes were rich but not ostentatious, for he was in truth a humble man, who sometimes seemed embarrassed by his kingship.

"Humans down there?" King Moross looked over the wall. If he was dismayed by what he saw—the vast army that was rapidly building an entire new city on the grasslands—he was careful to keep his expression impassive.

Onaset had never had a great liking for Moross, believing that the king cared too much about what people thought of him. Moross strove to please everyone, offend no one, and, because of this, he appeared indecisive and unreliable. When talking to two people, he would say what each person wanted to hear, which was fine, until the two came together to compare notes.

"Then this proves it. These monsters are being led by Karnuans," King Moross said, his brows coming together in anger.

"I don't see any signs of the Karnuans, Your Majesty," said Onaset, offering the king the spy glass. "Those are human mercenaries"— Onaset pointed to a group of soldiers he had spotted almost immediately, due to the fact they marched in traditional battlefield formation—"but they are probably ordinary sell-swords. What I believe the officer was referring to is the fact that these creatures have apparently taken human slaves." He directed the king to look in the direction of the nearest circle of tents.

Several humans moved around the interior of the enemy encampment. They were too far away to see clearly, but Onaset had the impression by the way they moved that the humans were manacled.

Moross cast an involuntary glance behind him, into the city of Dunkar that was home to thousands of men, women and children. He looked back to the tens of thousands of creatures making themselves at home in the desert and he blenched perceptibly. He motioned Onaset to come speak to him privately.

"What sort of monsters are these?" he asked in a low voice. "We've never seen anything like that on Loerem. Have you?"

Onaset shook his head. "No, Your Majesty."

"Then where did they come from?" King Moross was baffled, appalled.

"The gods know, Your Majesty," said Onaset solemnly, not blaspheming. "Perhaps you should consult with the High Magus. He is a most wise man—"

"The High Magus has left the city," King Moross said, biting a thumb-nail. "He left this morning immediately after the alarm sounded."

"Like I said—a wise man," Onaset remarked dryly.

Moross cast him a reproachful glance. "The High Magus is carrying word of this unprovoked attack by these creatures to the Temple of the Magi in New Vinnengael. He thinks that perhaps the wise among the magi there may know something of them."

"Considering that such a journey will take him six months—if he is for-tunate—I don't quite see how this benefits us, Your Majesty."

The king pretended not to hear, a trick of his when dealing with par-ticularly difficult problems. "They're setting up camps. Are they going to siege us, do you think, Seraskier?"

"Not unless their commander is an utter fool, Your Majesty," Onaset re-turned bluntly. "We are a port city. We could hold out against a siege al-most indefinitely, unless they blockade us. I would say, Your Majesty"—Onaset rubbed his bearded chin—"that these troops mean to attack and conquer. Look, here come their war engines."

Elephants came lumbering into view, hauling behind them enormous siege towers known as belfries. Mounted on four wheels, the towers stood as tall as the city walls and were made up of several stories that could be filled with armed soldiers. Archers mounted on top of the belfry kept the wall clear of defenders. When the belfry reached the wall, a gangplank could be lowered, allowing the soldiers to pour out onto the walls and from thence into the city. Other siege engines had strange hose-like de-vices mounted on top. The city's defenders feared these more than the bel-fries, for these housed the mechanism used to pump ork fire onto defenders and structures alike. The jelly-like substance burst into flame on contact, setting all it touched ablaze.

"Still, to attack a walled city will cost him dearly." Onaset glanced about at Dunkar's defenses and shook his head in amazement at this comman-der's temerity.

Having prepared to face Karnuans for years in a battle that had not yet come, Dunkar had built some of the best defenses of any city in the mod-ern age: mangonels and ballistae to hurl destruction at the enemy on the ground, well-trained bowmen on the walls, enormous cauldrons that could be filled with boiling oil and water to pour down on the heads of any trying to scale the walls, as well as their own version of ork fire that could set the belfries aflame, roast alive those hiding inside.

"Such a battle could take weeks and he will lose a vast amount of troops, men he can ill afford to lose, for if he takes the city he will have to hold it and I have already sent messengers to bring help from Amrah 'Lin."

"He? Who is he? This unknown enemy." King Moross gazed back out across the grasslands and muttered, "He must be working for Karnu."

Onaset was not convinced, although he could offer no other explanation. "He'll tell us in his own good time. We're not going anywhere." He paused a moment, coughed, then said, "I believe that our city can win this battle, Your Majesty. The gods know, though, that nothing is certain in this life save death and taxes. Your Majesty might want to have the Royal Barge ready—"

"No, Seraskier," returned King Moross with the first bit of decisiveness Onaset had seen in the man. "We will not flee and leave our people to face this threat alone."

One of the officers pointed out over the wall to where riders had appeared. "Seraskier, they are sending a herald."

"Good! At least we will find out what this is all about," King Moross stated. "Have him brought to the Royal Palace. Seraskier, come with us."

After a final glance over the wall at the rapidly increasing numbers of the enemy, Onaset accompanied his king to hear what his enemy had to say.

Raven was about to depart, when he heard the horns sounding the alarm. A Trevenici warrior, who had been on duty at the wall, came back to report. "There's an army out there." She shook her head gloomily. "Looks like a siege."

The Trevenici exchanged grim glances. Instead of glory on the battlefield, the Trevenici must endure months, perhaps years, of being under siege, trapped in these city walls that they detested, sleeping and eating with nothing to do except to exchange verbal insults with the enemy. Worst of all, with no way to return to visit their tribes.

"Well that's that," said one. "I'm not staying to die of starvation."

"You had better make haste, then," the warrior said. "The order has been given to close the gates."

At this dire news, Raven leapt onto his horse's back, kicked his heels into the animal's flanks. He knew better than to try the main gate. He knew of a wicket on the eastern side of the wall, one used by those who had business in the city after dark when the main gate had been closed. He would try that.

Unfortunately, word of the enemy had spread throughout Dunkar by this time, and the streets were clogged with people. The main street was impassable. Raven's horse was battle-trained, accustomed to the clash of arms and the smell of blood and the screams of the wounded and dying. The horse was not accustomed to small children darting under its belly, the shrill cries of gossip-mongers and the smell of fear. The horse pricked its ears, rolled its eyes and balked.

Then some drunkard had the bright idea that he should steal Raven's horse and use it to escape the city. The drunk grabbed hold of Raven's leg. Raven kicked at the fellow and sent him head over heels into the gutter.

Turning his horse's head, Raven managed to extricate himself from the mob. He tried another street, a narrow side street, and found that it was not as crowded. Still, he had to proceed slowly, keeping his horse under tight control, as people burst suddenly from doorways, crying out to know what was happening. Raven finally reached the wicket gate, to find that it was closed and barred.

"Open the gate," Raven called from horseback.

The soldiers glanced up at the sound of the order, but, seeing only a Trevenici, they shook their heads. Dunkargans are not adverse to having the Trevenici fight and die for them, but that doesn't mean that they have to like them.

"Go back to your rat-meat stew, Barbarian," said one shortly. "No one gets in or out. Seraskier's orders."

If Raven had been a Dunkargan himself, he would have tossed a few argents on the ground and the gate would have been opened for him with no more questions asked. The Trevenici had never been able to understand the concept of bribery, however. Raven slid off his horse's back and went to argue.

"The Seraskier's orders do not apply to the Trevenici," he said, which was perfectly true. "I am a Captain. You are obeying an order. You will not get into any trouble."

"I know I won't," said the guard, glowering. "Because I'm not opening the gate." He cast Raven a scathing glance. "You're not getting paid to run away."

Angry at the insult, desperate to leave this city, Raven laid his hand on his sword hilt and heard the rattle of steel behind him. He looked to find himself surrounded by six more guards, swords in their hands and dark expressions on their faces.

Trevenici are fearless in battle, but they are not foolhardy. Raven knew when he was beaten. He raised his hands, to show that they were empty, and then returned to his horse. Mounting, he galloped off back down the street, sending people leaping for the gutters or the alleys to escape the pounding hooves.

*   *   *

While Raven was trying to flee the city, the herald from the enemy was permitted to enter, passing through a wicket gate located at the main gate and into the city proper. The herald was a human, not one of the strange monsters—much to the disappointment of the townspeople, who had been hearing rumors about these creatures from those on the walls and wanted to see one for themselves.

Fearless and proud, the herald rode with calm dignity through a throng of angry Dunkargans, who had come to see and curse the enemy. He had a thatch of blond hair and a beardless chin. He might have been sixteen at best, but he already sported a battle scar on his face and he rode his horse and carried his sword like a man accustomed to warfare. He wore a tabard of rich material featuring the image of a phoenix rising from flames and he bore the same device on his shield. No one could recall ever having seen such a device before.

The herald was given a guard of the Seraskier's own hand-picked bodyguard, for the Dunkargans are a volatile people and every single one of them believed beyond doubt that the detested Karnuans had hired this army to attack them. There were shouted demands to behead the messenger and send his body back to Karnu. The Seraskier's men kept their swords out, struck with the flat of the blade at any citizen who drew too close. The herald regarded them all with a jaunty grin and a raised shield to deflect thrown vegetation.

He arrived at the palace and was not kept waiting, but was brought straight to the king. Moross sat on his throne in great state, attended by his ministers and members of the nobility. One and all, with the exception of the Seraskier, they expected the herald to state that he was from Karnu. Moross had his answer prepared, defiance to hurl into the teeth of the Karnuan king, who was, in fact, a distant cousin.

The herald entered with the same jaunty smile. He had been deprived of his sword and shield and boot knife. King Moross stared hard at the device of the phoenix on the tabard and glanced at his ministers, who shrugged. This was not a Karnuan device, at least that anyone recognized.

Advancing, the herald made a perfunctory bow. With elaborate ceremony, he drew forth a scroll, unrolled it, and began to read.

From Prince Dagnarus, son of King Tamaros of Vinnengael to His Most Serene Highness, etc., etc. Moross, King of Dunkarga.

I, Prince Dagnarus, as a son of Dunkarga, am grieved to see the state of war that exists between those who should be clasping each other by the hand and terming each other brother. This civil war has plunged a once great nation in ruin and made of Dunkarga, a land once proud and puissant, a shabby beggar in the streets of the world. I, Prince Dagnarus, propose to end this ruinous war and to raise Dunkarga once more to the level of strength and prosperity that will make all of Loerem look upon Dunkarga with jealous eyes and fear in their hearts.

The following are my terms: My troops and I will be permitted unopposed entry into the city. I will be named Seraskier and will be given command of all Dunkargan troops and the Dunkargan war fleet. The present king, my cousin, will continue to rule. I am to be consulted in all important decisions. In return, the city of Dunkar will be spared the ravages of war. Those citizens who support me will prosper. Those who oppose me will be given a chance to improve their opinion of me. If these terms are not accepted, my armies will launch their assault at dawn tomorrow. In that instance, the city and its people can expect no mercy.

King Moross listened in bemused amazement. Dagnarus. Who was Dagnarus? He could remember no Dagnarus who had any claim to Dunkarga. And yet there was something familiar about the name . . . He glanced about at his ministers, who looked offended and outraged, but also frightened. Seraskier Onaset was grim.

The herald fell silent, stared expectantly at the king. King Moross knew what his answer must be, but he did not intend to make it arbitrarily. In particular, he needed to talk to Onaset, who had made a sign to him.

"We will take this under consideration," said King Moross, cold and imperious.

"Do not consider long, Your Majesty," said the herald. "My lord is not a patient man and if I have not returned by sundown, he will begin the assault."

The ministers muttered angrily at being given this ultimatum and by the free and easy, sneering manner in which it was delivered.

Moross silenced them with a glance. He announced that the herald would have his answer when he was prepared to give it and not before. He then ordered that the herald be made comfortable and given food and drink. The herald bowed, turned on his heel, and departed. Moross was immediately surrounded by clamoring ministers, their voices raised in shrill and bellowing protestations that not so much as a single pebble from a Dunkargan alleyway be handed over to this bandit. Moross caught Onaset's eye. The Seraskier made a most emphatic sign that he needed to speak to the king in private. Moross dismissed the ministers, who expressed their support for His Majesty, and then departed. Their vociferations could be heard even after the great golden doors were closed with a resounding boom.

"Well, Seraskier?" King Moross asked. "What are we to make of this?"

"Did you note the name 'Dagnarus,' Your Majesty?"

"Yes, of course, I did," King Moross returned. Now that they were alone, the king dropped the royal "we," spoke man-to-man to his Seraskier. "I have been trying to think—"

"Prince Dagnarus, second son of King Tamaros of Old Vinnengael."

"Ah, yes." King Moross was relieved. "That is where I have heard it before. So that is how he claims to be a son of Dunkarga and my cousin. As I recall, Dagnarus's mother was Emillia, daughter of King Oglaf." Proud of his knowledge of his lineage, he was nettled that he had not recognized the name. "She was his second wife. Dagnarus was the one who reputedly brought down Old Vinnengael, if we are to believe the old legends. Quite appropriate that this bandit has taken that foul name. I suppose he could be some sort of great-great grandson," Moross continued, musing, interrupting Onaset who had sought to break in. "If I recall my history, the original Dagnarus could have populated a small village with his by-blows."

"What if this is the original Prince Dagnarus, Your Majesty?" Onaset asked. "As he claims."

King Moross looked severe. "Really, Seraskier, this is no time for levity—"

"Trust me, I am not joking, Your Majesty," said Onaset. "According to history, Prince Dagnarus was a Void worshiper. He was cursed by the gods, made Lord of the Void. He was said to be powerful in Void magic."

"Prince Dagnarus died in the destruction of Old Vinnengael," said Moross.

"His body was never found, Your Majesty."

"What are you saying, Onaset?" King Moross demanded impatiently. "That we are being attacked by a two-hundred-year-old Void lord?"

"I am saying, Your Majesty, that we may be under attack by the power of the Void. I urge Your Majesty to take this into account in your decision making."

"So you would have me surrender?" King Moross was astonished.

"I did not say that, Your Majesty—"

"I would be ruined. The people would be furious. You said yourself that this enemy will find it impossible to take this city—"

"Recall your history, Your Majesty. Old Vinnengael was a city ten times larger than Dunkar and ten times better fortified. And it fell to the power of the Void."

"They might cast some sort of evil spell on us?" King Moross asked uneasily. "Can they do that?"

"I don't know, Your Majesty. I don't know that much about Void magic, thank the gods. I do find it regrettable that the High Magus chose this time to leave. His advice in this matter would have been invaluable. Perhaps we could send a messenger—"

King Moross shook his head. "Impossible. I was sent word that he boarded a ship this morning and they sailed with the tide."

"You did not speak to him?"

"No, his departure was quite sudden."

"The High Magus sets sail at the first sign of this enemy," Onaset said. "Perhaps his sudden departure is his advice, Your Majesty."

Moross shook his head, but said nothing. Clasping his hands behind his back, he began to pace. "What a terrible decision, Onaset. If I go to war, I doom my people to the horrors of war and if I surrender I open the city to an army of Void monsters. We know that they have human slaves. What is to stop them from enslaving us all? Can I trust the word of a man who holds a knife to my throat? No, no, Seraskier. I will not even consider it."

He halted in his pacing, turned to Onaset. "Am I making the right choice?" he asked, almost pathetically.

"I believe so, Your Majesty," Onaset replied. "But we should seek assistance and advice from the magi of the Temple, those who remain."

"Yes, of course." King Moross paused a moment longer, then gave a sigh and straightened. "I will send this herald about his business. Arrogant wretch. Make what preparations you need to make to face the dawn attack, Seraskier."

"Yes, Your Majesty." Onaset bowed.

"And gods' fortune to us all," the king added.

"We will need it, Your Majesty," Onaset said.

In their camp, the Trevenici were also making preparations, although not the kind that the Seraskier would have approved. The Trevenici were making preparations to leave Dunkar.

The Trevenici warriors were never required to remain in Dunkar long. The Karnuans constantly sent raiding parties into the disputed no man's land that lay between Dunkar and the Karnuan city of Karfa 'Len and it was the Trevenici's duty to drive them back. Raven had been planning to lead his troop to take up patrol duty in the region this very week.

The Trevenici liked this assignment, for it left them free to roam the land, sleep in the open, show their courage in battle. Well-trained soldiers, the Karnuans were a superb military force. Fighting Karnuans meant that a Trevenici warrior had a chance to gain glory in battle and raise his standing in the tribe, not to mention the bounty money paid by the Dunkargans for Karnuan heads.

Raven arrived back at the Trevenici camp to find his people gathered together, taking stock of the situation. Heads turned at the sight of Raven and seeing his dark expression and lowering brows, one of their questions was answered.

"I take it they wouldn't let you leave," said one.

Raven shook his head. "The Seraskier has given orders that the gates are to be closed, no one in or out."

"Of course, he has to do that," said another disparagingly. "Else the entire Dunkargan army would head for the hills."

"I say we fight our way out," said a third, brandishing her sword.

"Fight! Hah!" another cried. "All we'd have to do is rattle our swords at them and they'll fall down and piss themselves."

"What about our tribes? Those monsters came from the west. Maybe they're already moving on our people," said another.

"I want to get out as much as any of you," Raven said and, at the sound of his voice, thick with weariness, and the sight of his haggard face, everyone knew that he spoke the truth. "But fighting is not the answer. On my way back, I heard that the enemy sent in someone to parley. You know Dunkargans. They'll talk for days. This night, we go over the wall."

"The walls will be heavily manned this night of all nights," one pointed out.

"And all eyes looking west," Raven answered. "We will go over the east wall."

"There is a full moon tonight."

"That is bad," Raven admitted, "but it cannot be helped."

"We will not have our horses—"

"Better we go on foot anyway. The enemy would hear the sound of hoofbeats."

"The Dunkargans will accuse us of being cowards, Ravenstrike. They will say we fled in the night."

Raven shrugged. "We know the truth, Sparrow Song. Does it matter to us what city dwellers say?"

No, it did not. Everyone agreed on that. After further deliberation, all decided that they should adopt Raven's plan. In the discussion, not one mentioned the fact that after they escaped the city, they would need to make their way either through or around the enemy lines. To the Trevenici, this was the least of their problems. They had never yet met a foe, not even the Karnuans, that any of the warriors considered a worthy opponent.

As the Trevenici made their plans to escape the city, Onaset made his plans to defend it. He ordered his soldiers to light the fires beneath the cauldrons of oil and water. He formed parties of willing civilians into brigades with orders to soak down with water any building made of timber or those with thatched roofs. Fortunately there were not many flammable buildings in Dunkar, for most buildings were made of stone or a mixture of sand, water and crushed limestone. He sent soldiers to quell a riot at the docks, where terrified citizens were trying to flee the city in boats and ships. When their captains began charging outlandish sums, people decided to take matters into their own hands and tried to steal the boats.

Onaset had the great satisfaction of declaring the port under martial law, stating that all shipping would be needed for the current emergency. He sent his soldiers on board, rounded up the wealthy passengers—the only ones who could afford to pay for their salvation—and marched them off to help in the city's defense.

Onaset went to his supper late that night. He ate alone in his quarters in the barracks. He was not married. He did not think it fair to a wife to have a soldier for a husband. Servants did the cooking for him. He sat down to a bowl of curried lamb stew, ate a spoonful and, while chewing, went over what remained left to do before dawn brought chaos and terror and death to the city of Dunkar.

The realization that he had been poisoned came to Onaset with the terrible burning pain that was like a fire in his vitals. Furious, appalled, fearful not for himself, but for his city, Onaset rose to his feet and tried to call out.

The pain increased. His throat closed. His heart seized, beat wildly, then stopped.

The Seraskier pitched forward onto the table, dead.

16

THE FLAMES OF TORCHES AND BONFIRES WERE BRIGHT SPLASHES AGAINST the purple black darkness. Torches burned up and down the walls. The fires beneath the cauldrons were kept stoked throughout the night. A red hot glow came from the giant braziers where they were heating refuse from the blacksmith's shop—iron scraps, bent nails, old horseshoes—to shower down on the enemy. Nervous soldiers patrolling the walls were shadows passing in front of the flames, shadows that blended into the night when they walked on.

Beyond, in the prairie itself, more fires burned—campfires. When the herald rode out the city walls and word reached the enemy that King Moross had refused the terms of surrender, the enemy soldiers moved closer to the city. Their numbers were incalculable, some estimated as many as ten thousand. The voices of the creatures came clearly to those on the walls, for the monsters were constantly talking or shouting at each other. Their language appeared to be comprised of grunts and clickings and crackling sounds, with explosive sizzling pops like wet wood blazing. Their harsh voices heard coming across the distance were unnerving, alien, strange and unknown.

There was no sleep for anyone in Dunkar that night. Excited, terrified, its citizens clogged the streets, spreading rumors that grew more fearsome with each telling. Captain Drossel had a difficult time walking the streets and wished that he had thought to wear his cloak over his uniform. He couldn't go three steps without some frantic civilian spotting him as a member of the military and latching onto him, begging him for news or to confirm the latest rumor.

Drossel shook them loose with an impatient, "King's business!" and continued on, cuffing or shoving those who were too persistent. He was going to be late and while that annoyed him—he was a meticulously punctual person—it didn't much bother him. His men weren't going to go anywhere or do anything without him.

Commander Drossel was forty years old, a Dunkargan by birth, born and raised in the capital city. He had joined the army at an early age, not out of a sense of loyalty to his country—he cared damn little about his country—but because he had heard that with cunning and a certain amount of cleverness, a fellow could do quite well for himself in the Dunkargan military. One had only to avoid the temptation to be a hero, for that could get a fellow killed. Drossel had survived in the army for more than twenty years by not being a hero. He took care to fight when his superiors were watching, took care of himself when they weren't. He had risen through the ranks by a judicious mixture of bribery and treachery. Everyone knew it, no one thought the worse of him for it. That's just the way things are done in the Dunkargan army.

He had turned to the worship of the Void fifteen years earlier after a love affair had gone bad. He had been walking the streets of Dunkar, his mind toying with the idea of poison in order to avenge himself on the little whore. With this in mind, he entered an alchemist's shop and told the proprietor he wanted something to kill rats.

Guessing at once the nature of the rat in question, the proprietor had asked a few questions and at length suggested a potion that would have a much better effect. The cost was dear, both in terms of his purse and his own hide, for Void magic takes a bit of one's life essence to work and causes pustules and lesions on the skin. Drossel was able to cover the worst of these with the flowing shirt the Dunkargans wore. He had never been a good looking man, being small and wiry in stature, dark-complected, with black hair and squinting black eyes. The pustules on his face were hidden by his beard.

The sacrifice had been worth it. The potion, slipped into her wine, had transformed the whore from a nubile and vain young beauty to a bony hag. The girl had known she had been cursed by the Void and she had guessed who had done it. She had tried to bring Drossel up on charges of being a Void worshiper, but he was a respected soldier and she was a whore and so no one believed her. Robbed of her looks and thereby her ability to make money, she had sunk lower and lower and was eventually found dead in the harbour.

Pleased with the power of the Void, Drossel had been indoctrinated into some of its secrets by a Void practitioner. Knowledge of those secrets and a way with potions led him to where he was today, a high ranking officer in the Dunkargan army, doing all he could to secretly undermine that army in the name of Dagnarus, Lord of the Void.

Drossel shoved his way through the panicked mobs, cursing them all heartily, and breathed a sigh of relief when he turned down a side street that was empty. The worst of the press was in the tavern districts, where people were accustomed to going for news. The merchant district, especially this part, was quiet. The shops had long been shuttered and those who lived above them had gone off to the taverns or to relatives to gorge on their fears.

He gave a moment's thought to what was in store for those clamoring in the streets and then shrugged the thought away. It wasn't his concern. A man had a right to take care of himself. Certainly no one had ever gone out of his way to take care of Drossel. His thoughts went from the people to the fat purse filled with silver argents he had hidden in a money belt secured tightly around his waist.

The street he walked was known as "Magi Street" due to the predominance of shops that catered to magi. The shops were closed, their windows shuttered and doors barred. The shop to which Drossel was headed was one of the more prosperous on the block. The shop had a white-washed façade and green shutters and the customary sign of the mandala representing "Earth magic" that was found on almost all the magi shops on this street.

Drossel turned down the alley next to the shop with green shutters. At the far end of the alley was another door. This shop was not marked, but everyone in Dunkar knew what was sold here: wares for those who practiced Void magic. Such a shop would not have been tolerated in New Vinnengael. The Church would have acted swiftly to shut it down, maybe even arrest the owner or, at the least, exile her. In Dunkar, the shop was just another shop.

The Dunkargan people did not like Void magic or Void magic users anymore than did the people of New Vinnengael, but Dunkargans held a pragmatic view of the matter. Dunkargans dislike anyone meddling in their affairs and consequently, they don't feel the need to meddle in other people's business. If a person wants to practice Void magic, it's his affair, not the king's—except to tax the shop owner—and certainly not the Church's. If a man is caught harming another through the use of an object of Void magic purchased in Dunkar, the Dunkargans will stone him to death—after they collect the taxes on the object he purchased. This dichotomy in thinking makes perfect sense to the Dunkargans, if to no one else in the world.

Drossel knocked three times on the door to this shop, counted to ten, knocked three more times. A panel slid open. An eye peered out.

"You're late," said a woman's voice.

The panel shut and the door opened. A woman stood inside the door holding a lighted lamp. The room was small and crowded with cabinets and tables displaying wares dedicated to the use of Void magic. A pungent smell scented the air—that of the ointments used by Void mages to spread over the pustules and skin lesions caused by the use of Void magic.

The woman gestured with the lamp for Drossel to come inside, shut the door behind him. She smelled of the ointment herself and he could see an oily patch on her cheek. Some believed the ointments worked, others did not, saying that those who did believe were fooling themselves. Drossel thought it eased the pain and the itch somewhat, but he couldn't tell that it improved healing time.

"Everyone is here," the woman told him. "In the back room."

"It's madness out there," he said, as an excuse for his tardiness.

"What did you expect?" the woman replied coolly, leading the way.

Drossel had no answer to that. He might have said he really hadn't had time to expect anything, since he'd only received his orders the previous night, but he kept his mouth shut. No matter what he said, he wouldn't phase Lessereti. She'd only come back with some rejoinder to make him feel like a fool and since she invariably got in the last word, he'd learned early on that it was easier just to let her have it from the beginning.

The woman named Lessereti was an avowed user of Void magic and the owner of this shop. Everyone in Dunkar knew of her and, although most would cross to the other side of the street rather than walk past her, those same people would not hesitate to call on her when they were in trouble. Lessereti was smart, careful and skillful in her work. She knew what jobs to accept and which ones to refuse, no matter how much money was in the offing. Thus she had managed to outlive many other Void magic-users in the city of Dunkar.

When he had first met her, Drossel had thought Lessereti a comely woman. She was only part Dunkargan, that much could be told by the fact that her complexion was not dusky, but more the color of milk laced with coffee. Her hair was brown, not black, like most Dunkargans, and she had one brown eye and one blue eye. She was in her early thirties or looked it. She never referred to her age or where she came from and no one—certainly not Drossel—had the effrontery to ask her. She was well built and but for the pustules on her face and the single startling blue eye that seemed to be able to stare into the dusty parts of a man's soul, she would have been considered attractive.

Drossel had found her attractive, at first. That notion had been dispelled for him after five minutes conversation with her. Lessereti had no use for men, viewed them all with scorn. He would soon discover that men were not singled out for special treatment. Lessereti had no use for women, either. She detested all mankind, looked upon her fellow travelers to the grave as fools and dunces and never failed to find cynical amusement in their follies.

"You're not going with us tonight?" Drossel asked, for she was not dressed as were the others he could see waiting in the inner room—all wearing the uniforms of the Dunkargan military. Lessereti wore long, draping robes, useful for hiding the marks her trade left on her skin.

"Of course not," she said. "I would be immediately recognized and then where would you be?" The words "you great idiot" were not spoken but implied in her tone.

Anger stirred in Drossel but he was careful not to show it. Captain Drossel was not afraid of anyone, with the single exception of Lessereti. Drossel had good reason to be afraid. He had been the one to drop Lessereti's poison in the Seraskier's lamb stew. Hiding in the kitchen, Drossel had witnessed first-hand Onaset's death. So fast-acting was the poison that the man had died with that first bite of meat still half-chewed in his mouth.

"So the Seraskier died like a lamb, did he?" Lessereti said, chuckling over her little joke.

"All went as you said it would," Drossel stated. "He had no time to cause a scene. He never even made a sound beyond a sort of startled gasp. The servant and I hauled him to his bed. The servant will tell anyone who comes looking for him that the Seraskier is asleep. When the attack comes, they'll find him, but—"

"—by that time it will be too late. You must make haste, Drossel. The servant has probably fled by now."

"I paid him enough—"

"Bah! You can never pay anyone enough. Well, here they are." Lessereti held the lamp high, motioned with her hand. "Stand up, gentlemen, stand up. Form into a line. You're supposed to be soldiers."

Twelve men wearing Dunkargan uniforms shuffled about in the inner room behind the shop. Lessereti did not like to live on the upper levels, as did most merchants, but preferred to live on the ground floor where she could quickly exit the building if she had to. Most people thought Lessereti rented her shop, but, in truth, Lessereti owned this building and also the one next to it.

Drossel looked each man up and down, making certain that all was correct and in order. He adjusted belts, smoothed folds, ordered one man to wipe the mud off his boots. They were not as good as he had hoped and he would have liked to have given them some training in impersonating soldiers.

"Don't worry, Drossel," said Lessereti impatiently, "by the time anyone figures out they're not what they seem, it will be all over."

"I hope so," Drossel said and cast her a grim glance. "Anything goes wrong and we're captured, it means my neck. And likely yours, as well, Lessereti. They won't have to torture me to find out who gave me my orders."

"Don't worry about me, Drossel," Lessereti replied. "If this fails, you won't live long enough to talk." She glanced around at the others. "None of you will. I've already seen to that."

Drossel felt a cold qualm shiver his gut. He recalled her comment that "you could never pay anyone enough." Lessereti was not one to make idle threats nor was she noted for her sense of humor. He looked askance at the other twelve men, but saw nothing in their faces to indicate whether they were fearful or not. Of course, they were all experienced Void magic-users, so perhaps this was a thing that was understood among them.

"We had best get going," Drossel said, his voice harsh to mask his uneasiness. "You, there. If you wear your sword like that, you're going to trip yourself. Shift it more to the left." He watched as the man struggled with the weapon. "It's not good, but it'll do, I suppose. Who's the leader?"

"Pasha," said Lessereti, indicating an older man whose face was so deeply scarred that it no longer resembled a face.

Drossel recognized Pasha. He had long served as a silversmith's assistant. His facial scars came presumably from an accident with molten silver. Drossel now understood that the scars came from his liaison with the Void.

"He knows his business?" Drossel asked nervously.

"Certainly," Lessereti returned. "Do you know yours?" The single blue eye was brilliant in the lamplight. "I'm beginning to wonder, Captain."

"I know mine," Drossel said. Fixing his thoughts on the bag of silver argents, he felt better.

"Good," said Lessereti. "You have only to take them close in. They will do the rest."

"And after that?"

"You needn't worry about them. They can take care of themselves."

"You put in a word for me?"

"I did," she replied. "Lord Dagnarus will be expecting you."

She lighted them out of her shop and into the alley. After they were gone, she shut and barred her door. Not a word of farewell, not a word to wish them luck.

Drossel had planned to form his squad into two lines and have them march behind him, but one glimpse of his "soldiers" and he knew that would never work. Not only would they not be able to keep in step, he could never train them to walk with the stiff and upright stance that marked the military man.

"Stay together," he said. "With luck, we'll look like a patrol just coming off duty. Keep your mouths shut. I'll do the talking. Any questions? Good. Move out. You, Pasha, come tell me what you and this bunch plan to do once we get there."

Pasha began to explain. Listening, Drossel glanced back at Lessereti's door, thinking she might be watching them.

The door was shut. No chink of light could be seen coming from beneath.

Drossel smiled ruefully at his notion. Lessereti didn't give a damn what they did or what happened to them. She had made her own arrangements for the future and was probably in her bed by now, sleeping quite peacefully.

The city of Dunkar was surrounded by a double wall made of stone with a thick layer of sand and rock in between. The wall had two main gates, one facing west and the other facing the harbor. The Harbor Gate, as it was known, had not been closed for as long as the eldest person in the city could remember. The last time had been during the devastating war with Karnu, over one hundred and seventy-five years ago. Fearing an attack by sea, Dunkar had strengthened its harbor defenses, adding infamous fire-hurling catapults.

The west gate, facing the Dunkar highway that led to the frontier outposts, was closed every night at sundown. The gate itself was massive. Made of iron, the two double doors were a marvel to all who saw them. The casting and mounting of the doors had required the combined efforts of all the blacksmiths in Dunkarga, as well as assistance from every magus with skills in Earth magic who could be persuaded to lend his arcane art. Earth magic continued to be required to keep the doors from rusting, only a minor problem, due to the dry climate.

The doors were so heavy that a team of twenty stout men were required to close them and open them in what had become a daily ritual. Timed by beating drums and their own chanting, the men divided into groups of ten each and, putting their hands on the doors, shoved them shut at night and thrust them open in the morning. After the doors had been shut, the twenty men lifted an enormous iron cross bar and, grunting and straining, wrestled it into place across the two doors. Then, each man grabbed a huge war hammer and beat on the bar until it fell into the pinions that held it firm.

They followed the same routine in the morning, removing the cross bar from the door and hauling it to where it stood during the day, resting on a hundred wooden trestles, watched over by city guards, who did little except keep children from playing on it and visitors from trying to scratch their names onto the iron.

The iron gate had been closed immediately the enemy army had come into sight, the enormous cross bar lowered into place. No battering ram on Loerem could smash down those gates, though it were wielded by an army of orks, and not even dwarven Fire magic could set the iron doors ablaze, so the Dunkargans believed, and probably with good basis for their belief.

The gate was normally heavily guarded, for the Dunkargans had little liking for foreigners, particularly those not of the human variety. The guard on the gate had been tripled with the sighting of the enemy. Drossel had never seen so many soldiers on duty all at one time.

The soldiers had cordoned off the area around the gate and the city walls, keeping the streets free of civilians so that troops and supply wagons could have access. Drossel had feared having to shove his way through a panicked mob of civilians in order to reach his objective. Now he had only to shove his way through a panicked mob of soldiers. Despite the Seraskier's efforts to improve matters, discipline in the Dunkar army was notoriously lax, with half its officers corrupt and the other half too incompetent to be corrupted.

"You're sure this is going to work?" Drossel asked Pasha.

The group had halted by mutual and unspoken consent in the heavy shadow cast by a statue of one of Dunkar's long-dead kings. Pasha stood regarding the gate with a frown that caused all the scars on his face to scrunch together.

"There is more light than usual," Pasha stated.

"Is this a problem?"

"It could be."

Glancing around at the group of Void wizards, Drossel saw nods of agreement. Heaving an exasperated sigh, he looked back at the gate. On a normal night, two torches burned on the walls near each of the two gatehouses, while a single lamp lit the interiors. This night, not only was there a bright, full moon and a cloudless sky, but all twenty wall sconces held a torch and several iron braziers filled with flaming charcoal had been brought in to stand near the gate.

The light illuminated a scene of confusion, with soldiers coming off duty stopping to talk to those who were coming on duty. Those soldiers who had no duty at all and who should have been back at the barracks milled about in front of the gate or tried to climb up the stairs to get a look at the enemy. Officers barked orders that no one heeded.

"There's not a damn thing I can do about the light—" Drossel began, only to find that no one was listening to him.

Pasha consulted with his fellows. They appeared to be hatching some sort of plan, for occasionally one or two murmured something in acquiescence. City bells began tolling the hour.

Drossel nudged Pasha.

"Midnight. It's time."

Pasha's eyes, deep set in the scarred face, were dark, calm. "We are agreed. We will proceed with the plan as I described it. You know what to do, Captain?"

"Yes, I bloody well know what to do," Drossel snapped. A veteran soldier who had done more than his share of killing—both on the field and off—he had not expected to be this nervous.

"Then I suggest you do it," Pasha said and he may have smiled; it was hard to tell for the scars.

"Wait a minute. This isn't going to work if there's no one on the other side of the gate."

"The taan will be there, Captain, have no fear."

"Taan? No one said I was relying on taan! What if they're spotted? What then?" Drossel was sweating. Accustomed to being in the lead, he didn't like this, relegated to a bit part. "What if they're seen?"

"They won't be," said Pasha and he actually was at ease enough to sound amused. "The taan cast the same Void spells we do, Captain." His mouth twisted. "Cast them better, from what I hear."

Drossel didn't believe it. He'd been told about the taan and from what he'd heard, they were beasts. He was sorry he'd let Lessereti talk him into this scheme. There had been no mention of the taan playing a major part until now. No amount of silver was worth this.

"How will these animals know when to act? How will we know they're out there?" He shook his head. "I don't like this. There's too much left to chance."

"I would think twice about backing out, Captain," said Pasha and he no longer sounded amused.

"I never said I wanted out," Drossel growled. "I'm just indicating where things might go wrong, that's all. I'll do my part, don't worry."

Muttering imprecations against Lessereti under his breath, he turned his back on the Void wizards and began to walk toward the gate. The distance he had to cover was not far, perhaps the length of a long city block, but it suddenly seemed furlongs to him. He walked alone. Pasha had given Drossel a strict injunction not to look back, not to try to see what the Void wizards were doing. Pasha warned that this might draw unwanted attention to them, and Drossel knew this was true, but he couldn't help it. He didn't trust them. He glanced over his shoulder.

Having left twelve "soldiers" wearing white tunics that would reflect the moonlight and be visible in all but the deepest darkness, Drossel was considerably startled not to see a single one of them standing beneath the statue where he'd left them. He passed his tongue over dry lips. Although he knew the plan, the thought that he'd been left in the lurch was too overwhelming. Twisting his neck, he sent a piercing gaze into the shadows and then he saw them.

The sight was unnerving and he wished he'd obeyed Pasha's orders and hadn't looked. The wizards' flesh withered as if they had been caught in a bubbling cauldron. They gave their substance to the Void and the magic seemed to be rendering their flesh as was done in the stockyards, where the animal fat is melted into tallow. The wizards' flesh melted into the Void. All that remained of the wizard was his shadow, a shadow cast by moonlight, a shadow that was gray and wavering and insubstantial, but could think and act like the man it had been.

Eleven of the wizards had already performed the transformation. Pasha was the last. As the leader, he had waited to make certain the spells the others had cast had worked, that his magic would not be required to assist any of them or to deal swiftly with a problem should someone's spell go bad, as occasionally happened. In that case, he might be left to dispose of a corpse, for Void magic was not merciful to those who mishandled it.

Drossel jerked his head forward, the sight of Pasha's scarred face melding grotesquely into its own shadow imprinted on the backs of his eyeballs. Drossel was not one for nightmares, but between the Seraskier's dead eyes staring accusingly at him and Pasha's living eyes dissolving, Drossel figured he'd be drinking himself to sleep the next few nights.

He shook off the chill that was creeping up his neck and wrenched his mind back to the job at hand. He kept walking, making his way toward the gate, shoving and cursing those who bumbled into his way. Someone called his name, wanting to know what he was doing here. He waved his hand to acknowledge that he heard, continued walking rapidly, as if on an urgent mission that could not be interrupted by idle conversation.

He darted a swift glance around to see if by chance he could detect any of the twelve Void wizards. Drossel thought he saw one man's shadow, slipping along the far wall opposite him, but there were so many people passing to and fro that he couldn't be certain. He breathed a sigh of relief. If he couldn't see them in this confusion and he was looking for them, he doubted if anyone else would notice.

Nearing the gatehouse, Drossel slipped his hand into the wide red belt that was part of the uniform and drew out a dagger that wasn't. He slid the handle of the dagger up into the long flowing sleeve of his shirt, holding the weapon by the blade, so that it would not be seen.

Much to his chagrin, he discovered that one officer had at last succeeded in restoring some sort of order at the gatehouse. The area was being cleared of idlers and that would include Drossel unless he had a reason to be here.

Walking up to the gatehouse guard, who was looking harried and uneasy, Drossel saluted.

"What do you want?" the guard demanded.

"I am looking for Seraskier Onaset. I have an urgent message for him."

"He's not here," the guard said shortly.

"I was told he would be here," said Drossel with obtuse stubbornness. "His aide said I would most certainly find him here."

"Well, he's *not* here, as you can plainly see if you've got eyes in your head," the guard returned.

"I will wait for him here," Drossel said and took up a position next to the gate near one of the enormous hammers used to pound the iron bar into place. He remained standing with his back straight, his eyes forward, his arms folded across his chest.

"Wait for him in the Void, for all I care," the guard muttered. He was clearly frightened. He kept glancing at the wall, as if he could see through it to the fearsome enemy beyond.

Someone shouted for the gate guard and he turned to discover what new crisis had presented itself.

Drossel remained standing until he was certain the guard had forgotten about him. As he stood there, he saw three disembodied shadows flow across the cobblestone street and approach the iron doors.

He looked nervously up at the battlements, at the soldiers walking the walls. Surely they must have heard or seen something? But no, they were pacing out the course of their patrol or standing staring out at the enemy, talking in low voices.

Drossel's mouth went dry as the pavement. He strained his ears to try to hear sounds from the opposite side of the door, any sort of sound to let him know that the taan who were supposed to be there were there.

Drossel shifted his gaze. The area around the gate was empty now, the shadows that had no corresponding bodies could be seen clearly. He told himself that this was because he knew what to look for and, indeed, that seemed to be the case, for one of the other gatehouse guards glanced in the direction of the gate and turned away.

More of the Void wizards arrived, the shadowy forms spreading out along the width of the gate, six to each door. Shadowy hands reached out to touch the enormous iron cross bar. Drossel tensed, listening for the sound Pasha had told him he would hear, the sound that was his signal to act. Unfortunately, at that moment, one of the soldiers who had been detailed to clear the area looked at the gate. Drossel could tell by the man's bulging eyes and gaping mouth that he had seen the disembodied shadows.

The soldier sucked in a breath to cry out, but the cry changed to a grunt of pain as Drossel drove his dagger into the man's ribcage. An expert at dagger work, Drossel hit the heart and the man died in Drossel's arms, the body sagging.

"You are in trouble, soldier," Drossel roared. "Drunk and disorderly at a time like this." He dragged the body into a dark corner and lowered it down, making certain that the small patch of blood on the man's uniform was hidden from view. The soldier's head slumped forward, his chin resting on his chest, his arms flaccid.

"Sleep it off, you reprobate!" Drossel growled and, looking disgusted, he took up his place again by the gate, thrusting the blood-stained dagger into his belt.

"Get on with it!" he hissed under his breath to the shadow nearest him.

A few soldiers had looked around at Drossel's roar. Seeing nothing except one of their own apparently inebriated, they went back about their business.

Shadowy hands rested on the cross bar and Drossel heard the whisper of the spell-casting words. He was wondering nervously if he would recognize the signal, but then it came, and he knew he need not have worried. The sound was unmistakable—as of someone stomping on broken glass.

"Now!" whispered a voice from the shadow nearest him.

Drossel grabbed hold of one of the immense war hammers that stood against the wall. Fear-laced excitement surged through him. The hammer was heavy, but he never noticed the weight. Grasping it convulsively, he swung the hammer at the iron cross bar. If the Void wizards had failed in their spell-casting, the hammer would strike the bar with a horrendous clang and send shattering and painful vibrations through Drossel's arms and shoulders. He thought of that and dismissed it in a fleeting instant. He was seized with a kind of euphoria that made him invincible.

He struck the cross bar. Altered by Void magic, the bar shattered as if it had been made of ice, not iron.

Drossel dropped the hammer and shoved with all his strength at one of the gates. He could not take the place of ten men, not even with the adrenaline pumping through his body, but he could open the gate a crack and that was enough.

Hands with long talons, covered with a thick leathery hide, thrust through the crack. Guttural voices called out and were answered by a single voice that sounded as if it were issuing an order. The hands grabbed hold of the door and pulled it open so swiftly that Drossel lost his grip and fell flat, face-down on the cobblestones.

He was in danger of being trampled, for the taan who had been waiting outside the gate now surged inside. Other taan were forcing open the other side of the gate.

Frantic voices shouted from the guardhouse, but the guards didn't have time to do much more than shout before the taan were on them. Wielding strange looking curved-bladed swords, spears or bludgeons, the taan slaughtered the guards with cruel efficiency, bashing in skulls, cutting off heads, impaling bodies on spears.

Scrambling to his hands and knees, Drossel realized that his fall had saved his life. He crawled swiftly outside the gate and crouched in the shadow of the wall, shaking with fear, for he knew as well as he'd ever known anything in his life that if the creatures spotted him, they would kill him. He had no way to communicate with them, no way to tell them he was on their side.

Ripping off the white uniform, he cursed himself, wondering why he hadn't foreseen this predicament, and he cursed the Void wizards, who, in their shadowy guise, would blend with the darkness and make good their escape across to the enemy lines. So far, no one had noticed Drossel in the chaos, but he knew his luck wouldn't last.

More and more taan poured through the open gate, a flood of death rushing into Dunkar. Blood-curdling yells rose from the plains outside Dunkar. The entire taan army was on the move, running to attack the city.

Siege ladders sprouted like evil weeds up and down the wall. The taan climbed them swiftly and surged over the walls as more taan continued to pour through the gate and now began to attack the battlements from the inside.

The taan were truly fearsome looking, seen up close. They walked upright like any human, and stood over six feet in height, some much taller. The bones of their arms were thick and their hands were enormous. Their faces were the faces of animals, with long snouts and mouths filled with razor-sharp teeth. Their eyes were small and wide-set on either side of the snout. Their hide looked tough and leathery and each creature was heavily scarred.

The scarification appeared to have been done deliberately, for the scars formed intricate patterns on the hide. Some wore armor, either chain mail or leather or a combination of both, while others marched into battle with little but a loincloth wrapped around their limbs. They fought fearlessly, but not recklessly, and handled their weapons with skill.

Drossel watched as a soldier on the wall tried to surrender to the taan who had him surrounded. The soldier knelt down and lifted his hands in supplication.

The taan sliced off the man's hands and cut off the soldier's head, then kicked the corpse off the wall. The headless body landed not three feet away from Drossel. Obviously, he realized, surrender is not an option.

Drossel drew his sword, hoping to take one of the Void-begotten fiends with him, when a voice from the shadows spoke right in his ear, nearly scaring him to death.

"An army of human mercenaries is located about twenty yards to the north," said the voice. "If you can make your way to them, you will be safe. Tell them you are Drossel and mention the name Lessereti. Good luck."

"Pasha?" Drossel cried, but there was no answer.

A shadow glided away from him across the moonlit ground, heading to the north.

Drossel wasted no more time. He had noticed that the taan attacked in waves and when one wave reached the gate, there was a slight lull in the action until the next wave surged forward. Taking advantage of this lull, Drossel made a dash for it. He flung away his sword, for it was weighing him down, and, after a struggle with himself, he threw away the bag of silver argents.

Dead men spend no coin, as the saying went.

17

ALMOST EIGHT HUNDRED TREVENICI MERCENARIES FOUGHT FOR THE Dunkargans, but there were rarely that many in the city at one time. Some were out on patrol, some were traveling to their villages. About five hundred Trevenici were in the city of Dunkarga the day the herald of Prince Dagnarus rode into the city to demand its surrender. A simple people, the Trevenici developed a simple plan for their escape. Moving through the city in small groups of no more than ten, they headed toward one of the three points designated to scale the eastern wall, their leaders dividing up the group in order to speed the escape, while the capture of one group would not mean the capture of all. Tribal members split up, so that if one was taken, the other might have a chance to escape and carry word to the tribe.

Trevenici tribes live isolated one from the other. Early in the history of the Trevenici, the tribes fought each other, for they are warriors born, the need to test oneself in battle is in the blood. This constant warfare proved ruinous. The Trevenici soon came to the realization that they might well wipe themselves out. A meeting of the tribal elders of the Trevenici was held in Vilda Harn, at which time it was determined that the tribes would be at peace with each other and at war with all the rest of the world. Since this was about the time the Vinnengaelean empire was on the rise and looking to expand, the Trevenici were not short on enemies.

Tribes live apart from each other and rarely have contact, but there are times when it is deemed necessary for one tribe to disseminate information to the others—in the case of a common enemy attacking their lands, for example. Thus it was that before they separated, the Trevenici warriors took blood vows to spread the news of this new and fearsome looking enemy among all the tribes.

Raven considered trying to pass along his warning to his tribe, but the more he thought about it, the more he wondered what he would say to them through another. He could not put a name and a face on his fear and so how could he relate it in terms his tribe would understand? The general warning that would go out to all the tribes would not suffice. The danger that shadowed his tribe was specific. It had to do with the accursed armor and the dying knight and his nephew, Jessan. Raven alone could say these things to his people. He had to escape, that was all there was to it.

The Trevenici left camp at just about the same time that Captain Drossel and the Void wizards headed to the gate. As did Drossel, the Trevenici discovered the streets to be crowded, but, unlike Drossel, the Trevenici did not find it particularly difficult to make their way through the crowds. At the sight of the tall, strong warriors, decked out in their gruesome trophies and carrying their weapons, the Dunkargans quickly made room for them to pass. The Dunkargans even raised a few cheers, thinking that the Trevenici were going to man the battlements.

The Trevenici reached their meeting points on time. Raven's group had chosen a place on the wall where a wealthy merchant had built a house whose upper stories extended to within a few feet of the wall. The Trevenici were prepared to deal with the merchant, but they discovered the house empty, the merchant and his family having been among the fortunate few to escape the city by boat.

This part of the city was dark and mostly deserted. Raven's eyes took a moment to adjust from the torchlight flaring in the streets to the moonlit darkness of this part of the city. He found other Trevenici already arrived. Silent and patient, they squatted in the shadows of the buildings. He looked up toward the wall, saw a few soldiers walking back and forth.

"How many are there?" Raven asked one of the warriors.

"Sixteen, maybe. Some left as you said they would. The moment they came on duty, they abandoned their posts."

"Anyone in the house?"

"No, it is empty. Fox Fang climbed to a window on the second floor, slipped inside. Food for supper was still on the table, clothes strewn all over. Whoever lived there left in a hurry. Fox Fang is in there now."

Raven stared intently at the wall. Those few guards who remained were nervous and fearful, constantly looking westward, trying to see something. One strange sound and they'd think they were under attack by the monsters and raise the alarm.

"I need eight warriors to go up there in advance of the main group to silence those guards," Raven said.

Eight warriors rose up and crossed the street to the house, keeping to the shadows. The front door of the house opened to them and they vanished inside. The rest of the Trevenici waited in the shadows.

As Raven headed for the house, he watched the silhouettes of the warriors materialize on the roof. They were about to make the leap from the house to the battlements, when a sound arose from the western part of the city, a sound that was strange enough and terrible enough to cause even the battle-hardened warriors to come to a startled halt, turn to stare westward.

Raven had never heard a sound like this before and he never wanted to hear it again. It was the sound of howls rising from a thousand throats, howls that were high-pitched and jarring and unearthly. The howls came from the throats of the taan and they were raised in battle-cries as the western gate fell to treachery and the taan launched their attack.

Raven blessed this assault, for at the very first cries, the guards who had remained at their posts took to their heels, some heading for the source of the howls, others running away as fast as their feet could carry them. The Trevenici could make all the noise they wanted to now and no one would pay heed to them. Once over the wall, they could take advantage of the chaos around the gate to slip off into the night.

The Trevenici raced for the wall, no longer needing to hide. They clambered up the stairs and onto the battlements. The first warriors on the wall were already tying ropes around the crenellations. Raven tested the knots to make certain that they would hold, then looked out across the moonlit plains to see if he could see any signs of the enemy. He saw movement, but could make nothing of it, for it was too far away. If it was a group of enemy soldiers, the group was small.

The Trevenici descended rapidly, lowering themselves down the rope hand over hand, using their feet to help propel them. The first down drew their weapons, faced outward, ready to protect the rest. Raven was the last man on the wall, having remained up above in case any of the guards decided to return. He could not see what was happening at the gate, the roofs of buildings blocked his view. He had excellent hearing, however, and he guessed from the screams and cries blending with animal-like howls that battle had been joined.

When the last man was down, Raven followed. The Trevenici set fire to the rope, once they'd reach the bottom, not wanting to leave any means for the enemy to ascend. Gathering his group together, Raven led them out across the plains, heading east, away from the fighting. They would eventually turn north, to reach Trevenici lands.

He took the lead, breaking into a long, loping run that he could keep up for hours, if need be. He looked out across the plains, saw only the grass waving in the moonlight. He could no longer see the signs of movement that he'd seen earlier from the wall and figured that any enemy that was out here would go toward the sound of fighting, not away from it. Raven heard some muttered comments behind him, warriors disappointed that they were missing what appeared to be a good battle. None had any thought of going to join it, however. Their thoughts were on their tribes, on home.

Raven's spirits soared as they always did when he was free of the confinement of the city walls, back to where he could feel the wind on his cheek and smell sage and wild garlic. Drawing in a deep breath, he noted another smell on the wind this night, a putrid smell, as of decaying flesh. The scent came and went, for the wind was blowing at his back, coming from the south. He took another step and felt a hand seize hold of his ankle. The hand yanked him off his feet.

Raven pitched face forward into the tall grass. The fall was so completely unexpected that he landed heavily on his stomach. The fall knocked the breath from his body and left him half-dazed. Raven heard sounds all around him, the cries of his people and the strange howls he'd heard earlier, only now right on top of them. Raven realized that he'd led his people straight into an ambush.

A guttural snarling came from directly behind him, and a scrabbling noise. As Raven scrambled to his feet, hands grabbed him from behind, sought his throat.

The taan's hands were powerful, his fingers strong. Seeing the purple and yellow stars that meant death burst in his eyes, Raven used what the Trevenici call the gods' own fear to find strength. Grabbing hold of his assailant's hands, he bent forward and flipped the creature over his head.

The move broke the taan's hold on him. Now the taan was the one lying on the ground, blinking up at the stars.

Gasping for breath, Raven fumbled for his sword. The taan regained his feet with speed and alacrity and Raven got his first good glimpse of the thing that had attacked him. The face was the face of a beast with a snout for a nose and rows of sharp teeth and the gleam of intelligence in its baleful eyes.

Raven drew his sword, fell back on the defensive, for he was still trying to catch his breath. A quick and agonized glance around him showed him the Trevenici were surrounded by hundreds of the taan. He could not look longer, for he dared not take his eyes off his attacker. The taan held his sword, but did not immediately attack. Instead, the creature pointed at Raven and, shouted something in his uncouth language.

Raven heard feet crashing through the grass behind him. He half-turned, ready to face this new enemy when he saw, out of the corner of his eye, his opponent hurl something at him. A net made of thick, heavy rope dropped over Raven's head and body, knocked the sword from his grasp. He fought to free himself, but the taan pulled the net tight around him, so tight that he could no longer move his arms. Raven continued to struggle ineffectually until the taan pulled his feet out from under him.

Taking hold of the end of the net, the taan dragged Raven through the grass like a cow going to slaughter.

Raven fought to free himself, but his struggles availed him nothing, except to annoy his captor. The taan halted, kicked Raven in the head.

The blow stunned Raven. The last thing he felt, before he lost consciousness, was the ground moving beneath him.

18

RAVEN DRIFTED IN AND OUT OF CONSCIOUSNESS, AWARE OF PAIN AND A
heavy weight around his neck. Bright orange light from a raging fire hurt
his eyes, voices that sounded excited made no sense. Every time he woke,
he tried to seize hold of consciousness and hang on to it, but the pain was
too great. He let slip his grasp and sank beneath the darkness.

Consciousness came with daylight and with it the hazy memory of
what had befallen him. He remained lying still with his eyes closed for
long moments, taking stock of his situation. First, his health. His head
hurt, but he was not sick to his stomach, nor, when he opened his eyes a
tiny bit, was his sight blurry. The kick had done little permanent damage,
seemingly. His body was a mass of bruises and welts, his skin rubbed raw
or missing altogether in places, a result of being dragged brutally over the
ground. Even the smallest movement caused him to wince in pain.

The heavy weight turned out to be an iron collar locked around his
neck. Opening his eyes another slit, he saw an iron chain running from the
collar to a stake driven into the ground. He reached out his hand, grunting at the pain caused by the movement, and grasped hold of the chain,
gave it a yank. The chain was secure, thick and strong.

Raven fell back, exhausted, eyes closed. Despair overwhelmed him. He
was a prisoner. The events of the previous night were a blur, but the one
thing he remembered clearly was the sound of the death cries of his people. Why, why, why had he not died with them? To be taken prisoner was
the worst disgrace that could befall a Trevenici. To their minds, a prisoner
of war was one who had not fought well enough or courageously enough.
Raven would be shamed, his family dishonored. Added to that, he had
failed in his duty to the tribe. Failure might have been forgiven him in
death, but he still lived. There was no excuse.

He could only hope that someone of the party had survived to carry the word to the Trevenici people that they were in danger. If any had survived, he hoped they had not seen him being hauled off like a deer carcass. Let them report his death. Better his tribe think him dead than a prisoner.

As for death, he trusted it would come to him soon. He had no care for his life anymore. He would not kill himself. To take by one's own hand the life the gods had given was the ultimate offense to the gods and would cause them to turn their faces from him. Raven would find solace in death, but he would die fighting and, the gods willing, he would take one or more of these creatures with him.

Raven had no thought of trying to escape. He must avenge his dishonor, though no one would ever know of it except himself and the gods. To do that, he must defeat the enemy who had bested him.

He sat up painfully and stiffly. The iron collar was heavy and chafed his skin and dug into his shoulder muscles. He grimaced at the thought of how much pain he would be in by nightfall. He would bear it, though, without a murmur. This was his punishment. He deserved no less.

Raven had been hauled back to a taan camp, where the taan were in a high state of excitement. A circle of tents formed an outside perimeter, inside which was a large open area. Another smaller circle of tents stood in the center. Fires burned and the smell of roasted meat filled the air, making Raven's mouth water. He could not remember when he'd last had a good meal.

Most of the taan appeared to be warriors, wearing armor and carrying weapons. Inside the circle, Raven could see taan who wore no armor. These tended the cook fires and what must be children, for there were younger and shorter versions of the creatures wandering about.

Raven wasn't the only prisoner. Other humans—both men and women—were held in a crude pen made up of spears driven into the ground in a circle. The prisoners were Dunkargans and they had been recently captured, to judge by their appearance. Horrible screams came from inside the tents of the monsters; other prisoners being tortured, most likely. Realizing what this meant, Raven shifted his gaze to the city walls that stood about a mile distant.

No sounds of battle came to him, borne across the prairie grass. The siege engines stood where they had been standing last night. Lines of soldiers could be seen marching into the city. The great iron gates stood wide open.

Dunkar had fallen.

Hearing shouts, Raven looked back. Most of the prisoners were women and girls, but there were a few men—most wearing the uniform of the Dunkargan army. One of the creatures, clad only in a loincloth, strode up to the spear-haft prison. He dragged behind him a human woman. Her face was bruised and battered, her clothing torn almost completely off. She was covered in blood and more dead than alive. Two of the taan stood guard over the prisoners. Looking at the woman, they made comments that caused her captor to grin. He shoved aside two spears and dumped the woman into the circle. Then he looked over the other terrified human women with the air of a man judging cattle.

Satisfied, he reached out his hand and seized hold of one—a girl of about sixteen. The girl cried out in terror and tried to pull away. A Dunkargan soldier caught hold of her and appeared to be pleading with the taan to let her go. The taan back-handed the soldier a brutal blow that felled him. Grabbing the struggling girl by her long black hair, the taan twisted her hair around his hand and hauled her off to his tent. Now Raven guessed who was screaming and why.

Some of the female prisoners seemed to be trying to help the injured woman, dressing her with what clothing they could spare and soothing her hurts. She was listless, seemed unaware that anything was being done to assist her. At the sight, the Dunkargan soldier snapped. Snatching a knife from his boot, he lunged through the circle of spears, intent on plunging the knife into the taan's back.

The taan guards were not in the least disturbed by this. They even paused a moment to exchange comments again, both of them snickering. Then, in a leisurely movement, one raised his spear and hurled it at the Dunkargan. The spear caught the man between his shoulder blades. He let out a cry and pitched forward onto the ground. The taan who had been his target glanced around without much interest and continued to walk back to his tent, which—Raven saw—stood in the inner circle.

Two of the taan who were not wearing armor hurried over to where the corpse lay. The two looked up questioningly at the guards and one of the taan motioned toward the cook fire. The two taan dragged away the corpse. Raven looked from the dead man to the meat roasting on the spit and he knew then what the creatures planned to do with the body. The smell of roasted meat that had set his mouth to watering now sent waves of nausea through him and he heaved and retched.

His retching sounds attracted attention. The taan guards glanced his direction—he was off to himself, staked out about six feet from the other prisoners. One of the guards gave a bellowing shout. A taan warrior inside the camp lifted his head, looked in Raven's direction.

The warrior motioned with his hand and said something to two of his fellows. All three came to stand in front of Raven. The taan looked down at him with their small, glistening eyes. Raven tensed, watched them warily, wondering what they planned to do to him. The warrior began to speak and, after a moment, Raven realized that the warrior was telling the tale of Raven's capture. The warrior told the story in words and in gestures, acting out what Raven had done, how he had flipped the taan warrior over on his back. The warrior did not appear to be embarrassed by this, but actually played up Raven's heroics.

Of course, the strength and cunning of his enemy made the taan warrior look good when he described how he had defeated Raven. He went through the motions of tossing a net over Raven's head. The two taan regarded their fellow with admiration, slapped him on the back and eyed Raven with undisguised envy.

Raven glared with fury at his captor, who appeared to take the glare as a tribute, for he looked inordinately pleased with himself as he walked away. Raven stared at the taan for as long as he could see him, taking care to memorize everything about him so that he could distinguish this one from all the others.

The taan warrior was about six and a half feet tall, with dark gray skin that was scarred and lumpy. At first, Raven thought the lumps were boils or welts, but, as he looked closely at the creature, Raven saw that the lumps were not natural. Some of them flashed or glittered as the sun caught them and Raven realized that the creature had shoved rocks underneath his flesh. The taan's hair was long and lank, the color of baked mud. He wore a breastplate made of metal with a symbol on it that Raven did not recognize. The taan had three teeth missing in the front of his mouth.

Raven kept the taan in sight as the warrior returned to camp. There, the taan spoke to another, smaller creature—one of those without armor— and gestured in Raven's direction. The smaller taan nodded quickly, cringing as if afraid a blow would follow. Snatching up a bowl, the smaller figure filled it with something from a bubbling pot and walked toward Raven.

The creature with the bowl came up to Raven and halted in front of him. He paid no attention at first. He was too busy watching his captor. But when his captor disappeared inside a tent, Raven shifted his gaze to the creature who now squatted near him, silent and patient as a dog waiting to be noticed.

Raven noted two things about this creature, noted them with shock. The first was that the creature was female. She wore only a loin cloth, her breasts were bare. The second was that although she had a nose similar to the snouts of the taan, her skin was smooth and brown. Her eyes and her mouth, her ears and the structure of her body were those of a human. Her age might have been around sixteen. She carried with her a crude bowl filled with a steaming liquid, and a bucket.

"Food?" she said to him, holding out the bowl.

He was surprised to hear her speak Elderspeak. He looked into the bowl, saw chunks of meat floating in broth. Almost gagging, he averted his head.

"Deer meat," she said, seeming to know what he was thinking. "Slaves like you are not given strong food to eat. Slaves eat weak food. Only the warriors eat strong food. Qu-tok would have eaten you"—she spoke hurriedly, as if fearing Raven might feel offended—"for you bested him in battle. But you are too valuable. Our god, Dagnarus, would be angry."

She set the bowl and the bucket on the ground within Raven's reach, taking care herself not to come near him.

"Water," she said, pointing to the bucket.

"Wait," said Raven. His head ached, his tongue felt thick and swollen. "Don't go."

The bucket was made of wood. He reached stiffly for the dipper, wincing at the pain. The girl stayed to watch him. Lifting the dipper, that was a hollowed-out gourd, he sniffed at the liquid, hesitantly tasted it. The water was tepid, but he noted no strange smell or flavor, other than that of the wooden bucket. He drank thankfully, gulping down huge draughts. When his thirst was slaked, the girl nudged the bowl of broth closer to him.

"My gods will be angry if I eat human flesh," he told her.

"I know," the girl said, nodding and squatting back down near him. "My mother told me this about humans, that they will not eat another of their own kind, no matter how strong the food is. The taan think this a sign of weakness and scorn humans for it. But our god says that this belief of humans must be honored and so the taan do as our god says. Besides, they would not feed you strong food anyway. You are a slave."

The broth certainly smelled like venison. Raven wasn't all that hungry after his bout of retching, but his body needed the food and he forced himself to take a sip. His hunger returned and he ate the entire meal. Between mouthfuls, he questioned the girl.

"What is your name?" he asked.

"Dur-zor," she answered. "You?"

"Ravenstrike."

"You are not like them." She glanced at the Dunkargans and back at Raven.

"No. I am Trevenici," he said. "There were more like me. More warriors. Do you know what happened to them? Are they prisoner somewhere else?"

Dur-zor considered, regarded him thoughtfully. "I am not sure, but I think that they are all dead. Qu-tok and the other warriors spoke of a good fight against worthy warriors, not whimpering dogs like these." She cast the Dunkargans a scathing glance. "Kroq said they slew a great many. Qu-tok was lucky to take such a strong prisoner."

Raven could not grieve for his people, who had died as warriors. He felt a brief flicker of hope that some had managed to escape, but the hope was snuffed out almost immediately, for no Trevenici would run in the face of the enemy.

"You call them taan," he said, speaking the word tentatively. "Is that what these creatures call themselves?"

"Yes, taan," she said.

"And you, Dur-zor?" He spoke the name haltingly. "You are not taan."

"I am half-taan," she returned.

"What is the other half?" he mumbled, chewing.

"Human," she replied.

Although his eyes had told him that already, he still could not believe it. He shook his head. "Elves and humans cannot breed. Dwarves and humans cannot breed. Snakes and humans cannot breed. These creatures and humans . . ." He cast the taan a look of loathing. "How is it possible?"

"I do not know how it is possible," the girl answered, shrugging. "I only know that it is so and has always been so. The taan say that long ago in their world of Iltshuzz-stan human slaves sometimes bore children that were neither taan nor human. In Iltshuzz-stan, half-taan children were slain, but here in this land our god forbids it. Such as me are valuable, he says, because we can speak the tongue of the humans and of the taan."

"The taan cannot speak human language?" Raven asked, thinking this information might be of use to him.

"No, although some of the taan shaman can understand it and write it." Dur-zor gestured to her face. "The mouth of the taan will not permit them to form the words of the humans and the throats of most humans cannot make the sounds of the taan. Elderspeak is the language of Dagnarus, our god, and also the language of many of the humans who fight for him. Thus there must be those of us who can carry the words of one group to the other and make ourselves understood."

A god who spoke Elderspeak. Raven mulled this over. He had never thought much about what the gods spoke. He supposed he had always assumed that gods had no need to speak. They could hear the words of the heart, the songs of the soul. They could make known their will through the whispers of the wind and the booming of the thunder. A god who was reduced to speaking with a human voice must not be much of a god, in Raven's opinion. He did not say such thoughts aloud, for he feared to offend this girl. He was glad to have found someone who could give him information.

"What will happen to me, Dur-zor?" he asked.

"You are to be given with the other valuable slaves to our god. In exchange for you, our god will give Qu-tok many wonderful gifts that will raise him in the eyes of the tribe. That is why you will not be killed. Not yet, anyhow." She said the last off-handedly.

"When will this occur?" Raven demanded, fearing that it might happen at any moment, before he could have a chance to avenge himself.

"Whenever our shaman deems that we celebrate a god day. On such a day, we pay homage to our god and, if we are fortunate, he walks among us. At that time, Qu-tok will present you to our god."

"When will this god day happen? Soon?" Raven persisted.

The girl shrugged. "Maybe soon. Maybe late. We do not know. That is up to the shaman."

Raven breathed a bit easier. He had time, apparently. "What of the others?" He glanced toward the circle of spears and the Dunkargans imprisoned within. The ravished girl lay with her head in another woman's lap, sobbing harshly.

"The females will be used as slaves around the camp and they will bear more half-taan, for that pleases our god. The men will be used for sport and, if they die well, the taan will honor them by eating their flesh. If they die poorly, their bodies will be fed to the dogs."

Raven thought this over. "Your mother, Dur-zor? What happened to her? Is she still alive?"

"No, but she lived longer than most." The girl spoke with pride. "She was strong and bore many half-taan, when most females die after the first. She was slain when I was eight for not speaking respectfully to a warrior. He crushed her skull."

A voice from the camp shouted something unintelligible. Dur-zor glanced back. A spasm of fear crossed her face, as she twisted to her feet. Without a word to Raven, she raced away. When she reached camp, she abased herself before one of the taan warriors, cringing and shrinking. Raven recognized the warrior as Qu-tok, the one who had taken him prisoner. Qu-tok cuffed the girl across the face, apparently for not responding to him quickly enough. She took the blow without a whimper, accepted it as her due.

Qu-tok jerked a thumb in Raven's direction. Whatever the girl answered, Qu-tok appeared satisfied, for he looked at Raven and smirked, lips parting in a tooth-filled grin. Qu-tok walked off, returned to his tent. Raven lost sight of the girl in the crowd of taan and half-taan. He had noticed, as she left, the scars of lash marks on her back.

One of the Dunkargan soldiers began shouting something at Raven, but the Trevenici paid the soldier no heed. Raven could do nothing to help them. He was sorry for them, but they were on their own. He lay down on the ground, squirming to find a comfortable position, which was not easy with the iron collar around his neck.

His belly was full and his thirst slaked. Now he needed rest. He had one goal in mind and that was to kill this Qu-tok, the taan who had brought this disgrace upon him. To accomplish that, Raven had to survive and that was what he was now putting his mind to—survival.

Raven was under no illusions. He had seen enough of the taan to guess that if he killed a warrior, his own death would follow and it wasn't likely to be an easy one. Once Qu-tok was dead, Raven would be content to die, ready to die. He only hoped that, if the taan ate him, they would get a raging belly-ache.

19

SHAKUR'S ORDERS WERE TO FIND THE VILLAGE FROM WHICH THE TREVENICI came, hopefully to find some clue about the Sovereign Stone. He had headed northward toward Trevenici lands immediately after leaving Dunkar. He had hoped to arrive before the mercenaries he had sent, or at least at about the same time, but two weeks had passed and he was still not anywhere near the village.

The fault was not Shakur's. He had dispatched the mercenaries, under the leadership of Captain Grisgel, northward within a few hours of his meeting with Dagnarus. Shakur provided Grisgel with what information the drugged Trevenici had given in regard to the village's location. The village was within a couple day's walk of Wild Town and there was a lake nearby. Not an ordinary lake, a lake concealing one of the magical Portals. Given that information and the fact that the bahk accompanying the mercenaries would be drawn to the magic of the Portal, the village should not be hard to find.

Grisgel and his trained bahk worked as a team. He'd been a highly successful highwayman until Shakur had run across him five years earlier. Shakur convinced Grisgel that he could provide him with a more secure way of life than robbing caravans. Grisgel and his bahk had undertaken several important jobs for Shakur and had more than fulfilled the Vrykyl's expectations. Shakur's last orders on this occasion had been emphatic.

"Do not kill all the inhabitants. Save several for me to question, preferably tribal elders."

Grisgel had promised he would do as ordered and he and his hand-picked squad of sell-swords had departed Dunkar just as the forces of Dagnarus were approaching the city. Grisgel carried a safe-conduct pass, but there was always the possibility that someone might shoot an arrow first and read his pass later, so he and his squad went out of their way to the east to avoid running into Dagnarus's army. Grisgel had told Shakur he expected to reach the Trevenici lands within twenty days' time.

Shakur had anticipated following shortly afterward. He had to make certain King Moross was suitably impressed, terrified and confused at the sight of Dagnarus's army and he had to lay the groundwork for his leaving the Temple, provide a plausible reason. There was not much possibility that he would ever be returning to Dunkar, but Shakur had learned over his brief lifetime and his longer death time that it was prudent not to burn your bridges behind you. He had given orders for the murder of Onaset, as being the one man in Dunkar who might conceivably be able to thwart the downfall of the city, and he had given Lessereti and her Void wizards their instructions on how to betray the city. This done, he had departed.

Although Shakur had gotten off to a late start, he could have still arrived at the camp well ahead of the mercenaries, who were human and therefore subject to the weakness of the flesh. The Vrykyl have no flesh, thus they have no need for rest. They can travel day and night without stop, hampered only by the mortality of their horses. The Vrykyl must first find a horse that will carry him, which is no small feat, for animals can sense the taint of Void and will flee as quickly as possible. A Vrykyl must exert his dominance over the horse and then cast a spell that will turn the animal into a shadow steed. The shadow steeds proved inadequate for Shakur's needs. He required a living horse, a trained war-horse. The shadow steeds were mere beasts of burden. He had developed the means to overcome the problem.

With the help of the powerful Void shamans of the taan, Shakur had created a caparison imbued with Void magic. He had only to fling the caparison over the horse and the animal would instantly obey the Vrykyl. In addition, the caparison would actually increase the beast's stamina and extend its period of usefulness, so that Shakur could ride for days before the beast foundered.

The only drawback was that the caparison always killed the horse, so Shakur had to take care to have another mount available when the one he was riding collapsed. Either that, or he must rest his horse, for with rest it could regain its strength. His horse would continue to survive until the caparison was removed, at which point it would die.

The caparison was beautiful to look at. Woven of silk by half-taan slaves, the caparison was red with golden trim around the edges that were cut to resemble flames.

Shakur made good time the first two weeks, covering far more territory than Grisgel's force could have in the same time span. But then Shakur arrived in the disputed no man's land north of Dunkarga and slowed his pace, for he was not likely to be able to find another horse in this unpopulated area. He was forced to halt to rest his mount. He hated the night, hated the long, boring hours when he could do nothing but pace back and forth beneath the trees, listening to the breathing of the sleeping animal, tormented by thoughts of the restful slumber Shakur had not known in over two hundred years.

This night, Shakur was further tormented by hunger pangs. This angered him. The need to feed would further slow his journey. Worse than the pain of the pangs of hunger were the pangs of fear. Dagnarus had promised Shakur that, as a Vrykyl, he would live forever. He would, only not as he expected.

Shakur noted that his strength waned more quickly. What remained of his corpse had started to deteriorate more rapidly. He was forced to feed more and more often to sustain the death that was his life. If he did not feed, and soon, he feared his power would wane to the point where he lacked the strength to feed and then he would sink into the Void, sink into nothingness, where he would know eternal hunger. For—or so he had come to realize—he would never truly die. When his body perished, his soul would live on in torment and he would have no way to feed it. And now here he was, in the middle of a deserted region, with the terrible hunger on him and not so much as a lonely farm house anywhere near.

The next morning, Shakur rode on. He had a bitter choice to make. He could ride swiftly and hope to reach the Trevenici camp before his strength waned. Once there, he could feed at his leisure. The camp was still days away, however, and the hunger pangs were growing more intense with each passing moment. If he rode slowly, he could search the plains for signs of life, a Karnuan patrol, perhaps, or a Trevenici hunting party.

Shakur was yet in the thralls of his dilemma when a thrill warmed his dead flesh. Somewhere another Vrykyl had taken a life. He felt the pleasure of drinking a soul through the bone knife. Whenever any Vrykyl uses the blood knife to kill and feed, all other Vrykyl feel and revel in the sensation. For an instant, all are bound together in a gruesome bond.

Shakur's delight changed to wonder and then exultation, for in that moment of pleasure he saw in his mind the image of Svetlana. Shakur saw her face clearly, as he had seen it the day the Dagger of the Vrykyl found her a suitable candidate and claimed her life.

Yet, Svetlana was gone to the Void. She was not the one using the blood knife, the knife she had made of her own bone.

Someone had found it. Someone had just used that knife to take life. Shakur reached out with his Void essence to gain an image of the person using Svetlana's knife. But he was slow to react. The sensation faded too quickly and he lost the image.

Halting his horse, Shakur considered the ramifications of this occurrence, what it meant to him and to his search for the Sovereign Stone.

Shakur could not sense the Sovereign Stone. He had never seen it or touched it. But he could sense the blood knife.

And now Shakur had a way to track the thief who had stolen the knife from Svetlana. The next time the blood knife was used, Shakur would be ready to seize hold of it. Through the power of the Void, he would reestablish a connection with Svetlana's knife. Once that happened, he would be able to enter the dreams of the person bearing the knife.

Dreams—the stuff of shadow, the perfect tool for a wielder of Void magic. One had to know how to sift through dreams, how to crack the shell of ever-shifting images and the wild illogic to find the kernel of truth that lay at the dream's heart. Once inside the dream, Shakur would come to know a great deal about the bearer of the knife. If the bearer had nothing to do with the Stone, Shakur would find that out and stop wasting his time in pursuit. If, on the other hand, the bearer proved to be a Trevenici who had something to do with a dead Dominion Lord, then Shakur would follow him to the ends of Loerem.

Shakur's hunger returned, but he no longer had to choose what to do. He could slow his pace, assuage his hunger, for it was not now critical that he reach the Trevenici village. He had only to wait for the bearer of the blood knife to use it again.

Shakur slowed his horse's mad gallop and proceeded at a less reckless pace. His patience was rewarded. Shakur came across hoof-prints. The horses were shod with iron shoes and he recognized a Karnuan patrol. The prints were fresh. The patrol was not far away. Shakur relaxed, pleased. Not only would he have a chance to feed, but he would find a fresh horse, as well.

The next morning, when the members of the Karnuan patrol woke with the dawn, they found one of their number had been murdered during the night. They were astonished, for they had heard nothing. Yet the man was dead of a single stab wound. The blade had pierced his heart, leaving only a small hole and little blood. He must have died instantly. He had seen his death coming, for his face was so contorted by terror that his fellows could not recognize the well-known features of their comrade in the twisted features of the corpse. Such was the fear this silent attack engendered among them that the Karnuans buried the man in haste and did not mark his grave. They rode all day and well into the night, fearful of halting. It would be many, many nights before any of them could sleep again.

Having fed well and taken on the illusion of the Karnuan soldier, Shakur passed through Wild Town. In the guise of the Karnuan soldier, he discovered that a mercenary band of soldiers had been here two days previous. A dealer in potions pointed out to Shakur the road they had taken. He followed the road, found the tracks where the band had turned off the trail. The bahk's enormous feet left behind clear imprints.

Shakur followed the tracks to the lake. He paused a moment, staring intently into the water, trying to see some sign of the Portal that lay beneath. He could see nothing, and might have doubted it, but that he could tell by the footprints on the bank that the bahk had entered the water, drawn to the magic within.

It was then Shakur saw the smoke.

Several gray-black tendrils spiraled up into the still summer air. Too much smoke for a cook fire. Shakur marked this as the smoke of destruction, the smoke of death.

Shakur spurred his horse forward and rode into the Trevenici camp at a gallop.

He reined in his horse sharply and looked around. Everything was as it should be, or so he thought at first. All the wooden hovels the barbarians called home had been destroyed. Here and there, a few still smoldered, creating the smoke. Most were burned out husks and charred thatch.

The village was empty. There was no one about.

"Grisgel?" Shakur shouted, rising up in the saddle to get a better look. "The Void take you, man! Where have you got to?"

No one answered. A breath of wind stirred, caused the smoke to drift through the empty village. Shakur turned his horse so that he could see in all directions. Nothing moved in that village except the smoke. He heard nothing, no sound at all.

Baffled, Shakur rode into the village. He looked left and he looked right and saw nothing. Then he came to a circle of white stones. Shakur halted, stared. Living and dead, he had been in this world almost two hundred and fifty years and he'd never seen a sight like this.

Shakur had found Captain Grisgel. He had found Grisgel's men and he had found the bahk. All dead.

Grisgel's body lay on the ground. The Trevenici had tied down his arms and legs, then driven a stake into his gut and left him to die. He'd been a long time at it, by the looks of it. His men lay around him, some with their throats cut, others with arrows through their eyeballs. In the very center of the circle, the head of the bahk stood mounted on a pole. The bahk's headless corpse was a bloody mass of wounds. Blood covered the ground, had splashed onto the stones.

The battle had been hard-fought. Many Trevenici must have died, but there was no sign of their bodies. There was no sign, either, of the pecwae, those strange beings who lived in proximity with the Trevenici. Shakur rode into the pecwae camp and found it deserted, as well.

The Trevenici had defeated Grisgel and his men and the bahk. Then the Trevenici had torched their homes, destroyed their village and fled, taking the pecwae with them. First, though, the Trevenici must have buried the bodies of their dead.

At least, thought Shakur, all may not be lost.

Familiar with the ways of the Trevenici, Shakur searched until he found the burial mound. As he had hoped and expected, the earth that sealed up the entrance was fresh packed. Shakur was not interested in the bodies of the Trevenici. Unless Shakur was very much mistaken, inside the burial mound he would find the body of the knight who had been the bearer of the Sovereign Stone. And while Shakur knew better than to think that he would find the Stone hanging about the corpse's neck, he did hope to discover who had the Stone and where it had been sent.

By the power of the Void, Shakur had the ability to raise the dead. He could not restore life to the dead, but he could animate a corpse, drag back the soul that had already traveled onward, be that soul with the gods or in the Void. Shakur was somewhat concerned about how effective such a spell might be. Generally the Void wizard who cast this must do so on a corpse that has not been dead over one or two days, whereas this knight must have been dead for weeks. No Void wizard and no other Vrykyl possessed the immense power of Shakur. He would wrestle with the gods themselves to seize this knight's soul.

Shakur approached the burial mound. He prepared to start digging.

A violent tremor shook the ground beneath the Vrykyl's feet. Shakur tried to remain standing, but the ground rocked and heaved and he lost his footing. The quake lasted for a good minute. At length, the tremors ceased. Shakur regained his feet and looked darkly at the burial mound.

Coincidence? Perhaps.

Shakur walked forward, placed his hand again on the mound—or tried to.

The quake was far more violent this time. The earth cracked open at his feet. Only a hasty backward leap saved him from plummeting into a chasm. The ground rolled and rippled beneath him. Shakur knew when he was beaten.

Shakur eyed the mound grimly. The chasm was wide and it was deep, yet the mound itself had not been harmed. Not a single clod of dirt had been dislodged. Shakur took the hint. He left the Trevenici and the knight to their rest. He hoped they were all eaten by rats.

Shakur returned to his horse. The beast was wild-eyed and terrified, but Shakur ignored it. What was he to do now? His search had come, quite literally, to a dead end. Shakur was thankful that his lord was busy with the occupation of Dunkar and the pursuit of his war. Dagnarus would think of Shakur eventually, however, for the Sovereign Stone was never far from his lord's mind. And when he did, Shakur would have no choice but to admit the truth, that he had failed.

Dagnarus did not take kindly to failure.

Then the person in possession of Svetlana's knife, the blood knife, used it.

Shakur was waiting. Suffused with the power of Void, Shakur reached mentally across the Void and laid firm hold on the hand whose fingers were wrapped around the hilt of the blood knife. For a fleeting instant, Shakur saw the person who wielded the knife. He saw a Trevenici youth use the blood knife to slit the throat of a rabbit.

The link established, Shakur kept tight hold so that he could invade the youth's slumbers. The memory of the Trevenici's face burned in his mind.

A great distance lay between them, hundreds of miles. Shakur could travel day and night, whereas the youth must rest. Shakur would easily close the gap.

He stood so long in thought that darkness crept over him and he did not notice. Shakur remounted his horse and started out on his journey, the face of the youth hanging before him. He would follow that face as orken sailors followed the star that shines in the north, the star they called the guiding star.

The Sovereign Stone travels north, Dagnarus said. *It travels north and it travels south.*

Shakur turned his horse's head north.

20

THE SOVEREIGN STONE IN ITS MAGICAL KNAPSACK, HELD BY THE PECWAE, traveled north. And so did the blood knife.

The bearer of sad news and a love token, Bashae had a solemn responsibility, but he did not let that stand in the way of enjoying the trip. Every day brought a wonderful new experience, new sights, new sounds. Whatever the day brought, Bashae never failed to thank the gods for it when he went to his rest, adding his prayers to the muttered prayers of the Grandmother, as he fell asleep to the clicking of her stones.

Jessan enjoyed himself, too, although not in the light-hearted manner of his friend. Jessan was always conscious of the burden of responsibility he carried, responsibility for the safety of the two pecwae, responsibility for the successful conclusion of the journey and the safe delivery of the token. He was the guide. He determined their course each day. He decided how far they should travel and when they could rest. He selected the night's camp site.

At the start of their journey, he wanted to set a watch, for evil beasts roamed the forests and sometimes evil men, both of whom preyed on the hapless traveler, alone in the wilderness. Bashae offered to split the night duties with Jessan.

The very first night, Bashae had every good intention of remaining awake and alert, but the hours of darkness are the time to visit the sleep-world. Jessan woke to find his friend curled up in a ball like a dormouse, slumbering soundly. Since Jessan could not stay awake all night and paddle the boat all the next day, he reluctantly abandoned the idea of setting a watch, adding that he thought it quite likely their throats would be cut while they slept.

"Bah!" the Grandmother stated. "What good is setting a watch anyway? Mortal eyes are blinded by the darkness and see too little. Mortal ears are open to every little sound and hear too much. The stick"—she pointed to the walking cane with the agate eyes—"sees no evil anywhere around us. You can trust the stick."

Jessan looked dubious.

"Very well," the Grandmother added, put out, "if it will make you sleep soundly in the night and not keep waking me up with your prowling about, I will insure that no one will disturb us."

That night, after they cooked their meal of fish, they laid out their blankets close together. The Grandmother insisted that they sleep near each other, in an open area. As Jessan watched, the Grandmother walked a circle around the blankets, muttering to herself and depositing, at fixed intervals, a turquoise stone.

"Twenty-seven stones," she said. "A circle of protection through which nothing with evil intent can pass."

Mindful of his uncle's decree that Jessan must treat the Grandmother with respect, he dutifully held his tongue each night after that, while the Grandmother went through her muttering and stone planting and he slept without a murmur inside the circle she created. But he slept with one eye and one ear open, as the saying went.

Whether it was the stones or Jessan's watchfulness or the Grandmother's mutterings, something worked, for during the weeks they traveled in their boat down the Big Blue river, they were not harmed by beast nor man.

The Big Blue river was narrow and swift flowing with occasional dangerous rapids. Whenever they came to a place where the water frothed and bubbled and crashed, they were forced to haul the boat out of the water and portage overland until they passed the raging water and could once more resume their journey. The Trevenici build boats that are lightweight and easy to carry—for two Trevenici. Hauling the boat out of the water and overland for sometimes several miles proved more of a challenge for one Trevenici and one pecwae.

Jessan took the prow and Bashae the stern. The pecwae didn't have the strength in his arms to lift the boat over his head and so he was forced to hoist the overturned boat on his rounded back. The first time Bashae tried this, he took five steps and then collapsed beneath the boat's weight.

"At this rate," Jessan said, extricating his friend from under the boat, "we will reach the elven lands when I am so old that I will be tripping over my beard. What are we going to do?"

The Grandmother began to sing.

She sang of thistles and cottonweed floating in the wind, of spider's webs and duck feathers and corn silks. As she sang, she ran her gnarled hand over the smooth planed wood that covered the boat and suddenly the boat was light enough that Bashae might have carried it all by himself and gone running away with it. After that, the trip down the Big Blue river was peaceful, idyllic. Every time they came to a portage, the Grandmother sang the boat up onto their shoulders.

More than once, as he walked along the portage path made by many feet over the hundreds of years his people had been navigating the Big Blue river, Jessan recalled how irate he had been when he'd first heard the Grandmother had decided to come with them. He had feared she would be a drag on them, a burden slowing them down. He had learned a valuable lesson. He was unfailingly respectful to the Grandmother after that and even helped her gather up her twenty-seven turquoise stones in the morning. If the Grandmother noticed this change and smiled, she was wise enough to smile her smile when Jessan had his back turned.

The Big Blue river flowed beneath thickly wooded banks. Tree limbs overhung the water that was dappled with patches of darkness and bright sunlight. Weeping willows clung to the shore. Bashae felt the delicate leaves brush his upturned face as the boat glided beneath them. Thanks to the fast flowing river and the Grandmother's assistance with the portage, this first part of their journey was the easy part.

Once they left the Big Blue river, they would have to travel north up the Sea of Redesh. Their going would be slower for they would not have the current to help them. And so Jessan decreed (much to his private regret) that they did not have time to waste to make a detour to Vilda Harn, the town the Trevenici claim as theirs.

Bashae might have tried to wheedle Jessan into changing his mind, but the pecwae was excited to see the Sea of Redesh for, he had been told, it was such a large body of water that it extended clear to the horizon. Jessan thought they were near the sea (that wasn't really a sea at all, but a large lake), although he had no way of knowing for certain. Raven had estimated that it would take them twenty days to travel down the Big Blue river. They were coming up on their twentieth sunrise.

"According to my uncle, before we enter the Sea of Redesh, we will pass between the Lovers—two enormous rock formations, many times bigger than a man, that stand one on either side of the Big Blue river," Jessan said that morning, as they took their places in the boat.

He sat at the rear, propelling the boat forward with strong, untiring strokes. The Grandmother sat in the center, saying little to the young men, but often murmuring or humming softly to herself. Sometimes she would hoist the stick with the agate eyes high into the air, turning it this way and that, giving each eye a chance to see. Satisfied, she would rest the stick carefully in the bottom of the boat. Bashae sat at the prow, sometimes helping to paddle if the current was very strong, but more often casting out a line and hook, baited with bread dough, to catch trout that he would wrap in leaves and cook on heated rocks.

The twelfth day, the Grandmother lifted the seeing stick up into the air and, after a moment, announced, "We are close. Very close. Around the next bend."

Jessan made a face. He knew better than to scorn pecwae magic, but he also knew with all the certainty of eighteen years that a stick was a stick and agates were rocks. He also guessed that they were close to the mouth of the river, but not because any agate eyeball told him. He could tell by signs the river was giving him—eddies and currents flowing in odd directions, strands of water that were a different color, the gradual widening of the banks.

Around the next bend, the Lovers came into view. The Grandmother snorted with satisfaction. Jessan smiled and shook his head and told the wildly excited Bashae to sit down or he was going to overturn the boat.

The two strange rock formations leaned toward each other, but did not touch, although they came close. The Trevenici had woven a legend around them, that they were two lovers from warring tribes who had been barred by sensible parents from having anything to do with each other. The lovers had disobeyed their parents and met on the river bank. Because of their disobedience to their parents, they had been turned to rock and made to stand here as a warning to rebellious children.

Bashae gazed up, open-mouthed in awe and wonder, as the boat slid beneath the towering rocks that leaned at a perilous angle and looked as if they might topple at any moment and crush those who sailed beneath. A gap of no more than five feet separated the rocks that were sheer, smooth-sided, with nary a hand- or foothold to be seen.

"My uncle says that whenever a group of our people travel this river, they halt their journey so that every warrior can test his courage by climbing the rock formation, then leaping across that gap," said Jessan.

After they shot past the rocks, Jessan headed immediately for shore, for Ravenstrike had warned him that once they passed between the Lovers, they must make landfall, for farther downstream the river tumbled over a small spillway. This would be their last portage and it would be the longest, about five miles. At the end, they would put the boat in the water of the Sea of Redesh.

Climbing out of the boat, the Grandmother hoisted the stick into the air to have a look around. Jessan hauled the boat up onto the bank, while Bashae went to talk to a group of deer who had come to the water's edge. Both the deer and the stick reported that no one had been in these parts in recent days. Jessan could tell the same from the lack of tracks in the damp mud along this popular portage site. Glancing at the sun, he concluded that they had plenty of daylight left. They could travel a couple of miles and camp closer to the Sea. The Grandmother sang her song. They hoisted the boat onto their shoulders and started off.

That day was the first day of the journey that Bashae had not had a chance to catch fish. When they made camp that night, the Grandmother cooked up a stew of wild onions and garlic with some sort of green leaves tossed in. She and Bashae were content to eat the resulting green sodden mass, but Jessan had worked hard that day and felt the need for meat. He went off to hunt.

He saw several squirrels, but they were too quick for him. Taking to the trees, they chattered at him in irritation and threw nut shells on his head. Padding soft-footed, he came upon a young rabbit feeding on some dandelion leaves. Jessan came quite close, before the rabbit heard him. Jessan pounced. The rabbit bolted and would have got away, but that it ran straight into a tangle of brambles.

Jessan caught the rabbit. Drawing the bone knife, he quickly ended its terror and its struggles by slitting its throat. The rabbit's warm blood flowed over the knife. Far away, the Vrykyl Shakur tasted the blood and saw an image in his mind.

Jessan had not used the bone knife up to this point; there had been no need. He was impressed to find how sharp it was, how cleanly it cut. Jessan dressed the rabbit, cooked it and ate it out of sight of their camp. He told himself he did this because he did not want to offend the pecwae by eating meat in front of them. This was only an excuse. The pecwae were used to the meat-eating habits of the Trevenici and with the pecwae's casual "live and let live" attitude toward life, neither would have been at all upset.

In truth, Jessan was loath to use the bone knife around the two pecwae, particularly the Grandmother. He cleaned the knife in a nearby stream and returned to camp just as the Grandmother was placing her twenty-seven stones around the campsite. She asked if he had eaten well and said that they had saved him some boiled greens, if he wanted some.

Jessan politely declined. They spread out their bedrolls in the protective circle and went to sleep.

Eyes were looking for him. Terrible eyes. Eyes of fire in a head of darkness. The eyes had been looking in another direction, but now they turned toward him. Jessan was afraid for the eyes to see him. He cowered in a bush, the body of a freshly killed rabbit in his hand, the blood pulsing warm from the rabbit. The eyes had almost found him . . .

Jessan woke with a start. Jumping to his feet, he looked around the campsite and beyond, into the woods, out to the river, to the dark water flowing past, murmuring quietly to itself. He listened and sniffed the air, but he sensed nothing unusual, nothing out of the ordinary.

Close by, Bashae and the Grandmother both slept. Bashae's sleep was deep and calm. The Grandmother was restless, however, tossing and crying out. Her hand reached for the stick with the agates, touched it. She seemed reassured when she found it, for she sighed and ceased to talk.

Jessan looked sharply at the agate stick. Lit by the lambent light of the stars and a pale, thin moon, the agates shone white, like eyes that are wide open. Perhaps it was these blasted agates that had caused the strange and disquieting dream.

Jessan lay back down on his blanket.

"Superstitious old woman," he said to himself grumpily.

Jessan rarely woke in the night and, when he did, he could always return to sleep easily. This night, however, he lay awake, staring at the stars until the gray light of dawn caused the stars' light to diminish.

They made a late start the next morning, due to the fact that Jessan slept past dawn. Bashae had to wake him to come to breakfast. This delighted the pecwae, for usually it was Jessan who was tossing water on Bashae's face, not the other way around.

Jessan woke in a bad mood. He did not see the joke. Scowling at Bashae, Jessan told him churlishly to act his age. He bade a cheerless good morning to the Grandmother, ate his food swiftly without seeming to taste it and fidgeted impatiently as she gathered up the turquoise protection stones. When she raised the sight stick into the air for the agate eyes to have a look at the morning, Jessan muttered something about seeing to the boat and stalked out of camp.

"What's wrong with him?" Bashae wondered, staring at Jessan's back. He went over to shake out Jessan's blanket, that he had forgotten. "Maybe he slept on ant hill."

The Grandmother said nothing. She stood staring at the sight stick, turning it this way and that, holding the stick in the air longer than usual. When she did finally lower the stick, she glanced, frowning, after Jessan.

"What is it, Grandmother?" Bashae asked, neatly rolling Jessan's blanket. "What do you see?"

She shook her head. The Grandmother helped Bashae break camp, but she was preoccupied, thoughtful and refused to heed Bashae's repeated questions. She told him sharply to cease pestering her.

Admiring the beauty of the sunlight glistening on the water, Jessan took himself to task for punishing his companions for his own sleepless night. When they came to meet him, he made an extra effort at good humor, his way of apologizing.

"A half-day's walk should bring us to a place where we can safely put the boat in the lake," he said cheerfully. "We should make good time. There is a trail. If you will sing the boat, Grandmother—"

"Evil walked close to our camp last night," the Grandmother stated abruptly.

Jessan's good mood vanished, shredded like the morning mists. He stared at her in shock, in sudden dry-mouthed silence, not knowing what to say.

"It passed by us," she continued, waving her hand to illustrate its passing. "But it was there."

Jessan opened his mouth, closed it again, moistened his lips. "I thought I heard something. I got up in the night but I couldn't see anything."

The Grandmother stared at him, as if she would sift his soul. Her gaze made him uncomfortable.

"At least, it's gone now," he said with a shrug and an attempt at nonchalance. He shifted his head, shaded his eyes with his hand to look up the trail.

"Yes," said the Grandmother. "It is gone. For now."

"What was it, do you think, Grandmother?" Bashae asked with interest. "A bear going to kill us? Wolves?"

"The bear and the wolf are not evil," the Grandmother returned in rebuking tones. "When they kill, they do so out of fear or out of hunger. Only man kills out of the darkness of his heart."

"No one tried to kill us last night," Jessan said impatiently, thinking this had gone far enough.

Snatching his bedroll from Bashae without so much as a thank you, Jessan slung the rope that held it together over one shoulder. "I looked for tracks this morning. There aren't any, as you can see for yourself."

"I did not say the evil walked with feet," the Grandmother retorted with dignity.

She began to sing in her high-pitched, reedy voice. After another long look at her, Jessan turned and lifted up his end of the boat.

"Well?" he demanded of Bashae. "Are you just going to stand there?"

Bashae looked from one grim face to the other. Tying on his own bedroll, he slung the knapsack over his shoulder and hoisted up his end of the boat. They set out along a trail that had been here for centuries. The Grandmother followed along behind, the stones that decorated her skirts clicking, the silver bells ringing, the stewpot that rode in a notch on the top of the sight stick clinking.

"His bed must have been crawling with ants last night," Bashae said, but he took care to say it to himself.

Sunshine and fresh air and exercise drove away the dream's horrors. Jessan relaxed and, after a few miles, began to sing a walking song. Bashae joined in the singing good-naturedly; pecwae dislike confrontation and are always quick to forgive and forget. The Grandmother kept silent, but she appeared to approve of the song, for she altered the rhythm of her walk to make the silver bells jingle in time to the steady beat.

Reaching the spillway, they halted to watch in silent awe the rush of water flowing over rocks that had long ago been worn smooth. This was not a fall, not a cascade. The water did not have far to drop and flowed in almost silence, with only a bubbling churning at the bottom. The water was clear. They could see the rocks through it, even see fish plunge over the spillway, presumably taking no harm, for there were fish in the water below, calmly swimming away.

Jessan said that his uncle had told him that during one part of the year, the fish actually swam upstream, leaping out of the water and flying up and over the spillway. Bashae smiled politely. Pleased that Jessan's good mood had returned, the pecwae said nothing to refute such an outrageous lie. He and Jessan lifted up the boat and they continued on, their pace quickening for now they were nearing the end of the first stage of their journey.

The sight of the Sea of Redesh was one that none of them would ever forget. They walked up a rise, looked out to the east and there it was. Blue water stretching to the sky, as far as the eye could see.

The Grandmother stood so still that nothing clinked or rang or rattled. She made no sound at all.

Bashae exhaled a long, tremulous sigh.

Jessan nodded and said softly, to himself, "Yes, so my uncle told me it would be."

They could have stood staring all day, but the launch site was still a ways distant, for Ravenstrike had warned them not to launch at the point where the water of the river and lake joined, for there the currents and eddies were wild and dangerous. They would put the boat in the calmer water farther down the shore.

They reached the place near midafternoon. The launch site was evidently popular, for a permanent camp had been built here. A stone ring could accommodate a fire and there were charred logs and a woodpile to testify to its use. The sandy beach was churned by the imprint of innumerable feet. White birds perched on a refuse pile, quarreling and squabbling over bones. Jessan said they were sea birds, who had flown all the way from the distant ocean.

Bashae had never seen birds of this sort and, after he had dropped his share of the boat by the water's edge, he ran over to talk to them. The birds were arrogant, however, disdainful of those who were land-bound, and told him rudely to go about his business. Disturbed in their meal, they flew away, showing off their graceful skill in flight by wheeling and diving above the water. To Bashae's awe, the birds landed on the water, settling down with folded wings to float upon the rippling waves.

He longed to join them, longed to put the boat into the lake and sail away that very moment, but Jessan decreed that they had best get a good night's rest and start fresh on the morrow. Sailing on the lake would not be as easy as sailing on the river, for the currents would not help them. Bashae gave in, reluctantly, but cheered up when Jessan suggested that they go for a swim.

Bashae caught several fish, standing quite still in the water as they came up to investigate him and nibble at his toes. Quick as lightning, his hands darted down and snagged them. He tied them to a string and left them in the water, to stay fresh. Tired and starting to chill, he and Jessan came out of the lake to lie on the warm sand and dry off in the sun. The Grandmother had set up camp, then gone off into the woods to replenish her herbs.

Bashae built a fire, keeping track of the wood he used, for Jessan said that by custom, all who camped here must replace whatever they took for the next traveler. Ordinarily Bashae cleaned the fish, but this evening Jessan took on that task, using the bone knife to gut fish and scrape off the scales. He washed the blood from the knife in the lake and had it safely back in its sheath before the Grandmother returned.

All were tired and went to their rest shortly after dinner. Jessan noted that the Grandmother took extra care in placing the turquoise stones and that brought back unwelcome memories of the dream, memories that had been banished by sunlight. Bashae went to sleep immediately, for that would hasten the coming of the morrow. The Grandmother was soon snoring contently. Jessan was bone tired. Sleep came, but it came slowly, and it was troubled.

That night, the eyes of fire found him. They fixed their terrible gaze on him, stared straight at him. Try as he might, he could not escape them.

And it was then he began to hear the hoofbeats. Far away, but moving steadily nearer.

21

WHILE THE SOVEREIGN STONE WENT NORTH, THE SILVER CASE THAT HAD held it traveled south and east. Wolfram and Ranessa had been on the road for nearly a month and were crossing the plains east of the Abul Da-nek mountains. They made good time, for now they both rode horses. After several days of riding pillion, Wolfram could take it no longer. Passing through Vilda Harn, he'd purchased his own mount—a short, stocky, shaggy-maned horse whose ancestors had undoubtedly once roamed the prairies of the dwarven homeland.

Dwarven-bred horses are expensive, for all in Loerem recognize their worth, and the beast cost Wolfram dear. But he was a landed nobleman now. He felt he could afford it. Having his own horse would speed their journey and he could not reach the monks fast enough, for there he would not only deliver the knight's message and gain his reward, but he would get rid of this crazy Trevenici.

The first week of their trip, she said never a word to him. She talked, but only to herself. Whenever he tried to join in the conversation—for Wolfram was a genial, social soul—she glared at him through the tangled mass of black hair and told him to hold his tongue or she would cut it out.

Firmly believing that she was capable of carrying out her threat, Wolfram used his tongue instead to curse the monks who had urged him to make this fiendish female his companion. He could have refused the burning pressure of the bracelet and he wondered repeatedly as the days passed why he had not. Curse his own greed and curiosity. Both were constantly getting him into trouble.

Another week passed, and Ranessa finally deigned to talk to him. This did not indicate a warming in their relationship, however, for she never opened her mouth but that she started an argument. She argued with him over everything. Whenever they came to a crossroads, she argued about the direction he chose. When he found a good campsite, she discovered something wrong with it. The previous night, she had even argued with him over whether it was better to stew gopher meat or roast it. She started in on him this morning. She was certain they were going the wrong way.

Turning around in his saddle, Wolfram halted his horse and fixed her with a baleful stare.

"Do you know where we are?" he demanded.

Taken aback, Ranessa darted a glance left and right and then said sullenly, "No, not really."

"Do you know where we are going?"

"Yes," she flashed. "To the Dragon Mountain."

"And do you know where that is?"

Ranessa hesitated, then jabbed a finger east. "That way."

"There's a lot of land lies *that way*," Wolfram said dryly. "The lands of the Karnuans lie that way. Past them you'll find the Tromek elves lie that way. Farther off, the lands of the Vinnengaeleans and farther still the lands of my people are that way. Most of the world lies that way, in fact, for we are on the western edge. A huge, vast world.

"I've no doubt," he added complacently, shifting on his saddle to a more comfortable position, "that you'll find what you seek. Oh, it might take you a good ten years, but you'll make it eventually and I'm sure they'll be pleased to see you. A good journey to you, Girl. The gods go with you. No one else will," he muttered under his breath.

Ranessa's eyes narrowed. She regarded him intently. He couldn't tell—due to the mass of hair in her face—whether there was hatred and fury in those eyes or sudden fear that he was truly abandoning her. He didn't know and he didn't much care. Yes, the bracelet was starting to grow warm, starting to remind him that it was his job to bring her to wherever it was she needed to be. Let her ride off, he thought. Let the bracelet that the monks affixed to my arm burn through to the bone. Let the heat consume my arm and leave me with naught but a charred stump. That would be better than having to put up with this obstreperous female for another single moment.

Ranessa shook back the hair. She put her hand on the hilt of her sword and for a heart-stopping moment Wolfram thought she meant to kill him.

"I cannot let you ride off alone," she said. "You are being followed, Dwarf. Something or someone searches for you. If I were to ride off and leave you to face the danger by yourself, I would be dishonored, my family disgraced. I will continue to accompany you."

"Followed?" was all Wolfram could manage to blurt between sputters. "What do you mean, we're being followed? I've seen nothing, heard nothing—"

"Neither have I," Ranessa said. She looked at him and for the first time since the start of their journey, her eyes lost the wild expression, became focused and clear. "Yet, Dwarf, I know that something is out there and that it seeks to find you."

Her voice was soft, her tone serious. The bright sunny day suddenly clouded over, the warmth of the midsummer morning air was tinged with a chill.

Nonsense! Wolfram told himself shakily. She's talking nonsense. She's mad, poggled. And she's trying to do the same to me.

"We should keep riding," she continued. "We're out in the open here, exposed." Pausing, she added coolly, without a blink of the eye, "You know the way, I take it."

Wolfram had so much to say that the words clogged his throat and he couldn't speak a single one. After a moment, he gave it all up and turned his horse's head and rode off in high dudgeon. He didn't believe it, not one whit. But he couldn't help but turn around every once in a while and look behind him long and hard.

The prairie land between the mountains of Abul Da-nek and Karnu was claimed by both Dunkarga and by Karnu and therefore in dispute. Both sides sent armed patrols into it. Wolfram had been fortunate thus far not to have run into any from either side. Not that he would have been in much danger. Traveling with a Trevenici had some advantages—both sides used them as mercenaries and neither side would want to do anything to make one angry. Yet, a dwarf never knew how soldiers might react and Wolfram was just as glad not to see any.

The ground was soft and flat, covered with long grass. The plains were not difficult to travel in broad daylight when both horse and rider could see any obstacles. With the light failing in late afternoon, Wolfram feared the horses might stumble into a gopher hole, for they'd come across many of the creatures during the last two days' ride. The horses were weary and in need of food and rest.

Sighting a grove of trees, usually an indication of a stream or a water hole, Wolfram slowed his horse and turned its head that direction.

"It's growing dark," he said. "We'll camp here for the night, get an early start in the morning."

"Dark!" Ranessa cried shrilly. "It is not dark! It is not anywhere near dark. We will keep riding."

"You're daft, Girl," Wolfram said, a statement that he made so often it had lost a lot of its luster. Sliding off his horse, he started walking toward the grove of trees. He expected that this action would effectively end the argument.

Damned if the crazy woman didn't kick her heels in her horse's flank and, gripping the beast's mane, order it to keep going.

Wolfram shook his head. Only hours ago she had stated that she had to keep near him. Now she was riding away. Good riddance.

Fortunately, between Ranessa and her horse, one of them at least showed some sense. The horse trotted forward, but only to follow Wolfram and his own horse to the stream.

Wolfram heard cursing in Tirniv. The girl used language that might have made her brother proud. She cursed the horse, kicking it in the flanks. Then she struck the horse. The blow was not hard. She used the flat of her hand against the horse's neck. But it was still a blow.

Wolfram rounded, faced her, stared her square in the eye.

"Strike me, if you want to hit something, Girl, but don't take out your anger on the poor beast, for he doesn't understand and he cannot hit back."

Ranessa's face flushed. She lowered her gaze in shame and stroked the horse with a gentle hand, muttering an apology in Tirniv. But she remained sitting on the horse.

"It is not dark, I tell you," she said through clenched teeth. Her fingers twined in the horse's mane, gripped it tightly. She glowered at him. "We could ride farther."

Wolfram said nothing. He merely pointed to the west, where the Abul Da-nek mountains were silhouetted against a backdrop of gold and red and the sky above them was purple, darkening to inky black.

She cast the red sky a furious glance, as if night was falling out of spite. With the abrupt movement with which she did everything, Ranessa swung her leg over and fell off the horse's back to land heavily on the ground.

Wolfram grit his teeth, looked away. He'd tried and tried to show her how to make a proper dismount, but she paid no attention. She either fell, leapt or slid. Mounting was even more a challenge, with Ranessa flinging herself bodily on the horse and scrabbling with her legs until somehow she finally managed to end up in the right position as the horse stood his ground, occasionally glancing back in bemusement.

It's a toss-up, Wolfram thought, which one of us is suffering the most— me or the poor beast.

"I suppose we *must* stop now," Ranessa said, casting the dwarf a withering glance as she walked past him toward the stream. "You've dawdled so long that there's no daylight left."

Wolfram led the horses to water, then, snatching a handful of the sweet smelling prairie grass, he rubbed his horse down first, then rubbed down Ranessa's. He spoke to the horses in dwarven, a language that held in it the dwarf's love and reverence for the horse, a language that horses everywhere in Loerem understand and find soothing and appealing.

After praising Ranessa's horse and commiserating with him, Wolfram turned the beasts loose to graze, knowing that the horses would not venture far from him, though he had no doubt that they'd leave Ranessa in a flash. He then went about setting up camp for the night, which meant clearing a place for their fire, finding wood, fetching water, cooking their food, catching their food, if that was necessary.

Ranessa never turned her hand. She spent the time pacing back and forth, back and forth, unable to sit still, always looking to the east. To teach her a lesson, the fourth night they'd been on the road together, Wolfram had caught a squirrel, skinned it, but not cooked it, planning to tell her if she wanted roast meat she could damn well roast it herself. To his amazement, he'd caught her about to eat the meat raw. When he demanded to know what she thought she was doing, she stared at the raw meat in her hands with a blank look as if wondering how it came to be there.

He couldn't figure her out. She wasn't lazy, nor did she consider herself above chores. If Wolfram asked her to do something, she would do it, although she wouldn't do it well and most of the time he'd have to do it over himself. It just never seemed to occur to her that there was any work to do. She walked and walked, staring into the eastern sky until she must have been on a first name basis with every single star. Wherever it was she went when she looked to the east, she left him behind.

This night was no different. She paced and Wolfram worked. He told her three times that food was ready if she wanted it. The third time, she halted her walk, glanced at him, and moved toward him.

"No fire, Dwarf?" she said, her brows drawing together in a scowl.

"We had cooked meat left over from last night," Wolfram said, waving a hunk her direction. "There's not that much wood to be found and it's mostly green."

He drank stream water, wished it was ale. Or something stronger.

Ranessa took the meat, ate it hungrily. She had the manners of an ork. After the meal, she did not return to her walking. She stared long and thoughtfully at him until he grew uneasy. Saying that he needed to attend to some private business, he rose to his feet.

"Wolfram," she said, and he was startled and wary. She'd never called him by name before. "How long will it take us to reach the Dragon Mountain? Will we be there in a few days?" She sighed deeply. "I grow weary of this traveling."

Wolfram's jaw dropped. "A few days! We have over eleven hundred miles to travel, Girl. With the gods' favor, I figure it will take us four months."

He might as well have shot an arrow into her heart. The blood drained from her face.

"Months," she said dazedly. "You mean that four times the moon must grow full before we . . . before we . . ."

"With luck," Wolfram emphasized. He had a sudden revelation. "Girl, if you thought you were coming with old Wolfram on a pleasure trip, you were sorely mistaken. The journey will be a long one and dangerous."

She stared at him bleakly.

"Those who make their living on the road know that it is a dangerous place," Wolfram continued, "and the danger does not always come from those who walk on two legs or even four. Bridges are guarded by trolls. Mistors travel on the wind. Hyrachor fly the air. Glyblin haunt old battlefields."

Wolfram's voice softened. "Return to your people, Girl. We are not that far but that you can find your way. You could reach Vilda Harn, at the very least."

She looked thoughtful and for an elated moment Wolfram thought that she might truly decide to turn back. He felt the bracelet warming and knew the monks wanted him to bring her. Why, he couldn't fathom, but that was the case. He had done nothing except tell her the truth, though. The monks could not fault him for that.

Ranessa slowly turned, looked to the eastern sky that was now studded with stars.

"No," she said. "I will go with you. The dreams have told me. But we must travel far each day. Rise early and ride late."

Wolfram stomped off in an ill temper to spend time with those he truly considered his traveling companions.

The horses were pleased with Wolfram's coming. They crowded forward to gain his attention, wanting their foreheads scratched, their ears tickled. They snuffled at him, nuzzled him, their breath warm on his face.

"Besides," Ranessa called after him, "someone *is* following us. Danger lies behind us as well as ahead."

Wolfram buried his head in his horse's flank, rubbed the animal's rump with a gentle hand. *The kildeer with the broken wing*—so the knight had said. Wolfram had discounted the warning. Gustav the Whoreson Knight and his mad quest! A good enough ale tale, the dwarf supposed. Nothing more.

Yet Wolfram believed Ranessa. He didn't know why. Perhaps because she was crazy and there are many among the peoples of Loerem—the orks, for example—who believe that lunatics are god-touched.

Privately Wolfram thought the gods might have been kinder to him and touched her a bit harder—hit her with a hammer, maybe. His was not to question, however. His was to obey. The monks wanted her—the gods themselves knew why—and the monks would have her. And not in four months. Especially not if someone was tracking them.

"We can reach Dragon Mountain in a month's time," he mumbled.

"What?" Ranessa demanded. His voice had been muffled against the horse.

"We can reach Dragon Mountain in a month's time. If we are lucky. That still plays into it. Luck plays into everything. But there is a way."

"How?"

Wolfram thrust forward his arm, bared his wrist. "Do you see this bracer I wear?"

Ranessa nodded.

"It is not just a bauble. It is a key. A key that unlocks certain doors to me and to me alone."

He was telling the truth, but not quite the entire truth. There were others who did the monks' bidding who had similar keys, but this Trevenici didn't accord him the respect he felt he deserved.

"What doors?" Ranessa looked skeptical. "I don't see how a door will help us."

"It will if it leads through time and space," said Wolfram smugly. "Do you recall your nephew talking about that magical door in the lake, the one the knight came through?"

"What are you talking about? What do doors have to do with lakes?" She frowned. "I'm beginning to think you're addled."

"I wouldn't doubt it," he returned, glowering. "Madness is probably contagious. Never you mind what doors have to do with lakes. I know and I have the key and that is what matters. You had best get to sleep. We've many long days' ride ahead of us yet before we get to where we're going."

"Where *are* we going?"

"Not that you'd know if I told you." Wolfram snorted. "It's a sea-port town in Karnu. Karfa 'Len."

"And is this door you speak of there?"

"One of them is," said Wolfram.

Someone was following them—the Vrykyl, Jedash. But he was having a hard time of it and for the life of him he couldn't figure out why.

"For the life of him" was an inaccurate statement. For the death of him would have been more appropriate, for Jedash had been dead for about fifty years. A former Void hedge-wizard in life, Jedash was one of the few who had made the transition from living man to animated corpse with no regrets, probably because he had not been much alive to start with.

Jedash had been sleeping in an alley when Shakur had quite literally stumbled upon him, mistaking the man for a pile of discarded rags. Fortunately for Jedash, Shakur had already fed or Jedash would have been one of the nameless, faceless souls stolen to keep Shakur's corpse from shuffling off its mortal coil. As it was, Jedash had been roused from his slumbers. Laying eyes upon the Vrykyl for the first time, Jedash had been moved to worship. He had prostrated himself before Shakur and asked to become his follower. Amused, Shakur had presented the man to Dagnarus.

Dagnarus had accepted Jedash, given him food and shelter and increased the hedge-wizard's knowledge of Void magic. Jedash's admiration for Dagnarus changed to adoration. Dagnarus had decided to reward Jedash by murdering the man, presenting him to the Dagger of the Vrykyl as a suitable candidate.

Unlike Shakur, Jedash had no fear of the emptiness into which he would eventually slip. He had known the emptiness of gnawing hunger, the emptiness of grinding poverty, the emptiness of living without hope of anything better. He had known chronic illness and chronic pain. He had known the bitter torment of ridicule, of being shunned, driven from the habitations of civilized men, persecuted, reviled. Thus Jedash did not find tedious the empty hours of the night. He did not long for sleep, because in life his sleep had never brought any comfort to him. He had comfort now in feeling nothing.

Assigned to follow the dwarf, capture him and bring him back to Shakur, Jedash assumed that this would be an easy task. Jedash went to the town of Vilda Harn, reasoning that the dwarf might well have stopped by the only place to purchase supplies between Nimorea and Dunkarga. Jedash was rewarded far beyond his expectations. Taking the form of a Dunkargan merchant he had once slain, Jedash picked up the dwarf's trail the very first place he stopped—a horse trader.

The horse trader remembered the dwarf quite clearly, for the dwarf was one customer who had known exactly what he wanted and, to the trader's chagrin, had seen through all of the horse dealer's best artifices in concealing defects or flaws in his animals. Wolfram had chosen the best animal of the lot and had then spent most of the day wearing down the trader until he had practically given the horse away.

The dwarf had a companion, the horse trader said in answer to Jedash's question. A Trevenici woman. Why they were traveling together, the trader could not say, for there appeared to be no love lost between the two of them. The trader thought the dwarf mentioned heading south for Karnu.

"They left only a short time ago," said the trader. "If you make haste, you can catch them."

A dirt road led out of Vilda Harn. Jedash mounted the shadow steed he rode and galloped off in pursuit, pleased that he would soon be able to provide his master with the dwarf and whatever it was the dwarf carried. The Vrykyl was sure he must soon overtake them, but he rode mile after mile and saw no signs of them. The dirt road dwindled to a dirt trail that turned into nothing more than two wagon ruts, leading south.

Due to the rumors of war, there were few travelers—a Karnuan patrol heading home, a caravan whose nervous drivers wanted only to reach Vilda Harn in safety. Taking the disguise of a Trevenici, claiming to be searching for his runaway sister, Jedash questioned everyone he encountered. Yes, they had seen the dwarf and the Trevenici woman, not long ago either. He had only to make haste and he would catch them.

Jedash made haste, but he did not catch them. They remained inexplicably out of reach. He started to grow angry.

The wagon ruts veered to the west, heading for the city of Amrah 'Lin. Jedash abandoned the useless road, struck off in an easterly direction. The dwarf would be trying to reach more civilized lands, not heading into the frontier. Finding a stream, the Vrykyl traveled alongside it until he came to two sets of hoofprints on the muddy bank, one of them belonging to the type of small horse the dwarf had purchased. These led him through the prairie grass to the remnants of a campfire.

The coals were still warm. The two were only a short distance ahead of him.

Jedash pressed on, confident of overtaking them. The Vrykyl was close. He smelled their blood. He heard the dwarf's gruff voice and the human female's shrill voice bickering over something. He urged his shadow steed up the next rise, certain that he would look down and see them.

He looked down, but they were not there.

From his position on the rise, Jedash gazed over the expanse of the vast prairie and the only living thing he saw was a hawk diving down to snatch up a mouse in its talons.

Furious, frustrated, Jedash was forced to ride in a wide arc across the prairie to see if he could find them once more, circling far to the east and to the west to discover if they had deviated from their southern course, veered off suddenly one way or the other. He lost two days in this search before he finally came upon their tracks.

The two had not veered off. They had continued on a southerly course. He did not understand how he could have missed them yet again. What magic were these two practicing that they should so confound his efforts?

Once more, Jedash set off in pursuit.

22

WHILE JESSAN ENJOYED HIS JOURNEY AND WOLFRAM ENDURED HIS, Raven's journey was one of misery and frustration. He remained chained to the stake, was never released. His chain was long enough so that he could relieve himself in a pit some distance from his post. Half-taan or human slaves covered the pit every other day with dirt and dug another. Raven was surprised at this cleanliness, but he noticed that while the taan were a cruel race, they were not a slovenly one.

The taan did not bathe—Dur-zor said that the taan had a great fear of water—but they rubbed their bodies with oil and then scraped off the dirt with the oil. Their smell that Raven found so sickening was not the smell of filth, but their own smell—a combination of musk and decayed meat. Taan liked the smell of humans, Dur-zor said, but Raven didn't find much comfort in that, for the taan were probably thinking only of their next meal.

The crude prison cell made of spears was dismantled. The male Dunkargans were now all dead. Their deaths had been horrible. They had been tortured for sport, their screams and writhings sending the taan into fits of merriment. Raven counted himself brave. He thought he could withstand anything, but the cries of the murdered men had been more than he could bear. He had closed his ears with dirt he scraped up from around his post. One man had lasted three days.

A few of the captured women had died. They were the fortunate ones. The rest were slaves of the taan, made to perform tasks the taan considered beneath them and even beneath half-taan. The women were raped repeatedly, beaten, kicked, slapped and whipped. Their faces haggard, often blood-stained, they looked toward Raven with pleading in their eyes, as if expecting him to do something to help them. He could not. He could not even help himself. He refused to meet their eyes and eventually they gave up.

Raven spent his time watching his captors, for it was said among the Trevenici that it is a wise warrior who makes a friend of his enemy. Raven could not understand the taan language, but the taan also relied on wild and often exaggerated gestures to emphasize their meaning and from these he could occasionally make out what was going on.

There was a definite hierarchy among the taan. Qu-tok and the other warriors constantly deferred to a fellow warrior, a female, and Raven eventually came to realize that this female was the tribal leader. She wore a crested helm of Dunkargan make and design, and it seemed that this marked her rank.

One day, the female warrior, accompanied by a proud Qu-tok, came to look at Raven. Qu-tok took great delight in showing off his prize to his leader.

Seeing the taan approach, Raven jumped to his feet and clenched his fists.

"Fight me, damn you!" he shouted. "Even with these chains on, I'll fight you, blast your lumpy hide."

Raven knew that Qu-tok could not understand a word he said, but the raised, clenched fists were a challenge to battle in any language. Unfortunately, Qu-tok was goaded to laughter rather than to rage or Raven presumed that was what the taan was doing, for he made a chortling sound in his throat and showed every razor tooth in his ugly head.

Qu-tok advanced to just outside of chain length and waved his hand at Raven with a gesture that was a perfect copy of one used by a performer exhibiting a trained bear. Realizing he was only putting on a show for the amusement of his captors, Raven grit his teeth and ceased to struggle.

Qu-tok pointed out some of Raven's finer points to the warrior, who eyed Raven with interest. She had an inordinate number of scars on her body, far more than Qu-tok or the others. Flashes of light glinted from beneath her hide. The warrior had gems embedded beneath her skin.

Having lived around the pecwae all his life, Raven was familiar with gemstones. He recognized the purple of amethyst, the pink of rose quartz and was astonished to see one large green gem that might well have been an emerald inserted beneath the hide of the warrior's right arm. He assumed these stones were merely decoration and thought it a strange and painful way to wear jewelry.

As if in reward for Raven's performance, Qu-tok tossed his prisoner a hunk of cooked meat. Raven bent and picked up the meat, closed his fingers around it. Qu-tok and the head warrior turned their backs, strode off. When Qu-tok was about six feet distant, Raven threw the meat as hard as he could. The meat struck Qu-tok squarely on the back of the head.

Feeling something splat, Qu-tok whipped around. He saw the meat on the ground, saw Raven standing with clenched fists, glowering at him.

"Come on, skink," said Raven grimly. "Fight me."

Qu-tok bent down to pick up the meat. He held the meat up before Raven's eyes, then slowly ate it, making a great show of enjoyment. Turning on his heel, he walked off, accompanied by the head warrior. Raven was given no food that night or the night after.

"I hit him in the back of the head in front of his chieftain," he said to Dur-zor when Qu-tok finally decided to feed him. "With a human, an ork, even one of the simpering Vinnengaeleans, that would have been a mortal insult. He should have fought me on the spot."

"Had another taan thrown the meat at him, that would have been an insult," Dur-zor said with a pitying smile for his ignorance. "You are a slave, Raven. Such a low worm can do nothing to insult him."

Dispirited, Raven slumped back against his post. He reminded himself of the many times he had lain concealed in a lair, sometimes for days on end, waiting for his prey to come to him, waiting for the elk to walk into the clearing so that he could get a clean shot or the wild boar to blunder into his nets. He was in much the same situation, he told himself. He had to be patient, bide his time, whatever time he had left.

"Tell me of this head warrior," he said.

"Dag-ruk," Dur-zor replied. "She is huntmaster. A renowned warrior, she has proven her skill in battle many times over and has taken many slaves. Our god himself gave her the helm she wears. Most think she will be named a nizam—the head of the battle group—this next god day."

"Is she anyone's mate?" Raven asked, thinking that her mate might be Qu-tok and wondering how this would affect his plans for revenge.

Dur-zor shook her head. "No, Dag-ruk does not want to be encumbered with the bearing of children. Thus she does not permit any to lie with her. It is said that she favors one of the shamans of the battle group."

Shamans, Raven had learned, were skilled in the practice of Void magic. They acted as sorcerers for the taan and they were shadowy and scary individuals. Even the taan feared them, or so it seemed, for whenever one entered the camp, all the taan—warriors included—went out of their way to accommodate him and rarely took their eyes off him.

At first Raven had found it difficult to distinguish the shamans. In fact, the first time he saw one, he mistook the shaman for a slave, for the taan wore no armor, but was wound about in strips of cloth that covered his breast, his loins, and his upper legs. He carried no weapon and had few scars on his arms or his head. Raven had been surprised to see the other taan make much of him and Dur-zor had explained that this was R'lt, the shaman of the battle group.

"He has the ritual scarring," Dur-zor assured Raven. "And a great many magical stones embedded beneath his skin. He has more scars and more stones than almost any other taan in the battle group. He does not show them, but hides them beneath his clothes. Thus when he goes into battle, his enemies mistake him for a weakling and fall easy prey to his magicks."

The taan war party remained camped outside the conquered city of Dunkar. Inside the walls, representatives of the taan's god brought the Dunkargan people under control, stocked up on supplies, and made ready to carry the war on to other lands. Raven had no knowledge of this first hand. His information came from Dur-zor.

Once a day, near evening, the half-taan female brought him food and water and was permitted to remain to talk to him. Raven knew that she received permission to talk to him, for he could see Qu-tok keeping an eye on them. Whenever he thought the conversation had gone on long enough, Qu-tok shouted for Dur-zor to return. She was quick to obey, often leaping up in the middle of a sentence to avoid being punished for dawdling.

"Why does he let you visit me, Dur-zor?" Raven asked this evening as she squatted down comfortably in the dirt. She never came within arm's length of him, was careful to remain outside his reach. He added wryly, "I can't think he does it out of the kindness of his heart."

"Oh, no," said Dur-zor with a smile. "Qu-tok says that I am a torment to you. That's why he sends me and why he lets me stay."

"A torment?" Raven was puzzled. "How do you torment me? You've never laid a hand on me."

"Qu-tok thinks you must want to lie with me," Dur-zor said, grinning. "And that when I am close to you, you are in torment because you want me and you cannot have me. I know this is not true," she added. "I know that you think I am ugly, a monster. But I tell Qu-tok what he wants to hear."

"I don't think you're a monster, Dur-zor," Raven protested uncomfortably. He had thought her monstrous the first time he'd seen her. And though her visits were the high point of his day, he could not look upon her bestial half-human features without a feeling of revulsion that made his belly shrivel. "As for being ugly, I'm not much to look at myself."

"I do not find you ugly," she said, looking at him with frank appraisal. Her brow crinkled. "Although I do not know how you humans smell anything at all with that lump of flesh you call a nose." She shrugged, amused. "I know you could not feel about me the same that you would feel about a female of your own kind. The taan consider us abominations. Humans consider us monsters. Our god says that if humans get hold of us, they will kill us."

"Some would, maybe," Raven was forced to concede, thinking that this didn't say much for humans, for it made them no better than the taan. "Others would say that your birth wasn't your fault. You have a right to live, same as any of the rest of us."

"Is that what you think?" Dur-zor asked curiously.

"I didn't at first," Raven admitted. "But I do now."

"That is the same with me," she said. "I thought you were a monster at first, but I don't now."

"What will happen to you, Dur-zor?" Raven asked. He could forget his own troubles, his own disgrace and dishonor, when he talked to her.

"One of the taan will kill me," she said matter-of-factly. "Maybe Qu-tok. Maybe another." She smiled at his shocked expression. "One day I will move too slowly or I will spill the water or not keep proper watch on a child. They will kill me and that will be that."

Raven felt such pity and anger that he could barely contain himself. What sort of terrible life was this?

"That is the fate of my kind," she added. "I know this. It is useless to fight against it. In this life, I serve my god and that is enough for me."

"Perhaps you will find a mate," Raven said, struggling to offer comfort, although—to be honest—the girl did not appear to require it. "You will have children."

"Half-taan cannot bear children, not with taan, not with humans, not with each other," she said with a shake of her head. "Our god wanted us to have children, but even he, a god, cannot cause us to be fertile. I have never lain with anyone and I do not expect to, since there is no reason to mate other than pleasure and slaves are not permitted to have pleasure."

"The taan don't . . . well, use you for their pleasure?" Raven asked.

Dur-zor stared at him, amazed. "The taan would find no pleasure in lying with us. They consider us monsters."

Raven began to have a glimmer of understanding. "The taan think human females are monsters, too, don't they? The taan don't find pleasure in them. They lie with humans only to subjugate them, to exert their power over them."

"In the old world," Dur-zor explained, "it was said that if the humans were permitted to do so, their population would grow like that of rabbits. They would soon outnumber the taan. The taan feared that and so they took measures to keep the human population in check. They needed humans for slaves, so they did not kill them. They abducted their women, forced them to bear half-taan children."

"What would you like to be, Dur-zor? If you could be anything you wanted?" Raven asked.

"A warrior," she answered promptly. "Becoming a warrior is one way in which a half-taan may gain some respect among the taan. It is even said that in another battle group, a half-taan has risen to become a huntmaster. That is far out of my reach, but I think I would make a good warrior. I have practiced with the kep-ker. I am skilled at it."

"The kep-ker? That is—"

"What you humans call a staff, except that it has a wooden ball at one end and a stone ball at the other. The wielder grasps hold of the wooden ball"—she demonstrated with an imaginary weapon—"and swings the staff like this."

Raven had seen the taan carrying such weapons. He had thought they used them like a quarterstaff, grasping the weapon in the center with both hands. He was surprised to learn this other method, but could see where it would have its advantages.

"They taught you to use a weapon?"

"Of course," Dur-zor replied. "When the warriors leave for battle, the taskers and the half-taan are left to keep watch over the camp. We have to know how to defend the children, should the camp be attacked."

This was something important to know. Taskers, he knew from Dur-zor, were taan who were not warriors, nor were they shamans. The taskers were those male and female taan who took care of the needs of the warriors: cooked the food the warriors brought in, kept the camp clean, tended to the young taan.

Although the taskers always treated the warriors with deference, the warriors respected the taskers, did not mistreat them as they did slaves or the half-taan. Still, Raven had never seen a single tasker carrying a weapon. He would keep this in mind.

He was about to ask more questions when Qu-tok, apparently thinking Raven had been tormented enough, called out. Dur-zor leapt to obey, but, as she was turning to run off, she said swiftly to Raven over her shoulder: "Tomorrow is a god day."

Raven jumped to his feet, lurched after her, tried to stop her, to question her further. His chain dragged him to a halt and he stared after Dur-zor with a frustration that highly gratified the watching Qu-tok, for he grinned widely and, laughing, pointed out Raven to his fellow warriors. Because he was in a good humor, Qu-tok did not strike Dur-zor, but merely kicked her as she knelt before him, dismissed her to go about her duties.

Raven slumped down beside his stake. He tried yet again to rend his chains—an exercise in futility and one that did nothing to relieve his frustration.

Tomorrow, a god day.

According to Dur-zor, on that day he would be sent off to some slave camp. Once that happened, he would lose the chance to gain his revenge on Qu-tok. He would die a slave, die in shame. He would never ride with the honored dead of his race, never join them to fight the battles of heaven as they had come together to fight for the soul of the dying knight. His fellow warriors would turn their faces from him.

He tried to think of a plan, but at last gave it up. He had no idea what was going to happen, what a "god day" entailed. Would he actually be confronting a god? Raven had no idea. He fell asleep, chained to his stake, resolving to be awake early on the morrow, watch for his opportunity, and seize it.

The entire taan encampment was up early on the god day, for next to fighting battles, these days were the high points in the lives of the taan. The warriors emerged from their tent wearing decorations of beads and feathers, skulls and scalps and every piece of armor they owned, polished to a high gleam. Those warriors who had not yet won glory in battle wore armor made of bones attached to a heavy leather backing or, in some instances, no armor at all, preferring instead to wear only a loincloth that showed off their ritual scarification and the gem stones that were lumps beneath their hide.

The warriors congregated together, male and female, and by their loud voices and hand gestures, Raven gathered that they were telling tales of past battles. The taskers and taan children, the half-taans and human slaves cleaned the campsite, even to the point of sweeping the ground with leafy boughs to remove rocks and sticks, gnawed bones and other refuse.

The shaman R'lt made an appearance, dressed in long black robes with the hide of a wild cat draped around his shoulders. He was attended by two young taan, who emulated his every move and gesture. R'lt joined the warriors, who were careful to make room for him and include him in their circle. The apprentices, if that's what the younger taan were, squatted at some distance outside the circle, keeping watch attentively on their master.

The camp clean, the taskers set about cooking. The taan had killed several wild boar in the past few days and these were being roasted in a pit. Wild boar are strong food, Dur-zor told Raven, worthy of being consumed on a god day.

The smell of the roasting boar meat was tantalizing to Raven, who would not eat until sunset and then he would not be given any of the boar meat. That would go to the warriors first and, if there was any left over, to the taskers and the children. Slaves and the half-taan were given weak food: rabbit, deer, squirrel. He kept close watch on the camp, hoping to see Dur-zor, hoping to catch her eye.

His hope was a faint one, for Dur-zor had never before looked his direction as she went about her daily tasks. He was amazed when she glanced at him this morning and pleased beyond measure when she came toward him.

"Qu-tok sent me," she said, placing a food bowl down just within

Raven's reach. "He wants you to eat this now so that you will look strong when the god's chosen come to judge the worthiness of the slaves taken in battle."

"Dur-zor," Raven pleaded, "stay for just a moment. Tell me what's going to happen."

Dur-zor paused, glanced uncertainly in the direction of Qu-tok. "I have much to do—" she began.

"If you don't stay, I will not eat," said Raven, spurning the bowl of steaming meat. He disliked doing that, for he knew that if he did not eat, Dur-zor would be the one who was punished. She would probably be punished, anyway, but he had no choice. He was desperate.

"Very well," she said, squatting down beside him. "This morning, the camp is cleaned and made ready for the presence of the god or his chosen, if the god is too busy to come. When the sun reaches its height, the kdah-klks will begin."

"What are those . . . things?" Raven could not have said the word kdah-klks without strangling himself.

"Contests between warriors. Long ago, in the taan home world, the nizam were chosen from the strongest warriors. To determine which was the strongest, the warriors would come together and fight for the honor of being chief of the tribe. The battle was to the death. If the loser didn't die, he was cast out of the tribe, which meant almost certain death. Our god said that this was a wasteful practice, that too many strong warriors were being killed. He said that from now on, the kdah-klks would be ceremonial in nature. Now warriors fight each other for prizes given by the god, for weapons or armor, and for their own honor. Do you understand?"

Raven didn't immediately answer. He was chewing more slowly, thinking. At last he spoke, "What will happen to me and the other slaves?"

"Usually our god or his chosen come to watch the kdah-klks, for our god always enjoys the contests. When the kdah-klks are ended, he will award prizes. He will then call for the slaves. The taan who captured slaves will bring them before our god, who will judge their worthiness, and then exchange armor and weapons for those slaves he wants to serve him. All the slaves he chooses are then taken to the mines or wherever else it pleases our god to take them. The human females will probably remain here. You are certain to be sent to the mines, for our god needs strong slaves to work there."

Was it his imagination or did she sound a little sorry that he was leaving? Raven had been wondering if their daily conversations had meant anything at all to her, if she had enjoyed speaking with him or if he was just another chore. He had guessed the latter, but now he was beginning to think he'd been wrong.

He was silent, slowly chewing the last of his meat. Dur-zor kept casting worried glances over her shoulder at Qu-tok. Fortunately, the warrior was deeply engrossed in listening to another warrior's story and appeared to have forgotten about them.

Finishing the last of his food, Raven reached a decision. He had no idea what this might gain him, but he could lose nothing by trying.

"Dur-zor," Raven said, "I want you to tell Qu-tok that I want to take part in the"—he stumbled over the name—"the kad-kill."

Her eyes widened in amazement. "The kdah-klks?"

"Yes, that thing," Raven said.

"Impossible." Dur-zor snatched at the bowl to try to retrieve it. "You are a slave."

"No! Wait, Dur-zor! Hear me out!" Raven held fast to the bowl, would not give it back and she dared not come close enough to him to take it. "Tell Qu-tok that I want to prove my worthiness as his slave by fighting in the contest. I would like to fight Qu-tok," he added and knew at once by the look on Dur-zor's face that such an honor was beyond the realm of possibility. "But if I can't fight him, I'll fight anyone he chooses. I'll fight any way he says, with a weapon or bare-handed."

Dur-zor was shaking her head.

"Tell Qu-tok that if I win, I will be worth my weight in armor," Raven continued.

"If you lose, if you are killed, Qu-tok will lose his prize."

"That's a risk he'll have to take. I take a risk, so does he. Is Qu-tok a gambler, Dur-zor?"

Dur-zor chewed her lip. "Do you truly want this, Ravenstrike?"

"I do, Dur-zor."

She sighed and he was afraid for a moment that she wasn't going to go along with this, then, suddenly, she smiled.

"Nothing like this has ever happened in the kdah-klks. Still, there is a chance they will go along. All taan are gamblers. I will tell Qu-tok what you have said."

Raven put down the empty bowl. Dur-zor picked it up and departed. Going over to the warriors' circle, Dur-zor knelt in the dirt some distance from them until one of them should deign to notice her. The shaman, R'lt, finally saw her and called Qu-tok's attention to the half-taan. He appeared highly irritated at being interrupted and, jerking her roughly to her feet, lifted his hand, about to strike her across the face.

Dur-zor spoke rapidly, gesturing repeatedly to Ravenstrike, who was standing on his feet, staring intently at Qu-tok.

The taan listened in astonishment. Several of the warriors began to laugh derisively, but not Qu-tok. Raven's hopes remained high. Qu-tok appeared intrigued. Perhaps he was a gambler, capable of risking all for high stakes. Qu-tok said something and the laughter of the warriors changed to shouts of outrage and anger.

The shaman, R'lt, kept silent. So, too, did the chieftain, Dag-ruk. Qu-tok appealed to her directly. Dag-ruk asked a question of R'lt.

Raven couldn't understand their language, but he could guess at the import of that question. Dag-ruk was asking her shaman if the god would have any objections. R'lt shrugged, shook his head. Dag-ruk looked at Qu-tok and gave a single nod.

Qu-tok was well pleased with himself. Raven guessed by the glum expressions on the faces of the other warriors that Qu-tok had gained some sort of advantage over them. Qu-tok gave Dur-zor a shove in the direction of Raven, then the taan warrior went back to his story-telling.

"Qu-tok agrees," Dur-zor reported. "The huntmaster has given her permission. The shaman says that our god will have no objection. The huntmaster will choose the weapons and who will fight. Probably one of the young warriors," she added, with a gesture to those young taan who wore no armor. Hanging about on the fringes of the warrior circle, they stared at their betters with undisguised longing and envy. "They would usually scorn to fight a slave, but they will want to gain favor with both Qu-tok and the huntmaster."

"When will it happen?" asked Raven, eager and impatient.

"When the huntmaster decides," Dur-zor replied. Her brows came together over her snout-like nose. "I know what you are trying to do, Raven." She pronounced his name oddly, rolling the r's.

"Do you, Dur-zor?" He eyed her, wondering if she would warn Qu-tok.

"You seek a quick death," she said. She shook her head. "I do not think that will happen. No matter what you do."

Raven relaxed, grinned. "Wish me luck, Dur-zor."

"Luck." She repeated the word with a shrug. "Luck is for the masters. For slaves and the likes of us, there is no such thing."

23

WHEN THE SUN BLAZED HIGH IN THE SKY, THE KDAH-KLKS BEGAN.

Acting under his instructions, R'lt's apprentices made a large circle outside the center circle of tents. For the first time, Raven saw the taan use Void magic. Under the watchful eye of the shaman, the apprentices ran their hands through the grass and, wherever they touched it, the grass blackened and withered and died. When the outer ring had been formed and the shaman approved, the young taan moved into the center, killing all the grass inside the ring and tamping the dead stalks smooth with their bare feet.

Raven's skin crawled in revulsion. He glanced around, thinking that some of the taan might be offended by the use of such heinous magic, saw all the taan watching with eager anticipation. It occurred to Raven that the taan were not shocked by the use of Void magic because that was the sort of magic they habitually used. The races on Loerem were skilled in the various magicks of creation. The taan, it seemed, were skilled in the magic of destruction.

For the first time since his capture, Raven thought of the rest of the people of Loerem, who would shortly be facing this army of savage monsters, skilled warriors and skilled wizards, dealing in death. How could the people of Loerem survive such an onslaught? He envisioned one proud city after another falling to these creatures and to their god, Dagnarus, the way Dunkar had fallen. The taan had beaten the Trevenici, the greatest warriors in the world. The rest did not stand a chance.

Once the circle was formed, R'lt took his place in the center and began to make a guttural hooting sound that might have been a chant, for his voice rose and fell. The taan gathered around the circle, the taskers holding onto small children, the warriors standing together. The half-taan were permitted to attend, taking their places behind the circle of taskers and children. Slaves were present as trophies, their chains held by the taskers. The human women watched dully, hopelessly, not caring what was going to happen.

The huntmaster came forward to stand in the center of the circle and spoke to the battle group. Many times had Raven seen one of his own tribal elders standing in the same place, announcing the rules of a contest, and he was overwhelmed with a feeling of homesickness that came near to unmanning him. Banishing the memory, he concentrated on the proceedings.

There were not many rules, apparently, for Dag-ruk did not speak long. She left the circle. He tensed, thinking that he might be called to fight, but two taan warriors took their places. They each bore a strange weapon—a sword with two blades that formed a V shape.

Raven never knew which struck first, for the fight was joined in a blur of speed. He had trouble seeing from his vantage point, for the taan blocked his view. Hearing howls and the clash of steel and what sounded like a really good fight, he strained to see and cursed those who got in his way.

He assumed that the fight would be contained within the circle, for this is how contests were run among the Trevenici. But the taan circle was nothing more than a staging area, apparently, for the fight was soon carried outside it. The battling warriors broke through the crowd, knocking down a few children who did not move swiftly enough to get out of their way. No one seemed to mind, least of all the taan children, who scrambled to their feet and returned eagerly to watch the battle.

The combat raged through the camp, the two slashing at each other with the fearsome looking weapons, smashing tents, upending pots and once coming perilously close to the fire over which the boar was roasting. Both had drawn blood, for their hides were spattered with red.

Raven had a good view now and he watched with grudging admiration, impressed with the skill of the warriors in handling what looked to him to be a weapon that could be as dangerous to the wielder as to an opponent. He noted that one taan appeared to be weakening. His foot slipped. He went down on one knee and did not leap back up as swiftly as he might have. He snatched a moment to try to catch his breath.

His opponent did not give him the opportunity, but pressed his attack, forcing the taan to lurch to his feet. The contest ended a short time after, with the stronger taan kicking the weapon out of his opponent's hand and then sending him crashing to the ground with a punch to the jaw.

The defeated taan lay blinking up at the sky, probably trying to remember who he was and why he was here. His fellow stood over him, weapon poised, just in case his opponent sought to keep fighting, but after a moment, the other taan pointed at the victor in a gesture of defeat.

There was cheering and hissing from the crowd, depending on who had wagered on whom. At a gesture from the shaman, his two apprentices hastened forward to tend to the wounded taan. Sitting up, he shook his head muzzily, and spurned their ministrations with an angry snarl. The winner strutted about, waving his arms and hooting. The loser limped back to the circle, where he refused to look at or speak to anyone.

Dag-ruk came forward, announced the next contest, and the fighting began again. This time the contest was between seasoned warriors. The two were evenly matched, wielding curved swords with serrated edges and carrying another strange looking device—two long sticks covered over with leather fastened together in such a way that they formed an X. Raven was intrigued to see that the taan used this as a human swordsman would use a shield in battle, holding the X in one hand, turning it this way and that to deflect blows and to try to trap an opponent's sword in the cross-bars.

Raven's admiration for these warriors increased. Caught up in the excitement, he forgot himself and at one point shouted, "Well struck! Well struck!" Some of the taan heard him and turned to stare. One of the human slaves cast him a glance of pure loathing. He knew he should be ashamed of himself, but a good hit was a good hit, no matter who swung the sword.

The fight looked as if it might go on all day and into the night, for neither opponent was making much headway. Both scored hits that drew blood. Neither was weakening and eventually Dag-ruk stepped in and halted the contest. She pronounced a winner by pointing at one of the taan. Raven approved her decision, but the loser did not take it well. The loser stomped her feet on the ground, threw down her shield and her sword and kicked dirt in the general direction of the huntmaster.

The taan went suddenly quiet. Dag-ruk stared hard at the loser, then very slowly and deliberately reached out to the victor, who handed over his sword and his shield to her. The huntmaster faced the loser. The warrior seemed at first prepared to accept the challenge, but then her anger cooled and logic prevailed. She cast a glance at Dag-ruk from beneath lowered lids, then raised her hand and pointed at the victor, though she would not look at him. Turning on her heel, the losing taan stalked back to her tent, disappeared inside.

Dag-ruk and the shaman R'lt exchanged glances. Several of the warriors looked severe, some of the taskers hissed. Raven guessed that the losing taan had forfeited more than the battle. She had lost her people's respect.

Raven tensed again. Like an old war horse, he was excited by the battle, by the smell of blood, the sounds of clashing steel. He felt himself ready for combat and hoped that he might be next. He was rewarded, for Dag-ruk said something to Qu-tok, who looked Raven's direction.

Raven hoped that Qu-tok himself would come to fetch his prisoner and they could settle matters between them then and there. Such menial duties as fetching a slave were beneath the dignity of a warrior. Qu-tok sent two tasker taan, both of them large males, to bring Raven.

The taskers removed the chain that attached Raven to the stake. They freed him of the iron collar around his neck, but left the manacles on his wrists, attaching the manacles with a length of heavy chain. They clamped manacles around his ankles and hobbled his feet together with another chain. Then they led him forward, moving awkwardly and slowly in his bonds, toward the circle of dead grass.

The other taan laughed and jeered derisively—at least that's how he translated the grotesque sounds they were making. He ignored them, kept his gaze fixed on Qu-tok, who remained some distance from the ring, standing with the other warriors near their huntmaster. The young warriors, those who wore no armor, clambered for his attention, shouting, jostling and shoving one another. A grinning Qu-tok looked them over, finally chose one. The young warrior gave a whoop, while his comrades looked glum and backed off.

The taan taskers shoved Raven into the circle of dead grass. Glancing around for Dag-ruk, Raven lifted up his manacled hands and gave the chains a shake, asking in dumb show that his bonds be removed. The huntmaster grinned and shook her head. The other taan found this amusing, for their chortling sounds grew raucous. A couple of the children tossed clods of dirt at him.

Raven looked in appeal to Dur-zor, but she only shook her head. There was nothing anyone could do. This was his idea. He had to play by their rules.

Grimly, Raven planted his feet and waited for his opponent. The chains were a liability, no doubt about it. But they could also be used as a weapon. He wondered if the taan were so stupid that they had not thought of that. Another glance at Qu-tok told Raven that the taan might have many faults, but stupidity wasn't one of them. Qu-tok's lips parted in a grin. Dag-ruk nodded, her eyes on Raven. Several other warriors spoke, perhaps making wagers, for Qu-tok nodded in agreement.

The young taan entered the ring. He was tall and stringy, all bone and muscle and tendon. His hide had some scarring, but not nearly as much as the elder warriors. He wore no armor and had only a few stones lodged beneath his flesh. The young taan looked smug, apparently thinking that this would be an easy fight. The huntmaster raised her voice, as she had done in the other contests, announcing the rules.

Raven shook his head to indicate he didn't understand. The huntmaster said something to Qu-tok, who found Dur-zor in the crowd and sent her forward with a gesture of his hand.

Dur-zor came to stand beside Raven, translated.

"The Kutryx has issued the rules of the contest. Lf'kk may not slay you, for you are the property of Qu-tok. If Lf'kk does accidentally slay you, he must make good your value to Qu-tok by serving him as a slave himself for a term of one sun cycle. This Lf'kk agrees to. As a slave—a derrhuth—you are not bound by such restrictions. You are free to try to kill Lf'kk."

Some of the half-taan, who understood Elderspeak, laughed heartily at this ludicrous notion.

"Lf'kk may not use the magic of his stones in the battle," Dur-zor continued. "That is customary in all kdah-klks."

Raven had no idea what this meant, but it seemed to be to his advantage, so he said nothing.

The young taan raised his hands and spoke. The crowd grinned and nudged each other.

"Lf'kk says he will fight you with his bare hands," Dur-zor explained. "He will not ruin one of his weapons by fouling it with the blood of a slave."

Raven grunted. "What do I get if I win?"

"Your life," said Dur-zor, looking puzzled.

"That's not good enough. I want something else. Tell Dag-ruk that if I win, I want to fight another battle."

Dur-zor translated the words to Dag-ruk, who eyed Raven narrowly.

"Tell her," Raven continued, "that if I win, I want to fight another battle against an opponent of my own choosing. Tell her."

The huntmaster considered. Qu-tok said something to her, but she ignored him, kept her gaze fixed intently on Raven. At last she spoke.

"Well?" Raven asked impatiently.

"The Kutryx says you amuse her and she agrees. If you defeat Lf'kk, you may fight another battle against the warrior of your choosing."

"That is all I ask," said Raven.

He cast a final glance at Qu-tok, then forced himself to settle down, to concentrate on this opponent. Raven would have to finish this fight quickly, for he couldn't afford to wear himself out. Not before the real fight began.

Lf'kk began to circle around Raven, who slowly shifted to face him, forced to take care that he didn't trip over the chain that bound his ankles. He kept his hands apart, waiting for the taan to make a move, certain now that this youth had underestimated him, would be overeager and careless.

Lf'kk leapt at Raven, hands reaching for his throat. Raven grasped hold of the chain that bound his wrists, formed a loop, and swung it with all his strength. The blow caught the taan in the midriff, knocked the wind out of him and probably broke a couple of ribs.

Lf'kk staggered, went down on one knee, gasping for air. Raven struck a blow at the taan's head with the chain, but the taan wasn't there. Having foreseen Raven's attack, Lf'kk flattened himself on the ground. Raven's chain whistled harmlessly over his head. The taan's strong hands seized Raven by the chain hooked to his ankles, jerked him off his feet.

Raven landed heavily on his back. Lf'kk jumped at him, grappling again for his throat. Raven brought up his knees, kicked Lf'kk in the chest, sent him flying backward to land ignominiously on his ass. Clumsily, Raven regained his feet, watching Lf'kk, who jumped up to face his opponent. The young taan was angry, his eyes blazed. His pride had been wounded by a slave. Lf'kk hurled himself at Raven, hoping to take him down bodily.

Raven side-stepped, not as swiftly as he might have done without the chains, but he managed to get out of the way. He flung the chain over Lf'kk's head, wrapped it around the taan's neck. Lf'kk reached his hands to the chain, tried to free himself. Raven twisted the chain, slowly strangling the taan. Lf'kk gurgled, choking. His hands tore at the chain, his eyes bulged in his head. The other taan had been cheering, but now they were silent except for a few hissing indrawn breaths. Raven kept twisting the chain. Lf'kk sank to his knees. His face was turning an ugly shade of blue, his tongue protruded from his mouth.

Raven kept twisting the chain. The young taan sank lower and lower. Raven lifted his head, searched for the slave woman who had given him a look of loathing. Her face was bruised, one eye swollen almost shut. She was practically naked, her dress hanging from her body in tatters. Her flesh was scratched and bore marks of the whip. She had been watching dully, but now her eyes met Raven's.

He yanked on the chain. There came a snapping sound and Lf'kk went limp, his neck broken.

Raven said nothing. The woman said nothing. She understood, though. In some small measure, he had avenged her wrongs. She smiled sadly, stood taller and straighter.

Raven released the chain, stepped back. The taan's body slid to the ground and lay there, lifeless eyes staring into the crowd. One taan started to make a gargling sound in his throat and then another and another and soon all joined in. They began stamping their feet on the ground. Some of the warriors who were wearing armor smacked the flat of their hands on their breastplates. If Raven had not found it too unbelievable, he would have said they were cheering him.

The taan began to shout and perhaps it was as well he did not understand, for it might have weakened his resolve.

The taan shouted, "Strong food! Strong food!"

Raven paid no attention to the cheers or shouts. He turned to face Dagruk. He had only one hope left—that the taan had some sense of honor. That she would be bound to keep her promise and let him fight an opponent of his own choosing.

"Kutryx Dag-ruk," he said. "I won the battle. I now claim my prize. I am free to choose my own opponent for the next fight. I choose him."

Raven pointed straight at Qu-tok.

Dag-ruk could not understand him, nor could any of the other taan, but there was no doubting what he had said. Dur-zor did not even bother to translate. Qu-tok understood and he didn't like it. The other warriors grinned, chuckled and made comments that appeared to infuriate Qu-tok, for he glared at them, snarled something in return and then stalked over to speak to the huntmaster. Pointing at Raven, Qu-tok began to argue vehemently.

Raven looked urgently at Dur-zor, silently asking her what was going on. With an uneasy glance at Qu-tok, Dur-zor moved a step or two into the circle, coming closer so that Raven could hear her over the commotion.

"By daring to claim you are the equal of Qu-tok, you have shamed him."

"Good," said Raven grimly.

"You do not understand. There is no reason for him to fight you. He would gain nothing, for there is no glory in killing a slave."

"I might kill him," Raven said, his fear of failure rising, his anger growing.

Dur-zor shook her head sadly. "You killed a boy who made a mistake. Qu-tok is a mighty warrior. He will not make mistakes."

Raven said nothing. He looked back at the huntmaster, who continued to listen to Qu-tok's spittings and snarlings.

Dur-zor stared at Raven intently and suddenly she understood. "You don't believe you can kill him, do you? You want him to kill you. You *want* to die."

"I want to die with honor," Raven said through grit teeth. He clenched his manacled hands. "Is that so hard for you to understand?"

"No," said Dur-zor softly. "No, it is not."

"Then tell me what I can do to make him fight me!"

"All right," Dur-zor said, considering, "I will tell you. You must—"

"Kutryx!" A stentorian shout rang throughout the camp, caused all heads to turn. "Kutryx!"

A taan came running through the long grass. He carried a spear in his hand and he brandished it to call attention to himself. "Kyl-sarnz! Kyl-sarnz!" Halting his run, he pointed with his spear behind him. "Kyl-sarnz!" he repeated.

"Kyl-sarnz," the other taan cried, sounding jubilant, elated.

The huntmaster began to snap orders. The taan dispersed in all directions, all of them talking excitedly. Children jumped up and down, creating a clamor. Qu-tok and his fellow warriors bellowed at taskers, who came hurrying forward to adjust their armor, polishing it with handfuls of grass and their own spit. Two taskers stepped into the circle to grab up Lf'kk's corpse and haul it away. Two more taskers approached Raven, who stood in the center of the blackened ring, staring about in bewilderment.

"What is happening, Dur-zor? What's going on?"

"The scout says that one of the kyl-sarnz is coming."

"What's that?" Raven demanded. "Is that your god? Is the god coming?"

"No," Dur-zor said. "Our god is far away in another land, we are told. But he has sent the kyl-sarnz and that is a very great honor. Kyl-sarnz means god-touched. The kyl-sarnz are those taan whom the god, Dag-narus, has chosen as his most trusted servants, commanders of his armies. One of them is coming to visit us this day. This is a rare occurrence and may mean that our battle group is being singled out for something special. That is why everyone is excited."

"Dur-zor," cried Raven desperately, as she turned to leave, "does this mean that the contests are ended?"

Dur-zor looked back over her shoulder. "You will not die this day, Raven. I am sorry."

Raven was a prey to such bitter disappointment that he was physically sick with it. Dizzy, nauseous, his belly and his bowels cramping painfully, he had no care what happened to him now. He had lost his chance of avenging himself. Another would be slow in coming; Qu-tok would see to that. The tasker taans hustled Raven back to his stake, dragging him when he could not walk fast enough to suit them. They dumped him into the dirt, chained him up. Raven doubled over, heaved up his breakfast.

Angered by the mess he had made, for it meant more work for them, one of the taskers struck Raven hard across the face while the other went to fetch a bucket of water. Raven vomited again, this time on the taan's feet. The tasker struck him again, savagely, and Raven achieved his goal. He lost consciousness.

Raven woke to a pounding head and intense stillness. He could hear nothing, no movement in the camp, no bird calls or the buzzing of bees, no clicking of grasshoppers. He could not even hear the sound of the wind rustling the grass. The taan were still here. He could see them quite clearly, gathered together in the center of the camp. For a moment Raven feared that the taan had done him some critical injury, caused him to go deaf.

Gritting his teeth against the pain in his head, Raven managed to strug-gle into a sitting position. The clank and rattle of his chains were loud in the stillness. He was relieved to hear them, even though some of the taan on the outskirts of the circle turned to cast him looks of anger. The silence had a reverent quality to it. The kyl-sarnz must be here. Drained of strength and emotion, Raven settled himself to watch, too weak and dispirited to do anything else.

A voice broke the stillness. Raven couldn't see the source of the voice, for it came from the center of the crowd of taan. The voice spoke the language of the taan, but it did not sound like the taan. The voice was strange, cold and hard. The taan language was an ugly language to listen to, harsh and guttural, bestial. It had warmth to it, though, a warmth of emotion, even if those emotions were oftentimes crude, cruel and savage. This voice was devoid of all emotion, devoid of warmth, devoid of life.

The voice ceased speaking. Another voice answered. Raven recognized the voice of the huntmaster. Dag-ruk sounded awed, respectful. When she ceased speaking, the other taan raised their voices, began to chant, "Lnskt, Lnskt," bending their bodies as they shouted, all of them bowing.

The circle of taan parted. A group of warriors appeared. Raven saw Qu-tok walking proudly among them. In their midst stood the kyl-sarnz.

At the sight, a shudder convulsed Raven's body. Fear shriveled his gut. His heart lurched, he could not breathe. Then adrenaline flooded his body and he felt the wild impulse to leap to his feet and run away, run even though he was chained to the stake. He had to flee this terror, though it meant he ripped his arms from their sockets.

The accursed armor that he had carried to the Temple of the Magi had come to life. The accursed armor walked and spoke.

Raven froze, paralyzed. He dared not move, for fear lest the armored being turn its hideous head and see him. He had never been so afraid in his life, had never known what true fear was until this moment. The sight of this being brought back the horror of that nightmare ride with the armor, the terror of the dreams in which the armor had come to life, claimed him, dragged him into endless, empty darkness.

The helm was fashioned in the likeness of the taan, the face made of metal far more fearsome and loathsome than the faces of the taan. Curved spikes protruded from the elbows and shoulders of the armor; the armor-covered hands ended in long, sharp talons.

The kyl-sarnz was accompanied by several taan shamans, whose robes were far more ornate than the robes worn by R'lt and were decorated with a fiery phoenix. A group of taan warriors walked behind the kyl-sarnz, forming an honor guard. These warriors wore elaborate armor that made the armor of which Qu-tok was so proud look poor and shabby by comparison. This armor had not been stolen from dead warriors, but had obviously been specially made for these taan. They were covered with scars, their hides lumpy with stones. Hideous to look upon, they appeared almost deformed. They were armed with sword, shield and spear and they walked with pride, heads held high. The other taan regarded them with reverence, awe and envy.

Accompanied by his entourage, the kyl-sarnz left the taan encampment. The taan continued chanting "Lnskt, Lnskt" until long after the

Vrykyl was out of sight and hearing. Then the huntmaster, Dag-ruk, gave a wild whoop and jumped straight into the air. The other warriors began to shout and jump and started to rampage about the camp, brandishing their weapons and hollering. Darkness fell. Fires burned bright. The taan feasted and celebrated far into the night.

Raven watched the taan dance, their bodies silhouetted black against the vivid orange of the fires. Exhaustion set in. He dozed some, but whenever he drifted off, a blood-curdling yell would rouse him from sleep, from a horrible dream that he was riding again with that black armor.

He woke to a touch on his arm. Starting violently, thinking it was a black armored hand, he thrust himself up off the ground and stood quivering, every muscle taut, ready to fight to the death. He stood blinking and shivering for a few moments, until he realized that the figure crouching in front of him, staring at him in astonishment, was not a Vrykyl, but only Dur-zor.

This was the first time she had dared come near him, the first time she had touched him.

Raven gave a shuddering sigh and sank back down into the dirt. "I'm sorry I scared you," he said. He shook his head. "Bad dream."

"Ah," she said and nodded. She held in her hand a wooden dish filled with roast boar meat. Dur-zor set the meat in front of Raven.

"What's this?" he asked, rubbing the sleep from his eyes. The pain in his head had subsided into a dull ache. His empty stomach rumbled, but he had no appetite. He feared the food would make him sick again. "You said slaves were not given strong food."

"Dag-ruk sent it," said Dur-zor and she smiled, pleased for him. "She says that you bring us luck. You brought the kyl-sarnz to our camp."

"No!" cried Raven in hollow tones, shrinking back. Chill sweat beaded on his forehead, trickled down his neck and breast. "No, don't say that!"

Dur-zor seemed puzzled by his reaction. "But why? The coming of a kyl-sarnz is good. Kyl-bufftt Lnskt has honored our tribe greatly. It is the will of our god that we be the ones to escort the slave caravan back to Taan-Cridkx. And when we return, Dag-ruk will be made a nizam, a high honor."

"You are saying that your warriors are going to escort the slave caravan back to this . . . wherever it is. Will Qu-tok be among them?"

"Of course," said Dur-zor. "Where else would he go?"

"Good," said Raven. He reached for the dish. "I will eat. Give Dag-ruk my thanks for the strong food."

24

THE BOAT TRIP NORTH UP THE SEA OF REDESH WAS A RELATIVELY EASY journey, though not a very comfortable one. Jessan unwittingly used the blood knife almost every night to kill his food and he continued to be haunted by nightmares—actual nightmares, for he could hear the beating of horses' hooves in his sleep. Every morning, the Grandmother wakened, raised the seeing stick and every morning, she eyed Jessan strangely.

Jessan resented her unspoken accusation. He'd done nothing wrong. He wasn't responsible for what some stupid stick thought it saw, nor was he accountable for his actions to an old pecwae woman. He might have shared the bad dreams with her or at least with Bashae, but, in truth, Jessan was ashamed of the dreams. He was striving to earn his name, to earn his place in the tribe as a powerful warrior and yet he woke up in the night quaking and shivering like a mewling brat who has lost its mama. He kept his guilty secret, for how could he admit that he was weak inside, a coward?

Depressed and unhappy, always tired from lack of sleep, Jessan plied his paddle in brooding silence, sorry he had ever agreed to go on this journey. The Grandmother was ill-at-ease and in a bad humor. She stared suspiciously into shadows along the banks, cried out in alarms that proved to be false, and fussed continually with her stones. Caught in the middle, Bashae tried to talk to Jessan, only to be coldly repulsed. When he tried to talk to the Grandmother, she snapped at him and told him to leave her alone, she hadn't come on this trip to be pestered. Shrugging his shoulders, Bashae sat at the front of the boat, paddled when he was told to, but spent most of his time indulging himself in the beauty and wonder of his ever-changing surroundings.

Boat traffic increased the farther north they traveled. Jessan was forced to keep close to the bank to avoid being run down by the immense ships

of all nations that sailed the Sea of Redesh. Awed at the sight of their col-
orfully painted sails and the hundreds of oars that swept through the water
in what seemed to be miraculous rhythm, Bashae thoroughly enjoyed the
trip and this did nothing to ease the tensions in the boat, for both the
Grandmother and Jessan felt Bashae had no right to be enjoying himself
when they were not and resented him deeply on that account.

Matters between the three of them grew easier, when they came nearer
the port city of Myanmin. They fell in with a party of Trevenici mercenaries, who were returning to their duties with the Nimorean military. The
Trevenici were interested to know why Jessan was ferrying two pecwae
about. Jessan told the Trevenici the knight's story and they were pleased
by it, as they would have been pleased by any story of a warrior who had
fought well and died well. They accorded the Grandmother marked respect, giving her a place of honor among them and serving her themselves. This put the Grandmother in a good mood and she actually started
speaking to Jessan and Bashae.

Jessan cheered up, as well. The Trevenici had plenty of food with them
and insisted on sharing it. Jessan no longer had to use the blood knife and
his bad dreams abated somewhat. The eyes of fire no longer seemd to
search for him and although he could hear hoofbeats, they grew distant.

In addition, he learned a great deal about the city of Myanmin, the capital of Nimorea.

"As cities go, Myanmin is fair to look upon," Eyes-Like-Dawn stated,
"for there are many elves who have homes and businesses in Myanmin and
elves can always be counted upon to be respectful of nature and not chop
it down or burn it up or brick it over or wall it in."

The other Trevenici nodded in agreement.

"Still," she concluded, "Myanmin is a city and there are a great many
buildings, all made of stone and wood, a great many streets and a great
many people. The Nimoreans do have one peculiar habit that they
brought with them into exile from Nimra. They build their temples to
their gods below ground like the ants."

Jessan was astonished. "How could the gods who dwell in the vastness
of the heavens be honored by a building that is nothing more than an
anthill?"

"They build like this for defensive purposes. Unlike the temples in
other cities, Nimorean temples are not open to outsiders, unless they have
received special dispensation from the priesthood to enter. Any who break
these rules may be put to death."

"As they should be," said Sharp Sword. "And their souls cursed to the
Void." He spoke sternly and the others agreed. The Trevenici are a devout
people, respectful of all gods, not just their own.

"But still some try," said Eyes-Like-Dawn, "for it is said that a vast quantity of jewels and golden statues and silver argents can be found in Nimorean temples. Some would consider the exchange of their souls for such wealth might be worth the gamble."

Jessan was uneasy at the turn the conversation had taken. The talk of souls being sold to the Void made him think of the eyes that had watched him in the night. He changed the subject, stating that he had business in Kite Makers Street and asking how to find it.

"What do they do in this street?" Bashae asked eagerly. "I know about the deadly kite spider. I even saw one once, floating in the air, waiting to drop down on someone. Do the Nimoreans spin kite webs on this street? Do they breed spiders there?"

If the Trevenici smiled, they did not allow the pecwae to see that they did so.

"No, they have nothing to do with spiders, Bashae," said Sharp Sword. "The kite spider takes its name from the type of kites that the Nimoreans produce in the Street of the Kite Makers. The kite is a device constructed of wood covered over with rice paper. When a kite is set loose upon the wind, the wind carries it up to the heavens. A length of rope attached to the kite permits a person on the ground to control it.

"Some kites are small and very colorful, being made in the shapes of birds or butterflies. Such kites are used to entertain children. Some kites are called 'fighting kites.' These have a knife blade on the end of the kite. The elves send the kites into the air to do battle, each elf trying to cut the string of the other. But some of the kites have a more serious purpose. Some are built as large as a house and are strong enough to carry people into the air. The elves often use these—what they call living kites—to spy on the enemy, for such kites can float over enemy positions and keep well out of the range of arrow fire."

Jessan listened politely, for these Trevenici were his elders and seasoned warriors. He truly thought they were mocking him, however, for he could not believe such wild tales. He was of a mind to be angry, but his mood soon lightened, for the Trevenici next began to tell stories of their battles and these he could believe. He listened eagerly and when it was time for sleep, he could grin at the thought of flying elves.

The Trevenici retired early to be up and away with the dawn. The Grandmother did not carry out her nightly practice of placing the twenty-seven turquoise stones around the camp. Since the Trevenici had done her honor, she felt she was obligated to return the compliment.

"In the presence of such brave and renowned warriors," she said with a bow that caused all the beads on her skirt to click together and the bells to ring, "I know that no evil will come to us this night."

Jessan was devoutly grateful for this, for although he knew the Trevenici would be outwardly respectful, he feared they would be in-

wardly laughing. His lack of sleep and the hard physical exercise of paddling the boat caused him to fall asleep almost immediately. He woke
again soon after, with the idea that someone was near him. He was disconcerted to find it was the Grandmother. He played possum, kept his
eyes closed, not wanting to talk to her. He hoped against hope she would
go away and leave him alone. The Grandmother did not wake him, did
not speak to him. She hovered near him and he could not figure out what
she was doing. Eventually, weariness overcame him and he slept.

Jessan woke with the dawn. Sitting up, he was startled and a little uneasy to find that the Grandmother had surreptitiously placed seven of the
turquoise stones around him.

They entered the city early in the morning, for Jessan wanted to find
this Arim in the Kite Makers' Street and be on his way immediately to the
elven lands. He figured that by the time they located Arim it would be
around noon, they should be started on their journey to Tromek by nightfall. They came into the city along with those bringing their goods to market, the most crowded time of day. This was probably well, for the busy
gate guards passed them through without much question, though they
stared hard at the pecwae, few of whom were seen these days outside of
the wilderness.

"Keep an eye on your little friends," one of the guards warned Jessan.
"It is illegal to trade in pecwae slaves, but there are some who don't mind
breaking the law if it's worth their while."

"Pecwae slaves," Jessan repeated, astonished. "What would anyone want
with a pecwae slave? The pecwae hasn't been born who has done an honest day's labor."

The guard chuckled. He was a retired soldier, had served with Trevenici
before and admired their blunt way of speaking. "The rich women of New
Vinnengael keep them as pets," he said. "They will pay dearly for them, so,
like I said, watch them, especially the young one."

Bashae had imagined that Myanmin might be like Wild Town, with
perhaps a few more buildings and a couple more streets. The pecwae was
completely unprepared for the immensity and the grandeur of the Nimorean city. He walked as one dazed as they passed through the city gate,
staring in bedazzled wonder at the stone buildings that were so tall—some
of them being three stories—they seemed to touch the sky. He gaped at
the Nimorean people, who had all of them seemingly painted their skin a
deep, rich, glossy black.

He saw in one instant more people than he had imagined could exist in
the world. He was deafened by the noise of carts rumbling over cobblestones, horses' hooves clattering, vendors hawking their wares or calling

out to friends, or voices raised to argue with other vendors. He felt weak in the knees and queasy in the stomach and light in the head and he could not move. He might well have taken root in one spot had not Jessan poked his friend in the back and ordered him sternly not to look like a gawking pecwae seeing a city for the first time.

"That's what I am," Bashae pointed out, aggrieved.

"You don't have to *look* like it!" Jessan told him. "Shut your mouth and keep moving."

If the Grandmother was intimidated, she did not show it. She advanced confidently into the crowd, skirts clicking, silver bells tinkling, her agate-eyed stick thumping the ground, her sharp eyes darting everywhere. Jessan was thankful for that, at least. He was himself secretly overwhelmed and amazed at the sights and sounds and smells, but with Trevenici stoicism, he took care not to show it. This confident image was somewhat marred when he was nearly run over by a horse cart, for he had no thought of looking before he stepped into the street.

Bashae pulled his friend out from beneath the horses' noses just in time. The cart driver swore at Jessan and flourished his whip as his cart went speeding past, shouting "barbarian" in Naru, the language of both Nimra and Nimorea, a language that fortunately Jessan did not understand.

"The fool should have gotten out of my way," Jessan stated, glowering after the cart and glowering still more at the people around him, some of whom had begun to snicker.

He looked around, secretly bewildered by the maze of streets spreading out before him, all of them bustling with activity.

The Trevenici had given him directions, but he could not find any of the landmarks they had named: a sign with a crow holding a coin in its beak, a building that was three dwelling houses stacked one on top of another. The instructions started to blur in his mind, he forgot which he was supposed to find first and was well and truly lost before he ever started out.

He could not show weakness in front of the pecwae, who were counting on him, and with a show of confidence but a sinking heart, he chose a street at random. He was cheered to find a sign with a crow on it, although the crow was holding a mug in its claw, not a coin in its beak. This led him only to a dead-end, however. They were forced to turn and retrace their steps, while Jessan muttered that he'd wanted to see what was at the back of the alleyway.

The sun rose high in the sky. They walked all morning and found no sign of kites or kite makers. Bashae was limping, his feet were rubbed raw from the stones on which they walked. The Grandmother continued on gamely, though she was starting to slow down, leaned more heavily on her stick. Jessan had reason to recall the guard's friendly warning, for the pecwae were attracting a good deal of notice and some of it seemed sinister. He kept his hand on Bashae's shoulder.

"Let's go find the kite maker, Jessan," said Bashae, stopping to stare in pity at some poor child who had been turned to stone and was spewing water out of his mouth.

He'd seen a lot of stone people in this city. He could only conclude that this was some sort of terrible punishment and he was fearful that he might accidentally break some law and end up that way himself.

"My feet hurt and I don't like this city."

Jessan did not like this city either. He was more than ready to see the kite maker, but he did not have a clue as to where he might be. The thought came to him that they could wander about this city for a lifetime and never find the way, for they had been walking all morning long and had yet to be in the same place twice. He was about to humble himself, bury his pride and admit that he was lost when, to his vast relief, he saw two of the Trevenici they had met the previous night.

Jessan waved. The Trevenici responded and came walking over to him. "By the gods," said Sharp Sword, "what are you doing in this part of town? The street you want is clear on the other side."

"They are taking in the sights," said Eyes-Like-Dawn. "We are going to the Street of the Kite Makers ourselves," she added, elbowing Sharp Sword when he would have spoken. She remembered what it was to be eighteen and proud. "Would you like to come with us?"

"After we've rested and had something to eat," Sharp Sword added, taking his mate's hint.

They squatted down beside the stone child to eat bread and dried meat, drinking the water that was clear and cold. Eyes-Like-Dawn allayed Bashae's worries by telling him that the child had not been turned to stone, but was carved out of stone, the way Bashae carved birds out of turquoise.

They reached Kite Makers' Street by mid-afternoon. Immediately Bashae forgot his sore feet and Jessan forgot his hatred of cities, for this street was a wonder.

The air was filled with kites of all shapes and descriptions: kites that were fish, kites that were birds, kites that were fantastical shapes made in every color of the rainbow and more, colors the gods themselves had not even thought of. The kite makers had been quite clever when it came to choosing a site for the location of their shops, for the narrow street acted as a wind tunnel for the almost continual breeze that flowed down out of the mountains to the west.

Apprentice kite makers posted out in front of every shop flew their wares, making the kites dip and dance and perform tricks in the air. At the very end of the street, one of the huge, man-bearing kites was on display for a potential buyer. The kite was in truth as big as a two story building and Jessan made a silent apology to the two Trevenici for doubting them.

"What is the name of the man you seek?" Sharp Sword asked.

While he and Jessan departed to ask one of the apprentices where they might find one called Arim, the pecwae remained standing in the street with Eyes-Like-Dawn. The Grandmother had been staring at the kites with gleeful wonder when suddenly she pointed a finger.

"What is that?" she demanded.

"An elf," said Eyes-Like-Dawn. "And his entourage."

The Grandmother drew in a deep breath and before the Trevenici could stop her, she walked over and planted herself directly in the lead elf's path.

A high-born noble of House Wyval, the elven lord was considering purchasing several of the man-bearing kites for his army. He was on his way to watch one being demonstrated, when he came to a startled halt, staring down at the small person blocking his way. His entourage of his military leaders and bodyguards clattered to a stop behind him. He raised his hand in warding as his guards instinctively drew their swords.

The Grandmother stood too close to him. She had unwittingly entered into the circle of the elf's aura, but the noble was too well bred to insult her by retreating. Seeing that she was elderly, the elven noble bowed politely to her, for the elves have a great reverence for any who have lived long in the world.

The Grandmother stared up at the elf with unabashed curiosity, taking in everything about him, from his long, thin nose to his almond-shaped eyes, his sleek black hair and his elegant robes. The noble elf was embarrassed at this scrutiny, which would have been considered extremely rude among his people. He did not know how to deal with the situation, for he could not thrust such an aged person out of his way, nor could he circle around her without appearing rude himself.

"Now I can die," said the Grandmother in Twithil, speaking with finality and thumping her stick on the ground.

"What does she say?" asked the bewildered elf of Eyes-Like-Dawn, who had come running up.

"She is a pecwae and she has never seen an elf before, Lord," Eyes-Like-Dawn replied, speaking Elderspeak, generally acknowledged to be a common language. "She says that now she can die for she has lived long enough to fulfill a dream."

"Ah, I see," said the elf, smiling faintly. He paused, thinking of a suitable rejoinder. "Tell her that I have never before beheld one of the pecwae race and that I have also fulfilled a life's dream."

Eyes-Like-Dawn translated the elf's words to the Grandmother, who laughed loudly, causing the elf to look askance, for laughing at another was even more rude. He beckoned to his aide. Drawing out a large purse, the aide fished out a silver coin and handed it with cold, stiff dignity to the Grandmother, who stared at it in wonderment, then licked it.

She opened one of the bags she wore on the belt around her waist, began to rummage around in it.

"She wants to give you something in return," said Eyes-Like-Dawn.

"Tell her that is not necessary—" the noble elf began, but the words halted on his lips as the Grandmother brought out a turquoise carved in the shape of a turtle.

The Grandmother held out the turquoise to him, made a bobbing bow in imitation of his. The elf at first declared he could not accept such a valuable gift, but the Grandmother insisted with a chuckle and peremptory wave of her hand. The elf argued only as long as politeness dictated and then accepted the turquoise with another, much deeper bow.

Eyes-Like-Dawn seized hold of the Grandmother, who was bowing again and seemed likely to go on bowing all day; dragged her out of the way, so that the elf and his retinue could continue down the street.

"So that is an elf," said the Grandmother.

Slightly dizzy from all that bowing, she seated herself comfortably on a doorstoop of a kite shop, completely blocking the entryway. The irate owner came out from behind his counter, bearing down on the Grandmother. Seeing the Trevenici warrior, he went back behind the counter, where he sat on a stool, emitting loud and doleful sighs.

"What did you think of them?" Eyes-Like-Dawn asked.

The Grandmother stared after the elves in their lacquered armor and elaborately embroidered silken robes. She pursed her lips in thought, thrust out her jaw.

"Liars," she stated. "But they mean well."

Sharp Sword, Jessan and Bashae had no difficulty at all locating Arim. Each merchant in the street was well-informed about his competitor's business and the very first apprentice they questioned immediately pointed out the shop where they could find Arim the Kite Maker.

They entered the shop that seemed dark after the bright sunlight and stood a moment in the doorway until their eyes adjusted. The owner had started to come forward with his best smile, but halted when he saw in the doorway two Trevenici and a small figure he mistook for a child. Rolling his eyes in exasperation, he jerked his thumb at the trio and one of his apprentices, a very large Nimorean, stepped forward to deal with the invasion.

"My master thanks you for honoring his shop but we are very busy right now as you gentlemen can undoubtedly see and he believes that you would find the shops of our competitors far more interesting . . ."

All the while he was talking, the apprentice used his arms and his body in an attempt to maneuver the trio back out the door, nearly trampling Bashae. Jessan flushed in anger. Catching hold of his friend, he steadied him and seemed about to say something to the apprentice that would almost certainly lead to a fight. Sharp Sword gave the young man a sidelong glance and a very slight shake of the head.

"A moment, friend," said Sharp Sword. Planting his feet firmly, he placed his hand on the chest of the Nimorean, brought the bigger man to a halt. "Tell your master that while it is true we have not come to buy his wares, we are not here out of idle curiosity. We seek someone."

The apprentice looked to his master for instructions. The master raised his hands in exasperation and said in Nimorean, "Anything to get them out of here. Barbarians. They will drive off my customers."

Sharp Sword, who understood Nimorean, grinned. Jessan, who didn't, frowned and looked at Sharp Sword. The warrior nodded, indicating that it was for Jessan to speak.

"We seek one Arim," said Jessan in Elderspeak. "Arim the Kite Maker."

The owner looked at them more closely, his gaze sharp, inquisitive. "Tell Arim he has visitors."

The apprentice left on his errand. The two Trevenici and the pecwae stood in the door, Bashae staring open-mouthed at the wondrous array of kites that hung from the ceiling like some brightly colored species of bat. Jessan was doing the same, then realized that while curiosity could be excused in a pecwae, it was beneath the dignity of a warrior. He emulated Sharp Sword, who stood with his arms folded across his chest, looking calmly at nothing and seeing everything.

The apprentice returned, accompanied by another Nimorean. He was tall, of slender build, with skin that was like soft black cloth dipped in blue dye. His eyes were brown and warm and gentle, as was his smile. His hands were delicate, their fingers long and supple and stained with paint. He held a small brush in his hand, wiped it with a cloth as he approached. He appeared mildly astonished to see the nature of those who wanted him and cast a brief interrogative glance at the owner, who shook his head and then jerked his thumb toward the door, as if to say, "I don't care why they're here, just get rid of them."

Arim smiled slightly in apology, then said in Elderspeak, looking uncertainly from one warrior to the other, "How may I assist you, gentlemen?"

Jessan stepped forward, spoke with characteristic Trevenici forthrightness. "A knight of Vinnengael, one Lord Gustav—"

Arim began to cough. The spasm was so severe that it doubled him over. He gasped for air, choking and wheezing. The apprentice looked alarmed. The owner asked if he needed water. Arim, looking embarrassed, gestured at this throat, finally gasped that it was the dust and whispered, between spasms, that he would feel better for some fresh air. He stumbled out the door.

"I have a poultice I can make for coughs," Bashae said, looking anxiously from Sharp Sword to Jessan. "It's made out of mustard seeds. I rub it on his chest. I could make it here, if I had some water and something to crush the seeds. Would you tell him that?"

"What do we do?" Jessan asked uncertainly.

Sharp Sword shrugged. "If he's the man you were sent to speak to, you must speak to him," he stated with irrefutable Trevenici logic.

Bashae began rummaging through his pack. The owner gestured hurriedly to the apprentice, who slammed shut the door, an indication to passersby that the establishment was closed for the day. The sun was starting to dip behind the mountains, casting long shadows in the street.

The day's customers made their final purchases. The apprentices began reeling in their kites, placing shutters over the windows and taking down the colorful awnings that shaded them from the sun. In an instant, a street of color and wonder was transformed into a street of the plain, the ordinary.

Arim stood in the street, gasping for breath and wiping his sweat-beaded forehead with the same rag he had been using to clean his brush.

"Forgive me, sirs," he said when he could speak. His voice still sounded raspy. "It is the rock dust. Some of the paints we use . . ." He could say no more, but raised his hand, begging their indulgence.

The Trevenici warriors looked helpless and embarrassed for the Nimorean's show of weakness. The street slowly emptied. Owners and their apprentices retreated behind closed shutters and closed doors.

The Grandmother came now, accompanied by Eyes-Like-Dawn.

"He needs a poultice," said Bashae, bringing out a small vial of yellow seeds.

Arim shook his head. "No," he croaked. "Please do not trouble—"

"I heard the commotion. What's the trouble?" Eyes-Like-Dawn asked. "We should be returning to camp," she added to Sharp Sword. "The commander will be wondering what happened to us. Will our friends be all right?"

"We will be fine," said Jessan immediately. "Thank you for your help, Sharp Sword, Eyes-Like-Dawn."

Sharp Sword cast a narrow-eyed glance at the Nimorean, then he and Eyes-Like-Dawn drew Jessan off to one side.

"I do not trust this one," said Sharp Sword. "Come back to camp with us. You can return in the morning, if you must."

Jessan hesitated. He wanted very much to leave this city with its noise and confusion and bad smells. He would have liked nothing better than to be with his people and spend a pleasant night listening to stories of courage and bravery and daring in battle. But he was duty bound, he had given his word to the dying Dominion Lord. He could almost feel his Uncle Raven at his shoulder, frowning at him with disapproval for even thinking of abandoning his mission.

"I thank you, Sharp Sword and you, Eyes-Like-Dawn," said Jessan. "But I made a promise and I must see it through. We will be all right."

The two Trevenici exchanged glances. Both of them were well aware of the dangers that hid in the city in night's shadows and they were starting to argue when the Nimorean came up to them.

"You are the one who needs to speak to me?" Arim asked, clearing his throat and looking at Jessan. "You and your pecwae friends?"

Jessan nodded.

Arim's gaze shifted to the two older warriors. "And you have been his guides and now must return to your duties. You are fearful of leaving your comrade in my care. Is that correct?"

He smiled. "Please have no concern for the young man. He and the pecwae will be honored guests in my house this night. I will guide them to your encampment on the morrow, if that is their desire."

"See to it that you do, Nimorean," said Eyes-Like-Dawn. "The Trevenici make very good friends, very bad enemies."

"Yes, I know," said Arim gravely. "You have my word that they will be safe. I swear it on the shining eyes of my Queen. May their blessed light avert from me forever if I fail in my trust."

Sharp Sword was impressed. He knew Nimoreans well enough to understand that this was a most solemn oath, for the Queen of Nimorea was not only the political ruler but the spiritual leader for her people. Arim the Kite Maker had essentially made of himself an outcast from both from his people and his religion if he broke his vow.

A simple and honorable people, who judge others by their own standards, the two Trevenici considered this oath quite sufficient, never stopping to consider that if Arim was a man with evil intent, he was probably damned already and had nothing to fear. The two warriors took their leave, breaking into a jogging run that would take them swiftly back to their encampment.

Jessan watched them depart and tried to keep his courage from departing with them. He was once more alone in this strange place with this strange man, responsible for those under his care. Jessan folded his arms, planted his feet, and got back down to business.

"Now, as I was about to say—"

"Please, sir," said Arim mildly. "What are you called, by the way?"

"I have not yet chosen my name," said Jessan, flushing, "but I am called Jessan. This is my friend Bashae and this is the Grandmother."

The Nimorean bowed gracefully to each of them in turn.

"I am Arim," he said. He made a graceful gesture. "My dwelling place is not far. If you would do me the honor to accompany me, we will find food and drink there and a place where we can speak without disturbing those around us."

The Grandmother gazed at the Nimorean steadily. He met her gaze, held it.

"I don't know about you, Jessan," she stated suddenly, "but I would like a place where I can soak my feet."

Reaching out, the Grandmother rubbed her finger on the Nimorean's arm. "Does that color come off, black sir?" she asked, peering at her finger in the fading twilight. "No, it doesn't." She sounded awed. "How do you people get the dye to stick?"

"My skin is not dyed, nor is it painted. Black is the color I was born with. All of the people of the Nimorean race have black skin."

"Now I can die," said the Grandmother with finality. "I have seen an elf and people with skin the color of midnight. Now I can die."

"I hope you will not die for a long time yet," said Arim politely.

"Ha!" The Grandmother chortled and poked at him again with her finger. "You and me both."

25

ARIM'S STREET CONSISTED ENTIRELY OF DWELLINGS—STONE AND WOOD houses that fit snugly together with nothing but the walls separating one house from another. They were built in this manner not only to conserve space—always a premium in a walled city—but to provide warmth in the winters that were harsh and chill this far north. Few of the dwellings had windows, for that would allow the cold to enter. All the houses looked alike, their stone walls chalk white in the darkness. Bashae asked sleepily how Arim knew which one was his, but his jaw-cracking yawn prevented him from hearing the answer.

Arim used a key to unlock his door, explaining that thieves were a sad fact of life, even in Myanmin. Jessan grimaced at the strange ways of city dwellers, wondered again why any person possessed of two feet would consent to stay in such a terrible place. He said proudly that Trevenici need no locks on their doors. Arim smiled and said that Jessan must be pleased to come from such a noble race.

Jessan always felt uneasy in houses, but more so in this one, that had no windows. The dwelling was small with only two rooms, a front room for living and the back room for sleeping. The rooms were beautifully decorated. Kites hung from the walls. Their rich colors sparkled in the light of a fire Arim built in a raised, conical fireplace that stood in the center of the room and was open on all sides. The floor was covered with beautiful, soft, thick rugs. Arim spread additional rugs down on the floor and bade his guests rest while he fixed dinner.

Bashae and the Grandmother lay down near the fire and were soon fast asleep. Jessan did not lie down but sat propped up against the door, as close to outside as he could possibly manage. He was fully determined not to sleep. He planned to keep an eye on this Nimorean. But the rigors of the day proved too much. The house was quiet, the thick stone walls shut out all noise from the city outside, the carpets helped muffle sounds inside.

Arim moved about the dwelling, murmuring that he would fix something for them to eat if they would honor him by being his guests and sharing his poor repast. He spoke softly, walked softly, his movements so graceful that he seemed to flow over the floor rather than place his feet upon it. Jessan found himself nodding off. His head slumped forward onto his chest and he slept.

He woke with a start, to Bashae's shrill voice and Arim's mellifluous tones. Bashae sat on a high stool made of rich, dark wood, polished to a gleaming gloss. The stool's legs were heavily carved with all sorts of fanciful designs. Arim stood at a counter, cooking fish, by the smell. The Grandmother slept; her snoring a backdrop to their conversation.

Angry at himself for having fallen asleep on watch, Jessan bounded to his feet and somewhat grumpily demanded to know what they were talking about.

Bashae turned to his friend. "Arim was about to tell me the story of how the first elf flew on a kite." He turned eagerly back. "Go ahead, Arim."

Arim formed the fish into small balls, then rolled them in ground meal laced with various leaves and spices that gave off a savory, pungent aroma. A pot holding some sort of liquid had been suspended over the fire and was starting to bubble.

Arim smiled over his shoulder at Bashae. "First you must know something about the elves. The elven land of Tromek is divided up among seven major noble houses. These houses are often at war with each other and the story I am about to tell took place many centuries ago during one of these wars. No one knows or remembers why the war started. House Sithmara had gone to battle against House Wyval. House Wyval proved victorious, defeated their enemies in a victory so stunning that they managed to capture the noble lord who was the leader of House Sithmara, and his wife and his son.

"The noble lord requested death, for he was dishonored, and this was granted him. Before his death, he asked to bid farewell to his wife and son. He said the customary words of good-bye aloud to his son, but he whispered in the young man's ear that he was to do all he could to survive and return one day to lead their House in vengeance against their enemies. The son promised he would do so.

"The nobles of House Wyval debated long what to do with the son and heir of House Sithmara. The young man was eighteen and full grown, but in the land of the elves, that is still considered to be a child and there is no crime more heinous among the elves than to slay a child, even the child of your enemy."

Jessan looked shocked at the idea of someone at age eighteen—his own age—being considered a child.

"You must remember that the elven lifespan is two hundred years or longer," said Arim by way of explanation. "An elf is not considered to come to manhood until he reaches the age of twenty-five years. Until then, he or she is dependent upon the parents and may not fight in battle or marry or have any say in politics."

"Tell about the kite," Bashae said, brushing aside the strange ways of elves.

"The nobles of House Wyval could not put the son to death, but they could exile him and that is what they did. They sent the young man and his mother to a small house on a small island in the middle of a vast lake. They were given a year's supply of food and firewood and then left alone to fend for themselves. The nobles of House Wyval were very proud of having thought of this idea, for it saved them from having to go to the expense of locking the two in some fortress prison where they would have to pay guards to keep watch. The water of the lake was the guard, for it was icy cold and perilously deep and the shore was far, far distant, so far away that they could not see it. Once every year, the nobles of House Wyval sent another year's supply of food and firewood, for they had left the prisoners no axes, for fear they would cut timber and build a boat. House Wyval meant to keep them captive for the rest of their lives.

"Now, the mother and son had not been given axes, but they had been given knives to cut their food. To while away the hours of boredom that hung so heavily on her hands, the mother cut sticks from the trees and made herself a kite out of some of the paper used to wrap their food. She wrote prayers to the gods on the paper of the kite and, using string from the sacks of rice, she sent the kite with the prayers skyward, hoping that the wind would carry them to the ears of the gods. The gods heeded her prayers, for one day while she was flying the kite, her son was given the idea of building a kite big enough to carry one of them to freedom."

The Grandmother woke up and joined them in listening to the tale. Arim took the fish balls and dropped them one by one into the bubbling pot, taking care not to splash any of the hot oil.

"They set to work the next day to build a gigantic kite, the likes of which had never been seen or imagined. They had to spoil some of the food in order to have enough paper and rope and they knew that, if this failed, they would starve. So certain were they that the gods were with them in this endeavor that they carried on.

"The day came when the giant kite was finished. They had decided that the mother would travel with the kite, for she was lighter in weight than the son and they would need his strength to guide the kite and keep fast hold of the rope. He lashed his mother to the wooden cross-bars of the

kite and the two bade each other the farewells of those who go to their
deaths.

"Then the mother and son cried out to the gods to hear them and answer their prayers. The gods did so, sending a great wind over the lake, a
wind that blew strong and lifted the kite carrying the noble mother up
into the air. The son guided the rope in his strong hands and soon the kite
was nothing more than a speck in the air. He held on until his arms trembled with weariness and his hands were raw and bleeding. He lost sight of
the kite and then, suddenly, the rope went slack. The kite had come down,
but whether over land or over water, he had no way of knowing. For all
he knew, his noble mother was dead and he would be alone on this island
till the end of his days.

"He kept track of time by cutting notches in a tree. The notches were
many, went up and down the bark several times. Months passed and his
hope began to wane. Then, one day, he was looking out over the water
when he saw a boat. His heart beat fast, for this was not the time that his
enemies were accustomed to bring them supplies. To make a long story
short," Arim said, "for the fish balls are cooked and should be eaten while
they are hot, in the boat was his noble mother and soldiers loyal to House
Sithmara. Led by his mother, the army had fought a great battle against
House Wyval and were victorious. The son was freed and went on to become a gallant leader of his people, while his mother is still honored as the
Lady of the Kite, the first elf to be given the gift of flight."

The Grandmother squatted on the floor, spread her bead skirt carefully
around her.

"Liars," was her pronouncement. "But they mean well."

Arim ladled out the steaming fish balls, placing them in lacquered
bowls decorated with pictures of flowers and beasts and filled with rice.
Accustomed to roasted meat for every meal, Jessan had been dubious
about eating this strange dish, but either he was extremely hungry or the
fish balls were delicious, for he devoured several of them and when those
were finished he was pleased to see Arim make more. He did not eat the
rice, which he found gooey and tasteless.

Jessan tried once again, in between fish balls, to tell Arim the story of
Lord Gustav, the reason they had come. But Arim said that business was
never discussed during meals, for it was harmful to the digestion. After he
had cleaned up, he brewed tea made of rose hips and hibiscus. This he
drank from a cup made of porcelain so thin that Bashae could see the fire-
light through it. He offered the tea to his guests. The Grandmother and
Bashae accepted. Jessan declined, said he would drink nothing but water.

"Now please tell me about Lord Gustav," Arim said, "and why he has
sent you to visit me."

Bashae told his tale. He would have started immediately with the fight by the lake, but Jessan, who liked things orderly, made him back up and tell how they had met the dwarf and to start from that point. Arim was a good listener. He kept his eyes fixed on Bashae and if he interrupted, it was only to ask for clarification of a detail.

Bashae came to his favorite part of the tale. "The lake water bubbled and boiled. Lord Gustav stared into the lake, his sword drawn. He warned us that something evil was coming right behind him, and that he must fight it and we were to keep well away. Then there came out of the water a knight wearing black armor that was terrible to look upon. It was so horrible that I was more afraid than I'd ever been in my life. Even Jessan was afraid, weren't you?"

Jessan said defensively, "The knight told us we were wise to be afraid for the thing was a creature of the Void, a Vrykyl—"

Arim sprang to his feet. His tea cup fell from his hand, landed on the carpet, so that it did not break, but the tea splashed over the Grandmother.

"A Vrykyl," Arim said in hollow tones. "Are you certain?"

"Yes. We did not know that was the name of the Void warrior at the time, but the dwarf told us later."

"A Vrykyl following Gustav," Arim said to himself. He bent down, picked up the empty tea cup and returned it to the counter. His hand was shaking. "Forgive my weakness. Please continue with your tale."

Bashae cast an uncertain look at Jessan, who shrugged, not knowing what to make of this. Bashae described Gustav's battle with the Vrykyl and their own roles in it. Arim smiled to hear that they had helped the Dominion Lord to kill the vile creature, but his smile was tremulous and he sighed deeply.

When Bashae came to the part about Jessan taking the Vrykyl's armor, Arim looked at Jessan and the Nimorean no longer smiled. His face was serious and grave.

"That was foolish," he said quietly.

"Why does everyone keep saying that?" Jessan demanded irritably. "It was good armor, the best I had ever seen. My uncle Raven said so."

"Where is the armor now?" Arim asked.

Jessan was not going to answer. It wasn't any of this man's business.

"Where is the armor now, Jessan?" Arim asked and the gravity in his voice compelled Jessan to reply.

"My uncle Raven has it," Jessan said. "He took it with him to Dunkar."

Arim said something in Nimorean.

"What does that mean?" Jessan demanded.

"I said, 'May the gods be with him,'" Arim replied, his voice somber.

Jessan flinched. He had discounted all notion that the armor could be evil. But now, after waking morning after morning from the debilitating nightmares, he was not so certain. Fear for his uncle chilled him, twisted his stomach so that the food he had eaten was suddenly cold, hard rock.

"I didn't know!" Jessan cried, jumping to his feet and pacing about the small room that seemed to be closing in on him. "It was just armor. Nothing more." He yanked open the front door, took in breaths of air that was not fresh, for it smelled of the city, but at least relieved his feelings of being trapped and caged. "Nothing more."

He stood a while longer in the open doorway, then turned slowly to look back inside. The Grandmother stared into the flames. Bashae regarded him with pity and understanding. Arim's face revealed nothing of what he was thinking. Jessan licked dry lips.

"What could the armor do? How can armor be evil? It's just armor, isn't it?" he repeated.

Arim sighed deeply. Rising to his feet, he walked over to where Jessan stood and laid his hand upon the young man's arm. Ordinarily, Jessan did not like to be touched by anyone, especially a stranger. But the man's hand was warm against Jessan's chill skin, the man's touch comforting.

"What a heavy burden to lay upon one so young," Arim said. "Still, the gods must have their reasons. Do not blame yourself, Jessan. You had no way of knowing. No, the armor of a Vrykyl is not merely armor. It is . . . their flesh, their bone, their skin. When the Vrykyl was slain, what happened? Inside the armor was nothing but dust, right?"

"Yes," said Jessan, amazed. "But how—"

"How do I know? I know about Vrykyl. To my sorrow, I know about them. A Vrykyl is not a living being, Jessan. It is dead and has been dead for perhaps a hundred years or more. A Vrykyl is a corpse that has been given the semblance of life by the evil magic of the Void, magic that is embodied in its black armor. The armor and the Vrykyl can never be separated, any more than you could be separated from your own flesh. When the Vrykyl is destroyed, the corpse crumbles to dust. The armor retains the essence of the Vrykyl, the magic of the Void."

Jessan was appalled. "What would it do to my uncle?" he asked fearfully.

"I don't know," Arim admitted. "I've never heard of anyone taking the armor of a Vrykyl, of anyone daring to do so."

Seeing Jessan's distress, Arim said, more cheerfully, "Your uncle is a strong warrior, a man of sense. Let us believe that he found a way to rid himself of the accursed armor."

"But if he didn't," Jessan demanded, jerking free of Arim's attempt to soothe him. "What could it do?"

Jessan's complexion was pale beneath his tan, his eyes were shadowed, haunted. He was afraid, and Arim realized suddenly that the fear was not all for the uncle. A suspicion came to Arim's mind.

"The armor is an artifact of the Void. It could draw another Vrykyl to your uncle. Or lure your uncle to one of them."

Jessan closed his eyes, leaned weakly against the door frame.

"What have I done?" he muttered.

Arim was alarmed, but he kept his voice calm. "What have you done, Jessan? Did"—he paused, thinking how best to phrase this—"did you take something else from the Vrykyl? Something you kept?"

"Tell me," Jessan said at last with a deep, shuddering sigh, "do the Vrykyl have . . . eyes of fire?"

"Show me, Jessan," Arim said softly.

Jessan's fingers wouldn't seem to work properly. He fumbled at the sheath, fumbled to open it. His hand shook. He clenched his fist and, with a great effort, regained mastery over himself. He drew forth the bone knife and held it in his palm. He had once thought it sleek and delicate. Now it looked hideous.

Bashae gasped and shrank back, as far from the knife as he could manage. Arim made no move to touch the knife. He looked down at it, looked back up at Jessan, whispered a blessing in Nimorean, then jerked Jessan back into the room. Leaning out the door, Arim searched intently up and down the street. He shut the door and bolted it and placed his back against it.

"Do you know what you hold, Jessan?" Arim asked and realized the moment he asked the question that, of course, the young man did not. To him, it was a knife, nothing more. The Void exploited such innocence. "The Vrykyl maintain their unhallowed existence by feeding on the souls of living beings. The knife you hold is called a 'blood' knife. When the victim has been claimed by the Void and transformed into a Vrykyl, the first action of the Vrykyl is to make a knife . . . out of his own bone."

Jessan stared, horrified. But did he truly understand?

"They use the knife to murder their victims," Arim said relentlessly. "To steal their souls."

Arim did not want to inflict more harm on this young man, yet he must understand the truth of what he had done. "In addition, the Vrykyl use this knife to communicate with each other, to keep in contact. They can speak to each other through the knife. Jessan, has this knife drawn blood?"

"Not human blood," Jessan said in a shaken voice. Sweat soaked his leather tunic. He wiped his forehead with his hand. "I didn't know. How could I?"

"But it has tasted blood?" Arim persisted.

"I killed a rabbit . . ." Jessan gasped for air, glanced around as if he could claw his way through a wall. "Maybe a couple. I don't know. That's when the eyes started looking for me. Eyes of fire. And the hoofbeats. I can't sleep. The ground shakes with them. Don't you hear . . ."

Jessan lunged forward and tossed the knife into the fire. Shrinking back, he grasped his right hand with his left, stared down at the palm. "It moved!" he gasped, panting. "I felt it twist in my hand like it was alive. It is evil. Cursed. Let it burn."

"I am afraid—" Arim began.

"Silence!" the Grandmother said sharply and, at her command, all of them were quiet, even Jessan, though his harsh breathing echoed loudly in the small house.

The Grandmother had taken no part in the conversation. She sat at her ease on the carpet, staring intently into the flames of the fire.

The bone knife lay on the glowing embers in the hottest part of the fire. The flames licked it, but could not consume it. The fire did the knife no damage. Staring at the knife, the Grandmother began to sing.

The song was in Twithil, the language of the pecwae, that usually had a merry, carefree sound, reminding the listener of the twittering of birds. But Twithil had its dark side, too, for the pecwae live close to nature and know that nature can be cruel, without compassion for weakness or care for innocence. The owl's sharp beak tears apart the mouse; the blue jay cracks the shells of the robin, devours the unborn; spiders build webs to trap butterflies. The Grandmother's song was eerie—the hooting of the owl, the harsh caw of the jay, the frantic beating of the butterfly's wings. As she sang, she pointed.

The others gathered near, stared into the flames.

A figure of darkness rode on horseback. Black armor reflected the light of the flames. Orange fire burned in the eye slits of the helm. The horse's hoofbeats were soft, muffled, but the hoofbeats were constant, did not stop.

"The Vrykyl!" said Bashae, awed. "The one the knight killed."

"No," said Arim. "This is another. He has tasted blood through the blood knife."

"He's coming after me, isn't he?" Jessan whispered. "He's coming to get the knife."

"So it would seem," Arim said. Reaching for the tongs, he gingerly lifted the blood knife, took it out of the fire, and dropped it into the coal scuttle. "These flames will not harm it. I doubt if even the sacred fires of Mount Sa 'Gra could destroy it." He looked with new respect at the Grandmother.

"I did not know pecwae magic was so strong," he said, bowing in apology in case he offended.

"The stick saw him coming," the Grandmother said, placing her hand reverently upon the stick decorated with the agate eyes. "They saw the evil, but they did not know what to make of it."

She gestured at the knife in the coal scuttle. "If this Warrior of Darkness wants the knife, give it to him. Then he will go away and leave Jessan in peace."

"I agree, Grandmother," said Arim politely. "Unfortunately, the matter is not that simple. Now that we know the worst, we can prepare for it. The knife must never taste blood again. The knife itself draws him. When it kills, it speaks to him, cries out to him. It is as if your friend, Bashae, were lost in a cave. You know he went into the cave and you have a general idea where to find him, but the search is easier if he shouts to you and you can follow the sound of his voice. That is what the knife does when it tastes blood. It shouts loudly for any Vrykyl to hear."

"You seem to know a lot about these creatures," Jessan said accusingly. He was starting to recover from his shock, the horror and the fright. Shamed by his weakness, he felt the need to regain ground that had been lost.

"Yes, I do," said Arim coolly. "But that is another story. Now I would like to hear the rest of *your* story, Bashae. Lord Gustav sent you to me. Why? Where is he? Why could he not come himself?"

"He is dead," said the Grandmother. "There was a great battle for his soul, but do not worry. The Trevenici fought at his side and his soul was saved. The Void did not take him."

"I thank your people for that, Jessan," said Arim. Hands clasped, he lowered his eyes, said a prayer in his heart. "Lord Gustav was my friend. A brave and true knight. He had one lifelong quest—"

Arim halted what he had been about to say. Could that be true? Could that be the reason? It made sense, but, if so, the gods help them. The gods help him!

"Please, Bashae, continue your story," Arim said, trying to still the sudden rapid beating of his heart. He blessed his dark complexion for he could feel the hot blood mount to his face and he did not want to show his agitation.

"Before Lord Gustav died, he asked me if I would take a love token to give to his sweetheart, an elf he called Lady Damra."

Bashae drew forth the knapsack as he spoke. Opening the knapsack, he brought out the silver ring set with the purple stone. "It's an amethyst."

"Yes, I know," said Arim, examining the ring. He recognized it, knew it to be Gustav's. But the ring was a family heirloom, of little value. Gustav would not have sent a messenger on a long and perilous journey to deliver an amethyst ring. Nor would a Vrykyl chase after a family heirloom. "Is there anything else in the knapsack?"

"No," said Bashae, and Arim's disappointment was acute.

"Did Lord Gustav give you nothing else? Tell you nothing else?" Arim asked.

"No-o-o . . ." Bashae drew out the word, squirmed beneath Arim's dark-eyed gaze.

"Ah!" Arim drew breath, understanding. "There is something more, but Lord Gustav said you were not to tell anyone except the Lady Damra. I won't ask you to reveal his secret. I would not have you break your vow."

"Lord Gustav said you could take us to the elf lady. He said that the elves would not let us into their country, but that you could make them let us in."

"Yes, I can gain you entry and I will serve as your guide. I have traveled much in elven lands. The Lady Damra is a friend of mine." Arim understood everything, or so he imagined. "You have done well, Bashae. Lord Gustav chose a brave and faithful messenger."

"The gods chose the messengers," said the Grandmother. "Both of them. Him." She gave a bird-like nod at Bashae. "And him." She gave another nod at Jessan. "They are meant to travel together."

Arim cast her a sharp glance. She had read his thoughts apparently, for at that very moment, he had been thinking how to separate the two. He intended to proceed into Tromek with Bashae and the Grandmother, leave Jessan among his warrior friends. Arim would warn them that the young man was in danger and that he should be guarded day and night. Jessan would never be safe so long as he carried the blood knife and Arim knew of no way Jessan could rid himself of the cursed Void artifact.

Arim owed his knowledge of the Vrykyl to Damra's husband Griffith, who was one of the Wyred, an elven sorcerer. The Wyred are required to be knowledgeable about all forms of magic and the last time Arim had visited the Lady Damra and her husband, two years previous, Griffith had been deeply involved in the study of Vrykyl.

The elves had extensive records on these Void knights, better than even those held by the Temple of the Magi in New Vinnengael, for the elves had gleaned their information from a first-hand source, one who had witnessed the creation of the Vrykyl, whereas all the others took their accounts from stories of those who had survived the destruction of Old Vinnengael.

Arim recalled the conversation as clearly now as if Griffith were seated beside him. He had thought little of it then, but it came back to him with dark foreboding.

Why do you study these Vrykyl when no one has paid attention to them for two hundred years? Arim had asked.

Because we have been warned to do so, Griffith had replied.

"We should sleep now," said the Grandmother. "I take it we'll make an early start in the morning, Kite Maker?" She cocked an eye at him, looking very much like an inquisitive sparrow.

Arim ceased his wool gathering, came back to the present. "Start where? For what? Oh . . . you mean that we will start for Tromek tomorrow." He shook his head. "I'm afraid that is impossible. I must speak to the elven ministers. We must obtain documents permitting us to travel in elven lands. Without them, we would be subject to arrest."

"A waste of time," Jessan exclaimed. "We have the ring. We have Lord Gustav's instructions. He told us to take this to this elf lady. Why do we need these—whatever you call them?"

"Documents. The elves are very careful about those they permit to enter their country. Especially humans. They think that all humans are there to spy on them. I have to convince them otherwise. The elves trust my people, as much as they can trust those of another race. Believe me," said Arim, guessing what was in Jessan's mind, "if you went to the border and attempted to enter on your own, they would stop you and probably imprison you."

"How long then?" Jessan demanded.

Weeks, Arim was about to say, but then he remembered the Vrykyl. "I will do what I can to convince them of the urgency," he replied, wondering despairingly just how he was going to do that without revealing the truth. Elven bureaucrats were not noted for their quickness of thought or the depth of their perception. They actually went out of their way to be obtuse.

"Days, perhaps. Maybe three or four. I have a friend in the ministry, but he may not be there or he may be busy. I will have to see. You can sleep in my room in the back," Arim added, rising to go prepare for their rest. "Make yourselves comfortable. Do not be alarmed if you hear me wandering about, for I am often up late. And I will probably be gone when you wake in the morning." He looked intently at Jessan. "For your own safety and that of your friends, I advise you not to leave my dwelling place."

Jessan muttered something and Arim had the feeling that his warning had fallen on deaf ears. He could do no more, short of locking them in the house, and he doubted if that would stop the Trevenici.

Jessan and Bashae went to the sleeping room, Bashae lugging the knapsack with him. Before she left, the Grandmother placed the stick with the agate eyes over the top of the coal scuttle.

"There," she said. "The eyes will keep watch. The Warrior of Darkness is still far away."

"But getting closer," said Arim.

"Yes." The Grandmother sighed. "That is true. Is there no way to stop him?"

"None that I know of. Perhaps the elves might. They loathe the Void and all things pertaining to it. We might be safer in elven lands, but I do not even know that for certain."

The Grandmother beckoned him with a finger. Arim stood almost six feet tall, the Grandmother was nearer four. He bent down, his face near to hers.

"The Warrior of Darkness is not after the amethyst, is he?" she asked in a hissing whisper.

"No," Arim confirmed softly, unable to lie to her. "He is not."

"He follows us for the bone knife?"

"I don't think so. I believe there is something more. The secret Lord Gustav shared only with Bashae." Arim spoke hesitantly. "Jessan places you and Bashae in peril."

"Don't tell *me*," said the Grandmother caustically. She pointed toward the heavens. "Tell the gods. They are the ones who chose him. Why do you think I decided to come along? Someone had to keep an eye on them."

Bidding Arim good-night, she gave the agate stick a final pat and an admonition to keep close watch and clicked and jingled her way to the sleeping chamber.

Arim doused the fire, so that the light would not disturb them, and poured himself a cup of honey wine from a flagon. He sat long, sipping the wine and staring at the dying embers, pondering what to say to the elven ministers, what to do about Jessan and the blood knife.

He reached a decision with the end of the wine. Rinsing out the cup so that the residue would not attract ants, he put away the cup and the flagon and went to check on his guests.

They were all asleep, deeply asleep. Bashae slept curled in a ball, one arm looped through the strap of the knapsack. Jessan slept fitfully, jerking and tossing on his mat. The Grandmother snored and snuffled. The little silver bells rang softly every time she moved.

Returning to the main room, Arim spread out his sleeping mat in front of the door. Opening an ornate chest decorated in ivory that stood in one corner, he removed a curved-bladed sword. He lay down in front of the door, the naked blade near his hand.

He lay awake, stared into the darkness. If he was correct, the most valuable artifact in all of Loerem had just come into his possession, his care. Arim fell asleep at last, but he did not sleep well.

26

BASHAE AWOKE TO DARKNESS. FOR LONG MOMENTS, HE WAS DISORIENTED, couldn't recall where he was or why he was here. Memory returned and with it a knowledge of his surroundings and with that the fear he'd felt last night. He lay on his pallet, staring into the darkness, wondering if it was the middle of the night or somewhere near dawn. He had just decided it must be night when he heard a bird chirp, reminding potential rivals that this was her nesting site and to keep away. She received a sleepy sounding response and then it seemed that the entire bird community was awake, their voices blending so that Bashae lost track of the various conversations.

The darkness in the room faded to gray. He glanced over at Jessan's mat and was not surprised to see it was empty. Hearing soft footsteps, Bashae swiftly closed his eyes and pretended to sleep. Jessan would be astonished to find his usually late-sleeping friend already awake. He would ask questions and Bashae didn't want to provide answers, mainly because he didn't have answers.

Bashae gave what he considered a very realistic start and grumble when Jessan shook him. Rolling over, blinking his eyes, Bashae yawned and said sleepily, "What time is it?"

"Dawn."

"Dawn! Go away." Bashae rolled back over. He truly hoped Jessan would leave. Not that Bashae wanted to go back to sleep. He couldn't do that. He wanted time to himself, time to think.

Jessan was persistent, however. Once he got an idea in his head, he never let go.

"Get up, you sloth!" he said. "I need your help."

Bashae sat up, rubbing his eyes. "Help? Help to do what?"

Jessan cast a glance at the slumbering Grandmother. "Not here."

Sighing deeply, Bashae rose to his feet and followed Jessan out to the main room. The fire had gone out, leaving only a pile of feathery ashes.

Bashae looked around. "Arim?" he called out softly.

"He's not here," said Jessan and his voice was grim.

"Why do you say it like that?" Bashae asked. He liked the Nimorean, liked his soft voice and his gentle demeanor, liked to watch him move. "He said he'd be gone before we were awake."

"I don't trust him," Jessan muttered.

"You Trevenici don't trust anyone," Bashae pointed out. "You're just angry because . . ."

Jessan rounded on him. "Because of what?"

"Nothing," said Bashae. Sometimes words have points sharp as knives. Such words can draw heart's blood and leave scars that will never heal. "What is it you woke me up to do?"

Jessan walked over to the coal scuttle, pointed down at it. "I want you to pick up that stick."

"Why?" Bashae wondered, coming over to join his friend.

"I want the knife," Jessan said. "That is—I don't *want* it," he added, answering Bashae's look of astonishment. "But I have to have it. If you must know, I'm going to get rid of it."

Bashae's spirits lifted. "Are you? What will you do with it?"

"I thought about it last night. I'm going to take it to the Temple our friends told us about."

"I think it's a good idea, Jessan," said Bashae, adding hesitantly, "But the Trevenici said only the Nimoreans are allowed in the Temple—"

"The gods chose me," said Jessan. "They can deal with it. I've staked my soul."

At this juncture, Bashae knew better than to argue. Once a Trevenici "stakes his soul," he will do what he says or die in the attempt.

"Do you know how to find the Temple? All these streets—" Bashae made a helpless gesture.

"Sharp Sword told me that there is one street called Queen's Row that runs through the center of Myanmin. The street leads from the wharves to the south to the temple in the north and goes past the military barracks. He told me about it in case I wanted to join them later. That street is only six streets west of Kite Makers' Street. All we have to do is to find it and follow it north to the temple."

"Won't Arim be worried when he comes back and sees that we're gone?"

"The Grandmother will be here," Jessan said shortly. "He knows we wouldn't go off and leave her."

Bashae thought this over and decided it sounded logical. He picked up the stick with the eyes. Jessan started to reach into the scuttle, to take the knife. He paused, straightened up, glared at the stick.

"Move it away," he ordered.

"But, Jessan—"

"I don't like it watching me."

Hiding his smile, Bashae carried the stick into the room where the Grandmother lay sleeping. He laid the stick down beside her hand. Mumbling to herself, she reached out, rested her hand on the stick and smiled in her sleep.

"There," Bashae said, returning. "It can't see you."

Jessan reached into the coal scuttle and, after a moment's hesitation, snatched up the knife. Grimacing, he thrust the knife swiftly into a leather pouch that he used to hold flints for making fires. His forehead was covered with sweat. He was pale around the lips.

"Let's go," he said.

Intent on not losing their way, both looked at the road ahead. Neither thought to look behind.

A devout people, the Nimoreans regularly consult the gods before almost any undertaking that is likely to have an effect on their lives. The gods are seen by the Nimoreans to take an active role in all aspects of life, from family affairs to business matters. The Nimorean Queen is also High Priestess, both political leader and spiritual.

The Myanmin Temple was located in the northern part of the city and was one of the oldest structures in the city, having been among the first to be built when the exiled Nimrans made their way north some three hundred years ago.

The street Jessan and Bashae followed ended at the city wall. A gate led through the wall into a pine forest. As they were about to enter beneath the tall trees, Bashae halted.

"What?" Jessan demanded.

"This forest is old," Bashae said, awed. "Old and magical. Can't you feel it? It makes my fingertips tingle."

"It's dark enough, that's for sure," said Jessan, eyeing the forest uneasily. "Does it seem angry?"

Bashae considered. "No, not at the moment. But I think it could be angry, if it wanted to be."

Jessan heaved a great sigh. "We've come this far . . ." His face dark, he plunged into the forest. Bashae followed, after nearly breaking his neck in an attempt to see to the very tops of the tall pines.

All along their route, people cast curious glances at the pair, some even pausing involuntarily to stare at the pecwae. The Nimoreans are a polite people, however, and no one interfered with them.

The two walked beneath the pine trees. Jessan ranged far ahead and kept gesturing impatiently to Bashae, who meandered along beneath the thick shadows, inhaling the sharp scent and running his hands through the pine boughs.

They emerged from the pine trees to see a wondrous sight, a sight that few others besides Nimoreans ever beheld. An area of green grass soft and smooth as silk encircled a vast canyon carved of magic and loving hands. The temple structure, built entirely below ground, was a half mile across and a half-mile deep. The top rim of the temple wall was made of granite that was carved in the shapes of animals, done in relief. It was said that every animal known to walk Loerem was represented in the carvings, all many times larger than life and so realistic that the lion seemed ready to pounce and the fawn ready to toddle off on unsteady legs.

Below the border of animals was a border done all of birds and winged creatures and below that were the fish and the animals who live in the sea. Interspersed among all the animals were the plants of the world and the sea.

At each of the four cardinal points was a dragon, one for each of the elements: earth, air, fire and water. The stone dragons kept watch over the stairs that led down into the Temple.

Nimorean males stood guard. Chosen for their height and stature and courage in battle, every one of them stood well over six feet five inches tall, with powerful arms and broad chests. They wore immense helmets, decorated with black feathers, that made them appear even taller. Each was clad in shining bronze armor of ancient design, but modern make. Each held a painted shield as big as he was and an enormous spear, also decorated with feathers. They held the spears together, tip-to-tip, to form an entryway through which every person seeking admittance into the temple had to pass. The guards said no word to anyone approaching the stairs, but looked over each with keen, glittering eyes.

The guards spotted Jessan and Bashae the moment the two walked out of the tree line. The guards' eyes flicked back to them constantly, never letting them out of their sight.

Jessan knew that if the gods did not dwell here, they were frequent guests. His steps slowed. The knowledge of his terrible burden weighted him down so that it seemed he wore shoes of iron.

Bashae, the fearful, the coward, was quite at his ease here. He was now the one who ranged ahead and he halted only when he realized that his friend had stopped walking. Bashae regarded Jessan in concern.

"What's the matter?"

"They know," was all Jessan could manage to say. "They know."

"Do you want me to go ahead?" asked Bashae.

Jessan couldn't reply, but he nodded.

Bashae walked toward the guards, but when he drew near, his own confidence lagged. He'd never seen people so big, didn't know that they came that way. He looked into the stern faces for some sort of sign, but although they watched him, their eyes gave nothing away. Knowing that Jessan was depending on him, Bashae gulped and walked forward, clutching the knapsack. He passed through the pointed spears. No one said a word. Turning, he grinned at Jessan and motioned for him to follow.

His face grim, his jaw so tight that it quivered, Jessan took a step forward. With a swift and sudden movement, the guards crossed their spears, barred his way.

"Let him pass," said a voice.

Jessan turned. So intent had he been on the guards that he had not noticed the sudden silence that had fallen over those behind him. He saw the Nimoreans sinking to the ground on one knee, placing one hand to the earth and the other over their hearts.

A Nimorean woman stood before him. She wore white silk robes threaded through with gold; a golden girdle, studded with emeralds; golden arm bracelets, warm against her ebony skin; gold ear rings and a golden band circling her head. Her black hair was shorn close, her eyes were large, wide set and luminous.

Jessan had never seen anyone so beautiful and the first thought that came to him was that she was one of the gods. This thought was confirmed by the fact that all the Nimoreans were down on their knees. He thought perhaps he should prostrate himself, as well, but he couldn't quite seem to make his body obey his brain's commands.

A flash of movement caught his eye. Arim appeared, emerging from the forest. Reaching Jessan's side, Arim knelt down before the woman.

"High Priestess, forgive him this sacrilege," Arim said. "He is my guest and does not know the ways of our people. Let his punishment fall instead upon me."

"No sacrilege here," said the priestess. "He comes in humility. His heart beneath the shadow is good. He and his friend may enter. You may come with them, Arim the Kite-Maker."

Breathing a relieved sigh, Arim rose to his feet. Bowing again to the priestess, he said, "First, I must make my explanation for my behavior to these gentlemen for following them without their knowledge."

The High Priestess inclined her head in gracious permission.

Arim turned to Jessan and Bashae. "I had to be certain of you both. I hope you understand."

Jessan's first inclination was to be angry, but the thought of the terrible object that he carried and the realization that he'd done little to earn anyone's trust caused him to swallow his bile. He nodded, his face rigid.

Bashae regarded Arim intently. "Can *we* be certain of *you?*"

Arim was taken aback for a moment. Because the pecwae was small, like a child, Arim had expected him to think like a child. He realized he had made a mistake.

"You can be certain of me," Arim said. "I swear by the gods in whose presence we now come."

"Good enough," said Bashae. "For now."

At the command of the priestess, the guards lifted their spears. The priestess indicated with a gesture of her hand that Arim and the Trevenici were to precede her.

The way down was long, the stairs steep, for they had been carved into the side of the cliff. At the bottom of the stairs was a vast courtyard, whose paving stones were made of white marble, flecked with gold. Benches and fountains provided solace and refreshment for those weary after their long descent. At the north end of the courtyard stood two double doors made of bronze, marked with the symbol of the Queen of Nimorea—a white bear formed of inlaid marble.

"I've never seen a white bear before," said Bashae and then he clapped his hand over his mouth, for his shrill voice rang throughout the court-yard.

"Yet, we have them in our country," the priestess answered him with a smile. "When our Princess Hykael led her people to this land, they came upon a white bear, blocking their path. The people were frightened, for they knew that the white bear had been sent by the gods. The people begged the Princess to flee the bear. The Princess refused to heed them. She walked forward to meet the white bear, saying that if it slew her, then she knew that the gods had punished her for her misdeeds. She came before the bear and knelt at its feet.

"The white bear turned and walked away. The Princess followed and so did all her people, though the white bear led them away from the main trail. The people heard a terrible noise, like thunder that was not in the heavens but on the ground. They found out later than an avalanche had swept down out of the mountains and wiped away the trail. Had they walked that path, they would have been killed, every one of them. The white bear had guided them to safety. Princess Hykael named the white bear sacred and it is death now to any who would slay one."

As she spoke, they crossed the great courtyard. People fell to their knees in reverence as she walked by.

"Are you the Queen?" Bashae asked, awed and abashed.

"No, I am not," said the priestess with a smile. "I am Sri, daughter to the Queen."

Sri led them through the bronze doors with their great white bears. No guards stood at the doors for if the guards upon the stairs felt threatened, they had only to jab the butt of the spear into the eye of a dragon to activate a mechanism that would cause the bronze doors to boom shut.

Peace and serenity reigned inside the temple. The music of flute and chimes and plashing water formed a soothing undercurrent to the prayers of the supplicants. Inside the bronze doors was a central altar, piled high with breads and fruit, bolts of silk cloth, carved wooden bowls and other offerings, some rich, some humble. The priestess stood to one side while Arim approached and left his offering, a gift of paper covered with pictures that he said the elves used as money.

"I didn't bring anything," said Jessan, stricken.

"I did!" Bashae said.

Reaching into his pouch, he brought forth a turquoise stone. He walked solemnly to the altar, and placed the stone upon it.

"Take care of that stone," said Bashae to the priestess. "It is very powerful. You can never have too much protection."

"I will do that and I thank you," said the priestess.

Bashae was never to know this, for he was never to see Nimorea again, but when Sri, priestess daughter of the Queen, came to rule some months later, she had the turquoise stone set into her crown. And perhaps the stone was powerful, for Queen Sri survived an assassination attempt made by a Vrykyl, the first and only person ever to do so. But that is another story.

After leaving their offerings, most of the Nimoreans went into the main chamber, there to kneel before the graven images of the gods and bring them their prayers. The three caught only a glimpse of these magnificent chambers, for the priestess led them down a smaller hallway.

The Temple was a veritable maze of tunnels, a small city beneath the ground. Here lived those who served the gods: priests and priestesses, their children, servants and acolytes. The Queen did not live here, but in the royal palace in Myanmin, a beautiful mansion of marble built on a promontory among the foothills of the Faynir Mountains. The Queen kept private chambers in the Temple, however; divided her time equally between matters spiritual and matters secular.

The doorways leading to the inner portions of the Temple were not readily visible. Most were secret doors, the trick to opening them known only to those who lived behind them.

Sri led them to a room at the very end of the corridor. At first, it seemed that they had entered a cul-de-sac, for the door was fashioned to look like part of the smooth-planed rock wall. She placed her hand on a certain area, palm flat against the rock, and pressed. The door opened, revolving silently on well-oiled hinges. She invited them inside.

Looking past her, Arim was awed, confounded. Reverently he lowered his eyes and almost immediately sank to his knees. He wished he could tell Jessan and the pecwae what a singular honor they were being accorded, but he dared not do so. If the priestess wanted them to know, it was for her to tell them.

"This is my private altar," said Sri. "I am pleased to welcome you and your friends, Arim the Kite-Maker."

"I thank you for this honor, Daughter of the Gods," Arim said.

His was a familiar face about the palace, for, under the guise of making and mending the royal kites, he had handled several delicate matters of state for the Queen. He had never seen Sri in the palace, had not known that the Princess was aware of him or his business. On reflection, he was not surprised. As heir to the throne, she would be kept apprised of all that was transpiring in her mother's realm.

Arim introduced his companions. He and the priestess both spoke in Elderspeak, as a courtesy to their guests. Bashae was awed into silence. Jessan could not take his gaze from Sri. He bowed, but said nothing.

The only light in the small chamber came from coals glowing red in a brazier standing on a raised dais. The room was heady with the scented oils the priestess Sri rubbed on her skin and with the lingering fragrance of incense.

Sri turned to face Jessan. "Do you know why the guards refused you admittance?"

Jessan's face flushed in the glowing light of the charcoal. "I—Yes," he said, after a moment's struggle. "I think I know."

"When the guards looked at you, they saw a fistula, an ulceration in your spirit. I know, for I see the same. The wound is not here." Sri placed her hand on his heart. Her touch was gentle, yet seemed to invoke pain, for his body trembled. "Nor is the wound here." She rested her long-nailed fingers lightly on his forehead. "Lift up your hands."

Jessan did so, turning his palms upward.

"The fistula is here," said Sri, indicating the palm of his right hand. She did not touch it.

Jessan closed the hand involuntarily, almost as if there were truly a wound there, though in reality the skin was unscarred.

"I have a knife, an artifact of the Void," he said. Looking into her eyes, he gave forth his very soul. "I took it from a creature of the Void, a thing known as a Vrykyl. I knew what I was doing was wrong. The dwarf warned me and so did the dying knight. But I wanted it and I would not listen. I knew it was wrong," he repeated, "but I didn't know the knife was evil. You have to believe me." He shuddered, his hands clenched. "I didn't know it was made of . . . of human bone. Now that I do know, I don't want to touch it or see it, ever again. I want to be rid of it."

"One of those Vrykyl is coming to get the knife back," Bashae added. "The Grandmother saw it in the fire and she showed it to us. Jessan's seen it, too."

"The knife is a blood knife," Arim explained. "A powerful artifact of the Void. Bashae is right. One of the Vrykyl does follow after them."

"I am putting those I was charged to protect in danger," said Jessan. "I didn't know what else to do. I came here because I hoped the gods would accept the knife and destroy it."

"We will see if the gods will accept it." Sri gestured to the brazier of glowing coals. "Drop the knife on the holy fire, Jessan."

Jessan slid the knife out of its sheath, handling it reluctantly, yet eager to be rid of it. The bone knife glimmered an eerie, ghostly white amid the red-tinged shadows. Holding the knife gingerly, Jessan approached the brazier and tried to drop the knife on the hot coals.

With startling swiftness, the knife blade altered form, wrapped around his hand.

Jessan's breath whistled through his teeth in horror. He gasped and tried to shake the knife free, but it held fast, not clinging to him in panic, but chaining him, making him a prisoner, claiming him for its own.

Crying out in pain, Jessan snatched back his hand. The moment the knife was away from the heat of the gods' anger, the blade reverted to its original shape and form.

Shuddering, Jessan hurled it to the floor.

"I have to get rid of it!" he cried in hollow tones, staring at the knife with loathing. "If the gods won't take it, I'll throw it in the Sea of Redesh—"

Sri shook her head. "The sea is not deep enough. The ocean is not deep enough. Every chasm has a bottom. An artifact such as this cannot be lost if it wants to be found. The other Vrykyl know that the blood knife still exists. They actively seek it. The knife would entangle itself in nets of some fisherman or wash ashore to be found by a child looking for sea shells. The knife would claim a new owner, some innocent, who does not know the nature of the evil. Is that what you want?"

Jessan shook his head. He could hear his uncle's voice. *A man must take responsibility for his own actions. It is the way of the coward to try to foist off blame onto another or to deny one's part for fear of retribution. The only act more cowardly is flight in the face of the enemy.*

"I know it will take great courage to continue to bear the bone knife, Jessan," Sri said, "but I believe you have that courage."

"I don't know if I do or not," Jessan said softly, anguished. "Every night I see the eyes, hear the hoofbeats. Every night I wonder if this will be the night the eyes see me. Every night I know the hoofbeats are coming closer. The worst part is that I am bringing the danger to those I care about."

Jessan squared his shoulders. "The burden is mine. It rests on me. I will keep the knife, but I will leave my friends to go on alone. I'll join my people, the other Trevenici—"

"But, Jessan," Bashae interrupted, "you can't. We were both chosen. Remember? Both of us together. I'm not afraid of the danger. Truly I'm not."

"You're not facing facts, Bashae! You're being stupid—"

"Then so are the gods being stupid," said Sri. "A cord binds you both, a cord woven of light and of darkness. Without the one, there is not the other. So it must be until your journey's end."

"I guess you're stuck with me, Jessan," said Bashae cheerfully.

Jessan did not smile. His expression was grim, his eyes shadowed.

"Have the gods answered *your* question?" she said suddenly, turning to Arim.

"Yes, Daughter of the Gods, they have," Arim replied.

"You will guide them to where they need to go?"

"Yes, Daughter of the Gods, I will guide them. And protect them."

Jessan's lip curled slightly at this. The young warrior glanced askance at the kite maker's slender build and delicate hands, fit for painting birds and butterflies. He said nothing, but thought to himself that here was one more burden, one more person he would need to look after.

"The gods be with you," said Sri. She pulled a ring off her finger, handed it to Arim. "Take this to the elven ministry. You will encounter no difficulty entering the lands of the Tromek."

Arim was thankful for the ring, for it bore the royal seal and would go far to smooth his way. "I would dare to ask one more boon of the gods before I depart."

"And that is?" Sri's eyes were warm, reflecting the glow of the coals.

"I would beg the gods' forgiveness for doubting their wisdom," Arim said humbly.

"You are forgiven," said Sri.

27

AFTER CROSSING THE SMALL RIVER KNOWN AS THE NABIR THAT FLOWED out of the Sea of Redesh, Wolfram and Ranessa traveled still farther south to the banks of the Sea of Kalar. Their journey was peaceful, too peaceful as far as Wolfram was concerned. They did not see a single person on this leg of their trip and this during midsummer, the best season of the year for traveling. Wolfram had been looking forward to falling in with some congenial companions as they drew close to their destination, the Karnuan seaport of Karfa 'Len, and he was disappointed as the days passed and they saw no one on the road. A journey shared is a journey shortened, as the saying went, and the dwarf had never wished for a shorter journey than this one.

Wolfram moped over this until Ranessa grew weary of hearing him complain and told him to shut up about it.

"There are no people on the road, so what?" she said. "There are too many people in the world as it is. I enjoy solitude and silence, especially silence."

Offended, Wolfram accommodated her. When he spoke, it was to his horse and then he took care that Ranessa should be out of hearing. As the days passed and the road continued to stretch empty before them, Wolfram's disappointment changed to unease. Caravans and merchants were kept off the road by only two things: snow and war. There was no snow. That left war.

Given the hatred that existed between Dunkarga and Karnu, the two waged war at the least provocation. Hundreds might die over a stolen chicken. Wolfram had no desire to be caught up in a civil war. He had nothing to fear from disciplined soldiers, but lawless gangs were quick to take advantage of the turmoil of civil war to raid and loot the countryside, prey upon hapless wayfarers.

Wolfram kept a sharp lookout. Ever since Ranessa's claim that someone was following them, the dwarf had felt eyes on the back of his head. More than once he'd wakened in the night with the feeling that someone was creeping up on him. The sound of an owl hooting in the night brought him bolt upright, breaking out in a cold sweat.

Wolfram blamed Ranessa. She was enough to spook anyone, with her fits of bad temper, her restless pacings and trance-like stares eastward. He'd be crazy as she was if they traveled together much longer.

The feeling of being watched abated somewhat as they traveled farther south. Wolfram had three good nights of sound sleep and felt better than he had in days.

"Whatever you claimed was following us must have lost us," he remarked to Ranessa that morning. "Likely we were too cunning for it. Gave it the slip."

He meant that to be sarcastic, but, as usual, Ranessa missed the gibe.

Leveling her gaze northward, she said gravely, "Yes, we have thrown it off the trail, but not for long." She turned her strange eyes upon him. "It comes for you."

He felt a chill right down to the marrow of his bones and was deeply sorry he'd ever spoken.

Wolfram was elated when they crossed the Nabir river, for that meant they were close to their destination. A half day's ride brought them to the walls of the city of Karfa 'Len. This was not the end of their journey, not by any means, but they had accomplished the first leg. Having settled in his mind that the country was in a state of war, Wolfram was not surprised to find the city gates shut and barred and under heavy guard. He *was* surprised to see that the Karnuan soldiers who lined the walls had their hands on their bows, and that they glared down at him and Ranessa suspiciously.

"What are they looking at me like that for?" Wolfram demanded. "Surely dwarves haven't declared war on Karnu."

He rode round to the postern that was some distance from the main gate. Dismounting, he told Ranessa to remain where she was and keep her mouth shut, then he walked over to the postern and rapped sharply at the iron-barred door.

A panel slid open, an unfriendly eye peered through it.

"What do you want?" a voice demanded in Karnuan.

"To come in," Wolfram growled. He spoke a smattering of Karnuan, enough to get by. "What do you think we want?"

"I neither know nor care," the voice returned coldly. "Ride on."

The panel started to slide shut. Wolfram was about to speak, when Ranessa shoved him to one side and thrust her hand inside the panel, preventing it from closing.

"We have business here," she stated in Elderspeak.

"Remove your hand from the door or I will remove it from your arm," said the voice.

In answer, Ranessa grasped hold of the wooden panel and ripped it off the door. She tossed it contemptuously to the ground and stood glaring through the opening.

Wolfram stared in open-mouthed wonder at the broken panel piece. The wood was thick as his thumb. A strong man might have grunted and heaved, expended all his effort and not ripped out that panel piece. The Karnuan on the other side of the door was no less amazed, both at the effrontery and at the show of strength.

Ranessa turned to Wolfram. "Tell him our business," she ordered peremptorily. Stepping back, she crossed her arms and stood waiting expectantly. If she thought she'd done anything remarkable, she did not show it by her calm demeanor.

Wrenching his gaze from the broken panel, Wolfram sidled forward. "I . . . uh . . . have business with Osim the Cobbler on Boot Street."

"The shops are closed. We are at war."

"I know that," Wolfram said impatiently. "Or at least I guessed it. What do you suspect me of? Do you think I have the Dunkargan army hidden in my pocket? You've been watching us for the last five miles. It's me and the girl, that's all. If you are at war, all the more reason to let us inside the walls where it's safe."

"Nowhere is safe," said the voice. "And we are not at war with Dunkarga."

The face disappeared, leaving Wolfram to wonder who in the name of the Wolf they were at war with then. He might have supposed the Vinnengaeleans, for Karnu had humbled and humiliated the empire by sweeping unexpectedly out of the south to seize the Vinnengaelean Portal located at Romdemer, now renamed Delak 'Vir. But the Karnuans had been in possession of the Vinnengaelean end of the Portal for many years now and although the Vinnengaeleans spoke heatedly of retaking it, they had yet to do more than issue empty threats.

The face returned. "You can come in," the soldier said grudgingly. "But you'll both be under escort, so watch your step."

Leading his horse through the postern into the bailey, Wolfram noted that the faces of the soldiers surrounding him were grim and stern and watchful. He might have added fearful, but that was hard to believe of Karnuans.

The postern gate shut behind them. Workmen arrived to repair the damaged panel. A guard was detailed to accompany them across the bailey to the main wall surrounding the city. The soldier was female, for in Karnu both men and women are trained to battle from their fifteenth year to their twentieth. The best warriors are accepted into the Karnuan army, the rest return to hearth and home to farm the land or take up a trade, raise their children to be future warriors. Their military training is put to good use, however, for they serve as the city militia, guarding their homes when the warriors are called to fight in other areas. The militia forces are not to be taken lightly, for they are well-trained and they fight with extra incentive—they fight to protect those they love.

"You rode from the north?" the soldier asked. Her speech was clipped. Her voice was tense. What little he could see of her face beneath her helm was drawn and taut.

"We did," said Wolfram.

"And saw no one? No *thing*?" she asked with a dire emphasis.

"No," said Wolfram, puzzled and increasingly uneasy. "The road was empty, except for her." He jerked his thumb back at Ranessa. "Unusual for this time of year. I feared something was up. One reason she and I elected to join forces, travel together."

He said this loudly. He sent Ranessa a piercing stare to indicate that she was not to contradict him. He had been able to think of no other way to explain the odd fact that a dwarf and Trevenici were companions.

Ranessa saw his look and absorbed it, but whether she intended to go along with his story or not, he couldn't tell. She gazed around her, so lost in wonderment that she'd dropped the horse's reins. Free to roam away, the horse trotted up to join Wolfram.

Retrieving the reins, Wolfram gave Ranessa a none too gentle prod in the shins with his boot. "Quit staring, Girl. You look like you've just fallen off the hay cart. You don't have to tell the world you've never been in a city before."

"It's here," she said, turning her gaze to the dwarf. "Close by."

"What's here?" Wolfram snapped.

"The thing that is following you."

Fumbling for his knife, Wolfram whipped around so fast that he made himself dizzy.

He saw nothing behind him except more city and more soldiers. Wolfram's racing heartbeat returned to normal.

"Don't do that to me, Girl!" he said angrily. "You've shaved ten years off my life at least. What do you mean telling me something's there when it's not?"

"It was," she said, shrugging. "It is."

The Karnuan soldier stood staring at him. "What ails you, Dwarf?"

"I'm just a little jumpy," he said lamely. "What with the talk of war and all. It makes me nervous."

The Karnuan cast him a scathing glance and rolled her eyes in disgust. Her already low opinion of dwarves was now even lower.

"I have been on the road for many months," Wolfram continued. Speaking to the soldier, he pointedly ignored Ranessa. "Up in Trevenici lands. I've heard no news. What is going on?"

The woman gave him a cool glance from out of the eye slits of her helm. "You have not heard, then, that the city of Dunkar has fallen?"

"What? Dunkar fallen! I suppose congratulations are in order," Wolfram said, then saw the woman was not pleased about her news.

"It did not fall to us," the soldier said bitterly. "It fell to this new enemy, hideous creatures who came out of the west, led by one who calls himself Dagnarus and claims to have the blood of the old Dunkargan kings in his veins. He maintains that he will return Dunkarga to her days of glory and he has attacked both the city of Dalon 'Ren and the Karnuan Portal."

Wolfram's jaw went slack. "I've heard nothing of this," he began and was nearly knocked down by Ranessa.

Bounding forward, she caught hold of the soldier's arm. "Dunkar fallen! Tell me—what of the Trevenici warriors? What happened to them?"

"She has a brother who fights with the Dunkar army," Wolfram added.

The soldier shook off Ranessa's nail-piercing grasp. "Unlike the sniveling coward Dunkargans, who surrendered in droves, we heard the Trevenici stood their ground and were wiped out to a man." She added the traditional Karnuan blessing for a fallen warrior, *Al shat alma shal*: "He died the death," meaning, "he died the death of a hero."

"I was unkind to him," Ranessa said softly. "I did not mean to be. I couldn't help myself." She clasped her arms, frantically ran her hands up and down her flesh. "My skin feels so tight sometimes!"

She spoke in Tirniv, for which Wolfram was thankful, not wanting their host to realize they had let a mad woman into their city. We'll not be here long, he reflected. Sounds like this part of the world is going to hell in a handbasket. The sooner we leave, the better.

They had just reached the main wall when a shout rang out. "Sails! Sails to the south!"

A second shout sounded on the echoes of the first.

"Orks!"

The soldier abandoned them in an instant, turned to run back to take her place on the outer wall. Wolfram tugged on the horses' reins and hurried forward toward the postern, urging the beasts along. Glancing back, he bellowed at Ranessa. She walked with her head bowed, her hair a tattered veil covering her face, seemingly oblivious to the commotion that was breaking out all around them.

"Make haste, Girl! Didn't you hear?"

She lifted her head. "What? Hear what?"

"Orks! The city's coming under siege!"

She had no idea what he meant, that was clear enough, but she did quicken her pace. They were admitted into the city without question, the

Karnuans being now far too preoccupied to concern themselves over a dwarf and a barbarian.

Bells rang throughout the town. People hastened to the walls or climbed up on their rooftops to see for themselves. Wolfram had no need. He'd seen ork ships before, seen their painted sails, the long sleek ships with rows of oars dipping up and down in a graceful, deadly motion.

The moment he and Ranessa set foot in the city, the first globs of the most feared ork weapon, flaming jelly, began to rain down on Karfa 'Len.

Flung from catapults mounted on the ork ships, flaming jelly is a combustible substance that sets fire to anything it touches, including human flesh. The worst part is that the flames cannot be doused. Water causes the flames to spread.

Wolfram cursed his luck. Had they arrived in the city an hour earlier, they would have been well out of this by now. As it was, he and the Trevenici were caught near the curtain wall, a place the orks would strike first, hoping to drive off its defenders. The orks launched boats, sent in their warriors to attack by land, while their ships kept up the bombardment from the sea.

Karnuan catapults began firing heavy boulders at the ork ships, hoping for a lucky hit to sink one. Wolfram conjured up a map of the city in his head. The orks would attack the port first, for the curtain wall did not extend over water. Massive logs roped together with heavy chains barred entrance into the harbor, but that would not stop the orks long. Worse luck, Boot Street was only a few blocks from the port.

"We have to get out of here!" Wolfram growled and, for once, Ranessa didn't argue with him.

He kept tight hold of the horses, for flames were starting to erupt around them. Smoke tinged the air. The horses rolled their eyes, nervous at the smell of burning and the fear that was palpable in the air. Wolfram stayed close to the heads of each animal, kept up a constant flow of soothing talk. The horses suffered him to lead them through the confusion and the cinders and smoke.

The streets of Karfa 'Len were crowded with people, but, unlike Dunkar, no one panicked. Every citizen was warrior-trained, knew what to do, where to go. Still, Wolfram and Ranessa had to make their way through streets clogged with soldiers running to reinforce the walls or dashing off to fight the fires that were now raging in various parts of the city. Their pace slowed to a crawl.

With the increasing smoke and noise, Wolfram had all he could do to keep the horses calm. He could not worry about Ranessa. Either she kept up with him or she didn't. Every passing moment brought the orks closer and while orks in general have friendly feelings toward dwarves, these orks wouldn't be having friendly feelings toward anyone they found in the city of their most hated enemy, those who had attacked and captured Mount Sa 'Gra, their sacred mountain, those who had taken many orks slaves.

He turned down one street, only to find it blocked. A wooden building had caught fire and collapsed, sending flaming rubble into the street. He retraced his steps, found another street, but he was now worried that he would end up lost. Not much liking Karnuans, who didn't have much liking for his kind, he never spent much time in Karfa 'Len. He knew his way to his destination and that was about it.

Ranessa kept close, her hand clinging to her horse's mane. He had no breath left to speak to her. Smoke burned his throat and stung his eyes. His arms ached. He coughed, blinked away tears, and kept trudging forward.

At the end of the next street, their way was blocked by a bucket brigade. A line of people stretched from the well to a burning house, passing along filled buckets and taking back empty ones to fill again. Wolfram kept going, determined to shove his way through if they would not let him by.

A glob of flaming jelly landed on the cobblestones near the Karnuans, splashing some of them, setting clothes and skin alight. Dropping buckets, they scrambled to get out of the way as the flaming jelly spread fire across the cobblestones. Some ripped off burning clothing, others screamed as the globules burned holes in their flesh. The fiery ooze struck closest to an old man. The burning jelly covered his chest and face, burned off his clothes in an instant, setting his very flesh afire. He shrieked in pain, staggered backward, clawing at the air with his hands.

His skin burned black, cracking and bubbling from the heat. His cries of agony were terrible to hear, resounded throughout the street. A young woman hovered near him, crying out that he was her father and begging someone to help him. His neighbors regarded him with pity and horror, but no one went near him. There was nothing they could do. If anyone touched him, the flaming substance would cling to him, set him ablaze, as well.

At last, one of the men—a veteran with a wooden leg—grabbed up a piece of timber that had fallen from the burning building and bashed the old man over the head. His skull crushed, he dropped to the ground. His screaming ceased.

"*Al shat alma shal,*" said the veteran.

Tossing aside the bloodied timber, he grabbed up a bucket and the water started flowing again, people edging gingerly around what remained of the flaming jelly. The old man's body continued to burn. His daughter stood over him for a moment with her head bowed, then she, too, returned to help pass buckets.

Wolfram had caught only glimpses of this. At the sight of the flames bursting up right in front of him, the horse reared in panic, nearly dragged Wolfram's arms out of their sockets. He spent a bad few moments struggling with the bucking and lurching beasts, trying desperately to calm them.

At last he had the horses under control. Exhausted, he stood panting, hoping to catch his breath, only to inhale smoke and spend the next few moments choking. Ranessa stood at his side, unmoving, staring.

"You might have at least helped me with the beasts, Girl!" Wolfram snarled, when he could talk again.

She turned and gave him the strangest look: as if she were seeing him from a far distance, as if she were standing on a mountaintop and he was in a valley below or as if she were somewhere up among the clouds and he was afloat on a vast ocean.

"Why do men do this to each other?" she demanded.

"Don't be daft, Girl," he said, exasperated. "The old man might have lingered for hours in terrible pain and suffering. The soldier did him a favor."

"Not just that," she said softly and, by her tone and her look, she had never before set eyes upon him. She spoke to a stranger. "All of it."

"Barking mad," said Wolfram to himself, shaking his head. He cast a glance at the body of the old man, now little more than a charred and smoldering lump. He looked at the burning building, the young woman passing buckets as the tears streamed unheeded down her cheeks, the veteran who continued to keep the water moving, even as he peered grimly over his shoulder in the direction of the harbor.

Nearby was a slave pen and an auction block. Several orks, chained together at the ankles, were being hastily moved to a place of safety. Their masters were not concerned over the orks' welfare, just over their profits. The orks lifted their heads, strained to see the harbor where lay freedom. They dared not cheer when a Karnuan house went up in flames, for the slave masters had whips in their hands. But they smiled.

"All of it," Ranessa said again.

Wolfram turned the horses. "Let's find another way."

The Vrykyl, Jedash, lost the dwarf and the Trevenici when they crossed over the Nabir river. He spent days combing the countryside for some sign of their trail. When at last he found it, the scent was cold. He estimated that they were at least three days ahead of him. Jedash was growing increasingly angry and frustrated over his failure. He had no answer to Shakur's insistent demands for information and now did his best to avoid Shakur. Jedash used the blood knife as infrequently as possible.

Jedash was well aware that Shakur was furious with him. Shakur cursed his lieutenant for being incompetent, could not understand why Jedash had not run such easy quarry to ground. Jedash had no explanation for his failure himself. It was as if he were chasing smoke. One moment he saw it clearly. The next moment came a puff of wind and it was gone.

Standing over the remnants of their camp, Jedash faced a difficult decision. He had an idea as to where they were headed. Karfa 'Len was the only major city in this part of Karnu and they were on the road leading to it. He could continue to traipse after them, wasting time meandering around the countryside in search of them, or he could place his money on his hunch that they were traveling to Karfa 'Len, could go there and wait for them. If he caught them in the city, they would be hard pressed to shake him.

Jedash decided that the odds were in his favor and he traveled to Karfa 'Len in haste. He avoided the main road, for he had not fed in some time and when a Vrykyl does not feed, the undead being has difficulty concealing its true nature.

The city had closed its gates by the time Jedash arrived, but he had no trouble obtaining entry. Waiting until nightfall, he used the power of his Void magic to scale the outer wall. His hunger was by now immense, verging almost on panic, for he could feel the magic that held the rotting parts of his body together start to weaken. He killed the first soldier he saw, thrust the blood knife into the man's heart. Jedash had a brief and fierce battle with the man's soul, but at last it succumbed to Jedash's will and he absorbed it into himself, strengthening the Void magic and assuaging his hunger.

He spent a difficult few moments answering to Shakur, who had been attracted to Jedash by the shared consciousness of the blood knife. Jedash assured Shakur that the two he sought could not escape him, not now.

Jedash disposed of the body by using a Void magic spell he had learned from taan shamans, a spell that accelerates decomposition of a corpse. The taan use such a spell to conceal from the enemy the numbers of their dead. Jedash found it useful in covering up his murders. Assuming the soldier's form, he finished the hours of his watch. All that was left of the corpse was a pile of black, moist dirt.

Jedash posted himself on duty at the gate, remained there day and night. His gamble paid off, his hunch was rewarded. He watched in satisfaction as the dwarf rode up to the gate, sought entry into the city.

Jedash looked for the dwarf's companion, the Trevenici female. Odd, but he had trouble seeing her. He was reminded of trying to look directly at the sun. It couldn't be done. Every time he tried, he was forced to avert his gaze. He couldn't understand it. Unlike the sun, the female didn't burn his eyes. No blinding light emanated from her. She appeared to be a perfectly normal human female, yet he could not keep her in view.

Jedash was about to leave his post, descend from the wall, when he realized that she was aware of him. She was searching for him. He froze in place. He felt her close to him and then her attention shifted suddenly away from him.

Relieved, he waited until the two had crossed the bailey and entered the next postern. By that time, the alarm had gone up that the orks were attacking. Jedash cared nothing about orks. He welcomed the confusion that would make snatching the dwarf that much easier.

Jedash raced across the bailey. He had to push his way through the soldiers crowding the postern and when he did, he ran into the street only to find no sign of the dwarf or his strange companion.

Jedash stared about in bafflement. They could not have escaped him! Not this time.

Cursing, the Vrykyl plunged into the crowd.

28

OLFRAM WAS LOST. THE LAST DETOUR HAD PROVED A MISTAKE. HE turned down a street that he thought led to the harbor, only to find it wound around to the south. Boot Street lay well west of his position. He could guess by the blaring sounds of the conch shells that the orks blew in battle that they had managed to fight their way ashore.

The orks set more fires as they surged into the city. Clouds of smoke billowed into the air. At least, their ships had quit hurling the flaming jelly, probably afraid that they'd hit their own people.

Wolfram was bone-tired. His throat was raw. His arms were so weak from hanging onto the reins that they shook. He did not have strength to fight a child, much less an ork. When he found a water trough, he gave a great sigh of relief. He led the horses to the trough, let them drink, while he splashed the cool water on his head and laved his neck and rinsed the smoke out of his mouth.

Feeling better, he assessed the situation. The streets in this part of the city were almost deserted, the inhabitants having rushed off to fight the orks at the harbor. This was a commercial street, the shops were shuttered. Faces of children peeped out of the windows above the shops. Occasionally an adult left behind to guard the children looked out as well, trying to see what was going on.

Wolfram sat down on the edge of the water trough, stuck his feet into the cool water.

"What are you doing?" Ranessa demanded.

"Soaking my feet."

"But . . . why have you stopped? Shouldn't we be going?"

"Nope," he said, shaking his head.

Ranessa glared at him, hands on her hips.

"Look, Girl, Boot Street, which is where we need to be, is hip deep in orks right now. If we went down there, we'd end up getting our throats cut if we were lucky or taken captive aboard an ork ship if we were not."

"But we can't just stay here!" Ranessa protested.

"Yes, we can," said Wolfram, complacently swishing his feet in the water. "I know ork raiders, Girl. They're here for three things: to do as much damage as possible, to steal as much loot as possible and to free all the ork slaves they can find. Once they've accomplished these goals, they'll go back to their ships and head for home. We just have to wait them out, that's all." He glanced around. "This seems as good a place as any."

Ranessa fidgeted and paced. Wolfram began to think he'd made a mistake. Ork voices, raised in gleeful howls or bellowing in pain, were coming closer, along with the clash of steel and officers shouting orders in Karnuan. The adults who had been looking out of windows came down to street level, stood in doorways, armed to the teeth, ready to defend their shops and their families.

One particularly gruesome cry caused Wolfram to flinch.

"Maybe you better go down to the corner of that street and take a look, Girl," he said nervously, pulling his feet out of the horse trough. "I'll stay with the horses."

"I told you," Ranessa returned, glaring at him.

"Told me what?" Wolfram demanded, but she was gone, running for a cross street about a block away. "Maybe, if I'm lucky, an ork'll snatch her—"

Glimpsing movement out of the corner of his eye, Wolfram put his hand on the hilt of his short sword and turned around.

By the Wolf, he *was* jumpy. It was only a Karnuan soldier, walking down the street. Wolfram relaxed, looked away, keeping half an eye on Ranessa, who was at the end of the street, about a block distant. Never fully trusting humans, Wolfram glanced back at the soldier. The Karnuan's walk was purposeful and his gaze was fixed on the dwarf.

Wolfram felt a twinge of unease, began to question the sudden appearance of this soldier. What was he doing here alone, away from his post? Away from the fighting? Ranessa's warning came back to Wolfram and, though he had put little credence in her words at the time, they now seemed etched in fire.

It's here. It's following you.

Wolfram drew his sword.

The Karnuan's walk quickened.

Wolfram's hand on the hilt grew sweaty. The soldier was coming for him, that much was certain. Perhaps the Karnuans had decided to arrest all dwarves or perhaps this was something worse, the something that had been trailing them across the plains . . .

A blood-curdling horn blast sent Wolfram leaping sideways, his heart clogging his throat. Guttural voices mimicked the horn blast. A group of orks appeared at the end of the street.

The orks held flaming torches and enormous curved-bladed swords. Their hands were bloodied to the elbows, their faces covered with grime and soot and smeared with blood. One of them lifted a conch shell to his lips and gave another blast. Some of the orks began breaking shop windows, tossing their torches through the broken glass. Others, sighting the Karnuan soldier, brandished their weapons and howled their battle cries. Karnuan citizens surged out of their doorways, weapons drawn.

The Karnuan soldier stood between Wolfram and the advancing orks. The soldier scowled, glanced from the orks to the dwarf and back to the orks. The gleeful orks descended on the soldier, caught out in the open, alone. They figured him to be easy pickings. Other Karnuans ran to the attack, but there were only five of them to about fourteen orks.

Calculating that the orks would keep the soldier occupied, Wolfram took to his heels. He raced down the street toward Ranessa, who was at the other end. Hearing howls and curses in two languages and the clash of steel, he assumed that the Karnuans and the orks had by now been formally introduced. He glanced over his shoulder.

The Karnuan soldier was gone. He should have been between Wolfram and the orks, fighting for his life. He wasn't there. The soldier had disappeared. An ork stood in his place. As Wolfram looked back at the ork, the ork looked at Wolfram and began to give chase.

Wolfram could not understand what had happened. He was so amazed that he forgot to watch where he was going. Tripping over his own feet, the dwarf went sprawling headlong onto the cobblestones.

The chill of death washed over him. Terrible memories of the Vrykyl came to his mind—of Gustav dying in torment, of the armor in the cave, oozing evil . . .

Wolfram leapt to his feet in a pounding heartbeat. He began to run as he was in the act of standing and he took off down the street.

His legs were short, the ork's legs were long, and the dwarf had lost precious time in his fall. Wolfram heard the ork's pounding feet right behind him. Wolfram sucked in a deep breath, let it out in a bellow.

"Ranessa! Help me! Hel—"

The ork seized hold of Wolfram, clapped a hand over his mouth and, with strength that was incredible even for an ork, he snatched up the heavy dwarf, hoisted him off the ground.

Ranessa stood at the end of the street that ran downhill, led to the harbor. She didn't know anything about battles or military strategy, but even she could see that the orks were leaving the battle field. Their purpose accomplished, their raid successful, the ork captains sounded the retreat.

The orks began to fall back. Disciplined, organized, they continued to set fires and grab up loot as they departed. They had with them freed ork slaves. The slaves still wore their chains, but they wouldn't be wearing them for long.

"Ranessa! Help me! Hel—"

Hearing Wolfram's cry, Ranessa turned to see an ork seize hold of Wolfram and lift him off his feet. The ork tucked the stout dwarf under one arm as easily as if he'd been a keg of ale and began to race down the street.

Rage swept over Ranessa. She didn't think much of the dwarf, but he was her dwarf and he was going to lead her to the Dragon Mountain. And now this ork had ruined everything.

Her anger swelled. The form of the ork wavered in her vision and then the ork disappeared. In its place stood a knight helmed and armored in death.

Ranessa recognized the Vrykyl, recognized the curse Jessan had brought into their camp. The curse that had brought doom upon Raven and the rest of her people.

Ranessa yanked her sword from her sheath.

More than once, Wolfram had tried to persuade Ranessa to abandon the heavy sword. This failing, he had then attempted to teach her to use it, so that at least she wouldn't cut off anything important to herself or to him. His teaching had proven only moderately successful. Ranessa was not athletic, nor was she particularly well coordinated. When she swung the sword, it was a toss-up whether she'd do more damage to herself or the enemy.

Ranessa let out a shrill scream that was like nothing that ever came from a human throat and ran straight at the Vrykyl, swinging the sword in clumsy, slashing arcs that came perilously close to gashing open her own thighs.

Jedash had not even seen Ranessa. All he cared about was the dwarf. Having fortunately killed an ork once, Jedash had shifted his image from Karnuan soldier to ork soldier. He was making good his escape, when he heard Ranessa's shriek.

The Vrykyl stumbled to a halt. Amazed, fearful, he stared at the thing that confronted him. He had not expected this. Not expected anything close to this.

He was certainly not going to fight it. Turning, he started to retreat, only to find that the true orks had all departed. Jedash in ork form was the lone ork on the street. Swords glinting in the light of the fires, the Karnuan citizens advanced on him, determined to vent their fury on the only ork around.

In his true form, the Vrykyl would have made short work of the Karnuans. He might have stood a chance with Ranessa, but that would be a hard-fought battle, one he was not yet prepared to wage. Jedash flung the dwarf at the advancing Karnuans. The howling Wolfram bowled into them, knocked them down like skittles. Freed from this threat, Jedash departed in haste, cursing Shakur, who had sent him on this ill-fated mission without providing him with all the details.

Ranessa gave chase, her one thought to catch the Vrykyl and slay the evil creature. Her sword grew increasingly heavy, however, and very nearly slipped out of her grasp, for her palms were wet with sweat. She was not accustomed to running. Her legs hurt and she had a severe pain in her side and no breath left in her lungs. With a final parting shout, that was both a victory yell and a challenge, she came to a halt, stood panting in the street.

Flinging the heavy sword to the pavement, wringing her aching hands in relief, she walked back to where Wolfram and the Karnuans were endeavoring to sort themselves out. Ranessa reached out her hand to help the dwarf to his feet.

Wolfram took hold of her hand. She gave him a yank that nearly upended him.

"Thank you, Girl," he said shakily. "You saved my life."

"I did, didn't I." She was gleeful. "Although I wish I'd had a chance to hit it with my sword. Are you hurt?"

Wolfram shook his head. He had a few bumps, his weak ankle ached, his ribs were bruised where the ork-thing had seized hold of him and he had a long, deep scratch down his arm made by a slashing Karnuan sword.

The Karnuans eyed Ranessa suspiciously. Far from being pleased that she'd helped them out, they grumbled that she'd stolen their opportunity for revenge. Knowing Karnuans and how they think, Wolfram guessed that it would be only a matter of time before it occurred to the Karnuans to take out their anger on the other foreigners in town.

"I'm all right," Wolfram said. "Let's get out of here."

Ranessa agreed. She'd spent time enough inside these walls. She wanted only to leave.

"That street leads to the harbor," she said, pointing.

Wolfram was pleased and gratified to find their horses still standing near the trough. For love of the dwarf, the horses withstood their instinctive terror of the Vrykyl. Taking hold of the reins, Wolfram limped down the road, heading for Boot Street.

Ranessa walked alongside him. The silence between them was a comfort to them both. Their shared encounter, their glimpse into the horrible maw of the Void, their unspoken fears and terrors twined about them, bound them together.

"Where are we going?" she asked at last. "To see a cobbler?"

"Osim," said Wolfram. "In Boot Street."

"Looks like most of that part of the city is on fire. Your cobbler may be nothing but ashes."

"Won't matter," said Wolfram. "It's nothing to do with him, really. In the back of his shop are the public privies." The dwarf grinned, his teeth white in his soot-covered face. "I don't think it likely the orks set fire to those. Inside the privies is a Portal, one of the magical tunnels through time and space. That's the real reason we came to the city."

"Will this tunnel take us away from here?"

"Yes," said Wolfram and he repeated it more emphatically. "Yes."

"Good," she said.

Wolfram noted something lacking.

"You dropped your sword, Girl," he said, slowing his steps. "Do you want to go back and fetch it?"

Ranessa shook her head. "No, I don't want it. The sword is too heavy for me. Too heavy for me to bear."

BOOK

II

THE OFFICIAL TITLE OF THE ELF LORD, GARWINA OF HOUSE WVYAL, WAS the Shield of the Divine. He was either the most powerful elf in the land of Tromek or second most powerful, depending on who you asked. This morning, Garwina did as he did every morning; he knelt before the household shrine dedicated to his Honored Ancestor.

Every elven household, from the lavishly furnished palaces of the Divine to the most humble hut of his most humble subject, has such a shrine. In the Shield's palace, the shrine was huge, expensive, elaborate. An altar made of black lacquered wood inlaid with ivory and decorated with silver stood on a raised dais secreted in an alcove hung with beautiful silks. The silk, specially hand-woven and hand-dyed by Nimorean craftsmen, bore the emblem of the Shield's house—a wyvern holding a thistle—embroidered in thread spun of gold.

On the table were arranged the possessions of the Honored Ancestor: his flute, his set of carved alabaster wine goblets, a silver pitcher taken in a raid from the castle of a Vinnengaelean lord, and other trophies and mementos, including his shield and his swords. A chair that matched the table stood behind it. Here the Honored Ancestor came on an almost daily basis to speak to his grandson.

Kneeling on the edge of the dais, the Shield lit the candles and made his offering—sugared wafers filled with honey and nuts. A favorite of the Honored Ancestor, the wafers had been made by the hands of his own wife, not those of a servant.

The Honored Ancestor appeared, a ghostly figure that wavered in the chair like candle smoke on a breath of air. The ancestor had died in his two hundred and sixtieth year of wounds suffered in battle. He wore the memory of his armor, in order to appear more intimidating. The old elf's hair had been silver gray when he died, but he remembered it as the shining black of his youth. His face was thin and gaunt and pale, resembled the face of his grandson—a trait of the members of House Wyval. The natures of the two were also very much alike. Both were stern, implacable, proud and unyielding. Always before they had sided together.

They did not side together now.

The Honored Ancestor ignored the sugared wafers. His ghostly hand did not reach for his flute, as it so often did, for though he could not touch it, he could remember the feel. He did not glance at the swords, although the Shield had ordered them newly sharpened and polished. Keeping both arms folded across his chest, he glowered at his grandson.

"Will you listen to what I have to say?"

"I will listen, Grandfather," said the Shield with a respectful bow.

"Listen but pay no heed," the Honored Ancestor said, sneering.

The Shield was annoyed. "Grandfather—"

"Enough! Hear me out. I have important information. This Dagnarus who now proclaims himself King of Dunkarga is in truth Dagnarus, son of old King Tamaros."

The Shield's expression hardened. "You think to make sport of me, Grandfather. That Dagnarus died in the fall of Old Vinnengael—"

"He did not die," said the Honored Ancestor. "He extended his life through the power of Void magic. He survived on lives he stole from others and thus he continues to survive. He is an abomination, a thing of evil. And this is the creature with whom you would ally yourself. Bad enough that he is a human. He is a human who uses magic to sustain his accursed life."

"He is also a human who has a chance of conquering New Vinnengael, of making himself King, of extending his control throughout the lands of the humans. He is the human who has promised me that if he is successful he will restore to the elves all the land now currently in dispute with the Empire. *All the land*, Grandfather! There is not a single elven House that would not be in my debt, for almost every one of them has some claim to some parcel along the border."

The Shield rose to his feet, began to pace, although he knew that this would highly annoy his Grandfather, who could pace only in memory. Unlike many of the dead, who were quite content to be dead, the Shield's Honored Ancestor was bitterly jealous of the living.

"The Divine himself is entitled to some five hundred acres of land south of MyrLlineth. He will be forced to come to me to beg for his land. He will be forced to humble himself before me, abase himself. Every elf in Tromek will see who is the true power in the nation. Does that mean nothing to you, Grandfather? That at last our House will receive the honor we are due?"

"And what is to be the cost of this magnanimity, Grandson?"

"I permit the troops of King Dagnarus to enter the Tromek Portal and I grant them safe passage through it. Have no fear, Grandfather. The humans will not remain on elven land. Once his troops are through the Portal, they travel south to capture New Vinnengael. The city will fall like rotten fruit to his plucking, for the eyes of the fool humans are turned to the west in terror of an invasion from Karnu. They will not be expecting an attack from the north."

"And you believe this man who has given his soul over to the evil magicks of the Void. That makes you more the fool. Dagnarus brought about the downfall of House Mabreton—"

"Of course I do not believe him. I have made my plans and if this is the same Dagnarus, as you insist, then he also brought about the downfall of House Kinnoth," the Shield observed coldly. The Houses of Kinnoth and Wyval had long been enemies.

"Bah!" The Honored Ancestor was not to be placated. "Kinnoth brought about their own downfall. Because of this Dagnarus, the House of the Divine came to power."

"Because of me, the Divine will lose it," said the Shield. "As to the Void magic . . ." He shrugged his shoulders. "I seem to recall that in the Battle of Tinnafah, you called upon the Wyred to use their magic—"

"I did not!" the Honored Ancestor stated furiously. "I would never be so dishonorable as to fall back on the use of magic in battle. The Wyred acted entirely on their own."

"Be honest with me, at least, Grandfather," the Shield returned coldly. "We elves have played this game for centuries. We do not admit to the use of magic, yet somehow the Wyred always seem to be in the right place at the right time to turn the tide of battle. I mention my plan for the use of magic to a certain member of my household, who mentions it to a certain member of his household, who sees to it that the Wyred find out about it. The next day I find a raven's feather lying on the path where I take my morning walk and I know that all is arranged. I have nothing to do with it. The magic does not touch me. In this instance, I rely on humans for the Void magic, not the Wyred. I see no difference."

"No, you do not. The Father and Mother help you," the Ancestor returned bitterly. "And your humans had better help you. I will not. For the last time, will you take heed of my words and disavow this evil man, break any and all ties to him?"

"I honor your memory, Grandfather," said the Shield evenly. "But you are dead and I am alive. You had your chance for glory. Now it is my turn."

"I will not be back!" the Honored Ancestor threatened.

The Shield silently bowed.

"The water of the snows of the mountains runs in your veins. Look to see me no more." The Honored Ancestor vanished.

"Good riddance," the Shield muttered, turning on his heel. "Meddle-some old fart."

Picking up the sugared wafers, he ate them himself.

After his midday meal, the Shield of the Divine took a digestive stroll in his garden at the hour of midday. He had a busy schedule this afternoon, for he had letters to write. Because elven missives are always written in the forms of elaborate poetry, his task looked to stretch forward well into the hours of evening. He did not have to compose the poems himself, praised be the ancestors. The Shield had not been blessed with a mind for words. He hired elven scribes, who are trained from childhood for such tasks.

He was about to summon the House poets when a servant came to stand at the end of the walkway, bowing and remaining in a prostrate position until the Shield should deign to acknowledge him. The servant was the Shield's own personal servant, a man who ranked as high in the small world of the Shield's household staff as the Shield ranked in his larger world. This servant was known as the Keeper of the Keys, for he kept in his possession all the keys to all the locks in the elven household, thus making him a very powerful individual.

Few elven rooms have locks on the doors. Few elven rooms have doors, for the elves prefer to live their lives in their gardens, which are elaborately constructed with many private alcoves and grottos, hedges, stands of trees and banks of flowers. The Keeper held the key to the chests containing the scrolls of the history of the family, the key to chests containing the family's wealth, the key to the cask containing jewels, the key to the cavern where the Shield kept his wine. In addition, the Keeper of the Keys was responsible for hiring all the other servants of the household, for knowing which ones were spies and for what Houses. He was responsible for the Shield's personal comfort and his business dealings, for arranging the Shield's daily schedule and for the planning of any trips the Shield might make.

Knowing that the Keeper of the Keys would not have interrupted unless the matter was of urgency, the Shield motioned the Keeper to come forward.

Advancing to the correct distance, the Keeper bowed and stated, "The Lady Godelieve has arrived, my lord. The Lady Godelieve knows how valuable is the time of Your Lordship and she knows that she is unworthy of taking up even a second, but she begs that you will overlook her unworthiness and grant her the favor of an audience. The matter is of the utmost importance or she would never dream of insinuating her insignificant self into your presence."

Insignificant self! The Shield smiled. The Lady Godelieve was one of the most beautiful and alluring women he had ever known. She was mysterious as she was beautiful, for she artfully avoided all discussion regarding her past. He knew very little about her, only that she was a member of House Mabreton, a House whose war with House Kinnoth following the fall of Old Vinnengael had effectively ruined both families. Mabreton had won, but the war had been costly in both lives and finances and, two hundred years later, Mabreton was still a House in ruins.

House Kinnoth was in worse condition, for one of its members had conspired with the elf who had then been Shield to murder two noble lords of House Mabreton and then participated in the seduction of a lady of that House by this very Prince Dagnarus, of whom the Ancestor had been speaking. This elf lord, whose name was Silwyth, and all members of House Kinnoth were cast out in disgrace. All titles, lands, and charters were stripped by the new Shield of the Divine (the aforesaid ancestor of this very Shield). The head of House Kinnoth "requested death," as was customary. The family name was removed from the roles of the Tromek.

Considered accursed, House Kinnoth had no protection under elven law. They were not permitted at either the court of the Divine or the Shield of the Divine. Denoted by the family tattoo that was ritually inscribed around the eyes, those members of House Kinnoth who ventured into other parts of the elven realm were shunned, thrown out of shops, refused admittance to taverns. Any who dared venture onto the lands of House Mabreton would be slain on sight. Thus would their punishment continue until some member of their House performed an act of either great heroism or great compassion. Then their case would be taken under advisement by the Divine, who might, in recognition, restore House Kinnoth to their rightful place in elven society.

As much as the members of House Mabreton hated those of House Kinnoth, they hated the members of the Divine's House of Trovale almost as much, for they blamed the Divine for their financial ruin. They were firm in their belief that much of their wealth had ended up in the coffers of the Divine.

According to Lady Godelieve (her name meant "beloved of the god" in elven), the Mabretons' plan was to bring about the downfall of the Divine, to recover what had been stolen. To further their plan, the Mabretons had joined forces with the human now calling himself King Dagnarus. The beautiful Lady Godelieve was the Mabretons' secret ambassador to Dagnarus. Acting in that capacity, she had come to enlist the Shield of the Divine on the side of the Mabretons.

"Where is the lady?" the Shield asked.

"In the tenth garden, my lord," the Keeper replied. "I know that she stands high your favor. She has been offered refreshment, which she declined, saying that she never takes food in the heat of the day."

"Escort her into my presence at once," said the Shield. "No, wait. Take her to the Island. I will meet her there."

The Keeper nodded and bowed his departure.

The most secluded area in the Shield's extensive land holdings was a large pool of crystal blue water surrounded by weeping willow trees. A barge moored in the center of the pool was known as "the Island." A wonder of craftsmanship, the barge was a floating patio, covered by a silken canopy to protect the occupants from the sun. A drawbridge extended from the shore to the barge. When the Shield and his guests had crossed the bridge, the bridge was raised. Guards stood at the bridge and around the pool. No one was permitted to cross on pain of death, thus providing the Shield and his party absolute privacy, something rare in large elven households, where eavesdropping is considered an art form.

The Shield reached the barge first. Seated beneath the silken canopy, he admired the beauty of the day and looked forward to admiring the beauty of Lady Godelieve. The Shield did not wait long. The Keeper of the Keys appeared, escorting the lady. She wore silken robes that were plain, not extravagant. As a member of an impoverished House, she knew her place, knew that to wear rich clothing would be seen as an attempt to rise above her station. Yet, such was her beauty that she might have dressed in sackcloth and been the most admired woman in the nation. Her complexion was flawless, pale with lips touched with carnelian. Dark rainbows shimmered in her long black hair. Her almond-shaped eyes were wide and entrancing, held secrets within their depths. Sorrowful secrets, or so the Shield guessed, for the Lady Godelieve never smiled.

The Shield received the lady with careful courtesy. She was profuse in her bows, acknowledged his generosity in seeing her with becoming humility. He seated her in the chair with the best view, made certain that she was comfortable and asked if she required anything to enhance her comfort. She protested that she was not worthy of such attention and begged him to be seated. He offered to have his servants bring her any delicacy she might desire, asked if she would take tea, for it was early in the day yet for wine.

The Lady Godelieve declined and he did not press her. After an hour exchanging the customary pleasantries that are required of almost every conversation among elves, the two were at last able to turn to matters of importance.

"His Majesty, King Dagnarus, expresses himself satisfied with the terms proposed by Your Lordship," said Lady Godelieve.

The Shield expressed his satisfaction with the King's satisfaction.

The Lady Godelieve made a seated bow, a graceful movement that put the surrounding willow trees to shame. "His Majesty King Dagnarus has asked that we once again go over the plan so that we are all of us in perfect accord."

A slight flush tinged the lady's pale complexion. "I am aware that Your Lordship has every right to consider such repetition an insult. I tried to explain this to His Majesty, but I could not make him understand. He has insisted."

The Shield's expression darkened. He *was* insulted, for he had dictated the terms and now he was going to be forced to hear them dictated back to him.

"I am not some schoolboy," he said coldly, "to sit through my lessons."

The Lady Godelieve rested her hand on his. Her marvelous eyes were soft with sympathy for him, pleaded for understanding.

"King Dagnarus is human, my lord. Take that into consideration and be generous. His Majesty says, and, I must admit, rightly so, that this is so very important to both of us that he wants there to be no mistake in his understanding."

The Shield took hold of her hand in his, softly stroked her slender fingers. "Ah, Lady Godelieve, such is the power of your exquisite beauty you could convince me that the moon is the sun, that day is night, that death is life."

The flush that had warmed her face vanished. She stared at him, her face gone bone white. If he had lifted his gaze to meet hers, he would have recoiled at the look in her eyes, a look expressive of loathing and disdain, that seemed to say, *What do you know of either death or life, you precious fool?*

She mastered her anger. By the time he lifted his gaze from admiring her hand, her eyes were limpid, still as the water.

"May I begin, Your Lordship?"

"Please, do," he said politely, thinking that, after all, this wasn't such a bad thing. The human was right. So critical, so dangerous was their plan that it was best to make certain both sides knew what was expected. And he could look at the Lady Godelieve forever.

"It is the intent of King Dagnarus to heap disaster after disaster upon the head of the Divine, so that he will finally collapse under the weight of them," the Lady Godelieve stated. "First, you will see to it that the elven Dominion Lords have no power to interfere with our plans. Those who do not side with you are either removed or rendered ineffective. This is most important to King Dagnarus."

"He has stated this before and I find it odd. His Majesty appears to have an irrational fear of Dominion Lords," said the Shield with some smugness. "They are mortal, for all their magical power."

"King Dagnarus does not fear anything in this life or the next," said the Lady Godelieve. "He respects Dominion Lords and the influence they wield over weak minds. He believes that you think too lightly of them, my lord, and he wants assurances that you take the threat they pose seriously."

"You can give him those assurances," said the Shield and not even the soothing effect of the lady's beauty could assuage his mounting anger. "Three of the lords, those of House Llywer, House Tanath and House Maghuran side with me. They feel the Divine is weak and too much under the influence of the Vinnengaeleans. Of the four Dominion Lords who oppose me, one finds himself embroiled in a peasant uprising in his homeland. Another has been sent on a mission to the land of the orks to study the state of the ork military, while yet another—"

"I know that already, my lord," interrupted Lady Godelieve coolly. "But what of the fourth—Damra of House Gwyenoc? She continues to be public in her disparagement of you and your policies. She is openly supportive of the Divine. We have information that the three who now side with you are starting to listen to her arguments."

"Her tongue will not wag for long, I assure you," said the Shield. "I have summoned Damra of Gwyenoc to my court. She arrives this day, in fact."

The Lady Godelieve was surprised. "What did you say to induce her to come here, my lord? Feeling as she does about you."

"It seems her husband has vanished," said the Shield. "A most unfortunate occurrence. I sent Damra a letter of condolence, in which I expressed my hope that her husband will soon be discovered safe and unharmed and that they will once more be reunited."

"Indeed," Lady Godelieve murmured, her gaze fixed intently on the Shield. "That is truly sad for her."

"I added in my letter that I had received information as to his whereabouts, information that I am loath to reveal in a missive, since it involves the Wyred. I suggested that she meet me here at my palace in Glymrae, where I would divulge the information and we would join forces, she and I, to see to it that her husband is recovered."

"I take it that the husband has been found," Lady Godelieve said with an arch of her delicate eyebrow.

"In truth," said the Shield, smiling, "he was never lost. Not to me, at least. He is being held captive by the Wyred of my own household."

"And she knows this?"

"Damra may be many things, but she is not a fool. She can read vinegar as well as ink. (A reference to the fact that elves often used vinegar to write secret messages which are invisible until held to the light.) Of course, she knows. Once she agrees to my terms, her husband will be released."

Lady Godelieve appeared skeptical. "Damra of Gwyenoc is said to be strong willed—"

"She has the misfortune to be in love with her husband," said the Shield dryly. "A destructive force—love. I do not know what the poets see in it. I am thankful to have escaped it myself."

The Shield made a signal to the Keeper of the Keys, and sent him to ascertain if Damra had arrived. So close were servant and master that the Shield had only to gesture for the Keeper to understand what he wanted. The Keeper bowed and left upon his errand.

"We were discussing love," the Shield said, turning back to his guest. "A destructive force, as I was saying—" He paused, alarmed. "My lady, are you ill?"

"No, no," Lady Godelieve said, but the words were inaudible, came from lips so stiff she could barely move them.

"You do not look well. I will have the bridge lowered at once." The Shield was on his feet. "Some wine . . . a honey posset . . ."

"Please, do not trouble yourself on my account, my lord." The Lady Godelieve reached out her hand, rested her cool fingers on his arm. "A sudden indisposition, nothing more. I am quite recovered. Let us continue with our business."

"If you are certain . . ." The Shield regarded her worriedly.

The lady assured him that she was and the Shield returned to his seat. He still had doubts, for she was extremely pale and he could plainly see marks upon her palm where she had driven her nails into her flesh. He did not question her further, however. One's health is a private matter among elves. Unlike humans, who delight in relating gruesome accounts of their latest gout attacks and the agonies suffered during a ruptured appendix, elves make no mention of illness in public and very little in private. The human greeting: "How are you?" is offensive to elves, who would never dream of questioning one another on something so personal. No matter how worried he might be about his companion, the Shield was bound by the dictates of politeness to continue on as if nothing had occurred.

"The Dominion Lords are not an issue," said the Shield. "Lady Damra will come around to my way of thinking. She will have no choice."

The Lady Godelieve looked as if she might have doubts on that score, but she said nothing, moved on to the next point—the attack on the Tromek Portal.

"The forces of King Dagnarus are in position along the Nimorean border," Lady Godelieve reported. "He keeps the taan in hiding, of course. When he receives word that the elven portion of the Sovereign Stone is in safe-keeping and out of the hands of the Divine, King Dagnarus will launch the attack against the Portal. You will see to it that he wins."

"Of course. How goes the war with Karnu?" the Shield asked. "Has the Karnuan Portal fallen yet?"

The Lady Godelieve frowned. Displeased, she favored the Shield with a cold glance. "The war with Karnu progresses slowly, but it progresses."

The Shield responded with polite wishes for the king's success, though privately he doubted if Karnu would fall. The Karnuan military was one of the best trained, best equipped forces on Loerem. The Shield's spies reported that King Dagnarus's war against Karnu was bogged down, that Dagnarus had badly underestimated the Karnuans' resolve and tenacity. The siege of the Karnu capital of Dalon 'Ren had been repulsed and Dagnarus had suffered heavy losses when a force from the neighboring city of Karfa 'Len had marched to the aid of the capital. Caught between hammer and anvil, the taan had been forced to retreat. The siege of the Karnuan Portal continued, but the Portal had yet to fall.

"Will King Dagnarus be sending reinforcements to Karnu?" asked the Shield. "I ask only because it seems to me that he is spreading his armies thin. I want to make certain that this attack on New Vinnengael will succeed. You can understand my concern, Lady Godelieve."

"Quite, my lord," she returned. "King Dagnarus believes that the numbers of his forces in Karnu are more than sufficient to achieve victory. That being said, once Dagnarus controls Vinnengael, he will be able to attack Karnu from the east, as well as the west. If Karnu falls now, or Karnu falls later, Karnu will still fall."

So, thought the Shield to himself, Dagnarus will not be sending in reinforcements. His troops in Karnu must make do with what they have. He wondered idly if those taan commanders knew that they were being flung to the wolves. Since he had heard that the taan monsters gloried in death in battle, perhaps they did not care.

"The Tromek Portal will fall. I will see to that," said the Shield. "In return, King Dagnarus pledges that he will move his troops straight through the Portal, that he will enter and exit our lands in the space of twenty-four hours and that he will relinquish control of the Portal once he has made use of it."

The lady found this talk of war boring. As she listened to the Shield, her gaze rested upon a pair of regal, white birds known as egrets. A mated pair, they strolled together through the crystal waters of the lake, their long, graceful legs lifting slowly and deliberately, their white head plumage fluttering in the wind. One, the male, spotted a fish. His head darted into the water, snagged it. Bringing it up, he presented it to his mate, who accepted it with delicate grace and gulped it down whole.

The lady watched the two birds a moment longer, then said, "King Dagnarus makes that pledge, my lord. Knowing that it is natural for two people who have never met face-to-face to hold doubts, I offer myself as hostage to the king's good faith. I will remain in Glymrae, in your keeping. Should King Dagnarus break his sworn word, you have leave to vent your wrath upon me."

"Then I have no more doubts," said the Shield with courtly gallantry.

"For I well know that King Dagnarus will never risk harm to such a beautiful lady, one whom he must hold in his highest esteem and regard."

The Lady Godelieve murmured her gratitude for the compliment and expressed her unworthiness. All the while she spoke, she did not look at him, but kept her gaze on the egrets.

"That leaves only the Sovereign Stone," said the Shield and with these words he won back the lady's attention. In this, she was vitally interested. "You run a great risk. I must own that I am reluctant to expose you to such danger."

"I do not make light of the danger, my lord, but I think you overestimate it. Our plan is a sound one. And," she added humbly, "should something go wrong, I am easily denounced. I am expendable."

"If you are determined—"

"I am, my lord. All is planned. It is too late to back out now."

The Shield yielded with a good grace, as he'd intended to do all along. "Very well. When the theft of the Sovereign Stone is discovered, I will send messengers throughout the realm, proclaiming that the gods themselves have given us this sign that they have turned their backs upon the Divine. You have arranged for a place of safe-keeping for the Stone?"

"Oh, yes," said the lady with calm composure. "On that you may rest assured."

The Shield regarded her long and hard. Much as he would like to ignore them, the words of his Honored Ancestor returned to him. *Dagnarus is an abomination, a thing of evil. And this is the creature with whom you would ally yourself.* The Shield admired the beauty of the Lady Godelieve, but he was not some moon-struck youth, to fall prey to the throbbing of his private parts and abandon common sense. The Shield was a tall man, counted thin even among the slender elves. His body ran to muscle and bone and ambition, as the saying went. He had a wife, taken by the customary elven practice of arranged marriage. The two of them had collaborated to produce the requisite number of children and, beyond that and appearing together at public functions, they had little to do with each other. He kept no mistresses, knowing that they could pose a danger to him. He measured everything in his life by one tape—his quest for political power—and he used that tape to take the measure of the Lady Godelieve.

"I remain in your keeping, Shield," said the lady quietly. "From this moment forward, my life is in your hands."

"You know, Lady Godelieve," said the Shield, "that it would grieve me deeply to harm you."

The lady made a seated bow.

"But it is a grief," he added gently, "from which I would soon recover."

"I would not cause you grief, my lord," said Lady Godelieve, "on any account."

The Keeper of the Keys appeared on the bank. Catching the Shield's eye, the Keeper made a gesture. The Lady Godelieve was quick to see this and rose to her feet, saying that as much as she was enjoying herself, she was certain the Shield had urgent matters to which he must attend. The Shield demurred, saying that he could gladly spend a month in the company of the lady and urged her to be seated. She insisted, however, and the Shield was at last forced to yield to her.

The bridge lowered. As the lady stepped upon it, the Shield came to escort her.

"I saw you admiring my birds," he said. "They are quite rare. I had them imported from the south. It would please me greatly to present them to you as a gift, Lady Godelieve."

"I thank your lordship very much," said the Lady Godelieve, without a glance at the birds, "but I have no luck with living things. In my care, they would surely die."

The Lady Godelieve declined a polite invitation from the Shield's wife to spend the remainder of the day with her. Since the Shield's wife was intensely jealous of the beautiful Lady Godelieve, the wife bore the lady's refusal with only a faint murmur of protest required by good manners.

Alone at last, Lady Godelieve was free to return to her small guest house, one of many guest houses that stood on the palace grounds. She noted that another guest house, not far from her own, was now occupied. Servants carried jugs of hot water for the customary bath taken after a long journey, bowls of fresh fruits and other delicacies. The Lady Godelieve paused a moment in the shadow of a flowering hedge to see if the newly arrived guest would appear.

A woman stepped to the door, looked out. Lady Godelieve had never before seen or met Damra of House Gwyenoc, but she had no doubt that this was her.

Although Damra was a Dominion Lord, she was not given the title "Lord" or "Lady," since elven Dominion Lords exist outside proper elven society. Dominion Lords are granted magical armor and are sometimes given the power to work magic. Magic is distrusted by the elves, its use in battle considered publicly to be dishonorable, its use anywhere else considered publicly to be suspect. Privately, the elves rely on magic, but they must be discreet when dealing with the powerful and mysterious elven wizards known as the Wyred.

When the elves were first given the opportunity over two hundred years earlier to create their own Dominion Lords through the magic of the elven portion of the Sovereign Stone, the elves were glad to have the ability to create knights who were blessed by the Father and Mother, capable of awesome power. At the same time, the elves were concerned as to how these knights would fit in the tight strictures of elven culture. The Dominion Lords were not Wyred and so did not fall in that category. They were not ordinary knights, however, and their ability to use magic at a whim gave many elves the horrors.

The Divine ruled that all elves who were granted the exalted honor of becoming Dominion Lords must make a sacrifice to attain that honor. This sacrifice was their position in elven society. Their property and houses would be forfeit to the lord of their House, who would find them a place to live. They could continue to collect revenue from those lands, but could keep only enough to live on. Any excess was given to the House to distribute to the poor. Unlike other elves, the Dominion Lords are free to travel without requesting permission of the head of their House. They can take no sides in any battle between the Houses, but must act as arbitrators and work to bring about peace.

These rules not only keep the Dominion Lords out of elven society but insure that such powerful knights do not become too powerful. Certainly the Father and Mother would choose only those people known for their loyalty and compassion, their courage and honor. Such knights are not likely to attempt to seize political power, but the elves are a cautious people and know that it never hurts to make sure.

All Dominion Lords wear a tabard to mark their exalted standing (and to brand them as different), the design of which dates back to the days of King Tamaros. The tabard features two blue griffins holding a golden disk. Damra wore such a tabard over the long flowing pants worn for travel. A wide sash encircled the lady's slim waist. She wore two swords—one the weapon of a Dominion Lord and the other the ceremonial blade of her House. The gods had denoted Damra the Lord of the Raven. She wore that emblem on the back of her tabard.

Elves honor the raven as being a bird of majesty and quick intelligence, fearless and proud. Supposedly this Damra was the embodiment of these characteristics. Lady Godelieve had no way of knowing that, but she did think to herself that perhaps the title had been inspired by the fact that Damra rather resembled a raven. She was not a beauty. She had her family's strong nose and piercing black eyes. Her shoulders were square and she walked with a man's gait—taking firm long strides, as opposed to the shorter, more graceful steps expected of well-born elven women.

Leaving her house, Damra passed quite close to where Lady Godelieve stood hidden amidst the flowers, allowing the Lady Godelieve a good look at the rebellious Dominion Lord.

The woman did not appear so rebellious at the moment. Pale and careworn, she cast a fleeting glance back at the guest house and sighed softly, giving the Lady Godelieve the impression that Damra wanted to be alone with her thoughts, wanted to escape the bustle and confusion of servants falling all over themselves to see to her comfort. The Lady Godelieve waited until the Dominion Lord was out of sight, then entered her own guest house.

She dismissed the servants, saying that she was going to pray and consult with her Honored Ancestor. Assured that no one would dare interrupt her now, Lady Godelieve closed the shutters on the windows and latched the door.

Safely alone, certain of not being interrupted (for the visit with the Honored Ancestor is a sacred ritual), the Lady Godelieve reached into the folds of the sash she wore and drew forth a knife made of smooth bone. Once the knife had been white and glistening. Now it was starting to yellow. The tip was stained black with blood.

Holding the knife, she softly caressed it. What appeared to be a black, viscous liquid oozed out of every pore in her skin. The drops of the liquid flowed together so that for an instant it seemed as if the lady's body glistened with black oil. The armor changed form, hardened so that it was stronger than the strongest steel made by the famed dwarven smiths.

Holding the knife in her hand, the Vrykyl knelt.

"My lord," she said.

"Valura!"

Dagnarus's response was immediate. She sensed his impatience, his eagerness, although such emotions did not normally register through the blood knife. She felt them because she knew him, knew him well, knew him and loved him. After two hundred years, she loved him still. More's the pity.

Valura had sacrificed everything for him, given him everything, her body, her honor, her soul. For him, she had murdered the innocent, would continue to murder them, for they fed her needs. She was his creation. He had made her into this evil thing that could find no rest, know no peace. She could not blame him. She had made the choice to accept the Void. When she had known that her death was upon her, she had begged him to transform her into a Vrykyl so that they could be together always. He drank her blood. She gave him her life essence. Theirs was an unholy marriage, not blessed by the gods, but cursed by them. The two were bound by the Void.

And in that moment they were joined, she lost him.

Dagnarus needed her. He relied on her. Of that she was certain. Next to Shakur, the eldest of his Vrykyl, Valura was the most powerful. Of them all, including Shakur, Valura was the most loyal to Dagnarus. He who had once loved her now hated her. Every time he looked at her, Valura saw the loathing in his eyes. He loathed her, but the true secret loathing was for himself and what he had become. Yet he could not stop himself. His ambition, fed by the Void, fueled the Void.

"Is everything arranged?" he demanded.

"Yes, my lord," she said. "The downfall of the Divine is assured. The Shield is everything you could want him to be—greedy, ambitious, with an inflated opinion of his own cleverness. He is clay to mold in your hands."

"What of that Dominion Lord, the one who threatens to thwart the Shield's plans?"

"Damra of Gwyenoc has been nullified, my lord. The Shield has taken her husband hostage. If she wants him back alive, she will keep silent."

"This sounds flimsy," Dagnarus said. "What assurance do we have that she will cooperate?"

"She has the great misfortune to love her husband, my lord," said Valura, softly repeating the Shield's words. "Through what I can only assume to be the machinations of the Void, Damra of Gwyenoc is here within the Shield's household. I could find a more permanent solution . . ."

"Yes, do that. But be subtle. Don't rouse suspicions."

"Rest easy, my lord. You may rely on me."

"I know I can." Dagnarus's voice was grim, ironic. "When do you take possession of the Sovereign Stone?"

"Tonight, my lord."

"Bring it straight to me. The human portion is found. The elven portion in my hands. It is all finally starting to come together, Valura. The dwarven Stone has been located and I have dispatched the Vrykyl after it. Shakur and Jedash are closing in on the human part. I lack only the orken, but I know where it is. I am close! So very close."

"Yes, my lord."

And what then, my lord? Valura asked him silently. When you have the Sovereign Stone, when it is yours, what then? Will it fill the emptiness inside you? Or will it be consumed by the darkness that has consumed everything else?

She was appalled to find herself thinking such things and banished the thoughts immediately, fearing he would read them through the blood knife. Dagnarus was too elated, too rapt in his own anticipated triumph to pay her any attention, however. Waiting a moment longer, to see if he had any further instructions, she realized that he had gone.

Valura rose from her kneeling position. The armor vanished, replaced by the illusion of what she had once been—an elven woman, beautiful and alluring.

The Lady Godelieve, loved of the god, went to find out from one of the spies she had planted in the household the time and location of the meeting between the Shield and Damra of House Gwyenoc.

2

DAMRA'S MEETING WITH THE SHIELD WAS SCHEDULED FOR THE TIME THAT is known as Idyllic Time, the hour before sunset. The timing was, itself, an insult, for that hour is the time when everyone is supposed to be relaxing after the rigors of the day. It is a time for the taking of light wine, walking in the gardens, admiring the sunset. Since the evening meal is always served with the lighting of the candles, this meant that the Shield had, in essence, imposed a time limit on their meeting.

Damra was under no illusions. She knew from the moment she read the Shield's effusive poem that her husband was being held hostage. Griffith had been missing for many months and, at first, Damra had not been overly concerned. As one of the Wyred for House Gwyenoc, Griffith often undertook secret missions for his lord. But although he could not speak of where he was or what he was doing, he could still communicate with her, sending her, by means of the Wyred, letters filled with his love for her. Through the same means, she could send letters to him, writing of her devotion and providing him with the latest court gossip.

When his letters stopped coming, she knew immediately that something was wrong. She was desperate enough to attempt to communicate with the Wyred directly, a feat that was not easy, even for a Dominion Lord. As the saying goes, the Wyred are smoke and moon shadow. She had no luck: the Wyred seemed to have disappeared off the face of the earth as far as she was concerned. She was growing frantic when the Shield's missive arrived.

House Gwyenoc had long sided with the Divine in his struggle for power against the Shield. Cedar of House Trovale was a progressive, a forward thinker. He saw the elven economy stagnating. He wanted to open elven lands to human, orken and dwarven traders. Faced with a growing population that was causing the walls of many elven cities to bulge and consuming more food than the land could deliver, the Divine wanted to encourage elves to migrate, to travel, to seek work in other nations.

The Shield and those who supported him were adamant in their refusal to even consider such an idea. They claimed much of elven culture would be lost by mingling with foreigners. Humans—a boisterous, loud, vulgar and disruptive people—would bring their evil ways into elven lands, rape their women and carry off their children into their frantic, fast-paced world.

The Divine knew to his sorrow that some of the dire events his detractors predicted might well come to pass, although he hoped that by limiting the numbers of foreigners through visas and other legal documents he could control those who entered his country. But if nothing was done, he could see a time when his country would fall in upon itself, like a house built with rotten timbers. One year of drought, of poor harvest, would bring famine and plague.

Why did the Shield not see the danger himself? Cedar had first thought that the Shield was simply oblivious to their peril or in denial, but Cedar was becoming more and more certain that the Shield knew disaster lay ahead and was cold-bloodedly planning to use such disaster to further his own ends. He began to see that Garwina was capable of sacrificing thousands of innocents to increase his own power.

Damra was a close friend of Cedar of Trovale and shared his suspicions concerning the Shield, one reason she had actively opposed Garwina in every move he made. She had expected him to retaliate, but had naively imagined that his anger would fall upon her. She had been prepared for that. She had not been prepared for him to strike her husband.

As she waited for her audience, she wondered bleakly what she would do, what she would say. He was clever, she had to give the Shield credit for that much. He had caught her in a web as transparent as gossamer and strong as steel. If she denounced him, he would claim innocence, and, since she had no proof, it was his word against hers. Because her husband was one of the Wyred, he was outside the laws of elven society and not even the head of House Gwyenoc (her husband's elder brother) could lift a finger to save him.

The Keeper of the Keys led Damra to the Blue Grotto. The location was another insult. Located a far distance from the palace, the Blue Grotto was where the Shield met with elves of the upper middle class: burghers, minor government functionaries, and the like. The Grotto was no place for a private conversation. Although the shallow cavern with its mass of lilies and its bubbling spring-fed fountain was a holy site, believed to have been created by the elven spirits known as the bywca, it was surrounded by tall hedges of holly and thickly planted pine trees, a perfect hiding place for any number of spies, most notably the Shield's own. If he needed witnesses to the content of their "private" meeting, he could always trot them out—servants who "just happened to be passing by."

Damra's greatest flaw was her temper and the Shield knew it, for she had failed that particular test in her trial to become a Dominion Lord, a trial he had helped judge. She was grateful to the gods for overlooking her flaw and granting her the honor despite it and she worked and prayed daily to overcome it. The Shield used these humiliations to try to provoke her and she was determined that in this, at least, he would not succeed.

The Shield was in attendance, but his back was turned—a terrible insult—under the pretense of admiring his lilies. Damra clenched her hand tightly around the hilt of her sword, so tightly that the hilt inflicted marks on her skin that would not fade for hours afterward. One of the Shield's bodyguards, who were never far from him, stepped forward.

"I must ask you to relinquish your weapons when in the Shield's house, Damra of Gwyenoc," said the guard.

Damra stared at him. "I am a Dominion Lord. I am exempt from such rules. The Divine does not require Dominion Lords to yield up their weapons." She cast a scathing glance at the Shield's back. "Why does his servant?"

That was nothing more than the truth. The Shield of the Divine was considered to serve the Divine and was required to swear an oath of fealty and homage on a yearly basis. Still, the Shield did not like to hear himself referred to as such. The jab told. He turned and favored her with a cold look.

"A man who wields influence and power must of necessity make enemies, Damra of Gwyenoc," said the Shield. "I envy the Divine his feeling of security."

"Don't give in. Don't let him do this to you," Damra said to herself.

She conjured up the image of her husband, his warm eyes, his gentle smile. The Wyred are taught to be soft-spoken, self-effacing, taught to be neither seen nor heard. Griffith must have possessed such characteristics from birth, so naturally did they come to him. He was the perfect complement to her. He was the silent falling snow that could douse her crackling fire. The fear of losing him twisted her heart. Nothing else mattered, certainly not her pride.

She removed both swords and handed them over in silence to the guard, who took them with a bow and backed out of their presence.

"I came in response to your letter, my lord," said Damra, adding impatiently, "You will forgive me if I dispense with the customary pleasantries about the weather and the fragrance of your garden. You may forgo praising my ancestors and exclaiming over my beauty. Our time is short and, as you may imagine, this matter is of paramount importance to me. You implied in your letter to me that you had news of my husband."

The Shield turned from perusing his lilies to gesture to a chair. Damra had no choice but to be seated. The Shield remained standing, looking down at her, placing her at a disadvantage. Fury roiled in her stomach. Keeping it in check made her physically ill.

"You are known to be blunt and forthright—characteristics I happen to admire. I also know that you consider me an enemy, Damra of Gwyenoc," the Shield added in sorrowful tones. "I am grieved by this. We do not agree on certain political matters, but show me two people who ever do? I would like you to think of me as your friend and that is why, when I heard that you were concerned over your husband's mysterious disappearance, I went to great trouble and no inconsiderable expense to discover what I could about him."

You mean you went to a lot of trouble and expense to capture him, you ruthless bastard, Damra thought but did not say. Not trusting herself to reply, she merely nodded her head once, abruptly, to indicate she was listening.

"Where your husband was and what he was doing, even I cannot say, for the Wyred never divulge their secrets. He is with my Wyred now, Damra. Your husband is among friends."

The Father and Mother help him, Damra prayed in despair. The Wyred are trained to their art in one central, secret location. They are raised together from childhood, but then each is sent to serve his or her own House. Their loyalties to the House come first. Griffith had often opposed the Wyred of the Shield's House. He was no more among friends than she was now, no matter how much the duplicitous Shield tried to convince her otherwise.

She watched the Shield warily, trying to figure out the man's game. He had gone out of his way to insult her. He was playing at being her friend. Naked steel in one hand, a turtle-dove in the other.

"Do you know what I enjoy most about this part of my garden, Damra of Gwyenoc?" the Shield asked. He made a significant pause, then said, "The babbling of the running water. It says nothing, yet I find the sound most soothing."

Damra understood. Either hand she chose, she lost and he won. If he provoked her into rage, he would claim she had threatened his life. He could have her arrested, escorted in ignominy and shame from his House (not even the Divine would be able to publicly forgive her that transgression). If she accepted the turtle-dove of silence in exchange for her husband's life, she forfeited not only her pride, but also her honor and her dearly cherished beliefs. Her defection would seriously weaken the Divine. Cedar would understand that she'd had no choice, but he would lose respect for her and she would lose the trust and esteem of a man she much admired.

Damra knew the torment of the prisoner on the rack, whose joints are pulled farther apart with every twist of the screw. The knowledge of what she should do bound her to the torture device and the knowledge of what she wanted to do turned the wheel. Griffith would want her to remain loyal to the Divine, though it would cost him his life. If she bought his freedom, he would be disappointed and she could not bear to lose his trust.

Yet, how she could go on without him—her steadfast friend, her most trusted advisor, her heart, her soul? Better she should die—

"Keeper? Why do you disturb us?" The Shield sounded startled, his tone was tense.

Damra had been staring unseeing into the flowing water, so wrenched by pain that she had not noticed the Keeper of the Keys approaching them. This must truly be an emergency, for no conversation with the Shield was ever interrupted.

"Forgive me for the intrusion, my lord," said the Keeper with his lowest bow, "but visitors have arrived in search of Damra of Gwyenoc. A Nimorean, accompanied by two pecwae and a barbarian human, carry a message to her from one who has recently gone to join his ancestors. The message to her is this man's dying request, my lord."

Damra was startled. She could think of no one she knew who would make a dying request of her, certainly not through such bizarre messengers. Her first thought was that this was another of the Shield's tricks and she shot a glance at him.

The Shield looked neither smug nor cunning, however. He was clearly displeased at the interruption and why not? He'd been certain of victory and now the moment had fled. He glowered at the Keeper. The Keeper cast his master a glance of apology. Among elves, the last request of the dying is considered sacrosanct and must be acted upon with the utmost reverence and respect. The moment the Keeper heard that the dead wanted to speak to her, he had been duty bound to find Damra and impart this news to her, just as she was duty bound to go meet with these people.

Whoever they are, the gods themselves must have sent them, Damra realized. She was not free of the rack, but her tormentors had left to go take tea. By turning over the hour glass, the sands of time are rearranged, those grains on the bottom end up on the top. Hopefully, with some breathing space, she could find the answer she so desperately sought.

She bowed her regrets. The Shield had no choice but to accept them. The guards returned her swords and Damra departed, accompanying the Keeper outside the palace grounds to the very first garden—the tradesman's garden—for even though they carried the request of the dead, such outré visitors would never be allowed anywhere near the Shield's palace.

The Shield cursed the Father and Mother, as Damra had blessed them. Garwina had had her where he wanted her and she had managed to escape him. On reflection, however, he grew calmer. Flutter as she might, she could not free herself of the web. She would meet his terms. He'd seen the suffering in her eyes. She would never sacrifice her husband.

"Pecwae . . . Trevenici . . ." Valura murmured to herself.

The lovely Lady Godelieve had been abandoned. Taking the form of an underling gardener she had killed in anticipation of just such a need, Valura had been eavesdropping on the Shield's meeting with the Dominion Lord. Kneeling in the dirt, pretending to pluck out the weeds growing beneath the bougainvillea, she was a person of no consequence, no significance, invisible to the eyes of most in the Shield's household.

Valura kept the illusion of the gardener and made her way to the first garden. She took the servants' route, for it would never do for her to be seen on the main walkway. The guards took notice of her, for the lowliest servant might be a hidden assassin. They made a routine search for weapons, but found nothing. The magic of the Void kept the blood knife invisible to prying eyes. Having taken the short route, Valura reached the garden well in advance of Damra and the Keeper.

Valura dropped to her knees behind a low stone wall and peered cautiously up over the edge. Spying the four waiting visitors, she placed her hand upon the blood knife.

"Shakur . . ." The name hummed through the knife.

She felt his response.

"Valura."

Shakur detested her. He was jealous of her standing with Dagnarus. She knew this and reveled in it; one of her few remaining pleasures. Bound together by the blood knife and, more importantly, through the Dagger of the Vrykyl, they had no choice but to work together. The time would come, perhaps, when one would be forced to destroy the other, but that time was not now. They worked for one goal—their lord's ascendancy.

"You spoke to me of a Trevenici youth and two pecwae. You said it was possible that they might have something to do with the human part of the Sovereign Stone."

"Yes . . . Why? Have you heard something about them?"

"Do you have a description? What do they look like?"

"A blasted Trevenici and two blasted pecwae is what they look like," Shakur returned.

"Is there nothing special about them?"

"One—the Trevenici—carries Svetlana's blood knife."

Valura peered over the wall. The Trevenici youth paced the garden, back and forth in a manner that was highly offensive to his elven host, for all who entered the gardens are supposed to be lost in wonder and admiration. The Nimorean spoke to him, rested a hand on his shoulder, tried to placate him. As a shark senses even the tiniest amount of blood spilled into the vastness of the ocean, Valura sensed the presence of the blood knife in the vastness of the Void. The knife was in the possession of the Trevenici.

"Yes, he has it, Shakur."

"I was following him by that means, for he foolishly used it to kill. He must have been warned, however, for he has not used it for many weeks now. Where are you? More important, where are they?"

"The Trevenici and his companions are inside the first garden of the Shield's palace in Glymrae."

"What in the name of the Void are they doing there?" Shakur was astonished.

"They have come to see a Dominion Lord—one Damra of Gwyenoc. They say they carry a request from a dying man—"

"That's it!" Shakur was exultant. "That's got to be the Sovereign Stone! Either that or at least knowledge of it. I am with our lord near the Tromek Portal. If I kill a few horses, I can be there in days—"

"Not soon enough," said Valura coolly. "Remain with our lord. I will deal with this."

She could not imagine her good fortune—to be able to present Dagnarus with two portions of the Sovereign Stone: the elven and the human. Particularly the human, the prize he'd sought for over two hundred years, the prize he'd murdered to obtain, the prize that he'd nearly died trying to possess. He would honor her for this, honor her and perhaps he might even love her again.

Shakur was furious. He, too, saw this as a way for her to rise to greater power. His rage was cold.

"This is too important for one of us to handle alone. I insist that you wait for me."

"You are not my master, Shakur," Valura said. "You are far away and I am near at hand. I will do what must be done."

He fumed, impotent, threatening. He knew she was right—time was of the essence—but her being right made him all the more angry.

"I will speak to our lord about this, Valura!"

"You do that, Shakur," she said and thrust the blood knife back into her belt. Retaining the image of the gardener, she crouched behind the wall, dug among the roots and bulbs, and listened.

Damra entered the first garden in company with the Keeper of the Keys. Her gaze swept the garden, took in everything, not a difficult task, for unlike the elaborate, maze-like gardens farther up the hill, the first garden was small and open to view. Concentric circles of colored flowers surrounded a sundial mosaic. By day, the stones gleamed in the sunlight. Time's shadow swept across the face of the sundial, lightly touching the marked hours before passing on. The sundial was in full shadow now, for the sun had set.

The evening dinner hour approached. Servants moved about the garden, lighting candles placed inside decorative wrought iron lamps that stood at intervals along the garden wall. The light shone on a pecwae female, squatting on her haunches, rummaging among the stones that formed the sundial. At this very great insult, the Keeper sucked in a shocked breath and was about to call the guards. Fortunately, the Nimorean became aware of the pecwae's unconscionable conduct. He left off speaking to the barbarian youth and moved hastily to remonstrate with the pecwae.

Damra might well have been dismayed by the sight of these uncouth visitors, except that she recognized the Nimorean. He was Arim the Kite Maker, a trusted and beloved friend. The sight of him warmed and soothed her like spiced wine, even as she wondered what urgent errand could have brought him here and in such strange company. The hope immediately came to her that he had some information about her husband.

Damra completed her inventory of the garden, noting one entrance and two exits. The Shield's guards stood at the entrance and both exits, keeping an eye on the guests. The guards were far away. Ostensibly they would not overhear any conversation, but Damra guessed that their helmets did not cover their ears, as the saying went.

In addition, she was acutely aware of the Keeper hovering near. He would not depart until he was certain that all guests of the Shield's, even unexpected ones in the first garden, had been made comfortable.

Arim straightened from speaking to the pecwae. The Nimorean bowed to Damra. His bow was formal and studied—the greeting of a stranger, a low-ranking stranger. She acknowledged the bow with a slight inclination of her head. She said nothing, looked at the Keeper.

If the Keeper was disappointed that she did not openly question her guests in front of him, he was too well-trained to show it. He came forward to introduce himself and to ask if the guests required food or drink. He took his time about it, going through an inventory of the larder in hopes of finding something that might appeal to the visitors. Damra fumed in impatience, even as she watched carefully the expressions on the faces of the two pecwae and the barbarian youth. The Keeper spoke in Tomagi, the language of the elves. Arim made the polite response in Tomagi, for almost all Nimoreans are fluent in that language. As for the other three, either they were excellent dissimulators or they did not understand Tomagi.

The male pecwae stared in awe at everything, from the garden to the magnificent house of the Shield that could be seen far above them, rising seven stories from the ridge on which it was built, exerting its authority over its surroundings. The female pecwae—an elderly example of that race, to judge by the wrinkles on the nut-like face—still slyly poked at the stones of the sundial with a bony foot when she thought Arim wasn't looking. The barbarian youth appeared as impatient as Damra felt. He could not keep still, but fidgeted about as humans will, for theirs is a race that must always be doing. When he caught sight of the guards, he stared at their weapons with an interest that they would shortly consider threatening. He took a step toward them. Fortunately, Arim noted and placed a restraining hand on the youth's arm.

This gave Arim the excuse he needed. Cutting smoothly through the Keeper's offerings of lemon water and barley cakes, Arim asked forgiveness for the rude behavior of his guests.

"I think it would be best, Keeper, if we gave our sad message and then departed," Arim said.

Having just seen the pecwae female wrap her incredibly long and agile toes around a stone and drag it away from the mosaic, the Keeper agreed, in a faint voice, that this would indeed be best. After a formal bow and another agonized glance at the Grandmother, the Keeper left.

"I am Damra of House Gwyenoc," said Damra with the formal bow of introduction.

"Arim the Kite Maker of Myanmin," replied the Nimorean in equally formal terms.

At such cool formality, the Trevenici looked surprised. He glanced from one to the other, as if thinking this was a strange way for old friends to conduct themselves. Arim said something in Elderspeak to the young man. The youth glanced at the guards and nodded, quick to catch on.

The youth was tall and well-muscled. He had the type of square-jawed, clean-planed face that showed every thought on it, a face that could not keep secrets and must be discovered in a lie. His eyes were clear and met hers without flinching. Something about him was repugnant to her. She did not want to touch him. Arim introduced him as Jessan of the Trevenici and when the young man extended his hand in the human custom of clasping hands upon being introduced, Damra pretended that she did not know the custom and kept her hands at her sides.

The Trevenici looked affronted, but Arim covered the awkward moment well. He glanced at Damra and she saw in his eyes that he understood. She saw also in his eyes a shadowed disquiet, an urgent need to speak to her in private.

Arim introduced the two pecwae, oddities to Damra, who had never seen any of their race before. They spoke in high-pitched voices, sounding very much like chirping sparrows. The elder pecwae, known as the Grandmother, had bright eyes that stared, unabashed, straight into Damra's.

"You've more fire in you than the others," said the Grandmother after this rudely appraising glance. "That's a compliment," she added brusquely.

"Thank you, Elder," said Damra gravely, for one must always be polite to the elderly.

The young pecwae was called Bashae. Damra dismissed him as a child, wondered why they had brought him on such a long journey. Perhaps that was the custom of pecwae.

"I would like to admire the setting of the sun," Damra said in a voice that was meant to carry to the guards. "Will you walk with me?"

Arim agreed and, with a glance, brought the others trailing after them. She led them to the wall that faced the west, as far from the guards as the garden would permit them to walk.

"Keep your back turned, Arim," Damra said in low tones in Tomagi. "They may be able to read lips."

"Even by lamplight?" Arim smiled.

"Even by lamplight," Damra said quietly. "My dear friend, it is so good to see you. You have no idea how you gladden my heart."

"We stopped first at your home, Damra," Arim said. "I spoke to your servant Lelo. He told me that Griffith is missing."

"Not missing, Arim," Damra said with an anguish she could not suppress. "I know exactly where he is." She cast a dark glance in the direction of the Shield's house. "I had hoped that perhaps your arrival meant that you had some news of him . . ."

"Alas, Damra," said Arim. "I did not know he was missing until I spoke to Lelo. I regret that I do not come to bring you relief from your burdens, but only to add to them."

Damra remembered the reason given for their arrival—the last request of the dead. For an instant the wildly irrational fear came to her that the dead man was Griffith, but after a stricken moment, logic prevailed. Arim had said he had not known Griffith was missing and Arim was one of the few people in this world that Damra could trust.

"You said you bore a request to me from the dead," Damra said. "Who has died? I cannot imagine—"

Yet, at that moment, she knew. "Gustav," she said.

The young pecwae's head jerked up at this, the first word he'd understood. "Is she talking about Lord Gustav?" Bashae asked Arim. "Am I supposed to tell her now?"

"I am sorry," said Damra, shifting to Elderspeak. "I have been thoughtless. Please accept my apology, all of you."

"I accept it," said Bashae. "What did you do wrong?"

"It is not polite to speak a language in front of others that they cannot understand," Arim explained. "I also add my apologies."

"Just get on with this," said Jessan impatiently. "You keep saying this is urgent, Arim. We half-killed ourselves to get here and now all we do is talk and bow. Give her the knapsack, Bashae, and the message and be done with it."

What is there about that young human that is so repulsive? Damra wondered. She found herself wishing he were not present, yet she would not trust him out of her sight.

"Keep your voice down, Jessan," said Arim in rebuking tones. He looked pleadingly at Damra. "I would not speak of this here."

"There is nothing I can do, my friend," she said helplessly. "The Shield's guards will stop us if we try to leave. I cannot take you to my guest house. I think we will be safe enough in the first garden. It is probably a good idea to continue to speak Elderspeak. I doubt that the guards know the language of Vinnengael."

Elves consider Elderspeak a crude language, one that is not only beneath their dignity to learn, but which could prove corruptive to the elven mind.

"Very well," said Arim with a sigh. "Although the story we have to relate is best told in the light, for it is darker than darkness. My heart speaks to you before my lips. You have guessed rightly. Lord Gustav, our dear friend, is dead. He died in the village of the Trevenici, this young man's village. The Trevenici treated him with the honor of a fallen warrior and gave him a hero's burial. His soul has gone to join with the soul of his beloved wife. We do not grieve him."

"We do not grieve him," Damra repeated, yet thinking of the wise and courageous friend she had lost, she did grieve his passing, grieved it sorely. "How did he die so far from his home? What dark deeds do you speak of?"

"He died of wounds received in battle with a terrible foe," said Arim. "A Vrykyl. These two"—he gestured to the pecwae and the Trevenici—"were witnesses to the battle."

The night air was suddenly chill, the night sky suddenly shadowed.

"His gods be with him," Damra said.

"They were, Damra," said Arim. He instinctively started to reach out to clasp her hand. Remembering where they were and who was watching, he let his hand fall. She understood. She, too, felt the need for the comfort of the warmth of another living being. The Trevenici lowered his eyes, stood staring grimly at the ground.

"He defeated his foe," Arim continued. "He cast it back to the Void that spawned it. Yet, not before the Vrykyl had managed to inflict his death wound."

"The Void tried to claim him," said the Grandmother, startling Damra, who had forgotten the old woman's presence. "But it did not succeed. The warriors who fight on the other side came together and joined with the knight. They were victorious."

"I thank you for that," said Damra, turning to Jessan, studying him intently. "I thank your people."

He muttered something, but did not look up. Damra glanced at Arim. He shook his head slightly and she let the matter lie.

"Lord Gustav knew his death was upon him. But he could not depart this world without completing what he had started," Arim continued. "His life's quest. I believe that he finished it."

Damra stared at her friend in disbelief. Gods of earth, wind, air and fire! This was no place to talk of this!

"I am so pleased for him," she said faintly.

"Bashae," Arim continued, taking his cues from her, "you may now present the lady with Lord Gustav's gift and the words that go with it. Say exactly what Lord Gustav told you to say."

Abashed and subdued, Bashae held out to Damra the knapsack he had been clutching close to him. "I memorized it," he said and now that she looked into his eyes, she realized he was no child. "Lord Gustav said, 'Tell her that inside the knapsack is the most valuable jewel in the world and that it comes from me, who searched for such a jewel a lifetime. I give it to her, to carry to its final destination.'"

Damra heard a sound. She could not identify it or the source, was not even certain she had heard it. The noise came from the opposite side of the wall surrounding the garden. Bowing her head, as one who is overcome with emotion, she sank down upon the stone wall and put her hand to her eyes. She cast a swift glance along the outside of the stone wall and caught a glimpse of a shadow disappearing into the night.

"What is it?" Arim asked softly.

"Someone was out there," Damra replied. She stood up briskly. "Not surprising. The Shield has spies everywhere. At least they could not possibly understand—"

She stopped talking. Arim and Jessan exchanged grim glances. Jessan averted his face, stared with a stone-cold expression out into the night.

"What?" Damra demanded.

"It might *not* be one of the Shield's spies," said Arim. "We are being followed. We thought we had shaken off pursuit, but perhaps . . ."

The Grandmother lifted her walking stick into the air. The stick was decorated with agates made to resemble human eyes and was the ugliest thing Damra had ever seen. The Grandmother twirled the stick this way and that. The agate eyes peered out into the darkness.

"Evil has been here," she announced. "It's gone now, but not far." Rapping the stick upon the wall, she glared at the agate eyes. "Now is a fine time to let me know. What good are you? The lot of you. Bad as my children."

The agate eyes appeared to blink, winced. Damra almost imagined them looking chagrined.

She shook off the fancy. "I don't understand—"

With a sudden jerking movement, Jessan yanked a knife from a leather sheath he wore at his waist.

"It's this," he said in tones that were wholly defiant, partly shamed. He held the knife reluctantly to the light.

The knife was made of bone, slender and delicate and stained dark with blood. Damra recognized the knife at once. She knew the full extent of their peril.

"A blood knife. A Vrykyl follows you." Damra's temper flared. "You knew this, Arim, yet you brought him! That was folly, madness—"

"No, it was faith," said the Grandmother sharply. "Jessan was chosen, as was Bashae. The gods bound them together."

"That is true, Damra," Arim confirmed. "The priestess confirmed it. Jessan took the knife unwittingly. He has accepted his burden. He might have cast the danger away, for some innocent to discover, but he bears his responsibility bravely, knowing that it may yet prove his doom."

Moving close, Arim said softly, "If the Vrykyl captured Jessan, Damra, he would lead the Vrykyl to us. He could not help himself. They would devour his soul to gain such information."

Jessan held out the knife, moved a step toward her. "You're a Dominion Lord, like Lord Gustav. He killed that thing. You could take this—"

"No!" Damra recoiled. She could barely look at the knife, for it seemed to wriggle and squirm in the young man's hand.

Jessan straightened his shoulders, lifted his head. His lips tightened.

"Never mind," he said tersely. "I can deal with it."

Damra was moved to pity. "My husband is one of the Wyred," she said. "An elven wizard. He has made aspecial study of these evil beings. He would know a way . . ."

Her voice died. Griffith would know a way, but he was far from here. Far from her. He was being held captive by the Shield, who was still waiting her decision. And what was she to do? Lord Gustav's lifelong quest had been the search for the human portion of the Sovereign Stone. If the Sovereign Stone was the jewel hidden in that knapsack, her sworn duty as a Dominion Lord was to take it with all haste to the Council of Dominion Lords in New Vinnengael.

The humans had been waiting for the stone's return for two hundred years. They were growing desperate. The number of Dominion Lords was decreasing. Some claimed this was due to the absence of the Stone, others to a dwindling of faith. Whatever the reason, the Stone's return would strengthen the Vinnengaeleans.

Anger stirred in Damra. The gods were using her for a toy, a pawn, a plaything. To fulfill one honor-bound trust she must abandon another. Yet it seemed she had no choice.

"I will take it," she said. Never had words come so reluctantly. She reached out her hands for the knapsack. "In the name of the gods, I accept—Hold the sack still," she ordered irritably. "This is no time for games!"

"I'm not doing anything." Bashae gasped. "It's moving by itself."

"This is ludicrous," Damra said angrily and made a snatch for the knapsack.

Startled, the pecwae let loose his hold on it. The sack fell to the ground at her feet. Damra bent to retrieve it and, as she did so, she became aware of the magic. Now that she was sensitive to it, she could feel the magic radiate from the knapsack, a force that repelled, but did not mean to harm. Not yet. The magic was like a cushion of thick, soft thistledown enveloping the knapsack. She might force her way past the magic, plunge her fingers through it, but she could sense the stinging prickle of nettles beneath.

Damra understood and began to laugh. She hoped the Father and Mother were laughing, too. Someone should find some amusement out of this.

Arim regarded her anxiously. Her laughter had a strange note to it.

"I can't take the sack, Arim," she said, when she was calm enough to speak. "I can't touch it. Earth magic surrounds it, protects it from me."

"But you're a Dominion Lord," Arim protested, dismayed.

"I am a Dominion Lord who is allied with the magic of the wild wind and the sea breeze, the blue sky and the towering clouds. Our magic is the magic of Air, not of Earth." Damra sighed heavily. "Gustav could not have known when he sent the Stone to me. He knew nothing of magic."

Bashae retrieved the knapsack and clutched it to his breast. He looked from one to the other. "What do we do now?"

"Sleep," said the Grandmother emphatically.

It was on the tip of Damra's tongue to say impatiently that there was no time to sleep, they must leave at once. That was her way. Take immediate action. Part of her was already thinking what excuses to make to the Shield, arranging for transportation to the Portal, planning what she would need to take with her. Once she made up her mind to do something, Damra wanted it done. She was a terrible mah jong player, throwing away a chance for a kong of dragons so that she could make a chow of simples. She was the same with life, forging ahead, never stopping to consider the consequences.

Never stopping to think of others.

Go slowly, Damra, she counseled herself. For once in your life, go slowly. Look at them. They are exhausted. They could not travel far this night. And you. You need time to think. The fact that the human part of

the Sovereign Stone has been discovered is a tremor that will crack wide
open the political landscape, rock the elven nation on its foundations. You
need to consider the ramifications, think what to tell the Divine and when
to tell him, think how best to keep this safe and keep it secret. This might
well gain you the advantage you need against the Shield. To save Griffith's
life, you must not choose the simples because they are quickest and easi-
est. You must wait patiently for the dragons.

"Do you have a safe place to spend the night?" she asked Arim.

He nodded. "The same place I always stay. You know of it."

"Let no one approach you," Damra cautioned. "No one. The Vrykyl can
take pleasing forms to ensnare the unwary."

"So Griffith told me once," Arim said quietly. "I understand."

"Good." She glanced at Jessan, at the bow and arrows he carried. "You
should buy him a sword. We need all the help we can get. We will meet
in the morning in the city of Glymrae, at the street of the Kite Makers."

Damra held out her hand to Jessan. He looked startled, but then, smiling, he clasped her hand in his. Damra shook hands with the Grandmother, like taking hold of a bird's claw. Last, she grasped Bashae's hand.

"I cannot bear your burden," she said, "but I can guard you until you
reach your final destination."

"Where is that?" Bashae asked.

The Grandmother poked him with her stick.

"Morning," she said and, turning, she walked out of the garden, considerably disconcerting the elven guards by raising her stick for a long look
at them as she marched past.

"May your ancestors watch over you this night," Damra said softly to
Arim as they parted.

They took care to appear to separate as acquaintances, not exchanging
the kiss of long-time friends.

"May your ancestors watch over you," Arim returned the ritual words of
farewell.

The eyes of the ancestors may well have been watching, but they were
not the only ones.

DAMRA RETURNED TO THE GUEST HOUSE TO FIND FIVE SERVANTS FROM THE Shield waiting patiently for her, four of them bearing trays and the fifth a message from the Shield that since she had missed the hour of dining, he had sent over delicacies from his own table. He expressed his regret that they had not been able to meet and talk again, but perhaps another meeting could be arranged in a few weeks. He was devastated that his busy schedule did not permit him to meet with her sooner. He would be delighted to read any message from her, however, and he wished her a safe and pleasant journey home on the morrow, should she decide to depart. If she decided to stay, he would most regretfully be obliged to shift her to a different guest house, since this one was needed for members of his wife's family.

This was telling her politely that she was to remove herself in the morning. If she chose to remain, he would be obliged to find her another place to stay, but that place would be uncomfortable and inconvenient, probably one of the temporary houses that were given over to human visitors, houses that were afterward torn down, for the stench left behind by humans was thought by elves to permeate the very walls. He made no mention of the strangers, for to do that would have been to pry into her personal business. He probably knew all about the meeting from his spies.

The servant asked Damra if she would take her meal outside in the guest garden or inside. Damra wanted to be alone and if any other guest happened to be in the garden, she would be forced to make polite conversation. She said she would dine inside. The four servants entered the guesthouse, where, under the direction of the fifth, they arranged the trays on a table and fussed over the food to make certain that it was beautifully and correctly presented.

The guest house was small, five people were a tight fit. Damra remained outside as they worked, walked in the guest garden alight with the small blazing sparks of fireflies. No lights glowed in the other guest houses. Damra recalled the servants telling her there was only one other guest visiting the Shield—a noblewoman of the House of Mabreton. Damra had seen the woman in passing and been struck by her beauty. Damra wondered idly if the woman's presence proved the Divine's growing suspicion that the Shield and the Mabretons were strengthening their alliance.

Damra's thoughts were a confused jumble and she attempted to sort them into some sort of order just as she sorted the mah jong tiles at the start of the game. This proved difficult, for so much had happened that she felt overwhelmed. She formed the tiles one way, then shifted them another: the Sovereign Stone, the Shield, the Divine . . . Griffith, always Griffith. She was so absorbed in her ponderings and anxieties that she did not notice the servants were finished, until, lifting her head, she saw one hovering on the edge of her vision. He indicated that the food was ready and asked if there was anything else they could do for her.

Damra dismissed them for the night. After another turn in the garden, she entered the guest house and closed the door behind her. She glanced at the food, that was quite sumptuous, but she was too pent-up to eat. She had a great deal to do and, characteristically, she wanted to be doing it. She started to remove the food, for she would need the table for writing. The tantalizing smell of ginger made her realize she was hungry. She had not eaten all day. The delicately phrased letter she must write to the Shield—a letter that must seem to give in to his demands and, at the same time, not give in to his demands—would take her hours to compose. She would need her strength and all her wits about her.

Damra sat down before the table. Selecting the very choicest morsels, she placed these in a small lacquered dish and then carried it to the shrine to the Honored Ancestor she had set up in a corner of the guest house. Since most elves rely upon their Honored Ancestors to offer counsel and advice, the guest house was already furnished with an area for a shrine. A screen of rice paper painted with birds in flight—to represent the souls of the ancestors—stood in a corner. Before that was a small folding table and a cushion. The guest could place personal effects on the table, light a candle and sit on the cushion for a comfortable commune with the Ancestor.

Unfortunately, neither Damra nor Griffith had been very lucky in their Honored Ancestors. Griffith's Ancestor was mortified to discover a member of the Wyred in the family and he had abandoned Griffith to devote all his ghostly energies to Griffith's elder brother.

Damra's Honored Ancestor was a benign old soul who had been quite fond of Damra when she was a child, but was baffled by Damra now that she was grown. When Damra became a Dominion Lord, her family did not know what to make of her and so chose to politely ignore her as much as possible. The Honored Ancestor remained in touch, but she made no secret of the fact that her warrior granddaughter was a sad disappointment to her. Whenever she visited, the ghost was always quick to remind Damra that her younger sister had sixteen children and another one on the way.

Damra lingered at the shrine a moment, arranging a spray of orchids in a vase and hoping that the Honored Ancestor would not choose this time for a visit.

The shrine remained empty.

Relaxed and calmer now, Damra sat down to her own meal. She lifted a spoonful of the highly spiced ginger pumpkin soup to her lips.

"Do not eat that, Damra of Gwyenoc," said a voice.

Damra was startled. The spoon jerked in her hand, spilling soup onto her lap. The voice had come from the vicinity of the small shrine, yet was not the voice of the Honored Ancestor. Damra looked that direction. Seeing no ghostly figure, she glanced swiftly about the room.

"Who are you and why do you speak to me from the shadows?" she demanded. "Show yourself to me and then tell me why I should not eat the food of my host."

A figure materialized from near the shrine, emerging from behind the screen. This was no ghost, friendly or otherwise. This was a mortal being, of flesh and blood. Damra was not fearful of assassins—the armor of the Dominion Lord would act immediately to protect her from danger, seen or unseen. Her first immediate thought was anger at herself for not having taken the time to search her room. She was, after all, in the house of the man who was holding her husband captive, threatening his life.

The elf advanced into the light cast by the single candle burning at the shrine. Damra looked first to the mask tattooed around the elf's eyes. She had very good eyesight, the eyes of the raven, but she could not make out the details of the mask that was tattooed around the eyes of every child to delineate his lineage. The elf was old, perhaps the oldest elf that Damra had ever seen. The tattoo mask was blurred by age.

Stoop-shouldered, his back bent beneath the burden of his years, the elf did not walk so much as creep. He leaned heavily on a well-worn wooden cane. His wizened face was like a withered apple, lined and crisscrossed with wrinkles. His head was bald, not a single hair remained. Two dark almond-shaped eyes peered at her from beneath lashless eyelids that were red-rimmed and stretched so thin she could see the lines of the veins. His eyes were clear, not webbed or fogged by the cataracts that often come with advanced years. The eyes revealed nothing, reflected back to her the steady, unwavering flame of the candle on her tray. He spoke no further word, but seemed content to wait for her to proceed.

At first annoyed and irritated, she was now pitying, thinking that the old man in his dotage had wandered into her guest house by mistake. Yet his voice had sounded clear and lucid, not wavering or confused. Senile or not, the old man was her elder and deserving of her respect.

"Honored Father, you come upon me by stealth in the night. You speak to me as if you know me and you bid me not eat my food. I ask that you explain these mysteries. Who are you, sir? What is your House, your name?"

The elf crept forward until he stood very close to the table. He moved slowly, with deliberation, placing the iron shod end of the cane on the floor with gentle care so that it did not thump. All the while, his red-rimmed eyes gazed at her intently.

"My House is the House of Kinnoth," the elf answered, his voice feeble, as if every breath were one to be measured out with care, not wasted on words when it might be needed to provide life. "The House accursed. As for my name, once it had meaning and honor, but those are lost to me. My name is Silwyth."

"Silwyth of House Kinnoth!" Damra repeated, amazed and shocked and disbelieving. She frowned. "I know of only one of that name and he lived many years ago. He died in dishonor."

"There is only one of that name and he yet lives in dishonor," returned the elf calmly.

"You are . . . Silwyth!" Damra stared at him. "Is that possible? You must be . . . near three hundred years of age."

"The gods have been kind to me," said Silwyth with a dark and bitter smile.

Damra shook her head. "Your life is forfeit here. You are an outlaw, the sentence of death is placed upon your head. I myself could slay you where you stand and I would be deemed a hero."

The old man nodded and shrugged. His hands were gnarled, the flesh stretched taut so that the smallest bones and tendons and veins were clearly visible. He was clad all in black in the rough clothes of a peasant: loose pants and long tunic, open at the neck. His feet were bare, the skin leathery, cracked and callused.

"My life is forfeit everywhere I walk. But I am not the one in immediate danger, Damra of House Gwyenoc." Lifting the cane, the old man used it to point to the soup. "If you had eaten that you would now be either dead or dying. The magical armor of a Dominion Lord protects against many weapons, but not against those that are ingested."

Damra laid down the spoon. She took care to wipe her fingers on the lap cloth. She looked back to the old man. If what was said of him was true, she was in the presence of one of the most treacherous elves ever to have been born.

"Garwina of Wyval is many things, most of them onerous, but he is not a murderer. At least," she amended, thinking of Griffith and the fact that his life was in peril, "the Shield would not murder a guest. His own House would rise against him if he committed such a heinous, dishonorable act. As for concealing the crime, that would be impossible. The servants have seen me. Many people know I came here, not the least of whom is the Divine. There would be questions asked—"

"And questions answered," Silwyth stated. "You died of heart failure, Damra of Gwyenoc. Foxglove has that effect. Such a death would be surprising in a woman your age, but not unknown. However, you are right. Garwina of Wyval did not commit this act against you. His is not a mind for such subtleties."

No, but yours is, apparently, Damra thought, eyeing the old man warily. Though he dressed like one, he was no peasant. She heard the mellow ring of culture in his voice, education, the kind attained only by the nobility, who have leisure to study. Silwyth of House Kinnoth, reviled in story and song, had been of noble blood.

"Why do you tell me this? Why warn me? What do you hope to accomplish?" Damra demanded.

"That my House may be restored to honor and to its place on the rolls of Tromek. My House can attain this goal through an act of great courage or an act of great compassion. I was responsible for the downfall of my House," said Silwyth. His voice lowered. "Not only that, but I was responsible for the destruction of a very beautiful, very noble lady. My time in this world is fast coming to an end. Before I leave to serve my sentence in the prison house of the dead, I would do what I can to make right the terrible wrongs that I caused in life."

"You choose to do this now, at the end of your life?" Damra's tone was scornful.

"I have worked toward this goal many long years," Silwyth returned. "I have traveled far distances with one aim in mind—to thwart the plans of the one who was once my prince, the one who is now Lord of the Void. Some small good have I done already, although few take note of it. The greater good I am now prepared to accomplish—with your help, Dominion Lord."

Damra pondered, not yet prepared to trust him, but ready to hear him out.

"Then who wants to kill me?" she asked.

"The one who watched you from behind the wall in the first garden this night."

"It seems that the person must be you, Silwyth of House Kinnoth," said Damra, folding the lap cloth and placing it on the table. She had most definitely lost her appetite. "How long have you been spying on me?"

"I was there," Silwyth admitted readily. "But not to spy on you, Damra of Gwyenoc. I came following another. The one I followed led me to you.

She and I both eavesdropped. I learned some most intriguing things. And so did she." He jabbed at the bowl again with the cane. "Thus, the fox-glove in the soup."

"You have admitted you are an outlaw, disgraced, dishonored. I do not know your game, but I begin to suspect that you want money." Damra rose to her feet. "I thank you for the warning. Whether it is true or not, you are due a reward for your trouble—"

"Do not dismiss me so lightly, Damra of Gwyenoc," Silwyth's voice hardened. "Valura thinks you are dead. She will be here soon, for she comes to steal the object in the knapsack. You heard her, behind the wall. You searched for her and she was forced to flee. Thus she did not see you try to take the knapsack from the pecwae and fail. That was good fortune, for otherwise she would be paying a visit to the pecwae and his friends this night. They would not survive the encounter. As it is, she came after you."

"Again, I thank you for the warning—"

"Do you know what she is, Damra of Gwyenoc? She is a Vrykyl. How frustrating it must have been for poor Valura." Silwyth smiled, dark, tight. "To find the prize Dagnarus has been seeking for two hundred years and not be able to take it. How she must have longed to slay you in the garden, seize the prize then and there. But she has other business this night, important business. She dared not risk a battle, one that would draw attention and involve the Shield's guards. Poisoning you was much easier, quicker, safer."

Damra was silent, troubled.

"You do not believe me," said Silwyth and he sounded more sad than offended. "My proof will walk through that door. What will you do when the Vrykyl comes?"

"If what you say is true—"

"It is."

"—then when this evil being comes, I will slay it—"

"No, that you must not do, Damra of Gwyenoc. As I said, Valura has other business this night, business she conducts for her lord Dagnarus. She must be allowed to proceed with that business, for then the plots and intrigues of Garwina of Wyval will be revealed and you will have the proof you need to force him to free your husband."

Damra's temper snapped. "You know a great deal about my personal affairs, old man. Too much!—"

"Far too much," he agreed, and there was pain in his voice, his eyes were shadowed.

Damra glared at him, frustrated. Heated words would gain her nothing and might lose her a great deal. Striving to calm herself, she looked away from the infuriating old man and looked back at the bowl of soup, now tepid. She looked at the screen behind which the old man had hidden.

She looked at the shrine of the Honored Ancestor, who had comforted the lonely little girl, but who was incapable of helping the woman, no matter how much Damra longed for it.

"Very well. I will do as you suggest. I will wait to see if this Vrykyl materializes." Once committed, Damra was ready to proceed. "When is she likely to appear?"

"With the depths of the night," said Silwyth. "She will expect to find you dead."

Damra gave an exasperated sigh. "This is ludicrous. The moment she touches me, she will discover that I am very much alive. The blessed armor will act to guard me from the Void. I will have no choice but to slay her." Damra pondered the problem. "I could use my power to create an illusion of death—"

"Illusions trick the living mind. The Vrykyl do not live. They are given existence by the Void and, as such, they can see through any illusion. But if you are adept at your part, Damra of Gwyenoc, Valura will not touch you or even come near you. She has no care for you. She comes for one thing, the thing that is to her more precious, more valuable than all the jewels and all the gold in all the world."

"The object is not as valuable as that," said Damra, off-handedly, not wanting to admit that she knew what the old man was talking about.

"To some, no. The Shield, for example, intends to use the Sovereign Stone to buy power. But to the Lady Valura"—Silwyth's voice softened—"she uses it to buy back something that was lost to her long ago. To her, its value is inestimable."

He gave a bobbing bow and stepped out of the candle light, heading for the door at his deliberate, slow-moving pace. "I will be close, should you have need of me."

You never followed anyone moving like a snail, Silwyth of House Kinnoth, Damra thought. That bent back of yours, those stooped shoulders are a lie. Everything about you is a lie. Yet I do not dare to eat the soup.

She did not hear the door open or feel the night air upon her face, yet when she called out, Silwyth made no answer. Was he gone or hiding again? Snatching up the candle, she searched the room, looked behind the screen, found no trace of him.

"What am I trying to prove?" she demanded of herself. "As he said, proof of his veracity will either walk through the door or it won't. If it does, I must be ready. If it doesn't, I will look an utter fool, but then, I should be used to that."

Should she blow out the candle? No. If she died while eating supper, the candle would still be burning. She knew of foxglove only that elven healers gave it in small doses to those who suffered from heart complaints. Large doses of it could prove fatal, yet she didn't know how it would act.

Some poisons worked swiftly. She did not think that foxglove would act that fast. She hoped not, at any rate, for she did not fancy the thought of lying sprawled across the table, her face in her soup bowl.

"Who knows how many hours I'll have to wait. I should be comfortable at least. On first feeling ill, what do I do? Lie down. I would have lain down and died in bed."

As Damra tried to arrange herself to look like a corpse, the silly aspect to this situation took hold of her and she started to giggle. Appalled, realizing she was giving way to nervous tension, she forced herself to calm down. She focused her thoughts on random things, one thought led to another.

Feigning death. Elven assassins know how to feign death, how to slow the breathing, slow the heartbeat, cause the blood to run sluggishly so that even the body's temperature dropped. No warrior would ever practice such dishonorable ways, but assassins had no honor and thus did not have to concern themselves. Damra wondered, suddenly, if Silwyth was trained as an elven assassin. That would explain much about him.

Much, but not all.

He was of noble blood and it was highly unusual for nobles to travel the dark and dismal road of the assassin. Unusual but not unknown, particularly for those elves whose Houses were impoverished or Accursed, for there are few honorable ways to make a living. Still, most elven nobles would choose to die honorably of starvation before they turned hired killer. The pain in his voice, the shadow in his eyes had been the pain and the shadow of regret, a luxury no cold-blooded hired killer can afford.

What was most convincing to her was the fact that Silwyth spoke knowingly of the Vrykyl. Few elves are even aware that the Vrykyl exist. The Wyred know, as they know all things pertaining to magic, but they keep their knowledge secret, for knowledge is power.

Damra knew about the Vrykyl, as did all Dominion Lords, for the Vrykyl are their dark opposites, tied to them in some mysterious way through the Sovereign Stone. Always curious, Damra had wanted to know more about the Vrykyl than she could find out through the Council of Dominion Lords. Her curiosity had sparked Griffith to make the Vrykyl an area of specialization, had led them both to meet and befriend the Whoreson Knight, Gustav, whose life had been dedicated to the study of the Sovereign Stone and all things pertaining to it. Through him, she had come into contact with Arim, who acted as a go-between for Damra and Lord Gustav, a Vinnengaelean and, as such, an enemy.

Gustav, slain by a Vrykyl, knew the Vrykyl were on the trail of the Sovereign Stone. Dying, he sent the Stone to her, knowing that she was the only member of the Council of Dominion Lords who would fully understand the danger. Silwyth of House Kinnoth would also know about the

Vrykyl. If he was what he claimed to be, he had been present during their unhallowed creation. He came to her, as Gustav had come to her.

The circle expands outward, touches the boundaries, and starts to flow back in . . .

Damra woke with a start, cursing herself for her lack of discipline. She lay frozen, for she thought she had heard a sound. Concentrating on listening, she heard the sound again, this time unmistakable—a hand slowly and stealthily sliding open the door.

The dead usually die with their eyes open, but Damra did not trust herself. She shut hers to a slit, so that she could see through her dark lashes. A woman entered her chamber, silk robes rustling—the beautiful Lady Godelieve. Damra was amazed. This beautiful, delicate woman a thing of evil? She would not have believed but for the evidence of her own senses. This woman was sneaking into the guest house at an hour of the night when decorum required that she should be in her own bed.

The lady moved into the light of the candle. Damra saw the expression on the beautiful face and she was no longer in doubt. Lady Godelieve gazed at Damra, gazed upon her victim and there was nothing in her expression. No sympathy, no pity. No hatred. Nothing. She cared not a whit for the life she had taken. Silwyth had been right.

Lady Godelieve turned her attention from her victim to searching for the Sovereign Stone. Now her expression altered, changed to hope, anticipation. Damra held perfectly still, made her breathing as shallow as possible. Her heartbeat seemed unnaturally loud, she feared it must give her away. She felt herself in the presence of powerful Void magic and it was all she could do to hold still, to keep from calling upon the magical powers of her holy armor, to keep from reaching for her swords.

The lady's search was thorough. She ravaged the shrine of the ancestor, overturned dishes, dumped out the water and peered inside the vase. She looked behind the screen. Damra wished her search ended, wished her gone. She could not endure the strain.

The Lady Godelieve stood irresolute, staring about her in a fury that Damra could feel.

"It is not here," said the Vrykyl in bitter tones.

Damra risked opening her eyelids a slit. Peering out from beneath her lashes, she saw that the lady held in her hand a slender knife, the blood knife.

"I have searched everywhere, my lord. It is not here, I tell you. Would I be likely to miss it?" The Vrykyl paused a moment, listening to that other voice, then said, "I did not feel it when I entered. Yes, I am certain that I would sense it. I saw it, remember. I was in the presence of both your father and your brother, Helmos." Another pause, then, "I do not care what Shakur says. He is a poltroon. What do you expect? I would feel it! I would!" Her voice quivered with passion, was low and desperate. "I would feel it as you would feel it, my lord."

The Vrykyl grew calmer, listening to the voice, and when she spoke again the tone was cold. "Perhaps I was mistaken. Perhaps the Dominion Lord did not take the Stone. If so, one of her confederates must still have it. I will acquire it in the morning. First the one," she said, "then the other."

She slid the knife back into the sash she wore around her robes. The Vrykyl cast Damra a final glance and this time the look was one of enmity, a look of vile loathing that transformed the beautiful face. For an instant, Damra caught a glimpse of the hideous visage of the Vrykyl, the gray and rotting flesh hanging to the skull, the eye sockets that held within them the darkness of the Void. And then the Vrykyl was gone, her departure causing the candle's flame to waver and go out.

Damra drew a shuddering breath. She was soaked with chill sweat, her body trembled. A wave of nausea swept over her. She sat up dizzily, afraid she was going to be sick. Never in her life had she known fear like that, horrible, debilitating fear that left her weak and shaking.

"Make haste, Damra of Gwyenoc," called the old man's voice from the doorway. "Throw off your terror. We must follow her."

Damra rose from her bed. Now that the Vrykyl was gone, her fear began to fade, replaced by a deep resolve to slay the creature and rid the world of its evil. The magical armor of a Dominion Lord flowed over her skin, and its blessed power brought back to her the love and strength she had felt flow from the Father and Mother during the Transfiguration.

Leaving the guest house, Damra glanced about the grounds. The Shield's palace stood shrouded in darkness, for although night's tide had come to the full and was now starting to recede, dawn was not yet a glimmer in the eastern sky.

The world itself seemed to slumber, for the silence was profound, yet not all in the Shield's household slept. Guards would be up and about, patrolling the grounds. Damra was known to be the Shield's enemy. Should they find her creeping about at this hour of the night, they would think the worst.

"Silwyth," Damra called softly to the darkness, for she could not make out where he had gone.

"I am here," he said and indeed he was, so close that she might have seized hold of him.

"Where is she going? What is she after?"

"The Sovereign Stone," Silwyth spoke the word with a hissing breath. "Not the stone bequeathed to you, Damra of Gwyenoc. Valura searched for that and failed to find it. She seeks now the stone bequeathed to the elves by King Tamaros, may the ancestors do him honor."

"Our Sovereign Stone! She could not possibly steal it," Damra protested, aghast. "The Stone is guarded day and night by soldiers loyal to the Shield and loyal to the Divine—"

"None of whom will prove much challenge for this Vrykyl," said Silwyth grimly. "It is up to you to stop her."

"The Sovereign Stone is kept secure in a hidden garden set in the very center of the Shield's property. Armed guards stand at every bend and turning between here and there. If I must fight them all I've no doubt I could defeat them," Damra added calmly, "but we are in for a very long night.

"As for my Raven's magic," she continued, forestalling what she presumed would be his next suggestion, since he knew so much about her, "my armor permits me to command the blessed air to lift me and carry me where I choose. Unfortunately, the Shield's Wyred will have blanketed the grounds with spells to disrupt elemental magicks and while my magic is powerful it is not infallible. I could not want to risk failure when I am level with the treetops."

"You are not infallible," Silwyth agreed. "And that is why you feel the need to pray at the Shrine of the Father and the Mother this night, Damra of Gwyenoc."

"Of course," Damra said, chagrined. "How stupid of me not to think of that. Where will you be?" she asked somewhat suspiciously.

"Where I need to be," he replied.

Bowing over his cane, he left her side, looked like an ancient, three-legged spider creeping into the darkness. Damra tried to keep him in sight, but the night absorbed him into itself.

She could not waste time wondering about Silwyth. Not any longer. He had spoken the truth thus far. She clasped a silver pendant she wore around her neck, a pendant that was in the form of a blazing sun held by two griffins, the symbol of the Dominion Lords. The magical armor she wore disappeared. Once more, she was clad in her tabard and flowing trousers. She would have to leave her battle sword behind, for one could not go into the shrine bearing weapons. However, she would be permitted to wear her ceremonial sword, for that is a symbol of honor, one granted to her by the ancestors, and thus could be worn into the sacred precincts.

The night air was mild. An owl called. Another, at a distance, answered. Damra walked swiftly from the area of the guest houses to the first of many gates she would need to pass in order to reach the Shrine of the Father and Mother. By elven law, no one could stop her.

4

THE HISTORY OF THE ELVEN PORTION OF THE SOVEREIGN STONE IS A bloody one; a sorrowful fact that the late King Tamaros never knew. The good man went to his death believing that the Sovereign Stone would bring the peoples of Loerem together in peace. If the gods are merciful, they still keep the truth from him.

When King Tamaros received the Sovereign Stone and announced that he would give each of its four sections into the hands of each of the four races, the Divine, the father of the current Divine, assumed that the Stone would come to him, as spiritual leader of the Tromek nation. He sent his representative, Lord Mabreton the Elder, to accept the Stone in the name of the Divine. The Shield of the Divine had other ideas. He recognized the extraordinary power the Stone would confer upon the one who possessed it.

With the aid of a minor elven lord, Silwyth, who was ostensibly Prince Dagnarus's chamberlain but was, in reality, a spy planted in the human court, the Shield caused Lord Mabreton to be secretly murdered. The Shield accepted the Sovereign Stone from the unwitting King Tamaros and refused all demands by the Divine to send it to him.

The Shield built a special garden to house the Stone, protected by cunning and powerful magical traps. The Stone did not reside there long, however. When Prince Dagnarus was transformed into the Lord of the Void, he declared war upon Vinnengael, upon his brother, King Helmos. The other races had agreed when they accepted the Sovereign Stone that if one race faced a threat, the other three portions of the Stone would come together in order to preserve peace. Helmos sent messengers asking each of the races to return their portions of the Stone. One by one, the others refused.

Fearful that the elven portion of the Stone might be in danger, the

Shield brought it into his own dwelling place. The Shield was secretly allied with Prince Dagnarus. Elven troops fought with Dagnarus and more stood on the border, ready to move in when Dagnarus was victorious, prepared to take over land that had been promised to them in return for their aid.

Many elves died in the destruction of Vinnengael. The Shield was called upon to answer for their lives before the Divine. Still the Shield might have managed to save himself, but that Silwyth came forward and revealed the Shield's crimes, starting with the murder of Lord Mabreton the Elder. The Shield saw himself surrounded by his foes. He requested death at the hands of the Divine, who gave that pleasure into the hands of Lord Mabreton the Younger. House Kinnoth was ruined from that day forward.

As to what happened to Silwyth, none ever knew. By bringing down the Shield, he encompassed his own destruction, for not even the Divine had the power to pardon him. Lord Mabreton the Younger spared no expense to find him, for it was Silwyth who had slain his brother and Silwyth who had helped Dagnarus seduce the Lady Valura, wife of Lord Mabreton. Lord Mabreton offered a reward that was equivalent to a king's ransom for Silwyth's head and many assassins tried their luck, but none ever found him. Now, after two hundred years, most assumed him to be dead, for how could a man survive that long with so many enemies and so few friends? Damra wondered that herself.

With the fall of the Shield's House, the Sovereign Stone was removed by the Divine to the Shrine of the Father and Mother in the Tromek capital city of Glymrae. Garwina of House Wyval, a lifelong friend of Cedar, was proclaimed Shield of the Divine. To honor his new status, the Divine presented Garwina with a royal palace in Glymrae. This magnificent palace encompassed the grounds on which stood the Shrine of the Father and Mother and the new garden that housed the sacred Sovereign Stone.

The Stone was guarded by soldiers loyal to both the Shield and the Divine. Even when relations between the Divine and his former friend began to sour, the Divine never feared the Sovereign Stone might be in danger. A man of honor and integrity, the Divine would not be able to conceive it possible that the mind of any man would be so corrupt as to consider stealing the sacred object for his own gain.

Damra could not conceive it. If Silwyth was right and the Shield was conspiring with the Vrykyl to steal the Stone for himself, the Shield was stealing not from the Divine, but the elven nation. The Shield had accepted the Stone to hold in trust for the elven people. He bound himself with sacred oaths. If he broke those oaths, the Father and Mother would turn their faces from him. His own ancestors would renounce him. Such a crime would be more heinous than those committed by House Kinnoth.

Garwina and his House would be ruined, disgraced, with perhaps no chance for reparation. Houses had been stricken from the rolls, but never had a House been dissolved, disbanded so that it ceased to exist. His might well be the first.

Much as Damra disliked the Shield and his politics, she could not wish such a terrible fate on him, for he would not be the only one to suffer. He would doom many thousands of innocents, those elves who looked to his House for protection. If he fell, he would take them down with him.

Damra came to the first of the many guardhouses that lay between her and the Shrine of the Ancestors. The guards were alert and wide awake. They halted her, regarded her with cool and wary looks. She told them she felt the need to pray this night. They passed her on, as they were bound to do. Glancing back unobtrusively as she continued on her way, she saw one of them depart, running toward the main house. He would report her movements to his superior. Would the superior report to someone higher up? How rapidly would the news eventually reach the Shield?

Damra quickened her steps. She followed the same routine at every guard post along the way. The grounds of the palace of the Shield were extensive, covering an area of perhaps twenty miles or more in diameter. Walkways and paths wound through the gardens from the palace to the Shrine.

The night was clear, lit by a silver moon and radiant stars. Damra had no difficulty finding her way. She walked alone. No one else was abroad this night. Spies might be lurking about, however, and so she dared not run, for that would look suspicious. She walked as rapidly as she could, slowing her pace to a pensive walk as she approached the guards. Impelled by a sense of urgency that increased the nearer she drew to the reliquary, Damra was forced to exert all her control to keep from snapping at the guards or, worse, to dash past them with unseemly haste.

She passed the last checkpoint with an overwhelming sense of relief. Topping a rise, she saw the Shrine of the Father and Mother below her. Elves believe that they are the children of the gods, most specifically, the Father and Mother, who watch over the family of the gods and the family of the dead, the elven ancestors. The elves feel close to their ancestors and thus take all manner of problems and complaints to them. Elves view the Father and Mother with reverence and awe. They seek their counsel only under dire circumstances.

The Divine is the nominal head of the Church, although the priests have their own hierarchy. Unlike the human Church that combines religion and magic, the elven Church works hard to separate the two. The priests have no great power, but they are important in that they are the only people who can cross the strict boundary lines of elven society. A priest, no matter how lowly his birth, may talk to anyone. A peasant who believes that he has been wronged could not take his grievance to the

Shield, for the peasant would not be permitted anywhere near the Shield. The peasant takes his grievance to the priest, who, even if he comes from peasant stock himself, can seek an audience with the Shield to relate to him the peasant's woes.

As a structure, the Shrine was not beautiful or imposing. It looked to be little more than a rock cairn with openings left among the stone blocks for windows and a larger opening that served as a door. The Shrine was one of the oldest structures standing on all of Loerem, for the earliest written histories of the elves speak of it as old even then. The rocks that form the walls of the Shrine are said to have been placed there by the hand of the Father and thus is it the holiest of holy sites in Tromek.

Bright light glowed from the windows. The Shrine was open day and night to anyone who sought guidance and counsel. A number of the priests could be seen silhouetted against the light, clustered in the open doorway, peering out into the night. At the sight of her, they called out in alarm. Something was wrong.

Not caring who saw her now, Damra broke into a run. She clasped hold of the pendant she wore around her neck. The armor of the Dominion Lord flowed over her. To reach the reliquary, she would have to pass through a grove of cedar trees, the first defensive barrier.

Arriving at the cedar grove, she halted, stared in consternation. Broken branches lay on the ground or hung, snapped and dangling, from the main trunks. One entire tree was split in two, as if it had been struck by lightning, yet there was no charring visible, no smoke rose from the splintered wood.

The air was tainted with Void magic. Damra could scarely breathe, so thick was the miasma. The Wyred had placed powerful magicks on the grove to keep out thieves. The magicks had been shattered. The power of the Void had destroyed them.

Gripping the handle of her ceremonial sword, Damra drew it, held it before her as she crept silently through the path of destruction created by her enemy. Having to watch where she placed every footfall, she had reason to bless the Raven Eyes that had been gifted to her by the gods. She reached the edge of the tree line, looked beyond to see the reliquary itself.

A crystal globe hung suspended on a wire made of beaten gold attached to the top of a cage whose bars were made of steel intertwined with gold. Inside the globe, the Sovereign Stone gleamed in the bright silver light that radiated all around it. The cage stood in the center of a mirrored floor that reflected the cage and the glittering stone hanging above. So smooth was the mirror's surface that the reflected objects were indistinguishable from the real. The mirrored floor extended outward from the cage for a radius of four feet.

Woe betide anyone who stepped on that surface without care, for unless one knew where to walk (and it was said that only two people in the Tromek knew the secret route, the Divine and the Shield of the Divine), the thief would step from solid ground onto nothing, for the mirrored surface was an illusion created by the Wyred. The thief would fall into a deep pit lined with razor-sharp iron spikes, to die a horrible death.

If one managed to safely cross the illusory floor, then one had to pass through the bars of the cage that were locked with seven locks (one for each of the seven major Houses) requiring the use of the seven keys—four keys held by the Divine, three held by the Shield. Then and only then could one reach the Sovereign Stone, held suspended in its crystal globe.

The bodies of several guards lay sprawled on the ground around the reliquary. Some wore the armor of House Trovale of the Divine, others wore the armor of the Shield of the Divine. The battle had been a bloody one, desperately fought on both sides. Guards loyal to the Shield had been victorious, six of them remained standing, but none had escaped unscathed. One guard clutched his bloody arm to his side. Another's face was slashed open to the bone. A third knelt beside a comrade, hastily tying a tourniquet around the man's upper thigh. No soldiers loyal to the Divine remained alive.

Damra could imagine the battle, imagine how vicious, how desperate it had been. Although loyal to different Houses, different causes, these men had served together for years. They must have become friends, comrades, some close as brothers. Then, in a single night of betrayal, some had turned on their friends, their comrades, their brothers. They had obeyed orders. Done their duty. None could reproach them, for duty to one's House took precedence over friendship, love, even family. Yet Damra felt sickened at the thought.

She watched warily, not rushing forward, taking in the situation. The guards appeared to be waiting for someone. They peered into the darkness. They were nervous, uneasy, hearing nothing but the accusing voices of the souls of their murdered victims. Damra began to be uneasy herself. The Vrykyl had blasted her way through the cedar grove. Where was she? Hiding in the shadows of the Void, watching, taking stock of the situation, even as Damra watched?

Movement caught Damra's eye. The soldiers raised their bloody swords, drew together for defense.

A figure emerged from the shadows of the cedars opposite to where Damra stood. The figure was that of a woman. Beautiful, fragile, she made her way with delicate grace across the blood-soaked and trampled grass. The guards lowered their weapons and stood back to let her pass.

Lady Godelieve scarcely noticed them. She looked neither to the left nor the right. Her gaze fixed upon the Sovereign Stone, glittering in its crystal globe.

Damra's first impulse was to rush from her hiding place, strike now, catch the creature in its weakest form. A Vrykyl can don its protective, magical armor as swiftly as a Dominion Lord, but Damra would have the element of surprise and that would count for something, particularly since the Vrykyl must believe her to be dead.

Damra was about to act on this impulse, even though it meant that she would also be fighting the Shield's guards. She gripped the hilt of her sword, shifted her weight forward.

A hand closed over her wrist.

Damra gave a violent start, turned her head.

Silwyth stood beside her.

"What—" she began in an angry, hushed whisper.

The grip on her wrist tightened. The aged hand was exceptionally strong. His lips formed a single word, "Wait."

Damra calmed her wildly beating heart, relaxed her stance. She had no idea how he came to be here, how he had managed to keep up with her, how he had made his way past the guards, who would have slain a member of House Kinnoth on sight. There was more to this aged elf than appeared on the surface.

The Lady Godelieve halted at the edge of the reliquary and summoned one of the guards.

"Stand watch," she ordered in her melodious voice.

The guard bowed low. His remaining men took up positions around the reliquary, facing the cedar grove, their swords drawn.

The Lady Godelieve walked around the rim of the illusory floor, looking closely at the edge of the stonework until she came to a certain point. Here, grasping the skirt of her robe that was stained with blood, she set her foot cautiously upon the smooth, mirrored surface. Finding safe purchase, she took another step and another and another, gliding across the mirrored surface as gracefully as a skater glides across shimmering ice. She reached the cage safely.

She would not have the seven keys, but bars of steel and gold would not stop a Vrykyl who had blasted her way through a forest. Still, Damra expected that the cage would cause the Vrykyl some difficulty, impede her way, if only for a moment. Damra stared in astonishment to see the Vrykyl slide her hand right through the bars, as if the cage did not exist.

Lady Godelieve lifted her head, looked up at the Sovereign Stone that hung above her. She gazed at it a moment, then knelt down upon the floor of the cage and reached for the reflection of the Sovereign Stone that glittered beneath her feet.

Only then did Damra see through the illusion. The Sovereign Stone did not hang suspended from the top of the cage. The Sovereign Stone was placed on a pedestal that thrust up from the bottom of the mirrored floor. The reflection was the reality, the reality the reflection. So powerful was the illusion that even when Damra understood how it worked, her eyes were still fooled and she had to struggle to reconcile what she saw with what her mind knew to be the truth.

Damra glanced at Silwyth. The aged elf stared intently at the Vrykyl, his expression fixed, unwavering.

"Was the living woman truly this beautiful?" Damra asked. Like the illusion, she was trying to reconcile what she saw with her eyes to what she knew with her mind.

"More so," he answered softly. "This is but a memory of her beauty."

A bitter memory, Damra thought, and turned her attention back to the Vrykyl.

The Lady Godelieve knelt on the floor of the cage. Reaching down with both hands, she plucked the crystal globe containing the Sovereign Stone from its pedestal. She gazed at the Stone for long moments. She did not smile. Her expression was one of quiet, complacent triumph.

"Now!" breathed Silwyth. "Take the guards, Damra. The Lady Valura is my responsibility."

Damra was about to argue that he could not possibly face down a Vrykyl, but then she saw the stooped body straighten. The hobbling gait changed to a swift run. Skilled, strong hands wielded the cane that had become a weapon. Silwyth was a blur of movement, a shadow darting across the bloody grass. One of the Shield's guards caught sight of him. The guard's shout alerted the others. The six began to converge on Silwyth.

Damra's silver armor shone with a holy radiance as she strode forth to do battle. The guards shifted their attention from Silwyth, who was little more than a dark blur, to this gleaming apparition, who seemed to come on them as a vengeful god. They stared at her in awe, as one thunderstruck.

Damra was quick to take advantage of their amazement. "As you have been the betrayer, so you are betrayed," she shouted. "You have been duped by a creature of the Void. Yield to me and I will spare your lives."

"I know her," a guard snarled. "Damra of Gwyenoc. This very night, the Shield deemed her a traitor to the realm. Her life is forfeit."

He was already holding his sword, and now he drew from his belt a dagger. All the Shield's warriors were expert in the use of two-handed fighting and these were among his most skilled soldiers. Five of them turned to seize her. A sixth chased after Silwyth.

Damra was armed only with a short sword that was more ceremonial than useful. She had a more potent weapon. Damra had her Raven magic and the raven is known to be a bird of tricks.

Suddenly the Shield's guards found themselves facing three Dominion Lords. Two illusions of Damra sprang up on either side of the guards, flanking them. The sixth guard, who was about to lay hands on Silwyth, heard a voice in his ear.

"Help me! I need your help!"

The voice was the melodious voice of the Lady Godelieve, or so the man thought. He halted, looked around, only to find that the Lady Godelieve's attention was fixed on the Dominion Lord, her beautiful face contorted in a scowl. He realized he'd been duped, but when he searched for his prey, the aged elf was nowhere to be found.

Damra deftly shifted position so that the elven guard attacked one of her illusions. His slashing sword blow whistled through the air, the momentum of his swing carrying him off balance. Damra caught him from behind, struck him a blow that drove him face first into the ground.

The illusions of herself were incredibly realistic, mimicking her in every way. One of the guards knew the moment his sword hit nothing solid that he battled air. He whirled about, saw Damra and an illusion of Damra and wasted a moment trying to figure out which was which. Damra's foot slammed into his chest, sent him flying backward. Hearing harsh breathing behind her, she recovered from her kick, turned, swinging her sword. Her blade sliced beneath the guard's armor at the waist and into his rib cage. Crying out in pain, he doubled over. She struck him on the jaw with the hilt of her sword, knocking him unconscious.

Turning swiftly to find other foes, she saw that one had fled; probably gone to fetch reinforcements. Another stood watching her warily, his eyes darting from one Damra to another, trying to make up his mind which to attack.

She searched for Silwyth, saw that he had reached the reliquary. He started to cross the illusory floor. Damra held her breath, expecting to see him plummet into the pit, but he had no difficulty. He crossed in the same place, in the same manner as had the Lady Godelieve. He crept up on the Vrykyl, who had her back turned. Valura kept watch on the Dominion Lord. The Vrykyl did not see Silwyth or hear him approaching.

Silwyth did not see one of the Shield's guards creeping up behind him. The guard knew the secret route, crossed the illusory floor with ease. Sword raised, he stood poised to stab the aged elf in the back.

"Silwyth!" Damra warned him. "Behind you!"

Silwyth turned, jabbed with the iron-shod heel of the cane to strike the guard in his midriff, below the breastplate. The guard lost his balance and tumbled, with a shriek, into the pit.

Valura heard danger behind her. Turning to face it, she took on the fearful image of the Vrykyl.

Damra could not worry about the Vrykyl or about Silwyth. Her shout effectively ended the illusion. The remaining guard moved warily to attack her.

"Must you rely on magic, Dominion Lord? Fight with honor," he jeered.

"You are one to talk of honor," Damra returned with scorn. "How many of the Divine's soldiers did you stab in the back?"

"The Shield proclaimed them traitors," the guard said angrily, defensively. "Traitors have no honor, as you yourself have proven."

"Look at the Sovereign Stone," Damra told him. "Witness the honor of the Shield."

"Another trick!" the guard snarled, but he was clearly shaken, unnerved. He had done his duty, obeyed orders, but he hadn't liked this night's treachery. He began to doubt.

Damra lowered her weapon, stepped back. "Look," she urged.

The guard held his weapons ready. He shifted his gaze, intending to glance swiftly at the Stone and then return to battle. He saw the Vrykyl, its dark armor absorbing the silver light of the mirrored floor, as if seeking to destroy the light from the heavens.

"Ancestors save us," he gasped, staring. "What evil has come upon us?"

"The perfidy of the Shield made manifest," Damra told him.

Calling upon the wings of the Raven, Damra lifted her arms and soared into the air. Hovering in front of the amazed guard, Damra kicked him in the teeth, smashed her foot into his face. He went over backward, blood spurting from his nose and mouth. Damra settled back to the ground.

"Those with honor I fight with honor," she told him, then turned to see how Silwyth fared.

Valura had not heard the fighting, she had not heard the shouting of the Shield's guards or the screams of the dying. She cared nothing about these mortals. They were as insects to her and whether they lived or they died was of no consequence. Her attention had been focused on the Sovereign Stone to the exclusion of all else. She held the crystal globe in her hands, stared, mesmerized, at the sparkling jewel inside.

"I have the Stone, my lord!" she cried.

Dagnarus's elation, his triumph, his pleasure surged through her, bringing back memories of long ago, when it had been her flesh that had given him pleasure, when his love had brought her joy. The memories were bitter now, filled with pain, and yet she kept fast hold of them, for they were the last connection to what she had once been. She had been about to smash the crystal globe, seize hold of the Stone, when she heard Damra's warning shout.

"Silwyth! Behind you!"

Silwyth! The name was part of Valura's most painful memories. Silwyth, Dagnarus's chamberlain, had connived at their illicit meetings. He had carried notes back and forth, brought her gifts from her lover. Silwyth had helped to deceive her deluded husband. Silwyth, who loved her for what she had been and pitied her for what she became.

His pity. She had seen his pity every time she had looked into his eyes and she hated him for it, even after all these years. She could endure Dagnarus's loathing of the thing she had become, though it hurt her as nothing, not even the pain of dying, had hurt her. She could not endure Silwyth's pity.

Valura's gaze shifted from the Sovereign Stone in her hands to the aged elf. Silwyth stood behind her, balanced precariously on the stone steps that led across the illusory floor.

Lady Godelieve disappeared, the illusion forgotten, abandoned. In its place stood the Vrykyl.

Armor darker than the darkest depths of her hatred flowed over Valura's skeletal body. Needle-sharp spikes jutted from her bony hands and from her shoulders. The hideous helm with its ravenous face of ever-hungry death covered her skull, lent eyes of fire to the empty sockets.

Silwyth was ancient, decrepit, the face wrinkled and wizened almost past recognition. But she knew him, knew it was Silwyth. She saw the pity in his eyes.

Valura flung the crystal globe to the platform on which she stood. The globe shattered. Amidst sharp, jagged shards of crystal, the Sovereign Stone lay gleaming at her feet. She paid no attention to the Stone; the prize was hers for the claiming. Drawing her sword, she sprang at Silwyth.

Valura brought her weapon down with a swift motion that should have cleaved her foe in twain. The sword blade struck the stones with such force that sparks flew, the rock cracked. The blade missed Silwyth, who now stood behind her.

A blow from Silwyth's staff struck Valura in the small of her back, nearly knocked her from the platform.

"Too long have you haunted me, dogged my steps," she cried, turning to end his life.

Blinded by her fury, she swiped at him with the sword. He evaded the blow with astonishing agility. She came at him. Savage blows drove him backward. His bare feet crunched on the shards of the broken crystal. Blood flowed.

"I have been aware of you, Silwyth," Valura said to him, pressing her advantage. "You have tracked me, trying to thwart my plans." She slashed at him again, drove him back another step. "Now you have a choice, old wretch. Die on my sword or die on the iron spikes below."

"You mistake me, Lady Valura," Silwyth said and his voice was soft with pity, curse him for that a million, million times. "I have sought you all these years in order to give you a gift."

"What is that?" she cried, swiping at him again.

He ducked beneath the whistling blow. Seizing hold of a long, sharp shard of crystal, Silwyth stabbed Valura in the stomach.

"Death."

The shard of crystal penetrated the armor of the Vrykyl, drove deep into the body that had long ago rotted away. The wound from the magical crystal that had been blessed by the Father and Mother severed the ties of the Void that bound Valura to this life. Screaming in fury and terror, she dropped her sword and clutched at the shard with both hands. She tried to drag it out.

"Accept my gift, Lady Valura," Silwyth urged her, his voice filled with pain, her pain, shared. "Let this tortured life that is no life slip away from beneath your fingers. Find rest and solace at last."

Darkness started to seep over Valura. She felt herself sink beneath it, as a person sinks beneath sweet sleep. The end of pain, the end of misery, the end of guilt, the end of . . . love.

The Sovereign Stone sparkled at her feet. Dagnarus's voice came to her.

"Valura? Do you have the Stone for me?"

With a shuddering cry, Valura yanked the crystal shard from her body. She lunged at Silwyth.

Spreading his arms, he took a step backward and fell into the pit.

She was glad. She listened for his death scream that would be sweet music. The scream did not come. He died in silence. Never mind. He was gone, would trouble her no more. The power of the Void began to mend her hideous wound. She reached for the Sovereign Stone.

She could not touch it. Valura tried to bring her hand close to the Stone, but an aura of magic shoved her hand away. Thwarted, she called upon the power of the Void and reached again for the Sovereign Stone. The magical aura surrounding the Stone shattered. Triumphant, Valura seized hold of the Stone.

The anger of the gods surged through her. A jolt of white-hot agony filled the Void within her, caused it to swell and burst apart. Bereft of her magic, Valura collapsed on the platform.

The Sovereign Stone rolled from her hand, came to rest upon the shards of broken crystal.

Damra hastened to the edge of the reliquary, thinking to intervene in the battle between the ancient, decrepit old elf and the powerful Vrykyl. Once there, she halted, amazed to see Silwyth dodge the Vrykyl's deadly, cleaving stroke, then leap into the air, twisting his thin body, to land behind her. He struck her in the back with his staff.

Damra could slay the Vrykyl from behind, but she had to first cross the illusory floor and she did not know the route.

"Winds of truth!" she cried, extending her hands. "Blow away the mists of deceit!"

The summoned magic caused the illusions that surrounded the Sovereign Stone to vanish before her eyes. The pool disappeared. Six round stone steps led to the platform on which the Vrykyl stood. Looking down into the pit, she saw the razor-sharp iron spikes imbedded into the floor. The body of one of the Divine's guards lay impaled on the spikes. His dead mouth remained open in a scream. The spikes protruded from his breast, his gut, his thighs and his arms. Blood covered the bottom of the pit.

Damra's stomach clenched at the thought of the horrible death the man had suffered. Concentrating on her footing, she had just managed to jump to the first of the six stones when Silwyth plunged the shard of glass into the Vrykyl.

The creature's scream froze Damra's heart, held her immobilized, balanced precariously on the stone. She saw Silwyth speaking to the Vrykyl. His words were soft, she could not hear what he was saying. The next moment, the Vrykyl wrenched the shard of glass free and dove at Silwyth.

Damra watched, horror-stricken, to see him step calmly from the platform. As the Vrykyl reached down to pick up the Sovereign Stone, Damra leapt to the next stone. She must reach the platform, battle the Vrykyl where there was room to maneuver.

The anger of the gods that came when the Vrykyl tried to seize the Stone manifested itself in a blast of white fire that shattered the stillness of the night with a tremendous boom. Damra averted her face from the blinding light. Her magical armor shielded her from the force of the hot, fierce wind that blew across the reliquary. When the wind died away and the light faded, Damra looked to see the Vrykyl lying on the platform, her body still and unmoving. The Sovereign Stone lay gleaming on the platform, near the edge.

Damra crossed the stepping stones. Reaching the platform, she drew her sword, held it poised above the Vrykyl. The creature did not stir. Damra circled around the black-armored figure and very nearly stepped on a bloody hand that clung to the platform.

"Help me," Silwyth gasped, reaching up another blood-stained hand.

Damra grasped hold, pulled Silwyth up over the edge of the platform.

"Why aren't you dead?" she demanded.

"A question many have asked," he replied with a half smile.

Bending down, he spoke to the Vrykyl.

"Lady Valura," Silwyth said in a voice so soft that Damra did not hear it so much as feel it touch her soul. "You were cruelly wronged by so many, myself among them. I ask you to forgive me."

The Vrykyl did not move. Sighing, Silwyth rose to his feet and took a step backward. Damra lifted her sword, brought it down upon the Vrykyl's neck, severed the head from the body. The helm rolled a slight distance from the trunk. Damra nerved herself to peer inside. Nothing, only darkness. Turning from the loathsome creature, she saw Silwyth's hand extended. In his palm rested the Sovereign Stone.

"Take the Stone, Damra of Gwyenoc," he said. "You have the elven part, the pecwae has the human. The gods have brought the two together."

"I cannot take this," Damra protested, aghast. "The Divine is the only one who may own the Sovereign Stone."

"No one may own it. No mortal," said Silwyth. "Listen to me, for we do not have much time. The Shield has been alerted that his plan has failed. He and his guards are on their way and we both should be gone before they arrive."

"I'm listening," said Damra reluctantly.

"The gods told King Tamaros when he was given the Stone that mankind was not yet wise enough to understand its use. He ignored their warning and sent the four parts of the Stone out into the world. There was murder done then over the Stone and murder done now." Silwyth gestured to the bodies of the soldiers that lay around them. "The Stone is drenched in blood."

Damra shook her head, unconvinced. "Without the Sovereign Stone, we lose the power to create Dominion Lords—"

"Take the Stones to the Council of Dominion Lords. Let them decide what to do with it," Silwyth urged, holding out the portion of the Sovereign Stone to her. "The power of Lord Dagnarus grows daily. I know, for I have seen the vastness of his armies. Their numbers are immense, his troops are devoted to him, for they believe he is a god. Ten thousand troops does he plan to send against New Vinnengael alone. Terrifying warriors, the taan are fierce in battle, for they are told that there is no greater glory than to lay down their lives for him. Already, these ten thousand troops march on the western gate of the Tromek Portal."

"The Portal will hold—"

"The Portal will fall. The Shield has promised Dagnarus access."

"The fool!" Damra said bitterly.

"The two parts of the Sovereign Stone must not remain in elven lands, Damra," Silwyth said earnestly. "The Divine is too weak to protect them."

"But what of my husband? I cannot leave him to die when it is in my power to free him. No, I will not—"

"Your husband is already freed," said Silwyth. "By my hand. He has been smuggled safely out of Tromek lands. He waits for you at a place in northern New Vinnengael called Shadamehr's Keep."

Damra stared. "I don't believe it. You said yourself I could use this information to free my husband. Yet you claim he is already free . . ."

"And so you did use it, Damra of Gwyenoc," Silwyth said, smiling.

"How can I trust you?" she demanded, frustrated and angry.

"I give you the Sovereign Stone," said Silwyth.

Damra hesitated, but there really wasn't much choice. She could not leave the Stone here, nor could she leave the Stone in the hands of Silwyth of House Kinnoth.

"Very well," she said.

Silwyth rested the Sovereign Stone gently on her palm. The Stone was sticky with his blood and no longer sparkled in the light.

"I ask one boon of you, Damra of Gwyenoc. Tell the Divine of what I have done this night. I ask no pardon for myself," Silwyth said. "I ask it for my family, for the young whose lives are ruined before they begin, for the old who die without dignity. Restore House Kinnoth to honor."

"If all you have said proves to be true, I will do so," was the best Damra could promise.

Apparently that was good enough, for Silwyth bowed and turned to depart. Before he left, he pointed.

The lights of flaring torches lit the darkness. The emblem of the Shield gleamed on the banners of the Shield's soldiers.

Concerned about Silwyth, Damra glanced around, but could not find him. She shrugged, dismissed him. He had proven adept at taking care of himself. She had other concerns.

Damra concealed the Sovereign Stone beneath the breastplate of her armor. She was still not certain of her ultimate decision. She required more information. Had the Shield truly sought to steal the Stone? Had he been in league with the creature of darkness? Damra retraced her steps across the stones, then crept into the guardian grove and waited to see what would happen.

THE SHIELD'S PERSONAL BODYGUARD ARRIVED ON THE SCENE FIRST, TO make certain that the Shield would not be exposed to any danger. The knights stared with unfeigned amazement at the gruesome sight and Damra concluded they had not been in on the plot. The first to notice the magic had been dispelled cried out that the Sovereign Stone was missing. Several started toward the reliquary on the run, but their officer brought them up short.

He ordered them to make certain the area was secure, to check to see if they could help the wounded, and to try to find someone among the wounded who could explain what had happened. The knights fanned out and Damra crept back farther into the shadows. She had cloaked the magic of her armor in the black plumage of the raven and she did not fear being seen, but there was always the possibility someone might bump into her.

The Vrykyl lay unmoving on the platform. The officer cast a single, piercing glance at the black-armored creature. He was obviously curious, but he was the cautious sort, as he must be with the life of the Shield in his hands. The Vrykyl was not moving and he was not about to send his men near it until he was certain that there were not more of the same lurking about. The knights searched the forest, but did not find Damra or anyone else. Posting guards in a ring around the perimeter, one returned to the officer to report that all was secure.

The guard Damra had kicked in the teeth sat up, holding his hand over his broken nose. The officer knelt beside the man, asked him what had happened. Mumbling through blood, spitting out teeth, the guard made some reply.

"He says he will speak only to the Shield," said the officer. He rose to his feet, surveyed the area. "One of you return to the barracks where the

Shield waits. He was warned by the ancestors that something like this might happen. Tell him what you have seen and ask if he will come."

The officer eyed the Vrykyl and looked about at the bodies of the soldiers of the Divine. Walking over to one, he placed his hand on the man's neck to feel for a pulse. He shook his head and his expression darkened.

"Warning from his ancestors," Damra muttered below her breath. "How convenient. But did they warn him of the Vrykyl?"

The officer walked over to the reliquary. He peered into the bottom, saw the body in the pit. Drawing his sword, he walked across the stepping stones and warily approached the Vrykyl. His men were silent, watchful. The night was so quiet that Damra could hear clearly the officer's boots crunch on the broken crystal and the sharp intake of his breath as he drew near the Vrykyl, which had the appearance of some sort of monstrous insect lying dead on its back. He reached out his hand to touch the armor, perhaps to see if the creature was still alive.

His fingers brushed the surface. He snatched back his hand and he wiped his fingers on the silk tunic he wore beneath his armor. He searched the platform, even stared into the pit in an effort to find the Sovereign Stone. When he could not find it, he looked again at the black-armored figure and kicked it with the toe of his boot to determine if perhaps the Vrykyl might be still holding it. Unable to locate the Stone, the officer walked back across the stepping stones. He continued to wipe his hand on his tunic.

Apparently the Shield had not remained in the barracks, but had followed on the heels of his guards, for he arrived far sooner than expected. Garwina was calm. He had his story prepared. He looked about sternly and was about to demand what had occurred, when he saw the Vrykyl.

Garwina was adept at concealing his true feelings. His was a face of clay that, once molded, would retain its shape indefinitely. At the sight of the black-armored creature, lying in the ruins of the shattered globe, the face cracked. The Shield's eyes widened, his jaw went slack. He stared, confounded.

"What . . . what is that?" he gargled.

"I do not know, my lord," said the knight officer. "I was hoping you could tell me."

At the dire tone of the officer's voice, the Shield looked at him sharply. All his knights wore grim expressions, stood regarding him with lowering brows. His gaze flicked from them to the dead soldiers to the wounded soldier to the reliquary. Damra could almost see the Shield's mind working.

"Isn't it apparent?" he said, his eyes flashing in anger at their suspicions. "The warning I was given was true. This was an attempt by the Divine to steal the Sovereign Stone. He sent that foul creature"—the Shield gestured to the Vrykyl—"to seize it. Our soldiers tried to halt them."

"What I see is that the soldiers of the Divine were stabbed in the back," said the officer. "Bring that man."

Two knights hauled the soldier with the broken nose before the Shield. "Tell us what happened," the officer commanded.

The man looked up at the Shield and went down on his knees, prostrated himself. "I failed in my duty. I request death, my lord!" the man cried.

The Shield drew his sword, quite happy to comply with the request, but the officer stepped in between the two of them.

"First you will speak the truth," the officer said to the soldier. "The position you held was a sacred one. You swore fealty to the Shield, to the Divine and to the Tromek nation. If you have broken that oath, your soul will go to the prison house of the dead, your family will be disgraced, dishonored for the next seven generations. Speak the truth and you may yet redeem your vow, save yourself and your family." The knight officer glanced at the Shield. "I am certain your lord will command you to be truthful."

The Shield tried to speak, but his face muscles were so stiff that his words were incomprehensible. The wounded man slid a glance at his lord, but saw nothing to help him. He began to speak.

"We were told that the Divine was plotting to steal the Sovereign Stone. We were ordered to slay his soldiers, before they killed us. We wondered at this, for they gave us no sign that they meant any treachery. They talked and laughed with us as always. They were our friends . . ." The man paused, his voice hardened. "We obeyed our orders, but it was hard. I had known Glath for many, many years. His son married my daughter. Yet, my duty was to my lord. I stabbed Glath in the back. My soul will always remember the look of shock on his face, that I had betrayed him. He died, cursing me."

The man hung his head. "I feared, then, that I was the one who had been betrayed. I did not want to admit it until the Dominion Lord came and—"

"Dominion Lord!" the Shield exclaimed. "What Dominion Lord?"

"I know her by sight, my lord," said the soldier. "I have seen her here in company with the Divine. But I do not know her name."

"I do," the Shield said, grinding his teeth.

"Continue," said the officer with a baleful glance at the Shield.

"We were told that a lady would come to take the Sovereign Stone to safety. She arrived and then she disappeared and that thing"—the officer pointed to the Vrykyl—"took her place. I don't know what happened after that, for the Dominion Lord struck me and I was unconscious for a short time. A blast awoke me. I saw the Dominion Lord standing over that creature and with her was an old man and then they were both gone."

"Did the Dominion Lord have the Sovereign Stone?" the Shield demanded.

"I . . . don't know, my lord," said the wretched man.

"She must have," said the Shield. He turned back to the officer. "There, you see? The Divine sent his agent to steal the Stone."

"It sounds to me more likely the Divine sent his agent to save it," said the officer. "The Dominion Lords are blessed by the gods. This thing"— he pointed at the Vrykyl—"is a creature of the Void."

The Shield's mouth worked. He was shaking with fury, but he could say nothing, dared not say anything until he had thought this through. The officer reached down and grabbed hold of the soldier, dragged him to his feet.

"You will tell your story to the Divine."

"It is my word against his," the Shield stated.

"There are other wounded here, who will corroborate his tale," the officer said. He did not look at the Shield, but kept his eyes averted.

The knights picked up the wounded and carried them off. The Shield was left alone, standing in the midst of the ruins of his plan, his arms crossed over his chest, his face once more the cold, stiff mask. He was, Damra could tell, still plotting.

Damra had heard all she needed to know. Her worst suspicions were confirmed. She should go to the Divine, tell Cedar the truth of the matter. Her steps tended that direction, but her pace was slow and eventually she halted altogether.

If she went to the Divine, she would have to hand over the Sovereign Stone. Silwyth's words, his urgency kept coming to her. This enemy, this lord Dagnarus. *I have seen the vastness of his armies. Their numbers are immense, his troops are devoted to him . . . The Divine is weak . . .* If she went to the Divine, she would become ensnarled in a political web of accusations, counter-accusations, recriminations, possibly even civil war. The Shield had been dealt a terrible blow, but he was not dead. Wealthy, powerful, clever, he might yet rise above this.

"Whatever else happens, I must take the pecwae and his companions to the Council of Dominion Lords. If I believe Silwyth, my husband waits for me at this place called Shadamehr's Keep in Vinnengael. My destiny lies in that direction. There is nothing here for me."

Damra looked around, at the conniving and manipulating Shield, at the bodies of those he had murdered, at the black-armored evil lying in the wreckage of the reliquary.

"Nothing now. Perhaps nothing ever."

Damra walked into the night.

*   *   *

Left alone, Garwina of House Wyval pondered his situation. His was a dispassionate, calculating nature, not given to mental hand-wringing. He had suffered a reversal of fortune. That happened in life and thus the gods blessed the cat with the ability to twist her body in the air and land on her feet. Like the cat, Garwina twisted.

The main problem, as he saw it, was this carcass of the strange creature of the Void. All else could be explained away, even the murders, for he had already provided himself with documents—innocent enough on the surface, but which could be altered here and there to implicate the Divine in an attempt to steal the Sovereign Stone.

Keeping an eye on the carcass, Garwina walked over to investigate it. He was not a coward but, like all elves, he deeply distrusted magic. Elves find Void magic particularly loathsome, for its use is an affront to the gods, an abomination. If the Divine were able to prove that Garwina was conspiring with Void wizards, the Shield would indeed be ruined. He might be forced to request death in order to salvage his honor and that of his House.

But what proof did the Divine have? Nothing except the word of some knights that they had seen such a creature, for the fools had departed without thinking to cart off the evidence. Garwina had only to get rid of this carcass and he would be able to claim that the knights were victims of an illusion created by the Dominion Lord. Garwina could see himself crawling out of the hole.

The Shield crossed the stepping stones and came to stand on the platform. He stared down at the black-armored thing that lay unmoving at his feet. He did not know where it came from and could only assume that the Lady Godelieve had employed it to steal the Sovereign Stone. The fact that she should be in league with the Void did not surprise him. She was in league with humans. Not a great leap from one to the other.

His stomach clenched and his skin crawled at the thought of touching the horrid object, but he had to haul away the black armor and the corpse inside it, bury it, burn it, somehow destroy it. Nerving himself to the dreadful task, Garwina grit his teeth and bent down to remove the helm, to get a look at the face.

A black-armored hand raised up and seized hold of Garwina's wrist.

The Shield's heart stopped. He could not breathe, he could not move. Stunned with terror, he stood staring as the Vrykyl rose to its feet. The creature retained a grip on the Shield's arm, a grip so tight that he gasped in pain. And then his gasp changed to one of astonishment as the Vrykyl melted away, dissolved back into the Void. The Lady Godelieve stood on the platform beside him, her delicate hand clasping his wrist.

The Shield pulled away from her, came perilously close to falling into the pit.

"You are dead! You had to be! Your head . . ." He could not finish.

"You are right. I am dead. I have been dead for over two hundred years. So wise are you, Silwyth. Yet you made a mistake. You did not strike to the heart." Her voice dropped. "Not as Dagnarus did, when he made me what I am . . ."

"What are you?" the Shield cried in terror.

The Lady Godelieve regarded him with disdain. "A force beyond your understanding. A powerful force. One that can help you." She took a step toward him.

Garwina saw her beauty but he also saw the hideous visage beneath the illusion. He saw the smooth skin and rotting flesh. He saw the high-planed cheekbones and the bleached bones of the skull. He saw the lovely eyes and empty sockets. He saw the curved, sensual lips part over the grin of the corpse. The Shield was horrified and, at the same time, intrigued. She was right. This was power. Immense power. And it had attached itself to him.

He repressed a shudder.

"What do you want of me?" he asked.

"Help me recover the Sovereign Stone," she answered.

DAMRA KNEW WHERE TO FIND ARIM. HE WOULD BE STAYING IN THE HOME of the Nimorean ambassador. Damra avoided the main house, slipped around to the guest quarters, located behind the main dwelling. A light burned in the window of one of the small houses, a signal Arim had left for Damra, in case she needed to find them. She knocked softly on the door and was immediately answered.

She whispered her name and added, "Let no one approach."

Arim opened the door, looked out. He held his sword in his hand.

"Something has happened," Damra said. "We must leave at once. Wake the others. Make haste!"

Arim wasted no time on questions. He disappeared into the darkness, leaving Damra to keep uneasy watch. Since Arim had told his companions to sleep in their clothes and they had few belongings, they took time only to gather up the twenty-seven turquoise stones the Grandmother had insisted on placing around them and which must be taken up one by one and counted over twice, no matter what the gravity of the situation. This done, they departed quickly and quietly.

Damra feared that they would badger her with questions, but none of them said a word. Pleased and grateful, she led them across country toward the city of Glymrae.

As they walked, she told Arim what had occurred. He listened in silence, amazed and disturbed. When Damra mentioned Silwyth of House Kinnoth, Arim frowned and shook his head. "I would not trust him."

"I thought so myself," Damra said. "But to see him, to hear him. Everything he foretold happened as he said it would happen."

Arim made no further argument. He was not an elf and had no right to criticize that which he did not understand. He was amazed almost beyond belief when Damra told him she had acquired the elven portion of the

Sovereign Stone and what she intended to do with it. He sympathized when she spoke of her worry for her husband, said nothing when she related that Griffith was supposed to be safe in Shadamehr's Keep. No need to remind her that this information came from an elf of a disgraced House, an unreliable source. The way she spoke indicated that though she wanted desperately to believe Silwyth, she was realist enough to know that he may have been saying this for his own purposes.

"What do you know of this Shadamehr?" she asked.

"Not much," Arim admitted. "Only that he is a Dominion Lord who is not a Dominion Lord. He passed the Tests," he said by way of explanation, "but he refused to undergo the Transfiguration."

Damra frowned. "I don't like that. It is dishonorable, if nothing else. An insult to the gods. Is the man a coward, then, that he could not go through with it?"

"I have heard the man termed many things: thief, rogue, outlaw, among others not so kind, but I have never heard anyone accuse him of cowardice. He is a mystery wrapped in an enigma, as the humans are fond of saying. His Keep is located near the eastern end of the Tromek Portal. If Griffith were to escape the Shield's Wyred, that would be a good place for him to go. Shadamehr has a reputation for welcoming people of all races and nationalities to his banner."

"Then I am resolved," Damra said. "We are close to the western entrance of the Portal. That is the fastest route to take to reach New Vinnengael and the Council of Dominion Lords. We will go there."

"But if what Silwyth said is true," Arim argued, "an enemy force under the leadership of the Lord of the Void has slipped unseen through Nimorea and crossed the border into elven lands with orders to seize the Portal. We may be walking into the cat's mouth." He quoted from an elven child's tale in which the cunning cat convinces the foolish mouse that the cat's mouth is the mouse's safe home.

"Wyred also guard the Portal's entrance—"

"And they are also of the Shield's House," Arim pointed out.

"Yet, they are Wyred. They will be appalled to hear about the Shield dealing with a creature of the Void. If I can convince them, they will turn from the Shield. They would never be a part of such treachery."

Arim shook his head. "Who can say but that they are the ones who advised him to do this? I do not think you should count upon their assistance, Damra."

"I must count upon something," Damra said briskly. "If not the Wyred, then the Father and Mother. The Portal is the quickest way to reach New Vinnengael and the Council of Dominion Lords. They must be apprised immediately of this dire situation. We cannot afford to waste three months in overland travel."

"There are the hippogriffs—" he began.

Damra cut him off. "I've already thought of that. We can make use of hippogriffs to fly us the short distance to the Portal, but they do not like making journeys much longer than that, for they do not want to be away from their young. Even if we were able to convince them to travel as far as Shadamehr's Keep, they would not prove to be much faster than horses, for they can fly for only a few hours each day while carrying a rider before they are required to rest."

"You know these creatures," Arim said. "I do not."

"Ah, Arim." Damra sighed. "I am trying hard not to let myself be influenced by the knowledge that Griffith may be at this Keep, although from what little you tell me of this Shadamehr, I think I am almost more worried than I was before. At least the Wyred are elven. I understand them. I will never understand humans, present company excepted, dear friend. I need Griffith's help and his wisdom. The burden of this responsibility is almost too heavy to bear."

She cast a glance back at their companions. In addition to feeling responsible for the lives of these people, Damra carried with her the elven portion of the Sovereign Stone. Not since its gifting from the gods had two portions been in such close proximity.

Not since the gifting had two been in such danger. The Trevenici carried with him the blood knife and although he was careful not to draw blood with it, the Vrykyl could be using it to track them. Damra had tried to think of some way to rid themselves of the blood knife, but since she knew next to nothing of Void magic, she feared she might do more harm than good. Griffith would know. Griffith would advise her. She longed to believe that Silwyth was telling her the truth.

"What are they talking about?" Bashae asked Jessan, the two of them trudging along several paces behind Arim and Damra.

"I don't know," he replied moodily. "I can understand only one word out of ten."

"They're speaking Elderspeak, aren't they?" Bashae sounded unsure. "Not elven?"

"They're talking Elderspeak, but the way the elf pronounces the words she might as well be using a foreign tongue."

"I like to hear her," said Bashae. "I always thought Elderspeak sounded like someone smashing rocks, but she makes it sound like birds singing. Almost like Twithil. Do you know where we're going?"

They hiked across rolling grasslands, following Damra, who had an objective in mind, judging by the firmness and rapidity of her steps. The Grandmother was hard pressed to keep up and occasionally lagged behind. She refused to complain, for that might slow their pace and the agate eyes saw danger everywhere. Jessan was forced to fall back now and then, take hold of her arm, and support her steps.

"Something about a stables," Jessan replied. Although by his expression, he was exasperated with her, his touch was invariably gentle and patient. "A good thing," he added pointedly. "We need horses."

"Yes, we do," said the Grandmother. "For I know you young ones have trouble keeping up with me."

Dawn was breaking when they came in sight of the highway that led into the capital city of Glymrae. Such a highway in human lands would have been paved, for humans use Earth magic to create their highways and maintain them. The elves, who are given to Air magic, disdain paved roads, considering them an insult to nature. Their highways are hard-packed dirt with plantings of trees, hedges and rosebushes along either side. Not only do the trees and hedges provide beauty for the traveler, they also have a strategic advantage in that any enemy army using the road to speed his march is subject to ambush from defenders hidden in the foliage.

Looking ahead, they could see numerous red tiled roofs shining in the early morning sun. Flags fluttered in the air. Damra called a halt.

"The castle you see before you is the fortress of the Divine. I am going there to acquire mounts for our journey to the Portal. I leave you in the care of Arim. He will tell you what has happened and what our plans are. I will not be gone long. Remain in hiding until you hear my signal."

She looked to Arim as she said this last. He nodded and, with a smile that was meant to be reassuring, Damra departed.

The group left the road, followed Arim's lead to a grove of trees. Here they sat down to rest. The Grandmother planted her stick in the soft ground, then cast a sharp glance at Arim.

"Tell us what happened to the Dominion Lord," she said. "Something went wrong, didn't it? That is why she came to us in the night."

"I am afraid so," said Arim, and he gave a concise account of all that Damra had told him.

"So we each have a part of the Sovereign Stone," Bashae said, when Arim was finished. The pecwae's voice was soft with awe and pride. "A Dominion Lord and me."

"I should clear out," Jessan said resolutely. "I am putting all of you in danger."

"Damra did consider that, Jessan," said Arim, reaching up his hand to detain the young man, who appeared ready to rush off that moment. "She considered leaving you behind. I tell you this because I do not want you to think we are making a foolish sacrifice in taking you with us. Will you listen to her reasoning?"

Jessan appeared irresolute, then he squatted back down. "I will listen. But I am not convinced. Every time I close my eyes, I see the red eyes, searching for me. It will be only a matter of time before they see me."

"If we left you on your own, without protection—"

Jessan stirred at this, but he kept silent.

"—the Vrykyl would almost certainly capture you. As it is, he knows only that you have the bone knife. He does not know about the rest of us, who we are, what we carry. If he did get hold of you, he would force you to tell him everything you know.

"I do not insult you when I say this, Jessan," Arim added, seeing Jessan's face flush. "I know that you are brave. Only a man of courage would offer to face this monstrous creature alone. But you would not be able to help yourself. The Vrykyl would slay you with the blood knife and then take over your body, your knowledge, your memories. He would use your body to find us and, disguised as you, he could come upon us and catch us unaware. Thus, Damra judges that we are safer together than apart. Do you find her reasoning sound?"

"Yes, I suppose," said Jessan. He was relieved, yet at the same time, disappointed.

The thought of leaving Bashae and the Grandmother in the care of others, striking out on his own, free and independent, seemed very attractive when considered in the light of day. A warrior from a race of warriors, he was not fool enough to think he could fight the Vrykyl. Yet he did think well enough of his woodland abilities to believe that he could keep out of the Vrykyl's way, at least until he found the means to destroy the knife.

Those were his daylight thoughts. At night, seeing those red eyes staring at him from the darkness of his dreams, he was glad to have his friends around him. He was even thankful for the twenty-seven turquoise stones.

Jessan lay down on the ground, stared up into the treetops and dreamed of home. The Grandmother dozed. Arim kept watch, as did the stick. Bashae sat holding the knapsack close to him, thinking of the heavy responsibility that was his. He wished that Lord Gustav had been truthful with him, and felt sad that the knight had not trusted him enough to tell him what he carried.

But then, Bashae asked himself, would I have trusted a total stranger with something this important? I didn't trust Arim enough to tell him.

"I understand, Sir Knight," Bashae said softly to the dead man's soul. "I'm sorry I doubted you."

Bashae then wondered if he was glad to know the truth or if he would rather not. He decided that he was glad Damra had been honest with him. He could make better decisions now. He looked back at the Bashae who had gone on this journey with such a light heart and that Bashae was a stranger. That brought to mind another question.

Edging over to the Grandmother, Bashae shook her by the shoulder.

"Grandmother," he whispered.

"Go away," she said, keeping her eyes closed. "I'm asleep."

"Grandmother," Bashae whispered again. "It's important."

Heaving a sigh, the Grandmother propped herself up on her elbow and glowered at him. "What do you want?"

"I was just wondering—did you know what it was the knight gave me? Is that why you wanted to come with us, because you thought that Jessan and I weren't wise enough to be trusted with it? I wouldn't blame you, if you did," he assured her.

The Grandmother lay down, flat on her back, but she didn't close her eyes. Clasping her hands over her chest, she said abruptly, "I didn't want to be buried there."

"What?" Bashae asked, startled. This was not the answer he'd expected. "What did you say?"

"Have you gone deaf? I said I didn't want to be buried there," the Grandmother repeated irritably.

She gazed up into the blue sky, twiddled her thumbs and moved her feet back and forth, so that the toes tapped together. The rhythmic movement set the bells on her skirt to jingling.

"I was born there. I lived there year after year after year. I knew every tree and every rock and they knew me." She didn't sound as if this had been an overwhelming pleasure. She sat back up. "Do you think I want to lie there staring at them for all eternity? A person needs a change," she stated defensively, as if she'd been accused of something. "A person likes to see something different."

She fixed a stern eye on Bashae. "So if I drop over, just plant me where I fall. Don't go hauling me back home."

"Yes, Grandmother," Bashae said, starting to smile and then thinking better of it.

"Good," she said and lay back down, twiddling her thumbs and smiling up at the sky.

With the daylight, travelers began to appear on the road. Arim cautioned his companions to keep still, make no sudden movement or any sound that would draw attention to themselves. Sitting in the shadows of the trees, they watched columns of soldiers march down the road, merchants traveling to market and a wealthy noble lady being carried in a palanquin, her retinue following along behind. Everything seemed normal, daily routine proceeded apace. Arim saw nothing to give any indication that a major upheaval in the politics of the elves had occurred during the night.

It was just a matter of time, though, before word spread. He glanced up at the sun that was rising steadily higher into the sky and began to worry. Damra had been gone four hours now.

Arim made a contingency plan. If she was not here by noon, he would have to leave, take the Sovereign Stone to New Vinnengael himself. He was thinking over the route they should take, when Jessan touched his arm, pointed.

"She's looking for us."

Arim saw Damra above the top of the hedge, her figure passing in and out among the trees that lined the roadway, and he gave a sigh of relief. Mounted herself, she led other steeds behind her. She set a leisurely pace, as if she were out for morning exercise, but every now and then she sent a sharp glance searchingly into the trees.

Warning the others to keep down, Arim walked out to meet her. As long as there were people in view, the two stood together on the road, talking pleasantly, as if they were fellow travelers who happened to meet along the way. The moment the road cleared, Damra entered the tree line, leading the animals she had brought behind her.

At the sight of the animals, the Grandmother lifted the agate-eyed stick. "Get a good look," she told it. "You won't see the like again."

"What are they?" Bashae stared.

"Griffin-horses," said Jessan nonchalantly, as if hippogriffs were creatures he encountered on a daily basis. "My uncle Raven told me about them. Elven warriors ride them into battle."

"I think I'd rather have a horse," said Bashae. "These griffin-horses look too clumsy to be of much use."

"They just look that way," Jessan replied, his voice warming with excitement. "They have talons in front. Their back legs are like those of a horse but they can run faster than any living horse. Using their wings to help them, they fly over the ground. And they don't have to stay on the ground. The elves use griffin-horses to attack from the air. They swoop down on the enemy, their front talons ripping and tearing. They can snap off a human's head in their strong beaks or lift him into the air with their talons. Then they drop him to his death."

"Do they do that on a regular basis, Jessan? Drop people to their deaths?" Bashae asked nervously.

"Just their enemies," Jessan said. "They don't drop their riders."

"But what if the riders dropped themselves. How do you stay on? I don't see any saddles."

"They'll tell us. No other Trevenici in our tribe has ever ridden a griffin-horse," Jessan stated with satisfaction. "I'll be the first. You'll likely be the first pecwae to ride one."

"Great," said Bashae.

Damra led the hippogriffs among the trees. She and Arim spoke together quickly, forgetting in the gravity of the moment to speak Elderspeak.

"As I predicted would happen, the Shield has managed to turn the knife blade that was at his throat so that now it points at the throat of the Divine."

"How did he do that?" Arim demanded, stunned. "You said that his own knights didn't believe him."

"Not all of them, apparently. He has rallied his forces and is now holed up in his fortress, challenging the Divine to attack him. He claims that the gods themselves took the Sovereign Stone, thus indicating their anger at the Divine. He says that if this is not true, if the Divine has the Stone, all he has to do is to return it."

"What will you do?"

"Keep the Stone, of course," she said as if amazed he could imagine anything else. Her voice hardened. "I am more assured than ever that I have made the right decision. These two see the Sovereign Stone now as nothing more than a piece in a game."

Horn blasts sounded in the distance, coming from the fortress of the Divine. Those on the road halted, listening. Some shook their heads. Others shook their fists. They had heard these sounds before and all knew what it meant. Merchants driving carts gave the reins a slap, sending their horses ahead at a gallop. Soldiers broke into a run, holding their swords to their sides to keep them from clanking. Some headed toward the castle of the Divine. Others turned in the opposite direction.

"I feared as much," said Damra. "The call to arms. The Divine has declared war against the Shield."

At the sound of the trumpets, the hippogriffs lifted their heads. Their bright eyes flashed at the sound, they gnashed their beaks. Their griffin talons ripped up the grass, their horse tails swished. Damra hurried to soothe them, running her hand over the soft plumage that extended from their griffin heads down to their withers.

"We must make haste," Damra said. "I borrowed these from the stables. I could only manage three. You and I will each take one of the pecwae with us."

Jessan came up to her. "What do the trumpet calls mean?"

"War," she said coolly. "Can you ride a horse?"

"Yes," said Jessan, affronted.

"Good. Then you can ride a hippogriff. Sit here, on the back. Don't touch their wings. They don't like that and they might take your head off. I had no time to saddle them, so we will have to ride bareback. The trick is to keep tight hold with your legs, press your thighs into the flanks, and lie forward. Wrap your arms around their necks. You have no need for reins. The hippogriffs know where they're going."

"I understand," said Jessan.

Walking over to one of the hippogriffs, he stood in front of the animal, gazed straight into her eyes. The hippogriff met his gaze, held it. Jessan said something to the animal in Tivniv. It is doubtful if the hippogriff understood, but she heard respect in the young warrior's tone and sensed no fear in him, only elation. She gave a nod of her proud head and held still to permit him to mount. Jessan took hold of the withers, swung himself up and his leg over. He looked to have been born on the back of the beast as he smiled in delight.

Damra was relieved. One worry gone. She had more than enough other worries to keep her from missing it, however.

Her skirts swinging, her beads clashing, the Grandmother halted in front of another hippogriff and spoke to him. Damra was not surprised by this, but she was amazed to find that the hippogriff lowered its head, appeared to be listening intently. Damra looked to Arim, who shrugged.

The Grandmother motioned to Bashae, who came reluctantly and placed his hand tremulously on the hippogriff's neck. The Grandmother and the hippogriff concluded their communication to the satisfaction of both, or so it appeared. The Grandmother walked over to Damra.

"We are afraid. We pecwae are always afraid. But the griffin-horse told us not to be. The distance is not far, the weather is fine for flying, and he will enjoy being up among the clouds, where the air is cleaner to breathe than the air down here that has been tainted by the snortings of the wingless."

"And that made you feel better?" Damra asked dubiously.

"Oh, yes," said the Grandmother. She held up the stick, twitched it all around. "We should probably be going. The eyes don't like what they see." She handed the stick to Damra. "Lash the stick onto my back. Make certain you fasten it tight."

Casting a bemused look at Arim, Damra did as the Grandmother ordered. Damra mounted her hippogriff, taking more than her usual care to be respectful of the animal. For some reason, Damra had always supposed that hippogriffs revered and honored the elves who had mastered them and she was nonplussed to find that the beasts apparently held "the snorting wingless" in contempt. She pulled the Grandmother up to sit behind her, cautioning her to keep fast hold around her waist.

Seeing that, despite the beast's assurances, Bashae had gone slightly green about the nose and mouth, Arim placed the pecwae in front of him, between the wings, and clasped one arm tightly around him. He nodded to show they were ready.

Damra gave the command to fly, feeling self-conscious as she did so, wondering if perhaps she should make the command a request. The hippogriffs obeyed, however. Planting their rear hooves firmly into the ground, they gave a convulsive leap, using their wings to lift themselves and their riders.

They soared up over the treetops. Jessan's face glowed. He gave a wild shout, forgot to lean forward, and came perilously close to falling off. A grab at the plumage saved him. The near disaster didn't bother him, though. Mouth open, he drank in the air that flowed around him and laughed for sheer joy.

Bashae kept his eyes squinched tightly shut. He shook his head violently when Arim urged him to look. Damra had no time to check on her fellow rider. She kept close watch on the ground, fearing that they might have been seen. Fortunately, the advent of war had captured everyone's attention. If anyone did notice three hippogriffs taking off from the woods, they must suppose that they were part of the current martial activity. They left behind the red tile roofs of the Divine's palace and Damra finally relaxed.

They had escaped. The way before her was clear and easy to travel. As the hippogriff had said, the weather was fine for flying.

THE SUN'S RAYS THAT SHONE ON TROMEK THAT MORNING HAD NOT YET brightened the land where Jessan's uncle Raven walked in shackles. Jessan was not thinking of his uncle. Raven was awake, and he was thinking of his nephew, thinking of all his family and those friends and comrades he would never see again.

Raven often woke before the dawn. He slept fitfully, the warrior part of him listening to all the sounds of the camp. The taan liked to make an early start and were always up with the sun, which meant that he and the other slaves were up, as well. These few moments before the taan stirred were the only moments of peace he was allowed.

Oftentimes his thoughts went to plots and schemes revolving around his one object in life. He spent these brief moments dreaming of the combat or thinking up ways to goad or trick Qu-tok into battling him. Thus far, none of the attempts had worked. Raven's insults afforded Qu-tok much amusement and ended up hurting only Raven, who was punished as a slave was punished. He was deprived of food or beaten, but he was not starved, nor was he ever seriously injured. As a human takes pride in a savage dog, Qu-tok took pride in Raven's rages. The half-taan Dur-zor told Raven that his fits of temper were often related with relish in the evening around the campfire to entertain the children.

Today, Raven's thoughts went to his nephew, traveling a far distant road. Perhaps somewhere Jessan watched the same sun that was struggling to lift itself up over the horizon. Watching the sun, Raven sent a silent blessing to his nephew and those under his care. Then his thoughts returned, like a horse chained to a waterwheel, to circle again the rutted track of his hatred.

The slave caravan consisted of about five hundred slaves, mostly human males, who were being transported to the mines to dig gold and silver to finance Dagnarus's war machine. The human women in the caravan were claimed by the taan. Their lives were a living hell, for they were brutally abused by night and by day forced to work for the taan at a variety of tasks. Many died along the route, either slain by the taan for some minor infraction or taken ill. The taan cast the sick aside to die alone on the trail, for the taan consider illness to be a weakness. One went mad and drowned herself in a river. The others did nothing but survive from day to day until the time when they must give birth to the wretched half-breed babies some now carried.

The males were treated better, for they were a valuable commodity and must reach their destination fit for hard labor. Most were young and strong, the elderly and infirm had all died. The men were chained together in long lines of twenty-five, forced to march in their shackles. If one proved too weak to march, his comrades supported him, for the taan would not cut him loose. When one of the slaves died on the march, his comrades were forced to carry his body or let it drag on the ground until nightfall, when the taan finally released the corpse and threw it in a pit. The taan covered thirty miles in a day, waking early and marching late, and nothing and no one was permitted to slow them up.

Raven alone was not chained together with the others. A length of chain was attached to the iron collar around his neck and he was led along by this chain like a dancing bear he'd seen once in a fair in Dunkar. Sometimes Qu-tok took the chain, showing off his slave. At these times, Raven yanked on the chain, dug in his heels, did anything he could to anger Qu-tok. He always failed, for Qu-tok only chortled and usually ended the contest by jerking Raven off his feet and dragging him along the ground. At other times, Qu-tok handed Raven off to some of the young warriors. These young taan teased and tormented Raven, hoping he would lunge at them or attack them, but they were always disappointed. Raven paid no attention to any of them. Only Qu-tok.

The other slaves looked on Raven with envy that bordered on hatred. Raven did not know this and he would not have cared if he did, for he never spoke to any of the other slaves, paid little attention to them. He had his own burdens and could not take on theirs.

What Raven saw as humiliation, the other slaves viewed as salvation. He was permitted to sleep by himself, chained only to a stake, not to twenty-four other miserable humans. He was permitted a greater share of food and the companionship of a female, even if it was only one of these perverted monsters. The other slaves soon regarded Raven as a traitor. They called him "lizard lover" and other names that were cruder. Raven ignored them.

He lost track of time, for one day melted into another, and last night, as he had watched the full moon rise, he was surprised to realize that they had been on the road for a month.

We must be nearing our destination, he thought. His desperation increased, for once the slaves had been delivered safely to the mines, Qu-tok would take his payment for Raven and depart.

"Yes," said Dur-zor that morning when she brought him his food, "we are within a few days' march of the mines. There was some talk that we would stop this day to allow the warriors to hunt, for we are running low on food, but Dag-ruk wants to push on. She is eager to deliver the slaves and return to the war and to her promotion to nizam."

The words were on the tip of Raven's tongue to ask Dur-zor to set him free, but he swallowed them now as he had swallowed them before. She had been a friend to him and he did not want to repay her friendship by asking her to do something that would cost her life. She had come to like him. He knew that and he would not take advantage of her liking. By freeing Raven she would be depriving Qu-tok of a valued possession and few things are more abhorrent to a taan than a thief. The taan would kill her, probably torture her to death.

Raven found her studying him intently and he feared she knew what he had been thinking. She proved it, by saying, "When I want something very much, I pray to our god Dagnarus to grant it. Have you prayed to your gods?"

"Constantly," said Raven. Eating his food, he eyed Dur-zor, who squatted comfortably in front of him. "Have you prayed to this god of yours to make you a warrior?"

"Oh, yes," she said, nodding her head violently.

"And you still bring me food every day and endure Qu-tok's beatings," said Raven with a shrug. "Your god must be as deaf as mine."

"I have faith," said Dur-zor. "I grow more skilled with the kep-ker every day. I do not think our god would grant me that skill if he did not intend for me to use it."

"So the gods would not have created Qu-tok if they didn't intend for me to kill him?" Raven said with a quirk of his mouth.

Dur-zor frowned. "Why do you jest about serious matters?"

"Jesting is a way humans have of dealing with serious matters," Raven explained, feeling uncomfortable. He thought that perhaps he'd gone a bit too far. "I'm sorry, Dur-zor. It's just that I'm losing hope—"

"Hope," she repeated. "What is that word? I have never heard it before."

Raven was confounded. Such a question might have confounded a Temple mage, and Raven was no scholar.

"Well," he said slowly, "hope means that we want something to happen. I hope it will rain, for example. Or I hope that a big rock will fall on Qu-tok's head—"

Dur-zor smiled at that, although she glanced guiltily over her shoulder before she did so. They did not have long to speak together. The taan had finished breaking their fast and feeding the slaves. They were packing up their camp, a job that did not take long. Everything a taan owned he had to be able to carry with him. This included his tent, his weapons, and supplies. Each taan bore his own burden, could not delegate it to a tasker or a slave. The most renowned warrior lugged his own tent. Dag-ruk, their chief, toted her own gear.

"Hope is something more than that, though," Raven added, as Dur-zor rose to leave. "It's not only a want. It's a need. A need to believe that our lives will be better. A need to believe that something will happen to change things for the better. You hope to be a warrior. That's what keeps you going, isn't it, Dur-zor? That's why you endure Qu-tok's beatings. We all have to have hope. It's like meat or drink to us. Without it, we die."

"But you want to die. You 'hope' to die." Dur-zor used the new word with pride.

"I hope to have my revenge on Qu-tok. If I die in the process . . ." Raven shrugged. "I could accept that. But it doesn't look like I'll have the chance."

From across the camp, Qu-tok gave a bellow. Dur-zor snatched up Raven's empty food dish and raced back to Qu-tok, who rewarded her tardiness with a buffet to the head that knocked her to the ground.

Raven watched her pick herself up and continue on about her duties. He couldn't count the number of times she had come to him with the side of her face bruised and swollen, her eyes blackened, her lip smashed and bleeding. Small wonder she had no hope for anything better. As far as she knew, there was nothing better. One day Qu-tok would hit her a little too hard and crack her skull and that would be that.

The taan ordered the slaves to line up and start moving, kicking and whipping those who did not obey quickly. Qu-tok sent two young warriors to fetch Raven. Qu-tok would not march with them today. He joined other warriors on point, walking about a half-mile ahead of the caravan, scouting for danger.

Raven could not imagine what danger the taan anticipated, for there was nothing in this godforsaken part of western Loerem. Dur-zor told him that their god Dagnarus warned them that gangs of giants lived in this area, but Raven scoffed at that. Exceptionally lazy and none too bright, giants preferred to live in populated areas, where they could plunder villages for food. A giant living out here would starve to death, for Raven saw no signs of civilization anywhere. Either this god of theirs knew nothing about giants or he'd said that to keep the taan on their toes.

Raven ignored the young warriors, who amused themselves along the route by jabbing him in the kidneys with the butts of their krul-uts—a weapon similar to a spear, except that it has three blades instead of one.

He plodded along glumly. He had grown stronger over the past month, had grown used to the weight of the iron collar so that he barely felt it. The taan had removed his ankle manacles, for the chains slowed the slaves' pace, and the taan were eager to reach their destination, receive their reward and get back to the fighting. The young warriors eventually lost interest in their tormenting Raven, for what fun is torment if the subject doesn't respond?

So absorbed was Raven in his thoughts that it took him some moments to realize something was wrong.

Shouts. Shouts coming from in front of them.

Raven looked swiftly to Dag-ruk, the chieftain. She raised her hand, brought the caravan to a halt. Silence fell among the taan, everyone listening. The young warriors on either side of Raven were tense, alert. Glancing about, Raven sought Dur-zor. If she had been near, he would have asked her what was going on, but she was far from him, marching in the back of the line with the other half-taan.

The landscape through which they traveled consisted of a series of rolling hills. The caravan was down in a depression of one of these hills. Another hill rose ahead of them, to the west, and another hill to the north. A small grove of trees was on the south. Qu-tok and the other warriors who had been scouting ahead of the group suddenly appeared at the top of the hill. Running full speed, they brandished their weapons, pointing to the north.

Pandemonium broke out among the taan. The two young warriors next to him let out hair-raising howls that sent a thrill up Raven's spine. Other taan began shouting and gesturing. Cursing his inability to understand what was going on, Raven kept his eyes on Dag-ruk as she snapped out commands. She was accustomed to strict obedience and her orders were immediately carried out. The taan warriors fanned out, forming a circle. Taskers and children and the valuable slaves were herded into the woods, to places of safety. The half-taan were left to fend for themselves. Some grabbed weapons. Dur-zor picked up the kep-ker, the staff she'd been practicing to use.

More shouts came from the other side of the ridge. Raven could not see anything, for at Dag-ruk's command the two young warriors seized hold of him and dragged him into the woods. They threw him to the ground, then raced back to take their places with the warriors on the perimeter. The enemy was bearing down on them from the north and, to judge by the racket they made, there were a lot of them. The slaves strained to see. They began to shout excitedly that this was Dunkargan cavalry, riding to the rescue.

Raven didn't think so. He'd never heard Dunkargans make such god-awful sounds as those coming from over the rise. The taan around him began to call out challenges. The enemy answered and that gave Raven an idea of what was happening.

The enemy topped the ridge and Raven saw that his suspicions were correct. An army of taan waving weapons and carrying the taan version of shields poured down the hill. The taan warriors under Dag-ruk's command raised their weapons, held their ground, and waited for the enemy to come to them. At the top of the hill, commanding the troops, stood one of the Kyl-sarnz—a Vrykyl.

The shouting and clashing of weapons stirred Raven's blood. He longed to at least see the battle and it was then, and only then, that he realized that the young warriors had forgotten, in their haste, to attach his chain to a stake.

Raven was free.

He was out in the middle of nowhere, with no idea where he was, surrounded by more taan than he could count, caught up in the middle of a fierce battle between forces who looked to be intent on killing each other and he had never known such joy. So heady was his elation that he gave a wild war whoop that would have made a taan proud. Rather late, he realized that he shouldn't call attention to himself. Fortunately, the taan had their own problems.

Raven lifted the heavy chain in his hands and slung it over his shoulder. He slunk along the fringes of the crowd, making his way stealthily to Dur-zor, who had taken up a position among the taskers.

He touched her on the shoulder.

Startled, she whipped around, raising her kep-ker to attack. Her eyes widened in astonishment, then narrowed at the sight of the chain dangling around his neck.

"Dur-zor," Raven said urgently, "tell me what's happening. Who are these taan? Why are they attacking?"

She turned away to watch the coming battle. She was probably wondering if she should report him or chain him back up. The front ranks of the taan met with a crash of weapons and howls of fury. She glanced back at him.

"There are taan who do not believe in our god Dagnarus. They say that he led us from our homeland and our old gods in order to use us for his own ends. He spills our blood for his gain and at the end he will betray us. These rebels set an ambush for us. They plan to steal our slaves and convert us to their way of thinking."

"Convert!" Raven repeated, amazed. The taan warriors hacked savagely at each other, taan blood ran freely. "Funny way to convert—"

He halted, sucked in a breath.

"Oh, no, you don't!" he shouted in fury. "He's mine."

"Raven! Stop!" Dur-zor cried, but he ignored her.

Pushing and shoving his way through the crowd, Raven sent taskers flying, knocked children aside. He paid no heed to the frantic calls of the
slaves, who begged him to cut their bonds, cursed him as he ran away.
Raven did not see the enormous Vrykyl standing on the top of the ridge,
looking down on the battle. Raven had one objective. He heard nothing
else, he saw nothing else. Nothing else mattered.

Nothing except fear that an enemy taan was going to slay Qu-tok.

Qu-tok faced off against another veteran warrior, a taan who had more
scar tissue than flesh. Both warriors used the tum-olt, a gigantic two-
handed sword with a serrated blade that was most effective in slashing
open a taan's thick hide. The combatants met with a crash and howls. The
sharp-toothed blades locked together. Fighting with the tum-olt is a test
of strength, as well as skill. The combatants struggled, each trying to rip
the sword out of the other's hand.

Digging their heels into the ground, Qu-tok and his opponent heaved
and shoved. The enemy taan kicked at Qu-tok's knee, trying to unbalance
him, but Qu-tok knew that trick and he used the enemy's move against
him, almost upsetting him. The enemy taan was quick and agile. He managed to regain his feet and keep his hold on the sword at the same time.

No other taan interfered in this contest. Taan fight one-on-one at the
start of a battle, each taan selecting his opponent. The winner is free to
find another enemy or to assist a fellow taan if he is in trouble.

Raven ran across the battlefield, ducking and dodging, intent upon Qu-
tok. The taan paid little attention to him. He was a slave, after all.

Raven reached the combatants. Qu-tok, grunting and groaning, shoved
against his opponent's sword. The other taan struggled against Qu-tok.
Their blades locked tight, sharp teeth biting into each other. Muscles
bulged. Their feet churned up the earth. Blood streamed down Qu-tok's
right arm. The other taan had gashed knuckles. The first taan who broke
would die.

Grabbing hold of the chain in both hands, Raven began to whirl it
around and around, then hurled the chain with all his strength at the
struggling taan. The chain wrapped around their locked sword blades.
With a single jerk, Raven wrenched both swords out of the hands of the
taan.

The expression on Qu-tok's face was almost laughable. The other taan
was also taken aback. Both stared, dumb-founded, to see their swords flying up into the air and away. Shrieking insults, swinging the chain, Raven
waded into the fray. The two taan stared at him. They looked at each
other and then both laughed.

"Derrhuth," said the enemy taan in disdain.

Reaching out a massive hand, the taan caught hold of the whipping
chain that was still attached to the iron collar around Raven's neck. The

taan gave it a jerk that dragged Raven off his feet and nearly snapped his spine. He stumbled to his knees. The enemy taan aimed a crushing blow at him. Raven saw his death coming. He couldn't move, the taan had a tight grip on his chain. Raven had failed, but at least he would die with honor . . .

A staff whistled past Raven's head, so close that it scratched his cheek. The butt of the staff struck the taan in his solar plexus. He doubled over, groaning.

Dur-zor stood protectively over Raven. As the taan fell, she bashed him hard on the head, knocking him to the ground. Another jab from the end of the kep-ker at the base of the skull broke the taan's neck.

Dur-zor grinned in elation. "I am a warrior!" she cried. "And you have hope. Fight your fight. I will watch your back."

Raven leapt to his feet, turned to face his enemy.

Qu-tok had been waiting for the other taan to dispatch the annoying slave, so that the true battle between equals could be resumed. Astounded beyond measure to see Dur-zor—a lowly creature—step in and slay his opponent, Qu-tok's astonishment mounted swiftly to fury. There would be those among his rivals who would be quick to take advantage of this, those who would say that Qu-tok had been losing his battle and that a half-taan had saved his life. And as if that were not insult enough, now he was being challenged to fight by his own slave. Nothing was more valuable to a taan than his honor and Qu-tok's honor had been besmirched.

Raven saw Qu-tok's eyes flash. Finally, Raven had gained Qu-tok's full attention. Seeing the spittle fly from the taan's gaping mouth and the fury in the taan's eyes, Raven knew that this time Qu-tok meant to kill him.

Snatching his knife from his belt, Qu-tok lunged at Raven, striking for the heart. Raven stood his ground, the heavy chain his only weapon. Swinging the chain, Raven struck Qu-tok's hand, trying to dislodge the knife.

The chain split open the hide on Qu-tok's fingers, but did no other damage. Still gripping the knife in his right hand, Qu-tok reached out his left, thinking to seize hold of Raven by the hair and then slash his throat.

Raven ducked the taan's grab and hurled himself bodily at Qu-tok. The two fell to the ground. Qu-tok landed on his back with a grunt. Raven jumped on top of him. Qu-tok tried to heave the human off him. Raven straddled the taan, locked him with his knees. Clenching his fist, he punched Qu-tok a blow on the jaw that would have killed a human.

Qu-tok did not even blink. Struggling to free himself, he slashed at Raven with the knife.

Raven caught hold of Qu-tok's knife-hand, slammed the taan's fist into the ground. Qu-tok rolled over, landing Raven on his back. Both of them grappled for the knife.

Dur-zor stood above Raven, holding the kep-ker with both hands, wielding it skillfully to ward off interference. At first, no one had paid any attention, but then the sharp-eyed Dag-ruk noticed what was going on. She shouted and surged forward to kill the rebellious slave.

Dur-zor cracked the huntmaster on the arm. Dag-ruk snarled in rage and advanced on Dur-zor, who proudly clutched the kep-ker and waited to die.

A voice rang out across the battlefield, a voice that was cold and deep and dark as a well of darkness.

"Intiki!"

The command brought the battle to a standstill. All taan from both sides halted in mid stroke, looked up in fearful respect. The taan Vrykyl stood atop the hill, his hand raised in command.

"Intiki!" he shouted again.

Two alone did not obey him. Raven did not hear the Vrykyl's call and would not have understood it if he had. Qu-tok heard, but he was too consumed with rage to listen.

The terrible eyes of the Vrykyl fell on Dur-zor. She dropped her staff and prostrated herself on the ground. Dag-ruk, standing beside the half-taan, did the same.

Behind them, Qu-tok and Raven rolled and grunted and kicked, bit and flailed and snarled and struggled for the knife.

"Intiki!" the Vrykyl roared again. "Let them fight!"

The taan lowered their weapons, but did not sheathe them, each taan watching his enemy warily, even as they looked to see what battle had drawn the Vrykyl's attention.

The slaves tried to see, but the taan were massed so thickly around the combatants that they could catch only glimpses. One gave a cheer, but the others immediately shushed him, not wanting to draw attention to themselves.

Raven knew nothing of any of this. His body was smeared with blood, his shoulder slashed open to the bone. His fingers were mangled. His arms were covered with welts from the chain and scratches from Qu-tok's talons. Raven felt no pain. All he could feel was the living flesh and bone and sinew of his enemy beneath his hands.

During their vicious struggles, the long chain wound around both warriors, binding them in links of iron. The chain wrapped around their legs and tangled their arms. Their flailings carried them over the ground. The watching taan backed up hastily to give them room. Raven spotted a large rock half-buried in the ground. He seized hold of Qu-tok's hand, that still clung to the knife, and brought the taan's hand down hard on the rock.

The knife flew from Qu-tok's fingers and Raven knew a moment's elation, a moment that ended when Qu-tok's strong hand grasped hold of the rock and wrenched it out of the ground. Wielding the rock, Qu-tok aimed a blow at Raven's head. The chain impeded his movements. He could not put much momentum behind the blow or aim it very well. Raven took the blow on the fleshy part of his upper arm.

Qu-tok brought his arm back for another strike and it was then Raven saw his chance. Qu-tok had left himself wide open. There was only one problem. Raven could not position himself and duck the next blow. He would have to take it. Seizing hold of the chain in both hands, Raven formed a loop in the chain, looped the chain around Qu-tok's neck.

Teeth grinding in fury, Qu-tok struck Raven with the rock.

Pain splintered through Raven's head, starbursts flared in the black night that began to fall over his eyes. He reeled from the blow and fought with all his being to retain his hold both on consciousness and on the chain.

Fortunately, Qu-tok had not been able to put his full muscle behind the blow. If he had, the taan would have smashed Raven's skull like a zarg nut. As it was, Raven's head throbbed, blood streamed into his left eye, but he did not lose consciousness. He was able to think and to act. Holding the loop of chain in each hand, using his last ounce of strength, Raven wrapped the chain around Qu-tok's throat and gave it a sharp yank.

Bone crackled beneath the chain. Qu-tok's eyes bulged; he gargled, choking on his own blood. Dropping the rock, he tried frantically to free himself of the chain that was crushing his windpipe. Raven continued to pull. He kept his eyes on the eyes of the dying taan and when he saw the light start to fade, he pulled harder.

"Die, damn you!" he said over and over. "Die!"

Blood drooled from Qu-tok's mouth. His heels drummed on the earth. The taan's body stiffened and then went limp. Qu-tok ceased to struggle. His eyes rolled back in his head. His arms and legs twitched and then he was still.

Not trusting him, Raven continued to pull on the chain.

"It is finished," said Dur-zor.

Raven didn't hear her. He let loose of the chain only because he was too weak to hold it any longer. The battle rage drained from him and Raven felt the pain he had not felt during the battle.

He didn't care. He would die soon. The other taan would kill him. He was only surprised they hadn't done so already and then it occurred to him that they were probably waiting to torture him to death for this crime.

He shrugged. Only one thing mattered to him at this moment. Raising his bloody hands into the air, Raven reared back his head and gave a Trevenici victory yell—the howl of a coyote over a kill.

Raven had never before known such elation, such satisfaction. His howl died away. His shoulders sagged. He slumped over the body of his dead foe and then toppled sideways, unconscious.

8

DUR-ZOR DROPPED HER KEP-KER AND BENT OVER RAVEN. PLACING HER FINger to his neck, she checked for the pulse, then looked up and announced proudly, "The beat is strong. He lives."

The taan looked at each other, then looked at the Vrykyl. No one was sure what to do. The taan warriors applauded Raven's courage and tenacity. They were impressed with the kill. But he was a slave, a slave who had dared raise hands against his master and, no matter how courageous, he must be punished. Normally the taan would have tortured him for days, as an example to other slaves, before they finally allowed him to die. After that, they would have done him the honor of eating his flesh, even fought over who got to devour his heart. Now the taan looked to the Vrykyl, grateful to him for having provided them with this show, but uncertain how he wanted them to proceed.

The Vrykyl's name was K'let, the most powerful of the taan Vrykyl, and the most revered. K'let left his hilltop. Accompanied by his bodyguards— immense taan, accoutered in rich armor—the Vrykyl walked among the taan, who parted at his coming. Many of his followers reached out to touch him as he passed. The Vrykyl's bodyguard was in truth an honor guard, for no taan, not even his enemies, would dare harm him, nor was it likely any taan could. The taan of Dag-ruk's tribe drew back as he approached, watching K'let with respect, but also distrust.

K'let stood over Raven, looked down upon the unconscious, blood-smeared human, who still wore the iron collar of a slave. His chain was now anchored to a corpse.

"This human has the heart of a taan," K'let announced and the other taan clicked their tongues against the roofs of their mouth in agreement. "He is strong food," K'let continued. "I myself would be honored to dine on his flesh."

The other taan concurred, some thumping their weapons against the ground or tapping them on their breastplates.

"I have known only one other human this strong," K'let said. "Dagnarus."

The taan who followed K'let grinned at each other. The taan who followed Dag-ruk fell silent, stood frowning. Dagnarus was not a human. He was a god who, for some strange reason, chose to take human form.

"Yes, I say Dagnarus is human," said K'let. He wore a dark helm that was the face of a ferocious, grimacing taan frozen in black metal, and he turned that fearsome visage to stare at the warriors of Dag-ruk's tribe. "I know that he is human. I was with him from the beginning. This is what I was then."

The Vrykyl armor dissolved. In its place stood a taan. He was tall and muscular, his body was covered with the scars of many battles. His hide was not the brown color of the hides of the other taan. K'let's hide was white. His hair was white, his eyes were brilliant red. None of the taan were surprised by this transformation. They all knew K'let's story, for his story was their god's story. Taan loved this tale, however, and had no objection to hearing it again.

"I was born with white skin, a shame to my parents. The tribe shunned me, threatened many times to cast me out. Then Dagnarus came among us. He was a human, but he was powerful. The most powerful human any of us had ever known. He fought and killed the nizam of our tribe. We did him honor and said that he would be our nizam. Dagnarus refused. He announced he would hold a contest to choose a new nizam. In those days, we fought to the death for the right to be leader. Not like these days, when the taan have grown weak."

K'let glared around, his eyes flaring. Some of the taan lowered their heads, but others—Dag-ruk among them—faced him defiantly.

"I went to Dagnarus," K'let continued. "I honored him then as did all the rest of the taan. I told him that I would take him for my god if he would grant me the strength to win the contest. He agreed, providing that I would agree to surrender my life to him any time he chose. I made the bargain. I won the contest. I defeated the other taan. I accepted Dagnarus as my god. I walked at his side as we traveled through our land, converting other tribes of taan to his worship. I fought at his side to prove our worth to the nizam of these other tribes. I helped convince the taan to choose Dagnarus as their god. I came with him to his world, to fight his battles. When he called upon me to fulfill my promise, I gave Dagnarus my life. He made me a Vrykyl.

"It was then, when the Void had taken me, that I saw Dagnarus for what he truly is. A human. A powerful human, a human who has been chosen by the Void, but a human all the same. In that moment, I knew myself to be more powerful than Dagnarus and in that moment, I knew he was not a god."

His followers lifted their voices, cried out K'let's name. Some of Dag-ruk's people looked uncertain and cast side-long glances at each other. Dag-ruk glowered around at them, said something to the shaman, R'lt, who lowered his eyes and shook his head. Dag-ruk looked troubled.

"Through the magic of the blood knife, Dagnarus felt my doubt," K'let continued. "He intended to prove to me that he was my master. He would make me see that I had no choice but to obey him, for he bound me to him by the Dagger of the Vrykyl. He ordered me to kill my mate, Y'ftil, and to feast upon her soul, depriving her of the chance to fight the final battle of the Gods War. The knife was in my hand. I saw my hand lift, I saw my feet carry my unwilling body toward Y'ftil. Dagnarus's will forced me on. My will fought against him in a struggle very much like the one we have witnessed this day, for we, too, were chained together, except that our chains were forged of the Void.

"I won," said K'let and his voice resounded in the sudden silence. "I defeated Dagnarus. I took the knife that he would have made me use on Y'ftil and I plunged it into the throat of one of his shaman. Then it was that I knelt before Dagnarus and I swore to him an oath of loyalty, not because I was forced to swear, but because I believed in his cause. I swore to follow him, so long as he treated the taan with honor. He promised me that he would give the taan this fat world with its forests and plentiful water to be our world. He promised me that we would feast on its people and have many slaves. He promised me the wealth of this world, its steel and its silver and its gold, its jewels to put into our bodies to give us strength."

K'let paused. The taan murmured agreement. All knew that Dagnarus had made such promises.

"One by one," K'let said, his voice quivering with anger, "Dagnarus broke his promises."

K'let jabbed a finger at the slaves. "Are you permitted to keep these strong slaves for your own use? No, you are not. You must give them to Dagnarus." He jabbed another finger at Dur-zor, who shrank back from him. "Are you permitted to destroy these abominations? No, we are forced to tolerate their kind among us. Are you permitted to fight to the death to choose your leaders? No, your leaders are now chosen for you. Are we permitted to worship the old gods, the gods who brought the taan to the world and gave us life? No, we are told that those gods are false gods and that this human is the only god. Are we permitted to return to our homeland? No, we are not. The Portal that would take us back to our world is guarded day and night. Those taan who try to re-enter it are put to death.

"Has Dagnarus kept his promise and given us this land for our own? No, we must fight yet another battle for him and yet another battle after that."

Dag-ruk stirred and then raised her voice defiantly, "Does Dagnarus care for the taan? Yes, he does!"

"No, he does not!" K'let thundered. "And I will prove it to you. He sent some of our people south to a land called Karnu, there to battle humans and seize a magical Portal. Our numbers were small, for Dagnarus told us that these humans were weak and that they would run before us like panicked rabbits. That was a lie. These humans proved to be strong like this one." He pointed at the unconscious Raven. "They had hearts like taan and fought like taan. We died on the field of battle and still we could not prevail against them. Our leaders went to Dagnarus and told him that the taan could defeat these humans, but only if he sent us more troops.

"His answer was no."

A silence fell that was thick, profound. The taan did not move, but stood rigid, staring.

"Dagnarus refused to send reinforcements. He said that he needed the troops for a more important battle, a battle in the land of the gdsr."

The taan scowled. The "gdsr" were elves, a people known to be weaker than humans, a people of no value whatsoever. If the taan capture an elf, they pull off his arms and legs, like an insect.

"Dagnarus said that our taan in the human land were on their own, must fend for themselves. They must stay and fight and either conquer or die."

Dag-ruk kept her unwavering gaze fixed on the Vrykyl, but all could see that doubt was upon her. R'lt, the shaman, began talking to her, whispering in her ear.

"It was then I told Dagnarus that if he was not loyal to the taan, I did not consider myself bound to be loyal to him. He laughed at me and said that I had no choice. I had defied him once, but he was stronger now. I dare not defy him again. He would destroy me."

K'let spread his arms. He raised his voice to the heavens and shouted, "Iltshuzz, god of creation, be my witness! I stand here before you unhurt, unharmed. Dagnarus could not carry out his threat. He tried, but I was too powerful. I turned from him and left him. Now I fight my own war in this land. I fight a war to free the taan. I fight to return the taan to the worship of the old gods. I fight a war against this human who dares to claim that he is a god."

"If you are so powerful, K'let," Dag-ruk said, shoving aside the warding hand of the shaman, "why did you not slay Dagnarus?"

K'let lowered his arms. He shifted his gaze from the heavens back to Dag-ruk. "A fair question, warrior. I can see why you are huntmaster."

Dag-ruk gave an abrupt nod to acknowledge this, but she was not to be ignored.

"Your answer?" she said insistently, if respectfully.

"Dagnarus is not a god. He is human, he is mortal, but he has many lives, lives piled on top of lives. Every life he takes through the power of the Dagger of the Vrykyl increases the span of his mortality. I could not kill him once. I would have to kill him many times over. He fears me. He keeps himself constantly surrounded by other Vrykyl, those who are still bound to him. I am the only one thus far who has managed to break away from his control. My time is not yet. It is coming, but it is not now."

Dag-ruk thought this over, made no comment one way or the other.

K'let abandoned the illusion of himself as he had been. Once more, he stood before them in his black armor. A powerful force, he looked around at his people. "It is wrong for us to kill each other. The blood of many fine warriors has been spilled in this battle and I am sorry for that. I am pleased I had this chance to speak to you. I ask you to put down your weapons and join me. For a time, we must continue to remain in this land, but I vow to you that the day will come when I will lead us back to our home. Back to the land you never knew, back to the true gods. Those who are willing to swear an oath of allegiance to me lay down their arms. Show your loyalty by handing over your slaves and by killing the abominations, those known as half-taan. If you choose not to join me, we will fight you in fair battle. I give you time to spend with your huntmaster to consider what you will do."

K'let turned back to look at Raven, who was starting to stir. "As for this human, I am pleased with him. I will take him as a member of my body-guard. He is to be treated with all honor. You"—he motioned to Dur-zor—"tell him what I have said."

Dur-zor knelt down beside Raven, helped him to sit up. He blinked, trying to see what was going on. One eye was gummed by dried blood and the other was swelling and starting to turn purple.

"I'm not dead," he said thickly, leaning weakly against her.

"No, you are not. You have been greatly honored," said Dur-zor and told him of K'let's command.

"Huh?" Raven had trouble understanding. "Who is K'let?"

Gritting his teeth against the pain the movement caused him, Raven looked up at the Vrykyl. The image took him back to the hideous black armor, that nightmare ride.

"No!" Raven cried, shuddering with horror. "No! I won't."

"You do not know what you're saying!" Dur-zor pleaded with him, aware of K'let watching them intently. "You must do this or he will slay you. Your death will be a terrible one, for your refusal will be an insult to him."

"I would rather die!" Raven mumbled through bruised and bloody lips.

"Would you?" Dur-zor asked, smiling, though her lips trembled. As one of the abominations, she knew her own death was not far off. "You did not fight Qu-tok like a man who wants to die. You fought to live."

"I fought to kill," said Raven. "There's a difference."

"And it was K'let who gave you the chance," said Dur-zor. "Do you think Qu-tok's fellow warriors would have permitted a slave to fight him in honorable contest? They were ready to kill you, but K'let ordered them to let you fight."

"He did?" Raven looked up at the Vrykyl. Unable to stand the sight of the grotesque creature, he hastily averted his eyes.

"You owe him Qu-tok's death," said Dur-zor. "Sit up so that I can see your shoulder wound."

Raven groaned. His head hurt. His shoulder was on fire. One of the taan shamans, after a glance at K'let, came forward and held out something in his hand to Raven.

"What's that?" Raven looked at it suspiciously.

"Tree bark," said Dur-zor. "It will ease your pain."

Taking some of the bark, Raven put it into his mouth, chewed down on it. The taste was bitter, but not unpleasant. He tried to clear his thoughts. Dur-zor's logic cut knife-like through the weariness and the pain. *You fought to live.* Apparently he wasn't as ready to die as he'd supposed.

"I'll do whatever he wants," Raven said and sucked in a sharp breath, for Dur-zor was examining the wound on his back, probing at it with her fingers.

"The blade slashed across the bone," she said, "but the bleeding has stopped. The wound will heal and leave you a fine scar."

Raven started to nod his head, thought better of it.

"I owe you something, Dur-zor," he said, chewing bark. "I owe you more than I owe that . . . K'let."

Taking hold of his hand, she began examining his mangled fingers. "Keep your voice down," she whispered.

"Why? K'let is a taan. He doesn't understand what we're saying."

Dur-zor slid the Vrykyl a sidelong glance. "I think perhaps he does. He has been around humans for a long, long time. K'let was once the favorite of our god."

Her voice held sadness in it, a sorrow Raven didn't understand. She lowered her head back to her task.

"I owe you, Dur-zor," Raven repeated earnestly. "I saw you kill that taan. If you hadn't stepped in, I'd be dead and Qu-tok would be munching on my toes."

He hoped this would win him a smile, but Dur-zor kept her head lowered so that he could not see her face.

"You fought well today, Dur-zor. You are a true warrior. No one can say otherwise."

She looked up at him and he saw that this had pleased her. "I know. I am glad." Slowly, carefully, so as not to hurt him further, she released his hands. "I do not think there is any serious damage, but you must watch to make sure that you do not fall ill with the stinking sickness."

By that, Raven understood her to mean gangrene. "If you fetch me some water, I'll wash the wounds. Dur-zor, what's wrong?"

"I might not be permitted to go fetch water for you," Dur-zor said quietly. "Things have changed. Look around."

Recalling that the taan had been in the midst of a pitched battle, Raven noted for the first time that the fighting had stopped. He wondered what had happened. Dag-ruk stood talking to her warriors, who were gathered around her and the shaman R'lt. They appeared to be in heated argument, yelling at each other and gesticulating wildly. The other taan, the enemy, tended to wounded, cleaned their weapons or picked their teeth. The slaves sat watching the taan warily, cognizant that their fate hung in the balance, not certain how or why. The half-taan had been herded together, were being guarded by the enemy taan.

"There seems to be more talking than fighting. Is this how the taan always conduct battle?" Raven asked.

"K'let asked our tribe to join the rebels," Dur-zor answered. "They are considering it. R'lt is in favor. Dag-ruk leans in that direction. Some of the warriors argue against it, but if Dag-ruk makes up her mind, that will be the end of it. They can either join or leave the tribe."

She rose to her feet, looked down at Raven. "I will ask if they will let me bring you water. If not . . ." She was quiet a moment, then she smiled, straightened her shoulders. "I was a warrior," she said proudly. "A good one. Our god will be pleased with me. He will take my soul into his army."

"What are you talking about?" Raven stood up. He felt better, seemed to be able to think more clearly, although there was a strange humming in his ears. The pain had been reduced to a dull ache now, with the occasional flash. "Taking your soul. What does that mean?"

"If Dag-ruk joins with the rebel taan, K'let has ordered that all half-taan be killed. We are abominations. We do not deserve to live."

Raven stared at her. She spoke calmly, matter-of-factly, as if she believed this herself.

"What? No! This is crazy!" He glanced groggily about. "Who do I talk to? K'let? All right, I'll talk to K'let." Reaching out with his bloody hand, he seized hold of her wrist. "Come with me."

Dur-zor stared at him blankly, too shocked to respond. When she understood that he truly meant to do what he said, she tried to free herself from his grasp.

"You are the one who is crazy!" she gasped, pulling and struggling against him.

He said nothing, but dragged her after him. His legs were weak, he wobbled like a drunkard after a three-day binge. He wasn't certain what was giving him the courage to face the Vrykyl. Perhaps it was the bark, perhaps it was the fact that he owed Dur-zor his life.

No, he thought grimly, I owe her more than that. I owe her my sanity. If it hadn't been for her, I would have gone mad long ago, ended up like that poor woman who drowned herself in the river.

K'let was at that moment speaking to one of the shamans who made up his retinue. The shaman's name was Derl and he was the oldest taan then living and one of the most revered. His scars showed he had held his own in battle. Gems of great value and worth were embedded in his hide. He used the power of Void magic to extend his life, although no one was certain how he managed to do so. He was not a Vrykyl, he was a living taan. His hair had turned white, his hide was a dull gray. These and the fact that he moved slowly and deliberately, as if conserving every ounce of his strength, were the only signs that he had been in this world one hundred and fifty years.

Derl and K'let discussed Raven.

"Why do you take this human as one of your honored guard?" Derl asked, not bothering to hide his disgust. "True he is courageous and strong—for a human. And I know it amuses you to have a human serve you, as you were once forced to serve a human. Still"—Derl shook his head—"such a vile creature will be more trouble than he's worth."

K'let regarded Derl with patient forbearance. "You do not look past the first bend in the road, my friend. True, the human will be some trouble now, but the day will come when he will serve me with unquestioning obedience. You know of the day I speak, do you not, Derl?"

The shaman's face creased into a grin. The grin was slow in coming, for he seemed to move even his face muscles stingily. "The day when the Dagger of the Vrykyl is yours—"

"I have sworn to Lokmirr, goddess of death, that I will make no taan into a Vrykyl," said K'let sternly. "Only humans. This one will be my second."

"If he is the second, who will be the first?" Derl asked slyly, as if he knew the answer.

"Who do you think?" K'let asked.

Derl gave a dry chuckle. "You truly believe that one stab of the Dagger of the Vrykyl will end Dagnarus's many lives?"

"I think it is worth a try," said K'let coolly. "You are a shaman of the Void. You tell me."

"I tell you that you are sucking on the bones before your victim is in the pot," Derl returned. "Dagnarus has the Dagger and he has named you a traitor, to be destroyed on sight."

"The day will come when he will rue those words," said K'let, magnificently unconcerned. "The day will come."

Derl bowed his head. "I will this night make an offering to Dekthzar, god of battle and mate to Lokmirr, that he hears your words and grants your prayer. But for now," Derl added, his cunning eyes shifting to a point behind the Vrykyl, "your pet human comes to speak to you."

K'let turned to see the human in the hands of his bodyguards. Raven struggled to free himself, cursed them all roundly. K'let could not speak the human language and he did not want to, for the words had a soft and slimy feel to them. Having been around humans for over two hundred years, K'let had learned to understand the language. He pretended that he did not, for he knew that in their careless arrogance, humans would speak their true thoughts before him.

"Let me go, you bastards. I'm his bodyguard, same as you. I have something to say," the human shouted.

Even as the human struggled with the guards, he kept fast hold of the wrist of one of the half-taan. She looked terrified.

"He speaks truly," said K'let. "I have named him one of my body-guard. Let him approach."

The human stumbled forward, dragging the half-taan with him. He still wore the iron collar that marked him a slave and dragged his chain behind him. Raising his eyes to K'let's face, the human immediately lowered them. A shudder went through his body. He held his ground, though, and spoke with grudging respect.

"Dur-zor says that you gave me the chance to kill Qu-tok and redeem my honor. For that, I thank you, K'let." He fumbled at the name.

K'let nodded and started to turn away. The human had said all that was needful to say or so he thought.

"Wait, uh . . . sir," the human cried.

Startled, K'let turned back.

The human stood with his eyes lowered, staring at his feet. "Dur-zor tells me that you say the half-taan are abominations and that you mean to kill them."

The human let loose of the half-taan, who flattened herself on the ground.

K'let pretended not to understand. He ordered the half-taan to translate. She did so in a faint voice, her forehead pressed into the dirt.

"I think that is a mistake," said the human doggedly. "Tell him what I said, Dur-zor," he ordered when the half-taan would not have translated.

She did so, looking up pleadingly at K'let and cringing, as if begging him to believe that such words were not hers.

"Ask him why this is a mistake," K'let said, intrigued.

"Dur-zor tells me that you are rebelling against this god of yours," said the human. He swayed where he stood, kept blinking his eyes. "Your army is not very big. You are vastly outnumbered. I would think you would want all the warriors you could get." He gestured at Dur-zor. "She's a damn good warrior. Don't waste her. Let her and the others fight your battle for you. After all, what harm can they do? They can't breed. They'll soon die off."

The human lifted his head and finally looked K'let straight in the eye. "It seems to me that if you don't want any more 'abominations,' maybe you should tell your people to quit making them."

K'let was pleased. He had chosen well. He found this human more amusing than he'd supposed.

"Have you rutted with him?" he asked Dur-zor.

Dur-zor was horrified. "Of course not, Kyl-sarnz! He is a slave."

"There is something in what he says. Humans are practical-minded, if nothing else. What is this human called?"

"Ravenstrike, Kyl-sarnz."

"He is called after a bird?" K'let was disgusted. "I will never understand humans. Tell this Ravenstrike that I like his suggestion and that I will do as he says. The half-taan will live, provided that they agree to fight for me."

"We are honored, Kyl-sarnz," said Dur-zor.

"You will make him a good mate. Tell him that." K'let gestured.

Dur-zor stared at K'let.

"Tell him," said K'let.

Dur-zor glanced back over her shoulder at Raven. She repeated K'let's words in a low voice.

Raven said nothing, his jaw tightened. Then, reaching down, he grabbed hold of Dur-zor's hand and pulled her to her feet.

"Thank you, Kyl-sarnz," said Raven.

He turned to walk away, but he had not taken more than four steps before his legs buckled and he collapsed onto the ground, out cold. The half-taan glanced worriedly back at K'let, fearing that perhaps this display of weakness might cause the Vrykyl to change his mind.

K'let waved his hand. He had more important matters to consider than this human. The last K'let saw of the human who was named for a bird, the half-taan was hauling him bodily down the hillside.

Raven woke with a start to the sound of a sharp metallic clank right in his ear. A firm hand on his shoulder held him down.

"Don't move," said Dur-zor. "We are removing your chains."

Raven relaxed. He'd been having terrible dreams and although he could not remember them, the blow of the hammer hitting steel seemed to fit right in. He held still, gritting his teeth, while another half-taan struck at the collar with a crude-looking hammer. Raven flinched at every blow, but, fortunately, the task did not take long. The collar fell away and with it, his chains. He sat up slowly, for his head still throbbed, and drew in a deep breath.

He was no longer a slave.

Darkness had fallen. He'd slept long. Sparks rose from a campfire in the distance. The sound of hooting and shouting and wild laughter came from the camp. The taan were celebrating, leaping around the fire, waving their weapons.

"I take it that this means Dag-ruk decided to switch sides?" Raven said. His hand had been cleaned and some sort of gunk smeared on it. His shoulder hurt with every move, as did his head. But he felt good. He could not explain his feelings any way other than that. He felt good.

"Yes," Dur-zor was saying. "Dag-ruk was not pleased to hear that our god—" She halted, then said softly, "I must stop calling Dagnarus that. Dag-ruk orders that we are not to think of him that way anymore. She says that we will return to the worship of the old gods. The shaman Derl will teach us of these. I don't think I will like these taan gods, though. They have no liking for half-taan."

"I will teach you of my gods," said Raven. He watched the sparks dance in the air, swirl up to heaven. "My gods honor brave warriors, no matter what race they belong to."

"Truly? Yes, I would like that," said Dur-zor. "We will keep that secret between us. Dag-ruk was angered to hear that Dagnarus abandoned the taan in the land known as Karnu. She will follow K'let. Our tribe will travel with him."

"What about the slaves?" Raven asked, feeling self-conscious. He looked around, but did not see them.

"K'let's warriors have taken them to the mines. The reward for them will go to the rebels. We will wait here a few days for the warriors' return, then we will move on."

"Where?"

Dur-zor shrugged. "Wherever K'let decides." She glanced sidelong at Raven. "Dag-ruk came to visit you while you were unconscious. She said that she would be honored if you stayed with the tribe. She will give you Qu-tok's tent, his weapons and his place in the inner circle. Will you like that?"

"Yes, I would like that," said Raven. "But I am to go off with that . . . thing. His bodyguard." He could not repress a shudder.

"K'let has many bodyguards," said Dur-zor off-handedly. "You will serve him only when he chooses to send for you. I hope that doesn't disappoint you?"

Raven breathed a sigh of relief. "No," he said heartily. "Not in the least. Did all the warriors decide to go with K'let?"

"Some of the young warriors did not agree. Dag-ruk told them they could leave, but they could take nothing with them, not even their weapons. And so they left with nothing. Their way will be hard, for as cast-outs they will not be readily accepted by other tribes."

They are alone in a strange land, Raven thought to himself. With no clear idea of where they are or how to return to what they had once been. And maybe there is no return. Certainly not now. Perhaps not ever.

"Raven," said Dur-zor softly, akin to his thoughts, "you are free. You can escape if you want to. You must not consider yourself bound to stay here because of me."

Dur-zor's gaze went to the fire, to the taan, who were stomping their feet and leaping into the air, to the half-taan, who were bringing the taan food and drink, minding the taan children, assisting the taskers.

"I could not imagine being a cast-out, leaving my people," she continued quietly. "That must seem strange to you, considering how we are treated."

No, it didn't. Not right now. Not at this moment. This moment was what mattered. None of those before, none of those that might come after.

Reaching out, Raven took hold of Dur-zor's hand and squeezed it tightly.

"Why do you do that?" Dur-zor asked, puzzled.

Raven smiled. "Among humans, that is a sign of friendship, of affection."

Dur-zor's forehead crinkled.

"Affection. Another word I don't know. What does it mean?"

Raven glanced over his shoulder, back into the grove of trees. "Come with me," he said, taking her in his arms, "and I will teach you the definition."

9

"**H**OW CLOSE ARE WE NOW?" RANESSA DEMANDED. "DO WE HAVE TO GO through another of those tunnels?"

"Be patient, Girl," Wolfram returned irritably. "We're a damn sight closer than we were a month ago and a whole heck of a lot closer than any other two-legged beast would be at this moment due to these very 'tunnels' as you call them. Their true names are Portals and you should be grateful to them instead of spitting on them."

"I did not spit on a Portal," Ranessa stated.

"You spit on the floor in front," Wolfram stated accusingly. "It's the same thing. A fine time I'll have explaining that away to the monks."

"They won't know!" she scoffed. "How could they?"

"They have ways," Wolfram muttered, rubbing the bracelet on his arm.

Ranessa looked a bit daunted. Following their successful escape from Karfa 'Len, Wolfram had spent much of their journey telling her about the monks of Dragon Mountain. He laid heavy emphasis on the monks' mysterious ways, their magical powers. He told her of the five dragons who guarded the mountain, a dragon for each of the four elements: earth, air, fire and water, and a dragon for the Void, the absence of all. He told her of the monastery in which the monks lived and of the library where the bodies of the monks were laid to rest and of how scholars came to study at the monastery and nobles and peasants came with questions and how the monks treated all as equals, gave every question serious consideration.

Wolfram told Ranessa that he worked for the monks, that he was a "purveyor of information" as he was fond of terming it. He had to do this, in order to explain how he came to know about the existence of these Portals and how he and other "purveyors" like him were the only ones who could enter them. If he embellished the truth a bit (describing the monks as such exalted and awful people that the gods themselves might have been leery of approaching them), Wolfram considered these fabrications necessary. First, he hoped that Ranessa might reconsider and decide to forgo the experience and second, if she persisted in her determination to travel to the mountain, he planned to impress upon the unpredictable female the need to behave herself, speak respectfully, and act with decorum.

A lesser man would have given up, but Wolfram continued to have hope.

"This is the last Portal we go through," he added testily, "if that's any comfort."

"It is," she said.

"I don't know what you don't like about them," Wolfram grumbled. "Many people find traveling through them to be quite soothing."

"I am *not* many people," Ranessa returned.

"There's a true statement," Wolfram said beneath his breath.

"You're always muttering. I can't stand it when you do that. What's the matter now? Have you lost the Portal?"

"No, I haven't lost it," Wolfram retorted, although, in truth, the entrance to the Portal was not where he thought it should be.

They had made their way across Karnu, covering over one thousand miles in a month. Once they left Karfa 'Len, their journey had been uneventful, for which Wolfram was grateful. They had avoided the southern part of Karnu, said to be overrun by horrible monsters who were trying to seize the Portal. Wolfram's secret Portal had saved them the perilous journey through the Salud Da-nek Mountains. Two weeks' hard riding had brought them to yet another secret Portal that had taken them to the Deverl river—the border between Karnu and New Vinnengael. During that time, they had seen not another living soul. Ranessa no longer had the feeling that they were being followed. The Vrykyl had given up the pursuit seemingly. Wolfram was thankful, but he couldn't help wondering why.

It was this second Portal that Ranessa had spit upon, drawing down Wolfram's ire. After crossing the Deverl river, they traveled another week through the forests of New Vinnengael, hugging the river bank, making their way south. Wolfram searched for the third and final Portal that would carry them to Dragon Mountain.

During this same time, Ranessa's brother Raven traveled with the taan and it was on the day previous to this one that he slew Qu-tok. Ranessa's nephew Jessan and his companions spent this morning journeying to the Tromek Portal in company with Damra. Not that Ranessa was thinking of either her brother or nephew. She had left them behind on the shore of her life, and as her journey carried her forward, they grew smaller and smaller, receding in the distance until now she could no longer see them.

In her thoughts and in her dreams loomed a mountain, Dragon Mountain. She saw it as a formidable jagged peak, dark and mysterious, silhouetted against the dawn of a purple and gilt-edged sunrise. Every morning she woke expecting to see this vision, and every morning she was disappointed. Bitterly disappointed. Ranessa was always in a bad mood in the mornings.

Dismounting, Wolfram walked through the forest, searching for the Portal. He had never been inside this one and he went over in his mind the directions the monks had given him. At a sharp bend in the Deverl river, he was to look for the black and white striped rock. Finding the rock, he walked five hundred paces due east as the crow flies to the cave with the pictures. That morning, they had reached a sharp bend in the river and there was the black and white rock—a gigantic boulder that stood on the shoreline.

Wolfram walked off five hundred paces, counting out loud or trying to, for he had to continually stop to tell Ranessa to shut up, her rambling talk distracted him. Trust the girl to travel in sullen silence for a week and then decide to talk the one time he didn't want her to. He was almost sure that due to her chatter, he had miscounted, and then there was the fact that he could never remember whether monk paces meant dwarf-sized paces or human-sized paces.

He came to a halt. This was the place, but where was the cave? He stumbled among the trees, pawed through the brush, prying and poking. The monks said that the entrance was hidden behind a stand of birch and he had yet to come across any birch trees.

Ranessa followed after him, holding onto the horses. At least, after all these weeks together, he had finally taught her how to ride so that she wasn't an embarrassment to him. The horses had come to tolerate her, if they didn't much like her. She had spent the last half-hour complaining loudly and bitterly about this aimless wandering and Wolfram, already on edge, was seriously considering braining her with a tree branch, when he lost his footing and fell flat on his face in a mud puddle.

Laughter rang out from behind him. This was the first occasion on which Wolfram had ever heard Ranessa laugh and at any other time he would have said she had agreeable laughter, deep and throaty. This time, since the laughter was at his expense, it only increased his ire. Lifting his head, he was about to wither Ranessa with a scathing comment, when he saw the entrance to the Portal right in front of him.

No one had used it in a long while, seemingly, for the entrance was so overgrown with brush and scrub trees that if he hadn't fallen on its doorstoop, so to speak, he might have never found it.

Wolfram clambered to his feet, wiped mud from his face.

"Bring the horses," he ordered. He'd spotted a nearby stream.

"Where now?" Ranessa demanded.

"I'm going to have a bath. And it wouldn't hurt you to have one either. You stink."

"So do the horses and you don't make them take a bath."

"That's different," said Wolfram. "That's a horsey smell. A good smell. You smell of . . . of . . ." He couldn't think what she smelled like. The smell wasn't unpleasant, not like some humans. It was unsettling. "Smoke," he said at last. "You smell of smoke."

She laughed again, but now her laughter was scoffing. "Next time we build a fire we should be certain to first wash the wood."

"Why won't you take a bath?" Wolfram demanded, rounding on her.

She glowered at him, then said in a low voice, "There is an ugly mark on my body. When I was little, the others pointed at it and shamed me. They said the mark was the gods' curse. Since then—But why do I bother? You wouldn't understand."

About shame and the gods' curse? "Oddly enough, Girl," said Wolfram gruffly, "I think I do. Bring the horses. They could use the water."

"Then we will look for the Portal," she said.

"Oh, that," said Wolfram nonchalantly. "I found it already. Back there." He waved his hand.

Ranessa stared at him, too stunned to speak.

Wolfram was pleased with himself. He'd finally gotten in the last word.

The journey through the Portal took some time, for it was a long one. Ranessa disliked the trip, but she kept quiet and did not complain. The magical Portals that cut through space and time are not threatening in appearance. Designed by the magi of Old Vinnengael, the Portals were built for travelers, for King Tamaros believed that knowledge of mankind was the most certain way to obtain peace. The Portal has a gray floor, with smooth gray sides and gray ceiling. The horses were not fearful, but plodded through the Portal as contently as if they were in their own pasture.

Ranessa didn't like it. The gray walls closed in on her. The ceiling pressed down on her. She felt squeezed. The other Portals had been short, she could see daylight at both ends and that had helped her through them. But in this one, she lost sight of daylight behind her and she could see nothing ahead but gray.

There wasn't enough air and she began to gasp and pant. Sweat beaded on her forehead and ran down her neck. Her stomach clenched, she thought she might be sick. She had to get out of this horrible place or it was going to collapse down around her and smother her.

Ranessa broke into a run. Wolfram shouted after her—something about being careful at the other end, for she never knew what might be out there—but she ignored him. She would gladly face even that evil black-armored thing than stay in this Portal another second.

Ranessa rushed out the end of the Portal and straight into darkness. It had been mid afternoon when they entered and now it was night. She looked up to see the vast dome of heaven over her, myriad stars shining brilliantly. The cool air of the waning summer eased her fever, she sucked vast quantities into her lungs. Ranessa had the impulse to fly, to lift into that star-dazzled sky and let the wind carry her up above the trees.

So strong was this impulse that she longed with all her soul to fulfill it. The realization that she couldn't wounded her to the heart. Devastated, she crumpled to the ground and wept out of frustration and the terrible pain of hopeless longing.

Finally emerging from the Portal, leading the horses, Wolfram looked about and could not find her.

"Where's that blasted girl got to now?" he demanded.

The horses had no answer and didn't much care. Weary, they wanted food and water and a rub down. Muttering curses, Wolfram led them to a stream, where one of the horses shied and jumped nimbly over something on the ground.

Looking down, Wolfram saw Ranessa. She lay huddled beneath a large tree, her body hidden by night's heavy shadows.

Fear compressed Wolfram's heart. Releasing the horses, he bent swiftly over her. He let out a deep sigh when he felt her heart beating strong and sure beneath his fingers. She was not dead. She was asleep. Brushing her hair gently from her face, he could see starlight glisten on the tears that were still wet on her cheeks.

"Girl, girl," he said to her softly. "What a trial you are. But the Wolf take me if I haven't come to care about you. I don't know why."

Wolfram sat himself down beside her. "I never cared for anyone before. Why should I? No one ever cared for me. Then the day comes when that black fiend attacks me and you run to save me. What a sight you were, Girl. Waving your sword about. Running to save Old Wolfram. As if I was worth the saving."

The dwarf sighed, shook his head. "What the monks want with you or you with them is beyond me. I guess we'll find out soon enough, for we're almost at our journey's end."

He fed and watered the horses and rubbed them down. He fed and watered himself, all the while keeping close watch on Ranessa, who slept through everything. He did not build a fire, for he was uneasy. He sat awake all night, keeping watch, waiting for the dawn.

Ranessa awoke and at first couldn't remember where she was. She looked around, puzzled. The sky was light. The tops of the trees were in sunlight, the trunks in shadow. Disoriented, she sat up and then she heard, close by, a rumbling snore. Wolfram had fallen asleep sitting up. Propped against a tree, he slumbered soundly with his chin on his chest.

Ranessa grimaced. He'd have a stiff neck this morning and he'd complain about it all day long. She wondered guiltily if he'd tried to wake her in the night for her turn at watch and then decided that if he had and he couldn't that was his fault, not hers. She was about to wake him, just for the pleasure of hearing him grouse and grumble, when a flash of light caught her eye.

Ranessa turned to the east. The sun rose from behind a jagged peak, silhouetted against the dawn of a purple and gilt-edged sky.

Dragon Mountain.

10

THE TRAIL THAT LED UP DRAGON MOUNTAIN WAS LITTLE MORE THAN A donkey path. Twisting and turning, the trail meandered around enormous red-rock boulders, twined along ridges and crawled around scraggly fir trees. Climbing it could take days. The Omarah, a tribe of humans who worship the monks and serve them, built small warming huts along the route for the comfort and protection of those travelers who find themselves benighted on the mountainside. The huts are simple structures, similar to those in which the Omarah live, and are always stocked with firewood.

Wolfram was familiar with this trail; he'd climbed it many times, and the journey usually took him three days on foot. Since horses do not fare well on the steep mountain trail, an enterprising group of Vinnengaeleans had established a small town at the base of the mountain, where they offered to board horses for those making the climb and rented out mules and donkeys. Wolfram boarded the horses with the Vinnengaeleans (although he considered the price they charged exorbitant), but he scorned to ride a donkey. Dwarves consider the donkey a horse-gone-wrong, use them only for hauling. Wolfram always made the climb on foot, taking his time. He had favorite huts along the route where he liked to spend the nights.

Ranessa, of course, turned his plans upside-down. If she'd had wings, she could not have reached the top fast enough to suit her. As it was, forced to rely on feet, she started up the mountain at a speed that soon had the dwarf huffing and gasping. She glowered whenever Wolfram stopped for breath and paced about in a fume of impatience, demanding every thirty seconds to know if he was ready to go yet or if he had taken root.

"The monastery has been there for centuries, Girl," the dwarf protested. "It's not going to sail off in the next high wind."

She refused to listen, but hustled him and badgered him so that he never knew a moment's peace. At one point, they passed some fellow travelers—a group of scholars from Krammes returning from a meeting with the monks. There is an unofficial custom on the mountain that groups who meet on the trail always stop to exchange pleasantries and the news of the world. These humans were extremely interested to hear that Wolfram and Ranessa came from the west. Was the rumor of war in Dunkarga true?

Wolfram would have dearly loved to have had a bit of a chat, but when he told Ranessa that he was going to visit with these fine people, she flew into a rage. Her angry shouts rebounded off the side of the mountain and her wild-eyed look caused the Krammerians to hastily change their minds and continue their journey. Wolfram regretted every kind thought he'd had toward Ranessa the night before.

The sun was dipping into the west when they reached the first of his favorite warming huts. Wolfram announced that they would be spending the night here. Ranessa was appalled and insisted that there were many more hours of daylight left. Wolfram was firm, however, for the next hut was half-a-day's journey farther up the mountain and he had no intention of getting caught on the slopes after dark. Exasperated, he told her she could keep climbing if she wanted. Ranessa looked for a moment as if she would, but then either she saw the wisdom of the dwarf's decision or she was more tired than she would admit. She hurled herself into the hut and plopped down on the floor, where she sulked for the remainder of the night.

At least when she sulked she was quiet. Wolfram considered this a blessing. Pleased with his victory, he prepared for sleep. He didn't bother to keep watch, for the trail was guarded by the Omarah. The dwarf fell asleep at once, which was good, for Ranessa had him up twice during the night, trying to convince him that it was dawn and time to start.

After another day traveling with Ranessa up the mountain, Wolfram decided that anything—even falling off the mountain—would be preferable to spending a single second longer with her. To her great joy, he agreed to continue their climb well past sunset. Fortunately, they happened to run into one of the Omarah, who walk the trail at all hours of the day and night. Taking the Omarah aside, Wolfram showed the woman his bracelet and said that he was on a mission of the utmost urgency and needed her help. She agreed to guide them the rest of the way.

The tallest humans on Loerem, the Omarah average seven feet in height and some may be taller. They are a silent, impassive people, who speak only when they have something to say and then they say it in the fewest possible words. Omarah are studiously polite, but are not given to casual conversation or idle chit-chat. They answer questions with a nod or a shake of the head and if the question cannot be answered like that, they don't answer it. No one knows much about them, for they never speak of themselves to any outsider. So far as anyone can tell, the only place that the Omarah have ever been seen is on Dragon Mountain. If they exist anywhere else in the world, no one knows of it.

The Omarah woman walked ahead of them. She wore leather armor and a fur cape and carried a gigantic spear that doubled as a walking stick. The climb proved to be relatively easy, for the air was clear as finest crystal and the stars so numerous that the sky seemed to be crusted with them. Topping a rise, the Omarah silently pointed.

A building, aglow with light, stood in front of them.

"Is that it?" Ranessa asked in hushed tones.

"That's it," said Wolfram, who was never more thankful to see any place in his entire life. "The monastery of the monks of the Five Dragons."

He thanked the Omarah, who refused to accept any payment, but turned in silence and stalked back down the path. Wolfram headed for the monastery, hot food, cold ale and a comfortable bed. He had walked a good many paces when he realized he was walking alone. Turning, astonished, he looked back to see Ranessa standing where he'd left her, staring.

"Are you coming?" he demanded.

She shook her head vigorously.

"What?" Wolfram roared. "After all your hustle and hurry that half killed me on that blasted trail now you're not coming?"

He stumped back toward her, so furious he could barely see straight.

"I'm afraid," she said, her voice quivering.

"Afraid!" He snorted.

Grabbing hold of her, planning to drag her if necessary, he was startled to feel her hand as cold as the hand of a corpse and that she was literally shaking with fear.

"What's there to be afraid of?" he asked, bewildered. "You wanted to come here. You've talked of nothing else for all summer!"

"I know," Ranessa whimpered. "I want to be here and I don't. I can't explain it. I don't understand. I . . . I think maybe I'll go back down the mountain."

"Oh, no, you don't," said Wolfram. The bracelet on his wrist was warming rapidly, but he had no need for its reminder. "We're going inside to find a bed and a meal. If you want to leave in the morning, that's your look-out." He glared at her. "Are you coming or must I carry you?"

"I'll . . . I'll come," she said meekly.

Meek! He never thought he'd see the day. Not trusting her, he kept a firm grip on her hand and led her to the monastery. She clung to him like a frightened child. Glancing at her as they entered the light, he was alarmed to see how pale she'd grown.

"Is it what I told you about the monks, Girl? Is that what's scaring you? It's possible I may have exaggerated. The monks are very kind. They wouldn't hurt a flea. You're a bit strange, Girl, but they're used to strange people. They see all kinds here. They'll make you feel welcome."

Ranessa paid no attention to his words of comfort. She stared at the monastery, her eyes so wide that he could see the immense granite structure with its many windows reflected in the dark pupils.

Unable to fathom what was wrong, keeping hold of her, lest she flee into the night, Wolfram brought her to a long wide porch and climbed the stairs to the entrance.

No guard stood at the door, for there was no door. No porter was present to answer a stranger's knock. Those who come to the monastery are not considered strangers. The windows have no bars or panes of glass, but freely admit the sunlight and the night, the wind and the water. Entering through the archway, Wolfram led Ranessa into the huge common room. An enormous fire pit stood in the center. Every day, the Omarah carried in huge logs for the fire pit. A fire always burned, even in summer, for the air was cool on the mountaintop. The monks kept refreshments for their guests. In the center of the room was a large wooden table spread with plain but nourishing food—bread and cheese and nuts, large jars of cold ale, a cauldron of steaming mulled wine.

Sleeping arrangements were simple. All who come to the monastery, from crowned king to rustic woodsman, were given a rush mat and a wool blanket and a space on the stone floor near the fire. In vain the important Karnuan general argued that he must have his own sleeping quarters. In vain the Vinnegaelean merchant offered silver argents for a room. Merchant and general ended up on the floor, along with everyone else. The rooms were for the monks, whose studies must not, on any account, be disturbed.

Once they were inside the monastery, Wolfram was relieved to see Ranessa relax. He stowed her near the fire with orders to warm herself, went to fetch her a blanket and wrapped it around her shoulders, fussing over her as if she were his only begotten daughter about to be married on the morrow. He ladled out a mug of the steaming wine and persuaded her to drink a sip. The wine restored some color to her cheeks. She stopped shivering, but she could not eat. Fortunately, there were no other visitors. He and Ranessa had the huge room to themselves.

After drinking the wine, Ranessa lay down upon the mat and closed her eyes.

Wolfram waited to make certain she was asleep, then he departed to the meeting room, there to make his report and to hand over the silver box that belonged to Lord Gustav, the Whoreson Knight.

Although the hour was extremely late, acolytes and several monks were still awake, studying and transcribing, listening to questions, providing information. An acolyte, smiling, came to greet him. Wolfram gave his name, showed the bracelet, and was about to say that he needed to speak to one of the monks on a matter of urgency, when the acolyte interrupted him.

"We have been awaiting you, Wolfram the Unhorsed," he said pleasantly. "Fire left word that you were to be sent to her immediately upon your arrival."

"Fire!" Wolfram grunted. "Well, well."

Five monks head the Order of the Keepers of Time, one monk for each element and one for the Void. The heads of the order are known by the name of that element, not by any name of their own, presuming they ever had names.

Each monk represents the race most identified with a particular element. Thus Fire is a dwarf, Air an elf, Earth a human, and Water an ork. No one knows to what race the monk of the Void belongs, for on those rare occasions when that monk makes an appearance in the monastery, it is hooded and cloaked in black that covers every portion of its body. Even the hands are wrapped in black cloth.

Few visitors to the mountain ever see the five monks that are the Heads of the Order, for they keep to themselves, rarely deigning to speak to the many visitors who come in search of advice or answers to questions. Wolfram had never seen the Heads of the Order and had not expected to see them this time. He was surprised, but, after a moment's reflection, decided that he shouldn't be.

Wolfram and the acolyte ascended the stairs to the very top part of the monastery, reserved for the Heads of the Order.

The acolyte showed Wolfram to a room and then left to inform Fire that the dwarf had arrived. Wolfram sat in the chair, kicked his heels on the legs and looked around. There wasn't much to see. A simple desk with nothing on it. Two wooden chairs of plain make and design. A window carved in the wall looked out at the stars.

The monk did not keep Wolfram waiting. A dwarf clad in bright orange robes entered the room. Wolfram started to stand, but she raised a hand to indicate that he could remain seated. She crossed the room, sat down behind the desk, and regarded him with eyes in which flickered a portion of the element for which she was named.

She greeted him in his own language, asked if he'd had a good journey.

Wolfram replied, warily, eyed her closely.

The monk was a dwarf, but there was something distinctly un-dwarf-like about her. What that was, Wolfram couldn't say. Perhaps it was the bright orange robes, a garb no self-respecting dwarf would have been caught dead wearing. Or perhaps it was the way she spoke Fringrese, as though she knew the language perfectly but was not quite familiar with it. Then there was the fact that no dwarf would voluntarily live her life in one single location, not unless she was Unhorsed and forced to do so.

Wolfram decided in that moment that the rumors he'd heard all these years about the Heads of the Order must be true. This was not a dwarf. This was a shape-changer who had altered form to look like a dwarf. He was immediately on his guard.

The interview started well. He handed over the silver box that Lord Gustav had given him, told Fire what Lord Gustav had told him to say.

"I'm the killdeer with the broken wing. The young ones went off in a different direction," Wolfram said. "His plan worked. Danger followed us." He explained to her about the Vrykyl. "I'm hoping the young ones got away safely," he added, hinting for more information.

Fire said nothing. She gazed at him expectantly. Her face was smooth and blank.

"Whatever is in that box must be extremely valuable," Wolfram said, trying again.

Fire smiled, took hold of the box and set it to one side. She gestured for him to continue with his tale.

Giving a shrug, Wolfram complied, providing a quick synopsis of the rest of his journey. He did not go into detail. He would do that when the scholar monks took down his description, tattooing it onto their bodies. Fire continued to listen without comment. He spoke casually of Ranessa, saying only that she was a Trevenici who had chosen to accompany him. He hoped that Fire would evince some sort of curiosity about this companion or make some mention of why they wanted to see her. If she did, Wolfram would have been able to parry her questions with a few of his own.

The monk said nothing on that score. Her silence placed Wolfram at a distinct disadvantage.

Finishing his statement, Wolfram sat back on his chair, his eyes on the box. Fire had set the box to one side, as if it were of no importance, but her hand continued to rest on the box. Her fingers caressed the box and sometimes her gaze strayed to it.

"You'll note the seal's unbroken," Wolfram pointed out.

Fire nodded. Breaking the seal, she opened the box.

Wolfram watched her closely. Lord Gustav had said there was a magical spell guarding the box, but, if so, Fire made short work of it. This confirmed Wolfram's suspicions that he was not in the presence of a true dwarf, who as a general rule dislike and distrust magic.

Fire withdrew from the box a vellum scroll tied neatly with a silken red ribbon. Untying the ribbon, she unfurled the scroll and read through it attentively.

Wolfram fidgeted with his bracelet. He should be tired and he was, but he wasn't. He was jittery and nervous and not quite certain why.

"All is correct and in order," said Fire at last, lifting her head from her reading. "We will, of course, honor Lord Gustav's dying request and hand over to you the title to his lands and castle. You are now a Vinnengaelean lord, Wolfram. And a wealthy man. The Wolf be praised."

She handed back the deed. Taking the scroll from her, Wolfram stuffed it in his belt. He didn't feel as pleased as he had anticipated. He kept his eyes on the box.

"Was that all there was?"

"Yes, Wolfram." Fire lifted the box, held it for him to see. "May the Wolf guard your sleep."

She rose to her feet. Wolfram was being dismissed, but he didn't feel like going yet. He remained seated.

"I know you must be weary," Fire added. "You may go to your rest now. One of the monks will come to you tomorrow to take down your story in detail."

"I think the Vrykyl was after the box," Wolfram stated abruptly.

Fire nodded. "Quite possibly."

"Why? What would a Vrykyl want with lands and a manor?"

"I believe you have figured out the answer, Wolfram," said Fire. "You knew Lord Gustav. You knew of his quest."

"Yes, I knew." He shifted in his seat. "So what of the young ones? Did they make it?"

"Much hangs in the balance," Fire replied.

Wolfram snorted. "What about Ranessa?" he demanded suddenly.

"What about her?" Fire repeated, regarding him with a mild expression.

"She's here." Wolfram jerked a thumb in the direction of the common room. "I brought her."

"Yes, I know." Fire frowned slightly. "If you expect some additional re-ward—"

"Reward!" Wolfram bellowed. "Is that what you think of me? That all I care about is gain? Here!" He yanked the title out of his belt and tossed it on the desk. Bouncing to his feet, he shook the arm with the bracelet in her face. "You've used me and I'm sick of it. You dropped me down in the Whoreson Knight's path. You bid me take the box. You bid me take Ranessa. Then you set the Vrykyl on me. If it hadn't been for the girl, the Wolf bless her, it'd be the Vrykyl standing on your doorstep with that box in his rotting hand and not me. Now the girl's lying down there scared out of her wits and I don't know what you want with her and all you talk about is reward! I won't stand for it anymore."

He began to pull and tug at the bracelet. "Take it off me," he raved. "Take it off me!"

Fire moved swiftly. Resting her hand on his arm, she wrapped her hand around the bracelet.

"I will do so, Wolfram," she said and her voice was gentle and soothing. "But first sit calmly and listen to me."

Wolfram glared at her, but eventually, satisfied that she meant to do as she said, he plunked himself back down in the chair.

"You won't talk me into keeping it," he said sullenly.

"I have no intention of trying to do so," Fire said. "Indeed, we were planning to take the responsibility from you, for your destiny now lies apart from us. I want you to understand what has happened to you and why we did what we did.

"We told you when you accepted this position of observer that the bracelet would guide you to places where we thought you might need to be. The choice is yours, Wolfram. You know that if you choose, you can ignore the bracelet. Its heat will subside and you will feel it no more."

"I can't ignore it if I want my pay," he muttered. Realizing the contradiction in what he'd just said, he kicked at the chair legs in irritation. "Very well, once I cared for nothing except my pay. Now it's different and I'm not exactly pleased with the difference. Answer me this."

Wolfram looked the monk in the eye. "This quest of Lord Gustav's. It's important. Really, really important. Maybe the most important thing to happen in centuries. Why didn't you send one of your monks to record it in person? Why did you have to send me?"

"It is true that our monks go out into the world, recording events as they happen. But we must be careful that we do not influence those events," Fire explained. "Thus we think long and hard before we send out the monks. For example, there was no monk at the city of Dunkar when the taan attacked. Why? If a monk had arrived, the people would have known something momentous was in the offing and would have reacted accordingly."

"They might have saved themselves," he said accusingly.

"Or their army might have marched off to attack Karnu, for they believed that the Karnuans were their worst enemy," the monk returned. "Or they might not have thought of war at all, but believed their king was going to fall ill and die."

Fire lifted a palm, turned it over. "A myriad possibilities, but if we cause even the most minor to occur, we interfere with the workings of the gods. Our observers were there, unnoticed. They marked down what occurred and reported back to us."

"Those who survived."

"Yes," said Fire. "Those who survived. They know the risks, as did you, Wolfram, when you agreed to work for us. It was up to them to run them, as it was up to you." The monk smiled. "It is not the heat of the bracelet that causes you annoyance, Wolfram. It is the heat of your own insatiable curiosity. That is what you cannot stand."

"Maybe," he said, not convinced. "Maybe." He put his hand on the bracelet and, to his surprise, it came off. He held it to the light, then laid it down with grudging respect in front of the monk. "I'm free of it now? Free to go about my life as I please?"

"You always were, Wolfram," said Fire.

He stood up. "You're not going to tell me about Ranessa, are you? About why you wanted me to bring her to you?"

Fire hesitated, then said, "You did not bring her, Wolfram. I want you to know that. You were her guide. You shortened her journey. In time, she would have found us for her desire to do so was strong. Whatever happens, I do not want you to blame yourself."

"Whatever happens . . ." Wolfram felt a chill. "Blame myself. Blame myself for what? What's going to happen?"

"A myriad paths lead us into the future, Wolfram," said Fire. "Among them lies the path that is finally chosen, but we have no way of knowing which one that will be. Go to your rest and leave the business of the gods to the gods."

This time, Wolfram's dismissal was final. The monk's voice was firm with a hint of coolness, warning that he risked raising her ire if he remained. He was frustrated enough and frightened enough that he might have done just that, but he caught movement out of the corner of his eye. One of the giant Omarah lingered in the hallway outside the monk's quarters.

The huge Omarah could pick up the dwarf by the scruff of his neck. Rather than endure this indignity, Wolfram departed. He would get no answers anyway. Not from that double-tongued, shape-changing thing that called itself a dwarf. And what a relief to be free of that blasted bracelet!

He was tired now, barely able to keep his feet and yawning so that he cracked his jaw. His interview had taken up the rest of the night. The advent of dawn was presaged by a faint gray light that brightened the shadowed halls. He'd check on Ranessa, then sleep the day through. He'd earned it. Clumping along, he remembered that he'd left the deed to Gustav's lands and manor lying on the monk's desk.

A dramatic gesture, but one he now regretted. He'd go back tomorrow, admit he'd made a mistake, ask for it back. He didn't want to be lord of the manor, but he could always sell the place and give the silver to a Vinnengaelean money dealer for safe keeping. He'd have enough to live on comfortably for the rest of his life.

"From now on, no more dickering for horses," he promised himself. "Only the best horse flesh for Lord Wolfram." He chuckled at his new title.

Entering the common room, he stopped dead in his tracks.

A pall of smoke hung in the air. The room was a wreck. Tables had been overturned. Blankets had been ripped to shreds, then burned. The rushes from the mats were strewn about the room. The straw had been set ablaze. Still smoldering, it lay charred and blackened on the floor.

An invading army might have done less damage.

Wolfram peered through the smoke to search for Ranessa.

She was nowhere to be found.

11

RANESSA FEIGNED SLEEP, PLAYING POSSUM UNTIL THE DWARF HAD GONE off, saying something to himself about having to see the monks to claim his reward. Lying on the mat, she stared up into the shadows that clustered thick around the ceiling. She had dreamed of this place for so long and now that she was here, she did not know why she had come. A voice tried to explain to her, but she couldn't understand what the voice said, for it spoke in a strange language.

The voice was patient, however, and kept repeating the words over and over, as one does to a very small child. Like a child, Ranessa grew frustrated with the voice. Throwing off the blanket, she jumped to her feet and shouted at the voice.

"I hear you, but I don't know what you want." She glared around in anger. "Speak plainly. Speak my tongue, damn you!"

The voice spoke again, quietly, patiently, but it was all gibberish.

Outraged, Ranessa ran to the long trestle table filled with food. Grasping the table, she gave a heave, tipped it over. Bread loaves tumbled to the floor. Wooden platters rattled on the stone bricks, wheels of yellow cheeses rolled into corners. Crockery pitchers slid off the table, smashed. Foaming ale flooded the room, filling it with a beery smell.

"Answer me!" Ranessa cried. "Tell me what you want of me!"

The voice spoke again, soothing as a long-suffering parent with a recalcitrant toddler. The words beat in Ranessa's head, but they made no sense. She tore at her hair and thought she would go mad with fury.

She stomped on the bread. She kicked the shards of the pitchers. Grabbing hold of the blankets, she ripped the cloth and threw the rags about the room. She tore apart the mats, shredded them and flung the bits of rushes into the air so that they fell around her like dusty rain. She ran to the fire, grabbed a burning brand, and hurled it into the pile of dry rushes. They burst into flame, filled the air with smoke.

The voice spoke again. Infuriated, Ranessa clutched at her head. She screamed and shrieked and ran blindly out the door and into the night.

The monks heard the commotion, but no one went to see what caused it. They paused in their studies or opened their eyes and sat up in bed. One by one, sighing softly, each returned to work or to sleep.

The Omarah put out the fire.

Appalled by the ruin, Wolfram stood in the middle of the smoke-filled room and tried to gather his wits. His first fearful thought was that Ranessa had been attacked and carried off. He abandoned that notion immediately. The Omarah were on constant watch. They would never permit such a violent act to occur in the monastery. But then, what had happened?

Where were the blasted monks? They must have heard this commotion. Why weren't they here? He recalled Fire's words "Whatever happens . . ."

"You did or said something to her," Wolfram said in angry accusation, speaking to the walls, for they were the only things around to hear him. "Something that upset her. It's your fault and, by the Wolf, if harm has come to the girl, I'll see to it that you pay!"

He dashed off into the night.

Ranessa roamed the mountaintop in the darkness. The voice dinned in her ears, still speaking that inexplicable language, a language that was sweet to her ears as a lullaby, or would have been, had she been able to make any sense of it. Unable to see, she stumbled over the uneven ground, blundered into boulders. She fell several times, scraped the skin off her knees and her hands. She kicked over a hay rick in the stables, terrorizing the gentle mules. The Omarah kept watch on her, to make certain she did not harm herself or anyone else in her rampage.

At last, exhausted, she collapsed onto the rocky ground and wept, painful, gulping sobs.

"I have disappointed you," she said, when the tears were dry and her sobbing had deteriorated into hiccups. "I am sorry. I don't know what you want of me. I never have!"

The sun rose from behind the mountain. Ranessa raised her head and the bright light struck her full in the face, dazzled her eyes that were red and swollen from weeping. She blinked in the light and lifted her hand to shade her eyes. A figure came into view, walking along the edge of the precipice.

Ranessa could not see clearly, for her eyes were blurred, but the figure was short and had the appearance of a dwarf, for its shoulders were broad and it was wide about the middle. The dwarf wore orange robes and, in Ranessa's dazzled vision, seemed to have borrowed the fiery garb of the morning sun.

The dwarf did not appear to see her and Ranessa kept quiet. She was too shamed to speak, too dispirited. She watched dumbly as the figure came to the very edge of the cliff. The dwarf spread her arms.

The arms were not arms but wings—wings of fire.

Slowly, Ranessa rose to her feet.

The voice spoke and this time, Ranessa understood.

"My child," said the voice, patient, kind and loving. "You are home."

Tears, soft tears, tears of the heart, flowed down Ranessa's cheeks. These tears did not blind her. These tears revealed to her the truth.

With a wild, glad cry, Ranessa spread her arms and leapt off the top of the mountain into the sunrise.

Time and again, Wolfram called out Ranessa's name. He had made his decision. When he found her, he would take her away from this place. He didn't know what he was going to do with her, but he'd see to it that no one hurt her or scared her, ever again. After all, she had saved his life. He owed her.

The sun had not yet appeared, but dawn was close. Light filled the sky behind the mountain with red and gold. Pausing to listen, Wolfram heard what sounded like sobbing. Hastily, he headed that direction. Rounding a corner of the building, he found himself near the ledge where the monks took their daily exercise. The view from this ledge was breathtaking. Far below, the river wound among the steep, towering red rocks, a twist of blue thread stitched into red cloth. Standing on this promontory, Wolfram often wondered if he were seeing the world as the gods saw it. If so, if he was down at the river's edge, he would not be able to see himself from the peak. He would not be so much as a speck. Yet he would be there. Conversely, if he stood on the river bank and looked up at the heights, he wouldn't be able to see himself either. Yet, he would be here.

"Thus," he often reasoned, "though I cannot see the gods I know they are there. And although they may not be able to see me, they know I am there."

He found this thought comforting.

Catching sight of movement, Wolfram saw the monk Fire taking her morning constitutional. Grunting his displeasure, Wolfram decided to confront her, demand to know what had happened to his companion.

At that moment, the sun lifted up from behind the mountain, its light warm and dazzling. Bathed in its fiery light, Ranessa rose up from behind a boulder.

Breathing a heartfelt sigh of relief, Wolfram hastened toward her. She did not see him. She started walking toward the monk.

Wolfram quickened his pace, hoping to intercept her before Fire noticed her.

"Girl," he began, the word sweet in his mouth.

Ranessa gave a wild shout that drove the word back down his throat. Spreading her arms, she ran straight toward the cliff's edge. He bellowed out her name. If she heard him, she paid no attention. Terrified, Wolfram broke into a run. He was too far away. He reached the ledge in time to see her fling herself over the precipice.

Wolfram gave a wild cry of grief that echoed among the mountain peaks and covered his face with his hands.

A voice spoke to him. "Open your eyes," said Fire. "Open your eyes and see the truth."

Wolfram peered out from behind his fingers. The monk that had taken the shape of a dwarf was gone. Wolfram's suspicions were confirmed. A dragon stood on the ledge, her wings spread, reveling in the sun of a new dawn.

The dragon's scales burned with the fire of the sunlight. The elegant head, with its elongated snout and rows of gleaming sharp teeth, lifted to the sky. The eyes looked to the heavens, searched out the very gods themselves. The dragon's wings were orange and the sun shone through them, shimmering as through silken curtains. The long tail curved gracefully about the shining body. The taloned feet dug deep into the rock. The head turned on its long, sinuous neck. The dragon's dark eyes looked intently at Wolfram.

Shuddering, not even pleased to know that he had guessed the truth about the Heads of the Order, Wolfram looked away from the dragon. He looked down below to where he expected to see Ranessa's body lying twisted and broken on the blood-stained rocks.

She was not there.

He blinked, stared about. He couldn't find her.

"Where is she?" he demanded hoarsely.

"There," said Fire and gazed out to the sky.

Wolfram lifted his eyes to look out over the mountain peaks. A young dragon, orange as flame, circled in the azure air. The dragon's scales gleamed new-made in the sunshine; the wings glistened, as if they were still wet from the hatching. Her flight was hesitant, tentative, for she was yet testing her strength, learning how to handle the new body. He did not know her and yet he knew her. When she soared past him, she looked down and saw him there. He looked into her eyes and he saw Ranessa.

"You didn't know?" Fire asked him.

"No," said Wolfram, bleakly. He was awed and proud, like a new parent, and yet lost and lonely, too. "No, how could I?"

"She bore the mark," said Fire. "As do we all."

Wolfram smiled then, and shook his head. "Is she your child, ma'am?" he asked humbly.

"Yes," said Fire. "She is mine and she has come home."

Young dragons do not hatch from eggs as do birds or other reptiles. The dragons of Loerem place their eggs inside the bodies of humans or elves, orks or dwarves. When the dragon child is born, the child takes on the appearance of the mother's race. The human mother knows no different, nurses the baby that she believes is her own. The young dragon knows no different, believes that it is human or elven or dwarven.

"Oftentimes, the children never know," Fire said, watching her glistening-scaled daughter with affectionate pride. "Such dragon children live their lives among humans or elves, dwarves or orks, and they are content and happy with their lot. These children are lost to us. We know that and we accept it, for these children were never meant to be what we are.

"Some children, the ones in whom the blood of our kind runs strong, know from their first conscious thought that they are not what they appear to be. They know they are different. They are often unhappy, that is true," Fire admitted. "But it is their unhappiness, their dissatisfaction with themselves that leads them to the knowledge of themselves. Ranessa is one of these. She yearned to know the truth, she actively sought it out."

"You make a lousy dwarf, Fire, you know that, don't you?" Wolfram groused. He made a rapid dash at his eyes with his hands.

Fire looked at Wolfram and her own dark eyes were soft with sympathy. "As I told you, you were merely her guide. You shortened her journey. Eventually, she would have found us herself."

"So you say," he muttered.

He thought he would leave. He would make his report to the monks and then depart, maybe go see what this manor of his was like. He'd have fun ordering the servants about, if nothing else. He'd have fun until that grew tiresome and his feet grew itchy and the manor house shrank until it was too small to hold him.

Wolfram thought he would leave, but he didn't.

He sat down on the sun-warmed rock and watched Ranessa learn to fly.

THE TROMEK PORTAL HAD ORIGINALLY BEEN CONSTRUCTED TO PROVIDE access from the human city now called Old Vinnengael to the elven capital of Glymrae. With the fall of Old Vinnengael and the shattering of the Portals, the Tromek Portal shifted its position. The Portal's disappearance from the city of Glymrae left the elves devastated, at first, for they had come to enjoy the benefits of trade with humans.

Most elves believed that the gods had destroyed the Portals, but the Wyred were not so certain. They knew that magic, once it is in the world, may be altered, but is next to impossible to destroy. In secret, the Wyred sent out parties to search for the Portals. Hearing through their spies in the human lands that the Karnuans had discovered a Portal outside the city of Delak 'Vir, the Wyred redoubled their efforts.

After a five-year search, the Wyred at last found the western end of the Tromek Portal in a heavily wooded area about fifty miles east of the border with Nimorea. Since no one knew where the other end was located, several of the Wyred volunteered to explore the tunnel to find out. Their journey was long, leading them to believe that the magic tunnel through time and space covered a great distance. When they emerged, they found themselves in the mountains.

Knowing they would be required to map this territory, they brought with them various tools used for navigation and mapping. They discovered that they were inside elven lands, only about forty miles north of the border of the reborn Vinnengaelean Empire, due north of what would many years later become the capital city, New Vinnengael.

The elves were immensely pleased to discover this: they had the only Portal that began and ended within the border of a single nation.

While elven merchants travel to other lands, they are wary of outsiders entering their domains and they built massive fortresses protected by magic and steel at both ends of the Portal. The Portal entrance was guarded by the Wyred and their magicks. The walls surrounding the Portal were protected by the warriors and their swords. The entire system of defense consisted of rings: a ring of stone walls and towers on the outside, rings of magic on the inside.

Using Nimorean humans to work Earth magic, the elves raised a double wall of granite around the outside of the Portal. These two walls were separated by a trench six feet wide and six feet deep. Inside this trench, they built a series of towers that provided an excellent view of the Portal and the surrounding countryside, an ideal location in which to post archers. Huge gateways, wide enough to accommodate large wagons, provided entry and egress into the Portal. The gates were well guarded, rarely closed. The elves obtained a great deal of revenue from those traveling the Portals and did not want to do anything to discourage business.

Everyone who entered the Portal was questioned. Human merchants were required to have papers signed by elven officials indicating that they were in good standing with their own Guilds and that they had permission to enter elven lands and permission to sell their wares. Elves traveling abroad must have papers signed by the head of their House proving that they had a valid reason for leaving their homeland and that they had received permission to do so. All wagons were inspected to make certain they were not carrying contraband. After the traveler paid the fee, he was permitted to enter the gate and sent on to the next ring, the ring guarded by the Wyred.

Most human travelers never knew that they were under the watchful eye of elven wizards. The traveler walked through a beautiful garden, with trees and streams and arched bridges, golden fish and flowers and paths of crushed stone that all led to the Portal. After such beauty, the Portal itself was a let-down to those who entered it the first time. The Portal looked like a pool of stagnant gray water set among a grove of flowering trees.

The Portal was real, but everything else around it—the trees, the garden, the flowers, the fish—were illusion. Cloaked in magic, the Wyred walked unseen among the travelers, eavesdropping on their conversations, searching them surreptitiously for hidden magicks. Those they mistrusted were spellbound and whisked away to caves hidden beneath the Portal, where they were questioned and then either freed to resume their journey or arrested and turned over to the military for further interrogation. The Wyred had devised other magicks for use against an invading army, but what these were, what lay beneath the illusion of the garden, no one knew.

The Portal was guarded by an army of one thousand elven soldiers, loyal to the Shield and House Wyval, and twenty-five Wyred, also loyal to the Shield. The soldiers lived in barracks that had been built near the Portal. Their duty was boring and onerous, for the Portal stood in the middle of nowhere. The closest civilization was a small village that had sprung up about five miles distant to serve the needs of travelers and soldiers.

The commander in charge of the Outer Ring defenses of the western Portal had been awakened before dawn by a messenger, who had flown to the Portal on hippogriff from Glymrae. Now, two hours later, as the sunlight gilded the tops of the trees with gold, Commander Lyall stood atop the vantage point located above the main gate and watched nine hundred of the one thousand elves supposed to be guarding the Portal marching away from it.

He looked from the line of soldiers winding along the highway to the letter the messenger had brought to him that morning. Lyall had already read it many times, in the faint hope that perhaps the reading of it would increase his understanding of it. The twentieth time proved no more illuminating than the first.

The elves often couch their messages to each other in flowery verse that is lovely, but sometimes open to misinterpretation. Military dispatches are not sent in verse, however, for they must be clearly understood, leaving no room for doubt. Gazing gloomily at the missive in his hand, Commander Lyall was left with no doubts at all. The Shield had ordered nine hundred troops to return immediately to Glymrae. He gave no reason. He did not have to. He was the Shield and he was in charge of the military defense of the nation. The messenger told Lyall what everyone in the capital city knew: the split between the Shield and the Divine was irreparable. The elven nation stood on the brink of civil war. The Shield needed every soldier loyal to him.

As for leaving men enough to guard the Portal, it had not been attacked in two hundred years. There was no reason to think that it would be threatened now.

"Hasn't he been receiving my reports?" Lyall demanded of the messenger.

The messenger was only a messenger. He couldn't say.

Lyall was a devoted follower of the Shield and rightly so, for the Shield had lifted Lyall from his obscure birth as the fourteenth son of a peasant farmer and elevated him to the rank of commander. Lyall had worked hard to attain his position. He had fought bravely in battle and had risked his life on numerous occasions. The number of battle scars he bore would have made a Trevenici warrior proud. He had been rewarded with this rank and this position.

Lyall knew, of course, that he would be expected to repay the Shield for his promotion. He knew that he had been placed in this position because the Shield wanted a man he could trust serving as commander of the Outer Ring. Lyall was that man. If not for the Shield, Lyall would now be yoked to a plow, trudging through the fields. Every night, when Lyall said his prayers to the Father and Mother, he included the Shield's name among them.

Still, there was a brief moment in the early morning darkness when Lyall was tempted to question his master's wisdom. The Shield had emptied the Portal of its manpower at the precise time when they might be needed most.

Only five days earlier, Lyall had sent the Shield an urgent dispatch stating his belief that a human army was hiding in the woods around the Portal. Scouts, both elven and Nimorean, who patrolled the area on a regular basis had seen nothing untoward, but several had gone missing. Alarmed, Lyall had placed his troops on heightened alert and doubled the guard in the towers. He had not informed the Wyred, for, as a soldier, he must turn a blind eye to the dishonorable and suspect workings of wizards. Besides, he was quite confident that the Wyred knew all about the presence of the enemy, perhaps more than he did.

He'd received no reply to his dispatch, and now this. Lyall couldn't understand. He could only obey.

The troops departed. Lyall had no time to bemoan their loss. Summoning what officers he had left, he made new plans for the defense of the Portal. He drew up new watch schedules. He did what he could to keep morale high, to make light of the matter, saying that they would certainly splurge on dinner that night, for they no longer had to share supplies with a thousand.

The officers weren't fooled, but they said what they were expected to say. All of them were thinking the same thought. What was out there in the wilderness? What had spooked the animals and caused the birds to vanish? What was picking off their scouts one by one?

No one knew the answers, but they all knew this: whoever was out there had just seen the garrison emptied of its defenders.

Lyall sent the men back to their duties, then sat at his desk and pondered his next move.

Presumably the Wyred had received the same orders Lyall had. Presumably the ranks of the Wyred had been similarly reduced. Lyall had no way of knowing for certain. He had never once spoken to the commander of the Wyred. On those rare occasions when they were forced to interact—usually when there was difficulty over someone trying to enter the Portal—the Wyred simply appeared with the offender and handed him over. Lyall didn't know the commander's name. He knew so little about the magic-users that he wasn't even certain the Wyred had a commander.

The situation was dire. He did not have time to follow the usual circuitous route used by warriors who must rely on the Wyred and yet must at the same time appear not to. He had to know what was going on, what he could expect in case of attack.

Other officers would have feared loss of honor. Lyall was a peasant. He had no honor to lose, or so he reasoned. Perhaps it was the peasant in him that tended to rank common sense higher than honor anyway.

Lyall walked from the Outer Ring across the open paved courtyard that divided one sphere of influence from another and entered the garden. He lingered among the azaleas and the bougainvillea, looking at everything in general and at nothing in particular.

Speaking to the azaleas or perhaps to the goldfish, Lyall said calmly, "I would talk with the master of the Wyred. The matter is of the utmost urgency."

He stood several more moments listening to the humming of the bees and watching the butterflies flit among the blossoms, then he strolled on, affecting nonchalance, though his nervousness grew. He could only guess that he'd been seen and heard. If he hadn't or if for some reason the Wyred refused to speak to him, he had no idea what to do next. Abandon this plan and come up with another one. But time was running out.

The path on which he walked ended at a fish pond. Lyall paused a moment to gaze at the fish, then turned to make his way back.

The Wyred stood in front of him, so close that Lyall might have touched her.

Lyall had not heard footsteps, had not sensed anyone coming up behind him. He gave a great start and took an involuntary step backward, a step that very nearly carried him into the pond. Recovering, Lyall felt a flash of irritation. Quick to swallow his annoyance, he made a bow.

"I thank you for coming. I am honored by this meeting."

"No, you are not," said the Wyred coolly. "You are dishonored by it. But that is neither here nor there. What is this matter of urgency that has caused you to break all the unwritten laws to come to me to discuss?"

He found himself staring, unable to take his eyes off the woman. The tattooed mask around the eyes marked her family, but in addition to that mask, she wore the tattoos that marked her as a Wyred. These were far more elaborate. Whorls and circles, lines and symbols extended down her cheeks and wrapped around her chin. Did these tattoos mark her standing among the Wyred? Did they have something to do with her magic? Were they nothing more than personal affectation? He had no way of knowing. He tried to wrench his mind back to the matter at hand, but he could not take his eyes from her face.

"You said the matter was urgent," she stated, growing annoyed at the delay.

Difficult to tell her age, due to the tattoos. Her eyes were opaque, unreadable. They did not give, they took. She stood with her hands tucked into long sleeves whose cuffs, made of brightly colored silk, extended to the floor. Her silk robes were decorated with fanciful designs of birds, each bird trimmed in golden thread.

"You have heard of the outbreak of war between the Shield of the Divine and the Divine?" Lyall began.

The Wyred raised an eyebrow, amazed at such forthrightness. "I have."

"You know that my force has been reduced from one thousand troops to one hundred," Lyall continued.

"I am aware of that, yes."

"Were you . . ." Lyall paused. This had to be phrased properly. "Were you required to make a corresponding reduction in your force?"

The Wyred seemed at first about to refuse to answer, then, after a moment's thought, she gave an abrupt nod of her head.

Lyall absorbed this news silently, then said, "You know that we have received reports of scouts going missing, of other strange occurrences in the forest. You know that the people of the village are uneasy and that many have departed. You know that our number of travelers from human lands has decreased markedly and those who come speak of war in Dunkarga and in Karnu, unrest in Nimorea and other human lands."

"I know this," she said. "And a great deal more. There is an army out there in the forest. Its numbers are vast. It is our belief that this is part of the same army that attacked Karnu and Dunkarga."

Lyall listened, appalled.

The Wyred continued. "The Shield knows about this army."

Lyall stared, appalled and astonished. "He knows! Then what—"

The Wyred shook her head. If she knew or guessed, she would not say.

"May I ask how you feel about this?" Lyall questioned her.

"The Shield of the Divine is of House Wyval. I am of House Wyval. My loyalty is to my Shield and my House," the Wyred replied and her voice was cold.

Lyall would have to be content with that. She was obviously not going to tell him anything more.

"You know, then, that I need your help," he said.

The Wyred raised the same eyebrow even farther. She waited for him to continue.

"If we are attacked, it must appear to the enemy that we have men enough to defend the Portal. Is this possible?"

He realized the moment he asked that question that he'd made a mistake.

The Wyred bristled. "Of course, it is possible. Creating such an illusion is simplicity itself. You realize that there is a danger in this, however. If your men are told it is illusion, they may have difficulty going along with it. Officers who lead illusory troops in a charge must do so knowing that in reality they face the enemy alone. Yet, troops who do not know the truth, who think that the illusions are real, may rely too heavily on illusory soldiers, only to find out at the last moment that their illusory comrade cannot come to their aid. I do not need to tell you that in such instances their trust in their officers and in each other will be damaged, not only now but in the future."

"I will tell the men," he said. "I have always told them the truth."

"I think that is best," she concurred and there was perhaps the slightest glimmer of respect in her eyes.

They'd said everything that was needful. He had much to think about, plans to make and he assumed that she did, too. He made another bow, indicating that he was about to take his leave. He was surprised to find her regarding him thoughtfully.

"We are to be sacrificed to save the shield's honor. You know that?"

What was this? Lyall wondered uneasily. A test of loyalty?

"It is my duty to obey the Shield," he replied carefully. "The Shield knows what is best for us. It is not my place to question his wisdom."

The Wyred regarded Lyall a moment longer, but he could read nothing in her expression. He met her gaze without flinching and she turned from him without comment. Walking calmly through the garden, she headed back toward the Portal.

Although Lyall had important duties to attend to, he remained to watch her, fascinated and repulsed at the same time. Lyall would have to explain matters to his officers, then he would speak to the troops—what troops remained. He would tell them the truth, but not all the truth. He would say nothing about the sacrifice.

They would figure that out for themselves.

In his command tent, Dagnarus, Lord of the Void and now self-proclaimed king of Dunkarga, met with his officers. His armed camp was located within striking proximity of the Tromek Portal. Taan scouts, perched high in the branches of the tall pine trees, could see the ring of stone in the distance. The heavy forest that the elves prized as part of their defense had proven to be more advantageous to their enemy. Dagnarus had used its cover to move ten thousand troops unobserved across the northern end of the Faynir mountains. He then marched south to the Tromek Portal with neither Nimorean human nor Tromek elf aware that an enemy had invaded their territory. Those few who did blunder across the taan army were swiftly dispatched, their bodies destroyed through Void magic that left nothing of the corpse behind.

"I am delaying the hour of our attack," Dagnarus told the assembled officers.

Some of the officers were humans, for there was a force of human mercenaries attached to his command. Most were high-ranking taan nizam, under the leadership of the taan Vrykyl, Nb'arsk. Shakur was there, as well. He hovered in the background, took no part in the proceedings. Most paid him little attention, assuming he was there as Dagnarus's bodyguard, in the absence of Valura.

"We were going to strike at dawn, but I have received information that has prompted me to change those orders. You will not attack at dawn, but will await my signal. Your troops will move forward to be in position, but they will remain hidden until the signal."

The taan warriors grumbled, not pleased at the delay. Dagnarus cast a grim glance about him and the grumbling ceased. He wore the black armor of the Lord of the Void, including his helm. The taan revered him as their god and feared him as their god, but he was well aware that he lost something of his stature among them when he appeared in his human form.

"Don't worry," he told the taan, "we have not marched all this way to sit in front of the Portal and watch elves travel in and out. We will attack. It may be an hour after dawn, it may be noon, it may be nightfall. But we will attack. All other orders remain standing. General Gurske, as we discussed, once we have seized the Portal, I will continue through it with the army to attack New Vinnengael. You and your forces will remain behind to retain our control of the Portal."

General Gurske nodded. He was a human, the officer in charge of the human contingent.

"Holding the Portal should be easy, General," Dagnarus continued. "The nearest elven force is at this moment marching back to Glymrae, the nearest human force is in Myanmin. The Shield will see to it that no elven troops are dispatched through the Portal to reinforce those few remaining to defend it. Any travelers who come to the Portal you will seize as slaves, confiscate their merchandise."

General Gurske nodded again. He knew his orders, foresaw no difficulty. He looked forward to being rid of the taan. His men had lived and fought alongside the taan for several years now, but the two races did not get along, had little respect for one another.

"The taan under the leadership of Nb'arsk will help in seizing and securing the Portal. Once that is accomplished, Nb'arsk will send an advance force through the tunnel to attack its elven defenders at the eastern end. The rest will then proceed through the Portal, where they will set up camp and await my orders."

Nb'arsk indicated that she understood. Dagnarus asked if there were questions, dismissed them when there weren't. He knew his troops, knew their value. When they had all departed, he motioned to Shakur.

The Vrykyl stepped out of the shadows, came to stand before his master.

"I take it you've heard something?" Shakur said.

"I have received word from Valura that both the human and the elven portions of the Sovereign Stone travel together. She thinks, and I concur, that they are headed for the Portal."

"I agree," said Shakur. "I sense the blood knife coming nearer every moment. The bearer of the knife is likely the one who bears the Sovereign Stone."

"Precisely. That's why I've postponed the attack. I do not want to frighten them away. You and a small force will enter the Portal disguised as merchant travelers. Remain there until you find these people. When you find them, signal me and I will launch the attack. During the confusion, you will seize them and bring them to me."

"Alive, my lord?"

"If possible. In case I have any questions for them." Dagnarus shrugged. "But it doesn't much matter. I will take the Stones either from their living bodies or their dead corpses. A word of warning, Shakur. Do not try to seize the Stones yourself. The Stones are imbued with elemental magic that guards them against the Void. Valura touched one and was very nearly destroyed."

"Then how will *you* take them, my lord?"

"You forget, Shakur," Dagnarus said. "I held the Stones. Each one was given into my hands by my father, King Tamaros. One by one, I carried each portion of the Sovereign Stone to give to the representatives of each race. *I* was the god's chosen. *Not* my brother, Helmos!"

Dagnarus's hand clenched, his voice rose in the intensity of his emotion. "When it came time for Helmos to call for the Stones, the other races would not relinquish them. The Stones were intended to come to me. These are the first two. The rest will follow."

Shakur grunted. "What will Valura be doing?"

Dagnarus knew his lieutenant. He knew this seemingly innocent question was intended to point out that Valura had bungled the job and it was left to Shakur to pick up the pieces.

The flesh rots away, the bones grow brittle, the brain and the heart turn to dust. Why does the soul survive? Dagnarus often wondered this about his Vrykyl and he often cursed the fact that it was so. How much less trouble for him if these creatures of his were automatons, thinking only what he taught them to think, reacting only as he taught them to react. True, it was these inconvenient souls that made them far more "human" and therefore far more valuable as spies, as infiltrators, as assassins and military leaders. But this "humanity" also meant that Dagnarus was forced to deal with the petty jealousies, lapses in judgment, and the outright rebellion of his servants. He sometimes regretted that he'd ever laid hands on the Dagger that created them. Such thoughts came to him more frequently these days since K'let's rebellion.

Dagnarus had no fear of the taan Vrykyl. K'let dared not challenge his master in battle. Yet K'let had succeeded in defying him and this disturbed Dagnarus far more than he admitted to himself. He was confident that all the rest of the Vrykyl remained under his control, but the very fact that he must constantly reassure himself of their loyalty was highly annoying, coming right at a time when he needed to concentrate his full attention on the war that would make him rightful ruler of Loerem.

"Valura obeys my orders," Dagnarus returned shortly. "As will you, Shakur."

Shakur bowed silently and departed.

Dagnarus turned back to his work. In his mind, the battle for the Tromek Portal was over. He began planning the battle he had looked forward to fighting for centuries—the battle to win New Vinnengael.

THE HIPPOGRIFFS FLEW THROUGHOUT THE REMAINDER OF THAT DAY AND into the night. The sky was crusted with stars, the air was clear, the moon half-full. The hippogriffs paused to rest, but only as needed, for if Damra was eager to reach the end of their journey, the hippogriffs were just as eager to complete their task and return to their young.

The Portal came into view as day dawned—a ring of white stone carved out of the verdant forest. Damra was about to tell the hippogriffs where to land, when the creatures began to circle in the air, calling raucously to each other.

"What do you suppose is the matter with them?" Damra asked Arim, puzzled. "What is wrong?"

The Grandmother poked her in the ribs, startling Damra, who thought her still asleep. The old pecwae had slept soundly through most of the trip, her head pressing against the small of Damra's back.

"They say there is a strange scent on the air," the Grandmother called out. "Unfamiliar. They don't like it."

Silwyth had warned of an army poised to seize the Portal. Damra looked closely, but could not see any sign of trouble on the ground. Yet even as she did so, she realized that an entire nation might be hidden in the shadows of the forests. Odd, though, that the hippogriffs wouldn't recognize the scent. They would certainly be familiar with humans. She gave them a sharp command to proceed. The hippogriffs continued to circle. One shook its eagle head, snapped its beak, and glanced back at her with a bright eye that had a grim look to it.

"They will take us there," said the Grandmother. "But after that we are on our own. They do not want to stay around here."

"I don't blame them," said Damra. "Very well."

The Grandmother spoke to the hippogriff in what Damra presumed was the pecwae language, for it was like them: its words short and quick and bright. The hippogriffs ceased circling and flew toward the Portal. They kept a close lookout on the ground, watchful for any signs of movement.

"Can you truly understand what animals say?" Damra asked, turning to speak to the Grandmother.

"Not what they say," the Grandmother replied. "That would be something!" She chuckled. "Listening to all that hooting and squawking, bleating and cawing. We pecwae know what animals are thinking. Most of the time."

"All animals?" Damra asked. The Grandmother was so matter-of-fact, it was hard to doubt her.

"Except fish. Stupid creatures, fish."

"If you understand the thoughts of animals, can you also understand the thoughts of people? Can you understand *my* thoughts?" The thought itself was not a comfortable one.

The Grandmother gave an emphatic shake of her head. "The thoughts of animals are clear and simple: fear, hunger, trust, distrust. The thoughts of people are a jumbled mess. Only the gods can read those and they're welcome to it."

They flew over the Portal. Damra scanned the area as closely as the hippogriffs. She saw only a merchant caravan approaching along the road—a single horse-drawn wagon that looked like a toy from the air and small toy dolls that must be its owners. When she asked the hippogriffs, through the Grandmother, if they saw anything, they indicated that they did not. But the beasts were not at ease, that much was clear. They descended rapidly, spiraling downward in ever tightening circles to land on a wide patch of cleared ground.

Once Damra and the rest had dismounted, the hippogriffs immediately departed. Leaping into the air, they spread their wings and were soon lost to sight, flying in the direction of Glymrae.

"There goes our way out of here," Arim stated ruefully as he watched them dwindle rapidly in the distance. "They might have at least remained until we safely entered the Portal."

"It can't be helped," Damra said. "You saw how uneasy they were. They wouldn't have remained even if I had ordered them. They are right. There is a strange feel to the forest. I am a city girl, born and bred, but even I sense it. Do you?"

"Yes. All the more reason I am sorry to see the hippogriffs depart," Arim said quietly.

"Like them, we will not linger," Damra said and walked toward the gate in the Outer Ring.

They were the only people at the Gate. The merchant caravan that

Damra had seen from the air had been admitted and was on its way through the Outer Ring. Damra expected trouble from the guards over the Trevenici and the two pecwae and she was not disappointed.

"Impossible," said the Portal guard, shaking his head. "I cannot authorize their entering the Portal."

"They have papers," said Arim, exhibiting their documents. "As you can see, all is in order. They were permitted to cross the border—"

"I cannot be responsible for what the border guards might do," said the Portal guard in a tone that implied the border guards were slackers who would allow two-headed trolls to cross with impunity. "You must speak to Commander Lyall."

"We will do so," Damra said crisply. "Tell him that Dominion Lord Damra of Gwyenoc requests admittance to the Portal for herself and her party."

The guard bowed perfunctorily in recognition of her honored title, but then he'd already known she was a Dominion Lord by her tabard and he obviously wasn't impressed. He escorted them to a waiting room in the gatehouse. The room had no windows, contained nothing but benches. It opened out onto a corridor.

"Where does that lead?" Jessan demanded, unable to sit still.

"He doesn't like to be closed in," explained Bashae, yawning.

"So I've noticed," said Damra, watching the young man pace about like a hungry cat. She was nervous herself and might have emulated him, but she wanted to maintain at least an outward appearance of composure. "The corridor ends in a staircase that leads up to the commander's offices, the dining hall and various other rooms."

"I can't breathe in here," Jessan said and headed toward the door. "I'll wait outside."

"Not alone," Damra said quietly. "Please remain in here with us."

Jessan turned to look at her, his expression dark and rebellious, and for a moment she thought he might refuse. She had carefully phrased her words as a request, knowing that he would resent an outright order. At length, with an ill-contented look, he slumped down on a bench. He was up again the next instant, pacing.

Arim slid over to speak softly to Damra, "This Commander Lyall is loyal to the Shield. Suppose he has been warned of our coming."

"No one knew we planned to come to the Portal, not even Silwyth," said Damra.

"No, but they could have easily guessed that we would head this way."

"And they probably did," said Damra.

Arim shook his head, settled back against the wall.

"Commander Lyall will see Damra of Gwyenoc," announced the guard.

Damra accompanied the guard upstairs.

Commander Lyall rose from behind his desk to greet her. The two bowed and exchanged the proper pleasantries. Damra noted immediately that Lyall was preoccupied, worried.

"I am traveling to New Vinnengael to meet with the magi of the Temple," said Damra. "I have made the interesting discovery that the old legends are true: pecwae can indeed speak to animals. My companion and I are conveying these two pecwae to the magi in hopes that we might study them and find out if they use magic or if this is something inherent to them as pec—"

"You are of House Gwyenoc," Lyall said abruptly, casting a sharp glance at the tattoos around her eyes. "You are known to be loyal to the Divine."

"As are all elves," Damra returned smoothly.

He would refuse them admittance. She steeled herself. To her amazement, Commander Lyall took up five passes, affixed his seal to each, and handed them back to her.

"Enter the Portal quickly and do not linger when you reach the other side," he said.

Damra started to express her thanks, but the commander turned his back on her, walked over to the window. She was being dismissed, rudely at that. She was not about to take offense, however.

As she was leaving, he remarked, "All that I am, I owe to the Shield." His voice sounded sad.

Damra did not know what to say in response. Eventually she concluded that she wasn't supposed to say anything. The man was talking to himself. She wasted no further time, but took the passes and ran downstairs, still puzzling over that enigmatic remark.

"We have permission to enter the Portal," Damra told her companions. "Gather up your gear. Keep together, follow me and let either Arim or myself do the talking."

Jessan and Bashae listened and both nodded. Neither had much gear to gather. Jessan wore the sword Arim had obtained for him, wore it proudly for it was the first sword he had ever owned. Bashae clutched the knapsack. He kept tight hold of it even when he slept. Damra's reference to "gathering" had been an oblique reference to the Grandmother, who had dozed off in a sunny corner.

"Damra," said Arim, speaking to her in a soft undertone, "I have been eavesdropping on the soldiers. Last night, their commander received an order to strip his garrison. Nine hundred troops marched out this morning, heading for Glymrae."

"So that explains it," Damra said softly, thinking of the commander's remark. She cast a glance up above her, wondered if he still stood by the window, watching for his death. "He is the babe cast to the starving wolves and he knows it. He warned us to make haste."

Damra showed the guard their passes. He pointed out the route they were to take. Damra led the way through the Outer Ring that was composed of two high stone walls separated by a grass-filled ditch. Eight stone towers, three stories in height, stood in the ditch between the two stone rings. Murder holes encircled every story. Occasionally Jessan caught a glimpse of light flashing off steel-tipped arrows or saw the shadow of an elven warrior pass by. Guards stood in plain sight on the top of the towers. Some kept watch over the surrounding countryside. Others kept an eye on what was happening inside. Their numbers were few, however. Woefully few. Damra increased their pace.

After passing through the Outer Ring, they entered a broad paved courtyard. Beyond was the Inner Ring of defense, the province of the Wyred. Damra wondered whether or not she should say something to the human and the pecwae warning them that the garden was magical. She decided against it. Most travelers—even elven travelers—had no idea the garden was more than it appeared to be. No need to rouse doubts, bring up questions. All was going smoothly. Only a few more minutes and then they would be safely inside the Portal.

Looking across the paved courtyard, Damra was disconcerted to see the caravan of human merchants parked in the center. They appeared to be having problems with their wagon, for two were peering underneath the wagon bed, gesturing at something. A fourth sat on the driver's seat, staring out at the horse's ears. Another reloaded boxes that had been taken out to lighten the weight while repairs were made.

The caravan should have been far ahead of them. The fact that they were still here made her uneasy. Probably her worries were groundless, but she was used to trusting her instincts. She led her companions across the courtyard at an angle that would take them well clear of the caravan. She kept close watch on the merchants. The one loading boxes ceased his work. He said something to the two inspecting the wagon. They straightened up and all of them turned to watch the small procession.

"Look, Jessan. Humans!" Bashae said, excited. "I wonder where they're from. Dunkarga, maybe. Perhaps they know your uncle—"

"Keep moving. Do nothing to draw attention," Damra said sharply.

The Grandmother came to a stop and lifted her agate-eyed stick in the air. Every single eye in the stick stared at the humans of the wagon.

"Evil!" the Grandmother shrieked in a shrill tone that reverberated throughout the courtyard.

Hearing her scream, the elven soldiers on guard in the towers turned to see what was going on inside their walls. From outside the walls, horns blared and drums boomed. Ten thousand taan voices lifted in a fierce yell, savage and thunderous. The shadows of the forest took on shape and form and began moving at a rapid pace toward the Outer Ring.

"They've launched the attack!" Damra shouted, trying to hurry along the Grandmother. "Quickly—"

"Damra!" Arim's voice cracked. His eyes stared over her head at something behind her.

Damra pivoted, one hand touching the medallion, the other grasping her sword. The silver armor of the Dominion Lord flowed over her body. She drew her blade in a smooth arc. Yet, at the sight of what they faced, she took an involuntary step backward.

A Vrykyl descended from the wagon, walked purposefully toward them. The Vrykyl's armor eclipsed the sunlight. A chill shadow fell on them. Though the sun shone everywhere else, they stood in darkness, the darkness of the Void. Void magic drained them of courage and of hope, emptied their souls.

The human merchants threw off their disguises, revealed themselves to be soldiers. Swords drawn, they ran ahead of the Vrykyl. The soldiers' attention was fixed on Arim and Jessan. They ignored Damra. The soldiers would leave a Dominion Lord and her magic to the Vrykyl.

An ambush, Damra thought ruefully. And I walked right into it. She looked back at her companions.

As the rabbit freezes at the sight of the coyote, the two pecwae froze at the sight of the Vrykyl. They stood staring, their faces drained of color, their small bodies quaking. Damra cried out Bashae's name thrice, but he didn't hear her. He made a whimpering sound. Damra reached back, gave him a vicious shake.

"Bashae!" she shouted.

His eyes were white-rimmed with terror. He stared at her in helpless fear.

"Run for the garden! The garden!"

She pointed emphatically. Bashae gulped. His horror-stricken gaze wavered, strayed to the garden, but flicked back in panic to the Vrykyl. Damra hoped he understood, for she had no more time to tell him anything else. Grasping her sword in her hand, she ran forward to intercept the Vrykyl, hoping to draw his attention from Bashae.

Pecwae are cowards. Born cowards, they are not ashamed of their cowardice, for it is only by being able to outrun the lion who seeks to devour them that they have survived as a race. The pecwae's instinct is to flee from danger and, after the first paralyzing effects of terror wear off, instinct takes hold.

All thoughts of loyalty to his comrades and affection for his friends departed from Bashae. He may have heard Damra or he may not. All he knew was that some distance away was a landscape that was familiar to him, a landscape that reminded him of home—trees to hide behind, rocks to crawl under, bushes that promised sheltering cover. Grabbing hold of each other by the hands, the two pecwae fled toward this safe haven with no clear, conscious thought except the urgent need to escape death.

Jessan was equally horrified at the sight of the Vrykyl, the creature of his nightmares come to life. He stood staring at it, unable to move or to think clearly. He might have turned and run in terror like his small friend, but then one of the humans raised a battle cry.

The cry roused the Trevenici warrior spirit in Jessan. An enemy of flesh and blood stood before him, a chance at last to prove himself in battle. The knowledge drove the horror of the Vrykyl from his mind. Raising his sword in the air, Jessan gave a hair-raising cry and launched himself at the enemy.

"Will the elves come to our rescue?" Arim shouted.

"They have their own problems!" Damra shouted back.

She could hear behind her the clamor of the garrison preparing to defend itself against the sudden onslaught. Officers shouted orders, elven troops came running from their quarters, dashing up the stairs to take their places inside the tower. The gates that led through the Outer Ring boomed shut.

Damra met one of the humans with a crash of steel. She fought him absentmindedly, her attention on the Vrykyl. The Vrykyl continued to advance, his fire-eyed gaze fixed on Damra. Even from this distance, she felt the heat of his hatred.

Good, she thought. Keep him focused on me.

Her opponent grew annoying. She had wounded him twice, but the blasted human would not die. Damra turned her full attention to the battle, watched for her opening. Finding it, she drove her sword through the man's leather armor and into his protruding gut. Wrenching her weapon free, she jumped over the body as it was still falling and hurled herself at the Vrykyl.

Jessan, to his chagrin, did not find his first battle as easy as he had expected it would be. The Trevenici are renowned for their courage and ferocity, not their skill. They have a simple strategy. They terrorize their opponent with a display of savage fury, then overpower him with their strength. Shrewd commanders put Trevenici forces in the front lines, use them to soften up the enemy, punch a hole in his ranks. The opponent able to withstand the initial Trevenici assault discovers that the Trevenici warrior is easily frustrated at this. Losing patience, they begin to make mistakes.

Jessan's opponent was a veteran of many campaigns. Having witnessed taan attacks, the soldier was not intimidated by this howling barbarian. The veteran knew the young man's fury would soon expend itself. All he had to do was survive until it did. He parried what blows he could, ducked the ones he couldn't, and kept on the defensive.

Jessan grew angered and, beneath the anger, he began to doubt himself. He should have slain this soldier easily, for Jessan was obviously the superior warrior. His opponent did nothing but duck and dodge and dance. Jessan brought down his sword again and again, aiming savage blows at the man's head, blows that would split his skull, once they connected. The man's sword was always in the way, however. Strong and big, the soldier was able by sheer brute force to hold off Jessan's attacks.

Out of the corner of his eye, Jessan saw the elf woman dispatch her opponent with an ease that was dazzling. Arim fought with a skill that amazed Jessan, who had discounted the lithe, slim Nimorean as weak. Arim's curved-bladed sword seemed to be everywhere at once. His opponent was covered in blood.

Enraged, Jessan slashed and pounded. The next thing he knew, the sword flew out of his hands. He stared in astonishment to find his enemy's blade at his throat.

Arim saw the young man's predicament. Dispatching his foe, Arim lunged at Jessan's soldier, shouting at the man to draw his attention. Facing a new enemy coming at him from the rear, the soldier was forced to turn away from Jessan. Another soldier ran up, took the place of the one Arim had killed. Arim fought both, but he was losing ground.

Jessan looked for his sword, saw that it was too far away for him to retrieve. He resorted instinctively to the only weapon he had left—the blood knife.

As Damra came within striking distance of the Vrykyl, she looked into his eyes as she looked into the eyes of any enemy, to gauge what he would do. That was a mistake. In the eyes, she saw power that was ancient, stemmed back to the time before time, when nothing existed, not light, not life.

The gods tore apart the Void to set the stars in the sky. The gods placed the sun and moon in the Void, brought life into the universe. But they could not banish the Void. The Void came before the beginning and it would be there at the end. In the empty eyes of the Vrykyl, Damra saw the Void and it was terrible to look upon.

Damra had known panic only once before, and that was during the Transfiguration, when she felt her flesh being consumed in the god-given magic of the Sovereign Stone. Then her panic had given way to ecstasy. Now she felt the opposite, panic giving way to despair.

Fighting to quell her fear, Damra's first instinct was to use her illusion magic to fight the Vrykyl as she had fought so many others. She recalled Silwyth's warning that the Vrykyl could see through illusion, but she was desperate.

The magic crumpled to dust like a dried rose, its petals falling brown and dead around her.

The Vrykyl struck at her with his sword. Damra met the blow, parried it with her own. He drew back, struck again. Again she parried, but now she realized that each time her blade touched his accursed weapon, the debilitating magic of the Void strengthened its hold on her. Desperately she fought, attacking again and again, praying for the Vrykyl to make one mistake, create one opening.

The Vrykyl made no mistakes. He matched her blow for blow, almost as if he could read her mind. The power of the Void caused the day to grow dark around her. Her strength flagged. Her courage started to seep from her like blood from a mortal wound. Her sword grew heavy in her hands, heavy as the knowledge of her own mortality.

She was compelled to look again and again into the empty eyes and each time she saw therein her own emptiness. So vast, so dark, she began to lose knowledge of herself. Memories, all memories, memories of who she was and what she was, memories of joy, love, sorrow and fear dwindled to nothingness and when all the memories were gone, she was left with only the memory of the single moment of her birth, a flame on a guttering candle that would vanish in a breath, her last breath.

A prey to Shakur's Void magic, Damra lost her will to survive. She lowered her sword and in the next instant, she would have dropped it. But then Jessan struck his enemy with the blood knife.

The knife tasted blood. The warmth flooded Shakur with a memory of his own. Turning, he saw Jessan, saw the blood knife in the young human's hand.

Whoever possesses the blood knife possesses the Sovereign Stone. Shakur was convinced of that. Still holding the Dominion Lord in his fell magical grip, Shakur turned his attention on the human who wielded the knife.

The elven warriors saw the Vrykyl materialize in the paved courtyard inside the Outer Ring. They knew it to be a creature of the Void, but they could not come to the aid of Damra and her companions. Those who saw had time for only one startled look, then the deadly buzz of arrows and the clamor of the enemy forced them to ignore what was happening inside the courtyard and concentrate on fighting for their lives.

An advance troop of humans led the attack on the Outer Ring. Lyall's men were prepared for that. They were not prepared for the second wave of troops—an immense army of monstrous creatures, who came shrieking and howling out of the shadows of the forest. The creatures walked like men but they had the faces of animals, with long snouts and gaping mouths filled with razor teeth. They carried bizarre looking weapons and attacked with ferocity and a complete lack of fear. They hurled themselves at the gate and the wall with wide grins on their hideous faces.

Thousands of them. Attacking a force of one hundred.

What is the Shield's plan? Lyall asked and answered himself. The Shield wants the Portal to fall, that much is clear. But he wants to make it look as if it fell by mischance. He can always claim in his defense that he had no way of knowing an enemy was anywhere within a thousand miles. My reports to the contrary will be conveniently misplaced. And there will be none left alive here to contradict him.

"Send a messenger through the Portal to the eastern end," he ordered his aide. "Tell them that we are under attack by a sizeable force. We will hold as long as we can, but they should make ready their own defenses."

The aide departed. Lyall went back to the window.

If I just knew why, he said to himself. If I only knew why. Perhaps that would make dying easier.

The taan raised siege ladders against the walls. Elves fought them, fought and lost. The taan surged over the walls, dropped down to land in the ditch. True to their word, the Wyred created the illusion of elven soldiers. They did their job well. Looking down, Lyall could not tell which troops were real and which were not.

A victim struck by an illusory arrow believes he has been struck by a real one. He sees blood, he feels pain. He may faint or fall down, but, eventually, he will come to realize that the wound is not real. The illusions might halt the enemy for a moment, but that was all. A moment.

A hundred taan wielding an enormous battering ram rushed at the gate. Elves fired a storm of arrows into their ranks. Some struck their marks. The taan fell, but that didn't stop the ram. The dead lay where they had fallen, their bodies trampled by those coming behind. The ram struck the iron gate a thunderous blow that caused the very ground to shake. The gate held, but the hinges loosened, jarred from their moorings. Howling in derision, the taan pulled back to have another go at it.

The gate must fall. Lyall had no way of stopping it. The enemy had as many troops carrying the battering ram as he had in the entire garrison. He gave the order for the elves at the gate to pull back, to man the towers. At least there, they could hold for awhile.

Although, what we're holding for is open to question, Lyall thought. Reinforcements won't come. The elves began to pull back, firing their arrows as they went. Lyall looked out into the forest. The shadows were alive with movement—more of these fiends running toward the Portal. The main gate gave way with a crash. Shrieking in triumph, the taan surged into the gatehouse.

Splayed feet pounded on the stairs. Lyall heard their raucous voices and smelled their rank stench. His bodyguard suggested bolting the door, stacking furniture in front of it, but that wouldn't stop the monsters for long. Gripping his sword, Lyall advanced to meet the enemy.

He was a peasant. He had no honor to lose. This day, he had honor to gain.

14

ERROR STOLE JESSAN'S BREATH AWAY. HIS HANDS LOST ALL FEELING, WENT numb. Tremors shook his body, his mouth dried, his tongue felt swollen. The Vrykyl of Jessan's nightmares walked toward him, his black-armored hand extended.

"The Stone," said a voice that splintered inside Jessan, sent shards of pain shooting through him. "I know you have it. I will find it if I have to sift through your living brain until you reveal it to me."

Jessan could have told the truth, that he didn't have the Stone, that Bashae carried it. He would never do so. Fear gnawed his bones, but it couldn't consume his heart. For generations, the Trevenici have watched over the pecwae, the small, gentle people who rely on the stronger humans. It was then, in that moment of terror, that Jessan's true name came to him. He might never have the chance to speak that name aloud, nor hear others do so. No one would ever know it. No one but him. At least he would die having achieved his name.

Defender.

Gripping the blood knife, Jessan gave a ragged cry and lunged at his foe. He attacked in cold blood. He had no thought of defeating the evil being. A knife made of bone could not penetrate armor made of metal. He hoped to goad the Vrykyl into slaying him quickly so that he could never be made to betray those who looked to him for protection.

Expecting the blade to shatter when it struck the Vrykyl's breast plate, Jessan was astonished past belief to feel the blade slide through the black metal. The Vrykyl flinched beneath Jessan's hand, as if the blade had pierced warm flesh.

Shakur felt pain, physical pain. Two hundred years ago, Dagnarus's hand wielding the Dagger of the Vrykyl struck Shakur in the back. He'd felt pain, tortured, searing agony that was unendurable. He'd been glad to die then, only to find that death's sweet oblivion had been denied him. The pain of that knowledge had been greater agony than the pain of the Dagger and now he felt the same. The bone knife struck to the core of Shakur's being. Acting as a lightning rod, the Void magic of the knife began to dissipate the Void magic that held together Shakur's existence.

A voice within him whispered to Shakur to let the knife drain him of the magic, to flow with it into the quiet darkness. A roar of fury drowned out the whisper. This boy, this mortal, this human insect had dared defy Shakur, had dared to try to destroy him.

The bone knife remained embedded in Shakur's chest. Jessan clutched the hilt, tried to drive it deeper. Shakur wrapped his hand around Jessan's, held him fast. With an immense effort of will, Shakur managed to turn the flow of Void magic, so that it no longer drained him.

The magic sought to drain Jessan.

Jessan screamed and writhed. He felt his life seeping away from him and struggled frantically to let go of the knife. Shakur held him fast in a bone-crushing grip.

Pain burned through Shakur's arm. He had forgotten the other warriors. Glowering around, he saw another human attacking him, a Nimorean, who wielded a slender curved blade that gleamed with a burning light. Only a blade blessed by the gods can do damage to a Vrykyl and this was such a blade. The Nimorean struck again, trying to force Shakur to release his hold on the young man.

Shakur ignored it. The pain was as a bee sting to him. Then he felt another blow, this one in his back and this time the pain was far worse. Grunting, still keeping his hold on Jessan, Shakur swung around.

The cursed Dominion Lord. He hadn't had time to properly finish her. He would destroy the young human, suck out his soul as a cat sucks a baby's breath, then he would deal with the rest.

The Dominion Lord struck him again. Shakur gasped and shuddered, but he held fast to Jessan. He was about to kill the Dominion Lord, blast her into obliteration, when a wind gust powerful as the sirocco hit Shakur, struck him with the force of a mailed fist. Seven of the Wyred advanced on him, their hands locked together, their eyes glittering inside the black markings of the tattoos. He felt their magic, felt the fury of the gods pent up, an indrawn breath, eager for release, eager to destroy him.

In his human form, Shakur had always known when to give in to superior odds, when to desert the battle, when to surrender in order to be able to continue the fight another day. He released the young Trevenici. Jessan fell to the ground. Shakur hoped he wasn't dead. Plucking the bone knife from his chest, Shakur tossed it contemptuously on the limp body of the young man.

"The curse stays with you," Shakur said. "As do I."

Invoking his power, the Vrykyl became one with the Void. He was nothing. He was empty. A shadow had more substance than Shakur. He vanished.

Damra killed the remaining human mercenary. Arim bent over Jessan, felt for a pulse. The Wyred ceased their spell-casting.

"Search for the Void creature," said their leader.

Two departed. The leader sent the others back to the Portal, while she looked in the direction of the Outer Ring. The sounds of battle came from all around them—the thunk of rocks flung from mangonels striking the towers, the screams of the wounded and dying, the strange howling of the monstrous enemy.

The Wyred turned to Damra.

"Dominion Lord, the Vrykyl came for you. We have to wonder why."

"Are the pecwae safe?" Damra asked, avoiding the question. She was exhausted, drained. The horror of her encounter left her shaken, barely able to think. Yet, she had to remain focused. She had to concentrate, determine her next move.

"They are safe," said the Wyred, and she eyed Damra intently. "For the time being, at least." Her gaze went to the Outer Ring, returned again to Damra. "You travel in strange company, Dominion Lord."

"With whom I travel is my business, not yours," Damra said, wearily sheathing her sword.

She did not think Bashae would reveal his secret to the Wyred, for they must have surely questioned the pecwae, but she could not be sure. The Wyred could be daunting, when they chose. Glad to have an excuse to avoid talking to the Wyred, she knelt down beside Jessan. Her action was rude, but then one could be rude to the Wyred. They were used to it.

"How is the young man?" Damra asked Arim. "I fear he has taken mortal harm."

"His pulse was weak at first, but it grows stronger. He's a tough one, this Trevenici. Some bones in his hand are broken, and he has lost blood from these cuts, but he will live."

Jessan stirred, his eyelids fluttered, then flared open. Giving a hollow cry of terror, he sat bolt upright, clutched at Arim's throat.

"Your foe is gone," Arim said, taking hold of Jessan by the shoulders and giving him a shake to bring him to his senses.

Jessan gasped in pain. Drawing back his injured hand, he cradled it in his arm. He looked around, shuddering. "What happened? Where did he go?"

"Back to the darkness that spawned him," Damra said. "That was a brave act, young man. I have never seen one so brave. Or so foolish." She smiled, to take the sting from her words. "He very nearly killed me. You saved my life."

Jessan flushed with pleasure at her praise, but he was bound to be honest. A true warrior knows his own worth, has no need to lie. "I wasn't brave. I was . . ." Jessan thought back, shivered at the memory. "I don't know what I was. I couldn't let him hurt Bashae. Where are they? The Grandmother and Bashae. Are they all right?"

Damra glanced obliquely at the Wyred, who undoubtedly had her ears stretched to hear every word.

"They're safe. They're waiting for us in the garden. Can you walk? If we stay much longer we're liable to find ourselves in the middle of a war. Once we reach the other side of the Portal, we'll have time to tend to your wounds. Both of you," she added, as Arim wrapped a strip of cloth torn from his shirt around a bloody gash on his upper arm.

"I can walk," Jessan stated as he would have stated if he'd had both legs hacked off.

He rose to his feet, wobbling slightly, but able to move under his own power.

"Here are our passes," Damra said, showing them to the Wyred. "We expect to enter the Portal without difficulty. Thank you for your help against the Vrykyl," she added grudgingly. She did not like to be beholden to House Wyval in anything.

Bowing to the Wyred, Damra started off at a moderate pace, keeping an anxious watch on Jessan. Shaking off his own horror of his encounter with the Vrykyl, he grew stronger with every step he took and Damra started to think that they might escape safely yet, when, to her ire, the Wyred began to walk alongside her.

"We don't want to take you from your duties," Damra said.

"Our defenses are in place," the Wyred replied. "We have done all we can. There are thousands of those creatures, all of them adept in the use of Void magic. We did not expect that."

"The Shield didn't think to mention it to you?" Damra retorted. "I can't imagine why."

As they entered the garden, Bashae came hurrying to Jessan.

"Are you hurt?" Bashae asked anxiously. "Here, let me see."

He took hold of Jessan's injured hand, examined it.

"That's my sword hand," said Jessan, clearly worried. "Can you heal it?"

"We have no time for healing," Arim said sternly. "We keep moving. Time for that later."

Bashae ignored him, continued to examine Jessan's hand. "Yes," he said, after a moment, "but not all at once and not here." He looked up. "Arim's right. We should go someplace quiet."

The Wyred turned to confront Damra, stood blocking her path.

"I could stop you from entering," said the Wyred.

"You could try," said Damra. "And what good will a battle between the two of us accomplish, except to give our enemies a belly laugh."

"The Portal is about to be overrun. You are a Dominion Lord. Your sword and your magic could be of help to us. If the Portal falls, the elven nation will be at risk."

"The Shield should have thought about that before he withdrew the Portal's defenders," Damra said sharply. "Do you really think he knew nothing about this army? Are you that gullible? Of course, he knew. He's made some deal with these humans. He's giving them what amounts to safe passage through the elven Portal, passage paid for with elven blood."

"The Shield is wise—" The Wyred began the old litany and then she stopped, fell silent.

Damra pitied the woman. She and the rest were the innocent victims of their master's perfidy, and perhaps they were just starting to figure that out.

"I would help you if I could," Damra said, her voice softening. "Despite the fact that your people were involved in the abduction of my husband." Seeing the Wyred's eyes flicker, she knew she'd struck the black center of the target. "But I have my own battle to fight, my own war to wage."

"Against the Shield," said the Wyred coldly.

"No," said Damra. She pointed back into the courtyard. "Against that Vrykyl, against creatures of the Void like that. They are the true enemy. Someday, the ancestors willing, we will all of us understand that and stop making war against each other."

"You live in a very pretty world, Dominion Lord," the Wyred said. "I wonder for how long."

Turning in anger, she stalked away.

"I wonder that myself," Damra admitted somberly. "Not long if we stay here. That can wait," she said firmly, jostling the Grandmother, who was knee deep in some sort of pecwae ritual, to judge by the screeching. They ran for the Portal, an oval of shimmering gray against a backdrop of trees and flowering bushes. They had almost reached it when they heard the howling sounds behind them grow in intensity and volume. Damra glanced over her shoulder. Hordes of taan ran across the courtyard, coming straight for them.

"Hurry!" she gasped. "The Vrykyl has sent them after us—"

A violent blast of wind tore the words from her mouth. The trees around the Portal dissolved, the flowers vanished. The gust was so strong that it knocked the pecwae off their feet. Bashae slammed into Jessan. Arim grabbed the Grandmother as she went flying past him, held fast to her while the wind threatened to tear her from his grasp.

The sky took on an eerie orange tinge. The garden disappeared and they stood in a desert landscape. Sand swirled around them, stinging their flesh and gumming their eyes, choking them. The magical helm of the Dominion Lord covered Damra's face, protected her from the worst of the sandstorm.

Jessan was bowed almost double. His long hair streamed behind him. He gripped Bashae with one hand, covered his eyes with the other. Buffeted by the wind, Arim held onto the Grandmother, who had wrapped herself around him like a scarf around a tree trunk. He shouted something at Damra, but she couldn't hear a word over the blasting wind.

"Lock hands!" she cried.

They couldn't hear her, but they could see her. The magical armor gleamed silver amidst the strange gray-orange darkness. Jessan grunted in pain as Bashae grabbed his broken hand, but he kept his hold. Linked together, they staggered toward the Portal. Damra was the only one who could see it. The rest could not lift their heads, but stumbled after her like a group of blind beggars.

Swirling sand obscured Damra's view, left her nearly as blind as the rest. She kept to her course, fixed her eyes on the location where she'd last seen the Portal. She watched for some sign of it, her eyes watering with the strain. Fear grew in her that they had missed it, that they wandered aimlessly.

She kept going in the direction she'd last seen the Portal, though the swirling sand soon had her dizzy and confused. Her strength started to wane. Those clinging to her were a dead weight. Grimly, she forged ahead. She thought she caught a glimpse of the Portal, a flash of gray, and the next moment, the winds parted the sand. The Portal appeared, right in front of them. With a sigh of relief, she plunged inside, half carried, half dragged the others with her.

The Portal's quiet enveloped them, blotted out the sounds of whipping wind and the eerie shriek made by the blasting sand. By mutual, unspoken consent, they halted just inside. Tears streamed down Bashae's grimy cheeks. He coughed and spluttered, but he held fast to the knapsack. Arim blinked his eyes and tried to free himself of the Grandmother's clutching hands. Her eyes were squinched tightly shut, she refused to open them. Jessan spit sand and looked ruefully at his bare arms, bleeding from a myriad tiny cuts, as if he'd been rubbed all over with salt. His hand was swollen, the fingers bent at odd angles.

"How long can the Wyred keep that up?" Arim asked, his voice rasping, his throat raw. He finally managed to pry loose the Grandmother's fingers.

"Depends on how many are spell-casting," Damra replied. "Several hours, perhaps. Not much longer."

"Still, that gives you time to reach the other side safely," said Arim.

"Yes, but we should not—" Damra stopped speaking. She'd just realized what he'd said.

Tearing a long strip of cloth from his shirt, Arim wound it around his nose and mouth.

"Arim, you can't go back out there," Damra said, appalled. "You heard the Wyred. There are thousands of those monsters—"

Arim's eyes gleamed. "I'm not a fool, Damra," he said, his voice muffled. "I don't plan to fight unless I have to. I'll slip away in the confusion, return to my home. I must bring word of this to my Queen. This war is not just among the elves."

"Arim," said Damra softly, shifting to elven, "you cannot do this. You will be throwing away your life. You cannot hope to win through—"

"I must try, Damra," said Arim quietly. "I must try. Give Griffith my warmest affection. The Mother and Father guard you."

"Arim," she began, but saw that arguing would be useless. She clasped her friend's hands, gave him a kiss on both cheeks. "The ancestors watch over you, Arim."

He turned to Jessan, whose face was gray with pain, and the two pecwae, who were staring at him in dismay.

"Where do you think you're going?" the Grandmother demanded.

"Back to my homeland," Arim said. "Someday, you will go back safely to yours. That is my dearest wish for each of you. Jessan, you are a valiant warrior. More than that, you have taught me the wisdom of the gods. If I had followed the thinking of my head and sent you and the blood knife away, we would all be dead now."

"I count you my friend. If you come to Trevenici lands," said Jessan, "you will be an honored guest in my house."

Arim bowed, touched. The gift of his friendship is the greatest gift a Trevenici has to bestow. Arim turned to Bashae.

"The gods chose well. You have proven a brave and true bearer."

"Thank you, Arim," said Bashae. That seemed so inadequate, but he didn't know what else to say. Certainly not the words in his heart, that were words of tears and ill omen.

"Take this, if you're set on going," said the Grandmother. Rummaging around in the pack that hung from the agate-eyed stick, she drew forth a turquoise.

"But that's one of your protection stones," Arim protested. "I couldn't take that."

"Twenty-seven, twenty-six, what's the difference?" the Grandmother said, pressing it into Arim's hand and folding his fingers around it. "You're going to need it more than I will."

Arim touched the stone reverently to his lips, clasped it tightly in his hand. "May the gods walk at your side with their arms around you."

Drawing his sword, he gave them a graceful wave and, before any of them could say another word, he ran back out of the Portal. He was immediately lost to sight in the shifting sands.

"What will happen to him?" Bashae asked. He stared intently out the Portal, hoping to catch a final glimpse of his friend.

When Damra failed to respond, Bashae looked directly at her. "He's going to die, isn't he? He doesn't have a chance. They'll catch him and kill him."

"No, they won't," Damra said, trying to sound reassuring. "Arim the Kite Maker is strong and cunning. Someday I will tell you a story of how he survived far worse peril than this."

"He will be safe," said the Grandmother, supremely confident. "I gave him my stone."

"Your stone, Grandmother?" said Bashae, suddenly troubled. "But you still have eight more, right? Nine for me and nine for Jessan and nine for you?"

The Grandmother chortled. "Hah! As if I needed nine protecting stones. There were thirteen for you and thirteen for him"—she jabbed her finger at Jessan—"and one for me. And I didn't really need it. He does." She gave an abrupt nod in the direction Arim had taken. "Foolhardy, that one," she said softly. "But he means well.

"And I won't hear another word about it," the Grandmother snapped, glowering at Bashae. She shifted the glower to Damra. "Shouldn't we be going? Or are we going to stand here and talk all day?"

"Yes, we should be going," said Damra, dispirited. She did not have much faith in the turquoise stone. "We have only a few hours to reach our destination before we find that army on our heels."

"Where are we anyway? A cave?" The Grandmother sniffed. "Doesn't smell like a cave."

"We are inside one of the magical Portals," Damra replied, shepherding her brood down the path.

The Grandmother's eyes widened. "A Portal," she repeated to herself in Twithil. She raised the agate-eyed stick. "Take a good look, boys. You won't see the like again."

"I can help your hand now," said Bashae to Jessan. "I can't set the bones, but I can ease the pain. We'll have to do this while we walk, so try to hold steady."

Jessan cradled his injured hand, while Bashae removed some green and red stones from his pouch. Carefully, muttering to himself, Bashae placed the bloodstones in the palm of Jessan's broken hand.

"Does that feel better?" he asked, eyeing it with the air of an expert. "Look, the swelling's going down. I'll set the bones when we stop for the night. Try not to move it, if you can."

"It does feel better," Jessan said. "Thanks." He paused a moment, then he said, almost shyly, "I have my adult name. It came to me when I fought the Vrykyl."

"Do you?" Bashae asked, pleased for his friend. "What is it?"

"Defender," said Jessan gruffly.

"It's kind of plain," Bashae said, disappointed. "Not like Chop-Their-

Heads or Ale Guzzler. Do you think you might get a better one? Something a little more exciting?"

Jessan shook his head. "I like this one."

"Well, all right. Should I call you Defender from now on instead of Jessan? It might take some getting used to."

"Not yet. The tribe has to decide if it is suitable."

"Good," Bashae said, relieved. "In the meantime, keep a look-out for another name, just in case."

Jessan didn't say anything to dash Bashae's hopes. Jessan knew he'd found his name. What he had to do now was to live up to it. He looked down at the bone knife, still at his side. The knife had saved his life and nearly cost him his life. Involuntarily, his hand closed over the hilt and he felt once again the blade stabbing through the armor of the Vrykyl. He felt the knife squirm in his hand, felt the white hot fury of the Vrykyl. He felt his own life begin to seep away, flowing through the bone knife to fill the Vrykyl's awful emptiness.

Jessan shuddered, a shudder that began in his bowels and spread throughout his body. He was sorry he remembered it and in that moment he knew that he would never forget. Every time he looked at the blood knife, he would hear the Vrykyl's words, *The curse stays with you. As do I.*

Damra pushed them mercilessly, permitting only the briefest halts for rest and to try to hear what was going on behind them.

Hearing nothing, she urged them on.

The Portal's defenders still held, but they would not hold it for long. The illusions ended. The Wyred fought their own battles in the Inner Ring. The elves had abandoned the gate, retreating back into the towers that stood in the Outer Ring. Once inside, the elves retracted the walkways that led from the towers to the walls and sealed up the doors that were located some six feet above ground level.

The elves who were holed up in the towers gained a brief respite. The taan did not immediately attack them. Lyall could not figure out why, at first, then the answer was obvious. The enemy commander had them trapped like rats. He had no need to bother with them. They could do him no harm. He held the Outer Ring and he sent his troops pouring through the gate and into the Inner Ring. Elven archers manned the murder holes, fired at the creatures as they moved past in a solid mass, thousands of them. The elves might hit one or two or twenty, but what was that? Like trying to drink the ocean dry a drop at a time. The archers were running short of arrows and Lyall ordered them to cease fire. They'd need what remained for the final assault.

He understood the enemy's plan clearly. Move the main body through the Portal. Leave behind a small force to mop up.

Lyall sat with his back against the wall, an apt pose, he thought to himself. He was wounded, but then so was every elf in the tower. The floor was slippery with their blood. He watched one warrior die before his eyes. The soldier made no sound, he did not groan, did not speak. Lyall hadn't even known the man was wounded until he looked over and saw the dead man's eyes frozen in his head.

"Sir!" One of the men roused him. "You should come see this."

Lyall rose stiffly to his feet, grimacing in pain, and limped over to the slit in the wall.

The warrior pointed. Several of the taan had broken away from the main body of the army and were walking toward the tower. They did not wear armor, but were clad in black robes. Some sort of strange ceremonial headgear covered their hideous faces.

"Shoot them," said Lyall immediately. "Don't let them come near."

He stepped back to allow the archers to come forward. The elves fired their precious arrows, taking their time, hoping to make every shot tell.

One taan shaman reached up a taloned hand and caught an arrow in mid-flight, plucked it out of the air. An arrow struck another taan in the chest, only to disappear in a flash of fire. The elves continued firing and an archer hit her mark. A shaman fell backward, clutching at an arrow in his throat, strangling on his own blood.

"An argent to the archer!" called out Lyall.

The elves cheered, but the cheering didn't last long. The surviving shamans paid no attention to their fallen comrade. Halting their advance, they raised their voices in an eerie-sounding wail. The elves increased their fire in order to try to stop the spell-casting, but had little success. The creatures were oblivious to the arrows, oblivious to the danger. One took an arrow in the thigh, but never missed a beat.

The elves waited tensely for the spell—earthquake, cracks in the stone, walls turning to mud. Such were the magic spells humans used.

Nothing happened.

The elves began to laugh. One said it reminded him of children playing at being wizards. Another said it reminded him of lizards playing at being wizards and that drew an even bigger laugh. Lyall smiled, but he did not join in the mirth. These creatures, hideous and bestial as they might appear, were in deadly earnest. There was a malevolent intelligence in the voices and in the eyes that was truly frightening.

Lyall felt a sudden tightness in his chest, as if he couldn't get enough air. He drew in a deep breath and was forced to work at it. He had to struggle to draw in another. Around him, his soldiers gasped for breath. They stared at him and at each other with dawning horror in their eyes.

The magic was sucking the air from the tower.

Lyall's chest burned. Starbursts stung his eyes. His soldiers slumped to the floor. Hoping to find air, Lyall staggered toward one of the slit windows. He could not make it. He sank to his knees. Pressing his hands against his chest, he gasped, panic-stricken, for the air he knew would not come.

"I hope it has been worth it . . ." was the last thought in his mind.

Several miles distant, high on a hilltop that overlooked the Portal, a thousand elven foot soldiers and a hundred mounted knights stood at the ready, watching, waiting. The elves wore armor that had been dipped in black paint. They carried a banner draped in black cloth. The trappings of the knights' horses were black. Their swords were sheathed in black, their spears and arrows were tipped in black. Soldiers and officers wore masks of black silk over their faces. Their hands were wrapped in black, their boots muffled in black. Theirs was a ghostly force, aligned with night's shadows. Those few taan scouts who had stumbled upon them were terrified, for to them it seemed that the darkness came to life.

The taan called out, "Hrl'Kenk, Hrl'Kenk," naming their ancient god of darkness. The elves had no knowledge of that, nor did they care what the taan said. The elves made short work of the creatures, ended the taans' cries by slitting their throats.

The elves had an excellent view of the Portal, of the fall of the Portal. They had a good view of the immense army of taan that poured into the Portal, their numbers so vast that they were beyond counting. The elves watched the enemy kill the pitiful few elves left to defend it. They watched the taan establish their defenses, then form into orderly ranks and march through the Portal. This took hours and by the time the last few started marching through the battered gate, dusk had fallen.

Smug in victory, General Gurske had not given any thought to attempting to repair that gate.

The elven officer, a young man, but already tested and proven in battle, smiled to see the great iron doors hanging off their hinges.

"So Grandfather said it would happen." His voice was grim. He did not take his eyes from the Portal.

"Do we ride?" asked his lieutenant. She found it hard to watch brave men die, even those who belonged to the House of her enemy.

"Not yet, but soon," said the commander. "We will let the main body of the army get well inside the Portal first."

"How many has he left to guard it, do you suppose?" the lieutenant asked.

"Not many," said the commander. "A few hundred. No more. All humans."

"Are you certain?" The lieutenant was skeptical. "We have heard that this Dagnarus is an able commander. Surely he would leave a large number to defend his only means of retreat."

"He will need all the troops he has with him and more to mount an assault against the city of New Vinnengael. That is his true target. And why not? Dagnarus imagines that he is safe, that there is no enemy within a thousand miles of him. For so the Shield has promised him."

The elves waited, continued to watch the Portal. Night stole across the land, the stars came out, the moon rose. Where this morning there had been the grating, clashing sounds of battle, now came the sounds of men celebrating their victory. The humans lit fires in the courtyard. The elves could see the soldiers silhouetted against the flames, coming and going with bottles in their hands. They heard drunken laughter.

Elven scouts returned to report that the humans had thrown some timbers across the broken gate to try to bolster it. A few guards walked the walls, bottles in their hands.

"They think themselves safe," said a scout.

The commander mounted his horse, a black destrier that he had bought in the human lands where he had been exiled for a hundred years. He turned to face his troops. Rising up in his stirrups, so that all could see him, he lifted his voice so that all could hear.

"We ride this night to restore the honor of our House."

Lifting his hand to the black mask that covered his face, the young man ripped off the mask, proudly revealed his tattoo, his lineage. He held his mask high in the air.

"Kinnoth!" he shouted.

"Kinnoth!" came the shout back.

Every elven warrior took hold of the mask of shame concealing the tattoos that marked him as belonging to that disgraced House and tore it off.

The standard bearer removed the black cloth from the banner of House Kinnoth. The wind caught hold of the banner and it rippled in the night air. The elves were heartened, for the wind is known to be the breath of the gods.

The young officer motioned to his squire, who brought forth a cloth and a bucket of water. The commander dipped the silk mask into the water. Raising the wet silk to the heavens, he then washed the black paint from his breastplate. The emblem of House Kinnoth gleamed white in the moonlight. This done, he held his hand poised high in the air, the black mask fluttering from his fingers. He dropped the mask and spurred his horse. He rode in the vanguard, his knights followed, charging down the hill. The foot soldiers came surging after. They sang no song, they shouted no battle cry.

Many elves of House Kinnoth would die this night, but they would die with honor, for the first time in two centuries.

BOOK

III

DAMRA AND HER COMPANIONS EMERGED FROM THE PORTAL INTO THE eastern fortress that guarded it. She was tense and nervous, not knowing what to expect—more questions, certainly, or perhaps a battle with the guards of House Wyval. She did not expect to find the Portal deserted.

No guards remained inside the vast fortress. The magic that had defended the Inner Ring had been lifted. No soldiers walked the ramparts. Everything was in disorder and disarray—papers still burned in the fire pits, half-eaten was food left on the table. Evidence that the elves had departed in haste. Either the Shield had ordered them to leave or they had made that decision themselves, on hearing reports of the army that was then marching through the Portal.

The silence of the empty fortress was unnerving. Damra did not linger. She and those in her care must put as many miles between them and the approaching army as possible.

She had hoped to borrow horses, but no horses remained and it was at that point she very nearly gave up. She was exhausted, as were the human and the pecwae. The Grandmother was gray with fatigue. She stumbled as she walked. Bashae yawned and blinked like an owl in the sunlight. Jessan made no complaint, but twice Bashae had been forced to put more healing stones on the young man's hand to help ease his pain.

"We cannot go much farther," Damra said to herself. "Yet we have to. We dare not stay here."

The eastern end of the Portal was located in the side of a mountain. A broad highway led from the fortress that surrounded the Portal to a valley below, not far from the headwaters of Arven river, where the elves had built a large harbor. Commerce in and out of the Portal traveled by boat.

Damra trudged wearily along the highway, wondering if it were actu-

ally possible to fall asleep on one's feet. She had about come to the conclusion that it was, when Jessan jostled her arm.

"What?" Damra lifted her head.

Jessan pointed. Four elves had ridden out of the woods. They did not
approach, but remained at the edge of the highway, watching her, waiting
for her to come level with them.

Damra eyed them warily. Were these the Shield's men? She recognized
the ritual masks, but those didn't tell her much about their allegiance, for
one was from House Tanath, another from a minor House, Hlae, and two
more were from another minor House, Sith-ma-Oesa. Any of those
Houses might be allied with the Shield.

Cautiously, hand hovering near her sword hilt, she continued on her
way. Coming near, she was about to give the requisite polite greeting and
keep going, but one of the elves urged his horse out from the woods to
block her path. She had no choice but to halt.

"Dominion Lord," he said, addressing her in respectful tones. "You and
your friends have come a long way. You must be hungry and tired. Our
master extends an invitation for you to rest and refresh yourselves at his
manor."

Damra was too exhausted to take the time for polite nothings. She
pointed behind her. "An army of creatures the likes of which have not
been seen in this world is coming through that Portal. Do you know that?"

"Yes," the elf said, "so we heard from the sons of cowards of House
Wyval who fled with their tails tucked between their legs. All the more
reason you should take advantage of our master's hospitality."

"Who is your master?" Damra asked.

"The Baron Shadamehr," the elf replied.

The elves had not brought extra horses, but two elves offered theirs,
saying that they had orders to stay behind, to see what this famous army
might do. Damra wondered how they planned to remain alive long
enough to report once they'd seen the army, but they did not seem concerned. She concluded that they must have some other means of transportation hidden away in the forest—hippogriffs, perhaps.

Mounting the horses, they rode to the harbor, where they boarded long
boats. Damra knew nothing of the journey. Lulled by the lapping of the
water and the knowledge that for once she was not expected to be in control of the situation, she fell asleep.

She woke to another ride overland and then a climb up the steep slope
of a cliff-face known, she was told, as the Imperial Escarpment. Above her,
she saw a castle, a towering structure of gray rock that seemed to float
among the clouds, for it was built on the highest point for miles around.

"What is that place?" she asked.

"Shadamehr's Keep," was the reply.

*   *   *

As Damra rode nearer to Shadamehr's Keep, Ulaf—once known many months ago as Brother Ulaf—was wandering about the bailey of the Keep, searching for his lord and master.

"Where is Shadamehr?" Ulaf demanded of everyone he met.

"I haven't seen him," was the invariable answer.

At last, Ulaf found a stable-hand, who made a vague gesture in the direction of the Keep. "I saw him go in there, but that was hours past. He came round to the stable, asking for all the rope we had on hand."

"Rope?" Ulaf repeated, puzzled. "What did he want rope for?"

The stable-hand shrugged and grinned. "You know his lordship."

"Indeed I do," muttered Ulaf. "All too well."

He hastened off across the stable yard, heading in the direction of an enormous castle that was known throughout the Vinnengaelean empire—sometimes with curses, sometimes with praise—as Shadamehr's Keep.

Built on the Imperial Escarpment that runs east of the Mehr Mountains, the original Keep had consisted of four walls, two towers and a gate. Constructed in the year 542, twenty years after the fall of Old Vinnengael and ten years after the founding of the city of New Vinnengael, the Keep stood at a strategic point in the northern part of the Vinnengaelean Empire, only about two hundred miles from the eastern end of the Tromek Portal.

Even back then, the Shadamehrs were considered to be "eccentric." The first Earl of Shadamehr had been an impoverished knight serving in the household of King Hegemon. Having nothing to give His Majesty except blood, Lord Shadamehr cheerfully shed that for His Majesty's cause during the Battle of the Plains, the war started by the dwarves when they discovered that the humans intended to build their new capital on land claimed by the dwarves.

Such was his heroism in battle—he saved the king's life—that Lord Shadamehr was named Baron Shadamehr and given an earldom. Instead of choosing land around the proposed city, as everyone else was doing, the Baron declared that he had seen a site not far from the elven border to the north that looked to him to be an excellent place to build a castle. He was very nearly laughed out of court, for there was nothing to the north but elves and giants, and relations were not so good with either that any man would choose to willingly live near them.

The king had tried to persuade Baron Shadamehr to accept an earldom that was more valuable, but the Baron persisted in his desire and, finally, the king gave in. Loading up several boats with men and supplies, the Baron traveled up the Arven, looking for a good place to build his Keep. He found it on a steep cliff about thirty miles from the headwaters of the

Arven. The escarpment being highly defensible, the baron set about building his castle.

A short time later, the elves announced that they had discovered a Portal through their lands, the eastern entrance of which Portal was within a day's ride of the Vinnengaelean border. Relations between humans and elves improved markedly when elven merchants began to clamor that they wanted to take their goods into the wealthy city of New Vinnengael. The river provided easy access. The Baron established an outpost on the river and charged a modest fee to those passing through his lands. The merchants might have balked at this, but, in return, Baron Shadamehr took care that river travelers were not molested by giants, dwarves or other nuisances. He was known to be a man of honor, whose word was good on anything, and even the elves spoke of him with grudging respect.

Certain envious barons, who watched the Earl grow wealthy almost overnight, said spitefully that Shadamehr must have known of the existence of the Portal in advance and that, if so, he should have told the king. Shadamehr would never say yea or nay to this, but since he always gave generously to the king whenever His Majesty was in need of funds, the king was not one to press the issue.

The Shadamehrs continued their eccentric ways down through the ages, scandalizing the New Vinnengaeleans with their outlandish mode of life. They married for love, not for money, for they had plenty of that. They raised healthy children who went out into the world and made names for themselves and were invariably loyal and loving to each other, disappointing those who had hoped to witness the family's disintegration.

The tolls they charged were modest. They were fair and open-handed in all their dealings.

The current Baron of Shadamehr's Keep had acted with an eccentricity that broke all previously held family records. A man known to everyone to be generous, brave, intelligent (some said too intelligent for his own good), and noble, he had been granted the very great honor of being permitted to take the tests to become a Dominion Lord. Shadamehr had taken the tests. He had passed them with ease, but for a few minor problems, dealing mainly with his tendency to speak a bit too lightly of the gods and to burst into laughter at solemn moments. He had been granted the right to undergo the Transfiguration. Everything was in preparation for the ceremony when, at the last moment, Shadamehr refused to take it, something no one had ever done in the glorious history of the Dominion Lords.

Shadamehr had a blazing row with the Council of Dominion Lords and another blazing row with the king, during which the Baron was stripped of his Earldom and ordered to cede his lands to the crown. Shadamehr responded by seceding. He removed his lands from under Vinnengaelean control, declared himself to be an independent nation, and challenged anyone to try to take his Keep from him. He then departed in high dudgeon.

The king in his fury did send one force to try to take the Keep, but his knights and barons, many of whom were friends of Shadamehr, either refused outright to fight or did so half-heartedly. The battle was a dismal failure. The king decided that it would be prudent from then on to simply ignore Shadamehr and pretend he didn't exist.

Some said that after his own wrath cooled, Shadamehr felt badly about the way he'd acted. He did not feel badly about refusing to undergo the Transfiguration. He rarely spoke of it, but when he did, he always made it clear that he had no regrets. He felt badly about severing his ties with the people of New Vinnengael and it was then that he began to do what he could to make reparation, to try to increase the safety and security of his people.

His interest in humanity began to extend to the rest of the world, to other races. He saw that the world could be a much better place if people would only learn to live together in peace. Most people thought this, or at least claimed to think it, but Shadamehr, with true eccentricity, decided that he would do something about it. He set about recruiting people of all races to help him attain this goal and whenever he heard rumors of war or discord, he sent in his agents to observe and report so that he might be able to do something to help defuse the situation. Sometimes he succeeded, other times he did not, but he never gave up hope.

The Keep was now a rambling structure that sprawled over the cliff face, various Shadamehrs having built towers, erected walls and added wings with little regard for fashion or architectural design. One Baron had been fond of spires and there were lots of these, sticking up all over the place, adding an air of whimsy to the building. Another Baron had taken a fancy to flying buttresses, while a third had delighted in stained-glass windows. The Keep was always bustling with activity, with agents and friends coming and going at all hours of the day and night.

Ulaf passed a group of orks gathered around their shaman, looking at him anxiously as he read the omens of some incident that had apparently just occurred, for more orks were coming at a run to hear the outcome. Ulaf glanced into the circle of large bodies, trying to see what was causing all the furor.

The orks were staring in consternation at a cat that had a live mouse in her mouth. Orks are fond of cats. Orks consider cats lucky and woe betide anyone who harms a cat in the presence of an ork. Whether or not this cat with the mouse was a good omen or a bad one, Ulaf couldn't tell. Ordinarily he would have stopped to ask, for he found orken superstitions highly diverting, but this day he had news of too much urgency to wait.

He entered the south door that was one of six leading into the Keep's main hall, an enormous chamber hung with tapestries and banners. A fire pit stood in the center. The ceiling was spanned by large beams, blackened from decades of smoke. The sun shining through the stained-glass windows made colorful splashes on the floor. The chamber echoed with the sound of raised voices and clashing steel. Several young knights practiced at swordplay in one corner, while a different group argued philosophy in another.

Or perhaps, Ulaf thought, those with the swords are arguing philosophy. Skirting both groups, he nabbed a young squire, who was watching the combatants with envy, and asked if he had seen Lord Shadamehr.

"I saw him go up the stairs with several large coils of rope," the squire reported. He had to repeat himself twice before Ulaf could hear over the uproar.

"What stairs?" Ulaf bawled, for there were as many staircases as there were entrances and each led to a different part of the castle.

The squire pointed. Ulaf wound his way up a staircase that carried the climber to the hall's third story. Having lived here off and on for five years, Ulaf could still get turned around. Reaching the top of the stairs, he searched the area, trying to regain his bearings and hoping to find Shadamehr.

He saw no sign of his lord, but he did recognize where he was. This corridor led to the Baron's private quarters. Several of his long-time friends had their sleeping rooms here, to be nearby in case they were needed.

Shadamehr's own bedchamber was at the end of this hallway. Cluttered with books and chests overflowing with all sorts of oddities he'd collected in his travels, the floor was strewn with his clothes, for he could never be bothered to take the time to put anything away and he refused to permit servants to go around "picking up after me."

Shadamehr was an energetic soul. Not much given to sleep and fond of study, he was known to beat upon someone's door in the still, dead hours of the night if he thought the person might provide him with an answer to one of his endless questions.

The room belonging to Shadamehr's seneschal, the long-suffering Rodney, was on this floor. Ulaf peered in through the open door, but Rodney of the Keep, as he was known, was not in his room, nor did Ulaf really expect him to be. Responsible for handling the vast estate and all that went with it, Rodney rarely saw the interior of his bedroom. It was often joked that there must be two or three of Rodney, for he was always to be found exactly where he was supposed to be, whenever anyone wanted him.

Two of the other rooms on the floor were occupied by members of the Revered Order of Magi. One room belonged to Rigiswald, who had been Shadamehr's tutor when he was young and was now his adviser and counselor. A dapper and polished old man with a neatly clipped, very black beard of which he was vain and which most believed he dyed, the sharp-tongued old man was the most feared person in the establishment. Ulaf hoped to goodness Shadamehr wasn't keeping company with his tutor, for then Ulaf would have to interrupt them, and while he had faced down many a monster during his travels through Loerem, he dreaded few things more in this world than a tongue-lashing from Rigiswald.

The mage's door was open. Ulaf peeped cautiously inside. The dour old man reclined in a chair near the fire with a goblet of wine in one hand and a book in the other. He was alone. Breathing a sigh of relief, Ulaf crept past.

The other room belonged to Alise, another member of the Revered Order of Magi and a long-time friend of Lord Shadamehr's. If Rigiswald was the most feared person in the household, Alise was the most loved. Almost every man who came into Lord Shadamehr's service found themselves dreaming of her fiery red hair and her vibrant green eyes. Shadamehr was not married and neither was Alise. There was much speculation about whether or not they were lovers and money had changed hands on the matter. No one had yet won or lost the bet, for if they were lovers, they were incredibly discreet. Ulaf tended to think they weren't, for he sometimes saw Alise look at Shadamehr with something in her eyes that was loving and at the same time not.

Ulaf concluded that Shadamehr must have come to visit Alise, for none of the other rooms in this wing was currently occupied. Alise's door was closed, however.

Wondering if the rumors were true, not wanting to disturb them if they happened to be together, Ulaf put his ear to the door. He didn't hear anything. He hesitated, but the news was really extremely important. Ulaf started to knock.

A strong hand clapped over Ulaf's mouth. A strong arm collared him and hauled him bodily across the hall, dragged him into the shadow of an enormous granite column.

"Don't say a word!" a voice spoke harshly in his ear, then added, "Promise?"

Ulaf couldn't speak, for the hand clamped shut his mouth, but he nodded. The hand slowly released its grip. Ulaf turned, glowering.

"You damn near gave me heart failure!"

Shadamehr raised a finger, pressed it against Ulaf's lips. "Shh! You promised." He pointed across the hall. "Watch!"

"My lord, I've been searching for you everywhere. I have urgent—"

Shadamehr shook his head. "Not now. Watch!" he intoned.

They heard the sound of footsteps, the gentle swish of a hemline on the floor, a woman's voice singing softly to herself an old folk tune.

Shadamehr's eyes glistened. He pulled Ulaf deeper into the shadows. "Keep your eyes on the door!" he breathed into Ulaf's ear.

Fuming, but knowing that the best way to accomplish his mission was to humor his lord, Ulaf did as he was told.

Alise walked to her door. Raising her hand, she spoke several words intended to remove the magic spell that kept the door locked. Then she stopped.

"That's odd," she said to herself. "I must have forgotten to cast the spell this morning."

Shrugging, she raised the black lever, pushed gently on the door and then halted with a gasp.

She stood staring in shocked amazement as every piece of furniture in her room moved rapidly away from her. Tables, couches, chairs, her desk, an ornate floor-standing candelabra went sliding and slithering over the floor, racing across the room in a mad dash that ended with all the furniture jammed up against an open window on the far wall.

Alise's face flushed as red as her hair. Clenching her fists, she shouted in a furious voice, "Shadamehr!"

His lordship collapsed with laughter onto the floor, where he lay kicking his heels, rolling back and forth, prostrate with mirth.

Spotting him, Alise pounced, nearly knocking down Ulaf in her attempts to seize hold of her lord. "How *dare* you? How dare you? Look at the mess—"

"Stop this infernal row!" Rigiswald shouted and slammed his door shut with a boom.

Still laughing, Shadamehr fended off Alise's pummeling and managed to regain his feet. "One of my better ones, don't you think? Come along!" Seizing hold of Alise with one hand and Ulaf with the other, he dragged them into Alise's room. "I'll show you how it's done."

"My lord," Ulaf tried again, carried along not so much by physical force as by the force of his lord's enthusiasm, "I have urgent news—"

"Yes, yes, someone always has urgent news. But this," Shadamehr pointed proudly. "This is really important. Do you see how I did it? I tied a length of rope to every stick of furniture in the room and then attached all the ropes to that great rock down there." Shadamehr hauled them bodily across the room to where the furniture stood in a jumbled heap, a veritable cobweb of rope tied around the legs. "Then I attached a last piece of rope to the door. When the door is opened, the weight falls and hauls all the furniture with it. I call it, 'The Vanishing Room.' Wonderful, don't you think?"

"I *don't* think!" Alise stated, glowering, though an astute observer might have seen her lips twitched with suppressed laughter. "Who's going to clean up the mess?"

"Oh, I will," said Shadamehr. "Ulaf will help me, won't you?"

Ulaf stared helplessly at his exasperating lord, who had once been described as "a human male of middle years with a nose like a hawk's beak, a chin like an ax-blade, eyes blue as the skies above New Vinnengael and a long, black mustache of which he is very proud and is constantly smoothing or twirling." Shadamehr stood twirling that very mustache.

"My lord, will you please listen to what I have to tell you?" Ulaf said desperately.

"If it's about the elves evacuating the eastern end of the Tromek Portal because some sort of great thundering army of monsters is supposed to come crashing through it, I've already heard," Shadamehr said, patting Ulaf on the shoulder. "But thanks for coming to tell me." He continued to gaze around with pride at his handiwork. "You should have seen your face, Alise."

"You should see yours with the marks of my fingernails in it," she returned calmly.

"You know about the army?" Ulaf demanded. "What are we going to do?"

"Can't tell yet," Shadamehr said, dabbing at the scratches with the lace cuff of his shirt sleeve. "Not enough information. As Rigiswald says, it is a capital mistake to theorize before you have all the evidence. It biases the judgment. You'll just end up having to revise your plans and then you've wasted all that time."

"Instead of spending all that time tying ropes to the legs of furniture," Ulaf growled.

"It *was* funny, admit it," said Shadamehr, nudging Ulaf in the ribs.

Voices called out from down below.

"My lord, there's a large rock dangling at the end of a rope—"

"My lord, an elven Dominion Lord has arrived. She came through the Portal and she—"

"Ah," said Shadamehr with a sigh. "Now we will have our evidence."

He put his arm around Ulaf's shoulder. "Let's go hear about this army of monsters. By the way," Shadamehr added, eyeing Ulaf critically, "your tonsure's growing out quite nicely."

"Thank you, my lord," said Ulaf. He gave up. "The Vanishing Room. It *was* funny, my lord."

"One of my best," said Shadamehr.

The elves believe that in the afterlife there is a prison house where those souls who have committed some terrible crime during their lifetime are sent for punishment. The souls are kept in the prison house, for they must not be permitted to return and wield influence over the living. The prison house of the souls is said to be a place of chaos and madness, for the souls are constantly trying to free themselves. Noble warriors, who have died honorable deaths, may choose to spend their eternal lives standing guard over these souls.

Upon first entering Shadamehr's Keep, Damra felt as if she had entered that same prison house, for everywhere she looked there was chaos and madness.

Elven households are tranquil, serene. Twenty elves may live in one small dwelling place, but the visitor would never be aware of it, for the elves know how to move silently and speak softly, make themselves unobtrusive. In this castle, noise erupted around Damra. Every single person had his mouth open, shouting and hallooing, exclaiming and questioning. Twenty people made noise enough for forty.

Arriving at the main gate to this prison house of lost souls, the elven guides handed Damra and her friends over to a human named Rodney. The elves departed, saying they must return to their duties.

Rodney escorted Damra and her companions to the outer courtyard, that resembled market day in Glymrae, only more confused. Stalls and lean-tos and ramshackle buildings filled the courtyard. Cattle, pigs, sheep, horses and chickens, adults of every type and variety, children of every manner and sort bellowed, hollered, bleated, baaed, clucked or screamed. Humans unwittingly entered Damra's aura, jostled and shoved her in good-natured enthusiasm. A group of children—two humans, an elf, an ork and a dwarf—gathered around to stare with wide eyes and friendly grins at the pecwae.

Damra was on the verge of leaving, when the crowd heaved and surged. People swirled around her, a voice shouted and a gap opened up. A man walked toward her. Some in the crowd applauded him, others cheered, a few laughed and called out to him in jest. He answered glibly, waving his hand, but not stopping. Two other humans accompanied him—a red-haired human female wearing the garb of a Temple mage and a dapper mage whose face was sour as if he'd bit into a briny pickle. By the calls and shouts, this man with the long mustache must be Baron Shadamehr.

Damra thought the baron ugly, but then she thought most Vinnengaelean humans ugly, for they seemed chiseled out of rock with all the rough edges left on. She much preferred the looks of the fine-boned, glistening-skinned Nimorean humans. The baron had an undeniable air about him, however. Born to lead, he was a born leader.

She stared at him with frank curiosity. After Arim had told her the story, she remembered hearing about Baron Shadamehr—the only Dominion Lord to have ever refused to undergo the Transfiguration. He had been the talk of the Council of Dominion Lords. They were still talking, although his refusal had taken place fifteen years ago. He'd been twenty at the time. He must be now about thirty-five.

Halting in front of her, the Baron made a flourishing bow that would have looked silly in most humans but oddly suited him.

"Baron Shadamehr, at your service, Dominion Lord," he said, and he sounded respectful.

She regarded him warily, not trusting him. He had refused a gift from the gods.

He seemed not to notice her coolness or her hesitation.

"My trusted advisers, Revered Brother Rigiswald and Revered Sister Alise. Whom might we have the honor of addressing?"

"Damra of House Gwyenoc," she said.

"Jessan," said Jessan briefly. He indicated the pecwae. "Bashae and the Grandmother."

Bashae bobbed his head.

The Grandmother thrust her stick at Shadamehr, let the eyes have a good look. "They approve," she stated.

"Thank you," said Shadamehr, glancing askance at the agate eyes. "I think."

He turned back to Damra. "House Gwyenoc. That name seems familiar to me, for some reason. You weren't on the Council when I was dilly-dallying with them, were you? No, I thought not. You're one of the new ones."

Hearing the term "dilly-dallying" used in reference to becoming a Dominion Lord, Damra was shocked almost past speaking. She was determined to remove herself from this madhouse as soon as possible, but she had one pressing question.

"I am looking for a man," she began.

"Oh, we have several about," Shadamehr replied with an ingratiating smile. He waved his hand. "Take your choice."

"You don't understand," Damra said, flushing. She did not like being made sport of. "He is my hus—"

"Damra!"

A voice she knew better than her own called her name. Arms that she loved better than her own enveloped her, held her close.

"Griffith!" she whispered in a choked voice, embracing her husband.

"*That's* where I've heard her name," said Shadamehr. "Poor man's talked of nothing else since he came here."

He watched the couple cling to each other with as much pride as if he'd created them himself. Then, resting his hand gently on Griffith's arm, Shadamehr said in apologetic tones, "I'm sorry I can't give you more time to enjoy your reunion. But I really do have to ask your wife about this enemy army that may be down around our ears at any moment."

DAMRA PROVIDED SHADAMEHR WITH INFORMATION ON THE ADVANCING taan army, telling him what Silwyth had told her. She was terse and concise, speaking the truth, but adding no embellishments. She sat close to Griffith as she spoke. The two did not touch, for elves consider public displays of affection to be boorish and intrusive, but she was intensely aware of Griffith's body so near hers. Whenever she answered a question evasively, she could feel him stir as if he would speak. He chose not to, but allowed her to tell her tale uninterrupted. She told Baron Shadamehr what she had seen and heard at the Portal, mentioning the Vrykyl as a creature of the Void, but not naming it.

She thought to find these humans amazed and perplexed by her news. Although they appeared concerned, they did not seem all that surprised. The Baron exchanged glances with the young man, who had been introduced as Ulaf.

"It seems that these Vrykyl are proliferating," said Shadamehr. "One finds them everywhere one turns around."

Damra glanced sidelong at Griffith, who smiled and said to her softly, "Shadamehr has first-hand knowledge of Vrykyl."

"To my everlasting sorrow," said Shadamehr. "But tell me, Damra of Gwyenoc, why did the Vrykyl attack you? From what we know of these creatures, the Void is in the area of the heart, not the brain. This Vrykyl knew you were going through the Portal. Why not just allow you to go?"

Shadamehr spoke the question in pleasant tones with the slight edge of mockery he used to speak of everything, as if nothing in this life could possibly be taken seriously. Damra didn't like him, she didn't trust him. She avoided the question by saying something to the effect that she could not possibly know what such monsters were thinking.

She found she could not look him in the eye when she said this untruth and that surprised her, for she had a very low regard for this human and could not understand why lying to him should bother her. Perhaps it was the eyes themselves. Gray in some lights, blue in others, Shadamehr's eyes were clear and alert. He listened to her with complete attention, quick to take note of every detail. She found such focused absorption disconcerting in a human.

Once again, she felt Griffith stir restlessly beside her. Reaching beneath her tunic, she found his hand and squeezed it tightly, promising him that she would tell him everything once they were alone together. He squeezed back, but his eyes, when they looked at her, were troubled.

As to Jessan, Bashae and the Grandmother, Damra had warned them before they arrived at the Keep to say nothing of the Sovereign Stones to anyone. She was worried, at first, thinking that among humans, they might feel inclined to talk.

Jessan sat silently, listened and watched, said nothing. Trevenici are known to be distrustful of strangers and are almost always reclusive and withdrawn until they come to know people. Shadamehr appeared to understand this about the young man, for, after offering one of the Revered Magi to heal his hand—an offer Jessan abruptly refused—Shadamehr said nothing else to the Trevenici, although he included him in the conversation by looking at him often.

As to Bashae and the Grandmother, they sat transfixed, unmoving. Bashae held his knapsack to his chest, the Grandmother held fast to the agate-eyed stick. They might have both been deaf and dumb, for they evinced no reaction to anything.

"I think we have enough information for the moment," Shadamehr said at last, rising to his feet. He looked at Damra and Griffith and smiled. "We'll let these two lovebirds have some time alone."

Damra would have left the baron's presence then and there, but Griffith lingered to speak to him.

"Shadamehr," he said, "what are we going to do? An army of ten thousand!"

"Yes, that does pose a bit of a problem, seeing that there are only about two hundred of us," said Shadamehr. "I'll have to give this matter some thought."

Reaching out a lanky arm, he draped it over the shoulder of the red-haired female mage, who promptly sought to escape.

"Round up the others, will you, Alise? Ulaf, take charge of our guests. All but Griffith and his lady love. They can likely manage on their own."

The moment the two elves were alone in Griffith's chamber—a small room located in the far west wing of the Keep—they made up for months of enforced absence with sweet kisses, pausing in their lovemaking to talk of what had happened, often speaking at the same time so that they were constantly interrupting each other.

"I would still be a prisoner of the Wyred, if it were not for Silwyth," said Griffith.

Tall and slender, Griffith was graceful and careful in his movements, as are all elves. He rarely raised his voice, yet there was a confidence about him that spoke of vast resources of energy and conserved power. Thus is the leopard still dangerous even when it sleeps. The elaborate tattooed mask of the Wyred emphasized his high cheekbones and made it seem as if his chin was more pointed than it really was. Damra ran her finger along that chin and kissed the point.

"Silwyth!" she exclaimed. "He told me he freed you, but I must admit that I found that difficult to believe. Why should he?"

Griffith regarded her in astonishment. "Why should he? Because you sent him to free me. He said that you had sent him and that I was to come here, where you would meet me when you had the chance. I was not to try to get in touch with you, for that would put both our lives in danger."

"Griffith," said Damra, sitting back to stare at him in equal astonishment, "I did *not* send him. I never even knew he existed before he saved my life from the Vrykyl. I had no idea where you were, what had become of you. For all I knew . . ."

She shuddered, and he clasped her tightly in his arms.

Theirs had been an arranged marriage, as are all marriages among the elves: high born or low. Considered societal outcasts, the Wyred often find it difficult to marry outside their own order. Yet such marriages are encouraged, in order that the Wyred receive an influx of fresh blood; the elves having discovered long ago that interbreeding of magi dilutes the magical powers of their offspring. No family will permit an eldest child, either son or daughter, to marry a Wyred, but perhaps a fifth or sixth child and especially a twelfth or thirteenth child may be married off to one of the outcasts without fear of damaging the family's honor. To make the marriage even more attractive, the Wyred always see to it that their members come well dowered.

Damra and Griffith had first met on their wedding day, customary among elves. Fortunately for both, they had been so smitten with each other that they disgraced their families by gazing at each other with lovesick eyes during the ceremony and then fleeing afterward in unseemly haste to the bedroom.

"We are together now, and that is what matters," said Griffith, smoothing her hair and gently kissing her tears from her cheeks.

"Yes," said Damra, wiping her face. "Yes, but I fear we're not going to be able to celebrate our reunion just yet. We have to leave here, Griffith. We have to leave immediately. We must go to New Vinnengael and we must reach there ahead of this army of the Void."

"Of course we must, my dear," said Griffith, "but there is no need to rush off at once, is there?" He watched his wife in some bemusement for she had left the bed on which they were relaxing and started stowing his clothes in her pack. "I would like to wait to hear what Lord Shadamehr plans to do. If he leaves, as well, we would be better advised to travel with—"

"No," said Damra, straightening. "No. You and I will leave together."

"My love—"

"You don't understand, Griffith!" Glancing back at the closed door, she came close to her husband. She took hold of his hands, held them fast and whispered in his ear, "I carry with me the elven portion of the Sovereign Stone."

Griffith was astounded. "What? How—"

"The Shield tried to steal it, or rather one of the Vrykyl tried. Garwina's working with the Vrykyl, Griffith. That's why they chased us in the Portal. Silwyth warned me this would happen. He took the Stone out of the dead hand of the Vrykyl and gave it to me. I must take it to the Council of Dominion Lords. And that is not all. Those people I came with. The young pecwae carries the human portion of the Stone."

Griffith regarded her in dazed confusion, helpless to say a word.

"So you see, Griffith, the heavy burden of responsibility that I bear. That is why we must leave at once. If these should fall into the hands of the Void Lord—"

Griffith rose from the bed. "We have to tell Shadamehr." He started for the door.

Damra caught hold of him, dragged him back. "What? Are you mad? I don't trust him—"

"Why ever not?" Griffith asked, puzzled. "He passed the Test for a Dominion Lord—"

"But he refused the Transfiguration. What kind of man does that?"

"A man who has questions and concerns, Damra," Griffith replied, his tone grave. "A man who feels that the Council is becoming too political. You yourself have said much the same. You said the Council should have taken action, should have spoken out when Karnu seized the orken holy site of Mount Sa'Gra."

"If I criticize the Council, I do so as one of them," Damra returned. "He abrogated that right with his cowardly refusal to humble himself to the gods."

"You may have a point there," Griffith admitted with a wry smile. "I can't imagine Baron Shadamehr humbling himself before anyone, the gods included. But you are wrong if you think him a coward, Damra, or anything less than honorable and loyal and just."

Griffith gestured to the door and the Hall beyond. "Ask those people out there and they will tell you tales of lives he has saved and injustices he has righted. He knows about the Vrykyl for he encountered one and barely escaped with his life. Whether he is a Dominion Lord or not, he is a true knight, not only of Vinnengael, but of all people everywhere."

"I think he has cast a spell over you, Husband," Damra said, half-jesting and half-concerned.

Griffith flushed. He had not meant to speak with such passion. "I have come to like Baron Shadamehr very much during the month I have spent here. I was doubtful as you when I first arrived, but I was able to do a small service for him. During the time when we were together I saw the courage and caring that lies below his devil-take-me attitude. Oh, he has his eccentricities. You have only to glance out the window to see a large rock hanging from the second story to know that. But his faults and foibles are of the gentler sort."

Griffith paused, observing his wife. She looked tired, weary to the point of dropping. Her shoulders were stooped as if the burden she bore was a physical one and she seemed to have aged years in the months during which they had been apart.

"I think you should tell him, Damra," Griffith said quietly. "If for no other reason than he knows the best and fastest way for us to travel to New Vinnengael, and he can provide us escort and protection." Griffith took his wife in his arms, kissed her forehead. "The decision is up to you, of course. I am merely your advisor."

"My best and most trusted advisor," said Damra, nestling into her husband's arms.

She rested her head against his breast, listened to the beating of his heart. Her expression was solemn, for this decision was hers alone to make. Silwyth sending Griffith here, Silwyth sending her here . . . all so strange and inexplicable. Silwyth himself, disgraced scion of a fallen House. He had by his own admission committed murder and worse. How could she trust him? Yet, how could she *not* trust him, for he had saved her life and saved the Sovereign Stone.

"You are tired," said Griffith. "Lie down and sleep and think no more of this until you are rested."

"I will lie down, but not to sleep," Damra said and taking her husband by the hand, she led him back to their bed.

Ulaf offered to escort Jessan, Bashae and the Grandmother to a guest hall where they could eat and drink and catch up on their sleep.

"And I will fix your hand," Bashae said to Jessan, who gave an abrupt nod.

As for the Grandmother, she thrust the stick in Ulaf's face, then said something in the pecwae language, that was like a twittering of birds. Apparently her opinion was favorable, for Jessan made a gesture that indicated Ulaf was to lead and they would follow.

They crossed a crowded courtyard, shoved their way past knots of people who stopped each other to ask if they'd heard the news, telling it if they hadn't and discussing it if they had. Some argued that Shadamehr should stay and fight, despite being vastly outnumbered, and others maintained that, no, he should evacuate the Keep. The merchants were already making preparations to depart. The soldiers eyed the walls of the Keep with martial interest and spoke knowingly of mangonels and belfry towers and boiling oil.

Ulaf kept up a one-sided conversation with his companions. Affable and easy-going, he had a gift for putting people at ease, one of the reasons Shadamehr had chosen him to go along with the newcomers.

Ulaf spoke of many topics, watching Jessan closely to see which might interest him. Trevenici lands are not far from Dunkarga. Many Trevenici fight for the Dunkargan military. Hoping to gain some information about what had happened in that land, Ulaf mentioned that he had recently been in Dunkar, saying that he'd been studying at the Temple of the Magi there. Seeing a flicker of interest in Jessan's eyes, Ulaf pursued the subject.

"I know some of the Trevenici warriors," he said. "There was a Captain whose name was Raven—"

Reaching out his good hand, Jessan grabbed hold of Ulaf. "Captain Ravenstrike? He is my uncle."

"Indeed," said Ulaf, his pulse quickening. He remembered quite vividly the captain riding into the Temple of the Magi and handing over the accursed armor of a dead Vrykyl. Now here was this young man, his nephew, who had been attacked by a Vrykyl in the elven Portal. All just a bit too coincidental. "We heard the city of Dunkar fell to a mighty army, perhaps the same army that threatens us. Have you any word of your uncle?"

Jessan shook his head disconsolately. "No, I know nothing of him. He will be fine, though," the young man added, lifting his head proudly. "He is my uncle."

"He would be proud of his nephew, I think," said Ulaf. "From what the Dominion Lord said, you fought the Vrykyl bravely and those creatures are truly terrifying. But then, that wasn't the first time you'd seen one, was it?"

Jessan cast Ulaf a sharp, suspicious glance.

"I say that only because your uncle spoke to me of some black armor he was carrying. Did he fight a Vrykyl?" Ulaf asked innocently.

Jessan seemed in two minds whether to answer or not. Finally, he said grudgingly, "It was the knight fought the Vrykyl. The Vinnengaelean."

"We helped," Bashae chimed in.

Ulaf was startled to hear the pecwae speak. He hadn't even been certain that they understood Elderspeak.

"Did you? That was very brave," said Ulaf. "What happened to the knight?"

"He died," said Bashae. "The Vrykyl wounded him and not even the Grandmother could help him. The knight was very old, though."

"His soul was saved," said the Grandmother. "The Void tried to claim him, but failed."

"I am glad for that, at least. What was his name?" Ulaf asked. "Perhaps I might have known him."

This was the wrong question, for some reason. The two pecwae went back to looking deaf and dumb. Jessan did not answer.

They continued on in silence, Ulaf trying to think of how to return to the topic, when Jessan halted and swung about to face him.

"What did he do with it? Did he have it with him?" Jessan demanded.

"Have what?" Ulaf said, not understanding. "Are you talking about the knight?"

"My uncle," Jessan returned impatiently. "The armor."

"Oh, of course. Don't worry," said Ulaf, seeing the fear in the young man's eyes, "he rid himself of it. He left it at the Temple for the magi to handle."

Seeing the young man's relief, Ulaf said nothing of the Vrykyl who had gone to seek out Captain Raven.

For long moments, Jessan was unable to speak and when he did, he uncharacteristically said too much.

"I am thankful," he said at last, gruffly. "I gave the armor to him. I didn't know it was cursed. Like this—" His hand strayed to his left side, but he suddenly seemed to recollect himself. His hand dropped. He turned away. His voice altered. "My friends and I are hungry. You said there would be food."

"Yes, this way," said Ulaf.

Even though Jessan had halted his movement, Ulaf had seen what the young man had been about to reveal. Ulaf knew it for what it was.

"A blood knife, my lord," Ulaf told Shadamehr. "He carries it with him. Not openly. It's in a leather sheath, but there was no mistaking the handle."

Shadamehr mulled this over. "They meet an elderly knight and help him fight a Vrykyl. The uncle ends up with the Vrykyl's cursed armor and takes it to the Temple of the Magi in Dunkar. This young man carries a Vrykyl knife and subsequently winds up in the elven kingdom traveling with a Dominion Lord through the Portal where they are attacked by a Vrykyl who tries to capture them alive. You see, of course, where all this is heading?"

"No," said Ulaf, feeling obtuse. "I don't."

"Don't you?" Shadamehr smiled. "Well, maybe I'm wrong."

"How do you know the Vrykyl was trying to take them alive?" Alise demanded.

"Because otherwise he would have simply slain them from a distance with a well chosen word or two, not risk his skeletal remains to duke it out with a Dominion Lord. She doesn't like me, you know," Shadamehr added plaintively.

"No one likes you," said Alise coolly. "I should think you would have realized that by now."

"Bah! Give her time and you'll have her eating cake from your hand. Twenty minutes should do it," said Ulaf.

"You're both mocking me," said Shadamehr. "My feelings are hurt and you mock me. There sits Rigiswald, looking severe. He thinks I'm being frivolous . . ."

"I'm thinking about those ten thousand taan warriors," Rigiswald said, glaring. "Give them a day to move through the Portal, another day to regroup and start their march." He pointed a well-manicured finger at Shadamehr. "They'll be eating supper here the evening after and all you can do is prattle on about some elf female not liking you."

"From what we know of the taan, it's far more likely that they'll be eating *us* for supper the day after," said Shadamehr. "Still, you do have a point, you annoying old man. We better decide what to do about these taan. Do we flee screaming into the night or stay and fight?"

Looking around at the others, at their grim and gloomy faces, Shadamehr smiled, slapped his knees and said, "Personally, I'm for staying and fighting. I have those new ballistae the orks designed for me. I've been hoping for a chance to try them out and this will be a splendid opportunity."

"Oh, do be serious for once in your life," Alise cried angrily. Rising to her feet, she walked over to the window and stood looking out to the north, in the direction of the elven Portal.

"I am very serious, Alise," said Shadamehr. "From all reports we've received, Prince Dagnarus's target is New Vinnengael. According to our history lessons Rigiswald has been teaching us, Vinnengael has been his target ever since he gave his soul to the Void. To reach New Vinnengael, Dagnarus will have to get past us first. Either he throws his entire army against us—"

"He won't do that," said Rigiswald tersely. "Might as well send in a giant to swat a gnat."

"I agree, Old Man. Dagnarus will have to commit a sizeable portion to fighting us, though, for he doesn't dare leave us here to cut off his path of retreat in case things go wrong for him in the city. Every taan fighting here is one less taan fighting in New Vinnengael. And he's going to need every one of those ten thousand to take the city."

"Unless he has some treachery in the works," said Ulaf. "Like what happened at Dunkar."

"Treachery takes intelligent people to work it and I fancy he'll have a problem finding anyone bright enough in the court of New Vinnengael to be treacherous," said Shadamehr. "So, let's plan out how to deploy our troops. We'll evacuate the noncombatants—"

"Stop it!" Alise shouted, turning to face him. "You're being crazy. Suicidal. Throwing away your life—"

"But think of the wonderful song it will make, my dear," Shadamehr interrupted her. He paused in thought, tugged on his mustache. "Except that nothing much rhymes with Shadamehr."

"Cavalier," suggested Ulaf.

"Yes, that might do. The Most Lamentable and Untimely but Immensely Heroic Death of Baron Shadamehr the Cavalier—"

Alise slapped him across the face. She slapped him hard, so that the sound resounded around the room and left him with a bright red imprint of her palm. Gathering up the skirts of her robes, she ran out the door, slammed it shut behind her.

"I'm not having much luck with women these days," said Shadamehr, putting his hand to his stinging cheek.

"Maybe she didn't like the rhyme," said Ulaf.

"Everyone's a critic. I'll have to have a talk—"

There came a soft knock at the door.

"Come in, Alise. I forgive you!" sang out Shadamehr.

The door opened, but it wasn't Alise.

"My lord?" Griffith looked in hesitantly. "Could we have a word with you? We would not bother you, but it is important—"

"Come in, come in. I was just about to send for all of you," said Shadamehr.

The two elves entered, bringing with them the Trevenici youth and the two pecwae. They had all of them heard the altercation, but the faces of the elves and the Trevenici were impassive, unreadable. The pecwae were clearly overawed, stared around in amazement at the high ceilings and ornate furniture and glittering tapestries. Pausing inside the door, the elves bowed to the assembled company. Shadamehr and Ulaf bowed to the elves. Rigiswald did not. He sat in his chair, ignoring them all.

"You said you were about to summon us, Baron?" Damra stated in Elderspeak. "May I ask why?"

"How very frank you are for an elf," said Shadamehr admiringly. "Right to the point. Very well, I will be equally frank with you, Damra of Gwyenoc." He shifted his gaze to Jessan and Bashae. "Which one of your friends is carrying the Sovereign Stone? My first thought was the Trevenici youth, but the longer I consider the matter, the more I tend to think that Lord Gustav gave the Stone to the pecwae."

Damra's jaw sagged. She stared at him in unblinking astonishment, then cast a reproachful glance at Jessan. He glared back at her.

"No, please, none of that," Shadamehr said to both of them. "Each of you has been true to his trust. But Jessan did let fall certain bits of information and it was not difficult for me to deduce the rest. An elderly knight, roaming alone, far from home in Trevenici lands. That could only be Gustav, the Whoreson Knight on his insane quest. I grieve to hear of his death, yet I am glad for him that he finally succeeded in fulfilling his lifelong dream.

"For he did succeed, didn't he, Jessan?" Shadamehr turned to the Trevenici, noting, as he did so, that his injured hand had been wrapped in a neat bandage and that he could actually move his fingers. "Gustav found the human portion of the Sovereign Stone. The Vrykyl knew he found it. One sought to slay him for it, but the creature managed only to wound him before he killed it. Knowing he was dying, Gustav entrusted the Stone to a messenger to deliver it to you, Damra of Gwyenoc. Jessan and Bashae and the Grandmother"—he bowed to the elderly woman— "bravely and intelligently completed their dangerous task. They brought the Stone to you and now you are responsible for seeing that it arrives safely in New Vinnengael.

"That has not been an easy task," Shadamehr continued, not allowing anyone to interrupt, "for the Vrykyl are bent upon recovering the Sovereign Stone for their lord Dagnarus. That is the reason the Vrykyl came after you and your charges in the Portal. I admit I'm a bit confused about why the Trevenici here is hauling about a blood knife, but I'm sure that can be explained."

Damra and Griffith exchanged glances. Griffith lifted an eyebrow, as if to say "I told you so." Jessan said something in Tirniv. The Grandmother gave a loud snort and thumped the butt-end of her stick on the stone floor, said something back to the two young men, also in Tirniv.

Ulaf translated, said softly, "The young man says that you are obviously a wizard and not to be trusted. The old lady says you are not a wizard, just a weasel."

"Weasel?" Shadamehr whispered, taken aback. "Are you sure?"

"Among the pecwae, the weasel is considered an animal of high intelligence," said Ulaf with a smile.

"Oh, well, that's better, then. My relations with the fairer sex are improving it seems. At least one of them likes me."

Shadamehr smiled benignly at the Grandmother.

Damra said a few words softly to her husband, then turned back to Shadamehr. She spoke defiantly, cold-eyed, her hand on the hilt of her sword.

"Obviously, Baron Shadamehr, it would be pointless for us to deny this. Our question is this. What do you intend to do now that you know?"

"Whatever you want me to do, Damra of Gwyenoc," said Shadamehr quietly. "You plan to take the Sovereign Stone to New Vinnengael to give it to the Council of Dominion Lords. I will be of as much help to you or as little as you require."

Damra's expression softened. She glanced sidelong at her husband and her companions.

"I see. I had not expected—" She fell silent, thoughtful.

"Twenty minutes," Ulaf whispered.

Shadamehr smiled, but said nothing. He kept his eyes on Damra and on the two young men, Jessan and Bashae. Other than Jessan's first remark about wizards, neither of them had yet spoken a word. They were leaving it to the Dominion Lord to do the talking.

"It is not quite as simple as you describe, Baron Shadamehr," Damra said finally. "Bashae carries the human portion of the Sovereign Stone. I carry the elven portion."

Now it was Shadamehr's turn to look astonished.

"Od's bodkin!" he exclaimed, almost reverently. "Any particular reason, or did you just happen to fancy it?"

Damra paled in anger. Hastily, her husband said something to her in Tomagi.

She glanced at Shadamehr, said stiffly, "My husband says that you meant no offense. He tells me you make a jest of everything, Baron Shadamehr—"

"Shadamehr, please. The 'baron' part doesn't suit me. Makes it sound as if I should be forty pounds overweight, have gout and wear a great gold chain around my neck. And I'm really harmless, truly. Ask anyone. Well, almost anyone . . . Now do tell me your story and I promise to behave. We'll start with you, Jessan. By the way, congratulations on holding your own against a Vrykyl. Few men I know have been as brave or done so well, myself among them. The first time I met a Vrykyl," Shadamehr added with blithe matter-of-factness, "I ran like a rabbit. If you didn't take your adult name from that encounter, you should have."

Jessan flushed, suspicious, yet intrigued by this strange man, who did not mind telling he'd run away in the face of a daunting enemy. Trevenici admire courage, and that includes the courage it takes for a man to reveal something detrimental to himself.

Shadamehr brought up chairs. He sat down, stretched out his legs as if he were in a tavern, with all the time in the world and nothing more important on his mind than the quality of the ale. "Now, tell me about Lord Gustav. Did you see his battle against the Vrykyl? I say that only because you carried away a prize—the blood knife. Tell me about that encounter."

Trevenici are generally only too happy to talk about a good fight. Jessan could see nothing wrong in this and he was glad to be able to talk about the knight's heroism. He began to speak, short and succinct at first, then gradually warming to his tale. Bashae forgot himself and spoke up, adding his part. The Grandmother chimed in, telling how the gods had chosen both young men to go on the journey, one to carry the Stone and one to guard it. At that, Shadamehr seemed a bit restless, squirming in his seat. But in general he was an attentive and interested listener, asking questions to draw them out, and soon all of them found themselves telling him more than they had ever intended.

They handed off the story to the elves. Damra told her tale, reluctant and halting, obviously uncomfortable about discussing elven politics with humans. Shadamehr asked several questions of her. To her amazement, he spoke fluent Tomagi and his questions indicated that he knew a great deal about the current elven political situation. He held the Divine in immense respect, and he did not mock the elves, as did many humans. Damra relaxed and was soon amazed to hear herself talking to him as if she had known him all her life.

"Well done, Damra of Gwyenoc," said Shadamehr approvingly at the end of her story. "A hard decision, but I think you made the right one. Garwina has lowered the Portal defenses to permit Dagnarus entry, undoubtedly in return for promised considerations. I'm certain Dagnarus agreed to relinquish the Portal once he has achieved his goal of capturing New Vinnengael. Unfortunately, when the time comes, Garwina will find Dagnarus reluctant to give the Portal back—"

A knock came on the door. "My lord!" called out a voice.

"Yes, what is it?" Shadamehr demanded, irritated at the interruption.

A head poked in the door. "My lord, our scouts report that the taan troops at the eastern end of the Portal are not marching as we feared they might. They're setting up camp on the banks of the river."

"Probably waiting to establish their supply lines. Unless—" Shadamehr turned to Rigiswald. "You don't think Dagnarus plans to sail down the river, do you?"

Rigiswald scowled, considering. "The taan hate water and fear it. They don't even like to get their feet wet. I doubt if there are any who can swim. Still, they worship Dagnarus as a god. Who knows what he could force them to do?"

"Taan?" Damra was confused. "What are these 'taan'?"

"The creatures that you saw entering the Portal. They fight for the army of Prince Dagnarus. From what information we've been able to glean, they come from a world on the other side of a Portal—"

"Continent," said Rigiswald sourly. "A continent. Not another world. Preposterous to even consider such a thing."

"Continent, then," said Shadamehr with a wink. "Now, then—"

"A desert continent," Rigiswald continued sententiously. "That's why they can't stand water."

"Thank you," said Shadamehr. "Now then, this gives us more time than I thought we had. What else, Rodney?" he asked.

"The scouts have retreated, my lord. They said it was too dangerous."

"Wise people. Nasty sort, the taan. Don't want to get too close. Anything else? Carry on, then."

The seneschal departed. Shadamehr turned back to the elves. "What are your plans, Damra of Gwyenoc?"

"We must reach New Vinnengael—"

"Yes, the faster, the better. And you can bring word of this army to the King, who probably knows nothing of the fact that he's about to be attacked by ten thousand monsters—"

He stopped speaking. Bashae was saying something to the Grandmother in Twithil.

"Is that their language?" Shadamehr said softly to Ulaf. "I've never heard it before."

"Nor have I, my lord."

"Sounds like a collection of crickets, doesn't it?"

The Grandmother responded tersely, shrugging her shoulders. Bashae looked at Jessan, who cast Shadamehr a glance that was intense and scrutinizing. At last, slowly, Jessan nodded his head.

Bashae came to stand before Shadamehr. Raising up the knapsack, the pecwae said, "Here. You take it."

Shadamehr leapt from his chair, backed off with as much haste as if the pecwae had presented him with a snake in a basket. Shadamehr put his hands behind his back.

"I appreciate the thought, but no. I couldn't possibly."

Rigiswald gave a dry chuckle.

Shadamehr cast him a cold glance. "Just shut up, Old Man. You don't know anything, so don't look so damn smug."

Bashae stared at Shadamehr in dismay. "You won't take it?"

"I . . . uh . . . That is . . . You see . . . It wouldn't be right," Shadamehr finished lamely.

"Why not?" Bashae asked. "Damra was going to take it, but she couldn't touch it because her magic is Air. But yours is Earth, like mine. I'd feel much better if you took it, sir. It's hard to sleep at night with so much responsibility," Bashae said and he was deeply in earnest.

"Don't you see, Bashae, the gods gave it to you," Shadamehr said, pointedly ignoring a snort from Rigiswald. "If they'd wanted me to have it, they would have chosen me, but they didn't. I'm afraid you'll have to carry the Stone a little longer. But," he added, his voice softening as he saw the pecwae droop, crushed and disappointed, "perhaps I could help guard the Stone. Would that be acceptable? You could use an extra hand, what with your friend here carrying around a Vrykyl magnet. The least I can do is go with you."

He looked at Damra. "Would my company be acceptable to you, Dominion Lord? I know the lands between here and New Vinnengael. No one knows them better. I could be your guide and I might also be of some use to you in a fight. In addition, I know several of the more popular elven love songs and I have a passable singing voice."

"My lord, we would be grateful for your company, your guidance and your protection. But I understood that you meant to stay here and defend your castle—"

"Castle!" Shadamehr waved his hand dismissively. "Damp place. I was considering having it remodeled anyway. You can't think how the ceilings leak in the rainy season. And the tapestries want cleaning. Did you get enough to eat and drink? There's plenty more, just help yourselves. Rodney will show you to the dining hall."

When the guests had departed, Shadamehr walked over to the window. Looking out at the castle and its grounds, he gave a deep sigh.

"My lord," said Ulaf. "You could go with them and the rest of us could stay behind, undertake the defense—"

"No, no. I wouldn't think of it, dear friend," said Shadamehr, turning to regard Ulaf with affection. "It wouldn't be fair—the lot of you having all that fun without me. I thank you for the offer, though. Besides, think how happy this will make Alise."

"We could leave traps behind," said Ulaf, hearing the wistful note in his lord's voice and hoping to cheer him.

Shadamehr's dejection disappeared. "We could, couldn't we? Cunning traps." His eyes shone. "The Vanishing Room—"

"I was thinking of something a bit more lethal," said Ulaf sourly.

"Yes, well, we'll see. We had best get to work immediately. Rigiswald, I'll require your magical help with the traps. Ulaf, tell Captain Hassan to assemble the troops. We'll split our forces, travel to New Vinnengael by various routes, some by land, others by water. Confuse the bejeebers out of anyone trailing us.

"As for me"—Shadamehr rubbed his hands—"I need more rope . . ."

"**F**EELING BETTER, SHAKUR?" DAGNARUS ASKED.

"Yes, my lord," Shakur responded in sullen tones.

"Tell me again how you managed to get stabbed with your own blood knife?"

"It was not my knife, my lord," Shakur returned, angry at the mockery.

"No matter," said Dagnarus, his voice cold. "I trust there will be no further comments from you regarding Vrykyl who bungle their assignments."

"I will go after the Stones, my lord. They are bound for New Vinnengael—"

"Of course they are. Where they will be in for a shock. This is how you will proceed. You will go to New Vinnengael . . ."

After Shakur had received his orders and departed, Dagnarus remained inside his command tent, which had been raised on the banks of the Arven, north of the border of the Vinnengaelean empire. Outside came the sound of ringing axes. The sound had not abated, not even during the night, as the taan continued to work by flaring torchlight. He had listened to that sound for two days now and so constant was the noise that he no longer heard it.

He went over his plans in his mind. A few setbacks—he had been annoyed to hear that a force of elves had attacked his human mercenaries at the western end of the Portal, taking them completely by surprise. The elves fought like ravening wolves, with small care for their own lives. So ferocious was their assault that there were only a few survivors of Guske's force who'd managed to make it through the Portal to report to him.

At first, Dagnarus had been worried that these elves might come through the Portal to attack the eastern end. Not that he feared he would lose to them, but such an attack would delay his march on New Vinnengael. Spies sent back through the Portal to study the situation reported that the elven numbers were too few. They appeared to be content with holding their ground. He would deal with that problem later. Or he would have the Shield deal with it, since it was obviously the Shield's blundering that had led to this debacle.

Then there was the report from his Vrykyl in the City of the Unhorsed that the dwarven part of the Sovereign Stone had been stolen. Try as he might, the Vrykyl could find out no information about who had taken the Stone. The dwarves refused to discuss it, even among themselves. They would say only that the Clan Chief was taking care of the matter. Knowing that the dwarves, who disliked and distrusted all magic, had never cared much about their portion of the Sovereign Stone, Dagnarus considered it likely that some dwarf had stolen the Stone for gain, probably hoped to sell it in human lands. Dagnarus ordered his Vrykyl to remain where he was and continue to nose about until he found out who had stolen the Stone and where the thief had taken it. Once provided with that information, Dagnarus would have little difficulty laying his hands on it. Perhaps, he mused, it was already on its way to Vinnengael right now. Such was the increasing power of the Void in the world.

All in all, Dagnarus was well satisfied. His plans proceeded on schedule. Not very long from now, he would be king of Vinnengael with the Sovereign Stone—all four parts, complete and whole—in his possession.

"Then you will see, Father," Dagnarus said quietly, speaking to the long dead King Tamaros. "You will see what sort of king I make."

In later days, when those who had served Baron Shadamehr were old men and women, they proudly spoke of knowing him. They recalled many adventures, terrible and dangerous, with laughter and tears. But few ever spoke of that wild dash to escape Shadamehr's Keep.

Most who recalled that horrendous journey remembered it as starting out in excitement and ending in pain, weariness, and a distinct desire to never set eyes on a horse again. Shadamehr divided his troops into three bands, sent one band circling east of the foothills of the Mehr mountains, while he and his group chose to ride straight through the foothills. The last band consisted of thirty orks who elected to travel by water, not willing to leave their boats behind for the taan to capture. Rigiswald went with the orks, for he was too old to ride, he said. Alise and Ulaf traveled with Shadamehr.

He placed the dwarves among his retinue in charge of setting the pace, telling them that they must cover no less than fifty miles a day and more if the weather held and the riding was good.

They emptied the stables of the Keep, bringing the extra horses with them so that the riders could change mounts frequently. Most of the horses were of dwarven stock—hearty and well accustomed to galloping long distances. They took no supply wagons, for those would slow them down. Each person carried what food he needed for the journey; Shadamehr quipping that by the end, hunger alone would spur them into New Vinnengael.

Every day, they were up with the dawn, riding for hours through the wind and rain of the coming autumn with only the briefest stops to rest and water the animals. The men suffered more than the beasts, for the dwarves took excellent care of the horses, pampering and making much of them, while the riders were expected to look out for themselves. By the end of the journey, even the stoic dwarves looked ragged and bleary-eyed.

If not for Shadamehr, none would have made it. He kept up their spirits, making them laugh with his pranks and practical jokes, singing them songs (he had a remarkable baritone), telling them stories to keep their minds off their exhaustion and discomfort. He made no secret of his own pain, complained loudly and often, to everyone's amusement. He ate his meals standing, for, he said, he was too saddle-sore to sit down. He was the first to rise, the last to sleep, and took more than his share of the watch detail.

They rode the last miles in a stupor; many having the feeling that this nightmare journey would never end, that they were doomed to gallop forever across a sea of grass that rolled to the horizon. On the tenth night, the Grandmother lay down and told them to bury her on the spot and be done with it. They eventually talked her out of it, but every single person in the group knew how she felt.

The last day, they had been riding only a few hours when a dwarf—one of the advance scouts—came haring across the plains with the news.

The walls of the city of New Vinnengael were in sight.

All of them stopped and looked at each other, immensely and humbly thankful, too tired to rejoice.

They had covered a thousand miles in sixteen days.

Taking the lead, Shadamehr guided his horse across one of the many bridges that led over the meandering river in the waterfront area of the city. He was almost across when he sighted an enormous ork, comfortably ensconced on an overturned boat, braiding rope.

The ork rose to his feet and stretched, yawned and scratched himself.

Shadamehr reined in his horse. "Keep riding," he said to Ulaf. "I'll meet you near the north gate."

Shadamehr moved off to the side of the road under the pretext of looking to see if his horse had come up lame. The ork sauntered over and struck up a conversation.

"I am glad to see that you and your group arrived safely," Shadamehr said in a low voice. "Was there any trouble? Did you find lodging?"

"Along the waterfront," the captain replied. "We arrived several days ago. I have been waiting for you ever since. We had no trouble on the journey down the river, but the omens are very bad, my lord. I waited to warn you."

"I could have guessed," Shadamehr said dryly. "What's happened now?"

"We had been traveling about three days when we saw an eagle flying high above us. The eagle circled three times and called to us and then flew away. At that moment, a wolf appeared on the bank of the river. The wolf howled at us and then it, too, ran away. Next, a fish leapt from the water and landed in the boat. It spoke to us and then it jumped back out again. The fish no sooner hit the water than a huge tree crashed down in front of us, barely missing striking our boat."

"And what does the shaman say this all means?" Shadamehr asked.

"It was a warning," the ork said solemnly. "A warning from the gods themselves. The eagle of the elves, the wolf of the dwarves, the fish of the orks, the tree of you humans. All of them crying out to us."

"I see," said Shadamehr thoughtfully.

"It was well they warned us," the captain continued. "Moments after the tree fell, those orks who had been in the rear came paddling up in great haste. The army of beast-men was not far behind us. Some of the beast-men are traveling by boat—great, huge rafts made of fresh-cut logs lashed together. Others come overland. The beast-men run swift as a galloping horse and they do not seem to tire. They kill animals as they run and devour them raw."

Shadamehr regarded the ork in consternation. Even if he believed only half of his tale—orks love to embellish a good story—this was dire news. "How far behind you, would you say?"

"Two days, maybe three at the most." The captain shook his hoary head, scratched himself on the chest. "There are a great many orken trading and fishing vessels at the waterfront. The shaman says we must warn them, but I wanted to speak with you first."

"Thank you, Captain. Yes, you can warn them, but tell them that if they leave New Vinnengael, to do so quietly. I don't want to start a panic."

The captain grunted. "We orks do not have so much love for humans these days that we would go out of our way to do them a good turn. Present company excepted," he added with a bob of his shaggy head. "Trade goods, that's the only reason the orks are here. Still I think even the stupidest human will start to notice something is wrong when they wake up tomorrow to find no more orks in the harbor."

"Yes, but by that time, I will have warned the king."

"The gods help us," said the ork, tugging on a lock of his hair on his forehead in respect. "What are your orders for us?"

Shadamehr considered his options. "I may need to leave this city in haste. I'll need a seagoing vessel, doesn't have to be large. Can you find one for me and keep it safe until you hear from me? I have money to pay for it—"

The ork waved his hand. "Not now. Maybe later. I know of such a ship and her captain owes me a favor. We'll be in the harbor. Send me word."

Shadamehr agreed and the two parted, the ork heading back down toward the harbor district. Shaking his head and sighing deeply, Shadamehr mounted his horse and continued toward the palace, increasing the animal's pace to a gallop.

As the citizens of New Vinnengael are fond of bragging, they live in the most magical city in the world.

Every important structure in the city, from the defensive walls to the palace, had been raised by Earth magic. New Vinnengael was the world's repository of magic. The Temple of the Magi located in the city's heart was the largest of its kind anywhere in Loerem. Humans interested in Earth magic came from all over the continent to study there and, since its library was considered the finest collection of arcane knowledge in the world, magi from the other elemental practices came to the Temple, as well. The beauty of the city itself was another kind of magic, for the New Vinnengaeleans were right when they claimed it to be the most wonderful city in Loerem.

Thanks to Earth magic, silver and gold and diamond mines spoon-fed wealth to the empire, that was growing fat and jolly and apoplectic as a result. For example, the New Vinnengaelean Navy was no match for the swift-sailing, far-ranging fleet belonging to the orks, but the New Vinnengaeleans knew that what they lacked in speed, maneuverability and fire power they made up for in panache.

The New Vinnengaelean military was the best equipped, with the best uniforms, the best armor, the best horses in Loerem. The soldiers looked particularly dazzling on parade. They were not so dazzling on the battlefield, as they had discovered to their discomfiture following their disastrous loss of their only Portal at the newly renamed Karnuan city of Delak 'Vir.

There were some in the city and in the empire who did not think that all was magic in New Vinnengael. They saw a citizenry who had put their wealth into buildings and temples and public edifices, erecting monuments to themselves, instead of investing the money in people. Some who thought this were a group of disenchanted military officers, who had left

New Vinnengael and moved to Krammes, far from the influence of the royal court. Here they sold their ornate and useless parade armor to raise money to found the Royal Cavalry School.

They hired the finest swordsmasters and riding masters. They bought the finest horses and the best horse trainers. They brought in the best instructors. They studied military history and strategy and tactics, often resorting to the shocking practice of examining those of the enemy. The best people in the military were quietly sent to Krammes to train as officers for a future military that might not be as dazzling as the current one, but would certainly be more effective.

That day was not here, however. Krammes was far from New Vinnengael, on the other side of the continent (only a few hundred miles south of the site of Old Vinnengael). Dagnarus's army of taan drew closer every moment. He would find the city a hard nut to crack. Its center might be soft, but its shell was formidable.

To those who first saw the city, riding from any direction, New Vinnengael seemed to be a star fallen to earth, floating on the water. Immense walls of dazzling white marble, built in the shape of an eight-pointed star, rose up from a peninsula that extended out into the Arven river. Designed to emulate and venerate Old Vinnengael, which had overlooked Lake Ildurel, the river created both a strong defense and a beautiful vista.

Immense towers, outfitted with impressive engines of destruction, guarded the city gates that were located at the northwestern end of the outer wall. Similar engines, designed for battling ships, guarded the waterfront. Soldiers walked the ramparts, glowering ferociously to intimidate the peasants and showing off their colorful uniforms to the giggling milkmaids, coming to sell their wares in the famous New Vinnengaelean market.

The notion of building the city in a star shape had been the idea of the famous architect, Kapil of Marduar, who had been hired to do the initial design. Pleased with the esthetic beauty and the fact that no other city in Loerem was built in the shape of a star, the king had been enthusiastic.

Eight major streets of New Vinnengael ran straight and true from each angle of the star, crossing at the center point that was the city's heart. In the center of the city, a vast magnificent circular mosaic, a half mile across, made of glistening, colorful stones, portrayed the sun, moon, stars, with Loerem in the center of the universe and New Vinnengael in the center of Loerem. The Temple of the Magi had been built on the north of the courtyard, to align with the stars. The Royal Palace stood on the south, to align with the sun. So straight were the streets that no matter where you stood on any one of them, you could see either the Temple or the Palace.

The streets divided the city into eight sections, that each had a name. Some were shopping districts, others were residential, each connected by narrow streets that ran at right angles to the eight major streets.

Bashae rode behind Ulaf, clasping hold of that long-suffering man's waist with a grip as constricting as a fat man's girdle. He looked up at the towers that rose to dizzying heights, seeming to brush the clouds, and he thought back to Wild Town. Gazing around him at the city of New Vinnengael, to see at every turning some new wonder, some marvel, Bashae found himself longing for the person he'd once been, the person who had been overawed by a shabby and sorry set of ramshackle hovels. He'd seen marvelous sights that he would remember the rest of his days, but he'd lost something, too. He wasn't certain what it was, but he felt its lack.

Jessan rode beneath the grand arches and immediately felt stifled. He paid little attention to the beauty of the city, but looked back wistfully to the green grasslands and forests they were leaving behind. The city held no wonder for him, only foul smells and gaping mouths and staring eyes.

None of the rest of Shadamehr's retinue paid much attention to the city. They'd been here before, many times, most of them, and were looking forward to a favorite inn, a favorite tavern, a proper meal, a mug of ale and a decent night's sleep.

Only the Grandmother was impressed. Only the Grandmother was awed. She was so enamored with the magnificence of what she saw that she forgot to show the agate-eyed stick, who was forced to catch what glimpses it could from the back of Damra's saddle.

Hearing the Grandmother softly sigh, Damra turned around to look at the elderly pecwae, riding pillion behind her.

"Why, Grandmother, what is wrong?" Damra asked, for she saw tears coursing down the wrinkled cheeks.

The Grandmother shook her head, snorted.

Not understanding, thinking the pecwae was either overawed or frightened or both, Damra said something soothing and comforting, to which the Grandmother merely snorted again.

Shadamehr joined his companions, who had waited for him outside the main city gate. Such was the flow of traffic into and out of New Vinnengael that two separate highways had been built to handle it, running beneath two enormous arches. Each highway was designed to handle one-way traffic only. Wagons and carts rumbled in opposite directions, entering the city on one highway, leaving it by the other. A large gatehouse was built into the center post of the arch. Guards asked routine questions of those entering and departing, gave the wagons a cursory search, and waved them on through.

The gate was congested, both inside and out, with throngs of people. A merchant, who had been required to unload his wagon to prove he carried nothing illegal, cursed the guards loudly. Street urchins ran underfoot, hopeful of earning a few pence to guide people to their destinations. Idlers leaned up against the walls, hands in their pockets, whiling away the hours until the taverns opened at sunset. Hawkers stood just inside the gate, shouting their wares. Cutpurses and shysters kept a sharp lookout for gawking farm lads and drunken noblemen.

All was not well in New Vinnengael, however. The Vinnengaelean Flag flew at half-mast and everywhere Shadamehr looked, pillars and statues were draped in black. Merchants and those of the lower classes wore black arm bands or sported large flowers made of black cloth pinned to their chests. Noble lords and ladies dressed entirely in black. The guards at the gate went about their business as usual, but there was a subdued air about them.

Shadamehr was well known in the city, by reputation, if not by sight, for he usually avoided the place like, as he put it "skunks, spiders and ambitious mothers with marriageable daughters." His coat of arms—a crouching leopard—that decorated his horse blanket was immediately recognized. The guards hailed him with pleased grins. Officers came out to shake his hand. People waiting in line for admittance to the city heard his name and stared at him, some asking their neighbors in fearful tones if he wasn't a notorious bandit and wondering whether the guards were going to apprehend him.

Street urchins, smelling money, surrounded him, shrieking at the top of their lungs and holding out grubby hands. Pickpockets took one look at the sharp gray eyes and went in search of easier prey. The idlers gathered closer, craning their necks, hoping for some excitement. Shadamehr's horse, a fierce, ill-tempered beast, grew skittish and nervous at the crowds and the noise.

Shadamehr dismounted to calm the horse and keep it from taking a nip at the street urchins. Thus involved, he did not see a person at the gate stare hard at him, then leap onto a waiting horse and vanish into the crowd.

Ulaf saw this, and so did Alise. She slid off her horse and motioned for Ulaf to do the same.

"I'm not staying up here alone!" Bashae said, and before Ulaf could stop him, he slid off the horse's back, landed on the street.

"Keep near me!" Ulaf ordered.

Bashae nodded, and did as he was told. Jessan, seeing Bashae in the street, dismounted his horse and moved to be near his friend. At Shadamehr's suggestion, they had disguised Bashae as a human child, with a cap to cover his pointed ears. No one in the crowd paid him any attention. He stared in amazement at the vast numbers of people.

The Grandmother poked Damra in the back.

"Let me off this beast."

Damra turned around. "I would not advise it, Grandmother. There are so many people and this city is large and strange. Should you become lost—"

"Bah!" the Grandmother scoffed. "Let me down. Someone has to keep an eye on the young ones."

She pointed at Jessan and Bashae with her stick and before Damra could react, the Grandmother slid backward off the horse to land nimbly on her feet. Unlike Bashae, she continued to wear her pecwae garb and several people stared at her and pointed.

Ignoring the stares, the Grandmother stumped over to Bashae and prodded him with a bony finger. "There's going to be trouble," she said to him in Twithil.

"I'm not surprised," said Bashae.

He had decided he did not like the jostling crowds, the immense buildings, the fetid air, or the tall guards with their bright armor and shining swords.

"Yes," she said. "The stick told me. But don't worry. I have found it."

"Found what?" Bashae asked.

"The sleep city," the Grandmother said in a loud whisper. "The city I visit every night. This is the place. My body and my spirit have met at last."

The Grandmother sighed contentedly and continued to look around her, smiling to herself now and then and nodding at each familiar sight.

"Truly, Grandmother? Your spirit comes here?" Bashae was stunned. "To this dreadful place?"

"Dreadful? What's wrong with it?" the Grandmother demanded, offended. "Where else should I go?"

"I . . . I don't know. Where I go, maybe. Walking beneath the willow trees that grow near the river—"

"Trees! River water! I've seen enough of them in my life." The Grandmother gave a disdainful sniff. "Now that." She pointed the stick at a man shoveling horse manure off the street and dumping it into a wagon. "That is something special."

"Yes," said Bashae, watching the man clean up after the horse. "That's something special."

"We best warn Shadamehr," Alise said to Brother Ulaf. "I'll come with you."

Ulaf nodded. Shoving his way through the crowd after Alise, he ordered the pecwae to keep near him, but was too preoccupied to look to see that they did so.

Jessan ordered Bashae and the Grandmother to stay close. Assuming the pecwae would do as they were told, the Trevenici pressed forward to get as close to Ulaf as possible, to find out what was going on.

Bashae started to follow Jessan. The Grandmother put her hand on his shoulder and jerked him back.

"The stick tells me we should leave," she said softly.

Shadamehr stood conversing with one of the officers, a Captain Jemid, whom he'd known in his youth.

After a few brief reminiscences centering around a tavern called the Cock and Bull, Shadamehr said casually, "The entire city seems plunged in mourning, my friend. Who died?"

Captain Jemid stared. "Haven't you heard? I assumed that's why you were here, my lord. To pay your respects."

"I've heard nothing but the sound of my horse's hooves the last sixteen days," Shadamehr said dryly.

"His Majesty the King. The gods rest him," the captain replied, removing his hat in respect.

"The King!" Shadamehr repeated, astonished. "Hirav was a young man. About my age. How did he die?"

"Heart failure, my lord. He was found in bed by his chamberlain. He had apparently died in his sleep. That would be about a fortnight ago. It was a shock, I'll say that." Captain Jemid shook his head. "A man fit and hale and in the prime of life to suddenly drop dead. Makes you stop and think."

"Indeed it does," said Shadamehr, troubled. "His son ascends the throne, I take it? How old is the boy?"

"Hirav the Second. He's eight years old, my lord."

"Poor lad," said Shadamehr quietly. "His mother died shortly after he was born. Now he loses his father and becomes king all in one day. I assume there is a regent?"

"The Most Revered High Magus Clovis, my lord."

Shadamehr cast a questioning glance at Alise, who raised an eyebrow and rolled her eyes.

Shadamehr's frown deepened. "Well, I will most certainly stop by the palace to offer my condolences, sign the book, that sort of thing. Best be on our way, then, Jemid. Good to see you again. Our first business is with the Council of the Dominion Lords. You wouldn't happen to know if they are in session—"

"I do happen to know that, my lord," said Captain Jemid. "The Council's been disbanded."

"You don't say," Shadamehr murmured.

"What was that, my lord?" Damra asked in Tomagi. Standing alongside Shadamehr, silent and observant, she was so shocked by what she'd heard that she wondered if she'd translated the words properly.

The officer glanced at her. Seeing her tabard with the insignia of the Dominion Lord, Captain Jemid bowed to her, then turned back to Shadamehr.

"The Council has been disbanded," he repeated, his voice and face impassive. "By order of the regent, High Magus Clovis. All Dominion Lords were told to leave the city or face arrest."

"I take it they left," Shadamehr said.

Captain Jemid looked uncomfortable. "There wasn't much they could do, my lord. There aren't that many human Dominion Lords to begin with and they are growing old. There hasn't been a new candidate to take the tests in fifteen years, my lord. You were the last. The orken Dominion Lords departed long ago, angry at what they considered our betrayal when the Karnuans seized their holy site. If there were ever dwarven Dominion Lords, I've never seen one, and this lady is the first elven Dominion Lord to come to the city in a year or more."

"I don't suppose you know why the High Magus disbanded the Council?" Shadamehr asked.

"I couldn't say, my lord," Jemid replied in a tone that indicated he could say, but not in public. He saluted. "I must be returning to my duties. If you need further assistance—"

"Make way!" a stentorian voice shouted. "Make way!"

A force of cavalry rode into view, trotting along the wide street that led from the Palace to the gate. Each cavalryman wore a highly polished cuirass, marked with the insignia of the Royal guard. They carried swords at their hips, every sword held at exactly the proper angle. An officer rode in front, his cuirass more elaborate than the rest, his tall helm adorned with brightly colored feathers.

The crowd scrambled to get out of the way. Wagon drivers shouted at their horses and steered their wagons off to the side of the road. Street urchins whooped and hollered and the cutpurses did a marvelous business for a frantic few moments during the confusion.

The cavalry officer's stern gaze searched the crowd. Spotting Shadamehr, the officer pointed at him.

"Isn't this kind of them," said Shadamehr. "They've sent a royal escort."

"I was going to tell you," Ulaf said hurriedly, "Alise and I saw someone by the inner gate who took an unusual interest in our arrival."

"I see. Tell me quickly, my dear"—Shadamehr caught hold of Alise by the hand, drew her close—"what do you know of this High Magus Clovis?"

"In a word: purity."

"A bit too brief," said Shadamehr. "You've lost me."

"She was always preaching purity: purity of thought, purity of motive, purity of deed, purity of the heart," Alise said, speaking in a rush. The cavalrymen had been forced to halt for a moment as a wagon filled with sacks of flour blundered across their path. "I'm not surprised she's disbanded the Council. She always maintained that because we did not have the Sovereign Stone, we humans should not have created Dominion Lords. It's not that she didn't believe in the Council. She believed too much. Unless the

Council could be pure and perfect, as it was when it was first created, the Council had no right to exist."

"Thank you, my dear. Now run along. You and Ulaf."

"Absolutely not—" Alise began, fire in her eye.

"If I am arrested you will be of much more use to me on the outside," said Shadamehr quietly. "Now go!"

The officer cursed at the wagon driver and finally ordered two of his men to grab hold of the horses' reins and lead the wagon off the road. This impediment cleared, the officer cantered forward, brought his horse to a halt directly in front of Shadamehr.

"Baron Shadamehr?" said the officer, dismounting. "I am Commander Alderman."

"Commander," said Shadamehr, bowing.

"Baron." The commander bowed. "A request has been made, my lord, that you and the elves"—his gaze shifted to Damra and Griffith—"proceed immediately to the Royal Palace. In accordance with that request, I am here to escort you."

"And I do appreciate you taking the trouble, Commander," said Shadamehr languidly. "You must have spit yourself dry polishing up your armor. But despite the fact that I haven't visited your city for fifteen years, I recall the way to the Royal Palace. Unless you've gone and moved it?"

Watching out of the corner of his eye, Shadamehr saw Alise and Ulaf melt into the crowd, taking the other members of his party with them. They did not go far. Posting themselves on the outskirts of the crowd, in strategic locations, his people patted their weapons, letting him know that they awaited his command.

"No, we have not moved the Palace, my lord," said the officer. "Now, if you will mount your horses and come with us, Baron, Dominion Lord and, er . . . Elven lord." He bowed to Damra and glanced askance at Griffith. "I am also to bring along the Trevenici." He pointed at Jessan.

"What's going on?" Jessan demanded. "What's this fool saying? I'm not going anywhere with—"

"Oh, yes, I think you will," said Shadamehr. Gripping Jessan's arm, he gave it a good squeeze and said softly, "The officer said nothing about bringing the pecwae. Keep quiet and don't cause trouble. Oddly enough, I think I know what I'm doing."

Jessan glanced about. True to form, the moment there seemed likely to be trouble, the pecwae had vanished. Jessan cast the officer a smoldering glance, but kept silent.

"Excuse us, Commander," said Shadamehr. "My Trevenici friend feels shy about having to appear in court—nothing fit to wear, you know. I've persuaded him that although he's a bit underdressed, the regent won't hold it against him. That's who we're going to see, isn't it? The regent?"

"In the name of the King," said the commander solemnly.

"Of course. Actually, my companions and I look forward to speaking to Most Revered High Magus Clovis. We were intending to call at the Palace ourselves. I was going to change clothes first, drape myself in black, but if you don't think there's time—"

"The King is expecting you, my lord," said the commander.

"Then far be it for me to keep the King waiting," said Shadamehr. "He probably wants his afternoon nap. I'll just explain to my friends what's happening. These elves don't speak our language. Unless you would rather tell them, Commander?"

"You go ahead, my lord. I don't speak elvish," said the officer.

Damra and Griffith caught on quickly. Shadamehr turned to them and they regarded him expectantly.

"It seems we're being arrested," he said in Tomagi. "I'm telling you that we're being taken to see the King, so if you could just smile and nod. That's it. Someone saw us riding in and took the trouble to report our arrival. The regent has asked these guardsmen to escort myself, the Trevenici and you two elves to the Palace. What does that tell you?"

"I'm not sure," said Damra cautiously.

"Who knows you have the elven Sovereign Stone? Who knows the Trevenici carries the blood knife? That's it, just smile and nod."

"The Vrykyl," Griffith said grimly.

"I fancy that's the case. We know that Vrykyl infiltrated the courts of Dunkarga and the Tromek. My guess is that one or maybe more have infiltrated this court—"

"Baron Shadamehr," said the officer, starting to grow impatient, "we are expected—"

"Yes, yes. Takes a bit longer to explain things to elves, you know. All the formalities one has to go through. We've just barely made it through discussing the weather."

Shadamehr turned back to the elves. "The King's been murdered—"

"Murdered!" Damra was aghast.

"Smile and nod, smile and nod. Not a doubt of it. The King was a hale and hearty man in his late thirties. He died in his sleep of his heart stopping. The same way you would have died, Damra of Gwyenoc, if Silwyth had not kept you from eating the soup."

"I see." Damra forgot about smiling and nodding. She cast the officer a dark glance. "Why are we going along with this, then?"

"Because," said Shadamehr, "there is an army of ten thousand monsters sweeping down on this city and an eight-year-old child in charge. I hope to find someone who will listen to us and heed our warning. And, if we can discover this Vrykyl and dispose of him, so much the better. Are you both with me?"

"We are, my lord," said Damra.

Griffith smiled and nodded.

Shadamehr grinned and turned to the officer. "My elven friends profess themselves to be overcome with rapture at meeting the regent. I mean, the King."

"I should think they would be," said the commander. He cast Shadamehr a sharp glance and gave his men a terse order to take up their positions.

Shadamehr mounted his horse. Jessan mounted his. He cast a quick glance around the crowd, searching for his friend and the Grandmother, but he couldn't find them. Suddenly a woman broke through the crowd, hurled herself at Shadamehr.

"Baron! I adore you!" Alise cried, reaching up to hand him a rose.

"Of course you do, my dear," said Shadamehr. Leaning down to take the flower, he said in an undertone, "Find the pecwae."

"The pecwae!" Alise gasped.

"Yes, I seem to have misplaced them."

"How did you—"

"Here, now, enough of that, you froward hussy," said the commander, edging his horse in between the two of them. He glowered at Alise. "And you a magus!" he stated, shocked.

At the officer's orders, the cavalry unit closed in around Shadamehr, moved him and the others off at a swift pace.

"How the devil did you lose the pecwae?" Alise asked his retreating back.

He glanced over his shoulder. Raising the rose to his lips, he kissed it, and then tucked it rakishly behind one ear.

"Rot in hell," Alise called after him.

"I love you, too!" he shouted.

4

ALISE STOOD IN THE MIDDLE OF THE STREET, LOOKING PUT-UPON, DIS-
gruntled and worried.

"What's up?" Ulaf asked, bringing along the rest of Shadamehr's retinue.
"What did he say?"

Alise waved her hand disgustedly in the direction of the disappearing
Shadamehr. "He's lost the pecwae."

"The pecwae?" Ulaf repeated, glancing down at the pavement, as if he
might find them underfoot.

"I think he did it on purpose, so they wouldn't be taken prisoner, but he
didn't have to be so bloody efficient about it," Alise said. "I don't see hide
nor hair of them and they shouldn't be hard to spot, what with the
Grandmother in that bell-ringing, stone-clicking skirt of hers."

"They're timid and shy, and they're in a strange city where they don't
know their way. They—"

"And one's carrying the Sovereign Stone," Alise interrupted, sighing.
"They were probably scared out of their wits by the soldiers."

Ulaf looked grave. "I was about to say that, being timid and shy, they
wouldn't go far, but if they're frightened they might just start running and
keep on running. And they're fast as rabbits, even the old one. How long
have they been gone? When did you last see them? Anyone?"

He looked at the group of Shadamehr's people gathered around. They
shook their heads. No one could recall.

"They were with us when we rode in the gate, but that's the last I remember seeing them," Alise said. "If they took off at the first sign of trouble . . ." She glanced at the sun that was high in the sky, nearing noontime.
"Then it's been about an hour. For all we know, they might have run back
out the gate."

"Bloody hell," said Ulaf with feeling. "I'll organize search parties. Everyone knows the pecwae by sight, that will be some help. We'll divide up the city in grids working from the gate inward. I'll send a team outside and alert the orks down by the waterfront."

"One of us will have to keep watch on the palace. That's where Shadamehr's been taken for an 'interview' with the regent. I'll do that," Alise offered.

"And someone's got to go to the Temple of the Magi and alert Rigiswald. He's in the great library boning up on the Sovereign Stone."

"I guess I'll have to do that, too," Alise said, adding with a harassed look, "It's just like Shadamehr to go and get himself arrested and leave us to do his dirty work."

"Cheer up," said Ulaf soothingly, patting her on the shoulder. "Maybe this time they'll hang him."

"That must be the hope that guides me," Alise said. "Everyone have his penny whistle?"

Reaching into her chemise, she drew out a small, bright silver flute attached to a silver chain. The rest of the group exhibited their own whistles. When placed to the lips, the whistle produced an unmistakable sharp, piercing screech that could be heard for blocks. Shadamehr's people used them routinely to contact each other in emergency situations. Ulaf split up the group, assigning each person to a different district and area in the city.

"You all know the signals," said Ulaf in conclusion. "Whistle only if you need help. Headquarters is the Tubby Tabby in Miller's Alley. Remember, the pecwae are probably frightened and confused, so be gentle. Don't scare them. And don't go asking about for them. We don't want to announce their presence in the city if we can help it."

Everyone nodded and took off, each heading for his or her own particular location.

"How do you think Shadamehr's going to get out of this one?" Alise asked Ulaf as he was about to depart.

"The gods know," said Ulaf with a smile and a shrug.

"About Shadamehr?" Alise said, amused. "You must be joking."

Shadamehr was right. There were Vrykyl in the city of New Vinnengael. One of them, Jedash, stood not far from the baron, observed his arrest.

Following his failure to capture the dwarf, Jedash was hauled before Shakur to answer why he should be permitted to continue his wretched existence. Jedash responded sullenly that Shakur's orders were to apprehend a lone dwarf, not a dwarf being guarded by a fire dragon.

Jedash explained his difficulty in tracking the dwarf, how he was never quite able to catch him. He knew now that he had been thwarted by the Trevenici woman, Ranessa, who was really a dragon in disguise. Dragons are powerful in magic, some more powerful than a Vrykyl. Having no orders concerning the dragon, and not willing to take on a dragon singlehanded, Jedash had deemed it best to immediately depart the premises and report back to his commander.

Much as Shakur would have liked to consign Jedash forever to the Void, that power belonged only to Prince Dagnarus and Shakur was loath to draw his lord's attention to yet another failure. Jedash escaped with a reprimand and was sent to New Vinnengael, there to await orders. Jedash was pleased with this assignment, for New Vinnengael was a large city with an immense population, a city where the body of a drunkard discovered in an alley with a stab wound to the heart was not considered anything out of the ordinary. Jedash fed well and occupied his time pleasantly. Then Shakur arrived and Jedash was forced to go to work.

Jedash's assignment was to remain by the front gate, day and night, and keep watch for an elven Dominion Lord traveling in the company of a Trevenici and two pecwae. The Vrykyl did as commanded, taking on the varied images of his many victims so that he did not draw attention to himself. He might be three different people in any one day, from a fat merchant to a flirting whore to a shambling peasant. He had no idea what Shakur was doing. Needless to say, Jedash was not in Shakur's confidence these days.

Jedash didn't care. He was not ambitious, but he did want to avoid the Void, wanted to keep the right to wield his blood knife and continue his survival. Aware that he was on probation, he hoped for a way to prove himself to Lord Dagnarus. Jedash had been at his post only a few days and had not even started to grow bored with his duty when the Baron and his party arrived. Jedash saw the messenger ride off in haste to the palace and observed the subsequent arrest in disappointment, thinking that his job was over.

Then he noted something. His instructions had been to find one elven Dominion Lord, one Trevenici and two pecwae. The Dominion Lord and the Trevenici were hauled off, but the guards had not taken the two pecwae. Jedash saw the two hover on the outskirts of the crowd, keeping watch to see what happened to their friends. When the soldiers escorted Shadamehr away, the two pecwae took to their heels.

Intrigued, Jedash followed after the pecwae. They did not move as if they were frightened. Quite the contrary. From the purposeful way the elder pecwae walked and the interested manner in which she pointed out the sights, she might have been bringing her grandson home for a visit. After trailing them for several blocks, Jedash clasped his hand over the bone knife and imparted this information to Shakur.

"Bring them to me," was the command.

"My pleasure," said Jedash.

The Temple of the Magi and the Royal Palace stood across from each other in the exact center of New Vinnengael. The Temple was designed to impress the viewer with the notion that this complex of buildings was the repository of the gods' power on earth, the holy and the ethereal made manifest. The Royal Palace was designed to impress the viewer with the idea that this single building was the center of man's power on earth, the temporal and the political made manifest.

Other races might and did quibble with this idea. The orks believed that the gods resided in Mount Sa'Gra. The Nimoreans saw the gods in every living thing. The elves scorned to think of the gods as being confined to a building of stone. But even the most inveterate detractor of New Vinnengael could not but feel awe at the magnificence of these structures. If nothing else, they were a testament to the creativity of mankind, to his love of beauty and his aching need to represent that love.

The centerpiece of the Temple complex was the temple itself, a building whose every line drew the eye to heaven. Tall spires pierced the clouds. Flying buttresses carried the earthbound dreams of man upward in graceful arches to the spires, that carried them to heaven. Huge double doors of beaten gold stood always open, day and night, to permit the worshipful to enter.

The University, the House of Healers, the Bibliotheca, and other buildings dealing with the workings and teachings of the magi were located behind the temple, amidst beautiful flowering gardens.

Directly across from the Temple was the Palace, an immense building formed in the shape of a crescent moon with its wings extending toward the Temple, as if to embrace it, yet never quite touching. Meant to give the impression of stable solidity, there were no fanciful, delicate spires on the palace, but thick, solid walls. The entire front of the building was a columned portico.

A favorite pastime of children and visitors was to try to count the number of columns. For some reason that could never be satisfactorily explained, the count either came out one thousand four hundred and ninety-nine columns or one thousand five hundred. The mystery of the vanishing column was one of the wonders of New Vinnengael. Treatises had been written on the subject by experts, who spoke of optical illusions or the position of the sun or the movement of shadows depending on the world's alignment with the stars. Each theory had its advocate, who could often be heard explaining the pet theory to visitors.

The Palace stood seven stories high with seven rows of seven hundred crystal windows that looked out to the east on one side and the west on the other. When the sun set, the light struck the myriad windows with a blaze of fire, so that one was nearly blinded by the sight. The banner of Vinnengael flew at the highest point on the palace, with the banners of its subject city-states ranged around it. All banners flew at half-mast this day, in honor of the death of the King.

Unlike the Temple, the palace was not open to all and sundry, for the political center of the Empire must be protected. When the Palace was first built, there had been thoughts of surrounding it with a high stone wall, but what is the use of building a marvelous structure if no one can see it? The Palace Guard had decided upon a fence made of twisted wrought iron topped by spikes, a fence that surrounded the entire palace and its gardens, front and back, and was enhanced by magical spells to repel any invading force. The Royal Guard mounted duty at the Palace Gate. Visitors gaped through the wrought-iron bars, hoping to catch a glimpse of the young King and trying to count the columns.

The Royal Cavalry handed off their prisoners to the Royal Palace Guard with dispatch and efficiency. The prisoners dismounted, their horses were led away to the stables. The cavalry officer saluted the Baron and the two elves, who smiled and nodded. The visitors, enthralled by the sight of the elves, clustered as near as they could, which wasn't very near, due to the guards, who hustled the party through the gate with alacrity.

Some know-it-all pronounced that these were representatives of the elf king coming to give homage to the young King and everyone immediately believed it.

The guards marched the prisoners across a courtyard that seemed as wide as the Sea of Redesh to Jessan. The palace was an enormous stone monster, its maw gaping wide, showing one thousand five hundred teeth and a myriad, gleaming eyes. At the thought of being swallowed up by this dreadful place, his steps faltered, his hands grew cold and clammy.

A longing for the silent, snow-filled forests, for the safe, warm, musky darkness of his uncle's hut filled Jessan's soul. He had borne with stoic fortitude the broken fingers of his hand, but this pain of longing for his home was too wrenching. Hot tears filled his eyes.

A hand gripped Jessan's arm.

"Steady, warrior," said Shadamehr. "You've done well so far, but you're about to face your greatest challenge. Quite likely, there's a Vrykyl in here, waiting for us. We don't know which one of these people it might be, although I have an idea. You must keep your nerve, watch me and act on my signal. Can you do that?"

Shadamehr regarded Jessan with confidence. Damra, walking on the other side of Shadamehr, smiled at Jessan. He realized suddenly that these strange people considered him an equal and his longing and his fears vanished.

"I understand," Jessan said softly. "What do you want me to do?"

"You're doing fine, so far," said Shadamehr with a grin. "Continue to act the part of the gawking rube and they'll discount you completely. They're going to take our weapons, once we're inside the palace. They won't find the blood knife, will they?"

Jessan shook his head, grateful to the man for crediting him with play-acting, when Shadamehr must have known Jessan's fears were very real.

"No, I guessed it had ways of keeping itself to itself. It's my thinking that the Vrykyl believes you carry the Sovereign Stone. Keep the Vrykyl thinking that, if you can. How's your hand? Can you use it?"

Jessan wiggled the fingers. "Stiff, but I can manage. What about Bashae and the Grandmother?"

"I have my people searching for them. They'll find them and keep them safe. Don't worry. Once we're finished here"—Shadamehr spoke blithely, as though they were going to have tea and crumpets and then depart—"we'll go retrieve them."

"And then what?" Jessan asked.

He'd been looking forward to reaching New Vinnengael, to getting rid of this Stone and the terrible burden he bore. Now that was impossible, or so it seemed. He began to think that he must carry the burden forever.

"One step at a time," said Shadamehr. "One foot in front of the other. One breath to the next."

"All is in the hands of the gods," said Damra.

"Good lord, I hope things aren't as bad as that," said Shadamehr.

The Royal Guards marched their prisoners across the stone paved courtyard. Eventually, after what seemed a journey of several days to Jessan, they reached the palace. They did not enter by the huge formal doors. Made of silver, the doors were opened only on special occasions. The last time had been just a week ago, to permit the coffin of the King to be carried out of the palace in solemn procession across to the Temple.

The guards took them in one of the innumerable side doors that gave access to the palace. The gate guard turned them over to the palace guard. The palace guard asked politely for Baron Shadamehr to surrender his sword, saying—quite truthfully—that no one was permitted to bear arms in the presence of the King.

Shadamehr handed over his sword, with the admonition that it had belonged to his great-grandfather and was quite valuable. The guards promised to keep it safe. An officer asked him if he would swear an oath to the gods that he carried no other weapons on his person.

"I'll swear at the gods anytime you like," said Shadamehr.

The guard flushed and said that was not quite what he'd meant.

"Oh, I understand," said Shadamehr. "Swear to the gods. Sorry for the confusion. What was it you wanted me to say?"

The officer was about to reply, when they were interrupted. It had suddenly occurred to the palace guard that there was no way they could really divest a Dominion Lord of her weapons. Although they could take her swords, they could not very well take away her god-given abilities. And, someone said, the only way to keep one of the Wyred from using his magic was to kill him and they had no orders concerning that.

"We are of the House of Gwyenoc, allies of the Divine, who is a friend to the King of New Vinnengael," Damra stated, as Shadamehr translated. "My cousin the Divine would take it amiss if something were to happen to either my husband or myself. I am a Dominion Lord. I am sworn to protect the innocent and the defenseless. I do not attack unless I am attacked. I would certainly never harm or seek to do harm to the King of New Vinnengael. You have my sacred oath on that."

"As for me," said Griffith, also speaking through Shadamehr, "I use my magic strictly for defensive purposes. To do anything else would not be honorable."

The officer bowed in respect to both elves, then motioned to an aide.

"Send to the regent," he said, unwilling to take this responsibility on himself. "Find out what we're to do."

While the aide was gone, Shadamehr exchanged gossip with the guards. The elves stood aloof and impassive. The guards searched Jessan, grimacing as they had to touch the greasy leathers he wore and making rude comments, as though he was deaf and dumb as well as a barbarian. His anger at this treatment effectively helped banish his fear. He did as Shadamehr had asked him to do—feigned ignorance. The guards did not find the bone knife, though one put his hand right on it.

The guard returned with the regent's aide—a Temple magus—who stated that the regent was quite capable of dealing with these people, if the Palace Guard was not. If the Palace Guard was fearful of two elves, they could double the number of men assigned to them. The officer exchanged grim glances with his men and muttered something beneath his breath.

No love lost between cloth and sword, Shadamehr noted with interest.

"Very well," said the officer tersely, "they are your responsibility."

The Temple magus stalked off, leading the way. The prisoners followed, escorted by four of the Palace Guard. The officer might have sent more, but he felt the honor of his men had been impugned by the magus.

Shadamehr had not been inside the Royal Palace for fifteen years. Having played here as a child when his parents came to visit, he knew his way around almost as well as if he'd been here yesterday. Some things had changed. New tapestries hung on the wall, new stands of armor replaced rusting ones, but a truly ugly statue of King Hegemon still held its ponderous place in an alcove and a large porcelain urn, inside which the young Shadamehr had once crawled during a game of hide and seek, was still in its corner.

Shadamehr noticed another change. He could not place it, at first, and then he realized what was different. The halls were usually filled with an assortment of sugared courtiers and self-important functionaries who clogged the royal arteries and kept the royal heart beating at a sluggish pace. The halls this day were empty.

"Quiet as a temple," said Shadamehr, puzzled. He realized the implication of his statement. "Od's bodkin. This *is* a temple."

The vast marble halls had once rung with laughter and the sounds of barking dogs and coins being tossed onto the marble floors in games of chance. By contrast, these halls were silent, the only sounds being the soft whisper of woolen robes, the soft shuffle of leather boots and the soft murmur of voices speaking of celestial matters.

A shiver ran over Shadamehr, starting at the base of his spine and rising up to his hair follicles. The thought came to him how easy it would be for a Vrykyl, in the guise of a High Magus, to populate the Palace with Void worshipers.

He had no way of knowing if these magi were what they appeared to be. Magi all looked alike to him, no matter how many times Alise had tried to explain the differences in the garbs of the various orders. He wished very much that she was here, for she was an expert—albeit reluctantly—in Void magic, and she might have been able to tell him if that sweet-faced young magus in the corner concealed the sores and pustules of Void magic beneath her robes.

Shadamehr assumed that they would be taken to the throne room, which was on the first level, but the magus disabused him of that notion by leading them up several marble staircases to the fifth level.

Shadamehr knew these rooms, the private quarters for the King and his family. He and the late King had been good friends as children, a friendship that had regretfully cooled as they grew older. The magus led them to an antechamber with chairs, a fireplace and thick, soft carpet. A door at the far end led to an inner chamber. The magus knocked on the closed door and was admitted by yet another magus. Shadamehr, the elves, Jessan and their guards were told to wait in the antechamber until the regent should deign to see them.

"My lord!" cried an astonished voice.

"Gregory!" Shadamehr said warmly, advancing to seize hold of the man's hand. "Thank the gods, I've found a living person! All these magi about, I thought I'd died, you know, and gone to the bad place."

"Baron Shadamehr!" Gregory stared at him, bewildered. "What are you doing here? If you've come for the funeral, you're too late. It was last week."

"I know. I heard. I'm dashed sorry, Gregory," Shadamehr said.

Gregory looked grieved, distraught. This was not surprising. He had been the King's chamberlain and confidant for well on twenty years.

Shadamehr drew the chamberlain off to one side, cast him a fond and worried glance.

"By the wretched way you look, we'll be attending your funeral next. When did you last get any sleep?"

Gregory shook his head. "I don't know. It doesn't matter. It's been awful. Simply horrible, my lord. I found him, you know. In his bed. He'd been fine the night before. He was in good spirits, though worried about these rumors of war coming out of the west. He canceled his annual hunting trip to his lodge because of it. I mulled his wine for him before bed; he liked me to make it, you know, instead of one of the servants. I left the cup sitting on the hob to keep warm, for he was writing in his journal . . ."

"So that's how they did it," Shadamehr said softly. "The mulling spices would conceal the taste of the poison."

"I beg your pardon, my lord," said Gregory.

"Nothing. Servants moving about the room, I suppose, turning down the bed covers, drawing the curtains, that sort of thing."

"Why, yes, my lord. The King was very well attended. The prince came in to bid his father good night and I left the two of them alone together . . ." He blinked red eyes. "That was the last time I spoke to him. I usually bid him goodnight and god's blessing on his rest, but I did not want to disturb him. I know it's foolish, my lord, but I sometimes think that if I'd asked the gods to watch over him—"

"Now, Gregory, be sensible," said Shadamehr with a kindly pat. "If you could truly invoke the power of the gods you'd be a wealthy man and not have to spend your days polishing His Majesty's shoes."

"I've quite enjoyed my work, my lord," said Gregory in wistful tones. "I shall miss it, when I'm gone."

"What's this?" Shadamehr said. "Are you being turned out?"

"Yes, my lord. Today is my last day. The regent decreed that only Temple magi are to be employed in the Palace from now on. She doesn't feel it's proper for His Majesty to come in contact with what she terms 'common people' such as myself."

"Good riddance to her, then, I say, Gregory," said Shadamehr.

"I suppose." Gregory sighed deeply. "But the palace has been my home, my lord. My father was the old King's chamberlain, you know. I shall miss His Majesty and I must admit that I am worried about him. He used to be such a happy and merry child. He rarely smiles at all now. It's as if the life has been crushed out of him by these blasted magi."

Gregory stopped talking. His face paled. "I beg pardon, my lord. I spoke before I thought."

"You spoke your heart, Gregory. Listen," Shadamehr added hurriedly, fearful that they might be interrupted, "where could I reach you, in case I needed you?"

"I have taken lodging in the White Hart Inn, my lord," Gregory said.

"Good, good. I may be around tonight to look you up. Depends on how things go here. You wouldn't mind coming to work for me, would you?"

"I would be honored, my lord," said Gregory, his face warming.

"The young King trusts you and likes you, I take it?"

"I should like to think so, my lord," Gregory replied, puzzled.

"Good, good." Shadamehr squeezed the man's hand. "Take care of yourself. Gods' blessing and all that."

Lightly, casually, Shadamehr turned away and sauntered across the room to where the two elves stood talking quietly together.

"Pretend we're admiring the furniture," said Shadamehr. "What do you say to a spot of kidnapping?"

Damra and Griffith stared at him, then exchanged conscious glances between themselves.

"Yes, amazing, isn't it?" said Shadamehr, shifting from Tomagi to Elder-speak. "This chair does not look thirty years old. I fancy it's been re-covered. However, if you will notice the right leg, you'll see my tooth marks. My mother was fond of saying that I cut my teeth on politics—"

Shadamehr leaned closer, shifted back to Tomagi, "If I am right, the Most High Revered Magus is, in reality, a Vrykyl. She has removed all the King's trusted servants, replaced them with her own people. It's my guess that she intends to hand New Vinnengael and the young King over to Dagnarus. We must rescue the King, smuggle him out of the city. Otherwise, I fear they will either imprison the child or kill him. What do you say?"

Damra and Griffith again exchanged glances. Griffith nodded.

"We've been thinking along the same lines, Baron Shadamehr," he said softly. "We noticed what was happening, but we weren't certain how to tell you. What is your plan?"

"For all of us to come out of this alive," said Shadamehr as the door to the inner chamber began to open. "With the possible exception of the Vrykyl."

The magus announced in sonorous tones:

"All bow to His Majesty, the Most High and Holy King of Vinnengael, Hirav the Second."

THE CHAMBER INTO WHICH THEY WERE USHERED HAD ONCE BEEN THE King's favorite in the palace, a place the King had liked to call his "working" room. Spacious and airy, the room was on the corner of the building at the northern horn of the crescent moon. Two crystal-paned windows provided a wondrous view of the city of New Vinnengael to the west and the rich farm lands along the Arven river to the north.

Passionately fond of hunting, Hirav had filled his room with souvenirs of his hunts. Shadamehr had not been in this room for fifteen years, but he remembered that there had been the white pelt of a deadly shnay on the floor. Heads of noble stags had adorned the walls, along with the King's favorite weapons and a stand for his hunting hawk, who often kept him company while he labored over affairs of state.

The room was undergoing transformation, Shadamehr noted with a pang. The stags' heads had been removed. The shnay pelt had been rolled up and stashed in a corner. The weapons were nowhere to be seen. The King's desk, that had once faced the windows—he liked to be able to look out into the sunlit meadows—had been turned so that it now faced the door. Heavy velvet curtains were being draped over the crystal windows to block out the sunlight. The job was only half completed.

Presumably this transformation was being undertaken at the behest of the Most Revered High Magus Clovis, the new regent. A heavy-set woman in her mid-sixties, she had eyes the color of pick-axes. The lines of the woman's face tended downward; no hint of a smile ever touched those thin, compressed lips.

Shadamehr stared intently at the woman, hoping to determine if she was the Vrykyl. He dared not look at his companions, but he knew they were doing the same, trying to see past the illusion of life in the iron-gray eyes to the reality of the dead emptiness of the Void. He did not see the Void, only stern disapproval.

Shadamehr casually shifted his gaze away from the High Magus to take note of other people in the room, to get a feel for the lay of the land, so to speak.

It was then he saw the other magus.

Shadamehr was born supremely confident in himself, in his cleverness, his skill and his courage. He rarely doubted himself or his abilities. At the sight of this magus, Shadamehr was forced to concede that they had a bit of a problem. The baron had been rather cocky over the fact that they were being guarded by four guards—one apiece. Take into account the King's two personal bodyguards and that was six guards—six to four. He would take those odds any day of the week and twice on High Holy days, especially in company with a Dominion Lord. He had not foreseen the lamentable fact that the Most Revered High Magus would bring along her pet war wizard.

Shadamehr sighed deeply. He knew the battle magus. His name was Tasgall, and he was a formidable opponent. The last time they'd been together, they had fought on the same side. Shadamehr favored Tasgall with a pleased grin of recognition, as one comrade to another.

Tasgall regarded Shadamehr with a stony look and Shadamehr remembered, rather late, that Tasgall had never really approved of him.

"If Tasgall's gone to the Void then we can all bend over and kiss our sweet behinds farewell," Shadamehr said to himself.

The most feared of all the magi, a battle magus is trained in the art of warfare, trained to use his powerful magicks to hinder or destroy the enemy. The battle magus relies not only on magical arts. He is also a skilled combatant, proficient in the use of steel as well as sorcery. Tasgall was all decked out in his war wizard best: plate and chain mail, marked with the emblem of the Battle Magi—a crushing mailed fist— and he sported a huge two-handed broadsword on his hip. Taller than average, Tasgall was powerfully built with massive shoulders and immense arms. He stood with his arms at his sides, poised and confident—the image of the veteran soldier, who has proven his worth in battle.

Shadamehr flicked a glance around the room, noted that despite the bright afternoon sunlight, a burning candle stood on the desk at Tasgall's side. The candle served to warn the prisoners that the war magus was capable of casting both Earth and Fire spells.

Tasgall's keen brown eyes sized up each of the prisoners as they entered the room and, although he kept all of them in view, his gaze went most frequently to Griffith, the Wyred, the battle magus's elven counterpart.

Last, Shadamehr noticed the Most High and Holy King of Vinnengael, Hirav the Second.

The child stood at one end of the desk. He had been fidgeting with a quill pen. At a word from the High Magus, the boy laid down the pen and turned to face them.

Hirav was a comely child, with brown-gold hair that gleamed like polished mahogany, and gold-flecked green eyes. Outlined by thick, dark lashes, the eyes' dancing glints were shadowed by thick dark brows. His face had the sickly pallor of one who is never permitted to go outside and play in the sunshine. He was dressed in all his finery, like a miniature adult, with tunic and silk hose and an ermine-collared cape that looked ludicrous on a little boy. He stood straight and tall and was trying very hard to look regal, although his red-rimmed eyes and pink-tipped nose gave signs that he'd been crying.

"By gods' arms," Shadamehr muttered to himself, a wave of pity and anger sweeping over him, "if I do nothing else, I'll see to it that this kid gets to play stickball outdoors in the sunshine."

They bowed to the King—the elves stiffly and Jessan not at all, until Shadamehr nudged him.

The King gave a slight nod of his head, after which his eyes slid to the High Magus, seeking her approval.

The workings of Shadamehr's mind proceeded with remarkable swiftness. He developed his plan in the time it took to bend his body for his bow and straighten himself again.

They were in the center of the room, about four feet from the desk. Clovis stood behind the desk, the King in front of the desk and slightly to the right. The prisoners' four guards stood directly behind them. The two royal bodyguards remained at the door, facing outward. The war magus took up a position almost directly across from Griffith. Damra stood beside Shadamehr, on his right. The elves were playing their parts well, looked elegantly outraged. Jessan was on Shadamehr's left.

What the Trevenici youth was thinking was impossible to tell. He stood stock still, looking outlandish and oafish with his long, straggling hair, his sun-darkened skin, his well-worn and not particularly clean fringed leather pants and bead-adorned tunic. The King's eyes widened at the sight of the young warrior and his glance strayed constantly to him. This was undoubtedly a new experience for the child, who had seen elves and noble barons by the score, but never a barbarian.

"The Wyred takes Tasgall, the Dominion Lord deals with the High Magus, the Trevenici and I dispatch the six guards," Shadamehr detailed his plan to himself. "I snatch the kid, use him as hostage—wouldn't really hurt him, but they don't know that, I'm a desperate character—and we high-tail it down the hall to a secret passage that, with my customary luck and good looks, still opens the same way it used to open thirty years ago and still leads to the same place which was, as I recall, somewhere down around the privies. Doesn't seem all that difficult."

The Most Revered High Magus rose up from behind her desk and walked around to stand at the side. If she hoped to daunt them by providing them with the full effect of her regalia that marked her as the highest authority in the Church, she was wasting her time. Shadamehr glanced at her with less interest than if she'd been the moth-eaten shnay pelt on the floor. Facing the King, Shadamehr said to him with a disarming smile, "We were brought here by your command, Your Royal Majesty. What is it you require of us?"

The child was taken aback. He had not expected this and he glanced beseechingly at the High Magus, who sallied forth to his rescue.

"I know you, Baron Shadamehr," she said in severe tones.

"Alas, Madam, you have me at a disadvantage," Shadamehr replied, still smiling at the young King.

"You *do* know me, I think." The High Magus's lips compressed. "I voted against you being given the opportunity to take the Tests for Dominion Lord. My opinion was ignored, more's the pity. I still believe that you passed by chicanery, although I could not prove it. I was not in the least surprised when you lacked the courage to assume the honor the gods saw fit to bestow on you."

"Ah, now, you see, Revered Magus," said Shadamehr, finally favoring her with a glance. "I thought that it was the gods who should be honored by my acceptance of the favor—an honor that I wasn't quite ready to grant them."

The High Magus's face suffused with anger. She swelled visibly and opened her mouth to respond, but Shadamehr had decided that the time had come to cease bantering with underlings. He returned his gaze to the King, who looked stunned.

"Your Majesty," said Shadamehr, ignoring the outraged splutterings of the High Magus, "my companions and I have ridden one thousand miles in sixteen days to bring you dire news. An army of ten thousand creatures of the Void is within two days' ride of New Vinnengael. This army is led by a Prince who has given himself to the Void and who intends to take Vinnengael and our people with him. Your Majesty must take action now to defend your city and the people who look to you for protection."

Shadamehr spoke to the King, but in reality he was imparting his warning to Tasgall. The veteran soldier took note. He shifted his gaze directly to Shadamehr.

As for the King, the child was dismayed. Apparently this wasn't in the script, for he had no idea what to do or say. He looked again to the High Magus.

Clovis's iron eyes flickered, then hardened.

"Flummery," she said.

Tasgall turned his head slightly, still keeping his eyes on his charges, but managing to regard her at the same time.

"High Magus," he said deferentially, "if this is true—"

"It isn't," said Clovis coldly, cutting him off. "This miscreant is trying to distract us from our goal." She advanced a step toward Shadamehr, held out her hand. "You will give me the two portions of the Sovereign Stone, the elven and the human."

Well, well, thought Shadamehr, how did you come to know about the Sovereign Stones, Most Revered High Magus? Through the blood knife?

"I assure you, Madam," he said aloud, "that the Sovereign Stones are the least of your worries." He pointed northward. "If you will look out that window, you'll see smoke on the horizon. I am willing to wager that the smoke is from the first of the outlying farms and villages being put to the torch—"

Tasgall shifted his gaze to the window. A frown line appeared between his eyes and he looked back at Shadamehr as if he would very much like to have a private talk with him. Tasgall was under orders, however, and could not very well depart from them.

"*You* are the enemy of the Empire, Baron Shadamehr," Clovis thundered. "You and the elves who conspire together. Enough of these lies! I am the head of the Church. Hand over the Sovereign Stones to me now. Both the human stone—that is in the possession of this barbarian—and the elven stone, that this false Dominion Lord stole from Tromek."

Shadamehr blinked. "Excuse me. Do I understand that you are accusing this noble Dominion Lord of being a base thief? If you'll allow me, Madam, I'll translate for her—"

Clovis clasped her hands in front of her robes, rocked back on her heels. "Damra of Gwyenoc is quite fluent in Elderspeak. Aren't you, Dominion Lord? If not, I am capable of doing my own translating." She shifted to Tomagi. "I am in contact with the Shield of the Divine. He sent an urgent messenger to inform the Temple that the Sovereign Stone was stolen in a bloody battle that left many of his men dead. He had reason to believe that the thief would come to New Vinnengael, there to try to deliver the Stone to the Council of Dominion Lords. As for the human part of the Stone, we know that it was discovered and that it was also en route to New Vinnengael. Do you deny this?"

"I see no reason to dignify this interrogation with a response of any kind," said Damra coolly.

The High Magus began to chant and, lifting her finger, she pointed at Damra's tabard. Clovis moved her finger in a circular motion, faster and faster, tightening the circle until finally she spread her hand and spoke the words, "True light."

A faint blue-white light shone from beneath the tabard. The light grew brighter and brighter, until its radiance dazzled the eyes. The image of the Sovereign Stone appeared, floating in front of Damra, who lifted her chin and stared unfazed at the Most Revered High Magus.

The High Magus turned to Jessan, pointed her finger at him.

"No," Jessan said through clenched teeth. "Stop her!"

"Easy, son," said Shadamehr quietly. "She won't hurt you. She can't."

The High Magus chanted and waved her finger. Jessan stood with his jaw clenched, his hands balled into fists.

No light gleamed.

"That's torn it," said Shadamehr softly. "She knows now that he's a decoy."

He reached swiftly into his boot, drew a poniard. Jessan snatched the blood knife from his belt. Damra touched the medallion of the Dominion Lord. Silver armor flowed over her body. She spoke words in elven and her husband nodded in response. Griffith filled his lungs with air, took a step toward the war magus.

"Guards to me!" the High Magus cried.

"Guards to the King!" Tasgall bellowed, glaring at the High Magus. "Protect the King!"

Seeing the barbarian draw a knife on the High Magus, the Royal Guards leapt to obey her. When they heard Tasgall countermand her order and shout for them to guard the King, they halted briefly, confused.

"The King, damn your eyes!" Tasgall shouted.

The guards obeyed. Shifting their attention to the King, they tried to reach the child, who was on the other side of the room, standing by the desk, his eyes wide and filled with terror. The guards halted, their way blocked by—unbelievably—three Dominion Lords.

The three Dominion Lords looked like Damra and fought like Damra. The guards knew in their heads that two of these were illusion, but they also knew that the third wasn't. The third was real and so was her weapon. Even as one of the guards endeavored to slip past what he thought was an illusion, Damra's sword pierced his shoulder. The man gasped in pain, blood spurted from the wound. The power of the mind is potent. The wound looked real and it felt real. Blood flowed down his arm. It was all he could do to keep his grip on his sword.

Shadamehr jumped in front of the King. "Don't be afraid, Your Majesty," he said swiftly to the child. "We're here to help you escape."

He turned to face two members of the Royal bodyguard, who advanced on him, their swords drawn. Shadamehr blocked the cutting stroke of one with his poniard. He kicked the man in the groin and, when he doubled over, gave him a clip on the ear with his fist. The second guard leapt at Shadamehr, swinging his sword. His mouth and eyes opened wide in astonishment. He gave a gasp. The sword fell from his hand. He slumped to the floor. Jessan stood over him, a blood-stained knife in his hand and a smile on his lips.

Shadamehr cast a quick glance around the room. The Dominion Lord and her illusions held their own. Not being certain which was Damra and which wasn't, he left that battle to the three of them.

Catching hold of Jessan's arm, Shadamehr gripped it tightly and shouted at him. "Cover me! I'm going to grab the King!"

He didn't know if Jessan understood him or not. The young man's eyes were pale and intent as those of a wolf seeking prey. Shadamehr couldn't take time to worry about it. He turned back to the child.

Tasgall had his spell ready to cast, but his attention had been distracted from his magic by his need to protect the King. He launched his magic, but he was just a few heartbeats too late.

Griffith breathed out all the air in his lungs. A cloud of noxious green gas flowed over Tasgall, enveloped him.

Tasgall's body froze, motionless. His mouth was wide open, but no sound came out. He could not move his hands or his feet or his head. Paralyzed, Tasgall dropped to the floor. He lay there, helpless, his torso twitching and jerking as he fought to try to free himself of the debilitating spell.

The paralyze spell is not meant to kill but to incapacitate, to give the spellcaster time to move on to round two. The spell would start to wear off in a few seconds, and then Griffith's enemy would be up and dangerous. Griffith moved in to take his enemy out for the duration of the battle. As he did so, he spared a glance for his wife.

Damra fought the guards with her usual spirit and skill, but another enemy, a more potent enemy than any Royal Guard, sneaked up on her from behind. High Magus Clovis was calling on the magic of the earth to halt the Dominion Lord.

"Damra! Look out!" Griffith shouted.

Damra smashed her mailed fist in her opponent's face, sent him reeling and turned around to face this new threat. Damra believed the High Magus to be a Vrykyl. Against a Vrykyl, Damra would need more than her powers of illusion. Her eyes went to the candle that had been placed upon the desk for the convenience of the battle magus. Other magi could utilize Fire magic, as well. Damra jumped forward, ran her hand through the flame of the candle, and called upon the gods to grant her the power of fire.

A ripple of Earth magic caused the floor to buckle beneath Damra's feet. She fought to keep her balance, but the magic was too potent. The Earth magic yanked the floor out from underneath her and she pitched forward to fall on her hands and knees. She felt a twinge in her wrist, a bone break.

Pain shot up her arm and her fingers went numb. She dropped her sword, unable to wield it. Her magic slipped away from her.

Griffith saw his wife in trouble. He also saw the spell he'd cast on the war magus start to wear off. No time to do this right. Bounding to Tasgall's side, Griffith leaned over the human and spit into his face.

Tasgall screamed. Covering his eyes with his hands, he rolled on the floor, kicking his feet and legs in agony. The pain was intense. His eyeballs seemed to be melting in his head. Blinded, he could do nothing, was more helpless than the child he was supposed to protect.

Griffith turned to his wife, intending to cast his magic on the High Magus. Unfortunately, the young King stood between them. Griffith was forced to halt his spell-casting, for the spell had the potential for harm and he did not want to hurt the child. Ethical and moral considerations aside, nothing would play into the Shield's hands more than a member of the Divine's faction killing the young King of Vinnengael.

Seeing that the High Magus was distracted by her fight with Damra, Shadamehr swooped in and grabbed hold of the King.

"I will not harm you, Your Majesty," Shadamehr said swiftly and earnestly, lifting the child in his arms. "I am your loyal subject. I will remove you to a place of safety—"

The High Magus cried out in fury. Searing pain glanced along Shadamehr's ribs, a pain that flashed swiftly, a pain he forgot in the sudden, riveting shock that drove all coherent thought and sensation from his mind.

Gasping, Shadamehr let loose his hold on the child. The King tumbled to the floor. Still staring at the child, Shadamehr stepped backward and collided with Jessan, who had obeyed Shadamehr's order to cover his back.

Jessan caught hold of Shadamehr, held onto him until the man could steady himself. Griffith had no idea what was going on. All he knew was that the young King had dropped to the floor and was safely out of harm's way. Griffith breathed the cloud of paralyzing gas onto the High Magus.

Clovis tumbled to the floor, lay there alongside the stunned child. The magic of the High Magus ceased. The floor quit shaking. Griffith helped his wife to stand.

"Shadamehr, are you hurt?" Jessan demanded, alarmed. The baron's cocky jauntiness had evaporated. He was white to the lips.

"We have to get out of here," Shadamehr said, struggling to breathe. He pressed his hand to his side. "The door. Run for it."

Damra looked at him, looked to her husband for an answer, but he could only shake his head. This was no time to bring the issue before a committee for a vote.

They ran toward the door, halted at the sound of shouts and running feet slamming down the hall.

"No good," said Shadamehr. He looked swiftly around for another way out. His gaze fixed on the crystal window.

"I think some magic would come in handy about now."

Damra guessed what he had in mind and looked to her husband.

"The High Magus will be paralyzed for only a minute," Griffith warned.

"I can deal with her," said Damra.

Lightning blazed in a blue-red arc over her head. She seized hold of the lightning. The bolt twisted and twined like a whip in her hand, crackled when she struck it against the floor.

"Take care of them, Griffith." Damra gave him a fond smile. "And yourself."

"No!" Jessan shouted, realizing suddenly what Shadamehr meant to do. Jessan struggled, tried to fight free. "You are mad! It's like jumping off the top of a cliff! I'll take my chances fighting—"

"Griffith!" Shadamehr shouted. "We're leaving!"

"There is a chance the spell might not work, my lord," Griffith shouted.

"Oh, balls!" Shadamehr said angrily. He clasped his arms around Jessan with a grip like an iron band.

Giving a roar, Shadamehr lunged shoulder-first through the window, five stories above the ground.

6

ALISE PACED BACK AND FORTH IN FRONT OF THE PALACE, WAITING AND watching for Shadamehr. Alternately fuming at him and worrying over him, it occurred to her that she had spent much of her twenty-eight years waiting and watching for Shadamehr.

The daughter of a goldsmith, Alise had been born to privilege and wealth. She had been expected to earn her position by marrying one of the sons of her father's business partner or some impoverished nobleman looking for funds to maintain his estate. A good many men, both old and young, merchant class and noble, were quite willing to take the gold-smith's beautiful red-haired daughter off his hands—until Alise made the mistake of opening her mouth, as her mother said in exasperation.

Quick-witted and sharp-tongued, Alise found books far more to her lik-ing than men. The Church was insistent that all children in New Vinnen-gael receive at least rudimentary schooling and so Alise had been taught to read and write. The Church had an ulterior motive in this. By issuing laws that all children attend Church-run schools, the magi were able to find out which children were gifted in magic. They immediately noticed Alise's intelligence and magical power, and when she was of age, the Church began courting her as assiduously as the young nobles, albeit for a different purpose. They hoped to persuade her to enter the Revered Sis-terhood.

Alise enjoyed her studies. The arcane art came naturally to her. She did not really want to become a magi, though, for she found the disciplined life of the Church too restrictive. Still, comparing that life to the boring life of a devoted wife, Alise decided that, all in all, the life of the magus did have its advantages. Over the tearful and vociferous objections of her parents, Alise entered the Church.

Once there, she was forever in trouble. She was caught sneaking out to go dancing, caught raiding the buttery, caught wearing pretty clothes in public, instead of the drab brown robes. Her glib tongue and her skill in magic saved her from being tossed out on her ear. One of her teachers, an irascible magus called Rigiswald, concluded that the girl was not really a troublemaker. She was bored. She needed a challenge and he was prepared to give her one. He recommended to his superiors that she be one of the chosen few permitted to study Void magic.

The Church had preached for centuries that Void magic was evil. The Church prohibited the unregulated study of Void magic. Unauthorized practitioners (usually hedge-wizards) were hunted down and either "persuaded" to discontinue the use of Void magic or face imprisonment or death. The Church did recognize (although not publicly) that Void magic had its place in the universe. Thus they permitted and encouraged a certain few of their own to study it, if for no other reason than that they could recognize it when they saw it and know how to deal with it.

Alise's teachers scoffed at the notion of the lovely young girl agreeing to work with Void magic, the casting of which takes its toll on the body. All elemental magic requires the use of an element to work the spell. A Fire magus must have access to flame, a Water magus must use water. The Void magus sacrifices a bit of his own life essence to work his magic. Void magic weakens a magus physically during spell-casting, pustules and sores appear on his flesh. Her teachers said that Alise was far too vain to do anything that would mar her rose-petal complexion.

Rigiswald knew Alise better than they. The idea of studying forbidden magic intrigued her. She did not like the magic of the Void, but she found it challenging, in a repulsive way, and she soon became adept at its use.

Observing her skill, the Church recommended that she join the Inquisition, those members of the Church who actively seek out Void magic practioners and bring them to justice. Because the Inquisition works in secret and in shadow, searching for heretics both within the Church and without, they are the most feared of all the Orders. Alise refused to have anything to do with them.

The Church insisted that she join or face retribution, for she was now a skilled practitioner of forbidden magic. Rigiswald helped her to escape and smuggled her safely out of New Vinnengael. He sent her to seek help from his friend, Baron Shadamehr.

When she'd first met Shadamehr, she'd thought him arrogant and silly and insufferable. She now added reckless and infuriating to the list, as well as brave and compassionate. She refused to acknowledge the last two, however, just as she refused to let herself fall in love with him. He could never take anything seriously, including love, and she knew she would end up deeply hurt. Meanwhile, they were good friends and comrades, except during those times when she hated and detested him. This was one of those times.

Before arriving at the Palace, Alise had slipped unseen into the Bibliotheca, avoided the Temple magi. (She was considered by the Church to be a rogue magus, and there was a warrant out for her arrest, but that is another story.) Finding Rigiswald among piles of books, she had warned him that the pecwae were lost in the city and that Shadamehr had been hauled off a prisoner to the Palace.

Grumbling at being interrupted, Rigiswald had asked tersely what else was new and had gone back to his reading.

Alise left the Bibliotheca to take up watch outside the palace. Fortunately for her, the large crowd that was almost always in attendance to gawk at the guards and stare through the iron bars was present this afternoon. Alise could loiter about herself and not attract undue attention. She kept her ears open for the sound of the penny whistles, but heard nothing and assumed that the pecwae had yet to be discovered. She paced back and forth, too restless to sit. For awhile, she tried to occupy her time by counting the columns, but she was too worried to concentrate and soon left off.

The sun dipped into the west, its red-hued rays seeming to melt the crystal windows into liquid fire. The crowds began to depart, heading for a warm hearth and cold ale. Alise was now one of the few people left in the street. She drew her hood up over her red hair, wrapped her cloak around her body, for the evening air was growing chill. Selecting a shadowy area near the iron fence at the north end of the palace, she stood against it, tried her best to blend in.

She had a pricking in her thumbs that something was wrong. Would they take Shadamehr and the others to the prison-fortress located on an island in the middle of the Arven river? She tried to remember what route the guards used to transport prisoners to the fortress. She wondered if she should post herself there or continue to wait here. She had about decided to leave, but she didn't.

Something kept her here, at the north end.

She had noticed before this an empathy developing between herself and Shadamehr, an empathy she disliked, for she could never make it work to her advantage. The empathy worked only to his. He never knew when *she* was in danger, but she always knew when something bad had happened to him.

She stared at the palace windows with an almost suffocating feeling in her breast and then she heard the sound of shattering glass.

Two bodies shot out of a fifth-floor window. Alise knew instantly that one of those bodies belonged to Shadamehr.

Alise could not move. Her heart ceased to beat. Her hands went cold, her feet numb. She knew he must die, his body broken on the stones, his head split open, and she could do nothing but watch in shock and in horror. She didn't notice the other person falling with him. Her eyes were only for Shadamehr and in that moment that she thought he was going to die, she whispered to him that she loved him.

As the words left her mouth, Air magic reached out a hand and caught hold of Shadamehr by the scruff of his neck. The magic held him suspended in midair for an instant, then gently lowered him, his long hair floating in the breeze, the sleeves of his shirt fluttering. Shadamehr's feet touched the paving stones with a gentle thump. The other person, the Trevenici, landed next to him and almost immediately collapsed.

Alise's heart started to beat again, her terror changed instantly to outrage. He'd done this for a lark, never mind that the fright had taken ten years off her life and probably made her red hair go white.

"I take it back," Alise muttered angrily, "I don't love you. I have never loved you. I've always despised you."

She was not the only person to hear the sound of glass shattering or see the astonishing sight of a nobleman and a Trevenici drift to the ground like thistledown on a spring breeze. The Imperial Guards at the front gate saw and heard. As stunned as Alise, they were slower to react.

Shadamehr looked around and she knew he was looking for her, confident that she would be there when he needed her. She cursed him for being confident and cursed herself for being there.

Pressing against the iron bars, she waved her hand, but he had already spotted her.

"Get us out of here!" he shouted, helping the Trevenici to his feet.

Just like that. Get us out of here.

Alise ran through the catalog of Earth-based spells she had memorized. Even as she did that, she knew what spell she had to use and it wasn't Earth-based. She detested using Void magic. She disliked the pain and the weakness and sickness that went with it. To add to her trouble, the spell she cast would be immediately recognized as a Void spell. Any magus happening to see it would know it for what it was and would alert the Church authorities.

To save Shadamehr, she would hurt herself, make herself sick, and place herself at risk of arrest. But then, as Rigiswald had said earlier, what else was new?

Calling the heinous words of the spell to her mind—words that felt like bugs crawling around inside her mouth—she rested both her hands on the iron bars and spoke the magic resolutely.

The iron bars began to rust. The corrosion spread rapidly, running up and down the iron. Alise moved her hands to two more bars and spoke the spell again. A wave of nausea swept over her. Feeling dizzy, fearful she might lose consciousness, she was forced to pause until the sick feeling passed. She clung to one of the bars until it disintegrated and hoped that four missing bars would be enough. She lacked the strength to do more.

The bars corroded rapidly. A large hole gaped in the iron work with a pile of rust beneath. Alise tried to call to Shadamehr, but she didn't have the energy. He wasn't watching. He had his back turned, looking up at the palace. One of the elves, the Wyred, came flying gracefully out of the window, landed in a flurry of robes alongside Shadamehr. Last came Damra, the Dominion Lord. Her silver armor caught the rays of the setting sun, she was bright as a meteor falling from the heavens. She alighted delicately as a bird on a bough.

Shadamehr turned. Seeing the hole in the bars, he pointed at it, and the four began to run toward it. The guards had figured out by now what was happening. They broke into a run, but they were a good distance away, clear back at the gate that stood opposite the center of the palace.

Raising her penny whistle to her lips, Alise blew three long notes. Instantly, other whistles answered hers. Some were near, some were distant, but Shadamehr's men were listening and they were already on their way to his aid.

Looking back, urging them to hurry, Alise saw with alarm that Shadamehr was having difficulty keeping up the pace set by the others. He had his hand pressed to his side and although he ran gamely, his steps faltered. At one point, the Trevenici youth halted to see if the baron needed help. Shadamehr grinned and waved him on.

"This is no time to play the fool, my lord," Alise growled in her throat. By the gods, did the man take nothing seriously?

"Can you do something to stop the guards?" Alise asked the two elves as they reached the hole in the bars.

The Wyred spoke his magic and waved his hand. The shattered glass lying on the paving stones lifted into the air, flashing red with the sunset. The elf made a motion with his hand, caused the glass to start to swirl. The glass whirled about, faster and faster. Another motion of the elf's hand sent the whirling cyclone of broken glass heading straight to intercept the guards.

Shadamehr reached the gate. He had to stop to catch his breath and then Alise saw that she had misjudged him. He had not been clowning. The side of his shirt was covered with blood.

"You're hurt!" Alise cried.

"A scratch, nothing more," Shadamehr said, straightening and giving her his usual infuriating smile.

Five of Shadamehr's men came dashing up, penny whistles in hand.

"What about the pecwae?" Shadamehr asked immediately. There was an odd catch in his voice, as if he were in extreme pain. He pressed his hand over his side. "Where is Ulaf?"

"I ran into him on Glover Street, my lord," one reported. "He said he was on the trail of the pecwae. They were only about a block ahead of him. I asked if he needed help, but he said no, they knew him and trusted him. He said that he would bring them to the Tubby Tabby and I was to meet him there, but that was over an hour ago. I waited for him at the Tabby, but he never came."

"Damn," Shadamehr muttered. He glanced back in the direction of the broken window, and Alise was alarmed to see a shudder run through his body.

"You're hurt worse than you think," she said, putting her arms around him. "I could use my magic to heal—No, damn! I can't! Not after I've cast a Void spell—"

"No time anyway, my dear," he said, and then caught his breath. Sweat broke out on his forehead. "Damra, you and Griffith go to the wharves. I have an orken ship waiting there. The orks know you. We'll join you as soon as we recover the pecwae."

"We don't like to leave you—" Damra began, looking at him in concern.

"I'm in good hands," said Shadamehr with a smile for Alise, a smile that tore at her heart. His face was livid, he was gray about the lips. "You are in danger here. The magi will be searching for two elves and you must admit that the two of you stand out in a crowd."

Damra looked as if she was going to refuse his suggestion.

"You have more than yourself to think about, Dominion Lord," Shadamehr said quietly. "You carry the hope of your people. That hope is in danger here."

Damra had only to glance about her to know he was right. Caught in a whirlwind of slashing glass, the guards stumbled about, trying to shield their faces from the shards. Horns were blowing, the alarm had sounded. More guards were coming. Damra had driven the High Magus into a corner with the lightning whip, but she was free now and would be tearing after them in a towering rage.

"What happened in there, Baron?" Griffith asked, with a gesture at the palace. "What made you alter your plans?"

Shadamehr hesitated, then spoke to them in Tomagi. Alise couldn't understand his words. The elves stared at him in dismay. "So you see," he finished, "you must go—quickly!"

The two elves regarded him with concern. He looked extremely ill.

"The Father and Mother be with you, Baron," said Damra at last. "The Father and Mother be with Vinnengael."

Glancing back up at the window of the Imperial Palace, Shadamehr looked away.

"There is no one to help Vinnengael," he said. "Not even the gods."

Damra clasped hold of her husband's hand. Their images wavered for a moment, then both the elves vanished, their magic cloaking them in shadow.

"Let's get out of here before company comes," said Shadamehr to his men. He kept hold of Alise's hand. "Split up. Meet at the Tubby Tabby. Keep an eye out for the pecwae and for Ulaf."

The red glow of sunset lingered in the sky. The sun's fire dimmed in the crystal windows, wavered like the glow of dying embers. One window, the broken window, was an empty black. The Temple and its attendant buildings cast deep shadows. Shadamehr's men departed, taking to their heels, their racing footfalls pounding loudly on the pavement, drawing off pursuit from their injured lord.

By the time the guards reached the gaping hole in the iron fence, they could find no sign of the miscreants. The Imperial Cavalry arrived, the officer shouting orders for the soldiers to split into groups, turn the city upside down and inside out in search of Baron Shadamehr and an elven Dominion Lord, outlaws who had dared lay hands on the young King.

Shadamehr, Alise and Jessan plunged into a shadowy byway. They dashed down one street, ran up another street, turned down a side street, darted into an alley. At the end of the alley stood a tavern. Shadamehr thrust open the door, ushered his friends inside.

Alise blinked, trying to make the adjustment from darkness to the bright light. Shadamehr did not give her time, but hustled her along. She had an impression of warmth, of the strong smells of beer, sweaty bodies, tobacco smoke and pea soup. Alise stumbled over chairs and feet, tripped over her robes. Shadamehr shouted at the barmaid, who shouted back and gave him a nod of her head. Making certain that Jessan was keeping up with them, Shadamehr herded them toward a door in the back of the tavern.

The door opened. A dark room swallowed up Alise. The door shut behind her. The room was pitch black. She couldn't see a thing and was about to ask Shadamehr why he hadn't thought to bring a lantern when there came the sound of a chair scraping across the floor and then a heavy crash.

"Shadamehr?" Alise called out, terror-stricken.

"He's over here," said Jessan.

"Jessan, we need light!" she cried desperately.

Reaching out her hands, cursing the darkness, Alise took a step forward and tripped over Shadamehr's legs. She knelt down beside him and placed her hand on his neck, feeling for a pulse.

His skin was cold and clammy, his heartbeat was wild and erratic.

"Shadamehr!" she cried to him, but no answer came to her from the darkness.

EPILOGUE

PATROLS OF SOLDIERS SEARCHED THE CITY OF NEW VINNENGAEL WITHOUT luck. Admittedly theirs was a daunting task, like trying to find a baron in a haystack, as one wit stated grumpily, but they kept at it, if somewhat half-heartedly. Rumors now spread among the soldiers that an enemy army, sprung from the Void, threatened the city. The terrible rumors bred like maggots in rotten meat and soon all of New Vinnengael was in an uproar, with people rushing out into the streets to hear the latest prediction of doom, further hampering the efforts of the patrols in their search for Baron Shadamehr and the outlaw elven Dominion Lord.

Adding to the hysteria, word went around that a monk from Dragon Mountain had arrived in New Vinnengael. Someone immediately recalled that a monk had ridden into Old Vinnengael prior to that city's destruction. Panic ensued.

Inside the palace, the battle magus Tasgall, his sight restored, argued with Most Revered High Magus Clovis. The battle magus believed Baron Shadamehr's warning. Tasgall was going to report to the Battle Magi and the High Magus would do well if she opened her eyes to the truth. He pointed to the north, where a sullen red glow lit the horizon.

Furious, the High Magus accused him of siding with rebels and thieves. Their argument ended abruptly when a Temple magus came rushing in to announce in breathless tones that one of the monks from Dragon Mountain had entered the city.

The High Magus went all pale and flabby. Tasgall stalked out.

In the excitement, no one remembered the King until a servant found him and took him to his room. The child asked what was happening, but was told that all was well. They fed him his supper and sent him to bed.

The child pretended to sleep, but the moment the servants departed, he threw aside the silken sheets. Climbing out of bed, he went over to stand in front of the window.

A voice spoke inside the child's head.

"Well, and what have you to report?"

"A monk has arrived from Dragon Mountain, my lord. The monk came this night. They have given him a room in the palace."

There was silence inside the child, then the voice replied, "That is gratifying news, Shakur. Immensely gratifying."

"I thought you would be pleased, my lord."

"It almost makes up for the fact that you have once again lost the Sovereign Stone."

The child reached his hand beneath the long, white nightgown that he wore to bed. The small hand of the eight-year-old caressed a knife made of bone that he wore strapped to his waist.

"They will not get far, my lord," said the boy in his childish voice. "They will not get far."